# UTTERLY UNCLE FRED

## ALSO BY P.G. WODEHOUSE

*Joy in the Morning*

*Very Good, Jeeves!*

*Right Ho, Jeeves*

*The Inimitable Jeeves*

*The Code of the Woosters*

*Blandings Castle*

*Summer Lightning*

*Heavy Weather*

*Leave It to Psmith*

*Uncle Fred in the Springtime*

### COLLECTIONS:

*Just Enough Jeeves*

*A Bounty of Blandings*

# UTTERLY UNCLE FRED

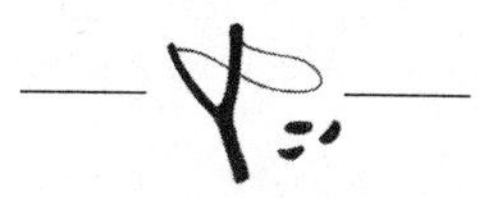

P. G. WODEHOUSE

W. W. Norton & Company
New York • London

Printed in the United States of America
First Edition

For information about special discounts for bulk purchases, please contact
W. W. Norton Special Sales at specialsales@wwnorton.com or 800-233-4830

Manufacturing by Courier Westford
Book design by Judith Abbate
Production manager: Louise Mattarelliano

Library of Congress Cataloging-in-Publication Data

Wodehouse, P. G. (Pelham Grenville), 1881–1975.
Utterly Uncle Fred / P.G. Wodehouse.
p. cm.
ISBN 978-0-393-34377-9 (pbk.)
1. Blandings Castle (England : Imaginary place)—Fiction. 2. Shropshire (England)—Fiction.
3. Nobility—Fiction. I. Title.
PR6045.O53U88 2012
823'.912—dc23
2012007004

W. W. Norton & Company, Inc.
500 Fifth Avenue, New York, N.Y. 10110
www.wwnorton.com

W. W. Norton & Company Ltd.
Castle House, 75/76 Wells Street, London W1T 3QT

1 2 3 4 5 6 7 8 9 0

# Contents

# UNCLE FRED FLITS BY

In order that they might enjoy their afternoon luncheon coffee in peace, the Crumpet had taken the guest whom he was entertaining at the Drones Club to the smaller and less frequented of the two smoking-rooms. In the other, he explained, though the conversation always touched an exceptionally high level of brilliance, there was apt to be a good deal of sugar thrown about.

The guest said he understood.

'Young blood, eh?'

'That's right. Young blood.'

'And animal spirits.'

'And animal, as you say, spirits,' agreed the Crumpet. 'We get a fairish amount of those here.'

'The complaint, however, is not, I observe, universal.'

'Eh?'

The other drew his host's attention to the doorway, where a young man in form-fitting tweeds had just appeared. The aspect of this young man was haggard. His eyes glared wildly and he sucked at an empty cigarette-holder. If he had a mind, there was something on it. When the Crumpet called to him to come and join the party, he merely shook his head in a distraught sort of way and disappeared, looking like a character out of a Greek tragedy pursued by the Fates.

The Crumpet sighed. 'Poor old Pongo!'

'Pongo?'

'That was Pongo Twistleton. He's all broken up about his Uncle Fred.'

'Dead?'

'No such luck. Coming up to London again tomorrow. Pongo had a wire this morning.'

'And that upsets him?'

'Naturally. After what happened last time.'

'What was that?'

'Ah!' said the Crumpet.

'What happened last time?'

'You may well ask.'

'I do ask.'

'Ah!' said the Crumpet.

Poor old Pongo (said the Crumpet) has often discussed his Uncle Fred with me, and if there weren't tears in his eyes when he did so, I don't know a tear in the eye when I see one. In round numbers the Earl of Ickenham, of Ickenham Hall, Ickenham, Hants, he lives in the country most of the year, but from time to time has a nasty way of slipping his collar and getting loose and descending upon Pongo at his flat in the Albany. And every time he does so, the unhappy young blighter is subjected to some soul-testing experience. Because the trouble with this uncle is that, though sixty if a day, he becomes on arriving in the metropolis as young as he feels—which is, apparently, a youngish twenty-two. I don't know if you happen to know what the word 'excesses' means, but those are what Pongo's Uncle Fred from the country, when in London, invariably commits.

It wouldn't so much matter, mind you, if he would confine his activities to the club premises. We're pretty broad-minded here, and if you stop short of smashing the piano, there isn't much that you can do at the Drones that will cause the raised eyebrow and the sharp intake of breath. The snag is that he will insist on lugging Pongo out in the open and there, right in the public eye, proceeding to step high, wide and plentiful.

So when, on the occasion to which I allude, he stood pink and genial on Pongo's hearth-rug, bulging with Pongo's lunch and wreathed in the smoke of one of Pongo's cigars, and said: 'And now, my boy, for a pleasant and instructive afternoon,' you will readily understand why the unfortunate young clam gazed at him as he would have gazed at two-penn'orth of dynamite, had he discovered it lighting up in his presence.

'A what?' he said, giving at the knees and paling beneath the tan a bit.

'A pleasant and instructive afternoon,' repeated Lord Ickenham, rolling the words round his tongue. 'I propose that you place yourself in my hands and leave the programme entirely to me.'

Now, owing to Pongo's circumstances being such as to necessitate his getting into the aged relative's ribs at intervals and shaking him down for an occasional much-needed tenner or what not, he isn't in a position to use the iron hand with the old buster. But at these words he displayed a manly firmness.

'You aren't going to get me to the dog races again.'

'No, no.'

'You remember what happened last June.'

'Quite,' said Lord Ickenham, 'quite. Though I still think that a wiser magistrate would have been content with a mere reprimand.'

'And I won't—'

'Certainly not. Nothing of that kind at all. What I propose to do this afternoon is to take you to visit the home of your ancestors.'

Pongo did not get this.

'I thought Ickenham was the home of my ancestors.'

'It is one of the homes of your ancestors. They also resided rather nearer the heart of things, at a place called Mitching Hill.'

'Down in the suburbs, do you mean?'

'The neighbourhood is now suburban, true. It is many years since the meadows where I sported as a child were sold and cut up into building lots. But when I was a boy Mitching Hill was open country. It was a vast, rolling estate belonging to your great-uncle, Marmaduke, a man with whiskers of a nature which you with your pure mind would scarcely credit, and I have long felt a sentimental urge to see what the hell the old place looks like now. Perfectly foul, I expect. Still, I think we should make the pious pilgrimage.'

Pongo absolutely-ed heartily. He was all for the scheme. A great weight seemed to have rolled off his mind. The way he looked at it was that even an uncle within a short jump of the loony bin couldn't very well get into much trouble in a suburb. I mean, you know what suburbs are. They don't, as it were, offer the scope. One follows his reasoning, of course.

'Fine!' he said. 'Splendid! Topping!'

'Then put on your hat and rompers, my boy,' said Lord Ickenham, 'and let us be off. I fancy one gets there by omnibuses and things.'

Well, Pongo hadn't expected much in the way of mental uplift from the sight of Mitching Hill, and he didn't get it. Alighting from the bus, he tells me, you found yourself in the middle of rows and rows of semi-detached villas, all looking exactly alike, and you went on and you came to more semi-detached villas, and those all looked exactly alike, too. Nevertheless, he did not repine. It was one of those early spring days which suddenly change to mid-winter and he had come out without his overcoat, and it looked like rain and he hadn't an umbrella, but despite this his mood was one of sober ecstasy. The hours were passing and his uncle had not yet made a goat of himself. At the Dog Races the other had been in the hands of the constabulary in the first ten minutes.

It began to seem to Pongo that with any luck he might be able to keep the old blister pottering harmlessly about here till nightfall, when he could shoot a bit of dinner into him and put him to bed. And as Lord Ickenham had specifically stated that his wife, Pongo's Aunt Jane, had expressed her intention of scalping him with a blunt knife if he wasn't back at the Hall by lunch time on the morrow, it really looked as if he might get through this visit without perpetrating a single major outrage on the public weal. It is rather interesting to note that as he thought this Pongo smiled, because it was the last time he smiled that day.

All this while, I should mention, Lord Ickenham had been stopping at intervals like a pointing dog and saying that it must have been just about here that he plugged the gardener in the trousers seat with his bow and arrow and that over there he had been sick after his first cigar, and he now paused in front of a villa which for some unknown reason called itself The Cedars. His face was tender and wistful.

'On this very spot, if I am not mistaken,' he said, heaving a bit of a sigh, 'on this very spot, fifty years ago come Lammas Eve, I . . . Oh, blast it!'

The concluding remark had been caused by the fact that the rain, which had held off until now, suddenly began to buzz down like a shower-bath. With no further words, they leaped into the porch of the villa and there took shelter, exchanging glances with a grey parrot which hung in a cage in the window.

Not that you could really call it shelter. They were protected from above all right, but the moisture was now falling with a sort of swivel action, whipping in through the sides of the porch and tickling them up properly. And it was just after Pongo had turned up his collar and was huddling against the door that the door gave way. From the fact that a female of general-servant aspect was standing there he gathered that his uncle must have rung the bell.

This female wore a long mackintosh, and Lord Ickenham beamed upon her with a fairish spot of suavity.

'Good afternoon,' he said.

The female said good afternoon.

'The Cedars?'

The female said yes, it was The Cedars.

'Are the old folks at home?'

The female said there was nobody at home.

'Ah? Well, never mind. I have come,' said Lord Ickenham, edging in, 'to clip the parrot's claws. My assistant, Mr Walkinshaw, who applies the anaesthetic,' he added, indicating Pongo with a gesture.

'Are you from the bird shop?'

'A very happy guess.'

'Nobody told me you were coming.'

'They keep things from you, do they?' said Lord Ickenham, sympathetically. 'Too bad.'

Continuing to edge, he had got into the parlour by now, Pongo following in a sort of dream and the female following Pongo.

'Well, I suppose it's all right,' she said. 'I was just going out. It's my afternoon.'

'Go out,' said Lord Ickenham cordially. 'By all means go out. We will leave everything in order.'

And presently the female, though still a bit on the dubious side, pushed off, and Lord Ickenham lit the gas-fire and drew a chair up.

'So here we are, my boy,' he said. 'A little tact, a little address, and here we are, snug and cosy and not catching our deaths of cold. You'll never go far wrong if you leave things to me.'

'But, dash it, we can't stop here,' said Pongo.

Lord Ickenham raised his eyebrows.

'Not stop here? Are you suggesting that we go out into that rain? My dear lad, you are not aware of the grave issues involved. This morning, as I was leaving home, I had a rather painful disagreement with your aunt. She said the weather was treacherous and wished me to take my woolly muffler. I replied that the weather was not treacherous and that I would be dashed if I took my woolly muffler. Eventually, by the exercise of an iron will, I had my way, and I ask you, my dear boy, to envisage what will happen if I return with a cold in the head. I shall sink to the level of a fifth-class power. Next time I came to London, it would be with a liver pad and a respirator. No! I shall remain here, toasting my toes at this really excellent fire. I had no idea that a gas-fire radiated such warmth. I feel all in a glow.'

So did Pongo. His brow was wet with honest sweat. He is reading for the Bar, and while he would be the first to admit that he hasn't yet got a complete toe-hold on the Law of Great Britain he had a sort of notion that oiling into a perfect stranger's semi-detached villa on the pretext of pruning the parrot was a tort or misdemeanour, if not actual barratry or soccage in fief or something like that. And apart from the legal aspect of the matter there was the embarrassment of the thing. Nobody is more of a whale on correctness and not doing what's not done than Pongo, and the situation in which he now found himself caused him to chew the lower lip and, as I say, perspire a goodish deal.

'But suppose the blighter who owns this ghastly house comes back?' he asked. 'Talking of envisaging things, try that one over on your pianola.'

And, sure enough, as he spoke, the front door bell rang.

'There!' said Pongo.

'Don't say "There!" my boy,' said Lord Ickenham reprovingly. 'It's the sort of thing your aunt says. I see no reason for alarm. Obviously this is some casual caller. A ratepayer would have used his latchkey. Glance cautiously out of the window and see if you can see anybody.'

'It's a pink chap,' said Pongo, having done so.

'How pink?'

'Pretty pink.'

'Well, there you are, then. I told you so. It can't be the big chief. The sort of fellows who own houses like this are pale and sallow, owing to working in offices all day. Go and see what he wants.'

'You go and see what he wants.'

'We'll both go and see what he wants,' said Lord Ickenham.

So they went and opened the front door, and there, as Pongo had said, was a pink chap. A small young pink chap, a bit moist about the shoulder-blades.

'Pardon me,' said this pink chap, 'is Mr Roddis in?'

'No,' said Pongo.

'Yes,' said Lord Ickenham. 'Don't be silly, Douglas—of course I'm in. I am Mr Roddis,' he said to the pink chap. 'This, such as he is, is my son Douglas. And you?'

'Name of Robinson.'

'What about it?'

'My name's Robinson.'

'Oh, your name's Robinson? Now we've got it straight. Delighted to see you, Mr Robinson. Come right in and take your boots off.'

They all trickled back to the parlour, Lord Ickenham pointing out objects of interest by the wayside to the chap, Pongo gulping for air a bit and trying to get himself abreast of this new twist in the scenario. His heart was becoming more and more bowed down with weight of woe. He hadn't liked being Mr Walkinshaw, the anaesthetist, and he didn't like it any better being Roddis Junior. In brief, he feared the worst. It was only too plain to him by now that his uncle had got it thoroughly up his nose and had settled down to one of his big afternoons, and he was asking himself, as he had so often asked himself before, what would the harvest be?

Arrived in the parlour, the pink chap proceeded to stand on one leg and look coy.

'Is Julia here?' he asked, simpering a bit, Pongo says.

'Is she?' said Lord Ickenham to Pongo.

'No,' said Pongo.

'No,' said Lord Ickenham.

'She wired me she was coming here today.'

'Ah, then we shall have a bridge four.'

The pink chap stood on the other leg.

'I don't suppose you've ever met Julia. Bit of trouble in the family, she gave me to understand.'

'It is often the way.'

'The Julia I mean is your niece Julia Parker. Or, rather, your wife's niece Julia Parker.'

'Any niece of my wife is a niece of mine,' said Lord Ickenham heartily. 'We share and share alike.'

'Julia and I want to get married.'

'Well, go ahead.'

'But they won't let us.'

'Who won't?'

'Her mother and father. And Uncle Charlie Parker and Uncle Henry Parker and the rest of them. They don't think I'm good enough.'

'The morality of the modern young man is notoriously lax.'

'Class enough, I mean. They're a haughty lot.'

'What makes them haughty? Are they earls?'

'No, they aren't earls.'

'Then why the devil,' said Lord Ickenham warmly, 'are they haughty? Only earls have a right to be haughty. Earls are hot stuff. When you get an earl, you've got something.'

'Besides, we've had words. Me and her father. One thing led to another, and in the end I called him a perishing old—Coo!' said the pink chap, breaking off suddenly.

He had been standing by the window, and he now leaped lissomely into the middle of the room, causing Pongo, whose nervous system was by this time definitely down among the wines and spirits and who hadn't been expecting this adagio stuff, to bite his tongue with some severity.

'They're on the doorstep! Julia and her mother and father. I didn't know they were all coming.'

'You do not wish to meet them?'

'No, I don't!'

'Then duck behind the settee, Mr Robinson,' said Lord Ickenham, and the pink chap, weighing the advice and finding it good, did so. And as he disappeared the door bell rang.

Once more, Lord Ickenham led Pongo out into the hall.

'I say!' said Pongo, and a close observer might have noted that he was quivering like an aspen.

'Say on, my dear boy.'

'I mean to say, what?'

'What?'

'You aren't going to let these bounders in, are you?'

'Certainly,' said Lord Ickenham. 'We Roddises keep open house. And as they are presumably aware that Mr Roddis has no son, I think we had better return to the old layout. You are the local vet, my boy, come to minister to my parrot. When I return, I should like to find you by the cage, staring at the bird in a scientific manner. Tap your teeth from time to time with a pencil and try to smell of iodoform. It will help to add conviction.'

So Pongo shifted back to the parrot's cage and stared so earnestly that it was only when a voice said 'Well!' that he became aware that there was anybody in the room. Turning, he perceived that Hampshire's leading curse had come back, bringing the gang.

It consisted of a stern, thin, middle-aged woman, a middle-aged man and a girl.

You can generally accept Pongo's estimate of girls, and when he says that this one was a pippin one knows that he uses the term in its most exact sense. She was about nineteen, he thinks, and she wore a black beret, a dark-green leather coat, a shortish tweed skirt, silk stockings and high-heeled shoes. Her eyes were large and lustrous and her face like a dewy rosebud at daybreak on a June morning. So Pongo tells me. Not that I suppose he has ever seen a rosebud at daybreak on a June morning, because it's generally as much as you can do to lug him out of bed in time for nine-thirty breakfast. Still, one gets the idea.

'Well,' said the woman, 'you don't know who I am, I'll be bound. I'm Laura's sister Connie. This is Claude, my husband. And this is my daughter Julia. Is Laura in?'

'I regret to say, no,' said Lord Ickenham.

The woman was looking at him as if he didn't come up to her specifications.

'I thought you were younger,' she said.

'Younger than what?' said Lord Ickenham.

'Younger than you are.'

'You can't be younger than you are, worse luck,' said Lord Ickenham. 'Still, one does one's best, and I am bound to say that of recent years I have made a pretty good go of it.'

The woman caught sight of Pongo, and he didn't seem to please her, either.

'Who's that?'

'The local vet, clustering round my parrot.'

'I can't talk in front of him.'

'It is quite all right,' Lord Ickenham assured her. 'The poor fellow is stone deaf.'

And with an imperious gesture at Pongo, as much as to bid him stare less at girls and more at parrots, he got the company seated.

'Now, then,' he said.

There was silence for a moment, then a sort of muffled sob, which Pongo thinks proceeded from the girl. He couldn't see, of course, because his back was turned and he was looking at the parrot, which looked back at him—most offensively, he says, as parrots will, using one eye only for the purpose. It also asked him to have a nut.

The woman came into action again.

'Although,' she said, 'Laura never did me the honour to invite me to her wedding, for which reason I have not communicated with her for five years, necessity compels me to cross her threshold today. There comes a time when differences must be forgotten and relatives must stand shoulder to shoulder.'

'I see what you mean,' said Lord Ickenham. 'Like the boys of the old brigade.'

'What I say is, let bygones be bygones. I would not have intruded on you, but needs must. I disregard the past and appeal to your sense of pity.'

The thing began to look to Pongo like a touch, and he is convinced that the parrot thought so, too, for it winked and cleared its throat. But they were both wrong. The woman went on.

'I want you and Laura to take Julia into your home for a week or so, until I can make other arrangements for her. Julia is studying the piano, and she sits for her examination in two weeks' time, so until then she must remain in London. The trouble is, she has fallen in love. Or thinks she has.'

'I know I have,' said Julia.

Her voice was so attractive that Pongo was compelled to slew round and take another look at her. Her eyes, he says, were shining like twin stars and there was a sort of Soul's Awakening expression on her face, and what the dickens there was in a pink chap like the pink chap, who even as pink chaps go wasn't much of a pink chap, to make her look like that, was frankly, Pongo says, more than he could understand. The thing baffled him. He sought in vain for a solution.

'Yesterday, Claude and I arrived in London from our Bexhill home to give Julia a pleasant surprise. We stayed, naturally, in the boarding-house where she has been living for the past six weeks. And what do you think we discovered?'

'Insects.'

'Not insects. A letter. From a young man. I found to my horror that a young man of whom I knew nothing was arranging to marry my daughter. I sent for him immediately, and found him to be quite impossible. He jellies eels!'

'Does what?'

'He is an assistant at a jellied eel shop.'

'But surely,' said Lord Ickenham, 'that speaks well for him. The capacity to jelly an eel seems to me to argue intelligence of a high order. It isn't everybody who can do it, by any means. I know if someone came to me and said "Jelly this eel!" I should be nonplussed. And so, or I am very much mistaken, would Ramsay MacDonald and Winston Churchill.'

The woman did not seem to see eye to eye.

'Tchah!' she said. 'What do you suppose my husband's brother Charlie Parker would say if I allowed his niece to marry a man who jellies eels?'

'Ah!' said Claude, who, before we go any further, was a tall, drooping bird with a red soup-strainer moustache.

'Or my husband's brother, Henry Parker.'

'Ah!' said Claude. 'Or Cousin Alf Robbins, for that matter.'

'Exactly. Cousin Alfred would die of shame.'

The girl Julia hiccoughed passionately, so much so that Pongo says it was all he could do to stop himself nipping across and taking her hand in his and patting it.

'I've told you a hundred times, mother, that Wilberforce is only jellying eels till he finds something better.'

'What is better than an eel?' asked Lord Ickenham, who had been following this discussion with the close attention it deserved. 'For jellying purposes, I mean.'

'He is ambitious. It won't be long,' said the girl, 'before Wilberforce suddenly rises in the world.'

She never spoke a truer word. At this very moment, up he came from behind the settee like a leaping salmon.

'Julia!' he cried.

'Wilby!' yipped the girl.

And Pongo says he never saw anything more sickening in his life than the way she flung herself into the blighter's arms and clung there like the ivy on the old garden wall. It wasn't that he had anything specific against the pink chap, but this girl had made a deep impression on him and he resented her glueing herself to another in this manner.

Julia's mother, after just that brief moment which a woman needs in which to recover from her natural surprise at seeing eel-jelliers pop up from behind sofas, got moving and plucked her away like a referee breaking a couple of welter-weights.

'Julia Parker,' she said, 'I'm ashamed of you!'

'So am I,' said Claude.

'I blush for you.'

'Me, too,' said Claude. 'Hugging and kissing a man who called your father a perishing old bottle-nosed Gawd-help-us.'

'I think,' said Lord Ickenham, shoving his oar in, 'that before proceeding any further we ought to go into that point. If he called you a perishing old bottle-nosed Gawd-help-us, it seems to me that the first thing to do is to decide whether he was right, and frankly, in my opinion . . .'

'Wilberforce will apologize.'

'Certainly I'll apologize. It isn't fair to hold a remark passed in the heat of the moment against a chap . . .'

'Mr Robinson,' said the woman, 'you know perfectly well that whatever remarks you may have seen fit to pass don't matter one way or the other. If you were listening to what I was saying you will understand . . .'

'Oh, I know, I know. Uncle Charlie Parker and Uncle Henry Parker and Cousin Alf Robbins and all that. Pack of snobs!'

'What!'

'Haughty, stuck-up snobs. Them and their class distinction. Think themselves everybody just because they've got money. I'd like to know how they got it.'

'What do you mean by that?'

'Never mind what I mean.'

'If you are insinuating—'

'Well, of course, you know, Connie,' said Lord Ickenham mildly, 'he's quite right. You can't get away from that.'

I don't know if you have ever seen a bull-terrier embarking on a scrap with an Airedale and just as it was getting down nicely to its work suddenly having an unexpected Kerry Blue sneak up behind it and bite it in the rear quarters. When this happens, it lets go of the Airedale and swivels round and fixes the butting-in animal with a pretty nasty eye. It was exactly the same with the woman Connie when Lord Ickenham spoke these words.

'What!'

'I was only wondering if you had forgotten how Charlie Parker made his pile.'

'What are you talking about?'

'I know it is painful,' said Lord Ickenham, 'and one doesn't mention it as a rule, but, as we are on the subject, you must admit that lending money at two hundred and fifty per cent interest is not done in the best circles. The judge, if you remember, said so at the trial.'

'I never knew that!' cried the girl Julia.

'Ah,' said Lord Ickenham. 'You kept it from the child? Quite right, quite right.'

'It's a lie!'

'And when Henry Parker had all that fuss with the bank it was touch and go they didn't send him to prison. Between ourselves, Connie, has a bank official, even a brother of your husband, any right to sneak fifty pounds from the till in order to put it on a hundred to one shot for the Grand National? Not quite playing the game, Connie. Not the straight bat. Henry, I grant you, won five thousand of the best and never looked back afterwards, but, though we applaud his judgment of form, we must surely look askance at his financial methods. As for Cousin Alf Robbins . . .'

The woman was making rummy stuttering sounds. Pongo tells me he once had a Pommery Seven which used to express itself in much the same way if you tried to get it to take a hill on high. A sort of mixture of gurgles and explosions.

'There is not a word of truth in this,' she gasped at length, having managed to get the vocal cords disentangled. 'Not a single word. I think you must have gone mad.'

Lord Ickenham shrugged his shoulders.

'Have it your own way, Connie. I was only going to say that, while the jury were probably compelled on the evidence submitted to them to give Cousin Alf Robbins the benefit of the doubt when charged with smuggling dope, everybody knew that he had been doing it for years. I am not blaming him, mind you. If a man can smuggle cocaine and get away with it, good luck to him, say I. The only point I am trying to make is that we are hardly a family that can afford to put on dog and sneer at honest suitors for our daughters' hands. Speaking for myself, I consider that we are very lucky to have the chance of marrying even into eel-jellying circles.'

'So do I,' said Julia firmly.

'You don't believe what this man is saying?'

'I believe every word.'

'So do I,' said the pink chap.

The woman snorted. She seemed overwrought.

'Well,' she said, 'goodness knows I have never liked Laura, but I would never have wished her a husband like you!'

'Husband?' said Lord Ickenham, puzzled. 'What gives you the impression that Laura and I are married?'

There was a weighty silence, during which the parrot threw out a general invitation to join it in a nut. Then the girl Julia spoke.

'You'll have to let me marry Wilberforce now,' she said. 'He knows too much about us.'

'I was rather thinking that myself,' said Lord Ickenham. 'Seal his lips, I say.'

'You wouldn't mind marrying into a low family, would you, darling?' asked the girl, with a touch of anxiety.

'No family could be too low for me, dearest, if it was yours,' said the pink chap.

'After all, we needn't see them.'

'That's right.'

'It isn't one's relations that matter: it's oneselves.'

'That's right, too.'

'Wilby!'

'Julia!'

They repeated the old ivy on the garden wall act. Pongo says he didn't like it any better than the first time, but his distaste wasn't in it with the woman Connie's.

'And what, may I ask,' she said, 'do you propose to marry on?'

This seemed to cast a damper. They came apart. They looked at each other. The girl looked at the pink chap, and the pink chap looked at the girl. You could see that a jarring note had been struck.

'Wilberforce is going to be a very rich man some day.'

'Some day!'

'If I had a hundred pounds,' said the pink chap, 'I could buy a half-share in one of the best milk walks in South London tomorrow.'

'If!' said the woman.

'Ah!' said Claude.

'Where are you going to get it?'

'Ah!' said Claude.

'Where,' repeated the woman, plainly pleased with the snappy crack and loath to let it ride without an encore, 'are you going to get it?'

'That,' said Claude, 'is the point. Where are you going to get a hundred pounds?'

'Why, bless my soul,' said Lord Ickenham jovially, 'from me, of course. Where else?'

And before Pongo's bulging eyes he fished out from the recesses of his costume a crackling bundle of notes and handed it over. And the agony of realizing that the old bounder had had all that stuff on him all this time and that he hadn't touched him for so much as a tithe of it was so keen, Pongo says, that before he knew what he was doing he had let out a sharp, whinnying cry which rang through the room like the yowl of a stepped-on puppy.

'Ah,' said Lord Ickenham. 'The vet wishes to speak to me. Yes, vet?'

This seemed to puzzle the cerise bloke a bit.

'I thought you said this chap was your son.'

'If I had a son,' said Lord Ickenham, a little hurt, 'he would be a good deal better-looking than that. No, this is the local veterinary surgeon. I may have said I looked on him as a son. Perhaps that was what confused you.'

He shifted across to Pongo and twiddled his hands enquiringly. Pongo gaped at him, and it was not until one of the hands caught him smartly in the lower ribs that he remembered he was deaf and started to twiddle back. Considering that he wasn't supposed to be dumb, I can't see why he should have twiddled, but no doubt there are moments when twiddling is about all a fellow feels himself equal to. For what seemed to him at least ten hours Pongo had been undergoing great mental stress, and one can't blame him for not being chatty. Anyway, be that as it may, he twiddled.

'I cannot quite understand what he says,' announced Lord Ickenham at length, 'because he sprained a finger this morning and that makes him stammer. But I gather that he wishes to have a word with me in private. Possibly my parrot has got something the matter with it which he is reluctant to mention even in sign language in front of a young unmarried girl. You know what parrots are. We will step outside.'

'We will step outside,' said Wilberforce.

'Yes,' said the girl Julia. 'I feel like a walk.'

'And you,' said Lord Ickenham to the woman Connie, who was looking like a female Napoleon at Moscow. 'Do you join the hikers?'

'I shall remain and make myself a cup of tea. You will not grudge us a cup of tea, I hope?'

'Far from it,' said Lord Ickenham cordially. 'This is Liberty Hall. Stick around and mop it up till your eyes bubble.'

Outside, the girl, looking more like a dewy rosebud than ever, fawned on the old buster pretty considerably.

'I don't know how to thank you!' she said. And the pink chap said he didn't, either.

'Not at all, my dear, not at all,' said Lord Ickenham.

'I think you're simply wonderful.'

'No, no.'

'You are. Perfectly marvellous.'

'Tut, tut,' said Lord Ickenham. 'Don't give the matter another thought.'

He kissed her on both cheeks, the chin, the forehead, the right eyebrow, and the tip of the nose, Pongo looking on the while in a baffled and discontented manner. Everybody seemed to be kissing this girl except him.

Eventually the degrading spectacle ceased and the girl and the pink chap shoved off, and Pongo was enabled to take up the matter of that hundred quid.

'Where,' he asked, 'did you get all that money?'

'Now, where did I?' mused Lord Ickenham. 'I know your aunt gave it to me for some purpose. But what? To pay some bill or other, I rather fancy.'

This cheered Pongo up slightly.

'She'll give you the devil when you get back,' he said, with not a little relish. 'I wouldn't be in your shoes for something. When you tell Aunt Jane,' he said, with confidence, for he knew his Aunt Jane's emotional nature, 'that you slipped her entire roll to a girl, and explain, as you will have to explain, that she was an extraordinarily pretty girl—a girl, in fine, who looked like something out of a beauty chorus of the better sort, I should think she would pluck down one of the ancestral battle-axes from the wall and jolly well strike you on the mazzard.'

'Have no anxiety, my dear boy,' said Lord Ickenham. 'It is like your kind heart to be so concerned, but have no anxiety. I shall tell her that I was compelled to give the money to you to enable you to buy back some compromising letters from a Spanish demi-mondaine. She will scarcely be able to blame me for rescuing a fondly-loved nephew from the clutches of an adventuress. It may be that she will feel a little vexed with you for a while, and that you may have to allow a certain time to elapse before you visit Ickenham again, but then I shan't be wanting you at Ickenham till the ratting season starts, so all is well.'

At this moment, there came toddling up to the gate of The Cedars a large red-faced man. He was just going in when Lord Ickenham hailed him.

'Mr Roddis?'

'Hey?'

'Am I addressing Mr Roddis?'

'That's me.'

'I am Mr J. G. Bulstrode from down the road,' said Lord Ickenham. 'This is my sister's husband's brother, Percy Frensham, in the lard and imported-butter business.'

The red-faced bird said he was pleased to meet them. He asked Pongo if things were brisk in the lard and imported-butter business, and Pongo said they were all right, and the red-faced bird said he was glad to hear it.

'We have never met, Mr Roddis,' said Lord Ickenham, 'but I think it would be only neighbourly to inform you that a short while ago I observed two suspicious-looking persons in your house.'

'In my house? How on earth did they get there?'

'No doubt through a window at the back. They looked to me like cat burglars. If you creep up, you may be able to see them.'

The red-faced bird crept, and came back not exactly foaming at the mouth but with the air of a man who for two pins would so foam.

'You're perfectly right. They're sitting in my parlour as cool as dammit, swigging my tea and buttered toast.'

'I thought as much.'

'And they've opened a pot of my raspberry jam.'

'Ah, then you will be able to catch them red-handed. I should fetch a policeman.'

'I will. Thank you, Mr Bulstrode.'

'Only too glad to have been able to render you this little service, Mr Roddis,' said Lord Ickenham. 'Well, I must be moving. I have an appointment. Pleasant after the rain, is it not? Come, Percy.'

He lugged Pongo off.

'So that,' he said, with satisfaction, 'is that. On these visits of mine to the metropolis, my boy, I always make it my aim, if possible, to spread sweetness and light. I look about me, even in a foul hole like Mitching Hill, and I ask myself—How can I leave this foul hole a better and happier foul hole than I found it? And if I see a chance, I grab it. Here is our omnibus. Spring aboard, my boy, and on our way home we will be sketching out rough plans for the evening. If the old Leicester Grill is still in existence, we might look in there. It must be fully thirty-five years since I was last thrown out of the Leicester Grill. I wonder who is the bouncer there now.'

Such (concluded the Crumpet) is Pongo Twistleton's Uncle Fred from the country, and you will have gathered by now a rough notion of why it is that when a telegram comes announcing his impending arrival in the great city Pongo blenches to the core and calls for a couple of quick ones.

The whole situation, Pongo says, is very complex. Looking at it from one angle, it is fine that the man lives in the country most of the year. If he didn't, he would have him in his midst all the time. On the other hand, by living in the country he generates, as it were, a store of loopiness which expends itself with frightful violence on his rare visits to the centre of things.

What it boils down to is this—Is it better to have a loopy uncle whose loopiness is perpetually on tap but spread out thin, so to speak, or one who lies low in distant Hants for three hundred and sixty days in the year and does himself proud in London for the other five? Dashed moot, of course, and Pongo has never been able to make up his mind on the point.

Naturally, the ideal thing would be if someone would chain the old hound up permanently and keep him from Jan. One to Dec. Thirty-one where he wouldn't do any harm—viz. among the spuds and tenantry. But this, Pongo admits, is a Utopian dream. Nobody could work harder to that end than his Aunt Jane, and she has never been able to manage it.

# UNCLE DYNAMITE

# PART ONE

# 1

ON the little branch line which starts at Wockley Junction and conveys passengers to Eggmarsh St John, Ashenden Oakshott, Bishop's Ickenham and other small and somnolent hamlets of the south of England the early afternoon train had just begun its leisurely journey.

It was a train whose patrons, sturdy sons of the soil who did not intend to let a railway company trouser more of their money than they could help, had for the most part purchased third-class tickets. But a first-class compartment had been provided for the rich and thriftless, and to-day it had two occupants, a large youth of open and ingenuous countenance, much sunburned, and a tall, slim, distinguished-looking man some thirty years his senior with a jaunty grey moustache and a bright and enterprising eye, whose air was that of one who has lived to the full every minute of an enjoyable life and intends to go on doing so till further notice. His hat was on the side of his head, and he bore his cigar like a banner.

For some ten minutes after the train had started, the usual decent silence of the travelling Englishman prevailed in the compartment. Then the young man, who had been casting covert glances at his companion, cleared his throat and said 'Er.'

The elderly gentleman looked up inquiringly. Deepening in colour, for he was of bashful temperament and was already wondering why he had been ass enough to start this, the sunburned youth proceeded.

'I say, excuse me. Aren't you Lord Ickenham?'

'I am.'

'Fine.'

The elderly gentleman seemed puzzled.

'I'm pretty pleased about it myself,' he admitted. 'But why do you rejoice?'

'Well, if you hadn't been—' said the young man, and paused aghast at the thought of what horrors might not have resulted from the wanton addressing of a perfect stranger. 'What I mean is, I used to know you. Years ago. Sort of. I was a pal of your nephew Pongo, and I came over to your place for tennis sometimes. You once tipped me five bob.'

'That's how the money goes.'

'I don't suppose you remember me. Bill Oakshott.'

'Of course I remember you, my dear fellow,' said Lord Ickenham heartily and quite untruthfully. 'I wish I had a tenner for every time I've said to my wife "Whatever became of Bill Oakshott?"'

'No, really? Fine. How is Lady Ickenham?'

'Fine.'

'Fine. She once tipped me half a crown.'

'You will generally find women loosen up less lavishly than men. It's something to do with the bone structure of the head. Yes, my dear wife, I am glad to say, continues in the pink. I've just been seeing her off on the boat at Southampton. She is taking a trip to the West Indies.'

'Jamaica?'

'No, she went of her own free will.'

The human tomato digested this for a moment in silence, seemed on the point of saying 'Fine,' then changed his mind, and enquired after Pongo.

'Pongo,' said Lord Ickenham, 'is in terrific form. He bestrides the world like a Colossus. It would not be too much to say that Moab is his washpot and over what's-its-name has he cast his shoe. He came into the deuce of a lot of money the other day from a deceased godfather in America, and can now face his tailor without a tremor. He is also engaged to be married.'

'Good.'

'Yes,' said Lord Ickenham, rather startled by this evidence of an unexpectedly wide vocabulary. 'Yes, he seems fairly radiant about it. I myself, I must confess, am less enthusiastic. I don't know if you have noticed it, Bill Oakshott, but nothing in this world ever works out one hundred per cent satisfactorily for all parties. Thus, while A. is waving his hat and giving a series of rousing cheers, we see B. frowning dubiously. And the same is true of X. and Z. Take this romance of Pongo's, for instance. I was hoping that he would marry another girl, a particular protégée of mine whom I have watched grow from a child, and a singularly fascinating child, at that, to a young woman of grace, charm and strength of character who in my opinion has everything. Among other advantages which she possesses is sense enough for two, which, it seems to me, is just the amount the wife of Reginald ("Pongo") Twistleton will require. But it was not to be. However, let us look on the bright side. Shall we?'

'Oh, rather.'

'Fine. Well, looking on the bright side, I haven't met this new girl, but she sounds all right. And of course the great thing is to get the young blighter safely married and settled down, thus avoiding the risk of his coming in one day and laying on the mat something with a platinum head and an Oxford accent which he picked up on the pier at Blackpool. You remember what a pushover he always was for the gentle sex.'

'I haven't seen Pongo since we were kids.'

'Even then he was flitting from flower to flower like a willowy butterfly. He was the Don Juan of his dancing class when he wore Little Lord Fauntleroy suits, his heart an open door with "Welcome" on the mat.'

'He'll chuck all that sort of thing now.'

'Let us hope so. But you remember what the fellow said. Can the leopard change his spots, or the Ethiopian his hue? Or is it skin? And talking of Ethiopians,' said Lord Ickenham, allowing himself to become personal, 'has someone been cooking you over a slow fire, or did you sit in the sun without your parasol?'

Bill Oakshott grinned sheepishly.

'I am a bit sunburned, aren't I? I've been in Brazil. I'm on my way home from the boat.'

'You reside in this neighbourhood?'

'At Ashenden Manor.'

'Married?'

'No. I live with my uncle. Or, rather, he lives with me.'

'What is the distinction?'

'Well, what I mean is, Ashenden really belongs to me, but I was only about sixteen when my father died, and my uncle came barging over from Cheltenham and took charge. He dug in, and has been there ever since. Running the whole show. You'd think from the way he goes on,' said Bill, stirred to unwonted loquacity by the recollection of his wrongs, 'that he owned the bally place. Well, to give you an instance, he's pinched the best room in the house for his damned collection of African curios.'

'Does he collect African curios? God help him.'

'And that's not all. Who has the star bedroom? Me? No! Uncle Aylmer. Who collars the morning paper? Me? No! Uncle Aylmer. Who gets the brown egg at breakfast?'

'Don't tell me. Let me guess. Uncle Aylmer?'

'Yes. Blast him!'

Lord Ickenham stroked his moustache.

'A certain guarded something in your manner, Bill Oakshott,' he said, 'suggests to me that you do not like having your Uncle Aylmer living at Ashenden Manor. Am I correct?'

'Yes.'

'Then why not bung him out?'

The truculence faded from Bill Oakshott's demeanour, leaving in its place embarrassment. He could have answered the question, but to do so would have involved revealing his great love for his uncle's daughter, Hermione, and agreeable old bird though Lord Ickenham was, he did not feel that he knew him intimately enough.

'Oh, well,' he said, and coyly scraped a shoe like a violin case along the floor of the compartment. 'No, I don't quite see how I could do that.'

'There are complications?'

'Yes. Complications.'

'I understand.'

It was plain to Lord Ickenham that he had stumbled upon a delicate domestic situation, and he tactfully forbore to probe into it. Picking up his *Times*, he turned to the crossword puzzle, and Bill Oakshott sat gazing out of the window at the passing scenery.

But he did not see the familiar fields and spinneys, only the lovely face of his cousin Hermione. It rose before him like some radiant vision, and soon, he reflected, he would be beholding it not merely with the eye of imagination. Yes, at any moment, now that he was back in England again, he was liable to find himself gazing into her beautiful eyes or, if she happened to be standing sideways, staring at her pure, perfect profile.

In which event, what would the procedure be? Would he, as before, just gape and shuffle his feet? Or would he, fortified by three months in bracing Brazil, at last be able to shake off his distressing timidity and bring himself to reveal a silent passion which had been functioning uninterruptedly for some nine years?

He hoped so, but at the same time was compelled to recognize the point as a very moot one.

A tap on the knee interrupted his meditations.

'Next stop, Ashenden Oakshott,' Lord Ickenham reminded him.

'Eh? Oh, yes. That's right, so it is.'

'You had better be girding up your loins.'

'Yes,' said Bill, and rose and hauled down his suitcase from the rack. Then, as the train puffed out of the tunnel, he gave a sudden sharp cry and stood staring. As if unable to believe his eyes, he blinked them twice with great rapidity. But they had not deceived him. He still saw what he thought he had seen.

Under normal conditions there is about the station of Ashenden Oakshott little or nothing to rouse the emotions and purge the soul with pity and terror. Once you have seen the stationmaster's whiskers, which are of a Victorian bushiness and give the impression of having been grown under glass, you have drained it of all it has to offer in the way of thrills, unless you are one of those easily excited persons who can find drama in the spectacle of a small porter wrestling with a series of large milk cans. 'Placid' is the word that springs to the lips.

But to-day all this was changed, and it was obvious at a glance that Ashenden Oakshott was stepping out. From the penny-in-the-slot machine at the far end to the shed where the porter kept his brooms and buckets the platform was dark with what practically amounted to a sea of humanity. At least forty persons must have been present.

Two, selected for their muscle and endurance, were holding aloft on poles a streamer on which some loving hand, which had not left itself quite enough room, had inscribed the words:

WELCOME HOME, MR WILLM.

and in addition to these the eye noted a Silver Band, some Boy Scouts, a policeman, a clergyman, a mixed assortment of villagers of both sexes, what looked like an Infants' Bible Class (with bouquets) and an impressive personage with a large white moustache, who seemed to be directing the proceedings.

From his post by the window Bill Oakshott continued to stand rigid and open-mouthed, like some character in a fairy story on whom a spell has been cast, and so limpid was his countenance that Lord Ickenham had no difficulty in analysing the situation.

Here, he perceived, was a young man of diffident and retiring disposition, one who shrank from the public eye and quailed at the thought of being conspicuous, and for some reason somebody had organized this stupendous reception for him. That was why he was now looking like a stag at bay.

Publicity was a thing from which Lord Ickenham himself had never been averse. He frankly enjoyed it. If Silver Bands and Boy Scouts had come to welcome him at a station, he would have leaped to meet them with a whoop and a holler, and would have been out taking bows almost before the train had stopped. But it was plain that this young friend of his was differently constituted, and his heart was moved by his distress.

The kindly peer had always been a practical man. He did not, as others might have done, content himself in this crisis with a pitying glance or a silent hand-clasp.

'Nip under the seat,' he advised.

To Bill it seemed like a voice from heaven. It was as if in the hour of deadly peril his guardian angel had suddenly come through with something constructive. He followed the counsel without delay, and presently there was a lurch and a heave and the train resumed its journey.

When he crawled out, dusting his hands, he found his companion regarding him with open admiration.

'As neat a vanishing act as I have ever witnessed,' said Lord Ickenham cordially. 'It was like a performing seal going after a slice of fish. You've done this sort of thing before, Bill Oakshott. No? You amaze me. I would have sworn that you had had years of practice on race trains. Well, you certainly baffled them. I don't think I have ever seen a Silver Band so nonplussed. It was as though a bevy of expectant wolves had overtaken a sleigh and found no Russian peasant aboard, than which I can imagine nothing more sickening. For the wolves, of course.'

Bill Oakshott was still quivering. He gazed gratefully at his benefactor and in broken words thanked him for his inspired counsel.

'Not at all,' said Lord Ickenham. 'My dear fellow, don't mention it. I am like the chap in Damon Runyan's story, who always figured that if he could bring a little joy into any life, no matter how, he was doing a wonderful deed. It all comes under the head of spreading sweetness and light, which is my constant aim.'

'Well, I shall never forget it, never,' said Bill earnestly. 'Do you realize that I should have had to make a speech, besides probably kissing all those ghastly children with the flowers?' He shuddered strongly. 'Did you see them? About a million of them, each with a posy.'

'I did, indeed. And the sight confirmed me in my view that since the days when you used to play tennis at my place you must have become pretty illustrious. I have knocked about the world long enough to know that infants with bouquets don't turn out for every Tom, Dick and Harry. I myself am a hell of a fellow—a first-class Earl who keeps his carriage—but have infants ever offered me bouquets? What have you been doing, Bill Oakshott, to merit this reception—nay, this Durbar?'

'I haven't done a thing.'

'Well, it's all very odd. I suppose it *was* in your honour that the affair was arranged? They would hardly have said "Mr Willm", if they had meant someone else.'

'No, that's true.'

'Have you any suspicions as to the ringleaders?'

'I suppose my uncle was at the bottom of it.'

'Was he the impressive citizen with the moustache, who looked like Clemenceau?'

'Yes. He must have got the thing up.'

'But why?'

'I don't know.'

'Search your memory. Can you think of nothing you have done recently which could have put you in the Silver Band and Boy Scout class?'

'Well, I went on this expedition up the Amazon.'

'Oh, you went on an expedition, did you, and up the Amazon, to boot. I didn't realize that. I assumed that you had merely been connected with the Brazil nut industry or something. That might account for it, of course. And why did you commit this rash act? Wanted to get some girl out of your system, I suppose?'

Bill blushed. It had indeed been the seeming hopelessness of his love for his cousin Hermione that had driven him to try a cure which, as he might have foreseen, had proved quite ineffective.

'Why, yes. Something of the sort.'

'In my day we used to go to the Rocky Mountains and shoot grizzlies. What made you choose Brazil?'

'I happened to see an advertisement in *The Times* about an expedition that was starting off for the Lower Amazon, run by a chap called Major Plank, and I thought it might be a good idea to sign on.'

'I see. Well, I wish I had known of this before. I could have stuck on a lot of dog on the strength of having met you as a boy. But we shall be at Bishop's Ickenham in a minute or two, and the question arises, what do you propose to do? Wait for a train back? Or shall I take you to my place and give you a drink and send you home in the car?'

'Wouldn't that be a nuisance?'

'On the contrary. Nothing could suit my book better. That's settled then. We now come to a matter to which I think we ought to devote some little attention. What story are you going to tell your uncle, to account for your non-appearance at the revels?'

A thoughtful look came into Bill Oakshott's face. He winced slightly, as if a Brazilian alligator had attached itself to the fleshy part of his leg.

'I was rather wondering about that,' he confessed.

'A good, coherent story will undoubtedly be required. He will be feeling chagrined at your failure to materialize, and he looked a dangerous specimen, the sort of man whose bite spells death. What is he? An all-in wrestler? A chap who kills rats with his teeth?'

'He used to be Governor of one of those Crown colonies.'

'Then we must strain every nerve to pacify him. I know these ex-Governors. Tough nuts. You didn't mention his name, by the way.'

'Bostock. Sir Aylmer Bostock.'

'What? Is that who he is? Well, I'll be dashed.'

'You know him?'

'I have not seen him for more than forty years, but at one time I knew him well. We were at school together.'

'Oh, really?'

'Mugsy we used to call him. He was younger than me by some three years, one of those tough, chunky, beetle-browed kids who scowl at their seniors and bully their juniors. I once gave him six of the juiciest with a fives bat in the hope of correcting this latter tendency. Well, the mystery of that civic welcome is now explained. Mugsy is to stand for Parliament shortly, my paper informs me, and no doubt he thought it would give him a leg up. Like me, he hopes to trade on his connection with a man who has extended the bounds of Civilization.'

'I didn't extend the bounds of Civilization.'

'Nonsense. I'll bet you extended them like elastic. But we are getting away from our discussion of what story you are to tell. How would it be to say that the warmth of the day caused you to drop off into a light slumber, and when you woke up blowed if you weren't at Bishop's Ickenham?'

'Fine.'

'You like it? I don't think it's so bad myself. Simple, which is always good. Impossible to disprove, which is better. And with the added advantage of having a historic precedent; the case, if you remember, of the lady who wanted to go to Birmingham and they were taking her on to Crewe.

Yes, I fancy it ought to get by. So that was young Mugsy, was it?' said Lord Ickenham. 'I must say I'm surprised that he should have finished up as anything so comparatively respectable as Governor of a Crown colony. It just shows you never can tell.'

'How long did you say it was since you had met him?'

'Forty-two years come Lammas Eve. Why?'

'I was only wondering why you hadn't run across him. Living so close, I mean.'

'Well, I'll tell you, Bill Oakshott. It is my settled policy to steer pretty clear of the neighbours. You have probably noticed yourself that the British Gawd-help-us seems to flourish particularly luxuriantly in the rural districts. My wife tries to drag me to routs and revels from time to time, but I toss my curls at her and refuse to stir. I often think that the ideal life would be to have plenty of tobacco and be cut by the County. And as regards your uncle, I look back across the years at Mugsy, the boy, and I see nothing that encourages me to fraternize with Mugsy, the man.'

'Something in that.'

'Not an elfin personality, Mugsy's. I'm afraid Pongo doesn't realize what he's up against in taking on such a father-in-law. It's his daughter Hermione that he's gone and got engaged to, and I see a sticky future ahead of the unhappy lad. Ah, here we are,' said Lord Ickenham, as the train slowed down. 'Let's go and get that drink. It's just possible that we may find Pongo at the old shack. He rang me up this morning, saying he was coming to spend the night. He is about to visit Ashenden Manor, to show the old folks what they've got.'

He hopped nimbly on to the platform, prattling gaily, quite unaware that he had to all intents and purposes just struck an estimable young man behind the ear with a sock full of wet sand. The short, quick, gulping grunt, like that of a bulldog kicked in the ribs while eating a mutton chop, which had escaped Bill Oakshott on the cue 'got engaged to', he had mistaken for a hiccough.

# 2

THE summer afternoon had mellowed into twilight and Bill Oakshott had long since taken his bruised heart off the premises before Pongo Twistleton fetched up at the home of his ancestors. One of those mysterious breakdowns which affect two-seater cars had delayed him on the road. He arrived just in time to dress for dinner, and the hour of eight found him seated opposite his uncle in the oak-panelled dining-room, restoring his tissues after a trying day.

Lord Ickenham, delighted to see him, was a gay and effervescent host, but during the meal the presence of a hovering butler made conversation of a really intimate nature impossible, and the talk confined itself to matters of general interest. Pongo spoke of New York, whence he had recently returned from a visit connected with the winding up of his godfather's estate, and Lord Ickenham mentioned that Lady Ickenham was on her way to Trinidad to attend the wedding of the daughter of an old friend. Lord Ickenham alluded to his meeting with Pongo's former crony, Bill Oakshott, and Pongo, though confessing that he remembered Bill only imperfectly—'Beefy stripling with a pink face, unless I'm thinking of someone else'—said that he looked forward to renewing their old friendship when he hit Ashenden Manor.

They also touched on such topics as the weather, dogs, two-seater cars (their treatment in sickness and in health), the foreign policy of the Government, the chances of Jujube for the Goodwood Cup, and what you would do—this subject arising from Pongo's recent literary studies—if you found a dead body in your bath one morning with nothing on but pince-nez and a pair of spats.

It was only when the coffee had been served and the cigars lighted that Lord Ickenham prepared to become more expansive.

'Now we're nice and cosy,' he said contentedly. 'What a relief it always is when the butler pops off. It makes you realize the full meaning of that beautiful line in the hymn book—"Peace, perfect peace, with loved ones far away." Not that I actually love Coggs. A distant affection, rather, tempered with awe. Well, Pongo, I'm extraordinarily glad you blew in. I was wanting a quiet chat with you about your plans and what not.'

'Ah,' said Pongo.

He spoke reservedly. He was a slender, personable young man with lemon-coloured hair and an attractive face, and on this face a close observer would have noted at the moment an austere, wary look, such as might have appeared on that of St Anthony just before the temptations began. He had a strong suspicion that now that they were alone together, it was going to be necessary for him to be very firm with this uncle of his and to maintain an iron front against his insidious wiles.

Watching the head of the family closely during dinner, he had not failed to detect in his eyes, while he was speaking of his wife's voyage to the West Indies, a lurking gleam such as one might discern in the eye of a small boy who has been left alone in the house and knows where the key of the jam cup-board is. He had seen that gleam before, and it had always heralded trouble of a major kind. Noticeable even as early as the soup course, it had become, as its proprietor puffed at his cigar, more marked than ever, and Pongo waited coldly for him to proceed.

'How long are you proposing to inflict yourself on these Bostocks of yours?'

'About a week.'

'And after that?'

'Back to London, I suppose.'

'Good,' said Lord Ickenham heartily. 'That was what I wanted to know. That was what I wished to ascertain. You will return to London. Excellent. I will join you there, and we will have one of our pleasant and instructive afternoons.'

Pongo stiffened. He did not actually say 'Ha!' but the exclamation was implicit in the keen glance which he shot across the table. His suspicions had been correct. His wife's loving surveillance having been temporarily removed, Frederick Altamont Cornwallis, fifth Earl of Ickenham, was planning to be out and about again.

'You ask me,' a thoughtful Crumpet had once said in the smoking-room of the Drones Club, 'why it is that at the mention of his Uncle Fred's name Pongo Twistleton blenches to the core and calls for a couple of quick ones. I will tell you. It is because this uncle is pure dynamite. Every time he is in Pongo's midst, with the sap running strongly in his veins, he subjects the unfortunate young egg to some soul-testing experience, luring him out into the open and there, right in the public eye, proceeding to step high, wide and plentiful. For though well stricken in years the old blister becomes on these occasions as young as he feels, which seems to be about twenty-two. I don't know if you happen to know what the word "excesses" means, but those are what he invariably commits, when on the loose. Get Pongo to tell you some time about that day they had together at the dog races.'

It was a critique of which, had he heard it, Lord Ickenham would have been the first to admit the essential justice. From boyhood up his had always been a gay and happy disposition, and in the evening of his life he still retained, together with a juvenile waistline, the bright enthusiasms and the fresh, unspoiled mental outlook of a slightly inebriated undergraduate. He had enjoyed a number of exceedingly agreeable outings in his nephew's society in the course of the last few years, and was pleasantly conscious of having stepped on these occasions as high, wide and plentiful as a man could wish, particularly during that day at the dog races. Though there, he had always maintained, a wiser policeman would have been content with a mere reprimand.

'As you are aware, if you were not asleep while I was talking at dinner,' he said, resuming his remarks, 'your aunt has left me for a few weeks and, as you can well imagine, I am suffering agonies. I feel like one of those fellows in the early nineteenth-century poems who used to go about losing dear gazelles. Still—'

'Now listen,' said Pongo.

'Still, in practically every cloud wrack the knowledgeable eye, if it peers closely enough, can detect some sort of a silver lining, however small, and the horror of my predicament is to a certain extent mitigated by the thought that I now become a mobile force again. Your aunt is the dearest woman in the world, and nobody could be fonder of her than I am, but I sometimes find her presence . . . what is the word I want . . . restrictive. She holds, as you know, peculiar views on the subject of my running around loose in London, as she puts it, and this prevents me fulfilling myself. It is a pity. Living in a rural morgue like Bishop's Ickenham all the time, one gets rusty and out of touch with modern thought. I don't suppose these days I could tell you the name of a single chucker-out in the whole of the West End area, and I used to know them all. That is why—'

'Now listen.'

'That is why the fact of her having packed a toothbrush and popped off to Trinidad, though it blots the sunshine from my life, is not an unrelieved tragedy. Existence may have become for me an arid waste, but let us not forget that I can now be up and doing with a heart for any fate. Notify me when you return to London, and I will be with you with my hair in a braid. Bless my soul, how young I'm feeling these days! It must be the weather.'

Pongo knocked the ash off his cigar and took a sip of brandy. There was a cold, stern look on his face.

'Now listen, Uncle Fred,' he said, and his voice was like music to the ears of the Recording Angel, who felt that this was going to be good. 'All that stuff is out.'

'Out?'

'Right out. You don't get me to the dog races again.'

'I did not specify the dog races. Though they provide an admirable means of studying the soul of the people.'

'Or on any other frightful binge of yours. Get thou behind me, about sums it up. If you come to see me in London, you will get lunch at my flat and afterwards a good book. Nothing more.'

Lord Ickenham sighed, and was silent for a space. He was musing on the curse of wealth. In the old days, when Pongo had been an impecunious young fellow reading for the Bar and attempting at intervals to get into an uncle's ribs for an occasional much-needed fiver, nobody could have been a more sympathetic companion along the primrose path. But coming into money seemed to have changed him completely. The old, old story, felt Lord Ickenham.

'Oh, very well,' he said. 'If that is how you feel—'

'It is,' Pongo assured him. 'Make a note of it on your cuff. And it's no good saying "Ichabod," because I intend to stick to my position with iron resolution. My standing with Hermione is none too secure as it is—she looks askance at my belonging to the Drones—and the faintest breath of scandal would dish me properly. And most unfortunately she knows all about you.'

'My life is an open book.'

'She has heard what a loony you are, and she seems to think it may be hereditary. "I hope you are not like your uncle," she keeps saying, with a sort of brooding look in her eye.'

'You must have misunderstood her. "I hope you *are* like your uncle," she probably said. Or "Do try, darling, to be more like your uncle."'

'Consequently I shall have to watch my step like a ruddy hawk. Let her get the slightest suspicion into her nut that I am not one hundred per cent steady and serious, and bim will go my chances of putting on the spongebag trousers and walking down the aisle with her.'

'Then you would not consider the idea of my coming to Ashenden as your valet, and seeing what innocent fun we could whack out of the deception?'

'My God!'

'Merely a suggestion. And it couldn't be done, anyway. It would involve shaving off my moustache, to which I am greatly attached. When a man has neither chick nor child, he gets very fond of a moustache. So she's that sort of girl, is she?'

'What do you mean, that sort of girl?'

'Noble-minded. High principled. A credit to British womanhood.'

'Oh, rather. Yes, she's terrific. Must be seen to be believed.'

'I look forward to seeing her.'

'I have a photograph here, if you would care to take a dekko,' said Pongo, producing one of cabinet size from his breast pocket like a conjurer extracting a rabbit from a top hat.

Lord Ickenham took the photograph, and studied it for some moments.

'A striking face.'

'Don't miss the eyes.'

'I've got 'em.'

'The nose, also.'

'I've got that, too. She looks intelligent.'

'And how. Writes novels.'

'Good God!'

A monstrous suspicion had germinated in Pongo's mind.

'Don't you like her?' he asked incredulously.

'Well, I'll tell you,' said Lord Ickenham, feeling his way carefully. 'I can see she's a remarkable girl, but I wouldn't say she was the wife for you.'

'Why not?'

'In my opinion you will be giving away too much weight. Have you studied these features? That chin is a determined chin. Those eyes are flashing eyes.'

'What's the matter with flashing eyes?'

'Dashed unpleasant things to have about the home. To cope with flashing eyes, you have to be a man of steel and ginger. Are you a man of steel and ginger? No. You're like me, a gentle coffee-caddie.'

'A how much?'

'By a coffee-caddie I mean a man—and there is no higher type—whose instinct it is to carry his wife's breakfast up to her room on a tray each morning and bill and coo with her as she wades into it. And what the coffee-caddie needs is not a female novelist with a firm chin and flashing eyes, but a jolly little soul who, when he bills, will herself bill like billy-o, and who will be right there with bells on when he starts to coo. The advice I give to every young man starting out to seek a life partner is to find a girl whom he can tickle. Can you see yourself tickling

Hermione Bostock? She would draw herself to her full height and say "Sir!" The ideal wife for you, of course, would have been Sally Painter.'

At the mention of this name, as so often happens when names from the dead past bob up in conversation, Pongo's face became mask-like and a thin coating of ice seemed to form around him. A more sensitive man than Lord Ickenham would have sent for his winter woollies.

'Does Coggs suffer from bunions?' he said distantly. 'I thought he was walking as if he had trouble with his feet.'

'Ever since she came to England,' proceeded Lord Ickenham, refusing to be lured from the subject into realms of speculation, however fascinating, 'I have always hoped that you and Sally would eventually form a merger. And came a day when you apprised me that the thing was on. And then, dammit,' he went on, raising his voice a little in his emotion, 'came another day when you apprised me that it was off. And why, having succeeded in getting engaged to a girl like Sally Painter, you were mad enough to sever relations, is more than I can understand. It was all your fault, I suppose?'

Pongo had intended to maintain a frigid silence until the distasteful subject should have blown over, but this unjust charge shook him out of his proud reserve.

'It wasn't anything of the bally kind. Perhaps you will allow me to place the facts before you.'

'I wish you would. It's about time someone did. I could get nothing out of Sally.'

'You've seen her, then?'

'She came down here with Otis a couple of weeks ago and left one of her busts in my charge. I don't know why. That's it, over there in the corner.'

Pongo gave the bust a brief and uninterested glance.

'And she didn't place the facts before you?'

'She said the engagement was off, which I knew already, but nothing more.'

'Oh? Well,' said Pongo, breathing heavily through the nostrils as he viewed the body of the dead past, 'what happened was this. Just because I wouldn't do something she wanted me to do, she called me a lily-livered poltroon.'

'She probably meant it as a compliment. A lily liver must be very pretty.'

'High words ensued. I said so-and-so, and she said such-and-such. And later that evening ring, letters and all the fixings were returned by district messenger boy.'

'A mere lovers' tiff. I should have thought you would have made it up next day.'

'Well, we jolly well didn't. As a matter of fact, that lily-livered sequence was simply what put the lid on it. We had been getting in each other's hair for some time before that and there was bound to be a smash-up sooner or later.'

'What were the principal subjects of disagreement?'

'For one thing, that damned brother of hers. He makes me sick.'

'Otis isn't everybody's money, I admit. He's a publisher now, Sally tells me. I suppose he will make as big a mess of that as he did of his antique shop. Did you tell her he made you sick?'

'Yes. She got a bit steamed up about it. And then there was more trouble because I wanted her to chuck being a sculptress.'

'Why didn't you like her being a sculptress?'

'I hated her mixing with all that seedy crowd in Chelsea. Bounders with beards,' said Pongo, with an austere shudder. 'I've been in her studio sometimes, and the blighters were crawling out of the woodwork in hundreds, bearded to the eyebrows.'

Lord Ickenham drew thoughtfully at his cigar.

'I was mistaken in saying that you were not a man of steel and ginger. You appear to have thrown your weight about like a sheikh.'

'Well, she threw her weight about with me. She was always trying to boss me.'

'Girls do. Especially American girls. I know, because I married one. It's part of their charm.'

'Well, there's a limit.'

'And with you that was reached—how? You had started to tell me. What was it she wanted you to do?'

'Take some jewellery with me when I went to New York and smuggle it through the customs.'

'Bless her heart, what an enterprising little soul she is. But since when has Sally possessed jewellery?'

'It wasn't for her, it was for one of her rich American pals, a girl named Alice something. This ass of a female had been loading herself up with the stuff in and around Bond Street and didn't like the idea of paying duty on it when she got back to New York, and Sally wanted me to run it through for her.'

'A kindly thought.'

'A fatheaded thought. And so I told her. A nice chump I should have looked, being disembowelled by port officials.'

Lord Ickenham sighed.

'I see. Well, I'm sorry. A wealthy husband like you would have come in very handy for Sally. I'm afraid that girl is on the rocks.'

Pongo's lower jaw dropped a notch. Love might be dead, but he had a feeling heart.

'Oh, I say!'

'I don't believe she gets enough to eat.'

'What rot!'

'It isn't rot. She seemed thin to me, and I didn't like the way she tucked into the lamb and green peas, as if she hadn't had a square meal for weeks. There can't be a fortune in sculping, if that's the right verb. Who the dickens buys clay busts?'

'Oh, that's all right,' said Pongo, relieved. 'She doesn't depend on her sculping. She's got a little bit of money an aunt in Kansas City left her.'

'I know. But I'm wondering whether something hasn't gone wrong with that sheet anchor. It's two years since she came to London to join Otis. He may have wheedled it out of her. A chap like Otis can do a lot in two years.'

'Sally's got too much sense.'

'The most level-headed girls often prove perfect mugs where a loved brother is concerned. At any rate, in answer to a recent communication of mine telling her that I hoped shortly to be in London and would like her to keep an evening free for dinner I got a letter saying she was glad I was coming up, because she wanted to see me on a very urgent matter. She underlined the "very". I didn't like the ring of that statement. It was the sort of thing you used to write to me in the old days, when you were having a passing unpleasantness with your bookie and hoped to float a small loan. Well, I shall be seeing her to-morrow, and I will institute a probe. Poor little Sally, I hope to God she's all right. What an admirable girl she is.'

'Yes.'

'You still feel that, do you?'

'Oh, rather. I'm frightfully fond of Sally. I tried to do her a bit of good just before I left for America. Hermione told me old Bostock wanted a bust of himself, to present to the village club, and I got her to put him on to Sally. I thought she might be glad of the commish.'

'Well, well. An impulsive girl would be touched by a thing like that. Yes, indeed. "The whitest man I know," one can hear her saying. I believe, if you played your cards right, you could still marry her, Pongo.'

'Aren't you overlooking the trifling fact that I happen to be engaged to Hermione?'

'Slide out of it.'

'Ha!'

'It is what your best friends would advise. You are a moody, introspective young man, all too prone to look on the dark side of things. I shall never forget you that day at the dog races. Sombre is the only word to describe your attitude as the cop's fingers closed on your coat collar. You reminded me of Hamlet. What you need is a jolly, lively wife to take you out of yourself, the sort of wife who would set booby traps for the Bishop when he came to spend the night. I don't suppose this Hermione Bostock of yours ever made so much as an apple-pie bed in her life. I'd give her a miss. Send her an affectionate telegram saying you've changed your mind and it's all off. I have a telegraph form in my study.'

A look of intense devoutness came over Pongo's face.

'For your information, Uncle Fred, wild horses wouldn't make me break my engagement.'

'Most unlikely they'll ever try.'

'I worship that girl. There's nothing I wouldn't do for her. Well, to give you a rough idea, I told her I was a teetotaller. And why? Purely because she happened one day to express the hope that I wasn't like so many of these modern young suction pumps, always dropping in at bars and lowering a couple for the tonsils. "Me?" I said. "Good Lord, no. I never touch the stuff." That'll show you.'

'So when you get to Ashenden—'

'—They'll uncork the barley water and bring on the lemonade. I know. I've foreseen that. It'll be agony, but I can take it. For her sake. I worship her, I tell you. If H. Bostock isn't an angel in human shape, then I don't know an angel in human shape when I see one. Until now I have never known what love was.'

'Well, you have had ample opportunity of finding out. I have watched you with the tender solicitude through about fifty-seven romances, starting with that freckled child with the missing front tooth at the dancing class, who blacked your eye with a wooden dumb-bell when you kissed her in the cloakroom, and ending with this—'

Lord Ickenham paused, and Pongo eyed him narrowly.

'Well? This what?'

'This gruesome combination of George Eliot, Boadicea and the late Mrs Carrie Nation,' said Lord Ickenham. 'This flashing-eyed governess. This twenty-minute egg with whom no prudent man would allow himself to walk alone down a dark alley.'

It was enough. Pongo rose, a dignified figure.

'Shall we join the ladies?' he said coldly.

'There aren't any,' said Lord Ickenham.

'I don't know why I said that,' said Pongo, annoyed. 'What I meant was, let's stop talking bally rot and go and have a game of billiards.'

# 3

## · 1 ·

It was with a light heart and a gay tra-la-la on his lips that Pongo Twistleton set out for Ashenden Manor on the following afternoon, leaving Lord Ickenham, who was not embarking on his metropolitan jaunt till a few hours later, waving benevolently from the front steps.

Nothing so braces a young man in love as the consciousness of having successfully resisted a Tempter who has tried to lure him into a course of action of which the adored object would not approve: and as he recalled the splendid firmness with which he had tied the can to his Uncle Fred's suggestion of a pleasant and instructive afternoon in London, Pongo felt spiritually uplifted.

Pleasant and instructive afternoon, forsooth! Few people have ever come nearer to saying 'Faugh!' than did Pongo as Lord Ickenham's phrase shot through his wincing mind like some loathsome serpent. The crust of the old buster, daring to suggest pleasant and instructive afternoons to a man who had put that sort of thing behind him once and for all. With a shudder of distaste he thrust the whole degrading episode into the hinterland of his consciousness, and turned his thoughts to a more agreeable theme, the coming meeting with Hermione's parents.

This, he was convinced, was going to be a riot from the word Go. He had little data about these two old geezers, of course, but he presumed that they were intelligent old geezers, able to spot a good man when they saw one, and it seemed, accordingly, pretty obvious that a fellow like himself—steady, upright, impervious to avuncular wheedlings and true blue from soup to nuts—would have them eating out of his hand in the first minute. 'My dear, he's *charming*!' they would write to Hermione, and bluff Sir Aylmer, whom he pictured as a sort of modern Cheeryble Brother, would say to Lady Bostock (gentle, sweet- faced, motherly), as they toddled up to bed at the conclusion of a delightful first evening, 'Gad, my dear, nothing much wrong with *that* young chap, what?'—or possibly 'What, what?' He looked forward with bright confidence to grappling them to his soul with hoops of steel.

It was consequently with some annoyance that he found on reaching his destination that there was going to be a slight delay before this desirable state of affairs could be consummated. The first essential preliminary to grappling a householder and his wife to your soul with hoops of steel is that you should be able to get into the house they are holding, and this, he discovered, presented unforeseen difficulties.

Ashenden Manor was one of those solidly built edifices which date from the days when a home was not so much a place for putting on the old slippers and lighting the pipe, as a fortress to be defended against uncouth intruders with battering rams. Its front door was stout and massive, and at the moment tightly closed. Furthermore, the bell appeared to be out of order. He leaned against the button with his full weight for a while, but it soon became clear that this was going to get him nowhere, and the necessity of taking alternative action presented itself.

It was at this point that he observed not far from where he stood an open French window, and it seemed to him that he had found a formula. A bit irregular, perhaps, to start your first visit to a place by strolling in through windows, but a kindly, hearty old boy like Sir Aylmer Bostock would overlook that. Abandoning the front door, accordingly, as a lost cause, he stepped through, and an instant later was experiencing the unpleasant shock which always came to people who found themselves for the first time in the room where the ex-Governor kept the African curios which he had collected during his years of honourable exile. Sir Aylmer Bostock's collection of African curios was probably the most hideous, futile and valueless that even an ex-Governor had ever brought home with him, and many of its items seemed to take Pongo into a different and a dreadful world.

And he had picked up and started to scrutinize the nearest to hand, a peculiar sort of what-not executed in red mud by an artist apparently under the influence of trade gin, and was wondering why even an untutored African should have been chump enough to waste on an effort like this hours which might have been more profitably employed in chasing crocodiles or beaning the neighbours with his knobkerrie, when a voice, having in it many of the qualities of the Last Trump, suddenly split the air.

'REGINALD!'

Starting violently, Pongo dropped the what-not. It crashed to the floor and became a mere *macédoine*. A moment later, a burly figure appeared in the doorway, preceded by a large white moustache.

## • II •

At about the moment when Pongo at Ickenham Hall was springing to the wheel of his Buffy-Porson and pressing a shapely foot on the self-starter, Sir Aylmer Bostock had gone to his wife's bedroom on the first floor of Ashenden Manor to mend a broken slat in the Venetian blind. He was a man who liked to attend to these little domestic chores himself, and he wanted to have it ready when the midday train brought Lady Bostock back from London, where she had been spending a week with her daughter Hermione.

In predicting that this old schoolmate of his would feel chagrined at Bill Oakshott's failure to co-operate in the civic welcome which he had gone to such trouble to arrange for him, Lord Ickenham had shown sound judgment of character. When an ex-Governor, accustomed for years to seeing his official receptions go like clockwork, tastes in a black hour the bitterness of failure and anti-climax, pique is bound to supervene. Fists will be clenched, oaths breathed, lower lips bitten. And this is particularly so if the ex-Governor is one whose mental attitude, even under the most favourable conditions, resembles, as did Sir Aylmer Bostock's, that of a trapped cinnamon bear. As he worked, his brow was dark, his moustache bristling, and from time to time he snorted in a quiet undertone.

He yearned for his wife's company, so that he could pour into her always receptive ear the story of his wrongs, and soon after he had put the finishing touches to the broken slat he got it. A cab drove up to the front door, and presently Lady Bostock appeared, a woman in the late forties who looked like a horse.

'Oh, there you are, dear,' she said brightly. In conversation with her consort she was nearly always obliged to provide brightness enough for both of them. She paused, sniffing. 'What a curious smell there is in here.'

Sir Aylmer frowned. He resented criticism, even of his smells.

'Glue,' he said briefly. 'I've been mending the blind.'

'Oh, how clever of you, darling. Thank you so much,' said Lady Bostock, brighter than ever. 'Well, I suppose you thought I was never coming back. It's lovely to be home again. London was terribly stuffy. I thought Hermione was looking very well. She sent all sorts of messages to you and Reginald. Has he arrived yet?'

On the point of asking who the devil Reginald was, Sir Aylmer remembered that his daughter had recently become betrothed to some young pot of cyanide answering to that name. He replied that Reginald had not yet arrived.

'Hermione said he was coming to-day.'

'Well, he hasn't.'

'Has he wired?'

'No.'

'I suppose he forgot.'

'Silly fatheaded young poop,' said Sir Aylmer.

Lady Bostock regarded him anxiously. She seemed to sense in his manner an anti-Reginald bias, and she knew his work. He was capable, she was aware, when in anything like shape, of reducing young men who had failed to arouse his enthusiasm to spots of grease in a matter of minutes, and she was intensely desirous that no such disaster should occur on the present occasion. Hermione, seeing her off at Waterloo, had issued definite instructions that her loved one, while at Ashenden Manor, was to enjoy the status of an ewe lamb, and Hermione was a girl whom it did not do to cross. She expected people to carry out her wishes, and those who knew what was good for them invariably did so.

Recalling all the timid young aides-de-camp whom she had seen curling up at the edges like scorched paper beneath his glare during those long and happy years in Lower Barnatoland, she gazed at her husband pleadingly.

'You will be nice to Reginald, dear, won't you?'

'I am always nice.'

'I don't want him to complain to Hermione about his unwelcome. You know what she is like.'

A thoughtful silence fell, as they allowed their minds to dwell on what Hermione was like. Lady Bostock broke it on a note of hope.

'You may become the greatest friends.'

'Bah!'

'Hermione says he is delightful.'

'Probably the usual young pest with brilliantined hair and a giggle,' said Sir Aylmer morosely, refusing to look for the silver lining and try to find the sunny side of life. 'It's bad enough having William around. Add Reginald, and existence will become a hell.'

His words reminded Lady Bostock that there was a topic on which an affectionate aunt ought to have touched earlier.

'William has arrived, then?'

'Yes. Oh, yes, he's arrived.'

'I hope the reception went off well. Such a good idea, I thought, when you told me about it. How surprised he must have been. It's so fortunate that he should have come back in good time for the fête. He is always so useful, looking after the sports. Where is he?'

'I don't know. Dead, I hope . . .'

'Aylmer! What do you mean?'

Sir Aylmer had not snorted since his wife's return and now it was as if all the snorts he might have been snorting had coalesced into one stupendous burst of sound. It was surprising that Pongo, at that moment driving in through the main gates, did not hear it and think one of his tyres had gone.

'I'll tell you what I mean. Do you know what that young hound did? Didn't get out at Ashenden Oakshott. Remained skulking in the train, went on to Bishop's Ickenham and turned up hours later in a car belonging to Lord Ickenham, stewed to the gills.'

One hastens to protest that this was a complete mis-statement, attributable solely to prejudice and bitterness of spirit. Considering that he had arrived there reeling beneath the blow of the discovery that the girl he loved was betrothed to another, Bill Oakshott had comported himself at Lord Ickenham's residence with the most exemplary abstemiousness. In a situation where many men would have started lowering the stuff by the pailful, this splendid young fellow had exercised an iron self-control. One fairly quick, followed by another rather slower, and he had been through.

It is true that on encountering his uncle his manner had been such as to give rise to misunderstanding, but something of this kind is bound to happen when a nervous young man meets an incandescent senior, of whom he has always stood in awe, knowing that it is he who has brought him to the boil. In such circumstances the face inevitably becomes suffused and the limbs start twitching, even if the subject is a lifelong abstainer.

So much for this monstrous charge.

Lady Bostock made that clicking noise, like a wet finger touching hot iron, which women use as a substitute for the masculine 'Well, I'll be damned!'

'A car belonging to Lord Ickenham?'

'Yes.'

'But how did he come to be in a car belonging to Lord Ickenham?'

'They appear to have met on the train.'

'Oh, I see. I was wondering, because we don't know him.'

'I used to, forty years ago. We were at school together. Haven't seen him since, thank God. He's a lunatic.'

'I have always heard that he was very eccentric.' Lady Bostock paused, listening. 'Hark. There's a car driving up. It must be Reginald. You had better go down.'

'I won't go down,' said Sir Aylmer explosively. 'Blast Reginald. Let him cool his heels for a bit. I'm going to finish telling you about William.'

'Yes, dear. Do, dear. He does seem to have behaved most oddly. Had he any explanation?'

'Oh, he had his story all ready, trust him for that. Said he went to sleep and woke up to find himself at Bishop's Ickenham. I didn't swallow a word of it. What happened, obviously, was that on seeing the preparations made for his reception he lost his nerve and remained in the train, the young toad, leaving me to get the Vicar, his wife, a Silver Band, ten Boy Scouts and fourteen members of the Infants' Bible Class back to their homes without any of them starting a riot. And let me tell you it was a very near thing once or twice. Those Bible Class infants were in ugly mood.'

'It must have been dreadfully disappointing for you all.'

'That's not the worst of it. It has probably lost me hundreds of votes.'

'Oh, but, dear, why? It wasn't your fault.'

'What does that matter? People don't reason. The news of a fiasco like that flies all over the county. One man tells another, it gets about that I have been placed in a ridiculous position, and the voters lose confidence in me. And nothing to be done about it. That is the bitter thought. You can't put a fellow of William's age and size across your knee and get at him with the back of a hairbrush . . . COME IN.'

There had been a knock on the door. It was followed by the entry of Jane, the parlourmaid.

'Your ladyship is wanted on the telephone, m'lady,' said Jane, who believed in respect to the titled. 'It's the Vicar, m'lady.'

'Thank you, Jane. I will come at once.'

'And I,' said Sir Aylmer with a weary snort, 'had better go and welcome this blasted Reginald, I suppose.'

'You won't forget about Hermione?'

'No, I won't forget about Hermione,' said Sir Aylmer moodily. He did not waver in his view that his daughter's future husband was bound to be a deleterious slab of damnation like all other young men nowadays, but if Hermione desired it he was prepared to coo to him like a turtle dove; or as nearly like a turtle dove as was within the scope of one whose vocal delivery was always rather reminiscent of a bad-tempered toastmaster.

He made his way to the drawing-room, and finding it empty was for a moment baffled. But ex-Governors are quick-thinking men, trained to deal with emergencies. When an ex-Governor, seeking a Twistleton, arrives in the drawing-room where that Twistleton ought to be and finds no Twistleton there, he does not stand twiddling his thumbs and wondering what to do. He inflates his lungs and shouts.

'REGINALD!' thundered Sir Aylmer.

It seemed to him, as the echoes died away, that he could hear the sound of movements in the collection room across the hall. He went thither, and poked his head in.

It was as he had suspected. Something, presumably of a Twistletonian nature, was standing there. He crossed the threshold, and these two representatives of the older and the younger generation were enabled to see each other steadily and see each other whole.

On both sides the reaction to the scrutiny was unfavourable. Pongo, gazing apprehensively at the rugged face with its top dressing of moustache, was thinking that this Bostock, so far from being the kindly Dickens character of his dreams, was without exception the hardest old gumboil he had ever encountered in a career by no means free from gumboils of varying hardness: while Sir Aylmer, drinking Pongo in from his lemon-coloured hair to his clocked socks and suede shoes, was feeling how right he had been in anticipating that his future son-in-law would be a pot of cyanide and a deleterious young slab of damnation. He could see at a glance that he was both.

However, he had come there grimly resolved to coo like a turtle dove, so he cooed.

'Oh, there you are. Reginald Twistleton?'

'That's right. Twistleton, Reginald.'

'H'ar yer?' roared Sir Aylmer like a lion which has just received an ounce of small shot in the rear quarters while slaking its thirst at a water hole, though, if questioned, he would have insisted that he was still cooing. 'Glad to see yer, Reginald. My wife will be down in a moment. What you doing in here?'

'I was having a look at these—er—objects.'

'My collection of African curios. It's priceless.'

'Really? How priceless!'

'You won't find many collections like that. Took me ten years to get it together. You interested in African curios?'

'Oh, rather. I love 'em.'

The right note had been struck. A sort of writhing movement behind his moustache showed that Sir Aylmer was smiling, and in another moment who knows what beautiful friendship might not have begun to blossom. Unfortunately, however, before the burgeoning process could set in, Sir Aylmer's eye fell on the remains of the what-not and the smile vanished from his face like breath off a razor blade, to be replaced by a scowl of such malignity that Pongo had the illusion that his interior organs were being scooped out with a spade or trowel.

'Gorbl . . . !' he cried, apparently calling on some tribal god. 'How the . . . What the . . . Did *you* do that?'

'Er, yes,' said Pongo, standing on one leg. 'Frightfully sorry.'

Sir Aylmer, not without some justice, asked what was the use of being sorry, and Pongo, following his reasoning, said Yes, he saw what he meant, supplementing the words with a nervous giggle.

Many people do not like nervous giggles. Sir Aylmer was one of them. On several occasions in the old days he had had to mention this to his aides-de-camp. Not even the thought of his daughter Hermione could restrain him from bestowing on Pongo a second scowl, compared with which its predecessor had been full of loving kindness. He lowered himself to the ground, and, crouched on all fours over the remains like Marius among the ruins of Carthage, began to mutter beneath his breath about young fools and clumsy idiots. Pongo could not catch his remarks in their entirety, but he heard enough to give him the general idea.

He gulped pallidly. A sticky moisture had begun to bedew his brow, as if he had entered the hot room of some Turkish bath of the soul. Governesses in his childhood and schoolmasters in his riper years had sometimes spoken slightingly of his I.Q., but he was intelligent enough to realize that on this visit of his, where it was so vital for him to make a smash hit with Hermione's parents, he had got off to a poor start.

It was as Sir Aylmer rose and began to say that the what-not had been the very gem and pearl of his collection and that he wouldn't have parted with it for a hundred pounds, no, not if the intending purchaser had gone on his bended knees to add emphasis to the offer, that there was a whirring sound without, indicating that some solid body was passing down the hall at a high rate of m.p.h. The next moment, Lady Bostock entered, moving tempestuously.

From Lady Bostock's aspect only Sherlock Holmes, perhaps, would have been able to deduce that she had just heard from the Vicar over the telephone that the curate was down with measles, but even Doctor Watson could have seen that her soul had in some way been badly jolted. So moved was she that, though a polished hostess, she paid no attention to Pongo, who was now standing on the other leg.

'Aylmer!'

'Well?'

'Aylmer . . . The Vicar . . .'

'WELL?'

'The Vicar says Mr Brotherhood has got measles. He wants us to go and see him at once.'

'Who the devil's Mr Brotherhood?'

'The curate. You know Mr Brotherhood, the curate. That nice young man with the pimples. He has gone and got measles, and I was relying on him to judge the babies.'

'What babies?'

'The bonny babies. At the fête.'

A word about this fête. It was the high spot of Ashenden Oakshott's social year, when all that was bravest and fairest in the village assembled in the Manor grounds and made various kinds of whoopee. Races were run, country dances danced, bonny babies judged in order of merit in the big tent and tea and buns consumed in almost incredible quantities. Picture a blend of the Derby and a garden party at Buckingham Palace, add Belshazzar's Feast, and you have the Ashenden Oakshott Fête.

One can readily appreciate, therefore, Lady Bostock's concern at the disaster which had occurred. A Lady of the manor, with an important fête coming along and the curate in bed with measles, is in the distressing position of an impresario whose star fails him a couple of days before the big production or a general whose crack regiment gets lumbago on the eve of battle.

'It's terrible. Dreadful. I can't think who I can get to take his place.'

Sir Aylmer, who believed in having a thorough understanding about these things at the earliest possible moment, said he was dashed if he was going to do it, and Lady Bostock said No, no, dear, she wouldn't dream of asking him.

'But I must find somebody.' Lady Bostock's eye, rolling in a fine frenzy from heaven to earth, from earth to heaven, picked on Pongo, now back on the leg he had started with, and she stared at him dazedly, like one seeing unpleasant things in a dream. 'Are you Reginald?' she said distractedly.

The emotional scene, following upon his chat with Sir Aylmer about what-nots, had left Pongo in a condition of such mental turmoil that for an instant he was not quite sure. Reginald? Was he Reginald? Was Reginald a likely thing for anyone to be? . . . Why, yes, of course. The woman was perfectly correct.

'Yes, I'm Reginald.'

'How nice to meet you at last,' wailed Lady Bostock like a soul in torment.

It is never easy off-hand to find the ideal reply to such an observation. Discarding 'Yes!' as too complacent and 'What ho!' as too familiar, and not being fortunate enough to think of 'I've been looking forward so much to meeting *you*,' Pongo contented himself with another of his nervous giggles.

A sudden light came into Lady Bostock's haggard eyes.

'Have you ever judged bonny babies, Reginald?'

'Me?' said Pongo, reeling.

Before he could speak further, an angel, in the very effective disguise of Sir Aylmer, intervened to save him from the ghastly peril which had so suddenly risen to confront him.

'You don't want Reginald,' he said, and Pongo, who a moment earlier would have scoffed at the suggestion that it would ever be possible for him to want to leap at his host and kiss him on both cheeks, was conscious of a powerful urge in that direction. 'I'll tell you who gets the job.'

After uttering the words 'I'm dashed if I'm going to do it' and receiving his wife's reassuring reply, Sir Aylmer had fallen into a silence, as if musing or pondering, and it was plain now that the brain work on which he had been engaged had borne fruit. His manner had become animated, and in his eye, which, resting upon Pongo, had been dull and brooding, there was a triumphant gleam.

It was a gleam which might have puzzled an untravelled beholder, but anybody who had ever seen a Corsican feudist suddenly presented with the opportunity of wreaking a sinister vengeance on a family foe would have recognized it immediately. It was that strange, almost unearthly light which comes into the eyes of wronged uncles when they see a chance of getting a bit of their own back from erring nephews.

'I'll tell you who gets the job,' he repeated. 'William.'

'William?'

'William,' said Sir Aylmer, rolling the word round his tongue like vintage port.

Lady Bostock stared.

'But William . . . Surely, dear . . . The very last person . . .'

'William.'

'But he would hate it.'

'William.'

'You know how terribly shy he is.'

'William. I don't want any argument, Emily. It's no good you standing there blinding and stiffing. William judges the bonny babies. I insist. Perhaps now he'll be sorry he skulked in trains and went on toots with old Ickenham.'

Lady Bostock sighed. But a habit of obsequiousness which had started at the altar rails was too strong for her.

'Very well, dear.'

'Good. Tell him when you see him. Meanwhile, you say, the Vicar wants us to go down to the vicarage and confer with him. Right. I'll drive you in the car. Come along.'

He darted through the French windows, followed by Lady Bostock, and after a few moments occupied in mopping his forehead with the handkerchief which so perfectly matched his tie and socks, Pongo followed them.

He felt he needed air. A similar sensation had often come to sensitive native chiefs at the conclusion of an interview with Sir Aylmer Bostock on the subject of unpaid hut taxes.

Sunshine and the pure Hampshire breezes playing about his temples soon did wonders in the way of restoring him to the normal. Presently, feeling almost himself again, he returned to the house, and, as always happened with those who had once seen Sir Aylmer's collection of African curios, there came over him a morbid urge to take another look at these weird exhibits, to ascertain whether they really looked as frightful as they had appeared at first sight. He passed through the French window into the collection room, and a pink policeman, who had been bicycling dreamily up the drive, uttered a sharp 'Ho!' and accelerated his pace, his eyes hard and his jaw protruding belligerently.

The policeman's name was Harold Potter. He represented the awful majesty of the Law in Ashenden Oakshott. His pinkness was due to the warmth of the weather, and he was dreamy because he had been musing on Elsie Bean, the Manor housemaid, to whom he was affianced.

It was in order to enjoy a chat with Elsie Bean that he had come here, and until he turned the corner and was in view of the house his thoughts had been all of love. But at the sight of furtive forms slinking in through French windows Potter, the Romeo, became in a flash Potter, the sleepless guardian of the peace. His substantial feet pressed on the pedals like those of a racing cyclist.

It looked to Harold Potter like a fair cop.

And so it came about that Pongo, his opinion of the intelligence of African natives now even lower than before, was disturbed in his contemplation of their fatuous handiwork by the sound of emotional breathing in his rear. He spun round, to find himself gazing into the steely eyes of a large policeman with a ginger moustache.

'Ho!' he cried, startled.

'Ho!' said Constable Potter, like an echo in the Swiss mountains.

## · III ·

It would be idle to pretend that the situation was not one of some embarrassment. It belonged to the type which would have enchanted Lord Ickenham, who enjoyed nothing better than these little variations in the calm monotone of life, but it brought Pongo out from head to foot in a sort of prickly heat.

Unlike most of his lighthearted companions of the Drones Club, who rather made pets of policemen, tipping them when in funds and stealing their helmets on Boat Race night, Pongo had always had a horror of the Force. That sombreness of his on the day at the dog races, for which Lord Ickenham had reproached him, had been occasioned by the fact that a member of that Force, who might have been this one's twin brother, had been attached to his coat collar and advising him to come quietly.

He smiled a weak smile.

'Oh, hullo,' he said.

'Hullo,' replied Constable Potter coldly. 'What's all this?'

'What's all what?'

'What are you doing on these enclosed premises?'

'I've been invited here for a brief visit.'

'Ho!'

It seemed to Pongo that he was not making headway. The situation, sticky at the outset, appeared to be growing progressively stickier. He was relieved, accordingly, when a third party arrived to break up the *tête-à-tête*.

This was a small, sturdy girl of resolute appearance with blue eyes and a turned-up nose, clad in the uniform of a housemaid. She regarded with interest the picture in still life before her.

'Hullo,' she said. 'Where did you spring from, Harold? And who's this?'

'Chap I've apprehended on enclosed premises,' said Constable Potter briefly.

Pongo, who had been dabbing at his forehead, waved his handkerchief in passionate protest against this too professional view.

'What's all this rot about enclosed premises?' he demanded with spirit. 'I resent the way, officer, you keep chewing the fat about enclosed premises. Why shouldn't I be on enclosed premises, when specially invited? Here, you, what's your name, my dear old housemaid—'

'Miss Bean, my fiancée,' said Constable Potter, frigidly doing the honours.

'Oh, really? Heartiest congratulations. Pip-pip, Miss Bean.'

'Toodle-oo.'

'I hope you'll be very, very happy. Well, what I was going to say was that you will be able to bear me out that I'm a guest at this joint. I've just arrived in my car to spend a few days. I'm the celebrated Twistleton, the bird who's engaged to Miss Bostock. You must know all about me. No doubt the place has been ringing with my name.'

'Miss Hermione is engaged to a gentleman named Twistleton.'

'Exactly.'

'And Jane heard them saying at dinner that he was expected here, Harold. I believe this is him.'

'Well spoken, young Bean,' said Pongo with enthusiasm. He had taken an immediate liking to this clear-reasoning girl. 'Of course I'm him. Look,' said Pongo, turning back the pocket of his coat. 'Read this definite statement by one of the most reputable tailors in London. "R. G. Twistleton." There you are, in black and white.'

'It could be somebody else's coat that you'd bought second hand,' argued Constable Potter, fighting in the last ditch.

Pongo gave him a look.

'Don't say such things even in jest, officer. Rather,' he said with a sudden flash of inspiration, 'ring up the Vicar and ask for Sir Aylmer, who is in conference with him on the subject of bonny babies, and put it squarely up to the latter—Sir Aylmer, I mean, not the bonny babies—whether he didn't leave me here only a few moments ago after a pleasant and invigorating chat.'

'You mean you've met Sir Aylmer?'

'Of course I've met Sir Aylmer. We're just like that.'

Constable Potter seemed reluctantly convinced.

'Well, I suppose it's all right, then. I beg your pardon, sir.'

'Quite all right, officer.'

'Then I'll be saying good afternoon, sir. How about a pot of tea in the kitchen, Elsie?'

Elsie Bean elevated her small nose.

'You can go to the kitchen, if you like. Not me. Your sister's there, calling on cook.'

'Ho!' Constable Potter stood for a moment in thought. The conflicting claims of tea and a loved one's society were plainly warring within him. One is sorry to report that the former prevailed. 'Well, I think I'll mooch along and have a cup,' he said, and mooched, as foreshadowed.

Elsie Bean looked after his retreating blue back with a frown.

'You and your sister!' she said.

The note of acerbity in her voice was so manifest that Pongo could not help but be intrigued. Here, he told himself, or he was very much mistaken, was a housemaid with a secret sorrow. He stopped mopping his forehead and cocked an inquiring eye at Elsie Bean.

'Don't you like his sister?'

'No, I don't.'

'Well, if there's any sort of family resemblance, I can fully comprehend,' said Pongo. With Constable Potter's departure Ashenden Manor seemed to him to have become a sweeter, better place. 'Why don't you like his sister? What's the matter with her?'

Elsie Bean was a friendly little soul who, though repeatedly encouraged to do so by her employers, had never succeeded in achieving that demure aloofness which is the hallmark of the well-trained maid. Too often in her dealings with the ruling classes, in circumstances where a distant 'Yes, sir,' or 'No, madam,' would have been more suitable, you would find her becoming expansive and conversational. And on the present occasion she regarded herself as a hostess.

'I'll tell you what's the matter with her. She goes on at him about how he mustn't leave the Force. It's "Don't you do it, Harold," and "Don't you let Elsie talk you into acting against your true interests," all the time. I haven't any patience.'

Pongo concentrated tensely.

'Let me see if I've got this straight,' he said. 'You want him to turn in his boots and truncheon? To cease, in a word, to be a copper?'

'R.'

'But his sister doesn't. Yes, I get the set-up. Why do you want him to turn in his boots and truncheon?' asked Pongo. A man who has been reading for the Bar for some years gets into the way of putting the pertinent question.

Elsie Bean seemed surprised that such a question should have been considered necessary.

'Well, wouldn't you? If you was a girl, would you like to be married to a policeman? Feeling your old man was hated by all. If I went home to Bottleton East and told my family I was going to get spliced to a copper, they'd have a fit. A nice thing for my brother Bert to hear, when he comes out in September.'

Pongo nodded intelligently. Until now, having supposed his companion to be a local product, he had failed to grasp the nub, but her last words made everything clear. He could quite see how a London girl, especially a child of the notoriously rather vivacious quarter of Bottleton East, might shrink from linking her lot with that of a professional tapper on shoulders and grasper of coat collars. In addition to this brother Bert—at the moment, it appeared, unhappily no longer with us—there were no doubt a number of Uncle Herbs and Cousin Georges in her entourage who, were she to commit such a *mésalliance*, would consider, and rightly, that she had inflicted a blot on the Bean escutcheon.

'I see what you mean,' he said. 'But what could he do if he resigned his portfolio? Not easy to find jobs nowadays.'

'I want him to buy a pub. He's got three hundred pounds. He won a football pool last winter.'

'The lucky stiff.'

'But he's scared of that sister of his, and I can't persuade him. "Now, listen, Harold," I keep saying, but he just hums and haws and chews his moustache. Oh, well,' said Elsie philosophically, 'I suppose it'll all come out in the wash. What's that mess on the floor?'

'It's what's left of a sort of gadget I happened to drop.'

'Does he know about it?'

'Oh, yes. The topic came up.'

'I wonder he didn't chew your head off.'

'He did look for a moment as if he were toying with some such idea. Rather a hard nut, what?'

'He's an overbearing dishpot,' said Elsie Bean.

Pongo wandered out into the hall. He had about as much as he required of the collection of African curios for the time being, and he wanted to pace up and down and ponder. He had already formed a reasonably accurate estimate of Sir Aylmer Bostock's character, but it was interesting to find it confirmed by the woman who knew.

An overbearing dishpot? The words had a disagreeable sound. His attitude towards overbearing dishpots resembled that of his companion's circle in Bottleton East towards officers of the Law. He disliked and feared them. It began to look to him as if union with Hermione Bostock, good though it might be in itself, carried with it certain disadvantages which wanted thinking over.

'And Lady Bostock?' he said. 'She flitted only briefly through my life, but she struck me as being slightly less of a man-eater.'

'Yes, she's better than what he is,' agreed Elsie Bean. 'But the one I like is Mr William.'

'Who would he be?'

'Their nephew. Mr Oakshott.'

'Oh, ah, yes. I was forgetting. I know him, or used to. Got a pink face, hasn't he?'

'Well, I'd call it more of a tomato ketchup colour. Owing to the heat of the sun in them parts. He's just come back from Brazil. He was telling me about Brazil this morning,' said Elsie, who had lost no time in buttonholing the returned wanderer and exchanging ideas with him. 'The natives there shoot birds with poisoned darts.'

'Poisoned darts?'

'R. Through blowpipes.'

Pongo was courteous, but he could not let this pass. Though it was some time since he had boned up on his Brazil, memories of 'The Boy Explorers Up the Amazon' still lingered in his mind.

'Not poisoned darts.'

'That's what Mr William told me.'

'He was pulling your leg. They keep those for their wives' relations. Use your intelligence, my dear old housemaid. When a Brazilian native shoots a bird, he does it with a purpose. He intends to employ that bird subsequently in broiled or fricassee form. Obviously, then, if he soaked it with a poisoned dart, he would be defeating his own ends, because no sooner had he bitten into the liver wing than he would kick the bucket in awful agonies. And Brazilian natives, while they may be asses, are not silly asses. If you really want to know how they shoot birds, I will tell you. They fashion a rude sling—thus,' said Pongo, taking out his handkerchief and unfolding it. 'They then look about them for a handy projectile, as it might be this paperweight, and stuff it into the rude sling. This done, they whirl the contraption round their heads and . . . Oh, my God! Where did that one go?'

It had not been his intention to give a practical demonstration. He had planned to stop short of the actual discharge of the projectile, merely indicating its effects verbally. But artistic enthusiasm had carried him too far. A rending crash, and something white in the shadows at the end of the hall was lying in fragments.

'Coo!' said Elsie Bean, awed. 'You aren't half breaking up the home, are you? You'll catch it when His Nibs gets back.'

For the third time since he had entered this house of terror, Pongo's brow grew warm and damp. With that get-together of theirs over the broken what-not still green in his memory, it seemed to him only too sickeningly certain that he would catch it when His Nibs got back.

'What was it?' he quavered, rightly speaking of the object in the past tense.

'It's a sort of sawn-off statue like, that he had presented to him when he give up being Governor of that dog's island out in Africa that he used to be Governor of. A bust, cook says it's called. He thinks the world of it.

The other morning he happened to come along while I was giving it a bit of a dusting, and you ought to have heard him go on, just because I kind of rocked it a little. "Be careful, girl! Be careful, girl! Mind what you're doing, my good girl!" Coo!'

Pongo's brow grew damper. A stylist would now have described it as beaded. And simultaneously he found himself chilled to the bone. He was a human replica of one of those peculiar puddings which lure the diner on into supposing that he is biting into a hot *soufflé* and then suddenly turn right around and become ice-cream in the middle.

Matters were even worse, he perceived, than he had feared. This was not one of those minor breakages which get passed off with a light apology on the one side and a jolly laugh on the other. It was as if Sir Aylmer Bostock had had a favourite child on whom he doted and he, Pongo, had socked that child on the occiput and laid it out good and proper. And coming right on top of the what-not misadventure, too! What would be the effect on his temperamental host of this second and possibly even more wrath-provoking outrage?

'Golly!' he moaned, sagging at the knees. 'This is a nice bit of box fruit. Advise me, young Bean. What do I do for the best, do you think?'

It may be that Bottleton East produces an exceptionally quick-witted type of girl, or perhaps all women are like that. At any rate, Elsie Bean, with scarcely a pause for thought, provided the solution hot off the griddle.

'Well, look,' she said. 'It's kind of dark in that corner, so maybe he won't miss his old bust for a bit. He's short-sighted, I know, and he won't wear specs because he thinks they'd make him look silly. Jane heard them talking about it at dinner. If I was you, I'd hop into that car of yours and drive lickerty-split to London and get another bust. And then you drive back and stick it up. Ten to one he won't notice nothing.'

For an instant Pongo's numbed brain was incapable of following her reasoning. Then the mists cleared, and he saw that it was red-hot stuff. This girl had found the way.

Drive lickerty-split to London? No need to do that. He could procure the substitute a dashed sight nearer than London. At Ickenham Hall, to be precise. His mind shot back to last night's dinner-table . . . Uncle Fred jerking a thumb at an object in the corner of the room and saying it was a bust which Sally had brought down and left in his charge, and himself—how ironical it seemed now—giving the thing a brief and uninterested glance. It wouldn't be an uninterested glance he would be giving it when he saw it again.

His spirits soared. Ickenham Hall was only a dozen miles away, and he had an owner-driver's touching faith in the ability of his Buffy-Porson to do a dozen miles, if pushed, in about three minutes and a quarter. He could be there and back and have the understudy on its pedestal long before his host had finished conferring with the Vicar.

He beamed upon Elsie Bean.

'That's the set-up. I'll go and get the car.'

'I would.'

'You, meanwhile, might be putting in a bit of earnest brush-and-pan work.'

'Right ho!'

'Fine. Great. Capital. Splendid,' said Pongo, and raced for the stables.

Elsie Bean, her errand of mercy concluded, was standing on the front steps when he drove up. He was conscious, as he saw her, of a twinge of remorse, for it had just come to him that he had churlishly omitted to chuck her so much as a word of thanks for her splendid resourcefulness.

'I say,' he said, 'I forgot to mention it in the swirl and rush of recent events, but I'm most frightfully obliged to you for the very sporting way you've rallied round and saved me from the fate that is worse than death—viz,' explained Pongo, 'getting glared at by that goggle-eyed old Jack the Ripper with the lip fungus.'

Elsie Bean said she was only too pleased, to be sure, and he took her hand in his and pressed it.

'But for you I should have been in the soup and going down for the third time. I owe you more than words can tell.'

He was still pressing her hand, and from that to kissing her in a grateful and brotherly manner was but a short step. He took it, and Bill Oakshott, coming round the corner after one of the long walks with which he was endeavouring these days to allay the pangs of frustrated love, was able to observe the courteous gesture from start to finish.

Pongo sprang into the car with a lissom bound, waved his hand and drove off, and Bill stared after him, stunned. Pongo belonged to the type of man which changes very little in appearance with the passage of the years, and he recognized him immediately.

Still, to make sure . . .

'Wasn't that Mr Twistleton? he inquired of Elsie Bean.

'Yes, sir,' said Elsie composedly. She had no inkling of the turmoil in his soul, and would have been astounded to learn that anyone was taking exception to that kiss. In Bottleton East everybody kisses everybody else as a matter of course, like the early Christians. 'He says you were wrong about the natives, Mr William.'

'The what?'

'Those natives in Brazil. They don't shoot birds with poisoned darts, only their wives' relations. They use rude slings.'

With an effort that shook his powerful frame to its foundations Bill Oakshott contrived to keep from saying something ruder about Brazilian natives than any sling fashioned by them. There was no room in his thoughts for Brazilian natives. All the available space was occupied by Pongo.

So this, he was saying to himself, was the man to whom Hermione had entrusted her happiness; a libertine who, once the Don Juan of his dancing class, now went about kissing housemaids on doorsteps. How right, how unerringly right, old Ickenham had been. Can the leopard change his spots, he had speculated. This leopard didn't even seem to want to.

'Gosh!' thought Bill, aghast at the stark horror of the thing.

A minor point presented itself.

'Where's he off to?' he asked, puzzled.

'London, sir.'

'London?'

'Yes, sir.'

'But he's only just arrived.'

'Yes, sir.'

'Did he say why he was going to London?'

Elsie Bean was a good accomplice, cautious, reliable, on the alert against verbal slips.

'No, sir. He just said "Coo! I think I'll go to London," and popped off.'

Bill Oakshott drew a deep breath. It seemed to him that in the years since he had seen him last, his old friend, never very strong in the head, must have become absolutely *non compos*. Do balanced men drive to country houses and immediately upon arrival say 'Coo! I think I'll go to London,' and drive off again? They certainly do not.

His heart, as he filled his pipe, was heavy. Sane libertines, he was thinking, are bad enough, but loony libertines are the limit.

# 4

It was at a quarter to eight that evening that Lord Ickenham, after a pleasant journey to London in his car and a bath and change at his club, arrived in Budge Street, Chelsea, to pick up Sally Painter and take her to dinner.

Budge Street, Chelsea, in the heart of London's artistic quarter, is, like so many streets in the hearts of artistic quarters, dark, dirty, dingy and depressing. Its residents would appear to be great readers and very fond of fruit, for tattered newspapers can always be found fluttering about its sidewalks and old banana skins, cores of apples, plum stones and squashed strawberries lying in large quantities in its gutters. Its cats are stringy, hard-boiled cats, who look as if they were contemplating, or had just finished perpetrating, a series of murders of the more brutal type.

It was a bit of luck, accordingly, for this dishevelled thoroughfare to be toned up by Lord Ickenham's ornamental presence. With his well-cut clothes and distinguished deportment he lent to the scene a suggestion of the enclosure at Ascot on Cup Day.

And he had not been there long, strolling up and down, when Budge Street had another slice of good fortune. Round the corner from the King's Road there came hurrying a small, alert girl in beige, whose arrival intensified the Ascot note. Nobody, not even Pongo at the very height of that unfortunate discussion about the tint of his liver, had ever attempted to deny that Sally Painter was pretty: and even if she had not been, there was a jauntiness in her carriage which would have gone far to create that illusion.

To Lord Ickenham she seemed like some spirit of the summer day. Watching her as she paused to tickle a passing cat and noting how under the treatment the cat became in an instant a better, more idealistic cat, his heart went out to her.

'Hoy!' he cried paternally, and she came running up, floating into his arms like a columbine.

'I hope I haven't kept you waiting, Uncle Fred. I had to see a man about a bust.'

'Not at all,' said Lord Ickenham. Odd, he was thinking, how everybody seemed to be seeing men about busts to-day. It was only a few hours since Pongo had come charging into his study, clamouring for one. 'Always see men about busts. It is the secret of a happy and successful life.'

Sally linked her arm in his, and gave it a squeeze.

'It's lovely seeing you again, angel.'

'I am always well worth looking at.'

'How wonderful of you to come. And how brave! How did you manage to sneak away?'

'What extraordinary verbs you employ, child.'

'Well, didn't Aunt Jane say she would scalp you with a blunt knife next time you were A.W.O.L.?'

'In her playful way she did say something of the sort. Odd, that craving of hers to keep me vegetating in the country. But your honorary Aunt Jane is at the moment on her way to the West Indies. This has eased the situation a good deal. I thought it a good opportunity of broadening my mind.'

'Or playing hooky.'

'That is another way of putting it, of course. Well, let's find a taxi and go and get some dinner. There's one,' said Lord Ickenham, as they turned the corner. 'Hop in. Barribault's,' he said to the driver, and Sally closed her eyes in a sort of ecstasy. A girl who as a rule dined sparingly in Soho, she found enchantment in the mere name of London's premier restaurant.

'Barribault's? We're not dressed.'

'Grill room. Ev. dress not oblig.'

'But do I look smart enough?'

'My dear, you look like Helen of Troy after a good facial.'

Sally leaned back against the cushions.

'Barribault's!' she murmured.

'We Earls step high,' Lord Ickenham assured her. 'The best is none too good for us.'

'It must be great being an Oil.'

'It's terrific. I often lie awake at night, aching with pity for all the poor devils who aren't.'

'Though I suppose you know you're an anachronistic parasite on the body of the State? Or so Otis says. He's just become a Communist.'

'He has, has he? Well, you can tell him from me that if he starts any nonsense of trying to hang me from a lamp-post, I shall speak very sharply to him. Doesn't he like Earls?'

'Not much. He thinks they're blood-suckers.'

'What an ass that boy is, to be sure. Where's the harm in sucking blood? We need it, to keep us rosy. And it isn't as if I hadn't had to work for my little bit of gore. People see me now the dickens of a fellow with five Christian names and a coronet hanging on a peg in the hats and coats cupboard under the stairs, and they forget that I started at the bottom of the ladder. For years I was a younger son, a mere Honourable.'

'Why have you never told me this?'

'I hadn't the heart to. A worm of an Hon. In Debrett, yes, but only in small print.'

'You're making me cry.'

'I can't help that. Do you know how they treat Hons, Sally? Like dogs. They have to go into dinner behind the Vice-Chancellor of the County Palatinate of Lancaster.'

'Well, it's all over now, darling.'

'The only bit of sunshine in their lives is the privilege of being allowed to stand at the bar of the House of Lords during debates. And I couldn't even do that, my time being earmarked for the cows I was punching in Arizona.'

'I didn't know you had ever punched cows.'

'As a young man, hundreds. I had a beautiful punch in those days, straight and true, like the kick of a mule, and never travelling more than six inches. I also jerked soda, did a bit of newspaper work, which was when I met your father, and had a shot at prospecting in the Mojave Desert. But was I happy? No. Because always at the back of my mind, like some corroding acid, was the thought that I had to go into dinner behind the Vice-Chancellor of the County Palatinate of Lancaster. In the end, by pluck and perseverance, I raised myself from the depths and became what I am to-day. I'd like to see any Vice-Chancellor of the County Palatinate of Lancaster try to squash in ahead of me now.'

'It's like something out of Horatio Alger.'

'Very like. But I'm boring you. I'm afraid we fellows who have made good have a tendency to go rambling on about our early struggles. Tell me of yourself. How are you doing these days, Sally?'

'Well, I still go into dinner behind fashion editresses, but aside from that I'm making out pretty satisfactorily.'

'Trade good?'

'Not so bad.'

The cab drew up at the ornate portal of Barribault's Hotel, and they made their way to the grill-room. As they took their seats, Sally was sniffing luxuriously.

'Heaven!' she said.

'Hungry?'

'I'm always hungry.'

Lord Ickenham looked at her a little anxiously.

'You're sure you're not hard up, Sally?'

'Not a bit. Busts are quite brisk. It's odd, when you think how hideous most people are, that so many of them should want to hand their faces down to posterity.'

'You wouldn't deceive me?'

'No, honestly. I'm opulent.'

'Then why did you send me that S.O.S.? What is the very urgent matter you wanted to see me about, with the "very" underlined?'

Sally was silent for a moment, but only because she was eating caviare. It did not often come her way.

'Oh, that? It's about Otis.'

'My God!'

'Well, it is. I'm sorry.'

'Otis again! A thing I've noticed all my life is that the nicest girls always have the ghastliest brothers. It seems to be a law of nature. Well, what's the trouble this time, and what do you want me to do?'

'I'll explain about the trouble later. What I want you to do is to ask Pongo to do something for me.'

'Pongo?'

'I can't very well approach him direct,' said Sally.

There was a sudden flatness in her voice which did not escape Lord Ickenham's quick ear. He leaned across and petted her hand.

'A shame about you and Pongo, Sally.'

'Yes.'

There was a silence. Lord Ickenham stole a glance across the table. Sally was gazing into the middle distance, her eyes, or so it seemed to him, suspiciously bright and with a disposition to moisture which disquieted him. It is rarely that an uncle is able to understand how a nephew of his can possibly cast a fatal spell and, fond as he was of Pongo, Lord Ickenham could not see him as a breaker of hearts. Yet it appeared plain that his loss had left a large gap in this girl's life. Her air was the air of one who was pining for Pongo, and it was a relief when the waiter, arriving with *truite bleue*, broke a tension which had begun to be uncomfortable.

'Tell me about Otis,' he said.

Sally smiled a rather twisted smile.

'You needn't be tactful, Uncle Fred. I don't mind talking about Pongo. At least . . . No, of course I don't. Have you seen him lately?'

'He left me this afternoon. He turned up yesterday and spent the night.'

'How was he looking?'

'Oh, very well.'

'Did he speak about me?'

'Yes. And when I cursed him for being ass enough to part brass rags with you, he told me the inside story.'

'About my wanting him to smuggle Alice Vansittart's jewels into America?'

'Yes.'

'I was a fool to get mad. And it was all so unnecessary, as it turned out.'

'The Vansittart decided on reflection to pay duty?'

'No. But I thought of a much better way of slipping the stuff through. I'm not going to tell even you what it was, but it's a peach of a way. It can't fail. Alice is crazy about it.'

She spoke with a girlish animation which encouraged Lord Ickenham to hope that her heart was, after all, not irretrievably broken. That bright, moist look had gone from her eyes, leaving in its place a gleam not unlike that of which Pongo had so disapproved, when he had seen it in the eyes of his Uncle Fred.

'She is, is she?'

'When I told her, she clapped her hands in glee.'

'You realize, of course, that it is very wrong to deceive the United States Customs authorities?'

'Yes, it makes me miserable. Poor darlings.'

'Still, there it is. So you and Pongo need not have split up at all.'

'No.'

'It was silly of him to take your breaking the engagement so seriously. My dear wife broke ours six times, and each time I came up smiling.'

'I ought to have remembered that Pongo does take things seriously.'

'Yes. A saintly character, but muttonheaded.'

'And now he's gone and got engaged to Hermione, only daughter of Sir Aylmer Bostock and Lady Bostock, of Ashenden Manor, Ashenden Oakshott, Hants. Oh, well. Do you know her, Uncle Fred?'

'No. I've seen her photograph.'

'So have I. It was in the *Tatler*. She's very good-looking.'

'If you admire that type of looks.'

'Pongo seems to.'

'Yes. For the moment you might describe him as being under the ether. But there will be a bitter awakening.'

'You can't know that just from seeing her photograph.'

'Yes, I can. She'll give him the devil.'

'Oh, poor angel.'

There was another silence.

'Well, what is it you want me to ask him to do for you?' said Lord Ickenham. 'I may mention that I'm pretty sure he will do it, whatever it is. He's still damned fond of you, Sally.'

'Oh, no.'

'He is, I tell you. He confessed as much, in so many words.'

A dazzling smile flashed out on Sally's face. The waiter, who was bringing chicken *en casserole*, caught it head-on and nearly dropped the dish.

'Did he?'

'And don't forget that he still retained enough of the old affection to send you a customer in the shape of Sir Aylmer Bostock.'

'Was it Pongo who got me that job? How like him,' said Sally softly. 'I love him for that. Though unfortunately it was through my doing that bust that poor Otis's trouble came about.'

'How did that happen?'

'Well, to begin at the beginning, I did the bust.'

'Quite.'

'And during the process, of course, my sitter and I talked of this and that.'

'Was his conversation entertaining?'

'Not very. He was rather inclined to compare my efforts to their disadvantage with those of a sculptor who did a bust of him when he retired.'

'The one that stands—or stood—in the hall at Ashenden?'

'Yes. However did you know?'

'Wait, my child. I shall shortly be telling you a story of my own. Go on. He conversed with you, but you did not find him very entertaining.'

'No. But he said one thing that gripped my attention, and that was that he had written his Reminiscences and had decided after some thought to pay for their publication. He spoke like a man who had had disappointments. So I said to myself "Ha! A job for Otis."'

'I begin to see. Otis took it on and made a mess of it?'

'Yes. In a negligent moment he slipped in some plates which should have appeared in a book on Modern Art which he was doing. Sir Aylmer didn't like any of them much, but the one he disliked particularly was the nude female with "Myself in the Early Twenties" under it. The first thing I knew about it was when he sent the bust back. Lady Bostock brought it round to my studio with a stiff note. And now he's bringing an action for enormous damages. If it comes off, it will smash Otis's poor little publishing firm. It's all rather unfortunate.'

'Most. But characteristic of Otis.'

'Poor lamb, he's dreamy.'

'Poor fish, he's a nightmare. I suppose you put up money for his publishing firm?'

'A certain amount.'

'Oh, heavens. Well, I'm sorry to say it, my dear, but if what you tell me is correct, any jury will give Bostock Otis's head on a charger.'

'I know. If the thing ever comes into court. That's why I need Pongo's help. I want him to use his influence with Sir Aylmer to get him to withdraw the suit. He might persuade him to settle for some smallish amount which wouldn't ruin Otis.'

'That would be the happy ending, of course. But is Pongo *persona grata* with him?'

'Surely?'

'I wonder. It all depends on how he has come out with that bust. Strange that Otis's future as a publisher, which I don't care a damn about, and your little bit of money, which I do, should depend on Pongo's ability to sneak a clay bust into Ashenden Manor and get away with it. Odd. Bizarre, you might say. Life can be very complicated at times.'

'What do you mean? What bust?'

'That is the story I am about to relate. Have you had enough to eat? Then let's go and have our coffee in the lounge. Yes,' said Lord Ickenham, when they had seated themselves in two of the luxurious armchairs which Barribault's Hotel provides for its patrons, 'very complicated indeed. I told you Pongo came to my place last night.'

'Yes.'

'To-day, after lunch, he started out for Ashenden, to fascinate the old folks. I waved him a tender farewell, and thought that that was the last

I should see of him for at least a week. I was wrong. He was back again in under two hours. Deeply agitated. More like a cat on hot bricks than anything human.'

'But why?'

'Because, in endeavouring to demonstrate to the Ashenden Manor housemaid how Brazilian natives shoot birds with rude slings, he had happened to break that bust in the hall, of which you were speaking just now.'

'Oh, golly.'

'Hullo! You agitated, too?'

'Of course I'm agitated. Don't you see, Uncle Fred? Sir Aylmer adores that bust. He'll be furious with Pongo—'

'Thus rendering Pongo in no position to plead for Otis? Yes, that seems to follow. But calm yourself. All may yet be well. His motive in coming to me was to borrow another bust to put on the bereaved pedestal, in the hope that the substitution would not be noticed.'

'That was bright.'

'Yes, much too bright for Pongo. It must have been the housemaid who suggested it. He isn't what I would call a quick-witted chap. I remember so well his confusion of mind when they were asking him his name that day at the dog races. He had got as far as "Tw—" when I was fortunately able to lean across and whisper to him that he was Edwin Smith of II Nasturtium Road, East Dulwich.'

'And what were you?'

'George Robinson, of number fourteen in the same thoroughfare. Yes, I think we may safely attribute to the housemaid any swift intelligence that was displayed on this occasion. Well, I gave him a bust and he drove off with it. We have no means of knowing as yet, of course, if the simple ruse has proved effective, but I think we may feel reasonably optimistic. He tells me it is darkish in the corner of the hall where the original used to stand, and I don't suppose Mugsy is in the habit of scrutinizing it too carefully. Just a casual glance in passing, and he toddles off to the garden to enjoy the sunshine.'

'Why do you call him Mugsy?'

'We always used to at school.'

'Were you and Sir Aylmer at school together?'

'For years.'

'Then couldn't you plead with him?'

'No, I could not. I was telling his nephew, whom I met in the train yesterday, that I once gave young Mugsy Bostock six with a fives bat, and no doubt the incident still rankles. Pongo is the one who must plead.'

'If everything has gone well.'

'I feel convinced that it has. He says Mugsy is short-sighted and won't wear spectacles, and he described the housemaid as staunch and true and not at all the sort to squeal to the big four.'

'You're a great comfort, Uncle Fred.'

'I try to be, my dear. Sweetness and light, that is my slogan.'

'It was lucky you happened to have a bust handy.'

'Extraordinarily fortunate. For one reason and another Ickenham Hall has never been very well provided with them. Statues, yes. If you came to me with a hurry call for a nude Venus, I could fill the order without any trouble whatsoever. My grandfather specialized in them. "Home isn't home," he used to say, running a thoughtful hand through his whiskers, "without plenty of nude Venuses." The result being that in certain parts of the grounds you have the illusion of having wandered into a Turkish bath on ladies' night. But busts, no. We Ickenhams have somehow never gone in for busts. So if it hadn't been for you providentially leaving one in my care—'

It is not easy to rise in a single bound from a Barribault armchair, but Sally had done so. Her face was pale, and she was staring with wide, horrified eyes.

'Uncle Fred! You didn't give him that one?'

'Yes. Why, what's wrong?'

Sally dropped back into her chair.

'It had Alice's jewels in it,' she said in a toneless whisper.

'What!'

'Yes. I slipped them in at the top of the plaster, and Alice was going to call for the bust next week and take it to America. That was the "way" I was telling you I thought of.'

'Well, dash my wig and buttons!' said Lord Ickenham.

There followed a pregnant silence. Having dashed his wig and buttons, Lord Ickenham, though nobody could have called him an unresourceful man, seemed at a loss. He scratched his chin, he twirled his moustache, he drummed with his fingers on the side of his chair, but without obtaining anything in the nature of an inspiration.

Finally he rose.

'Well, it's no good saying I'm sorry, my dear. Nor is there much to be gained by pointing out that I meant well. What you want is a policy, not remorseful bleatings. I think I'll take a turn up and down outside. The fresh air may assist the flow of thought. And the flow of thought would certainly seem to need all the assistance it can get.'

He went out through the revolving door, his head bowed, his hands clasped behind his back. When he returned some minutes later, it was with a message of hope. His face had cleared and he was his old bright self again.

'It's all right, my child. This little difficulty can be very simply adjusted. It just needed concentration. You did tell me Mugsy had returned that bust you did of him? You have it at the studio?'

'Yes.'

'Then all is well. We will go down to Ashenden to-morrow in the car, taking it with us, and I will substitute it for the one now in residence.'

'But—'

'Don't say "But".'

'How—?'

'And don't say "How". It's the sort of thing the boys in the back room used to say to Columbus when he told them he was going to discover America, and look how silly he made them feel. I'll find a way. Don't bother your head about the trifling details, leave them to me. You go home and pack a few necessaries and get a good night's rest, while I remain and iron out the one or two points I haven't got quite straight yet. More coffee? No? Then off you go. Bless my soul,' said Lord Ickenham with boyish relish, as he escorted her to the door, 'what a providential thing that this should have happened. Something on these lines was just what I was needing, to stimulate me and bring back the flush of youth. I feel as I did when Pongo and I started out last spring for Blandings

Castle in the roles of Sir Roderick Glossop, the brain specialist, and his nephew Basil. Did he ever tell you about that?'

'No.'

'Odd. I should have thought it would have been one of his dearest memories. You shall have the whole story to-morrow on the journey down. Well, good night, my dear,' said Lord Ickenham, assisting Sally into her taxi. 'Sleep well, and don't worry. You can trust me to look after everything. This is the sort of situation that brings out the best in me. And when you get the best in Frederick Altamont Cornwallis, fifth Earl of good old Ickenham, you've got something.'

# PART TWO

# 5

· 1 ·

It was the custom of Lady Bostock, when the weather was fine, to sit in a garden chair on the terrace of Ashenden Manor after luncheon, knitting socks for the deserving poor. A believer, like Lord Ickenham, in spreading sweetness and light, she considered, possibly correctly, that there is nothing that brings the sunshine into grey lives like a sock or two.

On the day following the events which have just been recorded the weather was extremely fine. Soft white clouds floated across a sky of the purest blue, the lake shone like molten silver, and from the adjacent flower-beds came the murmur of bees and the fragrant scent of lavender and mignonette. It was an afternoon to raise the spirits, lighten the heart and set a woman counting her blessings one by one.

Nor did Lady Bostock omit to do this. She recognized these blessings as considerable. It was pleasant to be home again, though she had never really enjoyed life in the country, preferring Cheltenham with its gay society. Mrs Gooch, the cook, had dished up an inspired lunch. And ever since the assignment of judging the bonny babies at the fête had been handed to his nephew William, Sir Aylmer had been in a mood which could almost be called rollicking, a consummation always devoutly to be wished by a wife whose life work it was to keep him in a good temper. She could hear him singing in his study now. Something about his wealth being a burly spear and brand and a right good shield of hides untanned which on his arm he buckled—or, to be absolutely accurate, ber-huckled.

So far, so good. And yet, despite the fineness of the day, the virtuosity of Mrs Gooch and the joviality of her husband, Lady Bostock's heart was heavy. In these days in which we live, when existence has become a thing of infinite complexity and fate, if it slips us a bit of goose with one hand, is pretty sure to give us the sleeve across the windpipe with the other, it is rarely that we find a human being who is unmixedly happy. Always the bitter will be blended with the sweet, and in this *mélange* one can be reasonably certain that it is the former that will predominate.

A severe indictment of our modern civilization, but it can't say it didn't ask for it.

As Lady Bostock sat there, doing two plain, two purl, or whatever it is that women do when knitting socks, a sigh escaped her from time to time. She was thinking of Sally Painter.

Budge Street, Chelsea, brief though her visit there had been, had made a deep impression on this sensitive woman. She had merely driven up in a cab, rung the bell of Sally's studio, handed her parcel to the charwoman and driven swiftly off again, but she had seen enough to recognize Budge Street for the sort of place she had read about in novels, where impoverished artists eke out a miserable existence, supported only by hope. How thankful, she thought, impoverished Miss Painter must have been to get the commission to model that bust of Aylmer, and what anguish must have been hers on having it thrown back on her hands.

She had mentioned this to Sir Aylmer as they were returning from their conference with the Vicar, and had been snubbed with a good deal of brusqueness. And now, though she was too loyal a wife to criticize her husband even in thought, she could not check a fleeting regret that he was always so splendidly firm.

Was there nothing, she asked herself, as she remembered the admirable luncheon which she had recently consumed and pictured Sally gnawing a dry crust and washing it down with a cup of water, was there nothing that she could do? Useless, of course, to make another attempt to persuade Aylmer to change his mind, but suppose she were to send the girl a secret cheque . . .

At this point her musing was interrupted and her despondency increased by the arrival of Bill Oakshott, who came heavily along the terrace smoking a sombre pipe. She eyed him with a sad pity. Ever since she had given him the bad news, the sight of him had made her feel like a soft-hearted Oriental executioner who, acting on orders from the front office, has had to do unpleasant things to an Odalisque with a bow string. It seemed to her sometimes that she would never be able to forget the look of horror and despair which had leaped into his crimson face. Traces of it still lingered on those haggard features.

'Hullo, Aunt Emily,' he said in sepulchral tones. 'Knitting a sock?'

'Yes, dear. A sock.'

'Oh?' said Bill, still speaking like a voice from the tomb. 'A sock? Fine.'

He stood there, staring before him with unseeing eyes, and she touched his hand gently.

'I wouldn't worry about it too much, dear.'

'I don't see how one could,' said Bill. 'How many of these frightful babies will there be?'

'There were forty-three last year.'

'Forty-three!'

'Be brave, William. If Mr Brotherhood could do it, you can.'

The flaw in this reasoning was so obvious that Bill was able to detect it at once.

'Curates are different. They train them specially to judge bonny babies. At the theological colleges. Start them off with ventriloquists' dummies, I shouldn't wonder. Forty-three, did you say? And probably dozens more this time. These blighters breed like rabbits. Gosh, I wish I was back in Brazil.'

'Oh, William.'

'I do. What a country! Nothing but flies and ticks and alligators and snakes and scorpions and tarantulas and a sort of leech that drops on you from trees and sucks your blood. Not a baby to be seen for miles. Listen, Aunt Emily, can't I get someone else to take this ghastly job on?'

'But who?'

'Yes, that's the snag, of course,' said Bill morosely. 'Mugs fatheaded enough to let themselves be talked into judging forty-three bonny babies, all dribbling out of the side of the mouth, must be pretty scarce, pretty scarce. Well, I think I'll be pushing along, Aunt Emily. It seems to help a little if I keep moving.'

He plodded off, listlessly puffing smoke, leaving behind him an aunt with an aching heart. And it was perhaps because Lady Bostock was now so near the nadir of depression that she thought she might as well make a complete job of it. So she began to think of Pongo.

It frequently happens that prospective sons-in-law come as a rather painful shock to their prospective mothers-in-law, and the case of Lady Bostock had provided no exception to the rule. Immediately on seeing Pongo she had found herself completely at a loss to understand why her daughter should have chosen him as a mate. From the very start she had felt herself to be in the presence of one whose soul was not attuned to hers. At moments, indeed, only her perfect breeding had restrained her from beating him over the head with the sock which she was knitting for the deserving poor.

Analysing his repellent personality, she came to the conclusion that while she disliked his nervous giggle, his lemon-coloured hair and the way he had of drooping his lower jaw and letting his eyes get glassy, the thing about him that particularly exasperated her was his extraordinary jumpiness.

Of this she had witnessed a manifestation only an hour or so ago, as they were leaving the dining-room after lunch. As they started to cross the hall, Aylmer had moved in the direction of that bust of his, as if to give it a flick with his handkerchief, as he sometimes did, and Reginald had bounded in his tracks with a soft, animal yelp, recovering his composure only when Aylmer, abandoning the idea of flicking, had moved on again.

A strange young man. Was he half—or even a quarter—witted? Or was his mind, if he had a mind, burdened by some guilty secret?

Speculations like these, indulged in on a warm day after a rather heavy lunch, are apt to induce drowsiness. Her eyelids began to flutter. Somewhere out of sight a lawn-mower was purring hypnotically. The west wind played soothingly on her face.

Lady Bostock slept.

But not for long. Her eyes had scarcely closed when the word 'EMILY,' spoken at the extreme limit of a good man's lungs, jerked her from her slumber as if a charge of trinitrotoluol had been exploded beneath her chair.

Sir Aylmer was leaning out of the study window.

'EMILY!'

'Yes, dear? Yes, dear?'

'Come here,' roared Sir Aylmer, like a bo'sun addressing an able-bodied seaman across the deck in the middle of a hurricane. 'Wantcher.'

## • II •

As Lady Bostock made her way to the study, her heart was racing painfully. There had been that in her husband's manner which caused her to fear unnamed disasters, and her first glance at him as she crossed the threshold told her that her apprehensions had been well founded.

His face was purple, and his moustache, always a barometer of the emotions, was dancing about beneath his laboured breath. She had not beheld such activity in it since the night years ago when the youngest and most nervously giggling of the aides-de-camp, twiddling the nut-crackers during the dessert course at dinner at Government House, had snapped the stem of one of his favourite set of wineglasses.

He was not alone. Standing at a respectful distance in one of the corners, as if he knew his place better than to thrust himself forward, was Constable Harold Potter, looking, as policemen do at such moments, as if he had been stuffed by a good taxidermist. She stared from one to the other, bewildered.

'Aylmer! What is it?'

Sir Aylmer Bostock was not a man who beat about bushes. When he had disturbing news to impart, he imparted it.

'Emily,' he said, quivering in every hair, 'there's a damned plot afoot.'

'A what?'

'A PLOT. An infernal outrage against the public weal. You know Potter?'

Lady Bostock knew Potter.

'How do you do, Potter?' she said.

'How do you do, m'lady?' said Constable Potter, coming unstuffed for an instant in order to play his part in the courteous exchanges and then immediately getting stuffed again.

'Potter,' said Sir Aylmer, 'has just come to me with a strange story. Potter!'

'Sir?'

'Tell her ladyship your strange story.'

'Yes, sir.'

'It's about Reginald,' said Sir Aylmer, to whet the interest of the audience. 'Or, rather,' he added, exploding his bombshell, 'the fellow who's posing as Reginald.'

Lady Bostock's eyes were already bulging to almost their maximum extent, but at these words they managed to protrude a little further.

'Posing?'

'Yes.'

'What do you mean?'

'What I say. I can't put it any plainer. The chap who's come here pretending to be Reginald Twistleton is an impostor. He isn't Reginald Twistleton at all. I had my suspicions of him all along. I didn't like his eye. Sly. Shifty. And that sinister giggle of his. What I'd call a criminal type. Potter!'

'Sir?'

'Get on with your strange story.'

'Yes, sir.'

Constable Potter stepped forward, his helmet balanced against his right hip. A glazed look had come into his eyes. It was the look which they always assumed when he was giving evidence in court. His gaze was directed some two feet above Sir Aylmer's head, so that his remarks seemed to be addressed to a bodiless spirit hovering over the scene and taking notes in an invisible notebook.

'On the sixteenth inst.—'

'Yesterday.'

'Yesterday,' proceeded Constable Potter, accepting the emendation. 'On the sixteenth inst., which was yesterday, I was proceeding up the drive of Ashenden Manor on my bicycle, when my attention was drawn to a suspicious figure entering the premises through a window.'

'The window of my collection room.'

'The window of Sir Aylmer Bostock's collection room. I immediately proceeded to follow the man and question him. In reply to my inquiries he made the statement that his name was Twistleton and that he was established as a guest at this residence.'

'Well, so he is,' said Lady Bostock, speaking a little dazedly.

Sir Aylmer waved an imperious hand.

'Wait, wait, wait, wait, WAIT. Mark the sequel.'

He paused, and stood puffing at his moustache. Lady Bostock, who had sunk into a chair, picked up a copy of the parish magazine and began to fan herself with it.

'We're coming to the part where he turns out not to be Twistleton,' said Sir Aylmer, allowing his moustache to subside like an angry sea after a storm. 'Carry on, Potter.'

Constable Potter, who had momentarily removed the glazed look from his eyes, put it back again. Raising his chin, which he had lowered in order to rest the neck muscles, he once more addressed the bodiless spirit.

'Having taken the man's statement, I proceeded to put searching questions to him. These appearing to establish his bona fides, I withdrew, leaving him in the company of Bean, a housemaid, whose evidence had assisted me in establishing the conclusion that his bona fides had been'—Constable Potter paused, searching for the telling verb—'established,' he said. 'But—'

'Here comes the sequel.'

'But I was not wholly satisfied, and I'll tell you why,' said Constable Potter, suddenly abandoning the official manner and becoming chatty.

'The moment I saw this chap, I had a sort of feeling that his face was kind of familiar, but I couldn't place him. You know how it is. And, what's more, I could have taken my oath that last time we'd met his name hadn't been Twistleton—'

'Or anything like it,' said Sir Aylmer, adroitly snatching the conversational ball from the speaker and proceeding to carry it himself. 'I must start by telling you . . . ARE YOU ASLEEP, EMILY?'

'No, dear. No, dear,' cried Lady Bostock, who had been rash enough to close her eyes for an instant in order to relieve a shooting pain across the forehead.

'I must start by telling you that before Potter came to Ashenden Oakshott he used to be a member of the London police force, and this afternoon, as he was smoking a pipe after his lunch—'

'Cigarette, sir,' interpolated the officer respectfully. He knew the importance of exactitude on these occasions. 'A gasper.'

'—It suddenly flashed on him,' went on Sir Aylmer, having given him a dangerous look, 'that where he had seen this fellow before was at some dog races down Shepherd's Bush way, when he had arrested him, together with an accomplice, and hauled him off in custody.'

'Aylmer!'

'You may well say "Aylmer!" It seems that Potter keeps a scrap album containing newspaper clippings having to do with cases with which he has been connected, and he looked up this scrap album and found that the chap's name, so far from being Twistleton, is Edwin Smith, of 11 Nasturtium Road, East Dulwich. Edwin Smith,' repeated Sir Aylmer, somehow contriving by his intonation to make it seem a name to shudder at. 'Now do you believe me when I say he's an impostor?'

Women, having no moustaches, are handicapped at moments like this. Lady Bostock had begun to pant like a spent horse, but it was not the same thing. She could not hope to rival her husband's impressiveness.

'But what is he doing here?'

'Potter's view is that he is the advance man of a gang of burglars. I think he's right. These fellows always try to simplify matters for themselves by insinuating an accomplice into the house to pave the way for them. When the time is ripe, the bounder opens a window and the other bounders creep in. And if you want to know what this gang is after at Ashenden Manor, it sticks out a mile. My collection of African curios. Where did Potter find this chap? In my collection room. Where did I find him? Again in my collection room. My collection fascinates him. He can't keep away from it. You agree, Potter?'

Constable Potter, though not too well pleased at the way in which he had been degraded from the position of star witness to that of a mere Yes-man, was forced to admit that he agreed.

Lady Bostock was still panting softly.

'But it seems so extraordinary.'

'Why? Its value is enormous.'

'I mean, that he should take such a risk.'

'These fellows are used to taking risks. Eh, Potter?'

'Yes, sir.'

'Doing it all the time, aren't they?'

'Yes, sir.'

'Dangerous devils, what?'

'Yes, sir,' said Constable Potter, now apparently resigned to his demotion.

'But he must have known that Reginald was expected here. How could he tell that he was not going to run into him?'

'My dear Emily, don't be childish. The gang's first step would, of course, be to make away with Reginald.'

'Make away with him? How?'

'Good Lord, how do chaps make away with chaps? Don't you ever read detective stories?'

Constable Potter saw his chance, and took it.

'They telephone 'em, m'lady, telling them to come to ruined mills, and then lock 'em up in the cellar. Or they—'

'—Slip drugs in their drink and carry them off on yachts,' said Sir Aylmer, once more seizing the ball. 'There are a hundred methods. If we looked into it, I expect we should find that the real Reginald is at this moment lying bound and gagged on a pallet bed in Limehouse. Eh, Potter?'

'Yes, sir.'

'Or in the hold of a tramp steamer bound for South America?'

'Yes, sir.'

'I shouldn't wonder if they weren't sticking lighted matches between his toes to make him write them cheques,' said Sir Aylmer dispassionately. 'Well, all right, Potter, that's all. We won't keep you. Would you like a glass of beer?'

'Yes, sir,' said Constable Potter, this time with real enthusiasm.

'Go and get one in the kitchen. And now,' said Sir Aylmer, as the door closed, 'to business.'

'Where are you going?'

'To confront this impostor and kick him out, of course.'

'But, Aylmer.'

'Now what?'

'Suppose there is some mistake.'

'How can there be any mistake?'

'But suppose there is. Suppose this young man is really Reginald, and you turn him out of the house, we should never hear the last of it from Hermione.'

## • III •

Something of the gallant fire which was animating him seemed to pass out of Sir Aylmer Bostock. He blinked, like some knight of King Arthur's court, who, galloping to perform a deed of derring-do, has had the misfortune to collide with a tree. Though keeping up a brave front, he, like his wife, had always quailed before Hermione. Native chiefs, accustomed to leap like fawns at a waggle of his moustache, would have marvelled at this weakness in one who had always seemed to them impervious to human emotions, but it existed.

''M, yes,' he said thoughtfully. 'Yes, I see what you mean.'

'She would be furious.'

'That's true.'

'I really don't know what to think myself,' said Lady Bostock distractedly. 'Potter's story did seem very convincing, but it is just possible that he is mistaken in supposing that this man who has come here as Reginald is really Edwin Smith.'

'I'd bet a million on it.'

'Yes, dear, I know. And I must say I have noticed something curiously furtive about the young man, as if he had a guilty secret. But—'

An idea occurred to Sir Aylmer.

'Didn't Hermione give some sort of description of this young poop of hers in that letter she wrote you saying she was engaged?'

'Why, of course. I had forgotten. It's in my desk. I'll go and get it.'

'Well?' said Sir Aylmer a few moments later.

Lady Bostock was skimming through the document.

'She says he is tall and slender, with large, lustrous eyes.'

'There you are! This chap hasn't got lustrous eyes.'

'Wouldn't you say his eyes were lustrous?'

'Certainly not. Like a couple of damned poached eggs. What else?'

'He is very amusing.'

'You see!'

'Oh!'

'What?'

'She says William used to know him as a boy.'

'She does? Then William's evidence will clinch the thing. Where is he? WILLIAM! WILLIAM!! WILLIAM!!!'

It is rarely that this sort of thing does not produce results. Bill Oakshott, who was still on the terrace, smoking his pipe and pondering over his numerous misfortunes, came clattering up the stairs as if pulled at the end of a string.

The fear—or hope—that his uncle was being murdered left him as he entered the room, but not his bewilderment at the summons.

'Hullo?' he said gropingly.

'Oh, there you are,' said Sir Aylmer, who was still bellowing out of the window. 'William, this fellow who calls himself Reginald Twistleton, how about him?'

'How about him?'

'Exactly. How about him?'

'How do you mean, how about him?'

'Good God, boy, can't you understand plain English? I mean How about him?'

Lady Bostock explained.

'We are terribly upset, William. Your uncle thinks that the man who came yesterday is not Reginald, but an impostor pretending to be Reginald.'

'What on earth gives him that idea?'

'Never mind what on earth gives me that idea,' said Sir Aylmer, nettled. 'You knew Reginald Twistleton as a boy?'

'Yes.'

'Good. That's established,' said Sir Aylmer, borrowing from Constable Potter's non-copyright material. 'Now, then. When you saw him yesterday, did you recognize him?'

'Of course.'

'Don't say "Of course" in that airy way. When had you seen him last?'

'About twelve years ago.'

'Then how can you be sure you recognized him?'

'Well, he looked about the same. Grown a bit, of course.'

'Have you discussed boyhood days with him?'

'No.'

'Have you asked him a single question, the response to which would prove that he had known you as a boy?'

'Why, no.'

'There you are, then.'

'But he answers to the name of Pongo.'

Sir Aylmer snorted.

'Of course he answers to the name of Pongo. Do you suppose that an impostor, when addressed as Pongo by somebody claiming to be an old friend of the man he was impersonating, would not have the elementary intelligence to dissemble? Your evidence is completely valueless.'

'Sorry.'

'No good being sorry. Well, I shall have to look into the thing for myself. I shall take the car and go over to Ickenham Hall. The real Reginald is Ickenham's nephew, so the old lunatic will presumably have a photograph of him somewhere on the premises. A glance at that will settle the matter.'

'What a splendid idea, Aylmer!'

'Yes,' said Sir Aylmer, who thought well of it himself. 'Just occurred to me.'

He shot from the room as if propelled from a rude sling in the hands of a Brazilian native, and hurried down the stairs. In the hall he was obliged to check his progress for an instant in order to glare at Pongo, who like a murderer returning to the scene of his crime, had come thither to gaze at the substitute bust and ask himself for the hundredth time what were its chances of getting by.

'Ha!' said Sir Aylmer.

'Oh, hullo,' said Pongo, smiling weakly.

Sir Aylmer eyed him with that blend of horror and loathing with which honest men eye those who call themselves Twistleton when they are really Edwin Smith of 11 Nasturtium Road, East Dulwich, especially when these latter smile like minor gangsters caught in the act of committing some felony. It seemed to him that if ever he had seen furtive guilt limned on a human face, he had seen it now.

'Ha!' he said again, and went off to get his car.

A few minutes after he had steered it out into the road, tooting fiercely, for he was a noisy driver, another car, coming from the opposite direction, drew up outside the gate.

At its wheel was Lord Ickenham, and beside him Sally.

# 6

## · 1 ·

Lord Ickenham cast an alert eye up the curving drive, and gave his moustache a carefree twiddle. His air was that of a man who has arrived at some joyous tryst. A restful night and a good lunch had brought his always resilient nature to a fine pitch of buoyancy and optimism. There is an expression in common use which might have been invented to describe the enterprising peer at moments such as this; the expression 'boomps-a-daisy'. You could look askance at his methods, you could shake your head at him in disapproval and click your tongue in reproof, but you could not deny that he was boomps-a-daisy.

'This might be the place, don't you think?' he said.

'It is.'

'You speak confidently.'

'Well, I've been here before. When I was doing the bust.'

'Didn't Mugsy come to the studio?'

'Of course not. Great men like him don't come to the studios of poor working girls.'

Lord Ickenham took her point.

'True,' he said. 'I can't get used to the idea of young Mugsy Bostock being a big pot. To me he remains permanently a pie-faced stripling bending over a chair while I assure him that what is about to occur is going to hurt me more than it does him. A black lie, of course. I enjoyed it. One of the hardest things in life is to realize that people grow up. Nothing, for instance, can convince me that I am not a sprightly young fellow of twenty-five, and, as for Pongo, the idea of him being old enough to contemplate marriage fills me with a perpetual astonishment. To me, he still wears sailor suits.'

'He must have looked sweet in a sailor suit.'

'No, he didn't. He looked foul. Like a ballet girl in a nautical musical comedy. But enough of this idle chatter. The time has come,' said Lord Ickenham, 'to discuss strategy and tactics.'

He spoke with the gay lilt in his voice which had so often in the past struck a chill into the heart of his nephew.

'Strategy and tactics,' he repeated. 'Here is the house. We have the bust. All that is needed is to effect an entry into the former, carrying the latter. This, accordingly, I shall now proceed to do. You spoke?'

'No, I only sort of gurgled. I was going to say "How?" but I mustn't, must I, because of Columbus and the boys in the back room.'

Lord Ickenham seemed amazed.

'My dear girl, you are surely not worrying yourself about the simple mechanics of the thing? There are a thousand ways, all child's play to one of my gifts. If I droop my moustache, thus, do I look like a man come to inspect the drains?'

'No.'

'If I turn it up at the ends, so, do I suggest the representative of a journal of rural interest, anxious to obtain Mugsy's views on the mangel-wurzel situation?'

'Not a bit.'

'Then I must try something else. I wonder if Mugsy has a parrot.'

'I know he hasn't. Why?'

'Didn't Pongo ever tell you of our afternoon at The Cedars, Mafeking Road, Mitching Hill?'

'No. What was The Cedars, Mafeking Road, Mitching Hill?'

'A suburban villa, heavily fortified and supposed to be impregnable. But I got in with absurd ease. One moment, I was outside its barred gates, lashed by an April shower; the next, in the sitting-room, toasting my toes at the gas fire. I told the maid I had come from the bird shop to clip the parrot's claws and slipped Pongo in with the statement that he was Mr Walkinshaw, my assistant, who applied the anæsthetic. I'm surprised he never mentioned it. I don't like the way he seems to have kept things from you. An unhealthy spirit. Yes, I think I may say with all due modesty that I am at my best when impersonating officials from bird shops who have called to prune the parrot, and I am sorry to hear you say that Mugsy has not got one. Not that I'm surprised. Only the gentler, kindlier type of man keeps a parrot and makes of it a constant friend. Ah, well, no doubt I shall be able to effect an entry somehow.'

'And what do you do then?'

'That's the easy part. I have the bust under my coat, I engage Mugsy in conversation, and at a selected moment I suddenly say "Look behind you!" He looks behind him, and while his back is turned I switch the busts and come away. So let's go.'

'Wait,' said Sally.

'Is this a time for waiting? The Ickenhams have never waited.'

'Well, they're going to start now. I've a much better plan.'

'Better than mine?' said Lord Ickenham incredulously.

'Better in every way,' said Sally firmly. 'Saner and simpler.'

Lord Ickenham shrugged his shoulders.

'Well, let's hear it. I'll bet I'm not going to like it.'

'You don't have to like it. You are going to stay in the car—'

'Absurd.'

'—While I take that bust to the house.'

'Ridiculous. I knew it was going to be rotten.'

'I shall try, of course, to put the deal through unobserved. But if I am observed, I shall have my story ready, which is more than you would have done.'

'I would have had twenty stories ready, each better than the last.'

'Each crazier than the last. Mine will be a good one, carrying conviction in every syllable. I shall say I came to see Sir Aylmer—'

'I wish you would call him Mugsy. It's friendlier.'

'I won't call him Mugsy. I shall say I came to see Sir Aylmer, bringing the bust with me, in the hope that I could persuade him to relent and accept it after all.'

'Loathsome.'

'I may even cry a little.'

'Revolting. Where's your pride?'

'The worst that can happen is that he will show me to the door and dismiss me with a cold gesture.'

'And then,' said Lord Ickenham, brightening, 'we will start all over again, this time putting the affair in older and wiser hands than yours. Well, all right. On that understanding I don't mind you trying your way. I don't like it. It's tame. It degrades me to the position of a super supporting a star, and you get all the fun. Still, carry on, if you must. I shall stay here and sulk.'

He lit a cigar, and watched her as she walked up the drive. At the point where it curved out of sight, she turned and waved her hand, and he waved back, filled with a not unmanly emotion. Good old Sally, he was feeling. What a girl!

Lord Ickenham was a man with many friends in the United States where he had spent twenty years of his life, and of all these friends the one of whom he had been fondest was the late George Painter, that amiable and impecunious artist with whom he had shared so many of the joys and sorrows of an agreeably chequered youth. He had loved George, and he loved his daughter Sally.

Sally was just the sort of girl that appealed to him most, the sort America seems to turn out in thousands, gay, grave, and adventurous, enjoying life with an almost Ickenhamian relish and resolutely refusing to allow its little difficulties to daunt her spirit.

How admirably, for instance, after the first shock, she had reacted to that unquestionably nasty wallop he had handed her in the lobby of Barribault's Hotel. No tears, no wringing of the hands, no profitless reproaches and recriminations. In the best and deepest sense of the words, a pippin of a girl. And why Pongo had let her go, simply from some finnicky objection to being disembowelled by New York port officials, baffled Lord Ickenham. It was one of the things that make a man who is getting on in years despair of the younger generation.

Time marched on. He looked at his watch. About now, he felt, she would be nearing the front door; about now, doing the quick glide through the hall and the rapid substitution of bust for bust. It would not be long before he saw her again, no doubt threading her way cautiously through the bushes that fringed the drive. He kept a keen eye riveted on those, but when she did appear she was walking in full view, and the first thing that attracted his attention was the fact that her hands were empty. At some point in her progress to and from the house, it would seem, she and her precious burden had parted company.

He could make nothing of this. His eyebrows rose in a silent query. Her face, he saw, was grave. It wore a strained look.

As she reached the car, however, her normal gaiety of disposition seemed to assert itself. She broke into a gurgling laugh, and his eyebrows rose again.

'We are amused?'

'Well, it was funny,' said Sally. 'I can't help laughing, though the absolutely rock-bottom worst has happened, Uncle Fred. We really are up against it now. You'll never guess.'

'I shan't try. Tell me.'

Sally leaned against the side of the car. Her face had become grave once more.

'I must have a cigarette first.'

'Nerves vibrating?'

'I'm shattered.'

She smoked in silence for a moment.

'Ready?'

'Waiting.'

'Very well, then, here it comes. When I got to the house, I found the front door open, which seemed to me about as big a piece of luck as I could want—'

'Always mistrust too much luck at the outset of any enterprise,' said Lord Ickenham judicially. 'It's simply part of Fate's con game. But I mustn't interrupt you. Go on.'

'I looked carefully over both shoulders. Nobody seemed to be about. I listened. I couldn't hear anybody in the hall. Everything was silent. So I sneaked in.'

'Quite.'

'And tiptoed across the hall.'

'You couldn't have done better.'

'And put the bust . . . Shall I call it Bust A., to distinguish it from Bust B.?'

'By all means.'

'You've got them clear? Bust A. was the one I was toting, and Bust B. the one with poor Alice's jewels in it.'

'Exactly.'

Sally drew at her cigarette. Her manner was absent, as if she were reliving an episode which had affected her deeply. She came to herself with something of the air of a sleeper awakening.

'Where was I?'

'Tiptoeing across the hall.'

'Yes, of course. Sorry to be so goofy.'

'Quite all right, my child.'

'I tiptoed across the hall and shifted Bust B. from its stand and put Bust A. in its place and gathered up Bust B. and started to come away . . . fairly quickly. No sense in hanging around, I mean.'

'None whatever. Never outstay your welcome.'

'And just as I got to the door of the room where Sir Aylmer keeps his collection of African curios, out came Lady Bostock from the drawing-room.'

'Dramatic.'

'I'll say it was dramatic. The memory of that moment is going to haunt me for the rest of my life. I don't suppose I shall sleep again for months and months and months.'

'We all sleep too much.'

'She said "Who's that?"'

'And you, I suppose, said "Me," meaning that it was you.'

'I hadn't time to say anything, because she suddenly leaped forward with a sort of pitying cluck—'

'A what?'

'A cluck. Of pity. Like a nice hen. She really is a good sort, Uncle Fred. I had never realized it before. When I was down here, doing the bust, she always seemed stiff and distant. But it was just her manner. She has a heart of gold.'

'A neat phrase, that. I must remember it. In what way did she exhibit this golden heart?'

'Why, by swooping down on me and grabbing the bust and saying in a hoarse whisper that she knew exactly why I had brought it and that she was terribly sorry for me and had begged Sir Aylmer to change his mind, but he wouldn't, so she would keep the bust and send me a cheque secretly and everything would be all right. And then she went into the collection room and locked it up in a cupboard, hurriedly, like a murderer concealing the body. And then she hustled me out. She didn't actually say "Fly!" but it amounted to that. And it all happened so quickly that there wasn't a thing I could do.'

'And there the bust is?'

'Yes. Locked up in a cupboard in Sir Aylmer's collection room with all Alice's jewels in it. Tie that for a disaster, Uncle Fred.'

All through the narrative, Lord Ickenham had been reviving like a watered flower. His air, as it reached its culminating point, was that of one hearing tidings of great joy.

'Disaster?' he said exuberantly. 'What do you mean, disaster? This is the most admirable thing that could have happened. I now have something I can get my teeth into. It is no longer a question merely of effecting an entry into the house, but of getting myself established there. And if there is one thing I enjoy more than another, it is getting established in other people's houses. It brings the roses to my cheeks and tones up my whole system. Here is the immediate procedure, as I see it. You will drive on to Ickenham, which will serve us as a base, and I will take my suitcase and put up at the local inn and weave my subtle schemes. Expect sensational results shortly.'

'You are really going to establish yourself at the house?'

'I am.'

'And I still mustn't say "How?"'

'You certainly must not. You just leave everything to me, confident that I shall act for the best, as always. But you look grave, my child. I hope not from any lack of faith in my vision and enterprise?'

'I was thinking of Pongo. What will he do, when you suddenly appear?'

'I should imagine he will get the start of his young life and skip like the high hills. And an excellent thing, too. Pongo is a chap who wants taking out of himself.'

The car drove off, and Lord Ickenham hoisted his suitcase and set off for the village. He was just wishing that he had thought of asking Sally to drop him at the inn, for it was a heavy suitcase, when something large and tomato-coloured loomed up before him, and he recognized Bill Oakshott.

## • II •

In Bill Oakshott's demeanour, as he approached, there was the suggestion of a somnambulist who, in addition to having blisters on both feet, is wrestling with an unpleasant nightmare. The scene through which he had recently passed, following so swiftly upon his election as judge of the Bonny Babies contest, had shaken to its foundations a system already weakened by the knowledge that Hermione Bostock loved another, and that other a libertine who kissed housemaids on doorsteps. In response to Lord Ickenham's whoop of welcome he stared dully, like a dying halibut.

'Oh, hullo, Lord Ickenham,' he said.

'Well, well, well!' cried the fifth earl buoyantly. The hour or two which he had spent with this massive youth had left him with a strong appreciation of his sterling worth, and he was delighted to see him again. 'Well, well, well, well, well! Bill Oakshott in person. Well met by moonlight, proud Oakshott.'

'Eh?'

'Adaptation of Shakespearian quotation. But let it go. It is not of the slightest importance. And how is every little thing with you, Bill Oakshott? Fine?'

'Well, to be absolutely accurate,' said Bill, 'no.'

Lord Ickenham raised his eyebrows.

'Not fine?'

'No. Bloody awful.'

'My dear chap, you surprise and shock me. I should have thought you would have been so glad to get back from a ghastly country like Brazil that life would have been roses, roses all the way. What's wrong?'

With his affairs in such disorder, Bill was in need of all the sympathy he could get. He decided to withhold nothing from this cordial and well-disposed old buster. It would not have taken much to make him sob on Lord Ickenham's chest.

'Well, to start with,' he said, touching on the most recent of the spiritual brickbats which had assailed his soul, 'my uncle's gone off his onion.'

Lord Ickenham pursed his lips.

'Nuts?'

'Completely nuts.'

'Indeed? That must jar you a good deal. Nothing spoils the quiet home atmosphere more than a goofy uncle on the premises. When did this tragedy occur?'

'Just now.'

'It came on suddenly?'

'Like a flash.'

'What caused it?'

'Pongo.'

Lord Ickenham seemed at a loss.

'You aren't telling me that a single day of Pongo has been enough to set a host sticking straws in his hair? If it had been two weeks . . . What were the symptoms?'

'Well, he gibbered a good bit, and now he's driven over to your place to get a photograph of Pongo.'

'Why?'

'To find out what he looks like.'

'Can't he see what he looks like?'

'He doesn't believe Pongo is Pongo.'

'But doesn't Pongo admit it?'

'He thinks he's an impostor.'

'Why?'

'I don't know. I tell you he's potty. I was out on the terrace and I heard him yelling for me, and I went to the study, and he said Hadn't I known Pongo when he was a kid? And I said Yes. And he said How did I know after all these years that this was the same chap and he was absolutely convinced that Pongo wasn't Pongo, and the only way to settle it was to drive to your place and get a photograph of him.'

Lord Ickenham shook his head.

'A fruitless quest. A man like myself, refined, sensitive, with a love for the rare and the beautiful, does not surround himself with photographs of Pongo. I could do him a nude Venus, if he would like one. Yes, it certainly looks as though you were right, Bill Oakshott, and that Mugsy's brain had come unstuck; the result, no doubt, of some sunstroke in the days when he was the curse of Africa. I'm not surprised that you are worried. The only thing I can suggest is that you give him plenty of aspirins, humour him in conversation and keep him away from razors, dinner knives and other sharp instruments. But apart from this everything is pretty smooth?'

Bill Oakshott laughed one of those hollow, mirthless laughs.

'Is it! If that was all I had to worry me, I should be singing like a lark.'

Lord Ickenham eyed him with concern. In his look, disappointment that he would not be able to hear his young friend singing like a lark was blended with distress at the news that he had further reasons for gloom.

'Don't tell me there is more? What else has happened, my ill-starred youth?'

Bill quivered, and for a moment could not speak.

'I saw Pongo kiss the housemaid,' he said in a low throaty voice.

Lord Ickenham was perplexed.

'But why shouldn't he?'

'Why shouldn't he? Dash it, he's engaged to my cousin Hermione.'

Lord Ickenham's face cleared.

'I see. Ah, yes, I understand. Her happiness is a matter of concern to you, and you do not like to think that she may be linking her lot with that of a Casanova. My dear chap, don't give the matter another thought. He does that sort of thing automatically. Where you or I would light a cigarette and throw off an epigram, Pongo kisses the housemaid. It means nothing. A purely unconscious reflex action.'

'H'm,' said Bill.

'I assure you,' said Lord Ickenham. 'You'll find it in all the case books. They have a scientific name for it. Housemaiditis? No. No, it's gone. But that ends your catalogue of woe? Apart from your uncle's strange seizure and this mannerism of Pongo's, you have nothing on your mind?'

'Haven't I!'

'You have? Is this the head upon which all the sorrows of the world have come? What is the next item?'

'Babies!'

'I beg your pardon?'

'Bonny babies.'

Lord Ickenham groped cautiously for his meaning.

'You are about to become a father?'

'I'm about to become a blasted judge.'

'You speak in riddles, Bill Oakshott. What do you mean, a judge?'

'At the fête.'

'What fête?' said Lord Ickenham. 'You are forgetting that I am a stranger in these parts. Tell me the whole story in your own words.'

He listened with interest while Bill did so, and the latter had no lack of sympathy to complain of when he had finished revealing the facts in connection with Sir Aylmer Bostock's hideous vengeance.

'Too bad, too bad,' said Lord Ickenham. 'But we might have foreseen something of the sort. As I warned you, these ex-Governors are tough eggs. They strike like lightning. So you are for it?'

'Unless I can find someone else to take on the job.' A sudden thought flushed Bill's brow. 'I say, will you do it?'

Lord Ickenham shook his head.

'Were the conditions right,' he said, 'I would spring to the task, for I can imagine no more delightful experience than judging a gaggle of bonny babies at a rural fête. But the conditions are not right. Mugsy would not accept my nomination. Between him and myself there is, alas, an unfortunate and I fear insurmountable barrier. As I told you on the train it is only the other day that he was curving his person into the posture best adapted for the receipt of six of the juiciest with a fives bat, and I was the motivating force behind the fives bat.'

'But, dash it, he'll have forgotten that.'

'Already?'

'Wasn't it forty years ago?'

'Forty-two. But you grievously underestimate the suppleness of my wrist at the age of eighteen, if you suppose that anyone to whom I administered six with a fives bat would forget it in forty-two years.'

'Well, if he hasn't forgotten it, what does it matter? You'll just have a good laugh together over the whole thing.'

'I disagree with you, Bill Oakshott. Why after your recent experience of his dark malignity you should suppose young Mugsy to be a sort of vat or container for the milk of human kindness, I cannot imagine. You must know perfectly well that in the warped soul of Mugsy Bostock there is no room for sweetness and light. Come now, be honest. Does he not chew broken glass and conduct human sacrifices at the time of the full moon? Of course he does. And yet you cling to this weak pretence that, with the old wounds still throbbing, he will forget and forgive.'

'We could try him.'

'Useless. He would merely scowl darkly and turn me from his door—or your door, didn't you tell me it was? And suppose he did not? Suppose he welcomed me? What then? It would mean starting an association which would last the rest of our lives. He would always be popping over to my place, and I would be expected to pop over here. Wife would meet wife, presents would be exchanged at Christmas, it would be appalling. Even to oblige you, my dear fellow, I could not contemplate such a thing. Did you say "Oh, hell!"?'

'Yes.'

'I thought you did, and it wrung my heart.'

There was a silence. Bill stared moodily at a passing beetle.

'Then I'm sunk.'

'But why? Have you no friends?'

'I've lost touch with them all, being away. The only one I could lay my hands on is Plank.'

'Who is Plank? Ah, yes, I remember. The head of the expedition you went on.'

'That's right. Major Brabazon-Plank.'

'*Brabazon*-Plank? You interest me strangely. I was at school with a fellow named Brabazon-Plank. He still owes me two bob. Is your Brabazon-Plank a pear-shaped chap, rather narrow in the shoulders and very broad in the beam?'

'Yes.'

'Practically all backside?'

'Yes.'

'Then it must be the same fellow. Bimbo we used to call him. Extraordinary what a mine of my old schoolmates you are turning out to be. You don't seem able to mention a name without it proving that of someone with whom in one way or another I used once to pluck the gowans fine. And you think you could contact Bimbo?'

'I have his address in London. We came back on the boat together. But it wouldn't be any use contacting him. If anyone suggested that he should judge bonny babies, he would run like a rabbit. He has a horror of them.'

'Indeed? The well-known baby fixation. See the case books.'

'All the way home on the boat he was moaning that when he got to England he would have to go and see his sisters, and he didn't know how he was going to face it, because all of them were knee-deep in babies which he would be expected to kiss. No, Plank's no good.'

'Then really,' said Lord Ickenham, 'it looks as if you would have to fall back on me.'

Bill, who had been staring dully at the beetle, transferred his gaze to his companion. It was a wide-eyed, gaping gaze, speaking eloquently of a mind imperfectly adjusted to the intellectual pressure of the conversation.

'Eh?'

'I say that you will be compelled, for want of anything better, to avail yourself of my poor services. Invite me to your home, and in return for this hospitality I will judge these bonny babies.'

Bill continued to gape.

'But you said you wouldn't.'

'Surely not?'

'Yes, you did. Just now.'

Lord Ickenham's perplexity vanished.

'Ah, I see where the confusion of thought has arisen,' he said. 'You misunderstood me. I merely meant that, for the reasons which I explained to you, it was impossible for that fine old English aristocrat, Frederick Altamont Cornwallis, Earl of Ickenham, to come barging in on an establishment of which Mugsy Bostock formed a part. What I am proposing now is that I shall throw a modest veil over my glittering identity.'

'Eh?'

'You do keep saying "Eh?" don't you? It is surely quite simple. I am most anxious to visit Ashenden Manor, of which I hear excellent reports, and I suggest that I do so incognito.'

'Under another name, do you mean?'

'Exactly. What a treat it is to deal with an intelligence like yours, Bill Oakshott. Under, as you put it so luminously, another name. As a matter of fact, I never feel comfortable going to stay at houses under my own name. It doesn't seem sporting.'

Bill Oakshott's was not a mind readily receptive of new ideas. As he stared at Lord Ickenham, his resemblance to a fish on a slab was more striking than ever.

'You'll call yourself something else?' he said, for he was a man who liked to approach these things from every angle.

'Precisely.'

'But—'

'I never like that word "But".'

'You couldn't get away with it.'

Lord Ickenham laughed lightly.

'My dear fellow, at The Cedars, Mafeking Road, in the suburb of Mitching Hill last spring I impersonated in a single afternoon and with complete success not only an official from the bird shop, come to clip the claws of the parrot, but Mr Roddis, lessee of The Cedars, and a Mr J. G. Bulstrode, a resident of the same neighbourhood. It has been a lasting grief to me that I was given no opportunity of impersonating the parrot, which I am convinced I should have done on broad, artistic lines.

Have no anxiety about my not being able to get away with it. Introduce me into the house, and I will guarantee to do the rest.'

The clearness with which he had expounded his scheme had enabled Bill to grasp it, but he was looking nervous and unhappy, like a man who has grasped the tail of a tiger.

'It's too risky. Suppose my uncle found out.'

'Are you afraid of Mugsy?'

'Yes.'

'More than of the bonny babies?'

Bill quivered. In every limb and feature he betrayed his consciousness of standing at a young man's cross-roads.

'But what's the procedure? You mean you just blow in, calling yourself Jones or Robinson?'

'Not Robinson. I have had occasion in the past to call myself Robinson, but it would not do now. You overlook the fact that the judge of a contest of this importance must be a man who counts. He must have authority and presence. I suggest that I come as Major Brabazon-Plank. It would give me genuine pleasure to impersonate old Bimbo, and I can think of no one more suitable. The whole thing is so plausible. You run into your old chief Plank, who happens to be passing by on a motor tour, and what more natural than that you should insist on him stopping off for a day or two at your home? And, having stopped off, what more natural than that he, learning of this very important and attractive job, a job which will render him the cynosure of all eyes and is in addition right up his street, he being passionately fond of babies, should insist on having it assigned to him? And the crowning beauty of the scheme is that I don't see how Mugsy can do anything about it. We've got him cold. It isn't as if Plank were just an ordinary man. Plank is a hell of a celebrity, and his wishes have to be deferred to. If you ask me, Bill Oakshott, if you care to have my unbiased opinion of the set-up, I think the thing's in the bag.'

Into Bill's fishlike eyes a gleam of enthusiasm had crept. His air was that of a red-faced young man who has been convinced by the voice of reason. He still feared the shape of things to come, should he fall in with his benefactor's suggestion, but he feared still more the shape of things to come, should he not.

Stamped indelibly on his mental retina was the memory of last year's fête, when he had watched the Rev. Aubrey Brotherhood preparing to embark on his duties in the big tent. Intrepid curate though he was, a man who could dominate the rowdiest Mothers' Meeting, the Rev. Aubrey had paled visibly at the task confronting him. Forty-three village matrons, holding in their arms in the hope of catching the judge's eye forty-three babies of almost the maximum repulsiveness . . .

'Right!' he cried with sudden resolution. 'Fine. Let's go.'

'Yes, let's,' said Lord Ickenham. 'You can carry the suitcase.'

They walked down the road. Bill, who had begun to think things over again, was a little silent and thoughtful, but Lord Ickenham was all gaiety and animation. He talked well and easily of this and that, and from time to time pointed out objects of interest by the wayside. They had just reached the Manor gates, when the uproar of an approaching car caused Bill to turn his head: and, having turned it, he paled beneath his tan and tottered slightly.

'Oh, golly, here comes my uncle. I say, do you think we really ought—'

'Tush, Bill Oakshott,' said Lord Ickenham, prompt in the hour of peril to stimulate and encourage. 'This is weakness. Stiffen the sinews, summon up the blood. Let us stand our ground firmly, and give him a huge hello.'

## • III •

Sir Aylmer Bostock had spent four minutes at Ickenham Hall, all on the front door step, and of these four minutes there had not been one which he had not disliked. Sometimes in our wanderings about the world we meet men of whom it is said that they have passed through the furnace. Of Sir Aylmer it would be more correct to say that he had passed through the frigidaire.

If you call at a country house where you are not known and try to get the butler to let you come in and search the premises for photographs of his employer's nephew, you will generally find this butler chilly in his manner, and Coggs, the major-domo of Ickenham Hall, had been rather chillier than the average. He was a large, stout, moon-faced man with an eye like that of a codfish, and throughout the proceedings he had kept his eye glued on Sir Aylmer's, as if peering into his soul. And anyone who has ever had his soul peered into by a codfish will testify how extremely unpleasant such an ordeal is.

The message in that eye had been only too easy to read. Coggs had not actually accused Sir Aylmer of being after the spoons, but the charge might just as well have been clothed in words. In a voice of ice he had said No, sir, I fear I cannot accede to your request, sir, and had then terminated the interview by backing a step and shutting the door firmly in the visitor's face. And when we say firmly, we mean with a bang which nearly jarred the latter's moustache loose from its foundations.

All this sort of thing is very galling to a proud and arrogant man, accustomed for years to having his lightest word treated as law, and it was consequently in no sunny mood that Sir Aylmer heard Lord Ickenham's huge hello. He was still snorting and muttering to himself, and a native chief who had encountered him in this dangerous mental condition would have called on his protecting ju-ju for quick service and climbed a tree.

Lord Ickenham was made of sterner stuff. He stepped out into the road and gave the huge hello, as planned.

'Hello, there, Mugsy,' he carolled. 'A very hearty pip-pip to you, my bright and bounding Bostock.'

It was probably astonishment at being addressed by a name which he supposed that he had lived down years ago, rather than the fact that the speaker was blocking the way, that caused Sir Aylmer to apply the brakes. He brought the car to a halt and leaned forward, glaring through the windscreen. Close scrutiny of Lord Ickenham afforded no clue to the latter's identity. All that Sir Aylmer was able to say with certainty was that this must be some old schoolfellow of his, and he wished he had had the moral courage to drive on and run over him.

It was too late to do this now, for Lord Ickenham had advanced and was standing with a friendly foot on the running board. With an equally friendly hand he slapped Sir Aylmer on the back, and his smile was just as friendly as his hand and foot. Sir Aylmer might not be glad to see this figure from the past, but the figure from the past was plainly glad to see Sir Aylmer.

'Mugsy,' he said with kindly reproach, 'I believe you've forgotten me.'

Sir Aylmer said he had. He contrived to convey in his manner the suggestion that he would willingly do so again.

'Too bad,' said Lord Ickenham. 'How evanescent are youth's gossamer friendships. Well, to put you out of your suspense, for I see that you are all keyed up, I'm Plank.'

'Plank?'

'Major Brabazon-Plank, Uncle Aylmer,' said Bill, emboldened by the suavity with which his accomplice was conducting these delicate pourparlers. 'Major Plank ran that expedition I went on to Brazil.'

Lord Ickenham was obliged to demur.

'Don't let him mislead you, Mugsy. In a strictly technical sense I suppose you might say I ran that expedition. Officially, no doubt, I was its head. But the real big noise was Bill Oakshott here. He was the life and soul of the party, giving up his water ration to the sick and ailing, conducting himself with cool aplomb among the alligators and encouraging with word and gesture the weaker brethren who got depressed because they couldn't dress for dinner. Chilled Steel Oakshott, we used to call him. You should be proud of such a nephew.'

Sir Aylmer appeared not to have heard these eulogies. He was still wrestling with what might be called the Plank angle of the situation.

'Plank?' he said. 'You can't be Plank.'

'Why not?'

'The Plank who was at school with me?'

'That very Plank.'

'But he was a fellow with an enormous trouser seat.'

'Ah, I see what is on your mind. Yes, yes. As a boy, quite true, I was bountifully endowed with billowy curves in the part you have indicated. But since those days I have been using Slimmo, the sovereign remedy for obesity. The results you see before you. You ought to try it yourself, Mugsy. You've put on weight.'

Sir Aylmer grunted. There was dissatisfaction in his grunt. Plainly, he was unwilling to relinquish his memories of a callipygous Plank.

'Well, I'm damned if I would have recognized you.'

'Nor I you, had not Bill Oakshott given me the office. We've both altered quite a bit. I don't think you had a white moustache at school, did you? And there's no ink on your collar.'

'You're really Plank?'

'None other.'

'And what are you doing here?'

'I'm on a motor tour.'

'Oh, are you?' said Sir Aylmer, brightening. 'Then you'll be wanting to get along. Good-bye, Plank.'

Lord Ickenham smiled a gentle, reassuring smile.

'That sad word will not be required here, Mugsy. Prepare to receive tidings of great joy. I'm coming to stay.'

'What!'

'I had intended to hurry on, but when Bill Oakshott became pressing, I could not refuse. Especially when he told me of this fête which is breaking loose shortly and promised that if I consented to be his guest at Ashenden Manor I might judge the Bonny Babies contest. That decided me. I would go fifty miles to judge bonny babies. Sixty,' said Lord Ickenham. 'Or make it a hundred.'

Sir Aylmer started like a tiger that sees its Indian villager being snatched away from it. His face, already mauve, became an imperial purple.

'You're not going to judge the bonny babies!'

'Yes, I am.'

'No, you're not.'

Lord Ickenham was a genial man, but he could be firm.

'I don't want any lip from you, young Mugsy,' he said sternly. 'Let me give you a word of warning. I see by the papers that you are about to stand for Parliament. Well, don't forget that I could swing the voting against you pretty considerably, if I wanted to, by letting an idealistic electorate in on some of the shady secrets of your boyhood. You won't like it, Mugsy, when questions about your boyhood are thundered at you from the body of the hall while you are outlining your views on the Tariff problem. Do I judge those bonny babies?'

Sir Aylmer sat brooding in silence, his Adam's apple moving up and down as if he were swallowing something hard and jagged. The stoutest man will quail at the prospect of having the veil torn from his past, unless that past is one of exceptional purity. He scowled, but scowling brought no solace. He chewed his moustache, but gained no comfort thereby.

'Very well,' he said at length, speaking as if the words were being pulled out of him with a dentist's forceps. His eye, swivelling round, rested for an instant on Bill's, and the young man leaped convulsively. 'Oh, very well.'

'Good,' said Lord Ickenham, his cheery self once more. 'That's settled. And now you shall take me home and show me the model dairy.'

'What model dairy?'

'Haven't you a model dairy? The stables, then.'

'I don't keep horses.'

'Odd. I was always led to believe that hosts at English country houses were divided into two classes: those who, when helpless guests were in their power, showed them the stables and those who showed them the model dairy. There was also, I understood, a minor sub-division which showed them the begonias, but that is a technicality into which we need not go. No model dairy, you say? No horses? Then perhaps I had better be going to the inn, where I have one or two things to do. These seen to, I will present myself at the house, and the revels can commence. And as you are doubtless anxious to hurry on and get my room—one with a southern exposure, if possible—swept and garnished, I won't detain you. You coming with me, Bill Oakshott?'

'I think I'll stay here and smoke a pipe.'

'Just as you please. We shall all meet then, at Philippi, and very jolly it will be, too.'

It was with a light and elastic step that Lord Ickenham made his way to the Bull's Head in Ashenden Oakshott's High Street. He was well satisfied with the progress of affairs. Something attempted, something done had, in his opinion, earned the spot of beer to which he had been looking forward for some considerable time, for this spreading of sweetness and light is thirsty work. After putting through a telephone call to his home and speaking to Sally, he sat down to a tankard, and was savouring its amber contents with quiet relish, when the door of the saloon bar burst open with a good deal of violence and Bill Oakshott entered.

That Bill was not at his serenest and most tranquil was indicated at once to Lord Ickenham's experienced eye by his appearance and deportment. His hair was ruffled, as if he had been passing a fevered hand through it, and that glazed look was back in his eyes. He was a young man who, when things went awry, always endeavoured, after the fashion of the modern young man, to preserve the easy repose of manner of a Red Indian at the stake, but it was plain that whatever had occurred to upset him now was of a magnitude which rendered impossible such an exhibition of stoicism.

'Ah, Bill Oakshott,' said Lord Ickenham affably. 'You could not have arrived at a more opportune moment. You find me enjoying a well-earned gargle, like Cæsar in his tent the day he overcame the Nervii. I stress the adjective "well-earned", for I think you will admit that in the recent exchanges I put it across the Nervii properly. Have you ever seen an ex-Governor so baffled? I haven't, and I doubt if anyone has. But you seem disturbed about something, and I would recommend some of this excellent beer. It will strengthen you and help you to look for the silver lining.'

He went to the counter, remained there a while in conversation with the stout blonde behind it, and returned bearing a foaming tankard.

'Nice girl,' he said paternally. 'I've been telling her about Brazil. Quaff that, Bill Oakshott, and having quaffed spill what is on your mind.'

Bill, who had been sitting with his head clasped in his hands, took a deep draught.

'It's about this business of your coming to the house as Plank.'

'Ah yes?'

'You can't go on with it.'

Lord Ickenham raised his eyebrows.

'Can't? A strange word to use to the last of a proud family. Did my ancestors say "Can't" on the stricken fields of the Middle Ages, when told off to go and fight the Paynim? As a matter of fact,' said Lord Ickenham confidentially, 'I believe lots of them did, as you can verify by turning up Richard Cœur de Lion's dispatches, so perhaps it is a pity that I asked the question. Why do you say I can't go on with it?'

'Because you jolly well can't. Shall I tell you what's happened?'

'Do. I'm all agog.'

Bill finished his tankard, and seemed to draw from it strength to continue.

'After you went away,' he said tonelessly, 'Uncle Aylmer drove off in the car, leaving me stuck there with the suitcase.'

'A low trick.'

'I yelled to him to stop and take the damned thing, because it weighed a ton and I didn't want to have to lug it all the way up the drive, but he wouldn't. And I was just starting off with it, when Potter came along on his bike.'

'Who is Potter?'

'The policeman.'

'Ah yes. Pongo spoke of him, I remember. A zealous officer.'

'So I said, "Oh, Potter" and he said "Sir?" and I said "You in a hurry?" and he said "No, sir," and I said "Then I wish you'd take this suitcase up to the house." And he said "Certainly, sir," and hoisted it aboard his bike.'

'I like your dialogue,' said Lord Ickenham critically. 'It's crisp and good. Do you ever write?'

'No.'

'You should. You'd make a packet. But I'm interrupting you.'

'You are a bit.'

'It shall not occur again. You had got to where Potter said "Certainly, sir." Then what?'

'I said "It belongs to Major Brabazon-Plank. He's coming to stay." And Potter said . . . Could I have another beer?'

'Had he already had some beer?'

'I mean, could I have, now? I think it might pull me together.'

Lord Ickenham repeated his trip to the counter.

'You were saying,' he said, having returned with the life-giving fluid, 'that you told Potter that the suitcase belonged to Major Brabazon-Plank. In response to which?'

Bill drank deeply, gasped a little and spoke with a sort of frozen calm.

'In response to which he said, his bally face lighting up joyfully, "Major Brabazon-Plank? Did you say Major Brabazon-Plank? Coo, I know him well. He comes from my old village. Played cricket with him, I have—ah, hundreds of times. If convenient, Mr William, I'll step up and shake him by the hand after I've had my tea." So now what?'

Lord Ickenham remained for a moment in thought.

'You're kidding me, Bill Oakshott. Nobody but a practiced writer could have told that story so superbly. Beneath your magic touch Potter seems to live and breathe. You publish your stuff secretly under another name. I believe you're one, if not more, of the Sitwells. But we can go into that later. "So now what?" you say. Yes, I agree that the problem is one that presents certain features of interest, but all problems can be solved with a little earnest thought. How did you articulate when you spoke the words "Brabazon-Plank"? Distinctly?'

'Yes.'

'You didn't mumble?'

'No.'

'So you couldn't say that what you had really said was "Smith" or "Knatchbull-Huguessen"?'

'No.'

Lord Ickenham reflected.

'Well, then, what we must do is tell him that I am your Plank's brother.'

'Do you think you could get away with that?'

'There are no limits to what I can get away with when I am functioning properly. We might go and call upon him now. Where does he live?'

'Just round the corner.'

'Then finish up your beer and let's be off.'

Except for the royal arms over the door and a notice saying 'Police Station', there was nothing about the residence of Constable Potter to suggest there here was the dreadful headquarters of Law and Justice. Like so many police stations in English villages, it was a cheerful little cottage with a thatched roof and a nice little garden, the latter at the moment occupied by Mr Potter's nephew Basil, aged nine months, who was taking a nap in his perambulator. Lord Ickenham, reaching the garden gate, cocked an inquiring eye at this vehicle.

'Is Potter a married man?'

'No. That's his sister's baby. She lives with him. Her husband's a steward on one of the South American boats. He's away most of the time. Of course, he comes back sometimes.'

'Yes, one guesses that.'

Through an open window there came the sound of a female voice, high and penetrating. It was touching on the subject of socks. How, it was asking, did the invisible person it was addressing contrive to get so many and such large holes in his all the time? The voice itself attributed the phenomenon to carelessness and a wilful lack of consideration for those who had to work their fingers to the bone, darning them. Lord Ickenham consulted Bill with a raised eyebrow.

'Would that be the lady speaking now?'

'Yes.'

'To Potter?'

'I suppose so.'

'She seems to be giving him beans.'

'Yes. He's scared stiff of her, so Elsie tells me.'

'Elsie?'

'The housemaid.'

'Ah, yes, the one Pongo . . . I forget what I was going to say.'

'I know what you were going to say.'

'Well, well, we need not go into that now. Let us saunter in, and let our first move be to examine this bonny baby more closely. It will all be practice for the great day.'

# 7

## · 1 ·

Inside the cottage, in the cosy little kitchen, Constable Potter, guardian of Ashenden Oakshott's peace, at his ease in his shirt sleeves, was enjoying high tea.

The word 'enjoying' is perhaps ill chosen, for he was partaking of the meal under the eye of his sister, Mrs Bella Stubbs, who, if not his best friend, had always been his severest critic. She had already told him not to put his elbows on the table, not to gollop his food like that and not to help himself to butter with his herringy knife, and at the moment when Bill and Lord Ickenham arrived had begun, as has been shown, to touch on the subject of his socks, one of which she held in her hand for purposes of demonstration.

Constable Potter was twenty-eight years old, his sister thirty-three. The simplest of mathematical calculations, therefore, will show that when he was seven she had been twelve, and a strong-willed sister of twelve can establish over a brother of seven a moral ascendancy which lasts a lifetime. In those formative years which mean so much, Harold

Potter had been dragged about by the hand, slapped, scolded and told by the future mother of George Basil Percival Stubbs not to do practically everything he wanted to do. She had even—crowning indignity—blown his nose.

These things leave their mark. It was the opinion of Elsie Bean, repeatedly expressed, that her Harold was a cowardy custard; and in the main, one feels, the verdict of history will be that Elsie was right. It is unpleasant to think of an officer of the Law cowering in his chair when a woman puts a finger through a hole in one of his socks and waggles it, but it cannot be disputed that while watching Mrs Stubbs do this Constable Potter had come very near to cowering.

To ease the strain, he bent forward to help himself to butter, being careful this time to use the knife allotted to that purpose, and the movement enabled him to see through the window the corner of the garden where George Basil Percival was taking his siesta.

''Ullo,' he said, glad to change the subject. 'There's somebody on the lawn.'

'Never mind about the lawn. I'm talking about this sock.'

'It's a tall gentleman.'

'Look at it. Like a sieve.'

'A tall gentleman with a grey moustache. He's poking your Basil in the stomach.'

He had said the one thing calculated to divert his companion's thoughts from the sock topic. A devoted mother, Mrs Stubbs held the strongest possible views on the enormity of gentlemen, whether tall or short, coming into the garden and poking her offspring in the stomach at a moment when his well-being demanded uninterrupted repose.

'Then go and send him away!'

'Right ho.'

Constable Potter was full to the brim. He had eaten three kippered herrings, four boiled eggs and half a loaf of bread, and his impulse would have been to lean back in his chair like a gorged python and give his gastric juices a chance to fulfil themselves. But, apart from the fact that his sister Bella's word was law, curiosity overcame the urge to digest.

Scrutinizing Lord Ickenham through the window, he had a sort of feeling that he had seen him before. He wanted to get a closer view of this mysterious stranger.

In the garden, when he reached it, Lord Ickenham, wearying of his attentions to Basil's stomach, had begun to tickle the child under the chin. Bill, who was not very fond of babies and in any case preferred them to look less like Edward G. Robinson, had moved aside as if anxious to disassociate himself from the whole unpleasant affair, and was thus the first to see the newcomer.

'Oh, hullo, Potter,' he said. 'We thought we'd look in.'

'I was anxious,' said Lord Ickenham, 'to make the acquaintance of one of whom I had heard so much.'

Constable Potter seemed a little dazed by these civilities.

'Ho!' he said. 'I didn't catch the name, sir.'

'Plank. Brabazon-Plank.'

There was a loud hiccough. It was Constable Potter registering astonishment; and more than astonishment, suspicion. There were few men, in Ashenden Oakshott at any rate, more gifted with the ability to recognize funny business when they were confronted with it, and here, it seemed to Harold Potter, was funny business in excelsis. He fixed on Lord Ickenham the stern and accusing gaze which he would have directed at a dog caught in the act of appearing in public without a collar.

'Brabazon-Plank?'

'Brabazon-Plank.'

'You're not the Major Brabazon-Plank I used to play cricket with at Lower Shagley in Dorsetshire.'

'His brother.'

'I didn't know he had a brother.'

'He kept things from you, did he? Too bad. Yes, I am his elder brother. Bill Oakshott was telling me you knew him.'

'He said you was him.'

'Surely not?'

'Yus, he did.' Constable Potter's gaze grew sterner. He was resolved to probe this thing to the bottom. 'He give me your suitcase to take to the house, and he said "This here belongs to Major Brabazon-Plank."'

Lord Ickenham laughed amusedly.

'Just a slip of the tongue, such as so often occurs. He meant Brabazon-Plank, *major*. As opposed to my brother, who, being younger than me, is, of course, Brabazon-Plank, *minor*. I can understand you being confused,' said Lord Ickenham with a commiserating glance at the officer, into whose face had crept the boiled look of one who finds the conversation becoming too abstruse. Three kippers, four eggs and half a loaf of bread, while nourishing the body, take the keen edge off the mental powers. 'And what renders it all the more complex is that as I myself am a mining engineer by profession, anyone who wants to get straight on the Brabazon-Plank situation has got to keep steadily before him the fact that the minor is a major and the major a miner. I have known strong men to break down on realizing this. So you know my minor, the major, do you? Most interesting. It's a small world, I often say. Well, when I say "often", perhaps once a fortnight. Why are you looking like a stuck pig, Bill Oakshott?'

Bill came with a start out of what appeared to be a sort of trance. Pongo, who had had so many opportunities of observing his Uncle Fred in action, could have told him that a trancelike condition was almost always the result of being associated with this good old man when he was going nicely.

'Was I?'

'Yes.'

'Sorry.'

'Don't mention it. Ah, whom have we here?'

Mrs Stubbs had made her appearance, coming towards them with a suggestion in her manner of a lioness hastening to the aid of an imperilled cub. Annoyed by her brother's tardiness in getting rid of these intruders, she had decided to take the matter in hand herself.

'Oh, hullo, Mrs Stubbs,' said Bill. 'We were just giving your baby the once over.'

Lord Ickenham started.

'Your baby? Is this remarkably fine infant yours, madam?'

His bearing was so courteous, his manner so reverent that Mrs Stubbs, who had come in like a lioness, began to envisage the possibility of going out like a lamb.

'Yes, sir,' she said, and went so far as to curtsy. She was not a woman who often curtsied, but there was something about this distinguished-looking elderly gentleman that seemed to call for the tribute. 'It's my little Basil.'

'A sweet name. And a sweet child. A starter I hope?'

'Sir?'

'You have entered him for the Bonny Baby contest at the fête?'

'Oh, yes, sir.'

'Good. Excellent. It would have been madness to hide his light under a bushel. Have you studied this outstanding infant closely, Bill Oakshott? If not, do so now,' said Lord Ickenham, 'for you will never have a better chance of observing a classic yearling. What hocks! What pasterns! And what lungs!' he continued, as George Basil Percival, waking, like Abou ben Adhem, from a deep dream of peace, split the welkin with a sudden howl. 'I always mark heavily for lungs. I should explain, madam, that I am to have the honour of acting as judge at the contest to which I have referred.'

'You are, sir?'

'I am, indeed. Is your husband at home? No? A pity. I would have advised him to pick up a bit of easy money by putting his shirt on this child for the Bonny Baby stakes. Have you a shirt, Mr Potter? Ah, I see you have. Well, slap it on the stable's entry and fear nothing. I have at present, of course, no acquaintance with local form, but I cannot imagine that there will be another competitor of such supreme quality as to nose him out. I see myself at the close of the proceedings raising Basil's hand in the air with the words "The winnah!" Well, Mrs Stubbs,' said Lord Ickenham, with a polished bow in the direction of his hostess and a kindly 'Kitchy-kitchy' to the coming champ, who was staring at him with what a more sensitive man would have considered offensive curiosity, 'we must be pushing along. We have much to do. Good-bye, Mrs Stubbs. Good-bye, baby. Good-bye, off—'

He paused, the word unspoken. Constable Potter had suddenly turned and was making for the cottage at a high rate of speed, and Lord Ickenham stared after him a little blankly.

'Gone without a cry!' he said. 'I suppose he forgot something.'

'His manners,' said Mrs Stubbs tartly. 'The idea!'

'Ah, well,' said Lord Ickenham, always inclined to take the tolerant view, 'what are manners, if the heart be of gold? Goodbye again, Mrs Stubbs. Good-bye, baby. As I say, we must be moving. May I repeat what a privilege it has been to get together with this superb child in what I may term his training quarters and urge you once more, with all the emphasis at my disposal, to put the family shirt on him for the big event. There could be no sounder investment. Good-bye,' said Lord Ickenham, 'good-bye, good-bye,' and took his departure, scattering sweetness and light in all directions.

Out in the road he paused to light a cigar.

'How absurdly simple these things are,' he said, 'when you have someone with elephantiasis of the brain, like myself, directing the operations. A few well-chosen words, and we baffle the constable just as we baffled Mugsy. Odd that he should have left us so abruptly. But perhaps he went in to spray his temples with eau-de-Cologne. I got the impression that he was cracking under the strain a little when I was dishing out that major and minor stuff.'

'How did you come to think of that?'

'Genius,' said Lord Ickenham modestly. 'Pure genius.'

'I wonder if he swallowed it.'

'I think so. I hope so.'

'You laid it on a bit thick about that ruddy baby.'

'Kind words are never wasted, Bill Oakshott. And now for Ashenden Manor, I think, don't you, and the warm English welcome.'

Bill seemed uncertain.

'Do you know, I believe I could do with some more beer.'

'You feel faint?'

'I do, rather.'

'All right, then, you push on to the pub. I must try to find Pongo. Would he be in the house?'

'No, I saw him going out.'

'Then I will scour the countryside for him. It is vital,' said Lord Ickenham, 'that I put him abreast of the position of affairs before he has an opportunity of spilling the beans. We don't want him charging in when I am chatting with Mugsy and calling me "Uncle Fred". Before we settle down to the quiet home evening to which I am looking forward so much, he must be informed that he is losing an uncle but gaining a Brazilian explorer. So for the moment, bung-ho. Where was it I told Mugsy that we would all meet? Ah, yes, at Philippi. See you there, then, when you have drunk your fill.'

## • II •

In times of spiritual disturbance there is nothing like a brisk mystery thriller for taking the mind off its anxieties. Pongo's first move after parting from Sir Aylmer Bostock had been to go to his room and get his copy of *Murder in the Fog*; his second to seek some quiet spot outside the grounds, where there would be no danger of meeting the ex-Governor on his return, and soothe himself with a good read. He found such a spot at the side of the road not far from the Manor gates, and soon became absorbed.

The treatment proved almost immediately effective. That interview with Sir Aylmer in the hall had filled him with numbing fears and rendered him all of a twitter, but now he found his quivering ganglia getting back to mid-season form: and, unlike the heroine of the tale in which he was immersed, who had just got trapped in the underground den of one of those Faceless Fiends who cause so much annoyance, he was feeling quite tranquil, when a shadow fell on the page, a well-remembered voice spoke his name, and he looked up to see his Uncle Fred standing before him.

If there is one occasion more than another when joy might be expected to be unconfined and happiness to reign supreme, it is surely, one would say, when a nephew in the course of a country ramble encounters an uncle who in his time has often dandled him on his knee. At such a moment one would anticipate the quick indrawing of the breath, the raising of the eyes thankfully to heaven and the meeting of hand and hand in a fervent clasp.

It is unpleasant, therefore, to have to record that in Pongo's bosom, as he beheld Lord Ickenham, joy was not the predominating emotion. He could scarcely, indeed, have appeared more disconcerted if the Faceless Fiend from the volume in his hand had popped from its pages to confront him.

'Uncle Fred!' he ejaculated. The burned child fears the fire, and bitter experience had taught Pongo Twistleton to view with concern the presence in his midst of Ickenham's fifth earl. One recalls the words, quoted in a previous chapter, of the thoughtful crumpet. 'Good Lord, Uncle Fred, what on earth are you doing here?'

Lord Ickenham, unlike Sir Aylmer Bostock, was a man who believed in breaking things gently. With a tale to unfold whose lightest word would harrow up his nephew's soul and make his two eyes, like stars, start from their spheres, he decided to hold it in for the time being and to work round gradually and by easy stages to what Pongo would have called the nub. With a gentle smile on his handsome face, he lowered himself to the ground and gave his moustache a twirl.

'Just pottering to and fro, my boy, just pottering to and fro. This road is open for being pottered in at this hour, I believe.'

'But I left you at Ickenham.'

'The parting was agony.'

'You told me you were going to London.'

'So I did.'

'You never said a word about coming here.'

'No, but you know how it is. Things happen. One's plans become modified.'

A passing ant paused to investigate Pongo's wrist. He flung it from him, and the ant, alighting on its head some yards to the sou'-sou'-east, went off to warn other ants to watch out for earthquakes.

'I might have known it,' he cried passionately. 'You're going to start something.'

'No, no.'

'Then what's up?'

Lord Ickenham considered the question.

'I don't know that I would go so far as to say that anything was actually *up*. The word is too strong. Certain complications have arisen, it is true, but nothing that cannot be adjusted by a couple of cool, calm men of the world who keep their heads. Let me begin at the beginning. I went to London and gave Sally dinner, and in the course of the meal she revealed why it was that she had wanted to see me so urgently. It seems that her brother Otis is in trouble again. She asked me to tell you all about it and endeavour to enlist your aid.'

As the story of Otis Painter and Sir Aylmer Bostock's Reminiscences unfolded itself, relief poured over Pongo in a healing wave. He blamed himself for having so readily fallen a prey to the agitation which the unexpected appearance of his Uncle Fred was so apt to occasion in him. Up to this point he had been standing. He now sat down with the air of a man who is at his ease. He even laughed, a thing which he was seldom able to do when in conference with his uncle.

'Rather funny,' he said.

'The matter is not without its humorous aspect,' Lord Ickenham agreed. 'But we must not forget that if the action goes through, Sally stands to lose a lot of money.'

'That's true. So she wants me to plead with the old boy and get him to settle the thing out of court. Well, I'll do what I can.'

'You speak doubtfully. Doesn't he love you like a son?'

'I wouldn't say absolutely like a son. You see, I broke one of his African curios.'

'You do break things, don't you? And this has rankled?'

'I fancy it has to some extent. When I met him in the hall just now, he gave me a nasty look and a couple of distinctly unpleasant "Ha's!" The slant I got was that he had been thinking me over and come to the conclusion that I was a bit of a louse. Still, he may come round.'

'Of course he will. You must persevere.'

'Oh, rather.'

'That's the spirit. Keep after him, exerting all your charm. Remember what it means to Sally.'

'Right ho. And is that really all you wanted to see me about?'

'I think so. Except . . . Now what else was it I wanted to see you about? . . . Ah, yes, I remember. That bust of Sally's. The one you borrowed from my place.'

'Oh, the old busto? Yes, of course. Well, everything went according to plan. I sneaked it in all right. A testing experience, though. If you knew what I went through, beetling across the hall with the thing in my possession, expecting every moment to feel old Bostock's hot breath on the back of my neck!'

'I can readily imagine it. I wonder,' said Lord Ickenham, 'if you know how these busts are made? Sally has been explaining it to me. It is a most interesting process. You first model the clay. Then you slap on it a coat of liquid plaster.'

'Oh, yes?'

'After that you wait a little while until the plaster becomes fairly hard, when you divide it into two neat halves and throw away the clay. You then fill the mould with plaster.'

'Very jolly, if you like that sort of thing,' said Pongo tolerantly. 'How was Sally looking?'

'At first, radiant. Later, somewhat perturbed.'

'About Otis, you mean?'

'About Otis—and other things. But let me finish telling you about the way busts are made. You fill the mould with plaster, leaving a small empty space at the top. This,' said Lord Ickenham, feeling that he had now broken the thing sufficiently gently, 'you utilize as a repository for any jewels that any friend of yours may wish to smuggle into the United States.'

'What!' Pongo shot up in a whirl of arms and legs. Another ant, which climbed on to his wrist in a rather sceptical spirit, took as impressive a toss as its predecessor had done, and might have been observed some moments later rubbing its head and telling a circle of friends that old George had been right when he had spoken of seismic disturbances. 'You don't mean—?'

'Yes. Inadvertently, intending no harm, we appear to have got away with the bust in which Sally had cached her friend Alice Vansittart's bit of stuff. The idea came to her, apparently, shortly after you had refused to help her out. It seems a pity now that you were not more amenable. Of course, as Hamlet very sensibly remarked, there's nothing either good or bad but thinking makes it so; still, a rather sticky situation has unquestionably been precipitated. The Vansittart sails for New York next week.'

'Oh, my gosh!'

'You see the drama of the thing? I thought you would. Well, there it is. You will agree with me, I think, that we are in honour bound to return these trinkets. Can't go snitching a poor girl's little bit of jewellery. Not done. Not cricket.'

Pongo nodded. Nobody could teach him anything about *noblesse oblige*. He shrank from repeating the dreadful performance to which he had forced himself on his arrival at the house, but he quite saw that it had to be done.

'That's right,' he said. 'I'll have to nip over to Ickenham and get another bust. Will Coggs be able to dig me out one?'

'No,' said Lord Ickenham. 'And if he could, it would not be any good. Another complication has occurred, which I must now relate to you. You remember the bust Sally did of Sir Aylmer, the one that was to have been presented to the village club, poor devils. Piqued as the result of this Otis business, he returned it to her, and I brought her down here this afternoon in my car and she crept into the house and substituted it for the one with Miss Vansittart's jewels in it. And just as she was getting away with the latter, Lady Bostock intercepted her, took it away from her and locked it up in a cupboard in the room where the African curios are. And there it now is. So—'

Pongo interrupted, speaking quickly and forcefully. There are limits to what *noblesse* obliges.

'I know what you're going to say,' he cried. 'You want me to sneak down in the middle of the night and break open the cupboard and pinch it. Well, I'm jolly well not going to do it.'

'No, no,' said Lord Ickenham. 'Calm yourself, my dear boy. I would not dream of burdening you with such a responsibility. I will do the pinching.'

'You?'

'In person.'

'But you can't get into the house.'

'I wish people wouldn't tell me I can't do things. It is all going to be perfectly simple. My young friend, Bill Oakshott, has invited me to stay at Ashenden Manor. He wants me to judge the Bonny Babies contest at a fête they are having here shortly. Why his choice fell upon me, one cannot say. I suppose he knew I was good. These things get about.'

Pongo gazed up at the reeling sky and sent his haggard eyes roaming over a countryside that had broken into a sort of Ouled Nail muscle dance. His face was drawn, and his limbs twitched. Lord Ickenham, watching him, received the impression that he did not like the idea of his, Lord Ickenham's, approaching visit to Ashenden Manor.

'You're coming to the house?' he gasped.

'I go into residence this evening. And, by the way,' said Lord Ickenham, 'another small point. I nearly forgot to mention it. My name during my visit will be Brabazon-Plank. Major Brabazon-Plank, the well-known Brazilian explorer. Don't forget it, will you.'

From between Pongo's hands, which he had clasped on either side of his head, as if to prevent it dividing itself into two neat halves like a plaster bust, there proceeded a low moaning sound. Lord Ickenham regarded him sympathetically and, in an endeavour to relieve the situation of some of its tenseness, began to chant in a pleasant baritone an old song hit of his youth. And he was interested some moments later to find that this, starting as a solo, seemed suddenly to have turned into a duet. Glancing over his shoulder, he perceived the reason. Constable Potter was riding up on his bicycle, shouting 'Hoy!'

## • III •

Lord Ickenham was always the soul of courtesy. You had only to shout 'Hoy!' at him from a bicycle to have him drop everything and give you his immediate attention.

'Ah, officer,' he said. 'You crave an audience?'

Constable Potter dismounted, and stood for a space bent over the handle-bars, puffing. His sharp ride, taken at a moment when he was loaded down above the Plimsoll mark with eggs, bread, tea and kippered herrings, had left him short of breath. Lord Ickenham, in his considerate way, begged him to take his time.

Presently the puffing ceased, and Harold Potter spoke.

'Ho!' he said.

'Ho to you,' replied Lord Ickenham civilly. 'Have a cigar?'

With an austere gesture Constable Potter declined the cigar. A conscientious policeman does not accept gifts at the hands of the dregs of the criminal world, and such he now knew this man before him to be.

Ever since that odd episode in the garden, the reader of this record, the chronicler is aware, has been in a fever of impatience to learn what it was that sent this splendid upholder of law and order shooting into his cottage with such curious abruptness. This can now be revealed. The social lapse which had caused Mrs Bella Stubbs to purse her lips and comment acidly on his lack of manners had been occasioned by the fact that he had got the goods on Lord Ickenham. He had remembered where he had seen him before, and he had hurried indoors to consult his scrap album and ascertain his name. Having ascertained his name, he had mounted his bicycle and ridden off to confront and denounce him.

He fixed Lord Ickenham with a gimlet-like eye.

'Brabazon-Plank!' he said.

'Why,' asked Lord Ickenham, 'do you say "Brabazon-Plank" in that strange tone, as if it were some kind of expletive?'

'Ho!'

'Now we're back where we started. This is where we came in.'

Constable Potter decided that the time had come to explode his bombshell. On his face was that hard, keen look which comes into the faces of policemen when they intend to do their duty pitilessly and crush a criminal like a snake beneath the heel. It was the look which Constable Potter's face wore when he was waiting beneath a tree to apprehend a small boy who was up in its branches stealing apples, the merciless expression that turned it to flint when he called at a house to serve a summons on somebody for moving pigs without a permit.

'Brabazon-Plank, eh? You call yourself Brabazon-Plank, do you? Ho!

You look to me more like George Robinson of 14 Nasturtium Road, East Dulwich.'

Lord Ickenham stared. He removed the cigar from his mouth and stared again.

'Don't tell me you're the cop who pinched me that day at the dog races!'

'Yus, I am.'

A bubbling cry like that of some strong swimmer in his agony proceeded from Pongo's lips. He glared wildly at the helmeted figure of doom. Lord Ickenham, in sharp contradistinction, merely beamed, like one of a pair of lovers who have met at journey's end.

'Well, I'll be dashed,' he said cordially. 'What a really remarkable thing. Fancy running into you again like this. I'd never have known you. You've grown a moustache since then, or something. My dear fellow, this is delightful. What are you doing in these parts?'

There was no answering cordiality in Harold Potter's manner as he intensified the gimlet quality of his gaze. He was taut and alert, as became an officer who, after a jog-trot existence of Saturday drunks and failures to abate smoky chimneys, finds himself faced for the first time with crime on a colossal scale.

For that this was the real big stuff he had no doubt whatsoever. All the evidence went, as he himself would have said, to establish it. On the previous afternoon that shambling miscreant, Edwin Smith, had insinuated himself into Ashenden Manor under the alias of Twistleton. This evening along came his sinister associate, George Robinson, under the alias of Brabazon-Plank. And here they were together by the roadside, plotting. If you could not call this the Muster of the Vultures, it would be interesting, Harold Potter felt, to know what set of circumstances did qualify for that description.

'What are *you* doing in these parts, is more like it,' he retorted. 'You and your pal Edwin Smith there.'

'So you've recognized him, too? You have an extraordinary memory for faces. Like the royal family. What are we doing in these parts, you ask? Just paying a country-house visit.'

'Oh, yes?'

'I assure you.'

'You think you are,' corrected Constable Potter. 'But a fat lot of country-house visiting you're going to do.'

Lord Ickenham raised his eyebrows.

'Pongo.'

'Guk?'

'I think the gentleman intends to unmask us.'

'Guk.'

'Do you intend to unmask us, Mr Potter?'

'Yus.'

'I wouldn't.'

'Ho!'

There was infinite kindliness in Lord Ickenham's voice as he went on to explain himself. You could see that he felt the deepest sympathy for Constable Potter.

'No, honestly I wouldn't. Consider what will happen. I shall be ejected—'

'You're right, you'll be ejected!'

'—And my place as judge of the Bonny Babies contest taken by another judge, less prejudiced in favour of your sister's little Basil. The child will finish among the also-rans, and in this event will not your sister make inquiries? And having made them and ascertained that it was through your agency that I was disqualified, will she not have a word or two to say to you on the subject? Think it over, my dear chap, and I fancy you will agree with me that the conditions for unmasking are none too good.'

It sometimes happens to a policeman that he is sharply censured by a bench of magistrates. When this occurs, he feels as if he had been kicked in the stomach by a mule and the world becomes black. The effect of these words on Constable Potter was to give him the illusion that he had been censured by half a dozen benches of magistrates, all speaking at once. His jaw drooped like a lily, and in a low voice, instinct with emotion, he uttered the word 'Coo!'

'You may well say "Coo!"' agreed Lord Ickenham. 'I know Mrs Stubbs only slightly, of course, but she struck me as a woman of high spirit, the last person to mince her words to the man instrumental in robbing her child of the coveted trophy. Potter, I would think twice.'

Constable Potter only needed to think once. For a long instant there was a silence, one of those heavy silences which seem to be made of glue. Then, still without speaking, he mounted his bicycle and rode off.

Lord Ickenham was a fighter who could always be generous to a beaten foe.

'Amazingly fine stuff there is in our policemen,' he said. 'You crush them to earth, and they rise again. You think you've baffled them, and up they pop, their helmets still in the ring. However, this time I fancy the trick has been done. There, in my opinion, pedalled a policeman whose lips are sealed.'

Pongo, always prone to the gloomy view, demurred.

'How do you know? He was heading for the house. He's probably gone off to tell old Bostock the whole story.'

'You say that because you do not know his sister. No, no. Sealed lips, my dear Pongo, sealed lips. You have now nothing whatever to worry about.'

Pongo uttered a mirthless laugh of a quality which would have extorted the admiration of Bill Oakshott, a specialist in that line.

'Nothing to worry about? Ha! With you coming to stay with Hermione's people under a—what's the word—'

'Pseudonym?'

'Pseudonym. And planning to prowl about busting open cupboards!'

'Don't let that trivial matter give you the slightest anxiety, my dear boy. I shall attend to that to-night, and then we can all settle down and enjoy ourselves.'

'To-night?'

'Yes. I phoned Sally from the inn, and everything is arranged. She will drive over in my car and be waiting in the garden outside the collection room at one ack emma. I shall secure the bust and hand it to her, and she will drive off with it. As simple as that.'

'Simple!'

'What can go wrong?'

'A million things. Suppose you're caught.'

'I am never caught. They know me in the Underworld as The Shadow.

I wish I could cure you of this extraordinary tendency of yours always to look on the dark side.'

'Well, what other sides are there?' said Pongo.

## • IV •

The dinner hour was approaching. In her room, Lady Bostock had finished dressing and was regarding herself in the mirror, wishing, not for the first time, that she looked less like a horse. It was not that she had anything specific against horses; she just wished she did not look like one.

Footsteps sounded outside the door. Sir Aylmer entered. There was a heavy frown on his face, and it was plain that something had occurred to disturb his always easily disturbed equanimity.

'Emily!'

'Yes, dear?'

'I've just been talking to Potter.'

'Yes, dear?'

'Dam' fool!'

'Why, dear?'

Sir Aylmer picked up a hairbrush, and swished it. There was a wealth of irritation in the movement.

'Do you remember,' he asked, 'the time I played Dick Deadeye in Pinafore at that amateur performance in aid of the Lower Barnatoland Widows and Orphans?'

'Yes, dear. You were splendid.'

'Do you remember the scene where Dick Deadeye goes to the captain to warn him his daughter is going to elope, and won't come out with anything definite?'

'Yes, dear. You were wonderful in that scene.'

'Well, Potter was like that. Mystic.'

'Mystic?'

'It's the only word. Kept hinting that I must be on my guard, but wouldn't say why. I tried to pin him down, but it was no use. It was as if his lips had been sealed. All I could get out of him was that he thought danger threatened us, probably to-night. What are you wriggling like that for?'

Lady Bostock had not wriggled, she had shuddered.

'Danger?' she faltered. 'What did he mean?'

'How the dickens should I know what he meant, when every time he started to say anything he stopped as if somebody had clapped a hand over his mouth? I believe the man's half-witted. But he did go so far as to advise me to be on the alert, and said that he was going to lurk in the garden and watch the house carefully.'

'Aylmer!'

'I wish you wouldn't bellow "Aylmer" like that. You've made me bite my tongue.'

'But, Aylmer—'

'Thinking it over, I have come to the conclusion that he must have found out something further about this impostor who calls himself Twistleton, but why he couldn't say so is more than I can imagine. Well, if this so-called Twistleton is planning to make any sort of move to-night, I shall be ready for him.'

'Ready?'

'Ready.'

'What are you going to do?'

'Never mind,' said Sir Aylmer, rather inconsistently for one who had reproached Constable Potter for being mystic. 'My plans are all perfected. I shall be ready.'

# PART THREE

# 8

## · 1 ·

The quiet home evening to which Lord Ickenham had so looked forward had drawn to a close. Curfews had tolled the knell of parting day, lowing herds wound slowly o'er the lea. Now slept the crimson petal and the white, and in the silent garden of Ashenden Manor nothing stirred save shy creatures of the night such as owls, mice, rats, gnats, bats and Constable Potter. Down in the village the clock on the church tower, which a quarter of an hour ago had struck twelve, chimed a single chime, informing Pongo, pacing the floor of his bedroom overlooking the terrace, that in just forty-five minutes the balloon was due to go up.

As Pongo paced the floor, from time to time quivering all over like a Brazilian explorer with a touch of malaria, he was still in faultless evening dress, for the idea of going to bed on this night of fear had not even occurred to him. A young man visiting the parents of the girl he loves, and knowing that at one sharp an uncle of the maximum eccentricity will be starting to burgle the house, does not hop between the sheets at eleven-fifteen and sink into a dreamless sleep. He stays up and shudders. Pongo had made one or two attempts to divert his thoughts by reading

*Murder in the Fog*, but without success. There are moments when even the most faceless of fiends cannot hope to grip.

In a past the contemplation of which sometimes affected him as if he had bitten into a bad oyster, Pongo Twistleton had frequently been called upon to tremble like an aspen when an unwilling participant in the activities of his Uncle Fred, but seldom had he done it more wholeheartedly than now. He was feeling rather as the heroine of *Murder in the Fog* was wont to do when she got trapped in underground dens, the illusion that his nerves were sticking two inches out of his body and curling at the ends being extraordinarily vivid. And it is probable that mental distress would have unstrung him completely, but for the fact that in addition to suffering agony of the soul he was also in the process of dying of thirst, and this seemed to act on the counter-irritation principle.

The thirst of which he was dying was one of those lively young thirsts which seem to start at the soles of the feet and get worse all the way up. Growing in intensity ever since his arrival at the house, it had reached its peak at eleven o'clock to-night, when Jane, the parlourmaid, had brought the bedtime decanter and syphon into the drawing-room. He was no weakling, but having to sit there watching his host, his uncle and Bill Oakshott getting theirs like so many stags at eve—he himself, in deference to his known prejudice against alcoholic liquor, having been served with barley water—had tested his iron control almost beyond endurance.

For some minutes he continued to pace the floor, cursing the mad impulse which had led him to tell Hermione that he never touched the stuff and sketching out in his mind the series of long, cool ones with which, if he ever got out of here alive, he would correct this thirst of his. And then, as he reached the end of the carpet and was about to turn and pace back again, he stopped abruptly with one foot in the air, looking so like The Soul's Awakening that a seasoned art critic would have been deceived. Two chimes had just sounded from the church tower, and it was as if they had been the voice of a kindly friend whispering in his ear.

'Aren't you,' they seemed to say, 'overlooking the fact that that decanter is still in the drawing-room? One merely throws this out as a suggestion.' And he saw that here was the solution of what had appeared to be an impasse. His guardian angel, for he presumed it was his guardian angel, had pointed out the way. Hats off to the good old guardian angel, was Pongo's attitude.

A minute later he was in the corridor. Three minutes later he was in the drawing-room. Three and a quarter minutes later he was pouring with trembling fingers what promised to be the snifter of a lifetime. And four minutes later, reclining in an armchair with his feet on a small table, he had begun to experience that joy, than which there is none purer, which comes to the unwilling abstainer who has at last succeeded in assembling the materials, when from immediately behind him a voice spoke.

All the voice actually said was 'Coo!' but it was enough. Indeed, in the circumstances, a mere clearing of the throat would have been sufficient. His knotted and combined locks parted, each particular hair standing on end like quills upon the fretful porcupine: his heart broke from its moorings and crashed with a dull thud against his front teeth: and with a wordless cry he shot toward the ceiling.

It was only some moments later, after he had hit the ceiling twice and was starting to descend to terra firma, that the mists cleared from his eyes and he was able to perceive that the intruder was not, as he had supposed, Sir Aylmer Bostock, but Elsie Bean, his old playmate of the rude sling days. She was standing by the door with a hand to her heart, panting a little, as housemaids will when they enter drawing-rooms at twenty minutes to one in the morning and find them occupied by the ruling classes.

The relief was stupendous. Pongo's equanimity returned, and with it a warm gush of the milk of human kindness. To a man who had been anticipating an embarrassing interview with Sir Aylmer Bostock in his dressing-gown Elsie Bean was like something the doctor had ordered. He had no objection whatever to Elsie Bean joining him, quite the reverse. A chat with one of the finest minds in Bottleton East was just what he was in the mood for. He beamed on the girl, and having released his tongue, which had got entangled with his uvula, spoke in a genial and welcoming voice.

'What ho, Bean.'

'What ho, sir.'

'It's you, is it?'

'Yes, sir.'

'You gave me a start.'

'You gave *me* a start, sir.'

'Making two starts in all,' said Pongo, who had taken mathematics at school. 'You must forgive me for seeming a little perturbed for a moment. I thought you were mine host. Thank God you weren't. Do you remember in your inimitable way describing him as an overbearing dishpot? You were right. A dishpot he is, and a dishpot he always will be, and to hell with all dishpots is my view. Well, come along in, young Bean, and tell me your news. How's the Harold situation developing? Any change on the Potter front?'

Elsie Bean's face clouded. She tossed her head, plainly stirred.

'Harold's a mess,' she said, with the frankness which comes naturally to those reared in the bracing air of Bottleton East. 'He's an obstinate, pig-headed, fat-headed, flat-footed copper. I've no patience.'

'He still refuses to send in his papers?'

'R.'

A pang of pity shot through Pongo. Nothing that he had seen of Constable Potter had tended to build up in his mind the picture of a sort of demon lover for whom women might excusably go wailing through the woods, but he knew that his little friend was deeply attached to this uniformed perisher and his heart bled for her. He was broad-minded enough to be able to appreciate that if you are enamoured of a fat-headed copper and obstacles crop up in the way of your union with him, you mourn just as much as if he were Gregory Peck or Clark Gable.

'He came round to-night after supper, and we talked for an hour and a half, but nothing I could say would move him.'

'No dice, eh? Too bad.'

'It's that sister of his. She won't let him call his soul his own. I don't know what's to come of it, I'm sure.'

A pearly tear appeared at the corner of Elsie Bean's eye, and she sniffed in an overwrought way. Pongo patted her head. It was the least a man of sensibility could do.

'I wouldn't despair,' he said. 'These things seem sticky at the moment, but they generally iron out straight in the end. Give him time, and you'll find he'll be guided by the voice of love.'

Elsie Bean, having sniffed again, became calmer. There was good stuff in this girl.

'What would guide him a lot better,' she said, 'would be being bopped on the nose.'

'Bopped on the nose?'

'R.'

Of the broad, general principle of bopping Constable Potter on the nose Pongo was, of course, a warm adherent. It was a thing that he felt should be done early and often. But he was unable to see how it could pay dividends in the present circumstances.

'I don't quite follow.'

'That would knock some sense into him. Harold's nervous.'

'Nervous?' said Pongo incredulously. He had detected no such basic weakness in the flatty under advisement. A man of iron, he would have said.

'That's why he got himself shifted to the country from London, where he used to be. He found it too hot being a rozzer in London. He had some unpleasant experiences with blokes giving him shiners when he was pinching them, and it shook him. He come here for peace and quiet. So if he found it was too hot being a rozzer here as well, he wouldn't want to be a rozzer anywhere. He'd give his month's notice, and we'd all be happy.'

Pongo saw her point. He could scarcely have done otherwise, for it had been admirably put.

'True,' he said. 'You speak sooth, Bean.'

'If only someone would bop him on the nose, he wouldn't hesitate not for a moment. *You* wouldn't bop him on the nose, would you?'

'No, I would not bop him on the nose.'

'Or squash in his helmet when he wasn't looking?'

Pongo was sorry for the idealistic girl, but he felt it due to himself to discourage this line of thought from the outset.

'A man like Harold is always looking,' he said. 'No, I wish you luck, young Bean, and I shall follow your future career with considerable interest, but don't count on me for anything more than heartfelt sympathy. Still, I fully concur in your view that what you require is an up and coming ally, who will drive home to Harold the risks of the profession, thus causing him to see the light, and I strongly recommend featuring your brother Bert in the part. It's a pity he doesn't come out till September. What's he in for?'

'Resisting of the police in the execution of their duty. He sloshed a slop on the napper with a blunt instrument.'

'There you are, then. The People's Choice. Tails up, my dear old housemaid. Provided, of course, that his sojourn in the coop has not weakened Bert as a force, you should be hearing the warbling of the blue bird by early October at the latest. Meanwhile, switching lightly to another topic, what on earth are you doing here at this time of night?'

'I came to get some whisky.'

All the host in Pongo sprang to life. He blushed for his remissness.

'I'm frightfully sorry,' he said, reaching for the decanter. 'Ought to have offered you a spot ages ago. Can't imagine what I was thinking of.'

'For Harold,' Elsie Bean explained. 'He's lurking in the garden. He chucked a stone at my window, and when I popped my head out he asked me in a hoarse whisper to bring him a drop of something. And I remembered Jane always took the whisky in here last thing before bed. Lurking in the garden!' she proceeded with bitterness. 'What's he lurking in gardens for? Doing some sort of copper's job, I suppose. If he'd give up being a copper, he could stay in bed like other folks. I've no patience.'

She sniffed, and Pongo, fearing another pearly tear, hastened to apply first aid.

'There, there,' he said. 'You mustn't let it get you down. Right will prevail. Have a cigarette?'

'Thanks.'

'Turkish this side, Virginian that,' said Pongo.

He had taken one himself a few moments before, and he proceeded now to light hers from his own. And it was while their faces were in the close juxtaposition necessitated by this process that Bill Oakshott entered the room.

## · II ·

Whether one is justified in describing Bill Oakshott and Pongo Twistleton as great minds is perhaps a question open to debate. But they had exhibited to-night the quality which is supposed to be characteristic of great minds, that of thinking alike. Pongo, yearning for a snootful, had suddenly remembered the decanter in the drawing-room, and so had Bill.

Ever since his meeting that afternoon with Lord Ickenham, Bill Oakshott's emotions had been rather similar to those which he would have experienced, had he in the course of a country walk discovered that his coat tails had become attached to the rear end of the Scotch express en route from London to Edinburgh. Like most of those who found themselves associated with the effervescent peer when he was off the chain and starting to go places, he was conscious of a feeling of breathlessness, shot through with a lively apprehension as to what was coming next. This had induced sleeplessness. Sleeplessness had induced thirst. And with thirst had come the recollection of the decanter in the drawing-room.

With Bill, as with Pongo, to think was to act, and only in a minor detail of technique had their procedure differed. Pongo, not knowing whether the bally things creaked or not, had descended the stairs mincingly, like Agag, while Bill, more familiar with the terrain, had taken them three at a time, like a buffalo making for a water hole. He arrived, accordingly, somewhat touched in the wind, and the affectionate scene that met his eyes as he crossed the threshold took away what remained of his breath completely. Elsie Bean, entering the room, had said 'Coo!' Bill for the moment was unable to utter at all. He merely stood and goggled, shocked to the core.

The theory which Lord Ickenham had advanced in extenuation of Pongo's recent kissing of this girl whose nose he was now so nearly touching with his own had not satisfied Bill Oakshott. It might have been, as the kindly peer had said, a mere mannerism, but Bill thought not. The impression he had received on the previous afternoon had been of a licentious clubman operating on all twelve cylinders, and that was the impression he received now. And at the thought that it was in the hands of an all-in Lothario like this that Hermione Bostock had placed her life's happiness his sensitive soul quivered like a jelly. The outlook, to Bill's mind, was bad.

Pongo was the first to break an awkward silence.

'Oh, hullo,' he said.

'Oh, hullo, sir,' said Elsie Bean.

'Oh, hullo,' said Bill.

His manner, as he spoke, was distrait. He was trying to decide whether the fact of Pongo not being, as he had at one time supposed, off his onion improved the general aspect of affairs or merely rendered it darker and sadder. It was plain now that Elsie Bean had been mistaken on the previous day when she had asserted that the other had said 'Coo! I think I'll go to London,' and had driven thither. He had merely, it appeared, taken a short spin somewhere in his Buffy-Porson, which was quite a reasonable thing to do on a fine afternoon. But was this good or bad? Bill had said in his haste that loony libertines are worse than sane ones, but now he was not so sure. It might be a close thing, but were you not entitled to shudder even more strongly at a libertine who was responsible for his actions than at one who was not?

On one point, however, his mind was clear. It was his intention, as soon as they were alone together, to buttonhole this squire of dames and talk to him like an elder brother—as, for instance, one could imagine Brabazon-Plank *major* talking to Brabazon-Plank *minor*.

The opportunity of doing this came earlier than those familiar with Elsie Bean and her regrettable tendency to be a mixer would have anticipated. It is true that all her instincts urged the gregarious little soul to stick around and get the conversation going, but though sometimes failing to see eye to eye with Emily Post she was not without a certain rudimentary regard for the proprieties, and her social sense told her that this would not be the done thing. When a housemaid in curling pins and a kimono finds herself in a drawing-room at one in the morning with her employer and a male guest, she should as soon as possible make a decorous exit. This is in Chapter One of all the etiquette books.

So with a courteous 'Well, good night, all,' she now withdrew. And it was not very long after the door had closed that Pongo, who had become conscious of a feeling of uneasiness, as if he were sitting in a draught, was able to perceive what it was that was causing this. He was being looked at askance.

The rather delicate enterprise of looking askance at an old boyhood friend is one that different men embark on in different ways. Bill's method—for while he was solid on the point that it was about time that a fearless critic came along and pointed out to Pongo some of the aspects in which his behaviour deviated from the ideal, he found it difficult to overcome his natural shyness—was to turn bright vermilion and allow his eyes to protrude like a snail's. He also cleared his throat three times.

Finally he spoke.

'Pongo.'

'Hullo?'

Bill cleared his throat again.

'Pongo.'

'On the spot.'

Bill took a turn up and down the room. It was not easy to think of a good opening sentence, and when you are talking like an elder brother to libertines the opening sentence is extremely important, if not vital. He cleared his throat once more.

'Pongo.'

'Still here, old man.'

Bill cleared his throat for the fifth time, and having replied rather testily in the negative to Pongo's query as to whether he had swallowed a gnat or something, resumed his pacing. This brought his shin into collision with a small chair which was lurking in the shadows, and the sharp agony enabled him to overcome his diffidence.

'Pongo,' he said, and his voice was crisp and firm, 'I haven't mentioned it before, because the subject didn't seem to come up somehow, but when I returned from Brazil the day before yesterday, I was told that you were engaged to my cousin Hermione.'

'That's right.'

'Congratulations.'

'Thanks.'

'I hope you will be very happy.'

'You betcher.'

'And I hope—here's the nub—that you will make *her* happy.'

'Oh, rather.'

'Well, will you? You say you will, but I'm dashed if I see how it's going to be done, if you spend your time hobnobbing with housemaids.'

'Eh?'

'You heard.'

'Hobnobbing with housemaids?'

'Hobnobbing with housemaids.'

The charge was one which few men would have been able to hear unmoved. Its effect on Pongo was to make him mix himself another whisky and soda. Grasping this, like King Arthur brandishing his sword Excalibur, he confronted his accuser intrepidly and began a spirited speech for the defence.

It was inaccurate, he pointed out, to say that he spent his whole time hobnobbing with housemaids. Indeed, he doubted if he could justly be said to hobnob with them at all. It all depended on what you meant by the expression. To offer a housemaid a cigarette is not hobbing. Nor, when you light it for her, does that constitute nobbing. If you happen—by the merest chance—to be in a drawing-room at one in the morning with a housemaid, you naturally do the civil thing, behaving like a well-bred English gentleman and putting her at her ease.

You chat. You pass the time of day. You offer her a gasper. And when she has got her hooks on it, you light it for her. That, at least, was Pongo's creed, and he believed it would have been the creed of Sir Galahad and the Chevalier Bayard, if he had got the name correctly, neither of whom had to the best of his knowledge ever been called hobnobbers. He concluded by saying that it was a pity that some people, whose identity he did not specify, had minds like sinks and, by the most fortunate of chances remembering a good one at just the right moment, added that to the pure all things were pure.

It was a powerful harangue, and it is not surprising that for an instant Bill Oakshott seemed to falter before it, like some sturdy oak swayed by the storm. But by dint of thinking of the righteousness of his cause and clearing his throat again, he recovered the quiet strength which had marked his manner at the outset.

'All that,' he said coldly, 'would go a lot stronger with me, if I hadn't seen you kissing Elsie Bean yesterday.'

Pongo stared.

'Kissing Elsie Bean?'

'Kissing Elsie Bean.'

'I never kissed Elsie Bean.'

'Yes, you did kiss Elsie Bean. On the front steps.'

Pongo clapped a hand to his forehead.

'Good Lord, yes, so I did. Yes, you're perfectly right. I did, didn't I? It all comes back to me. But only like a brother.'

'Like a brother, my foot.'

'Like a brother,' insisted Pongo, as if he had spent his whole life watching brothers kiss housemaids. 'And if you knew the circumstances—'

Bill raised a hand. He was in no mood to listen to any tale of diseased motives. He drew a step nearer and stared bleakly at Pongo, as if the latter had been an alligator of the Brazilian swamps whom he was endeavouring to quell with the power of the human eye.

'Twistleton!'

'I wish you wouldn't call me Twistleton.'

'I will call you Twistleton, blast you. And this is what I want to say to you, Twistleton, by way of a friendly warning which you will do well to bear in mind, if you don't want your head pulled off at the roots and your insides ripped from your body—'

'My dear chap!'

'—With my naked hands. Cut it out.'

'Cut what out?'

'You know what. This Don Juan stuff. This butterfly stuff. This way you've got of flitting from flower to flower and sipping. Lay off it, Twistleton. Give it a miss. Curb that impulse. Kiss fewer housemaids. Try to remember that you are engaged to be married to a sweet girl who loves and trusts you.'

'But—'

Pongo, about to speak, paused. Bill had raised his hand again.

The gesture of raising the hand is one which is generally more effective in costume dramas, where it always suffices to quell the fiercest crowd, than in real life: and what made it so potent now was probably the size of the hand. To Pongo's excited imagination it seemed as large as a ham, and he could not overlook the fact that it was in perfect proportion with the rest of his companion's huge body; a body which even the most casual eye would have recognized as being composed mostly of rippling muscle. Taking all this into consideration, he decided to remain silent, and Bill proceeded.

'I suppose you're wondering what business it is of mine?'

'No, no. Any time you're passing—'

'Well, I'll tell you,' said Bill, departing from a lifetime's habit of reticence. 'I've loved Hermione myself for years and years.'

'No, really?'

'Yes. Years and years and years. I've never mentioned it to her.'

'No?'

'No. So she knows nothing about it.'

'Quite. She wouldn't, would she?'

'And loving her like this I feel that it is my job to watch over her like a—'

'Governess?'

'Not governess. Elder brother. To watch over her like an elder brother and protect her and see that no smooth bird comes along and treats her as the plaything of an idle hour.'

This surprised Pongo. The idea of anyone treating Hermione Bostock as the plaything of an idle hour was new to him.

'But—' he began again, and once more Bill raised his hand, bigger and better than ever. In a dreamlike way, Pongo found himself wondering what size he took in gloves.

'As the plaything of an idle hour,' repeated Bill. 'I don't object to her marrying another man—'

'Broad-minded.'

'At least, I do—it's agony—but what I mean is, it's up to her, and if she feels like marrying another man, right ho! So long as it makes her happy. All I want is her happiness.'

'Very creditable.'

'But get this, Twistleton,' continued Bill, and Pongo, meeting his eye, was reminded of that of the headmaster of his private school, with whom some fifteen years previously he had had a painful interview arising from his practice of bringing white mice into the classroom. 'This is what I want to drive into your nut. If I found that that other man was playing fast and loose with her, two-timing her, Twistleton, breaking her gentle heart by going and whooping it up round the corner, I would strangle him like a—'

He paused, snapping his fingers.

'Dog?' said Pongo, to help him out.

'No, not dog, you silly ass. Who the dickens strangles dogs? Like a foul snake.'

Pongo might have argued, had he felt like going into the thing, that the number of people who strangle foul snakes must be very limited, but he did not feel like going into the thing. In a sort of coma he watched his companion look askance at him again, stride to the table, mix himself a medium-strong whisky and soda, drain it and stride to the door. It closed, and he was alone.

And he was just beginning to lose that stunned sensation of having been beaten over the head with something hard and solid which must have come to the policeman whom Elsie Bean's brother Bert had sloshed on the napper with a blunt instrument, when from across the hall, from the direction of the room where Sir Aylmer Bostock kept his collection of African curios, there proceeded an agonized cry, followed by the sound of voices.

Pongo, crouched in his armchair like a hare in its form, his eyes revolving and his heart going into a sort of adagio dance, was unable to catch what these voices were saying, but he recognized them as those of Sir Aylmer and Lord Ickenham. The former appeared to be speaking heatedly, while the intonation of the latter was that of a man endeavouring to pour oil on troubled waters.

Presently the door of the collection room slammed, and a few moments later that of the drawing-room opened, and Lord Ickenham walked in.

## · III ·

Whatever the nature of the exchanges in which he had been taking part, they had done nothing to impair Lord Ickenham's calm. His demeanour, as he entered, was the easy, unembarrassed demeanour of an English peer who has just remembered that there is a decanter of whisky in a drawing-room. As always at moments when lesser men would have been plucking at their ties and shaking in every limb, this excellent old man preserved the suave imperturbability of a fish on a cake of ice. It seemed to Pongo, though it was difficult for him to hear distinctly, for his heart, in addition to giving its impersonation of Nijinsky, was now making a noise like a motor-cycle, that the head of the family was humming lightheartedly.

'Ah, Pongo,' he said, making purposefully for the decanter and seeming in no way surprised to see his nephew. 'Up and about? One generally finds you not far from the whisky.' He filled his glass, and sank gracefully into a chair. 'I always think,' he said, having refreshed himself with a couple of swallows and a sip, 'that this is the best hour of the day. The soothing hush, the grateful stimulant, the pleasant conversation on whatever topic may happen to come up. Well, my boy, what's new? You seem upset about something. Nothing wrong, I hope?'

Pongo uttered a curious hissing sound like the death-rattle of a soda-water syphon. He found the question ironical.

'I don't know what you call wrong. I've just been told that I'm extremely apt to have my insides ripped out.'

'Who told you that?'

'Bill Oakshott.'

'Was he merely reading your future in the tea leaves, or do you mean that he proposed to do the ripping?'

'He proposed to do the ripping with his bare hands.'

'You amaze me. Bill Oakshott? That quiet, lovable young man.'

'Lovable be blowed. He's worse than a Faceless Fiend. He could walk straight into the Chamber of Horrors at Madame Tussaud's, and no questions asked. He also said he would pull my head off at the roots, and strangle me like a foul snake.'

'Difficult to do that, if he had pulled your head off. Assuming, as I think we are entitled to assume, that the neck would come away with the head. But what had you been doing to Bill Oakshott to stir his passions thus?'

'He didn't like my being in here with Elsie Bean.'

'I don't think I remember who Elsie Bean is. One meets so many people.'

'The housemaid.'

'Ah, yes. The one you kiss.'

Pongo raised a tortured face heavenwards, as if he were calling for justice from above.

'I don't kiss her! At least, I may have done once—like a brother—in recognition of a signal service which she had rendered me. The way you and Bill Oakshott talk, you'd think this Bean and I spent twenty-four hours a day playing postman's knock.'

'My dear boy, don't get heated. My attitude is wholly sympathetic. I recollect now that Bill told me he had been a little disturbed by the spectacle of the embrace. He has the interests of your fiancée at heart.'

'He's in love with her.'

'Really?'

'He told me so.'

'Well, well. Poor lad. It must have been a severe jolt for him when I mentioned in the train that she was engaged to you. I feel a gentle pity for Bill Oakshott.'

'I don't. I hope he chokes.'

'The astonishing thing to my mind is that a man like Mugsy can have a daughter who seems to fascinate one and all. One would have expected Mugsy's daughter to be something on the lines of the Gorgon, with snakes instead of hair. Did you happen to hear him just now?'

'Golly, yes. What was all that?'

'Just Mugsy in one of his tantrums.'

'Did he catch you going into the collection room?'

'He was there already. Sleeping among his African curios. All wrong, it seemed to me. Either a man is an African curio, or he is not an African curio. If he is not, he ought not to curl up with them at night.' A cloud came into Lord Ickenham's handsome face, and his voice took on a disapproving note. 'You know, Pongo, there is a kind of low cunning about Mugsy which I do not like to see. Can you conceive the state of mind of a man who would have his bed moved into the collection room and sleep there with a string tied to his big toe and to the handle of the door?'

'He didn't?'

'He certainly did. It's the deceit of the thing that hurts me. Naturally I assumed, when we all wished each other good night and went our separate ways, that Mugsy was off to his bedroom like any decent householder, so I toddled down to the collection room at zero hour without a thought of unpleasantness in my mind. A nice, easy, agreeable job, I was saying to myself. I sauntered to the door, grasped the handle, turned it and gave it a sharp pull.'

'Gosh!'

'I don't know if you have ever, while walking along a dark street, happened to step on an unseen cat? I once had the experience years ago in Waverly Place, New York, and the picture seemed to rise before my eyes just now, when that awful yowl rent the air.'

'What on earth did you say?'

'Well, Mugsy did most of the saying.'

'I mean, how did you explain?'

'Oh, that? That was simple enough. I told him I was walking in my sleep.'

'Did he believe it?'

'I really don't know. The point seemed to me of no interest.'

'Well, this dishes us.'

'Nonsense. That is the pessimist in you speaking. All that has happened is that we have sustained a slight check—'

'Slight!'

'My dear Pongo, there are a thousand ways of getting around a trifling obstacle like this. Mugsy is sleeping in the collection room, is he? Very well, then we simply sit down and think out a good method of eliminating him. A knock-out drop in his bedtime whisky and soda would, of course, be the best method, but I happen to have come here without my knock-out drops. Idiotic of me. It is madness to come to country houses without one's bottle of Mickey Finns. One ought to pack them first thing after one's clean collars. But I'm not worrying about Mugsy. If I can't outsmart an ex-Governor, what was the use of all my early training in the United States of America? The only thing that bothers me a little is the thought of Sally, bless her heart. She is out there in the garden, watching and waiting like Mariana at the moated grange—'

Pongo uttered a stricken cry.

'And so is that blighted Potter out there in the garden, watching and waiting like Mariana at the ruddy moated grange. I'd clean forgotten Elsie Bean told me so. She came in here to get a drink for him.'

Lord Ickenham stroked his chin.

'H'm. I did not know that. He's out in the garden, eh? That may complicate matters a little. I hope—'

He broke off. Shrilling through the quiet night, the front door bell had begun to ring, loudly and continuously, as if someone had placed a large, fat thumb on the button and was keeping it there.

Lord Ickenham looked at Pongo. Pongo looked at Lord Ickenham.

'Potter!' said Lord Ickenham,

'The rotter!' said Pongo.

# 9

## · I ·

It is a characteristic of England's splendid police force at which many people have pointed with pride, or would have pointed with pride if they had happened to think of it, that its members, thanks to the rigid discipline which has moulded them since they were slips of boys, are always able to bear with philosophic fortitude the hardships and disappointments inseparable from their chosen walk in life. They can, in a word, take it as well as dish it out.

If, for example, they happen to be lurking in the garden of a country house in the small hours, when even a summer night tends to be a bit chilly, and ask their friends to bring them a drop of something to keep the cold out, and after a longish wait it becomes evident that this drop is not going to materialize, they do not wince nor cry aloud. 'Duty, stern daughter of the voice of God,' they say to themselves, and go on lurking.

It had been so with Constable Potter. In their recent Romeo and Juliet scene Elsie Bean had spoken hopefully of whisky in the drawing-room, but he quite realized that obstacles might arise to prevent her connecting with it. And as the minutes went by and she did not appear, he assumed that these obstacles had arisen and with a couple of 'Coo's' and a stifled oath dismissed the whole subject of whisky from his mind.

In surroundings such as those in which he was keeping his vigil a more spiritual man might have felt the urge to try his hand at roughing out a little verse, so much was there that was romantic and inspirational in the garden of Ashenden Manor at this hour. Soft breezes sighed through the trees, bringing with them the scent of stock and tobacco plant. Owls tu-whitted, other owls tu-whooed. Add the silent grandeur of the fine old house and the shimmer of distant water reflecting the twinkling stars above, and you had a set-up well calculated to produce another policeman-poet.

But Harold Potter had never been much of a man for poetry. Even when alone with Elsie Bean in the moonlight he seldom got much further in that direction than a description of the effect which regulation boots had on his corns. What he thought of was beef sandwiches. And he was just sketching out in his mind the beef sandwich supreme which he would eat on returning to his cottage, when in the darkness before him he discerned a dim form. Like himself, it appeared to be lurking.

He pursed his lips disapprovingly. He had taken an instant dislike to this dim form.

It was not the fact that it was dim that offended him. In the garden of Ashenden Manor at one in the morning a form had got to be dim. It had no option. The point, as Constable Potter saw it, was that forms, dim or otherwise, had no business to be in the garden of Ashenden Manor at one in the morning, and he stepped forward, his blood circulating briskly. This might or might not be big stuff, but it had all the appearance of big stuff. 'Intrepid Officer Traps Nocturnal Marauder' seemed to him about the angle from which to look at the thing.

''Ullo,' he boomed. He should have said: 'What's all this?' which is the formula laid down for use on these occasions in 'What Every Young Policeman Ought to Know', but, as so often happens, excitement had made him blow up in his lines. ''Ullo. What are *you* doing here?'

The next moment any doubt which he might have entertained as to the bigness of the stuff was resolved. With a startled squeak the dim figure, which had leaped some six inches into the air on being addressed, broke into hurried flight, and with the deep bay, so like a bloodhound's, of the policeman engaged in the execution of his duty he immediately proceeded to bound after it. 'Night Chase in Darkened Garden', he was feeling as he dropped into his stride.

Into races of a cross-country nature the element of luck always enters largely. One notices this in the Grand National. Had the affair been taking place on a cinder track, few punters would have cared to invest their money on the constable, for he was built for endurance rather than speed and his quarry was showing itself exceptionally nippy on its feet. But in this more difficult going nimbleness was not everything. Some unseen obstacle tripped the dim form. It stumbled, nearly fell. Constable Potter charged up, reached out, seized something. There was a rending sound and he fell back, momentarily deprived of his balance. When he recovered it, he was alone with the owls and the stars. The dim form had disappeared, and he stood there with his hands full of what seemed to be the major part of a woman's dress.

It was at this point that he felt justified, despite the advanced hour, in going to the front door and ringing the bell. And it was not long afterwards that the door opened and he strode masterfully into the hall.

He found himself playing to a gratifyingly full house. He was, indeed, doing absolute capacity. You cannot punch front door bells in the small hours without attracting attention, and Ashenden Manor had turned out *en masse* to greet him. In addition to such members of his personal circle as Mrs Gooch, the cook, Elsie Bean, his betrothed, Jane, the parlourmaid, and Percy, the boy who cleaned the knives and boots, he noticed Sir Aylmer Bostock, looking like Clemenceau on one of his bad mornings, Lady Bostock, looking like a horse, and their nephew William, looking large and vermilion. There was also present, and a shudder ran through him as he saw them, the scum of the East Dulwich underworld in the person of the scoundrels George Robinson and Edwin Smith. The former was, as ever, debonair; the latter seemed agitated.

Constable Potter fondled his moustache. This was his hour, the high spot in his life when he was going to be fawned on by one and all. Or he thought it was until, just as he was about to speak, Sir Aylmer, who after the incursion of Lord Ickenham had managed to get to sleep again and had woken up cross, exploded like a bomb.

'POTTER!'

'Sir?' said the zealous officer, somewhat taken aback by his manner.

'Was it YOU making that infernal noise?'

'Sir?'

'Ringing the damned bell at this hour! Waking everybody up! Ruining my night's rest! WHAT THE DEVIL DO YOU MEAN BY IT?'

'But, sir, I've caught a marauder.'

'A what?'

'A nocturnal marauder, sir.'

'Then where is he? Don't tell me you let him get away?'

'Well, yes, sir.'

'Ass! Fool! Idiot! Imbecile!' said Sir Aylmer.

Constable Potter was wounded.

'It wasn't my fault, sir. The garments give when I clutched them.'

With the manner of Counsel putting in Exhibit A, he thrust beneath his interlocutor's eyes the flimsy fragment which he was holding, and Sir Aylmer inspected it closely.

'This is a woman's dress,' he said.

'A female's,' corrected Constable Potter, always indefatigable in his quest for exactitude. 'I observed her engaged in suspicious loitering, and when I up and apprehended her she come apart in my hands.'

At this dramatic recital of events which, even if colourlessly related, could scarcely have failed to chill the spine, there proceeded from the group of female members of the staff, huddled together for mutual support, a cry, or as Constable Potter would probably have preferred to put it, an ejaculation, consisting of the monosyllable 'OW!' Weighing the evidence, one would say that the speaker was not Elsie Bean, who would have said 'Coo!' but is more likely to have been Mrs Gooch or Jane the parlourmaid. The interruption had the unfortunate effect of attracting Sir Aylmer's attention to the group, and he started immediately to make his presence felt.

'EMILY!'

'Yes, dear?'

'What are all these women doing here?' Sir Aylmer's reddening eye passed from Mrs Gooch to Jane the parlourmaid, from Jane the parlourmaid to Elsie Bean. 'Good God! The place is full of damned women. Send 'em to bed.'

'Yes, dear.'

'Dishpot!' cried a clear young voice, this time unmistakably that of Miss Bean. She had been looking forward to spending most of the rest of the night in the hall, listening to tales of stirring events and commenting on them in her friendly way, and to get the bum's rush like this in the first five minutes was very bitter to her independent spirit. Not since the evening of her seventh birthday when, excitement having induced an attack of retching and nausea, she had been led out of the Bottleton East Theatre Royal half-way through her first pantomime, had she experienced such a sense of disappointment and frustration.

Sir Aylmer started. These were fighting words.

'Who called me a dishpot?'

'I did,' replied Elsie Bean with quiet fortitude. 'An overbearing dishpot, that's what you are, and I would like to give my month's notice.'

'*I* would like to give my month's notice,' said Mrs Gooch, struck by the happy thought.

'So would I like to give my month's notice,' said Jane the parlourmaid, falling in with the mob spirit.

Sir Aylmer clutched his dressing-gown. For a moment it seemed as if it were his intention to rend it, like a minor prophet of the Old Testament.

'EMILY!'

'Yes, dear?'

'Are you or are you not going to throw these women out?'

'Yes, dear. At once, dear.'

Briskly, though with a leaden heart, for none knew better than she the difficulty of obtaining domestic help in the country, Lady Bostock shepherded the rebels through the door. Of the wage-earning members of the household only Percy, the knives and boots boy, remained, a pimpled youth with a rather supercilious manner. He had lighted a cigarette, and his whole demeanour showed his satisfaction that the women had gone and that the men could now get together and thresh the thing out in peace.

Sir Aylmer drew a deep breath like a speaker at a public meeting after the hecklers have been ejected.

'Potter.'

'Sir?'

'Tell me your story again.'

The constable told his story again, even better than before, for he had been able to think of some new words, and Sir Aylmer listened frowningly.

'Where was this woman?'

'This Mystery Woman,' corrected Constable Potter. 'In the garden, sir.'

'What part of the garden?'

'Near the window of the room where you keep your thingamajigs, sir.'

'My *what*?'

'Those objects from Africa, sir. Curios is, I believe, the name.'

'Then call them curios.'

'Yes, sir.'

'Not thingamajigs.'

'No, sir.'

'What was she doing?'

'Lying in wait, sir.'

'What for?'

'Don't know, sir.'

Percy flicked the ash off his cigarette.

'If you arst me,' he said, throwing out the suggestion for what it was worth, 'she was expecting the arrival of her accomplice. This is the work of a gang.'

He would have done better to remain in modest obscurity. Compelled by his official status to accept meekly the recriminations of landed proprietors who were also members of the bench of magistrates, Constable Potter could be very terrible when dealing with knives and boots boys, and he had been wanting some form of relief for his feeling ever since Sir Aylmer had called him an ass, a fool, an idiot and an imbecile. To advance and seize Percy by the left ear was with him the work of an instant, to lead him to the door and speed him on his way with a swift kick the work of another. A thud and a yelp, and Percy had ceased to have a seat at the conference table. Constable Potter returned to his place, his air that of a man who has carried out a pleasant task neatly and well.

Percy's head appeared round the door.

'And so would I like to give my month's notice,' he said, and withdrew once more.

Lord Ickenham, who had been a genial spectator, spoke for the first time.

'A clean sweep, Mugsy. What, all my pretty chickens at one fell swoop! Too bad. Very difficult these days to get servants in the country.'

Sir Aylmer did not reply. The same thought had come to him independently, and he was beginning to be a little dubious as to the wisdom of his forthright policy in dealing with domestics. It was Constable Potter who now came before the meeting with a few well-judged words.

'Not but what there ain't a lot in what the lad said,' he observed. He was not fond of Percy, suspecting him of being the hidden hand which had thrown half a brick at him the other day as he cycled up the drive, but he could give credit where credit was due. 'About its being a gang, what I mean. Women don't conduct burglaries on their own hook. They have pals. Established inside the house as like as not,' he added with a significant glance.

It was Pongo who spoke next, as if impelled to utterance by a jab in the trouser seat from a gimlet or bradawl. In saying that Constable Potter's glance was significant, we omitted to state that it was at the last of the Twistletons that it had been directed, nor did we lay anything like sufficient stress on its penetrating qualities. It was silly of us to describe as merely significant something so closely resembling a death ray.

'What are you looking at *me* for?' he asked weakly.

Constable Potter, who could be as epigrammatic as the next man when he wanted to, replied that a cat may look at a king. And he was just smiling at his ready wit, when Sir Aylmer decided that the time for finesse and dissembling was past and that what was required here was direct frontal attack. All the evening he had been irked by the necessity of playing the genial host—or the fairly genial host—to this rat of the underworld, and now not even the thought of possible repercussions from his daughter Hermione could restrain him from speaking out.

'I'll tell you why he's looking at you, my man. Because he happens to be aware that you're a scoundrel and an impostor.'

'Who, me?'

'Yes, you. You thought you had fooled us, did you? Well, you hadn't. Potter!'

'Sir?'

'Tell your story about your previous meeting with this fellow.'

'Very good, sir,' said Constable Potter, quickly applying the necessary glaze to his eyes and starting to address the bodiless spirit in mid-air. 'Here's what transpired. On the . . . Coo! I've forgotten when it was, I'd have to look up my scrap album to establish the exact inst., but it was about a year ago, when I was in the C division in the metropolis and they'd put me on duty at the dog races down Shepherd's Bush way. Accused was drawn to my attention along of making himself conspicuous by conduct like as it might have been of a disorderly nature, and I apprehended him. Questioned while in custody, he stated his name was Smith.'

'Not Twistleton?'

'No, sir. Edwin Smith, of 11 Nasturtium Road, East Dulwich.'

'So what have you to say to that?' demanded Sir Aylmer.

Lord Ickenham intervened.

'My dear Mugsy, the whole thing is obviously an absurd misunderstanding. One sees so clearly what must have happened. Scooped in by the police and reluctant to stain the fine old Twistleton escutcheon by revealing his true identity, the boy gave a false name. You've done it yourself a hundred times.'

'I haven't!'

Lord Ickenham shrugged his shoulders.

'Have it your own way, Mugsy. The point is immaterial, and I would be the last man to awaken painful memories. But I can assure you that this is really Reginald Twistleton. Bill Oakshott happened to mention it only this afternoon. He was telling me that you had gone off your onion—'

'He was, was he?'

'—And when I inquired as to the symptoms, he explained that you had got this extraordinary idea that his old friend Reginald Twistleton was not his old friend Reginald Twistleton, whereas that is in reality what his old friend Reginald Twistleton is nothing else but. You will testify, Bill Oakshott, to the hundred per cent Twistletonity of this Reginald?'

'Fine. I mean, oh rather.'

'There you are, then, Mugsy.'

Sir Aylmer blew at his moustache.

'William on his own statement has not seen Reginald Twistleton for more than twelve years. How can he possibly claim to recognize him? Ha! William!'

'Hullo?'

'I see how we can settle this matter. Ask him questions.'

'Questions?'

'About your school days.'

'Pongo and I weren't at school together. I met him in the holidays at Lord Ickenham's place.'

'That alone would seem to be a guarantee of respectability,' said Lord Ickenham. 'A very exclusive house, that, I have always understood. By the way, how did you get on there this afternoon, Mugsy?'

'Never mind,' said Sir Aylmer shortly. 'What was he doing at Lord Ickenham's?'

'He was staying there.'

Sir Aylmer reflected. An inspiration came to him.

'Was there a dog there?'

'Eh?'

'A dog.'

'Oh, you mean a dog. Yes, a—'

'Don't tell him, don't tell him. Ask him.'

Lord Ickenham nodded.

'I see what you mean, Mugsy. Very shrewd. If he was staying at Ickenham Hall, he would remember the resident dog. Boys always remember dogs. Do you remember that dog, prisoner at the bar?'

'Of course I remember the dog. It was a sheep dog.'

'Correct, Bill Oakshott?'

'Absolutely.'

'Called—?'

'Mittens.'

'Accurate, Bill Oakshott?'

'Definitely. Right on the bull's eye. Want any more, Uncle Aylmer?'

'No,' said Sir Aylmer.

'I should hope not,' said Lord Ickenham. 'You've been making an ass of yourself, Mugsy.'

'Oh, have I?' said Sir Aylmer, stung. 'Well, let me tell you that I think the time has now come to ask you some questions.'

'Me?'

'Yes. How do I know who you are? You come here claiming to be Plank, and you don't look a bit like Plank, as I remember him—'

'But I explained about the absence of the billowy curves. Slimmo. In the small half-crown or the larger three-and-sixpence bottle. You mix it with your food, and it acts as a gentle, agreeable remedy for hypertrophy of the trouser seat, not habit-forming.'

'I don't believe you are Plank. How do I know that William did not pick up the first stranger he met and talk him into coming and judging the Bonny Baby contest, so that he could get out of it himself?'

'Ridiculous. You have only to look at that pure brow, those candid eyes—'

'There are some damned funny things going on here,' proceeded Sir Aylmer firmly, 'and I intend to get to the bottom—'

'Like Slimmo.'

'This afternoon a man I don't remember from Adam comes and insinuates himself into the house, saying he is an old schoolfellow of mine. To-night Potter catches a woman prowling in my garden—'

'Not so much prowling, sir, as lurking.'

'SHUT UP!'

'Yes, sir.'

'Potter catches a woman prowling in my garden, obviously trying to establish communication with some man in the house. Who was that man?'

'Ah.'

'It wasn't me.'

'One hopes not, Mugsy.'

'It wasn't William. It wasn't that boy who was in here just now, the one that cleans the knives and boots—'

'How do you know? If I were you, I would watch that boy, watch him closely.'

'It was presumably not Reginald, seeing that Reginald really is Reginald. That leaves you.'

'But, Mugsy, this is absurd. You say this woman was trying to establish communication with some man in the house. Why? What possible evidence have you of that? I see her as some poor, homeless waif who wandered into your garden trying to find shelter for the night in the tool shed or the byre, whatever a byre may be—'

'Poor, homeless waif be damned. And if she was trying to find shelter in the tool shed, why didn't she go there, instead of hanging about—'

'Loitering suspiciously, sir.'

'SHUT UP! Instead of hanging about outside the window of my collection room. She was one of a gang of burglars, that's what she was, and I'm going to find out who the rest of them are. You say you're Plank. Prove it.'

Lord Ickenham beamed.

'My dear Mugsy, why didn't you say so at first? Prove it? Of course I can prove it. But is not the fact that I have been calling you Mugsy from the start in itself a proof?'

'No. You could have found out somewhere that I used to be called that at school.'

'Then let us touch on some of the things which I could not have found out except by actual daily contact with you in those far-off days. Who pinched jam sandwiches at the school shop, Mugsy? Who put the drawing-pin on the French master's chair? Who got six of the best with a fives bat for bullying his juniors? And talking of bullying juniors, do you recollect one term a frail, golden-haired child arriving at the old seminary, a frail, wistful child who looked to you like something sent from heaven? You swooped on that child, Mugsy, as if you had been an Assyrian coming down like a wolf on the fold. You pulled his golden hair. You twisted his slender arm. And just as you had started twisting it, it suddenly uncoiled itself in one of the sweetest left hooks I have ever witnessed and plugged you in the eye. Ten minutes later, after we had helped you to bed, investigation revealed that the child was the previous year's public-school bantam-weight champion, who had been transferred to us from his former place of education because his father thought the air in our part of the world was better for his lungs. On another occasion—'

He paused. A horrible cackling sound, like a turkey with laryngitis, had interrupted the flow of his narrative. It was Constable Potter laughing. He was not a man who laughed easily, and he had not wanted to laugh now. He had, indeed, tried not to laugh. But his sense of the humorous had been too much for him.

'Uck, uck, uck,' he gurgled, and Sir Aylmer turned on him with all the fury of a bantam-weight champion whose arm has been twisted.

'POTTER!'

'S-sir?'

'Get out! What the devil are you doing, lounging about in here, when you ought to be finding that woman you were fool enough to let escape?'

The rebuke sobered Constable Potter. He saw that he had been remiss.

'Yes, sir.'

'What do you mean, Yes, sir?'

'I mean No, sir. I mean I'll start instituting a search instanter. It oughtn't to be so hard to find her. She'll be practically in the nood, as the expression is, and that,' said Constable Potter who, when he thought at all, thought clearly, 'will render her conspicuous.'

With a courteous inclination of the head he passed through the door, stern and vigilant, and Sir Aylmer prepared to follow his example.

'I'm off to bed,' he said shortly. 'It must be two o'clock.'

'Past two,' said Lord Ickenham, consulting his watch. 'How time flies when one is agreeably occupied. Then let us all go to bed.'

He linked his arm in that of Pongo, who was breathing stertorously like a fever patient, and together they made their way up the stairs.

## · II ·

The bedroom which had been allotted to Lord Ickenham was a spacious apartment on the second floor, looking out over the park. It was thither that he conducted Pongo, bringing him to rest on the chaise-longue which stood beside the window.

'Relax, my boy,' he said, tidying up his nephew's legs, which were showing a tendency to straggle and gently placing a cushion behind his head. 'You seem a little overwrought. You remind me of an old New York friend of mine named Bream Rockmeteller on the occasion one Fourth of July when somebody touched off a maroon beneath his chair. That same stunned look. Odd. I should have thought that the clearing up of that Edwin Smith misunderstanding would have made you feel as if you had just had a fortnight at Bracing Bognor.'

Pongo sat up, his legs once more shooting out in all directions.

'Come, come,' said Lord Ickenham, rearranging them. 'Are you a man or an octopus? One ought to tie you up with a system of ropes.'

Pongo ignored the rebuke. His eyes were stony.

'Uncle Fred,' he said, speaking in a low, metallic voice, 'I don't know if you know it, but you're Public Scourge Number One. You scatter ruin and desolation on every side like a ruddy sower going forth sowing. Life, liberty and the pursuit of happiness aren't possible when you're around. You're like the Black Death or one of those pestilences of the Middle Ages, taking their toll of thousands.'

His vehemence seemed to occasion Lord Ickenham a mild surprise.

'But, my dear boy, what have I done?'

'All that stuff about my giving a false name at the dog races.'

'Well, I'm dashed. I was looking on that as my day's good deed. But for my timely intervention—'

'I was just going to deny the whole thing, when you butted in.'

Lord Ickenham shook his head.

'You would never have got away with it. Heaven knows that there are few more fervent apostles of the creed of stout denial than myself—I have been practising it for thirty years with your aunt—but it would not have served here. The copper's word would have been accepted, and you would have been branded in Mugsy's eyes as a burglar.'

'Well, look what I'm branded in his eyes as now. A chap who goes on toots and gets pinched at dog races. What's Hermione going to say when he tells her about it? The moment the facts are placed before her, she'll sit down and write me a stinker, calling our engagement off.'

'You think so?'

'I can see her dipping the pen.'

'Well, that'll be good. If I were you, I would give three rousing cheers and let it go at that.'

'I won't give three rousing cheers. I worship that girl. Until now—'

'I know, I know. You have never known what love meant. Quite. Nevertheless, I stick to it that you would be well out of this perilous enterprise of trying to hitch up with a girl who appears to have the austere outlook of the head mistress of a kindergarten and will probably spend most of her married life rapping her husband on the knuckles with a ruler. But we mustn't sit yarning about your amours now. There are graver matters on which we have to rivet our attention.'

'Such as—?'

'My dear Pongo, Sally. Is it nothing to you that she is at this moment roaming Hampshire in her cami-knickers? Where's your chivalry?'

Pongo bowed his head in shame. No appeal to the *preux chevalier* in him was ever wasted. The thought that he had clean forgotten about Sally was a knife in his bosom.

'Oh, golly. Yes, that's right. She'll catch cold.'

'If nothing worse.'

'And may be gathered in by Potter.'

'Exactly.'

'Blast him.'

'Yes, I confess to feeling a little cross with Constable Potter, and in the deepest and truest sense it will be all right with me if he trips over a footprint and breaks his damned neck. In trying to cope with Constable Potter one has the sense of being up against some great natural force. I wouldn't have thought so much zeal could have been packed into a blue uniform and a pair of number eleven boots. Well, see you shortly, Pongo.'

'Where are you going?'

'Out into the great open spaces,' said Lord Ickenham, picking up a flowered dressing-gown. 'God knows where Sally is, but she can't have got far. As Potter said, she will be conspicuous.'

'Shall I come, too?'

'No,' said Lord Ickenham. 'We don't want the thing to look like one of those great race movements. You stay here and think calm, healing thoughts.'

He left the room, walking like one who intends not to let a twig snap beneath his feet, and Pongo leaned back against the cushion and closed his eyes.

'Healing thoughts!' he said to himself bitterly, and laughed one of his mirthless laughs.

But the human mind is capable of strange feats. You never know where you are with it. If questioned at the moment when the door had closed as to the chances of anything in the nature of a healing thought coming into a mind that was more like a maelstrom than a collection of grey cells, Pongo would have offered a hundred to eight against and been surprised if there had been any takers. Yet now, gradually, he discovered that one was beginning to shape itself.

As if painted in flame, the picture of the whisky decanter which he had left standing on the round table in the drawing-room, at least half of its elixir still within it, started to rise before his mental retina, and he sat up, the light of hope dawning in his eyes. He had tested the magic properties of that decanter before, and they had in no way fallen short of his dreams, and now there came upon him the urge to test them again. Reason told him that he would never need one for the tonsils more than in the present pass to which he had been reduced. In fact, added Reason, the first thing any good specialist, seeing him, would recommend—nay, insist on—was a little something in a glass.

Thirty seconds later he had begun his journey to the promised land, and a couple of minutes after that was sitting in his favourite armchair with his feet up, almost calm again.

It was very pleasant in the quiet drawing-room, very pleasant and restorative and soothing. At least, it was for perhaps a quarter of an hour.

At the end of that period Sir Aylmer Bostock entered in his dressing-gown. Tossing on his pillow after having had his beauty sleep twice broken, Sir Aylmer had bethought him of the decanter and it had drawn him like a magnet. Experience had taught him that the most stubborn insomnia can often be corrected by means of a couple of quick ones.

His emotions on beholding Pongo established at the fountain-head were sharp and poignant. Although he had been compelled to abandon his view of this young man as a rat of the underworld, he still considered him a rat, and the last thing he desired was a jolly party with him at half-past two in the morning, the glasses clinking and the conversation flowing free. Life, he was thinking, was difficult enough without finding Pongo under one's feet wherever one went. If Sir Aylmer Bostock after two days of his future son-in-law's society had been asked to sketch out a brief description of his ideal world, he would have replied that he was not a fussy man and did not expect perfection but that he did insist on one thing, that it should contain fewer and better Twistletons.

'Ugh!' he said. 'You!'

There are extraordinarily few good answers to the ejaculation 'You!' especially when preceded by the monosyllable 'Ugh!' Pongo could not think of any of them. The other's entry had caused him to repeat that sitting high jump of his, and on descending from the neighbourhood of the ceiling he had found his mind a blank. The best he could achieve was a nervous giggle.

This was unfortunate, for we have made no secret of Sir Aylmer Bostock's views on nervous gigglers. The ex-Governor had never actually fallen on a nervous giggler and torn him limb from limb, but that was simply because he had not wanted to get himself involved in a lot of red tape. But he definitely did not like them. He glared at Pongo, and as he glared observed the glass in the latter's hand, and it was as if someone had whispered in his ear 'What is wrong with this picture?'

'Gar!' he exclaimed, once more calling on one of those tribal gods. 'I thought you told me you were a teetotaller.'

'Eh?'

'Teetotaller.'

'Oh, yes, that's right.'

'How the devil can you be a teetotaller, if you sit swigging whisky all the time?'

'Medicinal.'

'What?'

'I take a drop occasionally for my health,' said Pongo. 'Doctor's orders.'

There are moments in life when, after offering frank and manly explanations of our actions, we are compelled to pause and wonder if they have got by. This was one of them. And it was while Pongo was anxiously scrutinizing his host's face and trying, without much success, to read in its rugged features an expression of childlike trust that Lady Bostock entered the room.

There are critics to whom it will seem one of those strained coincidences which are so inartistic that on this troubled night no fewer than six of the residents of Ashenden Manor should have been seized independently of each other with the idea of going to the drawing-room in order to establish contact with the decanter placed there earlier in the evening by Jane, the parlourmaid, while others will see in the thing that inevitability which was such a feature of the best Greek tragedy. Æschylus once said to Euripides 'You can't beat inevitability,' and Euripides said he had often thought so, too.

Be that as it may, it was the decanter which had brought Lady Bostock to the spot. Finding a difficulty in getting to sleep after the recent strain upon her nerves, she had thought that a weak whisky and water might prove the specific which she needed.

She, too, was surprised on discovering that she had boon companions.

'Aylmer!' she said. 'You here? And Reginald?' The glass in Pongo's hand attracted her attention, producing reactions identical with those of her husband. 'I thought you were a teetotaler, Reginald.'

Sir Aylmer snorted. A most unpleasant, cynical snort, a sort of nasal 'Oh, yeah.'

'He takes a drop occasionally for his health.'

'Oh, yes?'

'Yes,' said Sir Aylmer. 'Medicinal. Doctor's orders.' His intonation was so extremely disagreeable, suggesting as it did contempt, disgust and that revolted loathing which temperate men feel when confronted with the world's drink-sodden wrecks, that Pongo, though his sitting high jump had caused him to spill practically all the contents of his glass and he would much have liked to refill it, felt that this was not the moment. Stronger than his desire for one for the road was the passionate wish to be somewhere where Sir Aylmer and Lady Bostock were not.

'Well—er—good night,' he mumbled.

'You're leaving us?' said Sir Aylmer grimly.

'Er—yes. Good night.'

'Good night,' said Sir Aylmer.

'Good night,' said Lady Bostock.

There was an expression of concern on her face as the door closed. She looked like a horse that is worried about the quality of its oats.

'Oh, dear,' she said. 'I do hope Reginald is not a drinker.' A thought occurred to her, and she brightened. 'But, of course, I was forgetting. He isn't Reginald, is he? He's just somebody pretending to be Reginald.'

Sir Aylmer, though reluctant to present himself in the light of one who had been in error, felt obliged to put her abreast of his latest findings.

'Yes, he's Reginald. I've been into that matter, and it now seems pretty well established that he's Reginald all right. Apparently, at those dog races where Potter arrested him, he gave a false name and address.'

'That does not sound very nice.'

'It was not very nice. It wasn't nice at all. It was disgraceful and it throws a blinding light on the true character of Reginald Twistleton. Shows you what sort of a fellow he is. And as to him being a drinker, of course he's a drinker. You can tell it by those shifty eyes and that weak giggle. I knew there was something wrong with the young toad the first time I saw him. Dipsomaniac is written all over him. No doubt he has been absorbing the stuff like a sponge whenever our backs were turned. I don't suppose he has drawn a sober breath since he came here. God help Hermione, married to a chap like that. He'll be seeing pink snakes on the honeymoon. Orange spiders,' said Sir Aylmer, allowing his imagination free rein. 'Gamboge elephants. Purple penguins.'

It is never difficult to touch a mother's heart with this sort of thing. Lady Bostock uttered a stricken neigh.

'Hermione must be warned!'

'Exactly what I was about to suggest myself. You'd better write to her.'

'I'll go and see her.'

'Very well, go and see her.'

'To-morrow morning!'

'The sooner, the better. Well, if you're going to London in the morning, you'd better go to bed and get some sleep. Can't imagine why you aren't there now.'

'I came down to get a weak whisky. I couldn't sleep.'

'I came to get a strong whisky. I couldn't sleep, either. How the devil can anyone be expected to sleep in a house where fools are incessantly breaking in on you, saying they're somnambulists, and policemen ring door bells all the time? Did you get those women to bed?'

'Yes, dear. They kept giving their notices all the way upstairs.'

'Curse them. Say when, Emily.'

'When, O dear, O dear, O dear.'

'What's the matter now?'

'I was only thinking of Reginald,' said Lady Bostock. 'I wonder if the gold cure would do any good.'

Unaware of the exact nature of what was being said about him by the parents of the girl he loved, but suspecting that his case might have come upon the agenda paper after his withdrawal, Pongo had tottered up the stairs to his room. While not in tip-top form, he found himself enjoying the novel sensation of being separated for a while from members of the human race, a race for which the events of the night had caused him to acquire a rather marked distaste. 'Alone at last,' he was saying to himself, as he opened the door.

A moment later he saw that he had been too optimistic. Seated on the bed was his Uncle Frederick, enjoying a mild cigar, and in the armchair, clad in a flowered dressing-gown, a girl at the sight of whom his heart, already, as we have seen, on several occasions tonight compelled to rival the feverish mobility of a one-armed paperhanger with the hives, executed a leap and a bound surpassing all previous efforts by a wide margin.

'Ah, Pongo,' said Lord Ickenham. 'Come along in. Here's Sally. We climbed up the water pipe.'

## · III ·

It was not immediately that Pongo found himself able to speak. Strong emotion often has the effect of tying the vocal cords into a reefer knot, and he was in the grip of not one strong emotion, but two.

As always when confronted with some new manifestation of his uncle's activities, he was filled with a nameless fear, saying to himself, as so often in similar circumstances, 'What will the harvest be?': and in addition to this nameless fear he was experiencing the embarrassment which cannot but come to a young man of sensibility when he encounters unexpectedly a former fiancée from whom he has severed relations in a scene marked on both sides by raised voices and harsh words.

Fortunately women handle these situations more adroitly than the uncouth male. In Sally's demeanour there was no suggestion that she found in this meeting any cause for discomfort. Her eyes, bright and beautiful as he had always remembered them, shone with a friendly light. Her voice, when she spoke, was cordial. And she accompanied her words with a dazzling smile.

'Hullo, Pongo.'

'Hullo, Sally.'

'It's nice to see you again.'

'What ho.'

'You look very well.'

'Oh, rather,' said Pongo.

He spoke absently, for he was distrait. What with going to New York to attend to his financial interests and getting engaged to Hermione Bostock and all the other excitements of what had recently been a full life, he had rather allowed the peculiar properties of Sally's smile to fade from his mind, and getting it between the eyes like this had had a shaking effect, inducing a feeling somewhat similar to that which must have come to Lord Ickenham's friend Bream Rockmeteller in the course of those distant Fourth of July celebrations.

Sally's smile . . .

That smile of Sally's . . .

Yes, he had forgotten just what it could do to your system, suddenly flashing out at you like the lights of a village pub seen through rain and darkness at the end of a ten-mile hike and transporting you into a world of cosiness and joy and laughter. He blinked, and not even his great love for Hermione Bostock could keep him from experiencing a momentary twinge of nostalgia, a swift pang of that self-reproach which comes to a man conscious of having been on a good thing and of having omitted to push it along.

The weakness passed. He thought—hard—of Hermione Bostock, and it did the trick. It was a Reginald Twistleton who was himself again, a strong, firm Reginald Twistleton with not a chink in his armour, who now put the question which he would have put a good deal earlier but for the mental upheaval which we have just been analysing.

'What's all this?' he asked, and Constable Potter himself, addressing a suspicious loiterer, could not have spoken in a colder, more level voice. 'What's the idea, Uncle Fred?'

'The idea?'

'What's Sally doing here?'

'Seeking sanctuary.'

'In my room?'

'Just for the time being, till we can make other arrangements.'

Pongo placed a hand on either side of his head to shore it up. That old, familiar sensation that it was coming unstuck had swept over him.

'Oh, God!'

'Why do you say "Oh, God!" my boy? What seems to you to be the difficulty?'

'How the dickens can she stay in my room?'

'Why not? You will have a shakedown in mine. I can't offer you a bed, but you remember that very comfortable chaise-longue.'

'I don't mean that. I mean, well, dash it, what about people coming in?'

'Where?'

'Here.'

'When?'

'To-morrow morning.'

'Nobody will come in to-morrow morning except the housemaid. And before nightfall I hope to get the poor child safely away. She tells me she stowed the car in the local garage. I shall take it out and drive over to Ickenham first thing, and bring her back some of my wife's reach-me-downs. She will then be free to go where she lists. A word,' said Lord Ickenham thoughtfully, 'which I have never been able to understand. Why lists? How do lists come into it? However, that is neither here nor there. Getting back to what you were saying, nobody is going to muscle in except the housemaid, and all that is needed, therefore, is to square the housemaid. I wonder if you have ever reflected that if only he could square the housemaid, every visitor at a country house would be able to take in paying guests and make a good deal of money.'

'And how are you going to square the housemaid?'

'Odd how when one keeps repeating that it sounds like one of those forgotten sports of the past. Squaring the housemaid. One can picture William the Conqueror being rather good at it. My dear Pongo, have no uneasiness. The housemaid is already squared. Perhaps I had better tell you the story from the beginning. It won't bore you, Sally?'

'Not at all, Uncle Fred.'

'Capital. Well, when I left you, Pongo, I started to make a systematic search of the grounds, exploring every avenue and leaving no stone unturned. I was handicapped by having no bloodhounds, another thing which one ought always to bring with one to a country house, but eventually I located Sally in the potting shed, watering the geraniums with her tears.'

'I wasn't,' said Sally indignantly, and Lord Ickenham rose, kissed the top of her head paternally and returned to the bed.

'I was only making a good story of it, my dear. Actually, your attitude was heroic. I was proud of you. She laughed, Pongo, when she heard my voice. Laughed heartily.'

'I wish I could.'

'Can't you? Not at this happy ending?'

'What do you mean, happy ending?'

'Well, it looks like a happy ending to me. I see Sally as a little storm-tossed boat that has put into harbour after the dickens of a gruelling from the winds and waves, and can now take it easy for a bit. Where was I, Sally?'

'Potting shed.'

'That's right. I found her in the potting shed. I draped her in the dressing-gown, and we crept out into the night. Did you ever hear of Chingachgook?'

'No.'

'A red Indian of some celebrity in my younger days. I suppose nobody reads Fenimore Cooper now.'

'What about him?'

'I was only going to say that that was what we crept like; softly and silently, as if we were wearing moccasins. And while we were creeping, we heard voices.'

'And did I jump!'

'I, too. I soared up like a rocket. For one of the voices was Constable Potter's. The other was that of the housemaid, Elsie Bean. A rather pleasant feature of life at Ashenden Manor is the way you can always find housemaids sauntering about the grounds at half-past two in the morning. It was she who was doing most of the speaking. She seemed to be reproaching the officer for his professional activities. She was telling him that she had given her month's notice and that before her time expired he must make his decision about resigning from the Force. She said she hadn't any patience, and so alien did she appear to his aims and ideals that I felt that we had found a sympathizer. I was right. Presently, the constable left, his manner that of a man who has had his ears pinned back, and with a slight snort she turned, presumably to re-enter the house. It was at this point that we emerged and contacted her.'

'With a cheery "Hoy!"'

'With, as you say, a cheery "Hoy!" Well, after that everything went with the most delightful smoothness. I think she was a little surprised to see us—indeed, she stated later that that ghastly sound proceeding from the darkness had scared her out of a year's growth—but she soon recovered her poise and showed herself the soul of consideration. It was she who pointed out the water pipe and after I had helped Sally to climb it gave me that preliminary leg-up which a man needs at my time of life, if he is to negotiate water pipes successfully. I don't know when I have met a nicer girl, and I don't wonder you—'

'You don't wonder I what?'

'Oh, nothing. So here we are, thanks to her, and she has guaranteed that she will give us all the aid and comfort at her disposal. She said she would look in shortly and confer with us. I suppose she feels that there are one or two details which need discussing.'

Sally clasped her hands.

'My breakfast!'

'That, no doubt, was one of them.'

'I'm starving already.'

'Poor child. In a few minutes I will take you down to the larder and we will knock together a bite of supper which will keep you going till the morning. I could do with a couple of boiled eggs myself. These late hours give one an appetite. Ah, here is Miss Bean. Come in, Miss Bean. I think you know everybody. A cigarette?'

'Thank you, sir.'

'Give the lady a cigarette, Pongo. A chair, Miss Bean? And a footstool for your feet? That's right. And now, Miss Bean, tell us everything that is on your mind. I hope you have come to indicate to us in what way we may make some slight return for all your kindness to-night. Speaking for myself, if a fiver would be any good to you—and when I say a fiver I mean, of course, a tenner—'

Elsie Bean tossed her head, setting the curling pins leaping like Sir Aylmer Bostock's moustache.

'I don't want money,' she said, not actually referring to it as dross, but giving the impression that that was what she considered it. 'Thanking you all the same.'

'Not at all.'

'What I want,' said Elsie Bean, once more imparting life to the curling pins, 'is Harold bopped on the nose.'

She spoke with a strange intensity, her face hard and her blue eyes gleaming with a relentless light. That interview with her loved one in the garden seemed to have brought her to a decision. Here, you felt, was a housemaid who had been pushed just so far and could be pushed no further. Nor is the fact surprising. Tempers are quick in Bottleton East, and Constable Potter's way of replying 'Well, I dunno,' to her most impassioned pleadings would have irritated a far less emotional girl.

Lord Ickenham inclined his head courteously.

'Harold?'

'Harold Potter.'

'Ah, yes, our friend the constable. What did you say you wished done to his nose?'

'I want it bopped.'

'Struck, you mean? Socked? Given a biff?'

'R.'

'But why? Not that I want to be inquisitive, of course.'

'I was telling Mr Twistleton. There's only one way to make Harold be sensible and give up being a copper, and that's to dot him a good bop on the nose. Because he's nervous. He don't like being bopped on the nose.'

'Of course, of course. I see just what you mean. Your psychology is unerring. If I were a copper and somebody bopped me on the nose, I would hand in my resignation like a flash. The matter shall be attended to. Pongo—'

Pongo started convulsively.

'Now listen, Uncle Fred. All that's been arranged. This Bean and I have discussed it and are in full agreement that the bird to take the job on is her brother Bert. Bert, I may mention, is a chap who habitually sloshes slops on the napper with blunt instruments, so this will be a picnic to him.'

'But Bert doesn't come out till September.'

Lord Ickenham was shocked.

'Are you suggesting, Pongo, that this poor girl shall wait till September for the fulfilment of her hopes and dreams? It is obvious that time is of the essence and that we must rush to her assistance immediately. I, unfortunately, am a little too old to bop policemen on the nose, much as I should enjoy it, so the task devolves upon you. See to it as soon as possible.'

'But, dash it—'

'And don't say "But, dash it." You remind me of our mutual ancestor, Sir Gervase Twistleton, who got a bad name in the days of the Crusades from curling up in bed and murmuring "Some other time," when they asked him to come and do his bit at the battle of Joppa. I am convinced that this matter could not be placed in better hands than yours, and I would suggest that you and Miss Bean have a talk about ways and means while Sally and I go down to the larder and forage. It might be best if we took the back stairs. Can you direct us to the back stairs, Miss Bean? At the end of the passage? Thank you. I don't suppose we shall have any trouble in finding the larder. Is there a gas range in the kitchen for egg boiling purposes? Excellent. Every convenience. Then come along, Sally. I think I can promise you a blow-out on lavish lines. I have already tested Mugsy's hospitality, and it is princely. I shouldn't wonder if in addition to eggs there might not be a ham and possibly even sausages.'

With a bow of old world courtesy to Elsie Bean, Lord Ickenham escorted Sally from the room, speaking of sausages he had toasted at school on the ends of pens, and Pongo, who had folded his arms in a rather noticeable manner, found on turning to Miss Bean that her set face had relaxed.

'He's a nice old gentleman,' she said.

This seemed to Pongo such a monstrously inaccurate description of one who in his opinion was like a sort of human upas tree, casting its deadly blight on every innocent bystander who came within its sphere of influence, that he uttered a brassy 'Ha!'

'Pardon?'

'I said "Ha!"' said Pongo, and would have gone on to speak further, had there not at this moment occurred an interruption. Knuckles were rapping gently on the door, and through the woodwork there made itself heard a voice.

'Pongo.'

The voice of Bill Oakshott.

## · IV ·

In the literature and drama which have come down to us through the ages there have been a number of powerful descriptions of men reacting to unpleasant surprises. That of King Claudius watching the unfolding of the play of 'The Mouse Trap' is one of these, and writers of a later date than Shakespeare have treated vividly of the husband who discovers in an inner pocket the letter given to him by his wife to slip in the mail box two weeks previously.

Of all the protagonists in these moving scenes it is perhaps to Macbeth seeing the ghost of Banquo that one may most aptly compare Pongo Twistleton as he heard this voice in the night. He stiffened from the ankles up, his eyes rolling, his hair stirring as if beneath a sudden breeze, his very collar seeming to wilt, and from his ashen lips there came a soft, wordless cry. It was not exactly the Potter-Bean 'Coo!' and not precisely the 'Gar!' of Sir Aylmer Bostock, but a sort of blend or composite of the two. That intelligent Scottish nobleman, Ross, whom very little escaped, said, as he looked at Macbeth, 'His highness is not well,' and he would have said the same if he had been looking at Pongo.

Nor is his emotion hard to understand. When a sensitive young man, animated by a lively consideration for his personal well-being, has been told by a much larger young man of admittedly homicidal tendencies that if he does not abandon his practice of hobnobbing with housemaids in the drawing-room at one-thirty in the morning he, the much larger young man, will scoop out his insides with his bare hands, he shrinks from the prospect of being caught by the other entertaining a housemaid in his bedroom at two-forty-five. If Pongo said 'Gar!' or it may have been 'Coo!' and behaved as if an old friend whom he had recently caused to be murdered had dropped in to dinner with dagger wounds all over him, he cannot fairly be blamed. Those hands of Bill Oakshott's seemed to rise before his eyes like dreadful things seen in a nightmare.

But it was only for an instant that he stood inactive. In times of crisis blood will tell, and he had the good fortune to belong to a family whose members, having gone through a lot of this sort of thing in their day, had acquired and transmitted to their descendants a certain technique. A good many Twistletons, notably in the eighteenth and early nineteenth centuries, had been constrained by circumstances to think quick on occasions just such as this and, having thought quick, to hide women in cupboards. It was to the cupboard, therefore, acting automatically in accordance with the family tradition, that Pongo now directed Elsie Bean.

'Slide in there!' he hissed. 'And not a sound, not a yip, not a murmur. A human life hangs on your silence.'

He closed the cupboard door, straightened his tie and drawing a deep breath called 'Come in.' And it was while he was smoothing his hair and simultaneously commending his soul to God that Bill Oakshott entered.

'Oh, hullo,' he said.

'Hullo,' said Bill. 'I'm glad you're still up, Pongo. I—er—I wanted a word with you.'

The phrase is one that sometimes has an ominous ring, but it was not menacingly that Bill Oakshott employed it. His voice was soft, even winning, and Pongo was encouraged to see that though looking as large as ever, if not larger, he seemed pacific. Ross, or somebody like that who noticed things, would have said that Bill was embarrassed, and he would have been right.

It often happens that after talking to a boyhood friend like an elder brother a young man of normally kindly disposition, when he has had time to reflect, finds himself wondering if his tone during the interview was not a little brusque. It was so with Bill Oakshott. Musing in solitude and recalling the scene in the drawing-room, it had seemed to him that some of his remarks had taken too anatomical a trend. It was to apologize that he had come to Pongo's bedroom, and he proceeded now to do so.

It would have suited Pongo better if he had put these apologies in writing and submitted them to him in the form of a note, but he accepted them in a generous spirit, though absently, for he was listening to a soft, rustling sound which had begun to proceed from the cupboard. It made him feel as if spiders were walking up and down his back. The celebrated Beau Twistleton, in the days of the Regency, had once had a similar experience.

Bill appeared to have heard it, too.

'What's that?' he asked, pausing in his remarks.

'Eh?'

'That sort of scratching noise. In the cupboard.'

Pongo wiped a bead of perspiration from his forehead.

'Mice,' he said.

'Oh, mice. Lots of them about.'

'Yes, quite a good year for mice,' said Pongo. 'Well, good night, Bill, old man.'

But Bill was not yet ready to leave. Like so many large young men, he was sentimental, and this disinclined him to rush these scenes of reconciliation. When he healed rifts with boyhood friends, he liked to assure himself that they were going to stay healed. He sat down on the bed, which creaked beneath his weight.

'Well, I'm glad everything's all right, Pongo. You're sure you're not offended?'

'Not at all, not a-tall.'

'I thought you might have got the impression that I thought you were a foul snake.'

'No, no.'

'I ought never to have suggested such a thing.'

'Not keeping you up, am I, Bill?'

'Not a bit. It was just that when I found you and Elsie Bean in the drawing-room, I thought for a moment—'

'Quite.'

'You know how it is.'

'Oh, rather.'

'You see . . . I'd sock those mice, if I were you.'

'I will—to-morrow—with an iron hand. Regardless of their age and sex.'

'You see, your heads were a bit close together.'

'I was merely lighting her cigarette.'

'Of course, of course. I realize that now. I know that I can trust you.'

'Oh, rather.'

'I know that you love Hermione and will make her happy. You will look on it as a sacred duty.'

'You betcher.'

'Fine,' said Bill, clasping his hands and putting a good deal of soul into his expression. 'That's a bit of goose. I'm devoted to Hermione, Pongo.'

'Yes, you told me.'

'Hermione—'

'How about having a long talk about her in the morning?'

'Not now?'

'Bit late, isn't it?'

'Ah yes, I suppose you want to turn in. I was only going to say that Hermione is the . . . dash it, what are those things?'

'The berries?'

'Lode stars. She is the lode star of my life. I've been crazy about her for years and years and years, and her happiness means everything to me. How wonderful she is, Pongo.'

'Terrific.'

'You don't find many girls like Hermione.'

'Very scarce.'

'So beautiful.'

'Ah.'

'So clever.'

'What ho.'

'You've read her novels, of course?'

Pongo could not repress a guilty start. The question was an awkward one. He was uncomfortably conscious of having devoted to *Murder in the Fog* hours of study which would have been better employed in familiarizing himself with his loved one's output.

'Well, I'll tell you,' he said. 'Up to the moment of going to press, I haven't for one reason and another been able to smack into them to quite the extent I could wish. But she's given me her latest to read while I'm here, and I can see from the first page that it's the bezuzus. Strikes a new note, as you might say.'

'Which one is that?'

'I've forgotten the name, but I know it was called something.'

'How long has it been out?'

'Just published, I understand.'

'Ah, then I haven't seen it. Fine. That's a treat to look forward to. Isn't she amazing, Pongo? Isn't it extraordinary that she can write all those wonderful books—'

'Oh, rather.'

'—And still be a simple, healthy, out-of-doors country girl, never happier than when she is getting up at six in the morning and going for a long walk through the—'

Pongo started.

'Six in the morning?' He spoke in a thin, strained voice, and his jaw had fallen a little. 'She doesn't get up at six in the morning?'

'In the summer always.'

'And in winter?'

'Seven. I've known her to do a round and a half of golf before breakfast, and if she doesn't play golf it's a long walk through the woods and fields. I tell you, she's marvelous. Well, good night, Pongo, you'll be wanting to get to bed,' said Bill, and heaving himself up took his departure.

It was a pensive Pongo Twistleton who went to the door and listened and then went to the cupboard and extracted Elsie Bean. To say that Bill's words had weakened his great love would perhaps be going too far, for he still thought Hermione Bostock a queen among women and had no intention of replying in the negative when the clergyman said 'Wilt thou, Reginald, take this Hermione to be thy wedded wife?' But the discovery that he was engaged to a girl who habitually got up at six in the morning, and would presumably insist on him getting up at that hour also, had definitely shaken him. His manner as he de-Beaned the cupboard was distrait, and when his guest complained of being in the final stages of suffocation he merely said 'Oh, ah?'

His detachment displeased Elsie Bean. She displayed a captious spirit.

'What did I have to go killing myself in cupboards for? It was only Mr William.'

'Only!' said Pongo, unable to share this easy outlook. 'Do you realize that if he had found you here, he would have pulled my head off at the roots?'

'You don't say?'

'Not to mention scooping out my insides with his bare hands.'

'Coo! What a nut!'

'The word nut understates it. When roused—and finding you on the premises would have roused him like nobody's business—he's a menace to pedestrians and traffic. Gosh!' said Pongo, struck with an idea. 'Why wouldn't he be the man to bop your Harold on the nose?'

'But you're going to do it.'

'In case I can't manage to get around to it, I mean. You know how full one's time is. I believe Bill would be just the chap you want.'

Elsie Bean shook her head.

'No, I asked him.'

'Asked him?'

'R. I met him walking in the garden after I'd helped that nice old gentleman up the water pipe. He said he wouldn't.'

'Why not?'

'He doesn't believe in bopping coppers on the nose.'

It was a prejudice which Pongo shared, but nevertheless he found himself exasperated. One never likes to see a man stifling his natural gifts. The parable of the talents crossed his mind.

'But how on earth do you expect me to do it?' he demanded peevishly. 'The way everybody talks, you'd think it was the simplest thing in the world to walk up to a fifteen-stone policeman and sock him on the beezer. I can't see the procedure. How does one start? One can't just go and do it. It wants leading up to. And even then—'

Elsie Bean seemed to appreciate his difficulty.

'I've been thinking about that,' she said. 'How would it be if you pushed him into the duck pond?'

'What duck pond?'

'The one outside the front gate.'

'But he may not go near the bally duck pond.'

'Yes, he will. He always does, when he's on his beat. He goes and stands there and spits into it.'

Pongo brightened a little. It would be idle to pretend that he found the picture which his companion had conjured up attractive, but it was less repellent than the other.

'Creep up behind him, you mean?'

'R.'

'And give him a hearty shove?'

'R.'

'Yes. Yes, I see what you mean. Well, there is much in what you say, and I will give the matter my attention. It may be that you have found the solution. Meanwhile, go and peer cautiously up and down the passage and see if there's anybody about. If there isn't, pick up your feet and streak for your dug-out like a flash.'

But before she could reach the door, it had opened to admit Lord Ickenham and Sally. Both looked greatly refreshed, the former in particular wearing the contented expression of a man who has been steeping himself in boiled eggs.

'As good a little meal as I have ever tasted,' he said. 'Really, Mugsy does one extraordinarily well. And now bed, don't you think? The evening is wearing along. You had better be putting a few things together, Pongo.'

Pongo did not reply. He was staring at Sally. Lord Ickenham approached him and drove a kindly finger into his ribs.

'Ouch!'

'Start packing, my boy.'

'Eh? Oh, right ho!'

'Just a few necessaries. I can lend you a razor and my great sponge, Joyeuse.' Lord Ickenham turned to Elsie Bean. 'You two have settled things, I hope?'

'Yes, sir. Mr Twistleton is going to push Harold into the duck pond.'

'Capital, capital,' said Lord Ickenham heartily. 'An excellent idea. You'll enjoy that, Pongo. Don't forget that in pushing policemen into duck ponds the follow through is everything.'

Pongo, mechanically filling a suitcase, again made no reply. Though he had ceased to stare at Sally, she still occupied his thoughts. The sight of her coming through the door had acted upon him like a powerful electric shock, for her eyes, the eyes of a girl refreshed with tea and eggs, had seemed, if possible, brighter than ever, and once more she had flashed upon him that smile of hers. And this time, though he had immediately thought of Hermione Bostock, it was only to be reminded of her habit of rising at six in the summer and at seven during the winter months.

He closed the suitcase, and stood waiting. Strange thrills were shooting through his streamlined body, and his heart, which had been comparatively inactive recently, was again jumping and bumping. That consciousness of not having pushed a good thing along was now very pronounced.

'Well, good night, Sally,' said Lord Ickenham.

'Good night, Uncle Fred. Good night, Pongo.'

'Eh? Oh, good night.'

'And thanks for the sanctuary.'

'Eh? Oh, not at all.'

'Good night, Miss Bean.'

'Good night, sir.'

'You will be turning in yourself shortly, no doubt? A thousand thanks once more for all your sympathy and kindness. The duck pond, eh?' said Lord Ickenham thoughtfully. 'Yes, admirable, admirable. Come along, Pongo.'

Half-way along the corridor Pongo paused. Lord Ickenham eyed him inquiringly.

'Forgotten something?'

'Eh? Oh, no. I was only thinking about Sally.'

'What about her?'

'She looked dashed pretty in that dressing-gown.'

'Charming. By the way, she tells me she wants a lipstick. See to that to-morrow, will you.'

'Right ho,' said Pongo. 'Lipstick, one. Right.'

He resumed his progress musingly.

# PART FOUR

# 10

## · I ·

If you motor to Wockley Junction in the morning, starting from Ashenden Manor reasonably soon after an early-ish breakfast, you can get an express train which deposits you on the arrival platform at Waterloo at twelve-forty-three. The passage of the hours in no way having weakened her determination to visit her child and make plain to her the bleakness of the future awaiting any girl rash enough to put on a white veil and walk down the aisle with her arm linked in that of Reginald Twistleton, Lady Bostock had done this. Bill Oakshott drove her to the junction, and she reached the block of flats where Hermione had her London residence shortly after one, just as Hermione, outside its front door, was about to step into her two-seater.

Privileged to direct a square look at this girl as she stood there in the almost unbelievable splendour of her new hat, her best frock and her carefully selected shoes, gloves and stockings, the dullest eye would have been able to see that she had what it takes. Her father might look like a walrus and her mother like something starting at a hundred to eight in the two-thirty race at Catterick Bridge, but Hermione herself, tall and dark, with large eyes, a perfect profile and an equally perfect figure, was an Oriental potentate's dream of what the harem needed.

Hearing Lady Bostock's bleating cry, she turned and stared, incredulity blended in her gaze with the natural dismay of a daughter who, having said good-bye to her mother on a Monday afternoon after entertaining her for a week at her flat, sees her come bobbing up again on Wednesday morning.

'Mother!' she exclaimed in the rich contralto which for years had been stirring up Bill Oakshott's soul like an egg whisk.

'Whatever . . . ?'

'Oh, dear,' said Lady Bostock. 'Have you got to go? I came up specially to see you.'

'I must. I'm lunching at Barribault's and I'm late already. What did you want to see me about?'

'Oh, dear, oh, dear, oh, dear. Reginald.'

'Reginald?'

'Yes, dear. Your father—'

A smouldering gleam came into Hermione's fine eyes. Those words 'Your father', taken in conjunction with the name of the man to whom she had plighted her troth, had aroused her suspicions. They could only mean, it seemed to her, that in defiance of her explicit instructions Sir Aylmer had not been treating her nominee like an ewe lamb. And she was a girl who when she said ewe lamb meant ewe lamb.

'What has Father been doing to Reginald?' she demanded sternly. 'Has he been barking at him?'

'No, no. Your father never barks. He sometimes raises his voice.'

'Has he been raising his voice, then?'

'Scarcely so that you could notice it. No, what has happened . . . Oh dear, it's such a long story.'

'Then I really can't wait to hear it now. I'm terribly late. And I'm lunching with a publisher.'

'Mr Popgood?'

Hermione laughed a short, dry laugh. In an association which had lasted three years Augustus Popgood, the sponsor of her books, had never offered her so much as a cheese straw. Nor had his partner, Cyril Grooly.

'No,' she said. 'This is a new one. He wrote to me a few days ago, saying that he would like to have me on his list and suggesting luncheon. He seems a most enterprising man, quite different from Popgood and Grooly. He is the head of a firm called Meriday House, a Mr Pointer or Punter or Painter. I couldn't make out the signature on his letter. Goodbye, mother. I'll try to get back about three.'

'I'll wait for you, dear.'

'It's something important, you say?'

'Very, very important.'

'About Reginald?'

'Yes, dear. We find that he—'

'I'm sorry, mother,' said Hermione. 'I must rush.'

She was not without a normal girl's curiosity, but she was also an ambitious young authoress who believed that there is a tide in the affairs of men which taken at the flood leads on to fortune, and there was awaiting her at Barribault's Hotel a publisher who, judging from his letter, was evidently a live wire endowed with pep and ginger and all the other qualities which ambitious young authoresses like to see in those responsible for the marketing of their books.

The car moved off. Seated at the wheel, she gave herself up to agreeable thoughts about this pushful Mr Pointer.

Or Punter.

Or possibly Painter.

## • II •

Painter was the name. Not Pointer. Not Punter. Painter. It was Sally's brother Otis who was waiting for Hermione in the lobby of Barribault's Hotel, and at the moment when her two-seater joined the stream of traffic he had sprung from his chair, too nervous to sit any longer, and begun to stride to and fro, his eyes from time to time straying to his wrist watch. The coming luncheon marked a crisis in his affairs.

It was no mere coincidence that Otis Painter, in his capacity of publisher of the book beautiful, should have written to Hermione suggesting a meeting with a view to an agreement. The invitation had been the outcome of some very rapid thinking on his part.

Right from the start it had been plain to Otis Painter that if anything like a happy ending was to be achieved in that matter of the lawsuit which was brooding over him like a thunder cloud, Sir Aylmer Bostock would have to be pleaded with, and he had told Sally to tell Pongo to perform the task. And it was while he was in the grip of that unpleasant sinking feeling which always came to those who placed their affairs in Pongo's hands that he had happened upon the issue of the *Tatler* containing Hermione's photograph.

> 'Miss Hermione Bostock,' he read, 'daughter of Sir Aylmer and Lady Bostock of Ashenden Manor, Hants. In addition to being prominent in Society, Miss Bostock has written several novels under the pseudonym of Gwynneth Gould.'

The words had brought inspiration. His thoughts, as he gazed at the photograph and the caption beneath it, had run roughly as follows. And they seem to us to display an intelligence considerably above the average of what might have been expected in one who had been in his time both an interior decorator and a seller of antiques, besides running a marionette theatre in the Boulevard Raspail.

> Q. Who is the best possible person to plead with an old crumb who is threatening to bring a ruinous suit for damages against a shaky young publishing firm?
> A. Obviously the crumb's daughter, the apple of his eye to whom he can refuse nothing.
> Q. Get hold of the daughter, then, and enlist her in one's cause?
> A. Exactly.
> Q. But how?
> A. Easy. She's an author. Offer her a contract. Her interests will then be identical with those of her publisher, and she will exert her tremendous influence to save him from ruin. Better ask her to lunch.

Q. Right.

A. At Barribault's

Q. *What?* Have you ever been to Barribault's and seen the prices on the right-hand side?

A. No good spoiling the ship for a ha'porth of tar. You can't swing a deal like this on bottled beer, a mutton chop and two veg.

So now Otis was pacing Barribault's lobby, wondering why his guest did not arrive and what the lunch was going to set him back when she did. A few thoughtful words about acidity might steer her off champagne, but at a place like this even hock was likely to inflict a ghastly gash on the wallet.

Watching Otis Painter walk to and fro with his mouth ajar and his knees clashing like cymbals, for he had the misfortune to suffer from adenoids and to be knock-kneed, a spectator would have been surprised to learn that he was so closely related to Sally. But just as daughters have a way of being easier on the eye than their fathers and mothers, so are sisters frequently more attractive than their brothers. Otis was a stout young man with a pink nose, horn-rimmed spectacles and short side-whiskers, who looked like something from the Anglo-Saxon colony on the east bank of the Seine.

It was, indeed, to the east bank of the Seine that he had migrated immediately after graduating from the college where he had received his education, having sprouted a soul and the side-whiskers simultaneously towards the end of his sophomore year. From the *rive gauche* he had drifted to London, there to try various ventures with a uniform lack of success, and here he was, five years later, the directing executive of Meriday House, formerly Ye Panache Presse, waiting in Barribault's lobby to give lunch to Hermione Bostock.

The hands of his watch were pointing to twenty-seven minutes past one when through the glass of the outer door he saw the gaily apparelled official who stood on the threshold to scoop clients out of their cars and cabs suddenly stiffen himself; touch his hat convulsively and give his moustache a spasmodic twirl, sufficient indication that something pretty sensational was on its way in. And a moment later the door revolved and through it came a figure that made him catch his breath and regret that the pimple on the tip of his nose had not yielded to treatment that morning. There is nothing actually low and degrading about a pimple on the tip of the nose, but there are times when a susceptible young man wishes he did not have one.

He stepped forward devoutly.

'Miss Gould?'

'Oh, how do you do, Mr Pointer?'

'Painter.'

'Punter?'

'Painter.'

'Oh, Painter. I hope I'm not late.'

'No, no. Cocktail?'

'No, thank you. I never drink.'

Otis started. The wallet in his hip pocket seemed to give a joyful leap.

'What, not even at lunch?'

'Only lemonade.'

'Come right in,' said Otis with an enthusiasm which he made no attempt to conceal. 'Come right along in.'

He led the way buoyantly towards the grill room. Lemonade, he happened to know, was half-a-crown.

## · III ·

It was probably this immediate striking of the right note that made the luncheon such a success. For that it was a success not even the most exacting critic could have disputed. From the first forkful of smoked salmon it went with all the swing of a Babylonian orgy or of one of those conferences between statesmen which are conducted throughout in a spirit of the utmost cordiality.

Too often when a publisher entertains an author at the midday meal a rather sombre note tinges the table talk. The host is apt to sigh a good deal and to choose as the theme of his remarks the hardness of the times, the stagnant condition of the book trade and the growing price of pulp paper. And when his guest tries to cheer him up by suggesting that these disadvantages may be offset by a spirited policy of publicity, he sighs again and says that eulogies of an author's work displayed in the press at the publisher's expense are of little or no value, the only advertising that counts being—how shall he put it—well, what he might perhaps describe as word-of-mouth advertising.

There was nothing of that sort here to-day. Otis scoffed at the idea that the times were hard. The times, in his opinion, were swell. So was the book trade. Not a trace of stagnation. And as for pulp paper, you might have supposed from the way he spoke that they gave him the stuff.

He then went on to sketch out his policy as regarded advertising.

Otis, said Otis, believed in advertising. When he found an author in whom he had confidence—like you, Miss Gould, if he might say so—the sky was the limit. A column here, a column there. That sort of thing. The cost? He didn't give a darn about the cost. You got it all back on the sales. His motto, he said, coming through smoothly with the only bit of French—except *Oo-la-la*—which had managed to stick from the old left bank days, was *L'audace, l'audace, et toujours l'audace*.

It was a statement of faith well calculated to make any young authoress feel that she was floating on a pink cloud over an ocean of joy, and that was how Hermione felt as she listened. The sensation grew even more acute as her host spoke of commissioning her next three books, sight unseen, and paying royalty on them at the rate of twenty per cent, rising to twenty-five above three thousand. Even when uttered by a man with adenoids the words were like the strains of some grand anthem.

It is possible that the reader of this chronicle, misled by Bill Oakshott's enthusiasm, may have formed an erroneous idea of Hermione Bostock's standing in the world of literature, for her career had been a good deal less triumphant than he had appeared to suggest. She had published three works of fiction through the house of Popgood and Grooly, of which the first two had sold eleven hundred and four and sixteen hundred and eight copies respectively. The last, just out, was reported by Popgood, a gloomy man, to be 'moving slowly'. Grooly, the optimist of the firm, spoke in brighter vein of a possible sale of two thousand.

But even if you strung along with sunny young Grooly you could not say that figures like these were anything but a poor return for a great deal of hard toil, and Hermione attributed them not to any lack of merit in the books themselves, for she knew their merit to be considerable, but to the firm's preference for keeping its money in the old oak chest instead of spending it on advertisements in the papers. She had once taken this matter up with the partners, and Popgood had said that it was no use advertising in the papers, because the only form of advertising that counted was . . . how should he put it?

'Word of mouth?' suggested Grooly.

'Word of mouth!' assented Popgood, looking gratefully at the ingenious phrase-maker.

Little wonder, then, that as Hermione drank in Otis's intoxicating words, soft music seemed to fill the air and even the directing executive of Meriday House became almost beautiful. She listened as if in a dream, and the more he talked the more she liked it. It was only as she was sipping her coffee (two shillings, but unavoidable) that anything crept into his remarks that suggested that all was not for the best in the best of all possible worlds. Quite suddenly, after an eloquent passage surcharged with optimism, he struck a minor chord.

'Yay,' he said, 'that's how I feel. I admire your work and I would like to take hold of your books and push them as they ought to be pushed. But—'

He paused, and Hermione, descending from her pink cloud, looked at him with concern. When a publisher has offered you twenty per cent rising to twenty-five above three thousand and has been talking spaciously of column spreads in all the literate Sunday papers, you do not like to hear him use that word 'but'.

'But—?' she echoed.

Otis removed his horn-rimmed spectacles, polished them and replaced them on a nose which an excellent luncheon had turned from pink to scarlet. He also touched his pimple and polished that, and with a pudgy hand stroked his starboard whisker. The interview had reached its crux, and he wished to reflect before proceeding.

'But . . . Well, the fact is,' he said, 'there's a catch. I'm not so sure I'm going to have the money to do it with. I may go bankrupt before I can start.'

'What!'

'You see, I'm faced with a darned nasty legal action, and my lawyer tells me the damages may be very heavy.'

'But why do you speak as if you were certain to lose?'

'I am, if it ever comes into court. And I don't see how I'm going to stop it coming into court. This man Bostock—'

'Bostock?'

'Sir Aylmer Bostock. He used to be Governor of one of those African colonies, and he wrote his Reminiscences and got me to publish them—'

'But that was Ye Panache Presse.'

'I changed the name to Meriday House. Crisper. Why, say,' said Otis with natural surprise, 'you speak as if you know all about it. You do? Extraordinary how these things get around. Well, if you've heard what happened, I don't have to explain. The point is that this Bostock is showing a very vindictive spirit. And, as I say, if the thing comes into court, I shall be ruined.'

'Ah!' said Hermione.

Lord Ickenham, looking at this girl's photograph, had given it as his opinion that she was a potential eye-flasher. He had been correct. Her eyes were flashing now, and in that simple 'Ah!' there was all the sinister significance of Constable Potter's 'Ho!'

In earlier portions of this chronicle reference was made to the emotions of wolves which overtake sleighs and find no Russian peasant aboard and of tigers deprived of their Indian coolie just as they are sitting down to lunch. More poignant even than these are the feelings of a young authoress who, having just been offered twenty per cent rising to twenty-five above three thousand by a publisher who believes in column spreads in all the literate Sunday papers, learns that her father is planning to rob that publisher of the means to publish.

Hermione rose, grim and resolute.

'Don't worry, Mr Painter. I will see that the suit does not come into court.'

'Eh?'

'I ought to have told you earlier that Gwynneth Gould is merely my pen-name. I am Hermione Bostock. Sir Aylmer's daughter.' Otis was almost too amazed for words.

'His *daughter*? Well, fancy that. Well, I'll be darned. What an extraordinary thing.'

'I will talk to Father. I will drive down and see him at once.'

'How would it be if you took me along? In case you needed help.'

'I shall not need help.'

'Still, I'd like to be on the spot, to hear the good news as soon as possible.'

'Very well. While I am seeing Father, you can wait at the inn. So if you are ready, Mr Painter, let us be going. My car is outside.'

It was as they were nearing Guildford at sixty miles an hour, for she was a girl who believed that accelerators were made to be stepped on, that a thought which for some time had been groping about the exterior of Hermione's mind, like an inebriated householder fumbling with his latch-key, suddenly succeeded in effecting an entrance, and she gave a gasp.

'Pardon?' said Otis, who also had been gasping. He was finding his companion's driving a novel and terrifying experience.

'Nothing,' said Hermione. 'Just something I happened to remember.'

It was the circumstance of her mother's visit that she had happened to remember, that devoted mother who had now been waiting three hours at her flat to tell her something about Reginald. For an instant she was conscious of a twinge of remorse. Then she told herself that Mother would be all right. She had a comfortable chair and all the illustrated papers.

She pressed her foot on the accelerator, and Otis shut his eyes and commended his soul to God.

# 11

## · I ·

The afternoon sun, slanting in through the French window of what until the previous night had been Pongo's bedroom, touched Sally's face and woke her from the doze into which she had fallen. She rose and stretched herself, yawning.

The French window opened on a balcony, and she eyed it wistfully. It would have been pleasant on so fine a summer day to go and sit on that balcony. But girls who are known, if only slightly, to the police must be prudent. The best she could do was to stand behind the curtain and from this observation post peer out at the green and golden world beyond.

Soon exhausting the entertainment value of a patch of gravel and part of a rhododendron bush, she was about to return to the chaise-longue, when there appeared on the patch of gravel the tall, distinguished figure of Lord Ickenham, walking jauntily and carrying a small suitcase. He passed from view, and a moment later there was a thud as the suitcase fell on the balcony.

Her heart leaped. An intelligent girl, she realized that this must mean clothes. The fifth earl might have his frivolous moments, but he was not the man to throw suitcases on to balconies in a spirit of mere wantonness. She crawled cautiously on all fours and possessed herself of the rich gift.

Her confidence had not been misplaced. It was clothes, and she hastened to put on what she recognized as a white sports dress and red jacket belonging to Lady Ickenham with all the eagerness of a girl who likes to look nice and for some little time has had to get along with a man's flowered dressing-gown. And it was as she stood examining herself contentedly in the mirror that Lord Ickenham entered.

'So you got them all right?' he said. 'Not a bad shot for a man who has jerked very little since the old soda days. But if you have once jerked soda, you never really lose the knack. I like that red coat. Rather dressy.'

Sally kissed him gratefully.

'You're an angel, Uncle Fred. Nobody saw you, I hope?'

'Not a soul. The enemy's lines were thin and poorly guarded. Your hostess went to London soon after breakfast, and Mugsy is over at a neighbouring village, trying to sell someone a cow, I understand.'

Sally started.

'Then why not do it now? Get the bust, I mean.'

'My dear child, you don't suppose that idea did not occur to me? My first move on learning that the coast was clear was to make a bee-line for the collection room, only to discover that Mugsy had locked the door and gone off with the key. As I was saying to Pongo last night, there is a streak of low cunning in Mugsy's nature which one deplores. Still, don't worry. I'm biding my time. That's the sort of man I'm, as the song says. I shall arrange everything to your full satisfaction quite shortly.'

'Says you.'

'Sally! Don't tell me you're losing confidence in me.'

'Oh, darling Uncle Fred, of course not. Why did I speak those harsh words? Consider them unsaid.'

'They are already expunged from my memory. Yes, you look charming in that coat. Quite a vision. No wonder Pongo loves you.'

'Not any more.'

'More than ever. I was noticing the way his eyes came popping out last night every time they rested on you. Did you ever see a prawn in the mating season? Like that. And one of the last things he said to me was "She looked dashed pretty in that dressing-gown." With a sort of catch in his voice. That means love.'

'If he thought I looked pretty in a dressing-gown made for a man of six feet two, it must mean something.'

'Love, my dear. Love, I tell you. All the old fervour has started gushing up again like a geyser. He worships you. He adores you. He would die for one little rose from your hair. How are conditions at your end?'

'Oh, I haven't changed.'

'You love him still?'

'I'm crazy about him.'

'That's satisfactory. Though odd. I'm very fond of Pongo. In fact, except for my wife and you and my dog, George, I can think of nobody of whom I am fonder. But I can't understand anyone being crazy about him. How do you do it?'

'It's quite easy, bless his precious heart. He's a baa-lamb.'

'You see him from that angle?'

'I always have. A sweet, woolly, baa-lamb that you want to stroke and pet.'

'Well, you may be right. You know more about baa-lambs than I do. But this is official. If I were a girl and he begged me for one little rose from my hair, I wouldn't give it him. He'd have a pretty thin time trying to get roses out of me. Still, the great thing is that you love him, because I have an idea that he will very soon be at liberty to pay his addresses to you. This engagement of his can't last.'

'You certainly do spread sweetness and light, don't you, Uncle Fred?'

'I try to.'

'Tell me more. I could listen for ever. Why do you think the engagement won't last?'

'How can it? What on earth does a girl like Hermione Bostock want to marry Pongo for?'

'Maybe she likes baa-lambs, too.'

'Nonsense. I've only seen her photograph, but I could tell at a glance that what she needs is a large, solid, worshipping husband of the huntin', shootin' and fishin' type, not a metropolitan product like Pongo. Her obvious mate is her cousin, Bill Oakshott, who has been devoted to her for years. But he's too mild in his methods. He doesn't tell his love, but lets concealment like a worm i' the bud feed on his damask cheek. You can't run a business that way. I intend to have a very serious talk with young William Oakshott next time I see him. In fact, I'll go and try to find him now.'

'No, don't go yet. I want to tell you about Pongo.'

'What about him?'

'He's worried to death, the poor pet. My heart aches for him. He was in here not long ago, and he just sat in a chair and groaned.'

'You're sure he wasn't singing?'

'I don't think so. Would he have buried his face in his hands, if he had been singing?'

'No. You're perfectly right. That is the acid test. I have heard Pongo sing on several occasions at our village concert, and it is impossible to mistake the symptoms. He sticks his chin up and throws his head back and lets it go in the direction of the ceiling at an angle of about forty-five. And very unpleasant it is, especially when the song is "Oh, My Dolores, Queen of the Eastern Sea", as too often happens. So he groaned, did he? Why?'

'He doesn't like this idea of pushing the policeman into the duck pond.'

'Doesn't *like* it? Not when he knows it's going to bring happiness and wedding bells to the divine Bean?'

'The impression he gave me was that he wasn't thinking much about the divine Bean and her wedding bells.'

'Looking at the thing principally in the light of how it was going to affect good old Twistleton?' Lord Ickenham sighed. 'Young men are not what they were in my day, Sally. We were all Galahads then. Damsels in distress had merely to press a button, and we would race up with our ears flapping, eager to do their behest. Well, we can't have him backing out. We owe a debt of honour to Miss Bean, and it must be paid. And, dash it, what's he making such heavy weather about? It isn't as if this duck pond were miles away across difficult country.'

A strange look had come into Sally's face, the sort of resolute look you might have surprised on the faces of Joan of Arc or Boadicea.

'Where is it?' she asked. 'He didn't tell me.'

'Outside the front gate. A mere step. And I was speaking to Miss Bean this morning, and she tells me that when Potter arrives there on his beat he always stands beside it for an appreciable space of time, spitting and, one hopes, thinking of her. What simpler and more agreeable task could there be than to saunter up behind a spitting policeman, at a moment when he is wrapped in thought, and push him into a pond? To further the interests of a girl like La Bean, the finest housemaid that ever flicked a duster, I would have pushed twenty policemen into twenty ponds when I was Pongo's age.'

'But Pongo has such a rare, sensitive nature.'

'So had I a rare, sensitive nature. It was the talk of New York. Well, if the thing is to be done to-day, he ought to be starting. It is at just about this hour, I am informed, that Potter rolls along. Where is he?'

'I don't know. He drifted out.'

'I must find him at once.'

'Just a minute,' said Sally.

The resolute expression on her face had become more noticeable than ever. In addition to looking like Joan of Arc and Boadicea, she could now have been mistaken in a dim light for Jael, the wife of Heber, and Lord Ickenham, pausing on his way to the door, was impressed and vaguely disturbed.

'What's the matter?' he asked. 'You have a strained air. You aren't worrying about Pongo?'

'Yes, I am.'

'But I keep assuring you that the task before him is both simple and agreeable.'

'Not for Pongo. He's a baa-lamb. I told you that before.'

'But why should the circumstance of being a baa-lamb unfit a man for pushing policemen into ponds?'

'I don't know. But it does. I've studied this thing of pushing policemen into ponds, Uncle Fred, and I'm convinced that what you need, to get the best results, is a girl whose clothes the policeman tore off on the previous night.'

'Good God, Sally! You don't mean—?'

'Yes, I do. My mind is made up. I'm going to pinch hit for Pongo, and, if it interests you to know it, it is a far, far better thing that I do than I have ever done. Good-bye, Uncle Fred. See you later.'

She disappeared on to the balcony, and a scrabbling sound told Lord Ickenham that she was descending the water pipe. He went out, and was in time to see her vanish into the bushes on the other side of the terrace. For some moments he stood there staring after her, then with a little sigh, the sigh too often extorted from Age by the spectacle of Headstrong Youth doing its stuff, passed thoughtfully from the room. Making his way downstairs, still pensive, he reached the hall.

Bill Oakshott was there, balancing a walking stick on the tip of his nose.

· II ·

That the young squire of Ashenden in essaying this equilibristic feat had not been animated by a mere spirit of frivolity, but was endeavouring rather, as men will in times of mental stress, to divert his thoughts from graver issues, was made clear by a certain touch of the careworn in his manner. It is not easy to look careworn when you are balancing a walking stick on the tip of your nose, but Bill Oakshott contrived to do so.

At the sight of Lord Ickenham he brightened. Ever since he had escorted Lady Bostock to Wockley Junction that morning he had been wanting to see and seek counsel from one on whose judgment he had come to rely, and owing to the fact of having been obliged to fulfil a long-standing luncheon engagement with friends who lived on the Wockley road he had had no opportunity of approaching him earlier.

'Oh, there you are,' he said. 'Fine.'

Lord Ickenham reluctantly put Sally's affairs to one side for the time being. The sight of this massive youth had reminded him that he had a pep talk to deliver.

'The word "fine",' he replied, 'is happily chosen, for I, too, have been looking forward to this encounter. I want to speak to you, Bill Oakshott.'

'I want to speak to *you*.'

'I have much to say.'

'So have I much to say.'

'Well, if it comes to a duet, I'll bet I can talk louder and quicker than you, and I am willing to back this opinion with notes, cash or lima beans. However, as I am your guest, I suppose courtesy demands that I yield the floor. Proceed.'

Bill marshaled his thoughts.

'Well, it's like this. After breakfast this morning, I drove my aunt to Wockley to catch the express to London. I was feeling a bit tired after being up so late last night, so I didn't talk as we tooled along, just kept an eye on the road and thought of this and that.'

Lord Ickenham interrupted him.

'Skip all this part. I shall be able to read it later, no doubt, in your autobiography, in the chapter headed "Summer Morning Outings with My Aunt". Spring to the point.'

'Well, what I was going to say was that I was keeping an eye on the road and thinking of this and that, when she suddenly said "Dipsomaniac."'

'Why did she call you a dipsomaniac?'

'She didn't. It turned out she was talking about Pongo.'

'Pongo, egad? Was she, indeed?'

'Yes. She said "Dipsomaniac". And I said "Eh?" And she said "He's a dipsomaniac." And I said "Who's a dipsomaniac?" And she said "Reginald Twistleton is a dipsomaniac. Your uncle says he has not been sober since he got here."'

Lord Ickenham drew in his breath with a little hiss of admiration.

'Masterly!' he said. 'Once again, Bill Oakshott, I must pay a marked tribute to your narrative gifts. I never met a man who could tell a story better. Come clean, my boy. You are Sinclair Lewis, are you not? Well, I'm convinced you're someone. So your aunt said "Dipsomaniac", and you said "Eh?" and she said . . . and so on and so forth, concluding with this fearless *exposé* of Pongo. Very interesting. Did she mention on what she based the charge?'

'Oh, rather. Apparently she and Uncle Aylmer found him swigging whisky in the drawing-room.'

'I would not attach too much importance to that. Many of our noblest men swig whisky in drawing-rooms. I do myself.'

'But not all night. Well, you might say all night. What I mean is, I found Pongo in the drawing-room, swigging away, at about one o'clock this morning, and my aunt and uncle appear to have found him there, still swigging, at half-past two. That makes one and a half hours. Give him say half an hour before I came in, and you get two hours of solid swigging. And after my aunt and uncle left he must have started swigging again. Because he was unquestionably stinko after breakfast.'

'I decline to believe that anyone could get stinko at breakfast.'

'I didn't say he did get stinko at breakfast. You're missing the point. My theory is that he swigged all night, got stinko round about six a.m. and continued stinko till the incident occurred.'

'To what incident do you allude?'

'It happened just after breakfast. My aunt was waiting for me to bring the car round, and Uncle Aylmer made some unpleasant cracks about the hat she was wearing. So she went up to her room to get another, and as she reached the door she heard someone moving about inside. When she went in, there was nobody to be seen, and then suddenly there came a sneeze from the wardrobe, and there was Pongo, crouching on the floor.'

'She was sure?'

'Sure?'

'It wasn't a shoe or a bit of fluff?'

'No, it was Pongo. She says he smiled weakly and said he had looked in to borrow her lipstick. He must have been as tight as an owl. Because, apart from anything else, a glance at Aunt Emily should have told him she hasn't got a lipstick. And what I've been trying to make up my mind about is, oughtn't Hermione to be warned? Isn't it a bit thick to allow her to breeze gaily into a lifelong union with a chap who's going to spend his married life sitting up all night getting stinko in the drawing-room? I don't see how a wife could possibly be happy under such conditions.'

'She might feel rather at a loose end, might she not? But you are misjudging Pongo in considering him a non-stop swigger. As a general thing he is quite an abstemious young man. Only in exceptional circumstances does he go on anything which a purist would call a bender. At the moment he is under a severe nervous strain.'

'Why?'

'For some reason he always is when we visit a house together. My presence—it is difficult to explain it—seems to do something to him.'

'Then you don't feel that Hermione ought to be told?'

'I will have to think it over. But,' said Lord Ickenham, fixing his young friend with a penetrating eye, 'there is something she must be told—without delay, and by you, Bill Oakshott.'

'Eh?'

'And that is that you love her and would make her yours.'

'Eh?'

'Fight against this tendency to keep saying "Eh". You do love her, do you not? You would make her yours, wouldn't you? I have it from an authoritative source that you have been thinking along those lines for years and years.'

Bill had turned a pretty vermilion. He shuffled his feet.

'Why, yes,' he admitted, 'that's right, as a matter of fact. I have. But how can I tell her I would make her mine? She's engaged to Pongo.'

'What of it?'

'You can't go barging in on a girl, telling her you would make her yours, when she's engaged to another chap.'

'Of course you can. How about Young Lochinvar? He did it, and was extremely highly thought of in consequence. You are familiar with the case of Young Lochinvar?'

'Oh, yes. I used to recite the poem as a kid.'

'It must have sounded wonderful,' said Lord Ickenham courteously. 'I myself was best at "It wath the thschooner Hethperuth that thailed the thtormy theas." Well, let me tell you something, my dear chap. You need have no morbid scruples about swinging Hermione Bostock on to your saddle bow, as far as Pongo is concerned. He's in love with somebody else. Do you remember me speaking at our first meeting of a girl I had been hoping he would marry? I don't think I mentioned it then, but he was at one time engaged to her, and all the symptoms point to his wanting to be again. The last time I saw them together, which was quite recently, I received the distinct impression that he would die for one little rose from her hair. So you can go ahead without a qualm. Miss Bostock is in London, I understand. Pop up there and pour your heart out.'

'M'm.'

'Why do you say "M'm"?'

Once again Bill Oakshott shuffled his feet, producing on the parquet floor a sound resembling waves breaking on a stern and rockbound coast.

'It's so difficult.'

'What, to pour your heart out? Nonsense.'

'Well, I've been trying to do it for nine years, but not a ripple. I can't seem to get started.'

Lord Ickenham reflected.

'I think I see where the trouble lies. You have made the mistake of brooding in advance too much, with the result that you have pottered about and accomplished nothing. Swiftness and decision are what is needed. Don't hesitate. Have at her. Sweep her off her feet. Take her by storm.'

'Oh, yes?' said Bill flatly, and Lord Ickenham laid a kindly hand on his shoulder. He knew what was passing in the young man's mind.

'I can understand your feeling a little nervous,' he said. 'When I saw Hermione Bostock's photograph, I was struck at once by something formidable in her face, a touch of that majestic inaccessibility which used to cramp the style of diffident young Greek shepherds in their relations with the more dignified of the goddesses of Mount Olympus. She is what in my day would have been called a proud beauty. And that makes it all the more necessary to take a strong line from the start. Proud beauties have to be dominated.'

'But, dash it, Pongo can't have dominated her.'

'True. But Pongo, so I am informed, is a baa-lamb. Baa-lambs get their results by different methods.'

'You don't think I'm a baa-lamb?'

'I fear not. You're too large, too robust and ruddy of countenance, too obviously a man who does his daily dozen of a morning and likes roly-poly pudding for lunch. Where a Pongo can click by looking fragile and stammering words of endearment, you must be the whirlwind wooer, or nothing. You will have to behave like the heroes of those novels which were so popular at one time, who went about in riding breeches and were not above giving the girl of their choice a couple with a hunting-crop on the spot where it would do most good. Ethel M. Dell. That's the name I was trying to think of. You must comport yourself like the hero of an Ethel M. Dell novel. Buy her works, and study them diligently.'

A firm look came into Bill's face.

'I'm not going to sock her with a hunting-crop.'

'It would help.'

'No. Definitely no.'

'Very well. Cut business with hunting-crop. Then what you must do is stride up to the girl and grab her by the wrist.'

'Oh, gosh!'

'Ignoring her struggles, clasp her to your bosom and shower kisses on her upturned face. You needn't say much. Just "My mate!" or something of that sort. Well, think it over, my dear fellow. But I can assure you that this method will bring home the bacon. It is known as the Ickenham System, and it never fails. And now I fear I must be leaving you. I'm looking for Pongo. You don't happen to know where he is?'

'I saw him half an hour ago walking up and down on the tennis lawn.'

'With bowed head?'

'Yes, I believe his head was bowed, now you mention it.'

'I thought as much. Poor lad, poor lad. Well, I have tidings for him which will bring it up with a jerk. So good-bye for the moment. Oh, by the way,' said Lord Ickenham, reappearing like a benevolent Cheshire cat, 'in grabbing the subject by the wrist, don't behave as if you were handling a delicate piece of china. Grip firmly and waggle her about a bit.'

He disappeared again, and Bill could hear him trolling an old love song of the early nineteen hundreds as he started for the tennis lawn.

## • III •

On a shy and diffident young man, accustomed for years just to shuffle his feet and look popeyed when in the presence of the girl he loves, a pep talk along the lines of that delivered by Lord Ickenham has much the same effect as a plunge into icy water on a cold morning. First comes the numbing shock, when everything turns black and the foundations of the soul seem to start reeling. Only later does there follow the glowing reaction.

For some appreciable time after his mentor had taken his departure, Bill stood congealed with horror as he contemplated the picture which the other had limned for him. The thought of showering kisses on Hermione Bostock's upturned face set his spine crawling like something in the Snake House at the Zoo. The idea of grabbing her by the wrist and waggling her about a bit made him feel as he had once felt at his private school after eating six ice-creams in a quarter of an hour because somebody bet him he wouldn't.

And then suddenly, with considerable astonishment, he found that horror had given way to a strange exhilaration. He could now appreciate the solid merits of this Ickenham system, chief among which was the fact that it placed the wooing of Hermione Bostock on the plane of physical action. Physical action was his dish. Give him something to do with his hands, and he knew where he was.

So simple, too. Nothing intricate or elaborate about it. Run over it once more, just to make sure one hadn't forgotten anything.

Stride up and grab?

Easy.

Waggle about?

Pie.

Clasp to bosom and s.k. on upturned f.?

No difficulty there.

Say 'My mate'?

About that he was not so sure. It seemed to him that Lord Ickenham, brilliant as an arranger of stage business, had gone astray as regarded dialogue. Wouldn't a fellow be apt to feel a bit of a chump, saying 'My mate'? Better, surely, just to pant a good deal? Yes, that was the stuff. Stride, grab, waggle, clasp, kiss, pant. Right.

Under the stress of intense thought he had started to walk up and down the hall, his head bent over the fingers on which he was ticking off the various items on the list, and it was as he unconsciously accelerated his pace on getting that inspiration about panting that a bumping sensation and a loud roar of anguish told him that there had been a traffic accident.

Narrowing his gaze, he saw that he had rammed something substantial and white moustached, and narrowing it still further identified this as his uncle, Sir Aylmer Bostock. And he was about to offer suitable apologies, when all thought of injured uncles was wiped from his mind and his heart leaped within him like an adagio dancer trying out a new step. Behind Sir Aylmer, looking more unbelievably beautiful even than he had remembered her, stood Hermione.

Hermione smiled upon him dazzlingly. She was in the sunniest of moods. After dropping Otis at the Bull's Head in the High Street, she had arrived at the front door just in time to see her father driving up, and such was the force of her personality that she had settled that little matter of the proposed legal action of Bostock *v.* Painter in something under two minutes and a quarter. The future of the publishing firm of Meriday House, in so far as concerned civil actions on the part of the late Governor of Lower Barnatoland, was secure.

So she smiled dazzlingly. In an amused, sisterly way she had always been devoted to dear old Bill, and she was glad to see him again.

'Hullo, Bill,' she said.

Bill found speech.

'Oh, hullo, Hermione.'

Sir Aylmer also found speech.

'What the devil are you doing, you great clumsy oaf,' he said, standing on one leg and submitting the other to a system of massage, for the impact had been severe. 'Charging about the place like a damned rhinoceros. Why can't you look where you're going?'

Bill was staring at Hermione. In a dim way he was aware that words were proceeding from this old blighter, but he was unable to concentrate on their import.

'Oh, rather,' he said.

'What do you mean, oh, rather?'

'Yes, isn't it?' said Bill.

To a man who was good at snorting and to whom snorts came easily there was only one answer to this sort of thing. Sir Aylmer snorted, and stumped into the collection room, telling himself that he would go into the matter later on when his nephew seemed more in the mood. Useless to waste good stuff on one who, always deficient in intellect, seemed now to be suffering from some from of mental paralysis.

Hermione continued cordial.

'So you're back, Bill. It's jolly seeing you again. How was Brazil?'

'Oh, fine.'

'Have a good time?'

'Oh, yes, fine, thanks.'

'You're very sunburned. I suppose you had lots of adventures?'

'Oh, rather.'

'Snakes and so on?'

'Oh, yes.'

'Well, you must tell me all about it later. I've got to hurry off now. I have to see a friend of mine at the inn.'

Bill cleared his throat.

'Er—just a second,' he said.

This, he was telling himself, was the moment. Now, if ever, was his opportunity of putting the Ickenham system into practice. Here they were, alone together. A single stride would place him in a position to grab. And he was already panting. More ideal conditions could scarcely have been asked for.

But he found himself unable to move. All through those weary months in Brazil the image of this girl had been constantly before his mental eye, but now that he was seeing her face to face her beauty numbed him, causing trembling of the limbs and that general feeling of debility and run-down-ness which afflicts so many people nowadays and can be corrected only by the use of such specifics as Buck-u-Uppo or Doctor Smythe's Tonic Swamp Juice.

Had he had a bottle—nay, even a tablespoonful—of the tonic swamp juice handy, all might have been well. Lacking it, he merely shuffled his feet and looked popeyed, just as he had been doing for the last nine years.

'Well?' said Hermione.

('Stride, grab, waggle, clasp, kiss, pant,' urged Bill's better self. But his limbs refused to move.)

'Well?'

'Hermione.'

'Yes?'

'Hermione.'

'Well?'

'Oh, nothing,' said Bill.

He found himself alone. From outside came the sound of a car getting into gear and moving off. She had gone.

Nor could he blame her. Reviewing the late scene, recalling that horrible, bleating voice with its hideous resemblance to that of a B.B.C. announcer, he shuddered, marvelling that any being erect upon two legs and bearing the outward semblance of a man could have shown himself so wormlike a poltroon.

Writhing in anguish, he thought for a moment of bumping his head against the wall, but on reflection decided against this. No sense in dinting a good wall. Better to go to his room, fling himself on the bed and bury his face in the pillow. He did so.

## • IV •

Anxious to get to the Bull's Head and inform Otis as soon as possible of the happy outcome of her interview with her father, Hermione had started up her car and driven off with the minimum of delay. Had she postponed her departure for as long as a minute, she would have observed a wild-eyed young man without a hat making for the house from the direction of the tennis lawn at a feverish canter, his aspect that of a young man who has taken something big. Once before in the course of this chronicle we have heard Reginald Twistleton compared to a cat on hot bricks. It was of a cat on hot bricks that he would have reminded an onlooker now.

Skimming across the terrace, he reached the house and plunged over the threshold. Skimming across the hall, he flew up the stairs. Skimming along the first-floor corridor, he burst into what had formerly been his bedroom, and Sally, who was reclining on the chaise-longue like an

Amazon resting after an important battle, rose as he entered. Indeed, she shot up as if a gimlet had suddenly penetrated the cushions and embedded itself in her person. She was a girl of poise, who did not easily lose command of herself, but after pushing policemen into ponds even girls of poise experience a certain tautness of the nerves, and the abrupt opening of the door had given her a momentary impression that here came Constable Potter.

Recognizing her visitor, she became calmer, though still inclined to gasp.

'Oh, Pongo!' she said.

'Oh, Sally!' said Pongo.

To say that the story which Lord Ickenham had related to him on the tennis lawn, before going off to the Bull's Head for a drop of beer and a chat with the boys about Brazil, had stirred Reginald Twistleton would be to indicate but feebly the turmoil which it had created in his bosom. It had caused him to run what is known as the gamut of the emotions, prominent among them gratitude to a girl who could thus risk all on his behalf, shame that his own pusillanimity had rendered her stupendous act of heroism necessary and, above all, a surge of love such as he had never felt before—and he had been falling in love with fair regularity ever since his last summer but one at Eton.

His honourable obligations to Hermione Bostock had passed completely from his mind. He had no other thought than to find Sally and notify her of the trend of his views. Precisely as Bill Oakshott had done, he contemplated a future in which he would stride, grab and waggle, clasp, kiss and pant. With this difference, that whereas Bill, as we have seen, had planned to behave like an osteopath handling a refractory patient, he, Pongo, saw the set-up more in the light of abasing himself at a shrine. The word 'grab' is wrong. So is the word 'waggle'. But 'clasp', 'kiss' and 'pant' may stand.

He was panting now, and he lost no time in proceeding to the other items on the programme which he had sketched out. Bill Oakshott, had he been present, would have received a valuable object lesson on how this sort of thing should be done.

'Oh, Sally!' he said.

'Oh, Pongo!' said Sally.

Time stood still. In the world outside people were going about their various occupations. Constable Potter was in his cottage, changing into a dry uniform. Lord Ickenham, humming a gay stave, was striding along the road to the village. Hermione, half a mile ahead of him, was driving along the same road. Sir Aylmer was messing about with his African curios. Bill Oakshott was burying his face in his pillow. And up in London Lady Bostock, in her daughter's flat, had finished the illustrated papers and fallen into a light doze.

But Pongo and Sally were alone together in a world of their own, enjoying the scent of the violets and roses which sprouted through the bedroom floor and listening to the soft music which an orchestra of exceptional ability, consisting chiefly of harps and violins, was playing near at hand. Of Constable Potter, of Lord Ickenham, of Sir Aylmer Bostock, of Lady Bostock, of Bill Oakshott and of Hermione they recked nothing; though the time was to come when they, particularly Pongo, would be obliged to reck of the last named quite a good deal.

Presently Pongo, adjusting his arm more comfortably about Sally's waist, for they were now sitting side by side on the chaise-longue, began to speak remorsefully of the past, featuring in his observations the criminal idiocy of the oaf Twistleton, that abysmal sap who had allowed himself to be parted from the only girl on earth whom a discriminating man could possibly wish to marry. He contemplated with unconcealed aversion this mutton-headed Twistleton.

'Gosh, what a chump I was!'

'Not such a chump as me.'

'Much more of a chump than you. No comparison.'

'It was all my fault.'

'No, it wasn't.'

'Yes, it was.'

'It wasn't.'

'It was.'

The dispute threatened to become heated, but just as Pongo was about to say 'It wasn't' again he suddenly paused, and into his sensitive features there crept that look of horror and apprehension which they had worn fourteen hours earlier, on the occasion when Bill Oakshott's knocking had sounded in the silent night.

'What's the matter, precious?' asked Sally solicitously.

Pongo gulped.

'Oh, nothing. At least, nothing much, I just happened to think of Hermione.'

There was a pause. A quick twinge of anxiety and alarm shot through Sally. Much—indeed, her life's happiness—depended on the exact extent to which the Twistletons regarded their word as their bond.

'Oh, Hermione?' she said. 'You don't mean you're too honourable to break off the engagement?'

Pongo gulped again.

'Not too honourable exactly, but . . . You've never met Hermione, have you? Well, it's difficult to explain, but she isn't a frightfully easy girl to break off engagements with. It's a little hard to know how to start.'

'I should just go to her and tell her frankly that you find you have made a mistake.'

'Yes, that's one way.'

'Or you could write her a letter.'

Pongo gave a start, like some strong swimmer in his agony who hears a splash and observes that somebody has thrown him a lifebelt.

'A letter?'

'You might find it less embarrassing.'

'I might,' said Pongo, and, quivering with gratitude to his helpmeet for her timely suggestion, he clasped her to his bosom and showered kisses on her upturned face.

This would probably have gone on for some time, had not Elsie Bean at this moment entered softly with a tray in her hands containing a teapot, a cup, some slices of buttered toast and a piece of cake.

'Tea,' said Elsie, and Pongo, soaring ceilingwards, came down and regarded her wrathfully.

'Why the dickens can't you blow your horn?' he demanded with a good deal of heat.

Elsie remained unmoved. The passionate scene which she had interrupted had made little impression upon her. It was the sort of thing that was happening all the time in Bottleton East.

'Tea, toast and a bit-er-cake,' she said. 'Have you pushed Harold into the pond yet, Mr Twistleton?'

Sally took charge of the situation in her competent way.

'Of course he has pushed him into the pond. He said he would, didn't he? You don't suppose Mr Twistleton would fail you?'

'Did he go in with a splash?'

'With a terrific splash. You could hear it for miles.'

'Coo. Well, I'm sure I'm very much obliged to you, Mr Twistleton. Have you seen Miss Hermione?'

Pongo leaped an inch or two.

'She isn't here?'

'Yes, she is. I saw her drive up in her car.'

Pongo remained silent for a space. He was clutching his head.

'I think I'll go and walk up and down on the tennis lawn for a while,' he said. 'This wants brooding over.'

With a brief groan he left the room, once more with that suggestion in his manner of a cat on hot bricks, and Elsie followed him with a critical eye.

'Nice young gentleman, Mr Twistleton,' she said. 'A bit barmy, isn't he?'

'A bit,' agreed Sally. 'I love it.'

## · V ·

The Bull's Head was still standing in its old place in the High Street when Hermione drove up, but Otis was no longer on the premises. She was informed that he had stepped out some little time previously, but whither he had stepped was not known. Annoyed, for no girl bringing the good news from Aix to Ghent likes to find Ghent empty when she gets there, Hermione returned to her two-seater and started to drive back along the road by which she had come. It had occurred to her that, now that she was in the Ashenden Manor neighbourhood, she ought to take the opportunity of exchanging a few words with her betrothed. It was the first time since lunch that she had given him a thought.

But her annoyance did not last long, nor did the desire to seek out Pongo. She had just reached the first milestone when something seemed to hit her between the eyes. It felt like a thunderbolt, but actually it was the central idea for the first of that series of three novels at twenty per cent rising to twenty-five above three thousand which Otis Painter would now be in a position to publish. This sort of thing is always happening to authors. They are driving along or walking along or possibly just sitting in a chair, their minds a blank, when all of a sudden—*bing*.

And the first thing an author learns is that it is fatal on these occasions to pigeon-hole the inspiration away at the back of the mind, trusting that memory will produce it when required. Notes must be made immediately. Drawing up her two-seater at the side of the road, Hermione found an old envelope and began to write. She wrote rapidly, breathing tensely through the nose.

At about the same moment Lord Ickenham reached the Bull's Head and turned in at the door of the saloon bar.

## • VI •

It was with the easy assurance of one confident of his welcome that Lord Ickenham entered the saloon bar, for on his previous visit there he had had an outstanding social success. The stout blonde behind the counter, her uncle the landlord (Jno. Humphreys, licensed to sell ales, wines and spirits) and quite a number of the inn's clients had hung upon his lips. It is not often given to the natives of remote Hampshire hamlets to sit at the feet of a man who knows Brazil like the back of his hand, who has looked his alligator in the eye and made it wilt and who can talk of his adventures fluently and well.

To-day he saw that his audience was to be smaller. Indeed, at the moment only the barmaid was present. He seemed to have struck one of those slack periods which come to all saloon bars. With the best will in the world English villagers cannot be drinking all the time, and this appeared to be one of the times when those of Ashenden Oakshott had decided to allow their gullets a brief respite, no doubt on the *reculer pour mieux sauter* principle.

But your true artist will always give of his best, however thin the house. As Lord Ickenham placed an elbow on the counter and requested the stout blonde to start pouring, there was no suggestion in his manner that he was going to walk through his part. He resumed his saga of life on the Lower Amazon as if he had been addressing a crowded hall, and the barmaid listened with all the impressment which she had shown on the previous day.

'Well, I do call that a pity,' she said, as he paused for an instant to raise his tankard.

'A pity?' said Lord Ickenham, a little hurt, for he had been speaking of the occasion when a puma had only just failed to add him to its bill of fare. 'Ah, I see. You are looking at the incident from the puma's view-point, and your womanly sympathy has been aroused by its failure to get the square meal for which it had been budgeting. Yes, it was tough on the puma. I remember noticing at the time that the animal's eyes were wet with unshed tears.'

'A pity you should have missed that gentleman, I mean. There was a gentleman in here for a quick one not five minutes ago,' explained the barmaid, 'who was telling me he had just come from Brazil. He'd have liked to meet you.'

Lord Ickenham gave her to understand that this was an almost universal aspiration on the part of his fellow men, but privately he was relieved that he had not arrived five minutes earlier. In his present rather delicate circumstances he greatly preferred to avoid gentlemen who had just come from Brazil.

'Too bad,' he said. 'One of the boys, eh? It would have been delightful to have got together and swapped yarns.'

'Why, here he is,' said the barmaid.

The door had opened, revealing an elderly man of square build with a pugnacious, sunburned face. Such was the excellence of the Bull's Head beer that those who went out after having a quick one nearly always came homing back again to have another.

'This is the gentleman I was speaking of. Excuse me, sir,' said the barmaid, addressing the gentleman, who had approached the counter and placed an elbow on it and was now licking his lips in quiet anticipation, 'here's a gentleman you ought to know, you being from Brazil. He knows more about Brazil than you could shake a stick at. Major Plank, the great explorer.'

At this moment a voice from without, recognizable as that of Jno. Humphreys, licensed to sell ales, wines and spirits, made itself heard. It was bellowing 'Myrtle', and the barmaid, whose parents had inflicted that name on her, vanished with a brief 'Excuse me.' The voice had been urgent, and it was evident that stern experience had taught this niece that her uncle Jno. was a man who did not like to be kept waiting.

'Tell him about the puma, Major Plank,' she said, pausing for an instant in her flight.

Normally, Lord Ickenham would have done this without delay, for he enjoyed telling people about pumas and knew that he was good at it. But one of the things which a man of the world learns early in his career is that there are times when it is best to keep silent on the subject of these fascinating fauna. The gentleman was looking at him fixedly, and in his eye there was no spark of the encouraging light which indicates a willingness to be informed about pumas. There have been some bleak and fishy eyes scattered through this chronicle—those of Coggs, the butler at Ickenham Hall, spring to the mind—but none bleaker and fishier than the gentleman's at this juncture.

'Plank?' he said, speaking raspingly. 'Did I hear her call you Major Plank?'

'That's right,' said Lord Ickenham. 'Major Plank.'

'Are you Major Brabazon-Plank, the explorer?'

'I am.'

'So am I,' said the gentleman, evidently rather impressed by the odd coincidence.

# 12

## · 1 ·

When two strong men stand face to face, each claiming to be Major Brabazon-Plank, it is inevitable that there will be a sense of strain, resulting in a momentary silence. There was on this occasion. Lord Ickenham was the first to speak.

'Oh, are you?' he said. 'Then you owe me two bob.'

His companion blinked. The turn the conversation had taken seemed to have surprised him.

'Two bob?'

'If you have nothing but large bills, I can give you change.'

Major Plank's mahogany face took on a richer hue.

'What the devil are you talking about?'

'Two bob.'

'Are you crazy?'

'It is a point on which opinions differ. Some say yes. I maintain no. Two bob,' said Lord Ickenham patiently. 'It is useless for you to pretend that you do not owe me that sum, Bimbo. You took it off me forty-three years ago as we were crossing the cricket field one lovely summer evening. "Barmy," you said, "would you like to lend me two bob?" And I said "No, but I suppose I'll have to," and the money changed hands.'

Major Plank clutched the counter.

'Bimbo? Barmy? Cricket field?' He stared with terrific concentration, and his face suddenly cleared. 'Good God! You're Barmy Twistleton.'

'I was in those days, but I've come on a lot since then, Bimbo. You see before you Frederick Altamont Cornwallis, fifth Earl of Ickenham, and one of the hottest earls that ever donned a coronet. The boy you knew as a wretched Hon. is now a peer of the realm, looked up to like the dickens by one and all. Just mention to anyone that you know Lord Ickenham, and they'll fawn on you and stand you lunch.'

Major Plank took an absent sip from the tankard.

'Barmy Twistleton!' he murmured. It was plain that the encounter had affected him greatly. 'But why did you tell that girl you were me?'

'One has to say something to keep the conversation going.'

'Barmy Twistleton. Well, I'll be damned. After all these years. I wouldn't have recognized you.'

'Exactly what Mugsy Bostock said when we met. You remember Mugsy Bostock? Did you know that he lived in these parts?'

'I knew his nephew, Bill Oakshott, did. I motored down to see him.'

'You aren't on your way to Ashenden Manor?'

'Yes.'

'Turn round and go back, Bimbo,' said Lord Ickenham, patting his shoulder kindly. 'You must not visit Ashenden Manor.'

'Why not?'

'Because I am already in residence there under your name. It would confuse Mugsy and give him a headache if he were confronted with a couple of us. No doubt you will say that you can't have too many Brabazon-Planks about the home, but Mugsy wouldn't look at it that way. He would get bewildered and fret.'

Major Plank took another sip at the tankard, and when Lord Ickenham mentioned that he had paid for its contents and that if his old friend proposed to treat it as a loving cup he would be obliged to charge him a small fee, seemed disinclined to go into the matter. It was the earlier portion of the conversation that was engaging his mind.

'You're staying with Mugsy under my name?'

'Exactly.'

'He thinks you're me?'

'Precisely.'

'Why?' said Major Plank, going right to the core of the problem. 'Why are you staying with Mugsy under my name?'

'It's a long story, Bimbo, and would bore you. But have no uneasiness. Just say to yourself "Would my old crony do this without a motive?" and "Is his motive bound to be a good one?" The answers to these questions are "No" to the first, "Yes" to the second.'

Major Plank relapsed into a sandbagged silence. His was a slow mind, and you could almost hear it creaking as it worked.

'Good God!' he said again.

And then abruptly the full horror of the situation seemed to come home to him. No doubt he had been diving into the past and had brought memories of the boy Twistleton to the surface. It was not for nothing that this man before him had been called 'Barmy' at school. He had applied himself absently to the tankard once more, and his eyes above it suddenly grew round and wrathful.

'What the devil do you mean by staying with people under my name?'

'It's a good name, Bimbo. Got a hyphen and everything.'

'You'll ruin my reputation.'

'On the contrary. The image which I have been building up in the minds of all and sundry is that of what I should describe as a super-Plank or Plank *plus*. You ought to think yourself lucky that a man like me has gone out of his way to shed lustre on your name.'

'Well, I don't. So you had better get back to Mugsy's and start packing, quick. Because as soon as I've had some more of this excellent beer I'm coming up there to expose you.'

'Expose me?' Lord Ickenham's eyebrows rose reproachfully. 'Your old friend?'

'Old friend be damned.'

'A fellow you used to throw inked darts at?'

'Inked darts have nothing to do with the case.'

'And who once lent you two bob?'

'Curse the two bob.'

'You're a hard man, Bimbo.'

'No, I'm not. I've a right to think of my reputation.'

'I have already assured you that it is in safe hands.'

'God knows what you may not have been up to. If I don't act like lightning, my name will be mud. Listen,' said Major Plank, consulting his watch. 'I shall start exposing you at five sharp. That gives you twenty-three minutes. Better look slippy.'

Lord Ickenham did not look slippy. He stood regarding the friend of his youth with the same gentle commiseration which he had displayed when dealing, in somewhat similar circumstances, with Constable Potter. Essentially kind-hearted, he disliked being compelled to thwart these eager spirits who spoke so hopefully of exposing him. But it had to be done, so with a sigh he embarked on the distasteful task.

'Dismiss all ideas of that sort from your mind, Bimbo. It is hopeless for you to dream of exposing me. Bill Oakshott has told me all about you.'

'What do you mean?'

'You are a man with an Achilles heel, a man with a fatal chink in your armour. You suffer from a strongly marked baby phobia. If anyone points a baby at you, Bill tells me, you run like a rabbit. Well, if you betray my little secret to Mugsy, you will immediately find yourself plunging into a foaming sea of them. A fête is taking place here shortly, and among its numerous features is a contest for bonny babies. And here is the point. In my capacity of Major Brabazon-Plank I have undertaken to act as judge of it. You begin to see the hideous peril confronting you? Eliminate me, and you automatically step into my place.'

'Why?'

'Because, my dear fellow, some variety of Brabazon-Plank has got to judge those bonny babies. This has been officially announced, and the whole village is agog. And after my departure you will be the only Brabazon-Plank available. And if you imagine that Mugsy, a determined man, and his wife, a still more determined woman, will let you sneak away, you are living in a fool's paradise. You haven't a hope, Bimbo. You will be for it.'

His pitiless clarity had its effect. Major Plank's tan was so deep that it was impossible to say whether or not he paled beneath it, but he shuddered violently and in his eyes was the look that comes into the eyes of men who peer into frightful abysses.

'Why don't they get the curate to do it?' he cried, plainly struggling with a strong sense of grievance. 'When we had these damned baby competitions at Lower Shagley, it was always the curate who judged them. It's what curates are for.'

'The curate has got measles.'

'Silly ass.'

'An unsympathetic thing to say of a man who is lying on a bed of pain with pink spots all over him, but I can make allowances for your feelings, appreciating how bitter a moment this must be for you, my poor old Bimbo. I suppose there is nothing much more sickening than wanting to expose a fellow and not being able to, and I would love to help you out if I could. But I really don't know what to suggest. You might . . . No, that's no good. Or . . . No, I doubt if that would work, either. I'm afraid you will have to give up the idea. The only poor consolation I can offer you is that it will be all the same in another hundred years. Well, my dear chap, it's been delightful running into you again after all this time, and I wish I could stay and chat, but I fear I must be pushing along. You know how busy we Brabazon-Planks always are. Look me up some time at my residence, which is quite near here, and we will have a long talk about the old school days and Brazil and, of course,' said Lord Ickenham indulgently, 'any other subject you may wish to discuss. If you can raise it by then, bring the two bob with you.'

With another kindly pat on the shoulder he went out, and Major Plank, breathing heavily, reached for the tankard and finished its contents.

## · II ·

The plot of Hermione's novel was coming out well. As so often happens when an author gets the central idea for a story and starts to jot it down, all sorts of supplementary ideas had come trooping along, demanding to be jotted down too. It was not many minutes before the envelope proved quite inadequate to contain the golden thoughts which were jostling one another in her brain, and she had just started to use the back of her motor licence when, looking up, she perceived approaching an elderly man of distinguished appearance, who raised his hat with an old-world polish.

'Good afternoon,' he said.

In this lax age in which we live, it not infrequently happens to girls of challenging beauty to find themselves approached by hat-raising strangers of the opposite sex. When Hermione Bostock had this experience, her manner was apt to become a little brusque, so much so that the party of the second part generally tottered off feeling as if he had incurred the displeasure of a wild cat. It is a tribute, therefore, to Lord Ickenham's essential respectability that he gave her pause. Her eyebrows quivered slightly, as if about to rise, but she made no move to shoot the works.

'Miss Bostock, I believe? My name is Brabazon-Plank. I am a guest at your father's house.'

This, of course, made it all quite different. One of the gang. Hermione became cordial.

'Oh, how do you do?'

'How do you do? Could you spare me a moment?'

'Why, of course. How odd that you should have known who I was.'

'Not at all. Yours, if I may say so, are features which, once seen, cannot be forgotten. I have had the privilege of studying a photograph of you.'

'Oh, yes, the one in the *Tatler*.'

'Not the one in the *Tatler*. The one which your cousin, William Oakshott, carries always next to his heart. I should explain,' said Lord Ickenham, 'that I was the leader of the expedition up the Amazon of which Bill Oakshott was so prominent a member, and every time he got a touch of fever he would pull your photograph out and kiss it, murmuring in a faint voice "I love her, I love her, I love her." Very touching, I thought it, and so did all the rest of the personnel of the expedition. It made us feel finer, better men.'

Hermione was staring. Had she been a less beautiful girl, it might have been said that she goggled. This revelation of a passion which she had never so much as suspected had come as a complete surprise. Looking on Bill as a sort of brother, she had always supposed that he looked on her as a sort of sister. It was as if she had lived for years beside some gentle English hill and suddenly discovered one morning that it was a volcano full to the brim of molten lava.

'And don't get the idea,' proceeded Lord Ickenham, 'that he spoke thus only when running a temperature. It was rare for half an hour to pass without him whipping out your photograph and kissing it. So you see he did not forget you while he was away, as so many young men are apt, once they are abroad, to forget the girl to whom they are engaged. His heart was always true. For when he said "I love her, I love her, I love her," it seemed to me that there was only one construction that could be placed on his remarks. He meant that he loved you. And may I be allowed to say,' went on Lord Ickenham with a paternal smile, 'how delighted I am to meet you at last and to see at a glance that you are just the girl for him. This engagement makes me very happy.'

'But—'

'He will be getting a prize. And so, my dear, will you. I know few men whom I respect more than William Oakshott. Of all my circle he is the one I would choose first to be at my side in the event of unpleasantness with an alligator. And while it may be argued, and with perfect justice, that the part which alligators play in the average normal married life is not a large one, it is no bad thing for a girl to have a husband capable of putting them in their place. The man who can prop an alligator's jaws open with a stick and then, avoiding its lashing tail, dispatch it with a meat axe is a man who can be trusted to help fire the cook. So no one will rejoice more heartily than I when the bells ring out in the little village church and you come tripping down the aisle on Bill Oakshott's sinewy arm. This will happen very shortly, I suppose, now that he is back with you once more?'

He paused, beaming benevolently, and Hermione, who had made several attempts to speak, at last found herself able to do so.

'But I am not engaged to Bill.'

'Nonsense. You must be. How about all that "I love her, I love her, I love her" stuff?'

'I am engaged to someone else. If you are staying at the house, you will have met him.'

Lord Ickenham gasped.

'Not the pinhead Twistleton?'

Something of the chill which hat-raising strangers usually induced crept into Hermione's manner.

'His name is Reginald Twistleton,' she said, allowing her eyes to flash for a moment. 'I am sorry you consider him a pinhead.'

'My dear girl, it isn't that *I* consider him a pinhead. Everyone considers him a pinhead. Walk into any gathering where he is a familiar figure and say to the first man you meet, "Do you know Reginald Twistleton?" and his reply will be, "Oh, you mean the pinhead?" Good heavens, child, you mustn't dream of marrying Reginald Twistleton. Even had you not a Bill Oakshott on your waiting list, it would be madness. How could you be happy with a man who is always getting arrested at dog races?'

'What!'

'Incessantly, you might say. *And* giving a false name and address.'

'You're talking nonsense.'

'My dear, these are well-documented facts. If you don't believe me, creep up behind this young Twistleton and shout "Yoo-hoo, Edwin Smith, 11 Nasturtium Road, East Dulwich!" in his ear and watch him jump. Well, I don't know what you think, but to my mind there is something not very nice in going to dog races at all, for the people you meet there must be very mixed. But if a young man does go to dog races, I maintain that the least he can do is to keep from behaving in so disorderly a manner that he gets scooped in by the constabulary. And if you are going to try to excuse this Twistleton on the ground that he was intoxicated at the time, I can only say that I am unable to share your broad-minded outlook. No doubt he was intoxicated, but I can't see that that makes it any better. You knew, by the way, I suppose, that he is a dipsomaniac?'

'A *what*?'

'So your father tells me.'

'But Reginald is a teetotaller.'

'While your eye is on him, perhaps. But only then. At other times he shifts the stuff like a vacuum cleaner. You should have been here last night. He stole down when everyone was in bed and threw a regular orgy.'

Hermione had been intending to put an end to this conversation by throwing in her clutch and driving off with a stiff word of farewell, but now she saw that she would have to start later. A girl who has been looking on the man of her choice as a pure white soul and suddenly discovers that he is about as pure and white as a stevedore's undervest does not say 'Oh, yes? Well, I must be off.' She sits rigid. She gasps. She waits for more.

'Tell me everything,' she said.

As Lord Ickenham proceeded to do so, the grim expression on Hermione Bostock's lovely face became intensified. If there is one thing a girl of ideals dislikes, it is to learn that she has been nursing a viper in her bosom, and that Reginald Twistleton was a Grade A viper, with all the run-of-the-mill viper's lack of frankness and square shooting, seemed more manifest with every word that was spoken.

'Oh!' she said.

'*Well!*' she said.

'Go on,' she said.

The story wore to its conclusion. Lord Ickenham ceased to speak, and Hermione sat gazing before her with eyes of stone. She was doing something odd with her teeth which may have been that 'grinding' we read about.

'Of course,' said Lord Ickenham, ever charitable, 'he may simply be off his head. I don't know if you know anything of his family history, but he tells me he is the nephew of Lord Ickenham; a fact, surely, that makes one purse the lips dubiously. Do you know Lord Ickenham?'

'Only by reputation.'

'And what a reputation! There is a strong body of opinion which holds that he ought to have been certified years ago. I understand he is always getting flattering offers from Colney Hatch and similar establishments. And insanity so often runs in families. When I first met this young man Twistleton, I received a distinct impression that he was within a short jump of the loony bin, and that curious incident this morning, of which Bill Oakshott was telling me, has strengthened this view.'

Hermione quivered. She had not supposed that there was to be an Act Two.

'Curious incident?'

'It took place shortly after breakfast. Lady Bostock, going to her room, heard movements within, looked in the wardrobe and found Reginald Twistleton in it, crouching on the floor. His explanation was that he had come to borrow her lipstick.'

Hermione gripped her motor licence till the knuckles stood out white under the strain. Act One had stirred her profoundly, but Act Two had topped it.

In speaking of the dislike which high-principled girls have for vipers, we omitted to mention that it becomes still more pronounced when they discover that they use lipstick. That this erstwhile idol of hers should have feet of clay was bad, but that in addition to those feet of clay he should have, at the other end, a mouth that apparently needed touching up from time to time was the pay-off. People still speak of the great market crash of 1929, asking you with a shudder if you remember the way U.S. Steel and Montgomery Ward hit the chutes during the month of October: but in that celebrated devaluation of once gilt-edged shares there was nothing comparable to the swift and dizzy descent at this moment of Twistleton Preferred.

Hermione's teeth came together with a click.

'I shall have a talk with Reginald!'

'I should. I think you owe it to yourself to demand an explanation. One wonders if Reginald Twistleton knows the difference between right and wrong.'

'I'll tell him,' said Hermione.

Lord Ickenham watched her drive off, well content with the way she stepped on the gas. He liked to see her hurrying to the tryst like that. The right spirit, he considered.

He climbed the five-barred gate at the side of the road and lowered himself on to the scented grass beyond it. His eyes fixed on the cloudless sky, he thought how pleasant it was to spread sweetness and light and how fortunate he ought to reckon himself that he had been granted this afternoon such ample opportunity of doing so. If for an instant a pang of pity passed through him as he pictured the meeting between Pongo and this incandescent girl, he suppressed it. Pongo—if he survived—would surely feel nothing but a tender gratitude towards an uncle who had laboured so zealously on his behalf. A drowsiness stole over him, and his eyelids closed in sleep.

Hermione, meanwhile, had reached the house and come to a halt outside its front door with a grinding of brakes and a churning of gravel. And she was about to enter, when from the room to her left she heard her father's voice.

'GET OUT!' it was saying, and a moment later Constable Potter emerged, looking like a policeman who has passed through the furnace. She went to the window.

'Father,' she said, 'do you know where Reginald is?'

'No.'

'I want to see him.'

'Why?' asked Sir Aylmer, as if feeling that such a desire was morbid.

'I intend,' said Hermione, once more grinding her teeth, 'to break off our engagement.'

A slender figure pacing the tennis lawn caught her eye. She hastened towards it, little jets of flame shooting from her nostrils.

## • III •

Down at the Bull's Head the girl Myrtle, her conversation with her uncle concluded, had returned to her post in the saloon bar. The gentleman was still at the counter, staring fixedly at the empty tankard, but he was alone.

'Hullo,' she said disappointedly, for she had been hoping to hear more about Brazil, where might is right and the strong man comes into his own. 'Has Major Plank hopped it?'

The gentleman nodded moodily. A shrewder observer than the barmaid would have sensed that the subject of Major Plank was distasteful to him.

'Did he tell you about the puma? No? Well, it was very interesting. It was where he was threading his way through this trackless forest, gathering Brazil nuts, when all of a sudden what should come along but this puma. Pardon?'

The gentleman, who beneath his breath had damned and blasted the puma, did not repeat his observation, but asked for a pint of bitter.

'Would have upset me, I confess,' proceeded the barmaid. 'Yessir, I don't mind saying I'd have been scared stiff. Because pumas jump on the back of your neck and chew you, which you can't say is pleasant. But Major Plank's what I might call intrepid. He had his gun and his trusty native bearer—'

The gentleman repeated his request for bitter in a voice so forceful that it compelled attention. Haughtily, for his tone had offended her, the barmaid pulled the beer handle and delivered the goods, and the gentleman, having drunk deeply, said 'Ha!' The barmaid said nothing. She continued piqued.

But pique is never enough to keep a barmaid silent for long. Presently, having in the meantime polished a few glasses in a marked manner, she resumed the conversation, this time selecting a topic less calculated to inflame the passions.

'Uncle John's in a rare old state.'

'Whose Uncle John?'

'My Uncle John. The landlord here. Did you hear him shouting just now?'

The gentleman, mellowed by beer, indicated with an approach to amiability that Jno. Humphreys's agitation had not escaped his notice. Yes, he said, he had heard him shouting just now.

'So I should think. You could have heard him at Land's End. All of a doodah, he is. I must begin by telling you,' said the barmaid, falling easily into her stride, 'that there's a big fête coming on here soon. It's an annual fête, by which I mean that it comes on once a year. And one of the things that happens at this annual fête is a bonny baby competition. Pardon?'

The gentleman said he had not spoken.

'A bonny baby competition,' resumed the barmaid. 'By which I mean a competition for bonny babies. If you've got a bonny baby, I mean to say, you enter it in this bonny baby competition, and if the judge thinks your bonny baby is a bonnier baby than the other bonny babies, it gets the prize. If you see what I mean?'

The gentleman said he saw what she meant.

'Well, Uncle John had entered his little Wilfred and was fully expecting to cop. In fact, he had as much as a hundred bottles of beer on him at eight to one with sportsmen in the village. And now what happens?'

The gentleman said he couldn't imagine.

'Why, Mr Brotherhood, the curate, goes and gets the measles, and the germs spread hither and thither, and now there's so many gone down with it that the Vicar says it isn't safe to have the bonny baby competition, so it's off.'

She paused, well satisfied with the reception of her tale. Her audience might have been hard to grip with anecdotes of Major Plank among the pumas, but he had responded admirably to this simpler narrative of English village life. Though oddly, considering that the story was in its essence a tragic one, the emotion under which he was labouring seemed to be joy. Quite a sunny look had come into his eyes, as if weights had been removed from his mind.

'Off,' said the barmaid. 'By which I mean that it won't take place. So all bets are null and void, as the expression is, and Uncle John won't get his bottles of beer.'

'Too bad,' said the gentleman. 'Can you direct me to Ashenden Manor?'

'Straight along, turning to the right as you leave the door.'

'Thank you,' said the gentleman.

# 13

## · 1 ·

That Constable Potter, having returned to his cottage and changed into a dry uniform should then have proceeded without delay to Ashenden Manor to see Sir Aylmer Bostock was only what might have been expected. Sir Aylmer was the chairman of the local bench of magistrates, and he looked upon him as his natural protector. The waters of the pond had scarcely closed over his head before he was saying to himself that here was something to which the big chief's attention would have to be drawn.

He was unaware that in seeking an audience at this particular time he was doing something virtually tantamount to stirring up a bilious tiger with a short stick. No warning voice whispered in his ear 'Have a care, Potter!' adding that as the result of having been compelled to withdraw a suit for damages to which he had been looking forward with bright anticipation for weeks his superior's soul was a bubbling maelstrom of black malignity and that he was far more likely to bite a policeman in the leg than to listen patiently to his tales of woe.

The realization that this was so came, however, almost immediately.

He had been speaking for perhaps a minute when Sir Aylmer, interrupting him, put a question.

'Are you tight, you bloodstained Potter?' asked Sir Aylmer, regarding him with a sort of frenzied loathing. When a man has come to his collection room to be alone with his grief, to brood on the shattering of his hopes and to think how sweet life might have been had he had one of those meek, old-fashioned daughters who used to say 'Yes, papa!' the last thing he wants is policemen clumping in with complicated stories. 'What on earth are you talking about? I can't make head or tail of it.'

Constable Potter was surprised. He was not conscious of having been obscure. It also came as a shock to him to discover that he had misinterpreted the twitching of his audience's limbs and the red glare in that audience's eye. He had been attributing these phenomena to the natural horror of a good man who hears from another good man of outrages committed on his, the second good man's, person and it seemed now that he had been mistaken.

'It's with ref. to this aggravated assault, sir.'

'What aggravated assault?'

'The one I'm telling you about, sir. I was assaulted by the duck pond.'

The suspicion that the speaker had been drinking grew in Sir Aylmer's mind. Even Reginald Twistleton at the height of one of his midnight orgies might have hesitated, he felt, to make a statement like that.

'By the duck pond?' he echoed, his eyes widening.

'Yes, sir.'

'How the devil can you be assaulted by a duck pond?'

Constable Potter saw where the misunderstanding had arisen. The English language is full of these pitfalls.

'When I said "by the duck pond", I didn't mean "by the duck pond", I meant "by the duck pond". That is to say,' proceeded Constable Potter, speaking just in time, '"near" or "adjacent to", in fact "on the edge of". I was the victim of an aggravated assault on the edge of the duck pond, sir. Somebody pushed me in.'

'Pushed you in?'

'Pushed me in, sir. Like as it might have been someone what had a grudge against me.'

'Who was it?'

'A scarlet woman, sir,' said Constable Potter, becoming biblical. 'Well, what I mean to say, she was wearing a red jacket and a kind of red thingummy round her head, like as it might have been a scarf.'

'Was it a scarf?'

'Yes, sir.'

'Then why say "like as it might have been" one? I have had to speak before, from the bench, of the idiotic, asinine way in which you blasted policemen give your evidence. Did you see this woman?'

'Yes and no, sir.'

Sir Aylmer closed his eyes. He seemed to be praying for strength.

'What do you mean, yes and no?'

'I mean to say, sir, that I didn't actually see her, like as it might have been see. I just caught sight of her for a moment as she legged it away, like as it might have been a glimp.'

'Do you mean glimpse?'

'Yes, sir.'

'Then say glimpse. And if you use that expression "like as it might have been" once more, just once more, I'll . . . Could you identify this woman?'

'Establish her identity?' said Constable Potter, gently corrective. 'Yes, sir, if I could apprehend her. But I don't know where she is.'

'Well, I've not got her.'

'No, sir.'

'Then why come bothering me? What do you expect me to do?'

Broadly speaking, Constable Potter expected Sir Aylmer to have the countryside scoured and the ports watched, but before he could say so the latter had touched on another aspect of the affair.

'What were you doing by the duck pond?'

'Spitting and thinking, sir. I generally pause there when on my beat, and I had just paused this afternoon when the outrage occurred. I heard something behind me, like as it might have been a footstep, and the next moment something pushed me in the small of the back, like as if it might have been a hand—'

'GET OUT!' said Sir Aylmer.

Constable Potter withdrew. Crossing the terrace, he made for the bushes on the other side and there, lighting his pipe, stood spitting and thinking. And we make no secret of the fact that his thoughts were bitter thoughts and his expectoration disillusioned.

Just as a boy's best friend is his mother, so is a policeman's prop and stay the chairman of the local bench of magistrates. When skies are dark, it is the thought of the chairman of the local bench of magistrates that brings the sun smiling through, and it is to the chairman of the local bench of magistrates that he feels he can always take his little troubles and be sure of support and sympathy. Who ran to catch me when I fell and would some pretty story tell and kiss the place to make it well? The chairman of the local bench of magistrates. That is the policeman's creed.

Anyone, therefore, who when a boy ever went running to his mother with a tale of wrongs and injuries and instead of condolences received a kick in the pants will be able to appreciate this officer's chagrin as he passed the late scene under mental review. Sir Aylmer's attitude had hurt and disappointed him. If this was how a constable's legitimate complaints were received by those whose duty it was to comfort and console, then Elsie, he felt, was right and the quicker he left the Force, the better.

If you had approached Harold Potter as he stood there in his bush, smoking his pipe and spitting bitterly, and had said, 'Well, Constable Potter, how are you feeling?' he would have replied that he was feeling fed up. And there is little doubt that this black mood would have grown in intensity, had not something happened which abruptly wrenched his thoughts from their contemplation of the policeman's unhappy lot.

Through the branches before him he had a good view of the front of the house, and at this moment there appeared on the balcony of one of the windows on the first floor a female figure in a red jacket, wearing upon its head a red thingummy, like as it might have been a scarf. It came to the balcony rail, looked left and right, then went back into the room.

The spectacle left Harold Potter gaping. A thrill ran through him from the base of the helmet to the soles of his regulation boots. He started to say 'Coo!' but the word froze on his moustache.

Harold Potter was a man who could reason. A mystery woman in a red jacket had pushed him into the duck pond. A mystery woman in a red jacket was in that room on the first floor. It did not take him long to suspect that these two mystery women might be one and the same.

But how to make sure?

It seemed to him that there lay before him the choice between two courses of action. He could go and report to Sir Aylmer, or he could pop along to the potting shed, where there was a light ladder, secure this light ladder, take it to the side of the house, prop it up and climb to that first floor window and peer in. A steady look at close range would establish the identity of the red-jacketed figure.

He did not hesitate long between these alternative plans. Rejecting almost immediately the idea of going and reporting to Sir Aylmer, he knocked out his pipe and started for the potting shed.

## • II •

Sally, her tea and buttered toast long since consumed, had begun to feel lonely. It was quite a time now since Pongo had left her, and she yearned for his return. Seated on the chaise-longue, she thought what a baa-lamb he was and longed for him to come back so that she could go on stroking his head and telling him how much she loved him.

An odd thing, this love, and one about which it is futile to argue. If individual A. finds in individual B. a glamour which escapes the notice of the general public, the general public has simply got to accept the situation without protest, just as it accepted without protest, though perhaps with a silent sigh of regret, the fact of Mr Brotherhood, the curate, getting measles.

Seeing Sally sitting on the chaise-longue with clasped hands and starry eyes, her heart overflowing with love for Pongo, it would have been useless for a discriminating third party to tap her on the shoulder and try to persuade her that there was nothing in the prospect of a lifelong union with Reginald Twistleton to get starry-eyed about. Fruitless to attempt to sketch for her a picture of Reginald Twistleton as seen by the cooler-headed. She was in love, and she liked it.

The only cloud that darkened her sky was the fear lest a shrewd girl like Hermione Bostock, having secured such a prize, might refuse to relinquish it, but she need have had no anxiety. Hermione was relinquishing the prize at that very moment. When, some twenty minutes after he had left it, Pongo re-entered the room, there was a dazed look on his face as if he had recently been mixed up with typhoons, water-spouts and other Acts of God, but in his eyes shone the light which comes into the eyes of men who have found the blue bird.

Sally was not able to detect this immediately, her vision being obscured by the handkerchief with which he was mopping his forehead, and her first words were reproachful.

'Oh, angel, what a time you've been.'

'Sorry.'

'I went out on to the balcony just now to see if I could see you, but you weren't in sight. I know you had to brood, but need you have brooded so long?'

Pongo lowered the handkerchief.

'I wasn't brooding,' he said. 'I was chatting with Hermione.'

Sally gave a jump.

'Then you found her?'

'She found me.'

'And what happened?'

Pongo moved to the mirror and inspected himself in it. He seemed to be looking for grey hairs.

'Well, that I can hardly tell you,' he said. 'The whole thing's a bit of a blur. Have you ever been in a really bad motor smash? Or hit by an atom bomb? No? Then it's hard to explain. Still, the fact that emerges is that the engagement's off.'

'Oh, Pongo!'

'Oh, Sally!'

'Oh, Pongo darling! Then we can live happy ever after.'

Pongo applied the handkerchief to his forehead once more.

'Yes,' he agreed, 'after a brief interval for picking up the pieces and reassembling the faculties. I don't mind telling you the recent scene has left me a bit weak.'

'My poor lamb. I wish I had some smelling salts.'

'So do I. I could use a bucketful.'

'Was it so awful?'

'Quite an ordeal.'

'What did you say to her?'

'I didn't get a chance of saying anything to her, except, "Oh, there you are," right at the start. She bore the burden of the conversash.'

'You don't mean it was she who broke off the engagement?'

'And how! You know, Uncle Fred ought to be in some sort of home.'

'Why?'

'It appears that he met Hermione and spilled the beans with a lavish hand. He told her so many things about me that I wonder she remembered them all. But she did.'

'Such as—?'

'Well, getting pinched at the dog races and going down to the drawing-room last night to get a spot and being caught this morning in Ma Bostock's wardrobe. Things like that.'

'In the wardrobe? What were you doing there?'

'I had gone to her room to get you a lipstick, and—'

'Oh, Pongo! My hero! Did you really do that for me?'

'Not much I wouldn't do for you. Look what you did for me. Pushing Potter into that pond.'

'I think that's what's so splendid about us. Each helps each. It's the foundation of a happy married life. So Uncle Fred told her all that about you? Bless him.'

'Would you put it like that?'

'Well, he saved you from a girl you could never have been happy with.'

'I couldn't be happy with any girl except you. Yes. I suppose he did. I hadn't looked at it in that way.'

'He never minds how much trouble he takes, if he feels that he's spreading sweetness and light.'

'No. There have been complaints about it on all sides, and I still maintain that he ought to be in a padded cell with the board of Lunacy Commissioners sitting on his head. However, I agree that he has smoothed our path. I mean to say, here we are, what?'

'Here we are.'

'All our problems solved. Nothing to worry about any more.'

'Not a thing.'

'Oh, Sally!'

'Oh, Pongo!'

The embrace into which they fell was a close one, close enough, had it taken place in Hollywood, to have caused Eric Johnston to shake his head dubiously and recommend cutting a few hundred feet, but not so close as to deprive Pongo of a view of the window. And Sally, nestling in his arms, was concerned to notice that he had suddenly stiffened, as if he had been turned into a pillar of salt.

'What's the matter?' she asked.

Pongo gave a short gulp. He seemed to find a difficulty in speaking.

'Don't look now,' he said, 'but that blighter Potter has just stepped off a ladder on to the balcony.'

## · III ·

It was at about the moment when Constable Potter, having found the light ladder, was starting to lift it and Pongo, in the bedroom on the first floor, had begun his emotional description of the recent conference with Hermione that Major Plank turned his car in at the gates of Ashenden Manor and proceeded up the drive at a high rate of speed.

He had been progressing at a high rate of speed ever since leaving the Bull's Head. He would probably have driven fairly fast in any event, for he was one of those men who do, but what made him so particularly disinclined on the present occasion to loiter and look at the scenery was the fact that the full significance of Lord Ickenham's words in the saloon bar had just come home to him. He had remembered, that is to say, that the man whom he had known as Barmy Twistleton had told him that he was now Lord Ickenham.

There were circles in London where the eccentricities of Lord Ickenham were a favourite topic of conversation, and it was in these circles that Major Plank, when not among the alligators, was accustomed to mix. His old schoolmate's character and habits, therefore, were fully known to him, and he was able to form a vivid picture of what would be the effect on the reputation of anyone whom the other had decided to impersonate.

How long this public menace had been established at Ashenden Manor he did not know, but he felt very strongly that even a single day was too much and that anything like forty-eight hours would have caused a stigma to rest upon the grand old name of Brabazon-Plank which it would take a lifetime to remove.

There is probably no one who moves more slippily than a Brazilian explorer on his way to expose an impostor who has been causing stigmas to rest upon his name, and not even Hermione could have made better speed up the drive than did this fermenting Major. His was a large, flat, solid foot, admirably adapted for treading on accelerators, and he pressed it down with a will.

Arriving at the house, he was in far too great a hurry to ring the front door bell and wait till it was answered. Voices were proceeding from the open French window to his right, presumably that of the drawing-room, and he went thither and walked in. He found himself in the presence of his young subordinate, Bill Oakshott, and a rugged man of an older vintage who was puffing at a white moustache of the soup-strainer class. He had a feeling, looking at them, that they were upset about something.

Nor was he mistaken. Both Bill and his Uncle Aylmer had come to the tea table with their bosoms full of the perilous stuff that weighs upon the heart. The memory of his craven behaviour during that interview with Hermione had not ceased to torture Bill, and Sir Aylmer was still in the grip of the baffled fury which comes to men of imperious nature when their daughters tell them they must not bring actions against publishers, a fury which his conversation with Constable Potter had done nothing to alleviate. To say that William Oakshott and Sir Aylmer Bostock were human powder magazines which it needed but a spark to explode is not only clever, but true.

It is possible, however, that the soothing influence of tea, muffins and cucumber sandwiches might have succeeded in averting disaster, allowing the exchanges to confine themselves to harmless commonplaces, had not Sir Aylmer, too pleased to keep such splendid news to himself, chanced to mention that Hermione had told him that, her romance having sprung an unforeseen leak, he would not have to pass the evening of his life with Reginald Twistleton as his son-in-law. For this led Bill to exclaim 'Oh, gosh!' in an enraptured voice and, pressed to explain his elation, to say that the thought had crossed his mind that if Hermione was back in circulation again, there might be a chance for a chap who had loved her with a growing fervour for years and years and years: and this in its turn led Sir Aylmer to attack him with tooth and claw. There was a smile on his nephew's face which he considered a silly smile, and he addressed himself without delay to the task of wiping it off.

'Gar!' he said, speaking dangerously through a mouthful of muffin, and added that there was no need for Bill to grin all over his beastly face like a damned hyena, because whether free or engaged Hermione would not touch him with a barge pole.

'Why should she?' asked Sir Aylmer. 'You? She looks on you as a—'

'I know,' said Bill, with a return of gloom. 'A brother.'

'Not brother,' corrected Sir Aylmer. 'Sheep.'

A quiver ran through Bill's massive frame. His jaw fell and his eyes widened.

'Sheep?'

'Sheep.'

'*Sheep?*' said Bill.

'Sheep,' said Sir Aylmer firmly. 'A poor, spineless sheep who can't say boo to a goose.'

A more practised debater would have turned this charge to his advantage by challenging the speaker to name three sheep who could say boo to a goose, but Bill merely stood rigid, his fists clenched, his nostrils dilated, his face mantled with the blush of shame and indignation, regretting that ties of blood and his companion's advanced years rendered impossible that slosh in the eye for which the other seemed to him to be asking, nay pleading, with his every word.

'Sheep,' said Sir Aylmer, winding up the speech for the prosecution. 'She told me so herself.'

It was on this delicate situation that Major Plank intruded.

'Hullo there,' he said, striding in with the calm assurance of a man accustomed for years to walk uninvited into the huts of native chiefs. 'Hullo, Bill.'

It would be difficult to advance more conclusive proof of the turmoil into which Bill Oakshott's soul had been thrown by his uncle's words than by saying that the unexpected entry of the last man he would have wished to see in the drawing-room of Ashenden Manor did not cause so much as a gleam of horror to come into his eyes. He regarded him dully, his mind still occupied by that sheep sequence. Did Hermione, he was asking himself, really look on him as a sheep? And, arising from that, had she a prejudice against sheep? The evidence went to show that she had none against baa-lambs, but sheep, of course, might be a different matter.

It was left to Sir Aylmer to do the honours.

'Who the hell are you?' he asked, not unthankful that here was another object on which he could work off some of the spleen induced by the chit-chat of daughters and policemen.

Major Plank had had far too much experience of this sort of thing to be abashed by nervous irritability on the part of a host. Many of the householders on whom he had dropped in in his time had said it with spears.

'Who the hell are *you*?' he replied agreeably. 'I'm looking for Mugsy Bostock.'

Sir Aylmer started.

'I am Sir Aylmer Bostock,' he said, and Major Plank stared at him incredulously.

'You?' he said. 'Don't be an ass. Mugsy Bostock is younger than me, and you look a million. Have you seen your Uncle Mugsy anywhere, Bill?'

It was at this point that Jane, the parlourmaid, entered bearing strawberries in a bowl, for they did themselves well at tea-time at Ashenden Manor—cucumber sandwiches, muffins, strawberries and everything. Sir Aylmer addressed her in the carrying voice which was so characteristic of him.

'JANE!'

A lesser girl would have dropped the bowl. Jane merely shook like an aspen.

'Yes, sir?'

'Tell this son of a . . . this gentleman who I am.'

'Sir Aylmer Bostock, sir.'

'Right,' said Sir Aylmer, like the judge of one of those general knowledge quizzes which are so popular nowadays.

Major Plank said he was dashed.

'It's that ghastly moustache that misled me,' he explained. 'If you go about the place behind a whacking great white moustache, you can't blame people for taking you for a centenarian. Well, nice to see you again, Mugsy, and all that, but, cutting the guff, I came here on business. Plank's my name.'

'Plank!'

'Brabazon-Plank. You may remember me at school. I've just discovered that that raving lunatic, Barmy Twistleton—Lord Ickenham he calls himself now—has been passing himself off as me under your roof; and it's got to stop. I don't know what made him do it, and I don't care, the point is I'll be damned if I'm going to have people thinking that Barmy Twistleton is me. Good God! How would you like it yourself?'

There had been an instant, just after the words, 'Plank's my name,' when Sir Aylmer had given a quick and extraordinarily realistic impersonation of a harpooned whale, shaking from stem to stern as if a barb had entered his flesh. But as the speaker continued, this had given place to a frozen calm, the dangerous calm that heralds the storm.

'I can tell you what made him do it,' he said, allowing his eyes to play upon Bill like flame-throwers. 'He wished to be of assistance to my nephew here. We are holding our annual village fête shortly, and one of its features is a contest for bonny babies. My nephew was to have acted as judge.'

'Barmy told me he was going to be the judge.'

'That was the latest arrangement. My nephew persuaded him to take his place.'

'Very sensible of you, Bill,' said Major Plank cordially. 'Dashed dangerous things, these baby contests. The little beasts are bad enough themselves, but it's the mothers you want to watch out for. Look,' he said, baring his leg and indicating a cicatrice on the calf. 'That's what I got once in Peru for being fool enough to let myself be talked into judging a competition for bonny babies. The mother of one of the Hon. Mentions got after me with a native dagger.'

'The problem then arose,' proceeded Sir Aylmer, still speaking evenly and spacing his words with care, 'of how to introduce Lord Ickenham into my house. He was well aware that I would never allow him to enter my house, if I knew who he was. So he said he was Major Brabazon-Plank, the explorer, and my nephew endorsed this statement. What do you mean,' roared Sir Aylmer, suddenly abandoning the calm, judicial method and becoming a thing of fire and fury, 'what do you mean, you infernal young scallywag, by introducing impostors into my house?'

He would have spoken further, for it was obvious that the greater part of his music was still in him, but at this moment Bill exploded.

A good deal is always required to change a mental attitude which has endured for a number of years. From early boyhood Bill Oakshott had regarded this uncle of his with respectful awe, much as a nervous young prehistoric man might have regarded the leader of his tribe. He had quailed before his wrath, listened obsequiously to his stories, done all that lay in his power to humour him. And had this scene taken place at a time when he was in normal mood, there is little doubt that he would have folded like an accordion and allowed himself to be manhandled without protest.

But Bill was not in normal mood. His soul was seething in rebellion like a cistern struck by a thunderbolt. The interview with Hermione had left him raw and wincing. The information that she regarded him as a sheep had dropped vitriol on the wounds. And now, not once but three times, this white-moustached cuckoo in the nest had alluded to Ashenden Manor as 'my house'. At these emotional moments there is always something, generally trivial in itself, which fulfils the function of the last straw, and with Bill now it was this description of Ashenden Manor.

In the automatic, barely conscious fashion of the Englishman at teatime he had been continuing to eat and drink throughout his uncle's exposition, and for an instant a muffin prevented him expressing his views. He swallowed it, and was at liberty to proceed.

'"My house"?' he said. 'I like that. Where do you get that "my house" stuff?'

Sir Aylmer said that that was not the point, and was starting to indicate once more what the point was, when he was swept away as if by a tidal wave.

'"My house"!' repeated Bill, choking on the words like one who chokes upon a muffin. 'Of all the crust! Of all the nerve! It's about time, Uncle Aylmer, that we got this thing cleared up about who this ruddy house belongs to. Let's do it now.'

'Yes, let's,' said Major Plank, interested. A man with five sisters and seven aunts, he was well versed in family rows and thought that this one promised to be in the first rank and wanted pushing along. 'Whose house is it?'

'Mine,' thundered Bill. 'Mine. Mine. Mine. Mine. Mine.'

'I see,' said Major Plank, getting his drift. 'Yours. Then where does Mugsy come in?'

'He planted himself here when I was a mere kid, unable to do anything about it. I was only sixteen when my father died, and he barged over from Cheltenham and got into the woodwork.'

'What happened when you came of age?'

'Nothing. He stuck on.'

'You should have booted him out.'

'Of course I should.'

'That was the moment.'

'Yes.'

'Why didn't you?'

'I hadn't the heart.'

'Mistaken kindness.'

'Well, I'm going to do it now. I've had enough of this business of being a . . . what's the word?'

'Fathead?'

'Cipher in the home. I'm sick and tired of being a cipher in the home. You can jolly well clear out, Uncle Aylmer. You understand me? Buzz off. Where you buzz to, I don't care, but buzz. Go back to Cheltenham, if you like. Or Bexhill.'

'Or Bognor Regis,' suggested Major Plank.

'Or Bognor Regis. Go anywhere you like, but you're not going to stay here. Is that clear?'

'Quite clear,' said Major Plank. 'Very well put.'

'Right,' said Bill.

He strode out through the French window, and Major Plank helped himself to a muffin.

'Nice chap, Bill,' he said. 'I like a young fellow who knows his own mind. Extraordinarily good muffins, these, Mugsy. I'll have another.'

## · IV ·

Emerging through the French window, Bill passed along the terrace, walking rapidly towards the spot where the drive began. His eyes glowed. He was breathing stertorously.

The appetite grows by what it feeds on. So far from soothing him and restoring him to everyday placidity, his throwing off of the shackles had left Bill Oakshott in a mood for fresh encounters. He had tasted blood, and wanted more. It is often so with quiet young men who at long last assert themselves.

He was in the frame of mind when he would have liked to meet Joe Louis and pick a quarrel with him, and as he turned the corner and came into the drive there caught his eye something which seemed to have been sent in direct answer to prayer.

It was not Joe Louis, but it was the next best thing. What he had seen was a stout young man with a pink nose and horn-rimmed spectacles in conversation with Hermione Bostock. And just as he beheld him this young man suddenly folded Hermione in his embrace and started to kiss her.

Bill broke into a gallop, the glow in his eyes intensified, the stertorousness of his breathing still more marked. His general mental attitude was that of the war-horse which said 'Ha!' among the trumpets.

# 14

## · I ·

It is never easy for a high-strung young man whose whole future as a publisher of the book beautiful is being decided at a country house to sit in an inn two miles from that house, waiting patiently for news to be brought to him from the front. With each long minute that goes by his nervousness increases. The limbs twitch, the eyeballs roll, the illusion that there are ants in his pants becomes more and more pronounced, until eventually the urge to be closer to the centre of things grows so imperious that he yields to it.

That was why Otis Painter had been absent from the Bull's Head when Hermione arrived there. He had started to walk to Ashenden Manor. Like Edith of the swan's neck after the Battle of Hastings, he wanted to find out what had been going on.

When we say that Otis had started to walk to Ashenden Manor, it would be more correct to put it that he thought he had; in actual fact, having got his instructions twisted, he had turned to the left instead of to the right on leaving the inn, and it was only after he had proceeded a mile and three quarters through delightful country that he discovered that though he was improving his figure and getting lots of pure air into his lungs, he was diminishing his chances of reaching his destination with every step that he took.

Returning to the Bull's Head, he had borrowed a bicycle from the boy who cleaned the boots, a courteous and obliging lad of the name of Erbut with blacking all over his face, and after a couple of unpleasant spills, for it was many years since he had cycled and the old skill had rather deserted him, had found himself at the top of the drive. There, feeling that this was as far as it was prudent to penetrate into territory where there was a grave risk of meeting Sir Aylmer Bostock, he deposited his machine behind a tree, concealed himself in the bushes and resumed his waiting. And presently Hermione appeared, walking briskly.

As she drew near and he was enabled to get a clear view of her, his heart sank, for he could see that her lips were tightly set, her bosom heaving and her eyes bright and stormy. She looked, in a word, like a daughter who, approaching her father in the matter of withdrawing legal actions against publishers, has come up against something too hot to handle.

Actually, of course, Hermione's appearance was simply the normal appearance of a girl who has just been ticking off a viper. After a dust-up with a viper the female lips always become tightly set, and it is rarely that the bosom does not heave. But Otis did not know this, and it was with a mind filled with the gloomiest forebodings that he stepped from his hiding place. 'Here comes the bad news,' he was saying to himself.

'Well?' he said, uttering the monosyllable loudly and raspingly, as so often happens when the nerves are over-strained.

The briskness of her pace had taken Hermione past him, and it was from behind that he had addressed her. At the sound of a voice suddenly splitting the welkin where no voice should have been she left the ground in an upward direction and came to earth annoyed and ruffled.

'I wish you wouldn't pop out of bushes like that,' she said with a good deal of asperity.

Otis was too agitated to go into the niceties of etiquette and procedure. 'What happened?' he asked.

'I bit my tongue.'

'I mean,' said Otis, clicking his, 'when you saw your father.'

Hermione mastered her emotion. Her tongue was still paining her, but she had remembered that this man was a publisher who believed in column spreads in all the literate Sunday papers.

'Oh, yes,' she said.

The reply dissatisfied Otis. It seemed to him to lack lucidity, and lucidity was what he desired—or, as a literate Sunday paper would have put it, desiderated.

'What do you mean, Oh, yes? What did he say?'

Hermione's composure was now restored. She still disapproved of her sponsor's practice of popping out of bushes and speaking like a foghorn down the back of her neck, but was willing to let bygones be bygones.

'It's quite all right, Mr Painter,' she said, smiling kindly upon Otis. 'Father has withdrawn the suit.'

Otis reeled.

'He *has*?'

'Yes.'

'Gee!' said Otis, and it was at this point that he folded Hermione in his embrace and started to kiss her.

The last thing we desire being to cast aspersions on publishers, a most respectable class of men, we hasten to say that behaviour of this kind is very unusual with these fine fellows. Statistics show that the number of authoresses kissed annually by publishers is so small that, if placed end to end, they would reach scarcely any distance. Otis's action was quite exceptional, and Hodder and Stoughton, had they observed it, would have looked askance. So would Jonathan Cape. And we think we speak for Heinemann, Macmillan, Benn, Gollancz and Herbert Jenkins Ltd when we say that they, too, would have been sickened by the spectacle.

In defence of Otis there are several extenuating points to be urged. In the first place, his relief was so intense and his happiness so profound that he had to kiss something. In the second place, Hermione was a very beautiful girl (not that that would have weighed with Faber and Faber) and she had smiled upon him very kindly. And, finally, we cannot judge men who have lived on the left bank of the Seine by the same standards which we apply to those whose home is in London. If Eyre and Spottiswoode had taken a flat in the Rue Jacob, within easy reach of the Boul' Mich', they would have been surprised how quickly they would have forgotten the lessons they had learned at their mother's knee.

It was unfortunate that none of these arguments presented themselves to Bill Oakshott as he turned the corner. In Otis Painter he saw just another libertine, flitting from flower to flower and sipping, and we are already familiar with his prejudice against libertines. His impulse on seeing one, we recall, was to pull his head off at the roots and rip his insides out with his bare hands, and it was with this procedure in mind that he now advanced on the entwined pair. He gripped Otis by the coat collar and tore him from the clinch, and he would almost certainly have started to detach his head, had not Hermione uttered a piercing cry.

'Don't kill him, Bill! He's my publisher.'

And then, as she saw him hesitate, she added:

'He's doing my next three books and giving me twenty per cent rising to twenty-five above three thousand.'

It was enough. Practically berserk though Bill was, he could still reason, and reason told him that publishers of this type must be nursed along rather than disembowelled. Hermione's literary career was as dear to him as to herself, and he knew that he could never forgive himself if he jeopardized it by eviscerating a man capable of planning contracts on these spacious lines. He released Otis, who tottered back against a tree and stood there panting and polishing his spectacles.

Bill, too, was panting. His breath came in loud gasps as he strode up to Hermione and grabbed her by the wrist. There was in his demeanour now no trace of that craven diffidence which had marked it during their previous interview in the hall. Since then William Oakshott, with a victory over a tyrant under his belt, had become a changed man, and the man he had changed into was a sort of composite of James Cagney and Attila the Hun. He felt strong and masterful and in the best possible vein for trying out the Ickenham system. Otis Painter, peering at him through his spectacles, which he had now resumed, was reminded of a Parisian inspecteur who had once arrested him at the Quatz Arts Ball.

Nor was Hermione unimpressed. She was now being waggled about, and she found the process, though physically unpleasant, giving her a thrill of ecstasy.

Like all very beautiful girls, Hermione Bostock had received in her time a great deal of homage from the other sex. For years she had been moving in a world of men who frisked obsequiously about her and curled up like carbon paper if she spoke crossly to them, and she had become surfeited with male worship. Even when accepting Pongo's proposal she had yearned secretly for something rough and tough with a nasty eye and the soul of a second mate of a tramp steamer. And in the last quarter where she would have thought of looking she had found him. She had always been fond of Bill, but in an indulgent, almost contemptuous fashion, regarding him, as she had once mentioned to her father, as a sheep. And now the sheep, casting off its clothing, had revealed itself as one of the wolves and not the worst of them.

Little wonder that Hermione Bostock, as Bill having waggled her about, clasped her to his bosom and showered kisses on her upturned face, felt that here was the man she had been looking for since she first read *The Way of an Eagle*.

'My mate!' said Bill. Then, speaking from between clenched teeth, 'Hermione!'

'Yes, Bill?'

'You're going to marry me.'

'Yes, Bill.'

'That's clearly understood, is it?'

'Yes, Bill.'

'No more fooling about with these Pongos and what not.'

'No, Bill.'

'Right,' said the dominant male. He turned to Otis, who had been looking on at the scene with a sort of nostalgia, for it had reminded him of the old, happy days on the left bank of the Seine. 'So you're going to publish her books, are you?'

'Yes,' said Otis eagerly. He wanted there to be no mistake about this. 'All of them.'

'Giving her twenty per cent rising to twenty-five above three thousand?'

'Yes.'

'Why not a straight twenty-five?' said Bill, and Otis agreed that that would be much better. He had been on the point, he said, of suggesting it himself.

'Fine,' said Bill. 'Well, come along in, both of you, and have some tea.'

Hermione regretfully shook her head.

'I can't, darling. I must be getting back to London. Mother has been waiting for me at my flat since one o'clock, and she may be wondering what has become of me. I shall have to drive like the wind. Can I give you a lift, Mr Painter?'

Otis shuddered.

'I guess I'll go by train.'

'You'll find it slow.'

'I like it slow.'

'Very well. Good-bye, darling.'

'Good-bye,' said Bill. 'I'll be up in London to-morrow.'

'Splendid. Come and see me to the car. I left it outside the house.'

Otis remained, leaning against his tree. He felt a little faint, but very happy. Presently the two-seater, with Hermione bent over the wheel, whizzed round the corner and passed him at a speed which made him close his eyes and say to himself 'There but for the grace of God goes Otis Painter.' When he opened them again, he saw Bill approaching.

'Why not thirty?' said Bill.

'Pardon?'

'Per cent. For her books. Not twenty-five.'

'Oh, ah, yes. Why, sure,' said Otis. 'Thirty might be nicer.'

'You don't want to skimp.'

'That's right. You don't.'

'And publicity. You believe in lots of that, I hope?'

'Oh, sure.'

'Fine. She was always complaining that her last publishers wouldn't push her books.'

'The poor fish. I mean, fishes.'

'Used to stall her off with a lot of rot about all that counted being word of mouth advertising.'

'Crazy saps.'

'You intend to advertise largely?'

'In all the literate Sunday papers.'

'How about the literate weeklies?'

'In those, too. I also thought of sandwich men and posters on the walls.'

Bill had not supposed that he would ever be able to regard this man with affection, but he did so now. He still had him docketed as a libertine, but indulgence must be accorded to libertines whose hearts are in the right place.

'Fine,' he said. 'Posters on the walls? Yes, fine.'

'Of course,' said Otis, 'all that kind of thing costs money.'

'Well spent,' Bill pointed out.

'Sure,' agreed Otis. 'Don't get the idea that I'm weakening. But it begins to look as if I may have to dig up a little more capital from somewhere. There isn't any too much of it in the old sock. You wouldn't feel like putting a thousand pounds into my business, would you?'

'That's an idea. Or two?'

'Or three? Or, say, look why not five? Nice round number.'

'Would you call five a round number?'

'I think so.'

'All right,' said Bill. 'Five, then.'

Otis's eyes closed again, this time in silent ecstasy. He had had his dreams, of course. Somewhere in the world, he had told himself, there must be angels in human shape willing to put money into a shaky publishing firm. But never had he really supposed that he would meet one, and still less that, if he did, such an angel would go as high as five thousand.

Opening his eyes, he found that he was alone. His benefactor had either been snatched back to heaven or had gone round the corner to the terrace. He took his bicycle from behind the tree and flung himself on the saddle like a gay professional rider. And when, half-way down the drive, he had another of those unfortunate spills, he merely smiled amusedly, as one good-naturedly recognizing that the laugh is on him.

Life looked very good to Otis Painter. In the old left bank days he had been at some pains to cultivate a rather impressive pessimism, but now he was pure optimism from side-whiskers to shoe sole.

If Pippa had happened to pass at that moment, singing of God being in His heaven and all right with the world, he would have shaken her by the hand and told her he knew just how she felt.

• II •

Bill had not been snatched up to heaven. It was to the terrace that he had made his way on leaving Otis, and he had not been there many minutes when Lord Ickenham appeared, walking jauntily like a man whose forty winks in a field has refreshed him. At the sight of Bill he hurried forward with outstretched hand.

'My dear chap, a thousand congratulations.'

Bill gaped. This seemed to him clairvoyance.

'How on earth did you know?'

Lord Ickenham explained that his young friend's ecstatic expression, rather like that of a cherub or seraph on the point of singing Hosanna, would alone have been enough to tell him.

'But, as a matter of fact,' he said, 'I had the news from an acquaintance of mine whom I met bicycling along the road just now. Well, when I say bicycling along the road, he was lying in a ditch with his feet in the air, chuckling softly. He told me everything. It seems that he was a witness of the proceedings, and he speaks highly of your technique. You strode up and grabbed her by the wrist, eh?'

'Yes.'

'Waggled her about a bit?'

'Yes.'

'Then clasped her to your bosom and showered kisses on her upturned face?'

'Yes.'

'With the results that might have been anticipated. I told you the Ickenham system never fails. Brought up against it, the proudest beauty wilts and signs on the dotted line. It saddens you a little now, no doubt, to think of all the years you wasted on timid devotion.'

'It does, rather.'

'Timid devotion gets a lover nowhere. I was chatting with Miss Bean this morning, and she was telling me that she had a good deal of trouble at one time with Constable Potter owing to his devotion being so timid. She says that in the early days of his courtship he used to walk her out and chew his moustache and talk about the situation in China, but no real action. So one evening she said "Come on, my lad, get on with it," and he got on with it. And after that everything went like clockwork.'

'Fine,' said Bill absently. He had been thinking of Hermione. 'Potter?' he went on, his mind returning from its flights. 'That reminds me. You haven't a bit of raw steak on you, have you?'

Lord Ickenham felt in his pockets.

'Sorry, no. I seem to have come out without any. Why? You feel peckish?'

'Elsie Bean was out here a moment ago, saying she was in the market for a bit of raw steak. It's needed for Potter. Apparently someone has been sloshing him in the eye.'

'Indeed? Who?'

'I didn't gather. Her story was confused. I seemed to catch some mention of Pongo, but would Pongo punch policemen in the eye?'

'It seems unlikely.'

'I must have got the name wrong. Still, there it is. Someone has given Potter a shiner, and he's fed to the tonsils. You see, he got pushed into the duck pond this afternoon, and now on top of that comes this biff in the eye, so he feels he's had enough of being a policeman. He's chucking it up and buying a pub, Elsie tells me. She seemed rather braced about it.'

Lord Ickenham drew a deep, slow breath of contentment and satisfaction. He looked pleased with himself, and who shall blame him? A man whose mission in life it is to spread sweetness and light and to bring the young folk together may surely be forgiven a touch of complacency when happy endings start going off like crackers all round him and he sees the young folk coming together in droves.

'Great news, Bill Oakshott,' he said. 'This is . . . what is that neat expression of yours? Ah, yes, "fine!" . . . This is fine. You're all right. Pongo's all right. And now the divine Bean is all right. It reminds one of the final spasm of a musical comedy.' He paused and regarded his companion with some surprise. 'Are you wearing woolly winter underclothing?' he asked.

'Me? No. Why?'

'You keep wriggling, as though something were irritating the epidermis.'

Bill blushed.

'Well, as a matter of fact,' he confessed, 'I'm finding it awfully difficult to keep still. After what's happened, I mean. You know how it is.'

'I do, indeed. I, too, have lived in Arcady. You would like to go for a long, rapid walk and work off steam? Of course you would. Push off, then.'

'You don't mind me leaving you?'

'Well, one hates to lose you, of course, but better a temporary separation than that you should burst all over the terrace. Au revoir, then, and once more a thousand congratulations.'

Bill disappeared round the corner like a dog let off the chain, gathering momentum with every stride. His pace was so good and his preoccupation so intense that it was not until he was out in the open road a mile away that it suddenly came to him that he had omitted to inform Lord Ickenham of the arrival of Major Plank.

He paused, debated within himself the advisability of going back, decided that it was too late and walked on. And presently Lord Ickenham and Major Plank had faded from his mind and he was thinking again exclusively in terms of wedding bells and honeymoons.

## · III ·

As things turned out, it would have been unnecessary for him to retrace his steps, for almost immediately after his departure Major Plank came out of the house, wiping butter from his lips.

'Hullo, Barmy,' he said, sighting Lord Ickenham. 'You're too late for the muffins. I've finished them. And very good they were, too.' He replaced his handkerchief. 'You're surprised to see me here, aren't you? Thought you'd baffled me, eh? Well, what happened was that shortly after you left the pub that well-nourished girl behind the bar told me the bonny baby contest was off. So along I came.'

Lord Ickenham had given a slight start on seeing his old friend, but his voice, when he spoke, was as calm and level as ever.

'Off, is it? Why?'

'Outbreak of measles. Thousands stricken.'

'I see. And have you exposed me?'

'Exposed you is right.'

'Did Mugsy seem interested?'

'Most.'

'One sees how he might well be, of course. You're a ruthless old bird, Bimbo.'

Major Plank bridled.

'Ruthless be blowed. I merely took the necessary steps to protect my reputation. And what do you mean, "old bird"? I'm a year younger than you. My idea of an old bird is Mugsy. I was shocked when I saw how he had aged. He looks like that chap in the Bible, Methuselah, the fellow who lived to a thousand and ate grass.'

'Methuselah didn't eat grass.'

'Yes, he did.'

'He never ate grass in his life. You're thinking of Nebuchadnezzar.'

'Oh, am I? Well, the principle's the same. And now I suppose you'll be sliding off. You'd have done better to start packing when I told you to. Still, you're in luck in one way. You won't run into Mugsy. He's in that room over there, holding a court martial.'

'A what?'

'Court martial. There have been all sorts of stirring goings-on here. Just as I was finishing the muffins, a policeman with a black eye barged into the drawing-room with a tall, thin, light-haired young chap in one hand and a dashed pretty girl in a red jacket in the other, and said that the girl had pushed him into a duck pond and that when he was starting to apprehend her the light-haired young chap had biffed him in the eye. And Mugsy has taken them into that room there and is sitting on the case. I gather he's a magistrate or something and so is entitled to execute summary justice. I'm sorry for that young couple. It looks like a sticky week-end for them.'

Lord Ickenham gave his moustache a thoughtful twirl.

'Leave me, Bimbo,' he said. 'I would be alone.'

'Why?'

'I want to ponder.'

'Oh, ponder? Right ho! I'll go back and have some more strawberries,' said Major Plank.

He returned to the drawing-room, and Lord Ickenham, left alone, lost no time in giving himself up to that survey of ways and means which the other's presence had hindered. For some moments he paced up and down, his hands behind his back and a concentrated look in his eye. The tautness of his features showed that his agile brain was not sparing itself.

And presently it was plain that it had given service. His face cleared. The lips beneath the trim moustache curved in a contented smile.

He crossed the terrace and went into the collection room.

## · IV ·

Only Sir Aylmer was in the collection room when he entered. He, too, was wearing a contented smile.

For the first time that evening Sir Aylmer was feeling cheerful; as cheerful as a Colosseum lion which after a trying day when everything has gone wrong has found itself unexpectedly presented with a couple of Christian martyrs and has been able to deal faithfully with them. There is nothing which so braces up a chairman of a bench of magistrates in times of despondency as the infliction of a sharp sentence on a pair of criminals. It would be too much to say that he regarded Lord Ickenham amiably, but he did not bite him.

'Ha,' he said. 'It's you, is it?'

Lord Ickenham preserved his suavity.

'Ah, Mugsy,' he said. 'I understand you've met Bimbo Plank. How did you think he was looking? He thought you had aged. Where's Sally?'

'Who?'

'Bimbo told me she and my nephew Pongo were in here with you.'

Sir Aylmer started.

'You know that girl?'

'She is my honorary niece.'

A warm glow pervaded Sir Aylmer's system, as if he had been taking Doctor Smythe's Tonic Swamp Juice. This was even better than he had hoped.

'Oh, is she?' he said. 'Then it may interest you to know that I've just given her thirty days without the option, and your nephew the same. Potter's locked them up in the scullery while he has his eye bathed, and in a few minutes he'll be taking them off in custody.'

'A harsh sentence.'

'The only possible sentence. One of the most disgraceful cases that has ever come before me. She pushed Potter into the duck pond.'

'Well, what does a policeman expect, if he deliberately goes and stands on the edge of duck ponds? Girls will be girls.'

'Not while I'm sitting on the bench, they won't.'

'And how about the quality of mercy? It isn't strained, you know. It droppeth as the gentle rain from heaven upon the place beneath.'

'Damn the quality of mercy.'

'You'd better not let Shakespeare hear you saying that. Then you won't reconsider?'

'No, I won't. And now we'll discuss this matter of your coming here under a false name.'

Lord Ickenham nodded.

'Yes, I was hoping you would be able to spare me a minute to tell you about that. But before I begin, I would like to have a witness present.'

Lord Ickenham went to the door and called 'Bimbo,' and Major Plank came out of the drawing-room chewing strawberries.

'Could you come here a moment, Bimbo. I need you as a witness. I'm going to tell you a story that will shock you.'

'It isn't the one about the young man of Calcutta, is it? Because I've heard that.'

Lord Ickenham reassured him.

'When I said "shock", I meant that the tale would revolt your moral sense rather than bring the blush of shame to the cheek of modesty. Shall I begin at the beginning?'

'It sounds a good idea.'

'Very well. There was an American girl named Vansittart who came to

London and bought a number of trinkets in Bond Street, her plan being to take them back to America and wear them. All straight so far?'

'Quite.'

'What—?' began Sir Aylmer, and Lord Ickenham gave him a stern look.

'Mugsy,' he said, 'if you interrupt, I'll put you over that chair and give you six of the juiciest. I've no doubt Bimbo will be glad to hold you down.'

'Charmed. Quite like old times.'

'Good. Then I will resume. Where were we?'

'This American wench. Bought jewels in Bond Street.'

'Exactly. Well, when she had got them, the thought flashed upon her that on arriving with them in New York, she would have to pay heavy customs duty to the United States Government. She recoiled from this.'

'I don't blame her.'

'So in her innocent, girlish way she decided to smuggle them in.'

'Quite right. Don't pay the bounders a penny, that's what I say. They've got much too much money as it is.'

'Precisely what Miss Vansittart felt. She held that opinion very strongly. But how to work this smuggling project?'

'That's always the snag.'

'She mused a while,' said Lord Ickenham, interrupting Major Plank in what threatened to be rather a long story about how he had once tried to sneak some cigars through at Southampton, 'and was rewarded with an idea. She had a friend, a young sculptress. She went to her, got her to make a clay bust and put the jewels in its head, and was then all set to take them to America in safety and comfort. She reasoned that when the customs authorities saw a clay bust, they would simply yawn and say "Ho hum, a clay bust," and let it through.'

'Very shrewd.'

'So that was that. But . . . this is where you want to hold on to your chair, Bimbo . . . unfortunately this young sculptress was at that time modelling a bust of Mugsy.'

Major Plank was plainly bewildered. He stared at Sir Aylmer, studying his features closely and critically.

'What did Mugsy want a bust of himself for?'

'To present to the village club.'

'Good God.'

'During the sittings,' proceeded Lord Ickenham, 'Mugsy and the young sculptress naturally chatted from time to time, and in the course of these conversations she was rash enough to show him the bust that contained the jewels and to tell him that she was leaving it at my house a few miles from here until Miss Vansittart sailed. And Mugsy . . . I hardly like to tell you this, Bimbo.'

'Go on.'

'Well, you will scarcely credit it, but yesterday Mugsy nipped over to my house, effected an entrance and snitched the bust.'

'The one with the jewels in it?'

'The one with the jewels in it.'

Not even the menace of six of the juiciest could keep Sir Aylmer silent under this charge.

'It's an insane lie!'

Lord Ickenham raised his eyebrows.

'Is there anything to be gained by this bravado, Mugsy? Do you suppose I would bring such an accusation unless I could prove it to the hilt? Yes, Bimbo, he nipped over to my house, was admitted by my butler—'

'I wasn't. He wouldn't let me in.'

'That is your story, is it? It is not the one Coggs tells. He says he admitted you and that you roamed unwatched all over the premises. And, what is more, as you were leaving he noticed a suspicious bulge under your coat. Honestly, Mugsy, I wouldn't bother to persist in this pretence of innocence. It would be manlier if you came clean and threw yourself on the mercy of the court.'

'Much manlier,' agreed Major Plank. 'Whiter altogether.'

'I told you I could prove my accusation, and I will now proceed to do so. You have a nice, large foot, Bimbo. Oblige me by stepping to that cupboard over there and kicking in the door.'

'Right ho!' said Major Plank.

He approached the cupboard and drove at it with his brogue shoe. The niceness and largeness of his foot had not been over-estimated. The fragile door splintered with a rending crash.

'Aha!' he said, peering in.

'You see a clay bust?'

'That's right. Bust, clay, one.'

'Bring it here.'

Sir Aylmer was gaping at the bust like one who gapes at snakes in his path. He sought in vain for an explanation of its presence. His wife could have given him that explanation, but his wife was in London.

'How the devil did that get there?' he gasped.

Lord Ickenham smiled sardonically.

'Really, Mugsy! Good, that, eh, Bimbo?'

'Very good.'

'Break that thing's head.'

'Bust the bust? Right ho!' said Major Plank, and did so. Lord Ickenham stooped and picked from the ruins a chamois leather bag. Before Sir Aylmer's bulging eyes he untied the string and poured forth a glittering stream.

Major Plank's eyes were bulging, too.

'This must have been one of your best hauls,' he said, looking at Sir Aylmer with open admiration.

Lord Ickenham replaced the gems in the bag and put the bag in his pocket.

'Well, there you are,' he said. 'You were asking just now, Mugsy, why I had come here under a false name. It was because I hoped that if I could get into the house I might be able to settle this thing without a scandal. I knew that you were shortly to stand for Parliament and that a scandal would ruin your prospects, and I took the charitable view that you had yielded to a sudden temptation. As far as I am concerned, I am now willing to let the thing drop. I have no wish to be hard on you, now that I have recovered your ill-gotten plunder and can restore it to its owner. We all understand these irresistible temptations. Eh, Bimbo?'

'Oh, quite.'

'We need say no more about the matter?'

'Not a word.'

'You won't tell anyone?'

'Except for a chap or two at the club, not a soul.'

'Then the whole wretched affair can now be forgotten. Of course, this monstrous sentence which you have inflicted on my nephew and Sally Painter must be quashed. You agree to that, Mugsy?' said Lord Ickenham, raising his voice, for he saw that his host was distrait.

Sir Aylmer gave that impersonation of his of a harpooned whale.

'What?' he said feebly.

Lord Ickenham repeated his words, and Sir Aylmer, though evidently finding it difficult to speak, said, 'Yes, certainly.'

'I should think so,' said Lord Ickenham warmly. 'Thirty days without the option for what was a mere girlish—or, in Pongo's case, boyish—freak. It recalls the worst excesses of the Star Chamber. The trouble with you fellows who have been Governors of Crown colonies, Mugsy, is that you get so accustomed to giving our black brothers the run-around that you lose all self-restraint. Then let us go and notify Constable Potter immediately to strike the gyves from the young couple's wrists. We shall find them, I think you said, in the scullery.'

He linked his arm in Sir Aylmer's and led him out. As they started down the hall Major Plank could hear him urging his companion in the kindest way to pull himself together, turn over a new leaf and start life afresh with a genuine determination to go straight in the future. It only needed a little will-power, said Lord Ickenham, adding that he held it truth with him who sings to one clear harp in divers tones that men may rise on stepping stones of their dead selves to higher things.

For some moments after they had left, Major Plank stood where he was, regarding the African curios with the glazed look of a man whose brain is taking a complete rest. Then gradually there came upon him a sense of something omitted, the feeling which he had so often had in the wilds of Brazil that somewhere there was man's work to be done and that it was for him to do it.

Then he remembered. The strawberries. He went back to the drawing-room to finish them.

# COCKTAIL TIME

# 1

THE train of events leading up to the publication of the novel *Cocktail Time*, a volume which, priced at twelve shillings and sixpence, was destined to create considerably more than twelve and a half bobsworth of alarm and despondency in one quarter and another, was set in motion in the smoking-room of the Drones Club in the early afternoon of a Friday in July. An Egg and a Bean were digesting their lunch there over a pot of coffee, when they were joined by Pongo Twistleton and a tall, slim, Guards-officer-looking man some thirty years his senior, who walked with a jaunty step and bore his cigar as if it had been a banner with the strange device Excelsior.

'Yo ho,' said the Egg.

'Yo ho,' said the Bean.

'Yo ho,' said Pongo. 'You know my uncle, Lord Ickenham, don't you?'

'Oh, rather,' said the Egg. 'Yo ho, Lord Ickenham.'

'Yo ho,' said the Bean.

'Yo ho,' said Lord Ickenham. 'In fact, I will go further. Yo frightfully ho,' and it was plain to both Bean and Egg that they were in the presence of one who was sitting on top of the world and who, had he been wearing a hat, would have worn it on the side of his head. He looked, they thought, about as bumps-a-daisy as billy-o.

And, indeed, Lord Ickenham was feeling as bumps-a-daisy as he looked. It was a lovely day, all blue skies and ridges of high pressure extending over the greater part of the United Kingdom south of the Shetland Isles: he had just learned that his godson, Johnny Pearce, had at last succeeded in letting that house of his, Hammer Lodge, which had been lying empty for years, and on the strength of this had become engaged to a perfectly charming girl, always pleasant news for an affectionate godfather: and his wife had allowed him to come up to London for the Eton and Harrow match. For the greater part of the year Lady Ickenham kept him firmly down in the country with a watchful eye on him, a policy wholeheartedly applauded by all who knew him, particularly Pongo.

He seated himself, dodged a lump of sugar which a friendly hand had thrown from a neighbouring table, and beamed on his young friends like a Cheshire cat. It was his considered view that joy reigned supreme. If at this moment the poet Browning had come along and suggested to him that the lark was on the wing, the snail on the thorn, God in His heaven and all right with the world, he would have assented with a cheery 'You put it in a nutshell, my dear fellow! How right you are!'

'God bless my soul,' he said, 'it really is extraordinary how fit I'm feeling today. Bright eyes, rosy cheeks, and the sap rising strongly in my veins, as I believe the expression is. It's the London air. It always has that effect on me.'

Pongo started violently, not because another lump of sugar had struck him on the side of the head, for in the smoking-room of the Drones one takes these in one's stride, but because he found the words sinister and ominous. From earliest boyhood the loopiness of this uncle had been an open book to him and, grown to man's estate, he had become more than ever convinced that in failing to add him to their membership list such institutions as Colney Hatch and Hanwell were passing up a good thing, and he quailed when he heard him speak of the London air causing the sap to rise strongly in his veins. It seemed to suggest that his relative was planning to express and fulfil himself again, and when Frederick Altamont Cornwallis Twistleton, fifth Earl of Ickenham, began to express and fulfil himself, strong men—Pongo was one of them—quivered like tuning forks.

'The trouble with Pongo's Uncle Fred,' a thoughtful Crumpet had once observed in this same smoking-room, 'and what, when he is around, makes Pongo blench to the core and call for a couple of quick ones, is that, though well stricken in years, he becomes, on arriving in London, as young as he feels and proceeds to step high, wide and plentiful. It is as though, cooped up in the country all the year round with no way of working it off, he generates, if that's the word I want, a store of loopiness which expends itself with terrific violence on his rare visits to the centre of things. I don't know if you happen to know what the word "excesses" means, but those are what, the moment he sniffs the bracing air of the metropolis, Pongo's Uncle Fred invariably commits. Get Pongo to tell you some time about the day they had together at the dog races.'

Little wonder, then, that as he spoke, the young Twistleton was conscious of a nameless fear. He had been so hoping that it would have been possible to get through today's lunch without the old son of a bachelor perpetrating some major outrage on the public weal. Was this hope to prove an idle one?

It being the opening day of the Eton and Harrow match, the conversation naturally turned to that topic, and the Bean and the Egg, who had received what education they possessed at the Thames-side seminary, were scornful of the opposition's chances. Harrow, they predicted, were in for a sticky week-end and would slink home on the morrow with their ears pinned back.

'Talking of Harrow, by the way,' said the Bean, 'that kid of Barmy Phipps's is with us once more. I saw him in there with Barmy, stoking up on ginger pop and what appeared to be cold steak-and-kidney pie with two veg.'

'You mean Barmy's cousin Egbert from Harrow?'

'That's right. The one who shoots Brazil nuts.'

Lord Ickenham was intrigued. He always welcomed these opportunities to broaden his mind and bring himself abreast of modern thought. The great advantage of lunching at the Drones, he often said, was that you met such interesting people.

'Shoots Brazil nuts, does he? You stir me strangely. In my time I have shot many things—grouse, pheasants, partridges, tigers, gnus and once, when a boy, an aunt by marriage in the seat of her sensible tweed dress with an airgun—but I have never shot a Brazil nut. The fact that, if I understand you aright, this stripling makes a practice of this form of marksmanship shows once again that it takes all sorts to do the world's work. Not sitting Brazil nuts, I trust?'

It was apparent to the Egg that the old gentleman had missed the gist.

'He shoots things *with* Brazil nuts,' he explained.

'Puts them in his catapult and whangs off at people's hats,' said the Bean, clarifying the thing still further. 'Very seldom misses, either. Practically every nut a hat. We think a lot of him here.'

'Why?'

'Well, it's a great gift.'

'Nonsense,' said Lord Ickenham. 'Kindergarten stuff. The sort of thing one learns at one's mother's knee. It is many years since I owned a catapult and was generally referred to in the sporting world as England's answer to Annie Oakley, but if I had one now I would guarantee to go through the hats of London like a dose of salts. Would this child of whom you speak have the murder weapon on his person, do you suppose?'

'Bound to have,' said the Egg.

'Never travels without it,' said the Bean.

'Then present my compliments to him and ask if I might borrow it for a moment. And bring me a Brazil nut.'

A quick shudder shook Pongo from his upper slopes to the extremities of his clocked socks. The fears he had entertained about the shape of things to come had been realized. Even now, if his words meant what they seemed to mean, his uncle was preparing to be off again on one of those effervescent jaunts of his which had done so much to rock civilization and bleach the hair of his nearest and dearest.

He shuddered, accordingly, and in addition to shuddering uttered a sharp quack of anguish such as might have proceeded from some duck which, sauntering in a reverie beside the duck pond, has inadvertently stubbed its toe on a broken soda-water bottle.

'You spoke, Junior?' said Lord Ickenham courteously.

'No, really, Uncle Fred! I mean, dash it, Uncle Fred! I mean really, Uncle Fred, dash it all!'

'I am not sure that I quite follow you, my boy.'

'Are you going to take a pop at someone's hat?'

'It would, I think, be rash not to. One doesn't often get hold of a catapult. And a point we must not overlook is that, toppers being obligatory at the Eton and Harrow match, the spinneys and coverts today will be full of them, and it is of course the top hat rather than the bowler, the gent's Homburg and the fore-and-aft deerstalker as worn by Sherlock Holmes which is one's primary objective. I expect to secure some fine heads. Ah,' said Lord Ickenham, as the Bean returned, 'so this is the instrument. I would have preferred one with a whippier shaft, but we must not grumble. Yes,' he said, moving to the window, 'I think I shall be able to make do. It is not the catapult, it is the man behind it that matters.'

The first lesson your big game hunter learns, when on safari, is to watch and wait, and Lord Ickenham showed no impatience as the minutes went by and the only human souls that came in sight were a couple of shopgirls and a boy in a cloth cap. He was confident that before long something worthy of his Brazil nut would emerge from the Demosthenes Club, which stands across the street from the Drones. He had often lunched there with his wife's half-brother, Sir Raymond Bastable, the eminent barrister, and he knew the place to be full of splendid specimens. In almost no place in London does the tall silk headgear flourish so luxuriantly.

'Stap my vitals,' he said, enlivening the tedium of waiting with pleasant small-talk, 'it's extraordinary how vividly this brings back to me those dear old tiger-shooting days in Bengal. The same tense expectancy, the same breathless feeling that at any moment something hot may steal out from the undergrowth, lashing its top hat. The only difference is that in Sunny Bengal one was up in a tree with a kid tethered to it to act as an added attraction for the monarch of the jungle. Too late now, I suppose, to tether this young cousin of your friend Barmy Phipps to the railings, but if one of you would step out into the street and bleat a little . . . Ha!'

The door of the Demosthenes had swung open, and there had come down the steps a tall, stout, florid man of middle age who wore his high silk hat like the plumed helmet of Henry of Navarre. He stood on the pavement looking about him for a taxi-cab—with a sort of haughty impatience, as though he had thought that, when he wanted a taxi-cab, ten thousand must have sprung from their ranks to serve him.

'Tiger on skyline,' said the Egg.

'Complete with topper,' said the Bean. 'Draw that bead without delay, is my advice.'

'Just waiting till I can see the whites of his eyes,' said Lord Ickenham.

Pongo, whose air now was that of a man who has had it drawn to his attention that there is a ticking bomb attached to his coat-tails, repeated his stricken-duck impersonation, putting this time even more feeling into it. Only the fact that he had brilliantined them while making his toilet that morning kept his knotted and combined locks from parting and each particular hair from standing on end like quills upon the fretful porpentine.

'For heaven's sake, Uncle Fred!'

'My boy?'

'You can't pot that bird's hat!'

'Can't?' Lord Ickenham's eyebrows rose. 'A strange word to hear on the lips of one of our proud family. Did our representative at King Arthur's Round Table say "Can't" when told off by the front office to go and rescue damsels in distress from two-headed giants? When Henry the Fifth at Harfleur cried "Once more unto the breach, dear friends, once more, or close the wall up with our English dead", was he damped by hearing the voice of a Twistleton in the background saying he didn't think he would be able to manage it? No! The Twistleton in question, subsequently to do well at the battle of Agincourt, snapped into it with his hair in a braid and was the life and soul of the party. But it may be that you are dubious concerning my ability. Does the old skill still linger, you are asking yourself? You need have no anxiety. Anything William Tell could do I can do better.'

'But it's old Bastable.'

Lord Ickenham had not failed to observe this, but the discovery did nothing to weaken his resolution. Though fond of Sir Raymond Bastable, he found much to disapprove of in him. He considered the eminent barrister pompous, arrogant and far too pleased with himself.

Nor in forming this diagnosis was he in error. There may have been men in London who thought more highly of Sir Raymond Bastable than did Sir Raymond Bastable, but they would have been hard to find, and the sense of being someone set apart from and superior to the rest of the world inevitably breeds arrogance. Sir Raymond's attitude toward those about him—his nephew Cosmo, his butler Peasemarch, his partners at bridge, the waiters at the Demosthenes and, in particular, his sister, Phoebe Wisdom, who kept house for him and was reduced by him to a blob of tearful jelly almost daily—was always that of an irritable tribal god who intends to stand no nonsense from his worshippers and is prepared, should the smoked offering fall in any way short of the highest standard, to say it with thunderbolts. To have his top hat knocked off with a Brazil nut would, in Lord Ickenham's opinion, make him a better, deeper, more lovable man.

'Yes, there he spouts,' he said.

'He's Aunt Jane's brother.'

'Half-brother is the more correct term. Still, as the wise old saying goes, half a brother is better than no bread.'

'Aunt Jane will skin you alive, if she finds out.'

'She won't find out. That is the thought that sustains me. But I must not waste time chatting with you, my dear Pongo, much as I always enjoy your conversation. I see a taxi-cab approaching, and if I do not give quick service, my quarry will be gone with the wind. From the way his nostrils are quivering as he sniffs the breeze, I am not sure that he has not already scented me.'

Narrowing his gaze, Lord Ickenham released the guided missile, little knowing, as it sped straight and true to its mark, that he was about to enrich English literature and provide another job of work for a number of deserving printers and compositors.

Yet such was indeed the case. The question of how authors come to write their books is generally one not easily answered. Milton, for instance, asked how he got the idea for *Paradise Lost*, would probably have replied with a vague 'Oh, I don't know, you know. These things sort of pop into one's head, don't you know,' leaving the researcher very much where he was before. But with Sir Raymond Bastable's novel *Cocktail Time* we are on firmer ground. It was directly inspired by the accurate catapultmanship of Pongo Twistleton's Uncle Fred.

Had his aim not been so unerring, had he failed, as he might so well have done, to allow for windage, the book would never have been written.

# 2

HAVING finished his coffee and accepted the congratulations of friends and well-wishers with a modesty that became him well, the fifth Earl ('Old Sureshot') of Ickenham, accompanied by his nephew Pongo, left the club and hailed a taxi. As the cab rolled off, its destination Lord's cricket ground, Pongo, who had stiffened from head to foot like somebody in the Middle Ages on whom the local wizard had cast a spell, sat staring before him with unseeing eyes.

'What's the matter, my boy?' said Lord Ickenham, regarding him with an uncle's concern. 'You look white and shaken, like a dry martini. Something on your mind or what passes for it?'

Pongo drew a shuddering breath that seemed to come up from the soles of his feet.

'How crazy can you get, Uncle Fred?' he said dully.

Lord Ickenham could not follow him.

'Crazy? I don't understand you. Good heavens,' he said, a bizarre thought occurring to him, 'can it be that you are referring to what took place in the smoking-room just now?'

'Yes, it jolly well can!'

'It struck you as odd that I should have knocked off Raymond Bastable's topper with a Brazil nut?'

'It struck me as about as loopy a proceeding as I ever saw in my puff.'

'My dear boy, that was not loopiness, it was altruism. I was spreading sweetness and light and doing my day's kind act. You don't know Raymond Bastable, do you?'

'Only by sight.'

'He is one of those men of whom one feels instinctively that they *need* a Brazil nut in the topper, for while there is sterling stuff in them, it requires some sudden shock to bring it out. Therapeutic treatment the doctors call it, do they not? I am hoping that the recent nut will have changed his whole mental outlook, causing a revised and improved Raymond Bastable to rise from the ashes of his dead self. Do you know what the trouble is in this world?'

'You ought to. You've started most of it.'

'The trouble in this world,' said Lord Ickenham, ignoring the slur, 'is that so many fellows deteriorate as they grow older. Time, like an ever-rolling stream, bears all their finer qualities away, with the result that the frightfully good chap of twenty-five is changed little by little into the stinker of fifty. Thirty years ago, when he came down from Oxford, where he had been a prominent and popular member of the University rugby football team, Raymond Bastable was as bonhomous a young man as you could have wished to meet. The jovial way he would jump with both feet on the faces of opponents on the football field and the suavity of his deportment when chucked out of the Empire on Boat Race night won all hearts. Beefy, as we used to call him, was a fourteen-stone ray of sunshine in those days. And what is he now? I am still extremely fond of him and always enjoy his society, but I cannot blind myself to the fact that the passing of the years has turned him into what a mutual friend of ours—Elsie Bean, who once held office as housemaid under Sir Aylmer Bostock at Ashenden Manor—would call an overbearing dishpot. It's being at the Bar that's done it, of course.'

'How do you mean?'

'Surely it's obvious. A man can't go on year after year shouting "Chops! Gracious heavens, gentlemen, chops and tomato sauce!" and telling people that their evidence is a tissue of lies and fabrications without getting above himself. His character changes. He becomes a dishpot. What Beefy needs, of course, is a wife.'

'Ah,' said Pongo, who had recently acquired one. 'Now you're talking. If he had someone like Sally—'

'Or like my own dear Jane. You can't beat the holy state, can you? When you get a wife, I often say, you've got something. It was the worst thing that could have happened to Beefy when Barbara Crowe handed him his hat.'

'Who's Barbara Crowe?'

'The one he let get away.'

'I seem to know the name.'

'I have probably mentioned it to you. I've known her for years. She's the widow of a friend of mine who was killed in a motor accident.'

'Isn't she in the movies?'

'Certainly not. She's a junior partner in Edgar Saxby and Sons, the literary agents. Ever heard of them?'

'No.'

'Well, I don't suppose they have ever heard of you, which evens things up. Yes, Beefy was engaged to her at one time, and then I heard that it was all off. Great pity. She's lovely, she's got a wonderful sense of humour, and her golf handicap is well in single figures. Just the wife for Beefy. In addition to improving his putting, always his weak spot, she would have made him human again. But it was not to be. What did you say?'

'I said "Bad show".'

'And you could scarcely have put it more neatly. It's a tragedy. Still, let's look on the bright side. There's always a silver lining. If things are not all that one could wish on the Bastable front, they're fine in the Johnny Pearce sector. How much did I tell you about Johnny at lunch? I can't remember. Did I mention that your Aunt Jane, exercising her subtle arts, had talked Beefy Bastable into taking a five years lease on that Hammer Lodge place of his?'

'Yes, you told me that.'

'And that he's engaged to a delightful girl? Belinda Farringdon, commonly known as Bunny?'

'Yes.'

'Then you're pretty well up in his affairs, and you will probably agree with me that a bright and prosperous future lies before him. Far different from that which, if your young friends at the Drones are to be believed, confronts the athletes of Harrow-on-the-Hill. But here we are at the Mecca of English cricket,' said Lord Ickenham, suspending his remarks as the cab drew up at the entrance of Lord's. 'Golly!'

'Now what?'

'If only,' said Lord Ickenham, surveying the sea of top hats before him, 'I had my catapult with me!'

They entered the ground, and Pongo, cordially invited to remain at his uncle's side, shied like a startled horse and said he would prefer to be pushing along. It was his settled policy, he explained, never again, if he could avoid it, to be associated with the head of the family in a public spot. Look, he argued, what happened that day at the dog races, and Lord Ickenham agreed that the episode to which he alluded had been in some respects an unfortunate one, though he had always maintained, he said, that a wiser magistrate would have been content with a mere reprimand.

A good deal of walking about and hullo-ing is traditionally done at the Eton and Harrow match, and for some little while after parting from his nephew Lord Ickenham proceeded to saunter hither and thither, meeting old acquaintances and exchanging amiable civilities. Many of these old acquaintances had been contemporaries of his at school, and the fact that most of them looked as if they would never see a hundred and four again was a reminder of the passage of time that depressed him, as far as he was capable of being depressed. It was a relief when he observed approaching him someone who, though stout and florid and wearing a top hat with a dent in it, was at least many years from being senile. He greeted him warmly.

'Beefy, my dear fellow!'

'Ah, Frederick.'

Sir Raymond Bastable spoke absently. His thoughts were elsewhere. He was sufficiently present in spirit to be able to say 'Ah, Frederick,' but his mind was not on his half-brother-in-law. He was thinking of the modern young man. At the moment when Lord Ickenham accosted him, there had just risen before his mental eye a picture of the interior of the Old Bailey, with himself in a wig and silk gown cross-examining with pitiless severity the representative of that sub-species who had knocked his hat off.

When the hat he loved had suddenly parted from its moorings and gone gambolling over the pavement like a lamb in springtime, Sir Raymond Bastable's initial impression that it had been struck by a flying saucer had not lasted long. A clapping of hands and the sound of cheering from across the street drew his attention to the smoking-room window of the Drones Club and he perceived that it framed a sea of happy faces, each split by a six-inch grin. A moment later he had seen lying at his feet a handsome Brazil nut, and all things were made clear to him. What had occurred, it was evident, had been one more exhibition of the brainless hooliganism of the modern young man which all decent people so deplored.

Sir Raymond had never been fond of the modern young man, considering him idiotic, sloppy, disrespectful, inefficient and, generally speaking, a blot on the London scene, and this Brazil-nut sequence put, if one may so express it, the lid on his distaste. It solidified the view he had always held that steps ought to be taken about the modern young man and taken promptly. What steps, he could not at the moment suggest, but if, say, something on the order of the Black Death were shortly to start setting about these young pests and giving them what was coming to them, it would have his full approval. He would hold its coat and cheer it on.

With a powerful effort he removed himself from the Old Bailey.

'So you're here, are you, Frederick?' he said.

'In person,' Lord Ickenham assured him. 'Wonderful, running into you like this. Tell me all your news, my bright and bounding barrister.'

'News?'

'How's everything at home? Phoebe all right?'

'She is quite well.'

'And you?'

'I also am quite well.'

'Splendid. You'll be even better when you're settled in down at Dovetail Hammer. Jane tells me you've taken Johnny Pearce's Hammer Lodge place there.'

'Yes. I shall be moving in shortly. Your godson, isn't he?'

'That's right.'

'I suppose that is why Jane was so insistent on my taking the house.'

'Her motives, I imagine, were mixed. She would, of course, for my sake be anxious to do Johnny a bit of good, but she also had your best interests at heart. She knew Dovetail Hammer was just the place for you. Good fishing, golf within easy reach and excellent fly-swatting to be had in the summer months. You'll be as snug as a bug in a rug there, and you'll find Johnny a pleasant neighbour. He's a capital young fellow.'

'Young?'

'Quite young.'

'Then tell him to keep away from me,' said Sir Raymond tensely. 'If any young man attempts to come near me, I'll set the dog on him.'

Lord Ickenham regarded him with surprise.

'You perplex me, Beefy. Why this bilious attitude toward the younger generation? Doesn't Youth with all its glorious traditions appeal to you?'

'It does not.'

'Why not?'

'Because, if you must know, some young thug knocked off my hat this afternoon.'

'You shock and astound me. With his umbrella?'

'With a Brazil nut.'

'Who was this fiend in human shape?'

'All I know is that he belongs to the Drones Club, which to my lasting regret is situated immediately opposite the Demosthenes. I was standing outside the Demosthenes, waiting for a cab, when something suddenly struck my hat a violent blow, lifting it from my head. I looked down, and saw a Brazil nut. It had obviously been thrown from the room on the ground floor of the Drones Club, for when I looked up the window was full of grinning faces.'

Sir Raymond started. A thought had occurred to him. 'Frederick!'

'Hullo?'

'Frederick!'

'Still here, old man.'

'Frederick, I invited you to lunch with me at the Demosthenes today.'

'And very kind of you it was.'

'You declined because you had a previous engagement to lunch at the Drones Club.'

'Yes. Agony, of course, but I had no option.'

'You did lunch at the Drones Club?'

'Heartily.'

'Did you take your after-luncheon coffee in the smoking-room?'

'I did.'

'Then I put it to you,' said Sir Raymond, pouncing, 'that you must have seen everything that occurred and can identify the individual responsible for the outrage.'

It was plain that Lord Ickenham was impressed by this remorseless reasoning. He stood musing for a space in silence, a frown of concentration on his brow.

'Difficult always to reconstruct a scene,' he said at length, 'but as I close my eyes and think back, I do dimly recall a sort of stir and movement at the window end of the room and a group of young fellows clustered about someone who had . . . yes, by Jove, he had a catapult in his hand.'

'A catapult! Yes, yes, go on.'

'He appeared to be aiming with it at some object across the street, and do you know, Beefy, I am strongly inclined to think that this object may quite possibly have been your hat. To my mind, suspicion seems to point that way.'

'Who was he?'

'He didn't give me his card.'

'But you can describe his appearance.'

'Let me try. I remember a singularly handsome, clean-cut face and on the face a look of ecstasy and exaltation such as Jael, the wife of Heber, must have worn when about to hammer the Brazil nut into the head of Sisera, but . . . no, the mists rise and the vision fades. Too bad.'

'I'd give a hundred pounds to identify the fellow.'

'With a view to instituting reprisals?'

'Exactly.'

'You wouldn't consider just saying "Young blood, young blood" and letting it go at that?'

'I would not.'

'Well, it's for you to decide, of course, but it's rather difficult to see what you can do. You can't write a strong letter to *The Times*.'

'Why not?'

'My dear fellow! It would be fatal. Jane was telling me the other day that you were going to stand for Parliament at . . . where was it? Whitechapel?'

'Bottleton East. Frampton is thinking of retiring, and there will be a by-election there next summer probably. I am expecting the nomination.'

'Well, then, think of the effect of a letter to *The Times* on the electorate. You know what the British voter is like. Let him learn that you have won the Derby or saved a golden-haired child from a burning building, and yours is the name he puts a cross against on his ballot paper, but tell him that somebody has knocked your topper off with a Brazil nut and his confidence in you is shaken. He purses his lips and asks himself if you are the right man to represent him in the mother of Parliaments. I don't defend this attitude, I merely say it exists.'

It was Sir Raymond's turn to muse, and having done so he was forced to admit that there was truth in this. Bottleton East, down Limehouse way, was one of those primitive communities where the native sons, largely recruited from the costermongering and leaning-up-against-the-walls-of-public-houses industries, have a primitive sense of humour and think things funny which are not funny at all. Picturing Bottleton East's probable reaction on learning of the tragedy which had darkened his life, he winced so strongly that his hat fell off and got another dent in it.

'Well,' he said, having picked it up, 'I do not intend to let the matter rest. I shall most certainly do something about it.'

'But what? That is the problem we come up against, is it not? You might . . . no, that wouldn't do. Or . . . no, that wouldn't do, either. I confess I see no daylight. What a pity it is that you're not an author. Then you would be on velvet.'

'I don't understand you. Why?'

'You could have got these views of yours on the younger generation off your chest in a novel. Something on the lines of Evelyn Waugh's *Vile Bodies*—witty, bitter, satirical and calculated to make the younger generation see itself as in a mirror and wish that Brazil nuts had never been invented. But in your case, of course, that is out of the question. You couldn't write a novel if you tried for a hundred years. Well, goodbye, my dear fellow,' said Lord Ickenham, 'I must be moving along. Lot of heavy Hullo-there-how-are-you-old-boy-ages-since-we-met-ing to be done before yonder sun sets. Sorry I could not have been of more help. If anything occurs to me later, I'll let you know.'

He tripped away, and Sir Raymond was conscious of a mounting sense of indignation. He strongly resented that remark about his not being able to write a novel if he tried for a hundred years. Who the devil was Ickenham to say whether he could write a novel or not?

Anything in the nature of a challenge had always been a spur to Sir Raymond Bastable. He was one of those men who take as a personal affront the suggestion that they are not capable of carrying to a successful conclusion any task to which they may see fit to set their hand. Years ago, when a boy at school, he had once eaten seven vanilla ice creams at a sitting because a syndicate of his playmates had betted him he couldn't. It sent him to the sanatorium for three days with frozen gastric juices, but he did it, and the passage of time had in no way diminished this militant spirit.

All through the rest of the day and far into the night he brooded smoulderingly on Lord Ickenham's tactless words, and rose from his bed next morning with his mind made up.

Write a novel?

Of course he could write a novel, and he would. Every man, they say, has one novel in him, and he had the advantage over most commencing authors of being in a state of seething fury. There is nothing like fury for stimulating the pen. Ask Dante. Ask Juvenal.

But though his theme was ready to hand and his rage continued unabated, there were moments, many of them, in the weeks that followed when only the iron Bastable will kept him from giving in and abandoning the project. As early as the middle of Chapter One he had discovered that there is a lot more to this writing business than the casual observer would suppose. Dante could have told him, and so could Juvenal, that it does not come easy. Blood, they would have said, is demanded of the man who sets pen to paper, also sweat and tears.

However, as their fellow poet Swinburne would have reminded them, even the weariest river winds somewhere safe to sea: and came a day when Sir Raymond was able to point at a mass of typescript on his desk, the top sheet of which was inscribed:

COCKTAIL TIME
by
RICHARD BLUNT

and to point at it with pride. His whole soul had gone into *Cocktail Time*—a biting title with its sardonic implication that that was all the younger generation lived for—and he knew it was good. It was an infernal shame, he felt, that circumstances compelled him to hide his identity under a pseudonym.

As, of course, they did. No question about that. It is all very well for your Dantes and your Juvenals to turn out the stuff under their own names, but a man who is hoping for the Conservative nomination at Bottleton East has to be cautious. Literary composition is not entirely barred to those whose ambition it is to carve for themselves a political career, but it has to be the right sort of literary composition—a scholarly Life of Talleyrand, for instance, or a thoughtful study of conditions in the poppet-valve industry. You cannot expect to get far on the road to Downing Street if you come up with something like *Forever Amber*.

And he was forced to admit as he skimmed through its pages, that there was no gainsaying the fact that in both tone and substance *Cocktail Time* had much in common with Miss Winsor's masterpiece. Sex had crept into it in rather large quantities, for while exposing the modern young man he had not spared the modern young woman. His experiences in the divorce court—notably when appearing for the petitioner in the cases of Bingley versus Bingley, Botts and Frobisher and of Fosdick versus Fosdick, Wills, Milburn, O'Brien, ffrench-ffrench, Hazelgrove-

Hazelgrove and others—had given him a low opinion of the modern young woman, and he saw no reason why she, too, should not have her share of the thunderbolts.

Yes, he mused, *Cocktail Time* was unquestionably outspoken in one or two spots, particularly Chapter 13. A Raymond Bastable, revealed as the man behind Chapter 13 and in a somewhat lesser degree Chapters 10, 16, 20, 22 and 24, could never hope to receive the nomination for the impending election at Bottleton East. A prudish Conservative Committee would reject him with a shudder and seek for their candidate elsewhere.

# 3

INTO the early vicissitudes of Sir Raymond's brain-child it is not necessary to go in any great detail, for it had much the same experiences as any other first novel. He sent it from an accommodation address to Pope and Potter, and it came back. He sent it to Simms and Shotter, and it came back; to Melville and Monks, and it came back; to Popgood and Grooly, Bissett and Bassett, Ye Panache Presse and half a dozen other firms, and it came back again. It might have been a boomerang or one of those cats which, transferred from Surbiton to Glasgow, show up in Surbiton three months later, a little dusty and footsore but full of the East-West-home's-best spirit. Why it should eventually have found journey's end in the offices of Alfred Tomkins Ltd one cannot say, but it did, and they published it in the spring, with a jacket featuring a young man with a monocle in his right eye doing the rock 'n roll with a young woman in her step-ins.

After that, as is customary on these occasions, nothing much happened. It has been well said that an author who expects results from a first novel is in a position similar to that of a man who drops a rose petal down the Grand Canyon of Arizona and listens for the echo. The book had a rather limited press. The *Peebles Courier* called it not unpromising, the *Basingstoke Journal* thought it not uninteresting, and the *Times Literary Supplement* told its readers that it was published by Alfred Tomkins Ltd and contained 243 pp, but apart from that it received no critical attention. The younger generation at whom it was aimed, if they had known of its existence, would have said in their uncouth way that it had laid an egg.

But Fame was merely crouching for the spring, simply waiting in the wings, as it were, for the cue which would bring it bounding on stage to drape the chaplet about the brow of its favoured son. At two minutes past five one Tuesday afternoon the venerable Bishop of Stortford, entering the room where his daughter Kathleen sat, found her engrossed in what he presumed to be a work of devotion but which proved on closer inspection to be a novel entitled *Cocktail Time*. Peeping over her shoulder, he was able to read a paragraph or two. She had got, it should be mentioned, to the middle of Chapter 13. At 5.5 sharp he was wrenching the volume from her grasp, at 5.6 tottering from the room, at 5.10 in his study scrutinizing Chapter 13 to see if he had really seen what he had thought he had seen.

He had.

At 12.15 on the following Sunday he was in the pulpit of the church of St Jude the Resilient, Eaton Square, delivering a sermon on the text 'He that touches pitch shall be defiled' (Ecclesiasticus 13-1) which had the fashionable congregation rolling in the aisles and tearing up the pews. The burden of his address was a denunciation of the novel *Cocktail Time* in the course of which he described it as obscene, immoral, shocking, impure, corrupt, shameless, graceless and depraved, and all over the sacred edifice you could see eager men jotting the name down on their shirt cuffs, scarcely able to wait to add it to their library list.

In these days when practically anything from Guildford undertaker bitten in leg by Pekinese to Ronald Plumtree (II) falling off his bicycle in Walthamstow High Street can make the front page of the popular press as a big feature story with headlines of a size formerly reserved for announcing the opening of a world war, it was not to be expected that such an event would pass unnoticed. The popular press did it proud, and there was joy that morning in the offices of Alfred Tomkins Ltd. Just as all American publishers hope that if they are good and lead upright lives, their books will be banned in Boston, so do all English publishers pray that theirs will be denounced from the pulpit by a bishop. Full statistics are not to hand, but it is estimated by competent judges that a good bishop, denouncing from the pulpit with the right organ note in his voice, can add between ten and fifteen thousand to the sales.

Mr Prestwick, the senior partner, read the *Express*, the *Mail* and the *Mirror* in the train coming from his Esher home, and within five minutes of his arrival at the office was on the telephone to Ebenezer Flapton and Sons, printers of Worcester and London, urging Ebenezer and the boys to drop everything and start rushing out a large new edition. *Cocktail Time*, which Alfred Tomkins Ltd had been looking on all this while as just another of the stones the builder had refused, was plainly about to become the head stone of the corner.

But there was no corresponding joy in the heart of Sir Raymond Bastable as he paced the lawn of Hammer Lodge. Ever since he had read his morning paper at the breakfast table, his eyes had been glassy, his mind in a ferment.

To anyone who paces the lawn of Hammer Lodge, that desirable residence replete with every modern comfort, a wide choice of scenic beauties is available. He can look to the left and find his eye roving over green pasture land and picturesque woods, or he can look to the right and get an excellent view of the park of Hammer Hall with its lake and noble trees and beyond it the house itself, a lovely legacy from Elizabethan days. He can also, if it is a Monday, Wednesday or Friday, look in front of him and see a jobbing gardener leaning on a spade in a sort of trance in the kitchen garden. There is, in short, no stint.

But Sir Raymond saw none of these attractive sights or, if he did, saw them as through a glass darkly. His whole attention was riveted on the morrow and what it was going to bring forth. In writing *Cocktail Time*, he had had a malevolent hope that he would be starting something, but he had never expected to start anything of these dimensions, and the thought that chilled him to the very spinal marrow was this. Would that pseudonym of his be an adequate safeguard?

If there is one thing the popular press of today is, it is nosey. It tracks down, it ferrets out. Richard Blunt becomes front page news, and it is not long before it is asking itself who is this Richard Blunt? It wants photographs of him smoking a pipe or being kind to the dog and interviews with him telling the world what his favourite breakfast cereal is and what he thinks of the modern girl. It institutes enquiries and discovers that nobody has ever seen the gifted Blunt and that his only address is a sweets-and-tobacco shop in a side street near Waterloo station, and before you know where you are headlines have begun to appear. As it might be:

LITERARY MYSTERY

or

PHANTOM AUTHOR

or possibly

DICK, WHERE ART THOU?

and from that to exposure is but a step. At this very moment, Sir Raymond felt, a dozen reporters must be sniffing on his trail, and the contemplation of the appalling mess in which he had landed himself made him writhe like an Ouled Nail stomach-dancer.

He was still busily writhing when the voice of Peasemarch, his butler, spoke softly at his side. Albert Peasemarch always spoke softly when addressing Sir Raymond Bastable. He knew what was good for him. It is no pleasure to a butler to be thundered at and asked if he imagines himself to be a barrow boy calling attention to his blood oranges.

'I beg your pardon, Sir Raymond.'

The author of *Cocktail Time* came slowly out of the uneasy dream in which he had been sustaining the role of the stag at bay.

'Eh?'

'It is Madam, sir. I think you should come.'

'Come? What do you mean? Come where?'

'To Madam's room, sir. I am afraid she is not well. I was passing her door a moment ago, and I heard her sobbing. As if her heart would break,' said Peasemarch, who liked to get these things right.

A wave of exasperation and self-pity flooded Sir Raymond's tortured soul. Phoebe, he was thinking, *would* start sobbing at a time like this, when he needed to devote every little grey cell in his brain to the problem of how to elude those infernal reporters. For an instant he was inclined to counter with a firm refusal to go within a mile of Madam's room. He had just been deriving a faint consolation from the thought that, she having breakfasted in bed and he being about to take train and spend the day in London, he would not have to meet her till late tonight, by which time, he hoped, his agitation would be less noticeable. Phoebe, seeing him now, would infallibly ask what was the matter, and when he assured her that nothing was the matter would say 'But what *is* the matter, dear?' and carry on from there.

Then kindlier feelings prevailed, or possibly it was just the curiosity and urge to probe first causes which we all experience when told that someone is crying as if her heart would break. He accompanied Peasemarch back to the house and found his sister sitting up in bed, dabbing at her eyes with a liquid something that looked as if it might have been at one time a pocket handkerchief.

Except that her ears did not stick up and that she went about on two legs instead of four, Phoebe Wisdom was extraordinarily like a white rabbit, a resemblance which was heightened at the moment by the white dressing jacket she was wearing and the fact that much weeping had made her nose and eyes pink. As Sir Raymond closed the door behind him, she uttered a loud gurgling sob which crashed through his disordered nervous system like an expanding bullet, and his manner when he spoke was brusque rather than sympathetic.

'What on earth's the matter?' he demanded.

Another sob shook the stricken woman, and she said something that sounded like 'Cosh him'.

'I beg your pardon?' said Sir Raymond, clenching his hands till the knuckles stood out white under the strain, like the hero of an old-fashioned novel. He was telling himself that he must be calm, calm.

'Cossie!' said his sister, becoming clearer.

'Oh, Cosmo? What about him?'

'He says he's going to shoot himself.'

Sir Raymond was in favour of this. Cosmo Wisdom, the fruit of the unfortunate marriage Phoebe had made twenty-seven years ago, long before he had become influential and important enough to stop her, was a young man he disliked even more than he disliked most young men in these days when the species had deteriorated so lamentably. Algernon Wisdom, Cosmo's father, had at one time sold secondhand cars, at another been vaguely connected with the motion pictures, and had occasionally acted as agent for such commodities as the Magic Pen-Pencil and the Monumento Mouse Trap, but during the greater part of his futile career had been what he euphemistically described as 'between jobs', and Cosmo took after him. He, too, was frequently between jobs. He was one of those young men, with whom almost all families seem to be afflicted, who are in a constant state of having to have something done about them. 'We must do something about poor Cossie,' were words frequently on his mother's lips, and Sir Raymond would say in the unpleasant voice which he used when addressing hostile witnesses that he had no desire to be unduly inquisitive, but would she mind telling him what precisely she meant by the pronoun 'we'.

The most recent attempt on his part to do something about poor Cossie had been to secure him a post in the export and import firm of Boots and Brewer of St Mary Axe, and the letter his sister was reducing to pulp announced, he presumed, that Boots and Brewer had realized that the only way of making a success of importing and exporting was to get rid of him.

'What has he been doing?' he asked.

'What, dear?'

Sir Raymond took a turn about the room. He found it helped a little.

'Why have Boots and Brewer dismissed him? They have, I take it?'

'He doesn't say so. He just says he wants two hundred pounds.'

'He does, does he?'

'And I haven't *got* two hundred pounds.'

'Very fortunate. You won't be tempted to throw it down the drain.'

'What, dear?'

'Letting Cosmo have it would be tantamount to that. Don't give him a penny.'

'He doesn't want a penny, he wants two hundred pounds.'

'Let him want.'

'But he'll shoot himself.'

'Not a hope,' said Sir Raymond, with a wistful little sigh as the bright picture the words had conjured up faded. 'If he tries, he'll be sure to miss. For heaven's sake stop worrying. All that letter means is that he thinks he may get a tenner out of you.'

'He says two hundred pounds.'

'They always say two hundred pounds. It's common form.'

'What, dear?'

'Phoebe, in the name of everything infernal, *must* you put your head on one side like a canary and say "What, dear?" every time I speak to you? It's enough to madden a saint. Well, I can't stand here talking. I shall miss my train. Take an aspirin.'

'What, dear?'

'Take an aspirin. Take two aspirins. Take three,' said Sir Raymond vehemently, and whirled off like a tornado to the car which was waiting to convey him to the station.

# 4

Of the several appointments he had in London that day the first was lunch with Lord Ickenham at the Demosthenes Club. Arriving there, he found the place its old peaceful self, the smoking-room full of the usual living corpses lying back in armchairs and giving their minds a rest. He eyed them with distaste, resenting this universal calm at a time when he himself was feeling like a character in a Greek tragedy pursued by the Furies. Though he would have said, if you had asked him, that far too much fuss was made about being pursued by Furies. The time to start worrying was when you were pursued by reporters. Curse their notebooks and pencils and damn their soft hats and raincoats. He could see them in his mind's eye, dozens of them, creeping about like leopards and getting nosier every moment.

His guest was late, and to while away the time of waiting he went to the centre table and picked up a paper. One glance at its front page, and he had dropped it as if it had bitten him and was tottering to the nearest chair. It was not often that he indulged in alcoholic stimulant before lunch, but he felt compelled now to order a double dry martini. What he had seen on that front page had made him feel quite faint.

He had just finished it when Lord Ickenham was shown in, all apologies.

'My dear old Beefy, you must be feeling like Mariana at the moated grange. Sorry I'm so late. I started walking here in plenty of time, but I met Barbara in Bond Street.'

'Who?'

'Barbara Crowe.'

'Oh?'

'We got talking. She asked after you.'

'Oh?'

'Affectionately, I thought.'

'Oh?'

Lord Ickenham regarded him disapprovingly.

'It's no good saying "Oh?" in that tone of voice, Beefy, as if you didn't care a damn. You know perfectly well that one word of encouragement from her, and you would be at her side, rolling over on your back with all your paws in the air.'

'Well, really, Frederick!'

'You think I am showing a little too much interest in your private affairs?'

'If you like to put it that way.'

'I'm fond of you, Beefy, stuffed shirt though you have become after a promising youth and young manhood. I wish you well, and want to see you happy.'

'Very good of you. Cocktail?'

'If you'll join me.'

'I have had one.'

'Have another.'

'I think I will. Phoebe upset me this morning. Her son Cosmo appears to have been getting into trouble again. You know him?'

'Just sufficiently well to duck down a side street when I see him coming.'

'He is trying to borrow two hundred pounds.'

'You don't say? Big operator, eh? Will he get it?'

'Not from me.'

'Is Phoebe distressed?'

'Very.'

'And I suppose you yelled at her. That's your great defect, Beefy. You bark and boom and bellow at people. Not at me, for my austere dignity restrains you, but at the world in general. Used you to bellow at Barbara?'

'Shall we change—'

'I'll bet you did, and it was that that made her break off the engagement. But from the way she was speaking of you just now, I got the impression that your stock was still high with her and you've only to stop avoiding her and never seeing her to start things going again. For heaven's sake, what's a broken engagement? Jane broke ours six times. Why don't you look her up and take her out to lunch and make a fuss of her. Show yourself in a good light. Dance before her. Ask her riddles.'

'If you don't mind, Frederick, I really would prefer to change the subject.'

'Do simple conjuring tricks. Sing love songs accompanied on the guitar. And, just to show her you're not such a fool as you look, tell her that you are the author of the best-selling novel, *Cocktail Time*. That'll impress her.'

It is very rarely that the smoking-room of a club in the West End of London suddenly springs into spasmodic life, with its walls, its windows, its chairs, its tables, its members and its waiters pirouetting to and fro as if Arthur Murray had taught them dancing in a hurry, but that was what the smoking-room of the Demosthenes seemed to Sir Raymond Bastable to be doing now. It swayed and shimmied about him like something rehearsed for weeks by a choreographer, and it was through a sort of mist that he stared pallidly at his companion, his eyes wide, his lower jaw drooping, perspiration starting out on his forehead as if he were sitting in the hot room of a Turkish bath.

'What . . . what do you mean?' he gulped.

Lord Ickenham, usually so genial, betrayed a little impatience. His voice, as he spoke, was sharp.

'Now come, Beefy. You aren't going to say you didn't? My dear fellow, to anyone who knows you as I do, it's obvious. At least three scenes in the thing are almost literal transcriptions of stories you've told me yourself.

You've used the Brazil nut episode. And apart from the internal evidence we have the statement of Jane.'

'Jane?'

'She came to London one day on a shopping binge and thought it would be the half-sisterly thing to do to look you up and slap you on the back, so she called at your house. You were out, but Peasemarch let her in and parked her in the study. After nosing about awhile, she started, as women will, to tidy your desk, and shoved away at the back of one of the drawers was a brown paper parcel from the publishing house of Simms and Shotter, despatched by them to Richard Blunt at some address which has escaped my memory. She mentioned this to me on her return. So you may as well come clean, Beefy. Denial is useless. You are this Blunt of whom we hear so much, are you not?'

A hollow groan escaped Sir Raymond.

'Yes. I am.'

'Well, I don't see what you're groaning about. With all this publicity you ought to make a packet, and if there's one thing in the world that's right up your street, it's money. You love the stuff.'

'But, Frederick, suppose it comes out? You haven't told anyone?'

'My dear fellow, why would I? I assumed from your having used a pseudonym that you wanted it kept dark.'

'And Jane?'

'Oh, Jane's forgotten all about it ages ago. It just happened to stick in my mind because I remembered saying something to you once about writing a novel. But what does it matter if it comes out?'

'Good heavens, it would mean the end of any hope I have of a political career.'

'Well, why do you want a political career? Have you ever been in the House of Commons and taken a good square look at the inmates? As weird a gaggle of freaks and sub-humans as was ever collected in one spot. I wouldn't mix with them for any money you could offer me.'

'Those are not my views. I have set my heart on getting that nomination for Bottleton East, Frederick. And there isn't a chance that they will give it to me, if it's in all the papers that I wrote a book like *Cocktail Time*.'

'Why should it be in all the papers?'

'These reporters. They find things out.'

'Oh? Yes, I see.'

Lord Ickenham was silent for some moments. From the frown of concentration on his forehead he appeared to be exercising that ingenious brain of his.

'Yes,' he said, 'they do find things out. I suppose that's what worried Bacon.'

'Bacon?'

'And made him, according to the Baconians, get hold of Shakespeare and slip him a little something to say he had written the plays. After knocking off a couple of them, he got cold feet. "Come, come, Francis," he said to himself, "this won't do at all. Let it become known that you go in for this sort of thing, and they'll be looking around for another Chancellor of the Exchequer before you can say What-ho. You must find some needy young fellow who for a consideration will consent to take the rap." And he went out and fixed it up with Shakespeare.'

Sir Raymond sat up with a convulsive jerk, spilling his glass. For the first time since breakfast that morning he seemed to see dimly, like the lights of a public-house shining through a London fog, a ray of hope.

'Don't you know any needy young fellows, Beefy? Why, of course you do. One springs immediately to the mind. Your nephew Cosmo.'

'Good God!'

'You say he wants two hundred pounds. Give it him, and tell him he can stick to all the royalties on the book, and the thing's in the bag. You'll find him just as willing and eager to co-operate as Shakespeare was.'

Sir Raymond breathed deeply. The ray of hope had become a blaze. Across the room he could see old Howard Saxby, the Demosthenes Club's leading gargoyle, talking—probably about bird-watching, a pursuit to which he was greatly addicted—to Sir Roderick Glossop, the brain specialist, who was usually ranked as the institution's Number Two gargoyle, and it seemed to him that he had never beheld anything so attractive as the spectacle they presented.

'Frederick,' he said, 'you have solved everything. It's a wonderful idea. I don't know how to thank you . . . Yes?'

A waiter had materialized at his side, one of the waiters who a short while before had been dancing the shimmy with the walls, the tables and the chairs.

'A gentleman to see you, sir.'

As far as was possible in his seated position, Sir Raymond himself did a modified form of the shimmy. A reporter? Already?

'Who is he?' he asked pallidly.

'A Mr Cosmo Wisdom, sir.'

'What!'

'Beefy,' said Lord Ickenham, raising his glass congratulatorially, 'it's all over but the shouting. The hour has produced the man.'

# 5

It was in uplifted mood and with buoyant step that Sir Raymond a few moments later entered the small smoking-room, which was where visitors at the Demosthenes were deposited. He found his nephew huddled in a chair, nervously sucking the knob of his umbrella, and once again experienced the quick twinge of resentment which always came to him when they met. A social blot who was so constantly having to have something done about him had, in his opinion, no right to be so beautifully dressed. Solomon in all his glory might have had a slight edge on Cosmo Wisdom, but it would have been a near thing. Sir Raymond also objected to his beady eyes and his little black moustache.

'Good morning,' he said.

'Oh—er—hullo,' said Cosmo, standing on one leg.

'You wished to see me?'

'Er—yes,' said Cosmo, standing on the other leg.

'Well, here I am.'

'Quite,' said Cosmo, shifting back to the first leg. He was only too well aware that there he was.

It was as the result of a telephone conversation with his mother that the young man had ventured into the Demosthenes Club this morning.

Phoebe, sobbingly regretting her inability to produce more than fifteen shillings and threepence of the two hundred pounds he required, had made a constructive suggestion. 'Why don't you ask your uncle, dear?' she had said, and Cosmo, though he would greatly have preferred to enter the cage of a sleeping tiger and stir it up with a short stick, had seen that this was the only way. A *tête-à-tête* with Sir Raymond Bastable always made him feel as if he were being disembowelled by a clumsy novice who had learned his job through a correspondence school, but when you are up against it for a sum like two hundred pounds it is necessary to sink personal prejudices and go to the man who has got two hundred pounds. Charm of manner, after all, is not everything.

So now, having taken one more refreshing suck at the umbrella knob, he stiffened the sinews, summoned up the blood and said:

'Er—uncle.'

'Yes?'

'Er—uncle, I don't want to bother you, but I wonder if you could . . . if you could manage . . . if you could see your way to letting me have . . .'

'What?'

'Eh?'

Sir Raymond adopted the second of the two manners that got him so disliked by witnesses in court, the heavily sarcastic.

'Let me refresh your memory, my dear Cosmo. After expressing a kindly fear that you might be bothering me—an idle fear, for you are not bothering me in the least—you went on to say "I wonder if you could . . . if you could manage . . . if you could see your way to letting me have . . ." and there you paused, apparently overcome with emotion. Naturally, my curiosity aroused, I ask "What?" meaning by the question, what is it you are hoping that I shall be able to see my way to letting you have? Can it be that your visit has something to do with the letter I found your mother bedewing with her tears this morning?'

'Er—yes.'

'She was somewhat incoherent, but I was able to gather from her that you need two hundred pounds.'

Actually, Cosmo needed two hundred and fifty, but he could not bring himself to name the sum. And anyway, though his bookmaker, to whom he owed two hundred, must be paid immediately, his friend Gordon Carlisle, to whom he was in debt for the remainder, would surely be willing to wait for his money.

'Er—yes. You see—'

Sir Raymond was now enjoying himself thoroughly. He reached for his coat-tails as if they had been those of a silk gown and gave a sidelong glance at an invisible jury, indicating to them that they had better listen carefully to this, because it was going to be good.

'With the deepest respect,' he said, 'you are in error. I do not see. I am at a loss. Boots and Brewer pay you a good salary, do they not?'

'I wouldn't call it good.'

Sir Raymond shot another glance at the jury.

'You must pardon me, a rude unlettered man, if by inadvertence I have selected an adjective that fails to meet your critical approval. One is not a Flaubert. I have always considered your emolument—shall we say, adequate.'

'But it isn't. I keep running short. If I don't get two hundred quid today, I don't know what I shall do. I'm half inclined to end it all.'

'So your mother was telling me. An excellent idea, in my opinion, and one that you should consider seriously. But she, I believe, does not see eye to eye with me on that point, so as I have a great fondness for her in spite of her habit of putting her head on one side and saying "What, dear?" I am prepared to save you from making the last supreme sacrifice.'

Cosmo came up from the depths. It was always difficult to understand what his relative was talking about, but there had been something in that last remark that sounded promising.

'You mean—?'

'Two hundred pounds is a lot of money, but it is just possible that I might be able to manage it. What do you want it for?'

'I owe it to a bookie, and he—er—he's making himself rather unpleasant.'

'I can readily imagine it. Bookies are apt to get cross on occasion. Well, I think I can help you out.'

'Oh, uncle!'

'On certain conditions. Let us speak for a while of current literature.

Have you read any good books lately, Cosmo? This novel *Cocktail Time*, for instance?'

'The thing there was all that in the *Express* about this morning?'

'Precisely.'

'No, I haven't read it yet, but I'm going to. It sounds hot stuff. Nobody seems to know who wrote it.'

'I wrote it.'

This was so obviously a whimsical jest that Cosmo felt it only civil to smile. He did so, and was asked by his uncle not to grin like a half-witted ape.

'I wrote it, I repeat. I assume that you can understand words of one syllable.'

Cosmo gaped. His hand, as always in moments of surprise and bewilderment, flew to his upper lip.

'That moustache of yours looks like a streak of ink,' said Sir Raymond malevolently. 'Stop fondling it and listen to me. I wrote *Cocktail Time*. Is your weak mind able to grasp that?'

'Oh, rather. Oh, quite. But—'

'But what?'

'Er—why?'

'Never mind why.'

'Well, I'll be damned!'

'And so shall I, if it ever comes out.'

'Is it as bad as all that?'

'It is not bad at all. It is frank and outspoken, but as a work of fiction it is excellent,' said Sir Raymond, pausing to wonder if it was worth while to quote the opinions of the *Peebles Courier* and the *Basingstoke Journal*. He decided that they would be wasted on his present audience. 'It is not, however, the sort of book which a man in my position is expected to write. If those reporters find out that I did write it, my political career will be ruined.'

'It's a bit near the knuckle, you mean?'

'Exactly.'

Cosmo nodded intelligently. The thing was beginning to make sense to him.

'I see.'

'I supposed you would. Now, the thought that immediately flashes into your mind, of course, is that you are in a position on parting from me to hurry off and sell this information to the gutter press for what it will fetch, and I have no doubt that you would leap to the task. But it would be a short-sighted policy. You can do better for yourself than that. Announce that you are the author of *Cocktail Time*—'

'Eh?'

'I want you to give it out that it was you who wrote the book.'

'But I never wrote anything in my life.'

'Yes, you did. You wrote *Cocktail Time*. I think I can make it clear even to an intelligence like yours that our interests in this matter are identical. We both benefit from what I have proposed. I regain my peace of mind, and you get your two hundred pounds.'

'You'll really give it me?'

'I will.'

'Coo!'

'And in addition you may convert to your own use such royalties as may accrue from the book.'

'Coo!' said Cosmo again, and was urged by his uncle to make up his mind whether he was a man or a pigeon.

'These,' said Sir Raymond, 'in light of the publicity it is receiving, should be considerable. My contract calls for ten per cent of the published price, and after all this fuss in the papers I should imagine that the thing might sell—well, let us be conservative—say ten thousand copies, which would work out—I am no mathematician, but I suppose it would work out at between six and seven hundred pounds.'

Cosmo blinked as if something had struck him between the eyes.

'Six and seven hundred?'

'Probably more.'

'And I get it?'

'You get it.'

'Coo!' said Cosmo, and this time the ejaculation passed without rebuke.

'I gather,' said Sir Raymond, 'from your manner that you are willing to co-operate. Excellent. Everything can be quite simply arranged. I would suggest a letter to each of the papers which have commented on the affair, hotly contesting the bishop's views, which you consider uncalled for, intemperate and unjust, and revealing yourself as Richard Blunt. If you will come to the writing-room, I will draft out something that will meet the case.'

And having done so, Sir Raymond returned to the smoking-room to tell Lord Ickenham that the thing, as he had predicted it would be, was in the bag.

# 6

As might have been expected, the announcement, appearing in the papers two days later, that Cosmo Wisdom was the author of the novel *Cocktail Time*, now at the height of its notoriety, did not pass unnoticed. One of the first to notice it was J. P. Boots of Boots and Brewer, and it was the work of an instant for him, on arriving at his office in St Mary Axe, to summon the young man to his presence and inform him that his services, such as they were, would no longer be required. Import and export merchants, whether of St Mary Axe or elsewhere, have the reputation of the firm to think of and cannot afford to retain in their entourage employees capable of writing Chapter 13 of that work. J. P. Boots did not in so many words bid Cosmo go and sin no more, but this was implied in his manner.

It was, however, only this importer and exporter who struck the jarring note. Elsewhere the reactions were uniformly pleasant. Alfred Tomkins Ltd wrote Cosmo an affectionate letter, telling him to come up and see them some time, and an equally affectionate letter came from Howard Saxby of Edgar Saxby and Sons, the literary agents, recommending him to place his affairs in the hands of the Saxby organization (offices in London, New York and Hollywood). This Cosmo, feeling that the situation in which he had been placed was one of those where a fellow needs a friend, decided to do, though wincing a little at the thought of that ten per cent commission.

Two little girls, Ava Rackstraw, aged ten, and Lana Cootes (12) wrote asking for his autograph, saying that he had long been their favourite author and they had read all his books. He was invited to address the Herne Hill Literary Society on 'Some Aspects of the Modern Novel'. Six unpublished authors sent him their unpublished works with a request for a detailed criticism. And Ivor Llewellyn, president of the Superba-Llewellyn motion picture company of Hollywood, about to return to California after a visit to London, told his secretary to go out and buy a copy of the book for him to read on the plane. Mr Llewellyn was always on the lookout for material which, if he could ease it past the Johnston office, would excite the clientele, and *Cocktail Time*, from what everyone was saying about it, seemed likely to be just the sort of thing he wanted.

And, finally, Mrs Gordon Carlisle, breakfasting in the sitting-room of the flat which she shared with her husband, opened her morning paper, looked at page one, started, said something that sounded like 'Cheese!' and lifting her attractive head shouted 'Hey, Oily!'

'Yes, sweetie?'

'Cummere,' said Mrs Carlisle, and there entered from the bedroom a tall, slender, almost excessively gentlemanly man in a flowered dressing-gown, who might have been the son of some noble house or a Latin-American professional dancer.

Actually, he was neither. He was a confidence trick artist whose virtuosity won him considerable respect in the dubious circles in which he moved. American by birth and residence, he had brought his wife to Europe on a pleasure trip. After years of strenuous work he proposed to take a sabbatical, though of course if something really good came up, he was always prepared to get back into harness again. The Carlisles did not spare themselves.

'Yay?' he said, hoping that his loved one had not summoned him to tell him he must wear his thick woollies. She had a way of doing so when the English summer was on the chilly side, and they tickled him. ''Smatter, sweetie?'

'Want to show you somef'n.'

Gertrude ('Sweetie') Carlisle was a strapping young woman with bold hazel eyes and a determined chin. These eyes were now flashing, and the chin protruded. It was plain that what she had read had stirred her.

'Listen, Oily. Didn't you tell me you won fifty pounds from a guy named Cosmo Wisdom the other night?'

Mr Carlisle nodded. It was the sombre nod of a man reluctant to be reminded of a sad experience.

'I did, yes. But he didn't pay me. He turned out to be one of these forty-dollar-a-week city clerks. The woods are full of them over here. They fool you by dressing like dukes, and when it's too late you find they're office boys or something. That's what you get for coming to a strange country. It would never have happened back home.'

'What did you do?'

'I didn't do anything.'

'I'd have busted him one.'

Mr Carlisle could well believe it. Impulsiveness and a sturdy belief in direct action were the leading features of his mate's interesting character. Some time had passed since the incident occurred and the bump had gone down now, but there still remained green in his memory the occasion when a fancied misdemeanour on his part had led her to hit him on the back of the head with a large vase containing gladioli. It had, in his opinion, spoiled the honeymoon.

'Well, too late to do anything now,' he said moodily. 'Just got to write it off as a bad debt.'

'Bad debt nothing. He was playing you for a sucker.'

Mr Carlisle started. His *amour-propre* was wounded.

'A sucker? *Me*?'

'Certainly he was. He was holding out on you. Read this.'

'Read what?'

'This.'

'Which?'

'This stuff in the paper here about him having written this book they're all talking about. He's got oodles of money. It's a best seller.'

Mr Carlisle took the paper, scanned it and said 'Well, I'll be darned!'

Gentlemanliness was his aim in life, for he had found it his best professional asset, and he seldom used any stronger expletive.

'Looks like you're right.'

'Sure, I'm right.'

'Unless,' said Oily, struck by a damping thought, 'it's some other Cosmo Wisdom.'

His wife scoffed at the theory. Even in England, she reasoned, there couldn't be two men with a name like that.

'Where does he live, this guy?'

'Down Chelsea way. One of those side streets off the King's Road.'

'Then have a bite of breakfast and go see him.'

'I will.'

'Don't come back without those fifty smackers.'

'I won't.'

'Get tough.'

'You betcher.'

'And wear your thick woollies.'

'Oh, sweetie! Must I?'

'Certainly you must. There's a nasty east wind.'

'But they make me want to scratch.'

'Well, go ahead, then. They can't jail you for scratching.'

'Oh, hell!' said Oily.

It was not a word he often employed, but it seemed to him that the circumstances justified it.

It was getting on for lunch time when he returned to the little nest, and there was nothing in his face to indicate whether his mission had had a happy ending or the reverse. The better to succeed in his chosen career, Oily Carlisle had trained his features to a uniform impassivity which often caused his wife annoyance. Though recognizing the professional value of a dead pan, she wished that he would not carry it into the life of the home.

'Well?' she said.

'Rustle me up an old-fashioned, will you, sweetie?' said Oily. 'My tongue's hanging out.'

Mrs Carlisle rustled him up an old-fashioned, and having done so said 'Well?' again.

'Did you see him?'

'I saw him.'

'What did he say?'

'Plenty.'

'Did you get the fifty?'

'No. Matter of fact, I lent him another twenty.'

'For heaven's sake!'

'But I got something a darned sight better than fifty pounds.'

'What do you mean?'

'I'll tell you.'

In Oily's demeanour as he took another sip of his cocktail and prepared to speak there was a suggestion of that Ancient Mariner of whom the poet Coleridge wrote. Like him, he knew he had a good story to relate, and he did not intend to hurry it.

'Yes, I saw him, and I said I'd been expecting to hear from him before this, because wasn't there a little matter of a hundred and fifty dollars or so he owed me, and he said Yes, that was right, and I said it would be righter, if he'd come through with it, and he said he hadn't got it.'

'The nerve!'

Oily took in the last drops of his old-fashioned, lit a cigarette and put his feet on the table.

'And he couldn't raise it, he said. Oh, no? I said. How about this book of yours you can't pick up a paper without seeing all that stuff about it? I said. The money must be pouring in like a tidal wave, I said.'

'What did he say to that?'

'Said it wasn't any such thing. These publishers pay up twice a year, he said, and it would be months before he could touch. I said Well, why didn't he get something from them in advance, and he said he'd just been trying to and they'd told him it would be foreign to their policy to anticipate the customary half-yearly statement.'

'Do what?'

'They wouldn't bite. Said he'd have to wait.'

'So what did you say?'

'I said "Too bad".'

A bitter sneer marred the beauty of Gertrude Carlisle's face.

'Got all fierce, didn't you? Scared the pants off him, I shouldn't wonder.'

'I said "Too bad",' proceeded Oily equably, 'and I said "Sweetie will be vexed", I said, and he said "Who's Sweetie?" and I said "Mrs Carlisle". And when Sweetie's vexed, I said, she generally hits people over the head with a bottle. And I told him about you and me and the vase.'

'Oh, honey, we've forgotten all that.'

'I haven't. Forgiven, yes. Forgotten, no. I can remember, just the same as if it had been yesterday, how it feels to get hit on the back of the head with a vase containing gladioli, and I described the symptoms to him. He turned greenish.'

'And then?'

'Then I came away.'

Mrs Carlisle's lips had closed in a tight line, and there was a sombre glow in her fine eyes. Her air was that of a woman thinking in terms of bottles and making a mental note to set aside the next one that became empty.

'What's this guy's address?'

'Why?'

'I thought I'd call around and say Hello.'

'You won't need to. Relax, sweetie. You ain't heard nothing yet. When I told you I came away, I ought to have said I started to come away, because he called me back. Seemed worried, I thought. He was gulping quite a good deal.'

'I'll gulp him!'

'And then he came clean and spilled the whole works. You know what he said? He said he didn't write that book at all.'

'And you believed him?'

'Sure I believed him, after I'd heard the rest of it. He said his uncle wrote it. His uncle's a guy called Sir Raymond Bastable. Big lawyer and going in for politics and knew that if it came out that he had written this *Cocktail Time* thing, he'd be ruined.'

'Why?'

'Seems in England you can't mix writing that sort of book with standing for parliament, which is what he's set on. So he got our Mr Wisdom to say he'd done it. Well, I needn't tell you what I said to myself when I heard that.'

'Yes, you need. What did you say to yourself?'

'I said "Here's where I touch the big money."'

'I don't get it.'

Oily smiled an indulgent smile.

'Look, sweetie. Use your bean. You're this Bastable character. You write a book, and it's too hot to handle, so you get your nephew to take the rap, and the papers run a big story about it's him that wrote it. All straight so far?'

'Sure, but—'

'Well, what do you do when you get a letter from the nephew saying he's been thinking it over and his conscience won't let him go on with the ramp, so he's going to tell the world it wasn't him who done it, it was you? Here's what you do—you pay up. You say "How much do you want, to keep this under your hat?" And you get charged as much as the traffic will bear.'

Mrs Carlisle's eyes widened. Her lips parted. She might have known, she was feeling, that she could have trusted her Oily. Gazing at him reverently, she expressed her emotion in a quick 'Gosh!'

'But will he do it?'

'Will who do what?'

'This Wisdom fellow. Will he write the letter?'

'He's done it. I've got it right here in my pocket. I said I'd mail it for him. I explained the idea, and he saw it at once. Very enthusiastic he was. He said his uncle's got all the money in the world—you know what they pay these big lawyers—and there isn't a chance that he won't cough up prac'lly anything.'

'Protection money.'

'That's right, protection money. So I dictated the letter and brought it away with me. That's when I loaned him that twenty pounds. He said he wanted to celebrate. Now what?' asked Oily, noting that a cloud had passed over the face of the moon of his delight.

'I was only feeling what a pity it is you'll have to split with him. You will, I guess?'

'That's what he guesses, too, but, ask me, he's guessing wrong. I'm taking the letter to this Bastable after lunch—he's living in the country at a place called Dovetail Hammer—and I shall want the money right down on the counter. Well, of course, it's just possible I may decide to give Wisdom his half of it, but I doubt it, sweetie, I doubt it very much indeed.'

'Oily,' said Mrs Carlisle, her eyes shining with a soft light, 'there's no one like you. You're wonderful.'

'I'm pretty good,' agreed Mr Carlisle modestly.

# 7

THE 3.26, Oily decided, having consulted the railway guide, was the train to take to Dovetail Hammer. It would, he pointed out, give them nice time for lunch at the Ritz and Gertie, all enthusiasm, begged him to lead her to it. Too often in her past luncheon had had to be a thing of sandwiches and dill pickles on the home premises, and she was a girl who, like the fifth Earl of Ickenham, enjoyed stepping high, wide and plentiful.

It was at about the moment when they were sipping their coffee and Oily had lighted a seven-and-sixpenny cigar that Lord Ickenham, who had been taking the mid-day meal with his nephew Pongo at the Drones preparatory to going and visiting his godson at Hammer Hall, looked out of the smoking-room window at the Demosthenes across the way and heaved a sigh.

'Boo!' said Pongo.

'I beg your pardon?'

'Just trying to scare you. Said to be good for hiccups.'

'It would take a lot more than that to scare an intrepid man like me. Chilled Steel Ickenham they used to call me in the old regiment. And, anyway, that was not a hiccup, it was a sigh.'

'Why were you sighing?'

'Because I felt a pang. No, sorry, three pangs. What caused one of them was the thought that, going off to stay with Johnny, I shall be deprived for quite a time of your society and those pleasant and instructive afternoons we have so often had together. It would have been delightful to have remained in London, seeing the sights with you.'

'You don't see any ruddy sights with *me*. I know you when you're seeing sights.'

'My second pang—Pang B you might call it—was occasioned by looking across the street at the Demosthenes Club, for it brought my semi-brother-in-law, Beefy Bastable, to my mind. I found myself thinking of something that happened last summer. You have probably forgotten the incident, but about a year ago, seated in this window, I shot his topper off with a Brazil nut.'

'Gosh!'

'Ah, I see you remember. Well, I had hoped that the experience would have proved a turning point in his life, making him a gentler, kinder Beefy, a sweeter, softer Bastable, more patient with and tolerant of his sister Phoebe. I was too sanguine.'

'Isn't he patient with and tolerant of his sister Phoebe?'

'Far from it. My well-meant effort appears to have had no effect whatsoever. According to Peasemarch, his butler, with whom I correspond, his manner toward her is still reminiscent of that of Captain Bligh of the *Bounty* displeased with the behaviour of one of the personnel of the fo'c'stle. Of course, he could make out a case for himself, I suppose. Phoebe, poor lost soul, has a way of putting her head on one side like a canary and saying "What, dear?" when spoken to which must be very annoying to a man accustomed to having one and all hang upon his lightest word. It is when she has done this some six or seven times in the course of a breakfast or luncheon that, according to Peasemarch, he shoots up to the ceiling in a sheet of flame and starts setting about her regardless of her age and sex. Yes, I can see his side of the thing, but it must be very bad for his blood pressure and far from pleasant for all concerned. Peasemarch says it wrings his heart to listen with his ear to the keyhole. You don't know Bert Peasemarch, do you?

'No.'

'Splendid chap. About as much brain as you could put comfortably into an aspirin bottle, but what are brains if the heart be of gold? I first met him when he was a steward on the Cunard-White Star. Later, he came into some house property and left the sea and settled down in a village near Ickenham. Then, if you remember, war broke out and there was all that bother about the invasion of England, and I joined the Home Guard, and whom should I find standing shoulder to shoulder with me but Bert Peasemarch. We saw it through together, sitting up all night at times, chilled to the bone, but with our upper lips as stiff as our hip joints. Well, two men don't go through all that without becoming buddies. I grew to love Bert like a brother, and he grew to love me like a brother. Two brothers in all. I got him his job with Beefy.'

'I thought you said he came into house property.'

'Quite a bit of it, I understand.'

'Then why did he want to buttle?'

'Ennui, my dear boy, the ennui that always attacks all these fellows who retire in their prime. He missed the brave tang of the old stewarding days. Years of life on the ocean wave had left him ill-fitted to sit on his fat trouser seat and do nothing. Well, a steward is practically a butler, so I advised him to make a career of that. My Coggs down at Ickenham coached him, and when Coggs said the time was ripe, I unloaded him on Beefy.'

'How did he get on with him?'

'I think he found him something of a trial. But that was before Beefy moved to the country. Who knows that living in the country will not improve him out of all knowledge. The quiet rural life does have a wonderful effect on people. Take me. There are times, I admit, when being cooped up at Ickenham makes me feel like a caged skylark, though not of course looking like one, but there is no question that it has been the making of me. I attribute to it the fact that I have become the steady, sensible, perhaps rather stodgy man I am today. I beg your pardon?'

'Eh?'

'I thought you spoke.'

'I said "Ha!" if you call that speaking.'

'Why did you say "Ha!"?'

'Because I felt like saying "Ha!" No objection to me saying "Ha," is there?'

'None whatever. This is Liberty Hall.'

'Thanks. Well, I can't see it.'

'See what?'

'All this about old Bastable becoming a different man. According to you, he still bites pieces out of his sister.'

'Merely because he is always coming up to London and bullying witnesses in court. This makes his progress slower than one could wish. But I am confident that the magic of Dovetail Hammer will eventually work. Give him time. It isn't easy for leopards to change their spots.'

'Do they want to?'

'I couldn't say. I know so few leopards. But I think Beefy will improve. If Barbara Crowe hadn't returned him to store, he would already have become a reformed character. I am convinced that, married to her, he would today be the lovable Beefy of thirty years ago, for she wouldn't have stood that Captain Bligh stuff for a minute. Too bad the union blew a fuse, but how sadly often that happens. When you get to my age, my dear Pongo, you will realize that what's wrong with the world is that there are far too many sundered hearts in it. I've noticed it again and again. It takes so little to set a couple of hearts asunder. That's why I'm worried about Johnny.'

'Isn't he all right?'

'Far from it.'

'Doesn't he like being married?'

'He isn't married. That's the whole trouble. He's been engaged to Bunny Farringdon for more than a year, but not a move on his part to set those wedding bells ringing out in the little village church. She speaks to him of buying two of everything for her trousseau and begs him to let her have the green light, but all she gets is a "Some other time". It gives me a pang.'

'Pang C?'

'Pang, as you say, C. Good heavens,' said Lord Ickenham, looking at his watch. 'Is it as late as that? I must rush. I'm catching the 3.26.'

'But half a second. Tell me more about this. Isn't she getting fed up?'

'Distinctly so. I was having lunch with her yesterday, and the impression I received was that she was becoming as mad as a wet hen. Any day now I expect to see in *The Times* an announcement that the wedding arranged between Jonathan Twistleton Pearce of Hammer Hall, Dovetail Hammer, Berks, and Belinda Farringdon of Plunkett Mews, Onslow Square, South Kensington, will not take place.'

'What do you think's at the bottom of it? Money? Johnny's pretty hard up, of course.'

'Not too well fixed, I agree. The cross he has to bear is that Hammer Hall is one of those betwixt-and-between stately homes of England, so large that it costs the dickens of a lot to keep up but not large enough to lure the populace into packing sandwiches and hard-boiled eggs and coming in charabancs to inspect it at half-a-crown a head. Still, what with running it as a guest-house and selling an occasional piece of furniture and writing those suspense novels of his, he should be in a position to get married if he wants to. Especially now that he is getting quite a satisfactory rent from Beefy for the Lodge. I don't think money is the trouble.'

Pongo drew thoughtfully at his cigarette. A possible solution of the mystery had occurred to him. Devoted to his Sally, he personally would not have looked at another female—no, not even if she had come leaping at him in the nude out of a pie at a bachelor party, but he was aware that there were other, less admirable men who were inclined to flit like butterflies from flower to flower and to run their lives more on the lines of Don Juan and Casanova. Could it be that his old friend Jonathan Pearce was one of these?

'I don't often get together with Johnny these days,' he said. 'It must be well over a year since I saw him last. How is he as of even date?'

'Quite robust, I believe.'

'I mean in the way of staunchness and steadfastness. It just struck me that the reason he's jibbing at jumping off the dock might be that he's met someone else down at Dovetail Hammer.'

'Do you know Dovetail Hammer?'

'Never been there.'

'I thought you hadn't, or you would not have made a fatuous suggestion like that. It isn't a place where you meet someone else. There's the vicar's daughter, who is engaged to the curate, and the doctor's daughter, betrothed to a chap who's planting coffee in Kenya, and that, except for Phoebe and Johnny's old nurse, Nannie Bruce, exhausts the female population. It's not possible for his heart to have strayed.'

'Well, something must have happened.'

'Unquestionably.'

'You'd better talk to him.'

'I intend to, like a Dutch godfather. We can't have this playing fast and loose with a young girl's affections. Letting the side down, is the way I look at it. And now, young Pongo, stand out of my way, or I'll roll over you like a Juggernaut. If I miss that train, there isn't another till five-forty.'

# 8

UNLESS your destination is within comfortable walking distance—the Blue Boar, let us say, or the Beetle and Wedge, both of which are just across the street from the station—the great thing to do on alighting from the train at Dovetail Hammer is to nip out quick and make sure of getting the station cab. (There is only one—Arthur Popworth, proprietor.)

Lord Ickenham, who had been there before and knew the ropes, did this. The afternoon was now warm, and he had no desire to trudge the mile to the Hall carrying a suitcase. He had just bespoken Mr Popworth's services and was about to enter the vehicle, when there emerged from the station a gentlemanly figure crying 'Hey, taxi!' and registering chagrin on perceiving that he had been forestalled. Oily Carlisle had lingered on the platform seeking from a porter with no roof to his mouth information as to where Sir Raymond Bastable was to be found.

Lord Ickenham, always the soul of consideration, turned back and beamed with his customary geniality. He did not particularly like Oily's looks, but he was humane.

'If you are going my way, sir,' he said, 'I shall be delighted to give you a lift.'

'Awfully kind of you, sir,' said Oily in the Oxford accent which he had been at some pains to cultivate for professional purposes. 'I want a place called Hammer Hall.'

'My own objective. Are you staying there?'

'No—I'm—'

'I thought you might be. It's a guest-house now.'

'Is that so? No, I'm returning to town. Just run down to see a man on business. Hammer Lodge the porter said the name of his house was, and it's somewhere near the Hall.'

'Just before you get there. I'll drop you.'

'Frightfully kind of you.'

'Not at all, not at all. It all comes under the head of spreading sweetness and light.'

The cab made a noise like an explosion in a boiler factory and began to move. There was a momentary silence in its interior, occupied by Lord Ickenham in wondering what business this dubious character, whose fishiness his practised eye had detected at a glance, could have to conduct with Beefy; by Oily in massaging the small of his back. For a long time now the heavy underclothing on which his loved one had insisted had been irking him.

'Warm day,' said Lord Ickenham at length.

'I'll say,' said Oily. 'And can you beat it?' he went on, having reached the stage of exasperation when a man has to have a confidant, no matter who he be. 'My wife made me wear my thick woollies.'

'You shock me profoundly. Why was that?'

'Said there was a nasty east wind.'

'I hadn't noticed it.'

'Me, neither.'

'You have a sensitive skin?'

'Yes, I have. Very.'

'I suspected that that was the reason why you were behaving like a one-armed paperhanger with the hives. Watching you at work, I was reminded of the young lady of Natchez, whose clothes were all tatters and patches. In alluding to which, she would say, "Well, Ah itch, and wherever Ah itches, Ah scratches." If you wish to undress, pay no attention to me. And Mr Popworth, I know, is a married man and will take the broad view.'

A feeling of irritation, the spiritual equivalent of the one he was feeling in the small of the back, began to grip Oily. He found his companion's manner frivolous and unsympathetic and was conscious of an urge to retaliate in some way, to punish this scoffer for his untimely gaiety, to wipe, in a word, that silly smile off his face. And most fortunately he possessed the means to do so. In his vest pocket there nestled a ring made of what looked like gold, in which was set a large red stone that looked like a ruby. It seemed the moment to produce it.

Oily Carlisle had not always been a man at the top of his profession, selling stock in non-existent copper mines to the highest in the land and putting through deals that ran into five figures. He had started at the bottom of the ladder as the genial young fellow who had found a ruby ring in the street and was anxious to sell it, the darned thing being of no use to him, and a touch of sentiment led him to carry on his person always this symbol of his beginnings. He regarded it as a sort of charm or luck piece.

Fingering it now, he said:

'Take a look at this.'

Lord Ickenham did so, and felt a pleasurable glow stealing over him. His, in the years before he had succeeded to the title and was an impecunious younger son scratching for a living in New York, Arizona and elsewhere, had been a varied and interesting career, in the course of which he had encountered a considerable number of what are technically known as lumberers, and he had always obtained a great deal of spiritual uplift from their society. To meet once again an optimist who—unless he was sadly wronging this sleek and shiny fellow-traveller—hoped to sell him a ruby ring he had found in the street carried him back to those good old days and would have restored his youth, had his youth needed restoring.

'My word!' he said admiringly. 'That looks valuable. How much did you give for that?'

'Well, I'll tell you,' said Oily. 'It's rather an odd story. You're not a lawyer, by any chance, are you, sir?'

Lord Ickenham said he was not.

'Why I asked was, I was walking along Piccadilly this morning, and saw this lying on the side-walk, and I thought you might be able to tell me if findings are keepings in a case like that.'

'Speaking as a layman, I should say most certainly.'

'You really think so?'

'I do indeed. The advice I always give to young men starting out in life and finding ruby rings in the street is "Grab the money and run for the train." You want to sell it, I suppose?'

'If it's not against the law. I wouldn't want to do anything that wasn't right.'

'Of course not. Naturally. About how much were you thinking of charging?'

Oily, too, had now begun to feel a pleasurable glow. This was pretty elementary stuff, of course, and he knew he ought to have been a little ashamed of himself for stooping to it, but it was giving him something of a nostalgic thrill to be back in the days when he had been a young fellow starting to break into the game.

'That's where I can't seem to make up my mind,' he said. 'If it's genuine, I suppose it's worth a hundred pounds or so, but how's one to tell?'

'Oh, I'm sure it's genuine. Look at that ruby. Very red.'

'That's true.'

'And the gold. Very yellow.'

'That's true, too.'

'I think you would be perfectly justified in asking a hundred pounds for this ring.'

'You do?'

'Fully that.'

'Would you buy it for a hundred pounds?'

'Like a shot.'

'Then—'

'But', proceeded Lord Ickenham, 'for the fact that as a purchaser of ruby rings from chance-met strangers I am unfortunately situated. Some time ago my wife, who is a woman who believes in a strong, centralized government, decided to take over the family finances and administer them herself, leaving me just that little bit of spending money which a man requires for tobacco, self-respect, golf balls and so on. So I have to watch the pennies. My limit is a shilling. If you would care to settle for that, you have found a customer. Or, as this warm friendship has sprung up between us, shall we say eighteen pence?'

Oily was too much the gentleman to use bad language, but the look he gave his companion was not at all the sort of look he ought to have directed at anyone with whom he had formed a warm friendship.

'You make me sick,' he said, speaking the words from between clenched teeth with no trace of an Oxford accent.

It was in jovial mood that some moments later, having dropped the stowaway outside Hammer Lodge, Lord Ickenham stepped from the station cab at the door of Hammer Hall. He was genuinely grateful to his recent buddy for having given him five minutes of clean, wholesome entertainment, free from all this modern suggestiveness, and he wished him luck if he was planning to sell that ring to Beefy.

The ordinary visitor to the ancestral home of the Pearces, arriving at the front door, stands on the top step and presses the bell, and when nothing happens presses it again, but these formalities are not for godfathers. Lord Ickenham walked right in, noting as he passed through the spacious entrance hall how clean, though shabby, everything was. Nannie Bruce's work, he presumed, with a little assistance, no doubt, from some strong-young-girl-from-the-village.

Externally unchanged in the four hundred years during which it had housed the family of Pearce, internally, like so many country mansions of the post-second-world-war period, Hammer Hall showed unmistakable signs of having seen better days. There were gaps on the walls where tapestries had hung, hiatuses along the floor where chests and tables were missing. A console table which was a particular favourite of his, Lord Ickenham observed, had folded its tents like the Arabs and silently stolen away since his last visit, and he was sorry to see that that hideous imitation walnut cabinet, a survival from Victorian days, had not gone the same way, for it had always offended his educated eye and he had often begged his godson to get rid of it.

He sighed a little, and with a fourth pang added to the three he had mentioned to Pongo made his way to the room down the passage where Johnny Pearce, when not interrupted by Nannie Bruce, wrote those suspense novels which helped, though not very much, to keep Hammer Hall's head above water.

It was apparent that she had interrupted him now, for the first thing Lord Ickenham heard as he opened the door was her voice, speaking coldly and sternly.

'I've no patience, Master Jonathan. Oh, good evening, your lordship.'

Nannie Bruce, a tall, gangling light-heavyweight with a suggestion in her appearance of a private in the Grenadiers dressed up to play the title role in *Charley's Aunt*, was one of those doggedly faithful retainers who adhere to almost all old families like barnacles to the hulls of ships. As what she called a slip of a girl, though it was difficult, seeing her now, to believe that she had ever had a girlish sliphood, she had come to Hammer Hall to act as nurse to the infant Johnny. By the time he went off to his first school and the need for her services might have been supposed to have ceased, the idea of dispensing with them had become an idle dream. She was as much a fixture as the stone lions on the gates or the funny smell in the attic.

'You are in your old room, your lordship,' she said. 'I'll be going and seeing to it. So I'll be glad if you would kindly speak to her, Master Jonathan.'

'She does her best, Nannie.'

'And a poor best it is. She's a gaby, that one. Verily, as a jewel of gold in a swine's snout is a woman which is without discretion. That's what Ecclesiastes wrote in the good book, Master Jonathan,' said Miss Bruce, 'and he was right.'

The door closed behind her, and Johnny Pearce, a personable young man with a pleasant but worried face, sat jabbing moodily with his pen at the sheet of paper on which he had been writing of Inspector Jervis, a fictional character to whom he was greatly addicted. Lord Ickenham eyed him with concern. If vultures were not gnawing at his godson's bosom, he was feeling, he did not know a vulture-gnawed bosom when he saw one. Only the thought that Belinda Farringdon was having similar vulture-trouble and that he had come here to talk to Johnny about it like a Dutch godfather restrained him from condoling and sympathizing.

'What was all that?' he asked.

'The same old thing. Another row with the cook.'

'She has them frequently?'

'All the time.'

'Has the cook given notice?'

'Not yet, but she will. Cooks never stay here more than about five minutes. They can't stand Nannie.'

'She is a bit testing, I suppose, though a useful person to have around if you want to brush up your Ecclesiastes. However, it is not of Nannie and cooks and Ecclesiastes that I wish to speak,' said Lord Ickenham, getting down to it. 'Far more urgent matters are toward. I saw Bunny yesterday.'

'Oh, did you?'

'Gave her lunch. Smoked salmon, *poulet en casserole* and a fruit salad. She toyed with them in the order named. In fact, the word "toyed" overstates it. She pushed her plate away untasted.'

'Good Lord! Isn't she well?'

'Physically, yes, but spiritually considerably below par. It's in the soul that it catches her. She is fretting and chafing because you keep postponing the happy day. Why the devil don't you marry the girl, Johnny?'

'I can't!'

'Of course you can. Better men than you have got married. Myself for one. Nor have I ever regretted it. I'm not saying I enjoyed the actual ceremony. I had the feeling, as I knelt at the altar, that the eyes of everybody in the ringside pews were riveted on the soles of my boots, and it bathed me in confusion. I have a foot as shapely as the next man and my boots were made to order by the best booterers in London, but the illusion that I was wearing a pair of those things people go hunting fish under water in was very strong. That, however, was but a passing *malaise* and the thought that in about another brace of shakes the dearest girl in the world would be mine bucked me up like a week at Bognor Regis. Honestly, Johnny, you ought to nerve yourself and go through it. It only needs will power. You're breaking that pen,' said Lord Ickenham, 'and what is far, far worse, you are breaking the heart of a sweet blue-eyed girl with hair the colour of ripe corn. You should have seen her yesterday. I am a strong man, not easily shaken, but as I watched her recoiling from that *poulet en casserole*, as if it had been something dished up by the Borgias, my eyes were wet with unshed tears. I blush for you, Johnny, and am surprised and hurt that you seem incapable of blushing for yourself. To think that any godson of mine can go about the place giving the woman who has placed her trust in him the sleeve across the windpipe like this makes me realize that godsons are not what they were.'

'You don't understand.'

'Nor does B. Farringdon.'

'I'm in a hell of a jam.'

Johnny Pearce quivered as he spoke, and passed a feverish pen over his brow. The sternness of Lord Ickenham's demeanour softened a little. It had become evident to him that he was the godfather of a toad beneath the harrow, and one has to make allowances for toads so situated.

'Tell me the whole story in your own words, omitting no detail, however slight,' he said. 'Why can't you get married? You haven't got some incurable disease, have you?'

'That's just it. I have.'

'Good heavens! What?'

'Nannie Bruce.'

It seemed to Lord Ickenham that the toad raising a haggard face to his was a toad who spoke in riddles, and he said so.

'What on earth do you mean?'

'Have you ever had a faithful old nurse who stuck to you like a limpet?

'Never. My personal attendants generally left at the end of the first month, glad to see the last of me. They let me go and presently called the rest of the watch together and thanked God they were rid of a knave. But what have faithful old nurses got to do with it? I don't follow you.'

'It's perfectly simple. Nannie Bruce has been here for twenty-five years—damn it, it's nearer twenty-seven—and she has become the boss of the show. She runs the place. Well, do you suppose that, if I get married, she's going to step meekly down and hand over to my wife? Not a hope.'

'Nonsense.'

'It isn't nonsense. You saw her in action just now. A perfectly good cook melting away like snow on a mountain side, and why? Because Nannie will insist on butting in all the time and criticizing. And it would be the same with Bunny. Nannie would make life impossible for her in a million ways. I'd call her high-spirited, wouldn't you?'

'Nannie?'

'Bunny.'

'Oh, Bunny. Yes, very high-spirited.'

'Well, then. Is she going to enjoy being interfered with and ordered around, told not to do it that way, do it this way, treated as a sort of half-witted underling? And her sniff. You know the way she sniffs.'

'Bunny?'

'Nannie.'

'Oh, Nannie. Yes, she does sniff.'

'And that hissing noise she makes, like a wet thumb drawn across the top of a hot stove. It would drive a young bride potty. And there's another thing,' said Johnny, vigorously plying the pen. 'Do you realize that every single discreditable episode in my past is filed away in Nannie's memory? She could and would tell Bunny things about me which in time would be bound to sap her love. How long could a wife go on looking on her husband as a king among men after hearing an eye-witness's account of his getting jerked before a tribunal and fined three week's pocket money for throwing rocks at the kitchen window or a blow-by-blow description of the time he was sick at his birthday party through eating too much almond cake? In about two ticks I should sink to the level of a fifth-rate power. Yes, I know. You're going to say why don't I get rid of her?'

'Exactly,' said Lord Ickenham, who was. It seemed to his alert mind the logical solution.

'How can I? I can't throw her out on her—'

'Please, Johnny! There are gentlemen present.'

'Ear.'

'Oh—ear. Sorry. But couldn't you pension her off?'

'What with?'

'Surely she would not want a fortune. A couple of quid or so a week . . .'

'I know exactly what she wants. Five hundred pounds.'

'In a lump sum?'

'Cash down.'

'It seems unusual. I should have thought a weekly dole . . .'

A sort of frozen calm descended on Johnny Pearce, the calm of despair.

'Let me tell you my story, omitting, as you say, no detail, however slight. I did offer her a weekly dole.'

'And she refused?'

'No, she accepted. That was when I felt justified in proposing to Bunny. I ought to have told you, by the way, that she's engaged to the policeman.'

'Bunny?'

'Nannie.'

'Oh, Nannie. What policeman would that be?'

'The one in the village. There's only one. His name's McMurdo.'

'Short-sighted chap?'

'Not that I know of. Why?'

'I was only thinking that it would be very difficult to be attracted to Nannie Bruce while seeing her steadily and seeing her whole. However, that is neither here nor there. Policemen are paid to take these risks. Proceed with your narrative.'

'Where was I?'

'You had just offered her a weekly sum, and she had accepted it. Which sounds to me like the happy ending, though obviously for some reason it was not. What came unstuck?'

'McMurdo won a football pool last winter. Five hundred pounds.'

'And why was that a disaster?' asked Lord Ickenham, for his godson had made this announcement in a hollow voice and was looking as if his was the head upon which all the ends of the world had come. 'I could do with winning a football pool myself. Wasn't Nannie pleased?'

'No, she wasn't. Her pride was touched, and she said she wasn't going to marry any man who had five hundred quid salted away unless she had the same amount herself. She said her aunt Emily had no money and married a man with a goodish bit of it and he treated her like an orphan child. She had to go to him for everything. If she wanted a new hat, he'd say hadn't he bought her a hat only five or six years ago and get off nasty cracks about women who seemed to think they'd married into the Rothschild family. None of that for her, Nannie said.'

'But, dash it, my dear Johnny, the two cases are entirely different. Musing on Emily, one draws in the breath sharply and drops a silent tear, but Nannie, with a weekly income, wouldn't be in her position at all. She would be able to make whatever kind of splash seemed fit to her. Didn't you point that out to the fatheaded woman?'

'Of course I did, but do you think it's possible to make Nannie see reason, once her mind's made up? Either she had five hundred pounds, or all bets were off. That was final. And that's how matters stand today,' said Johnny.

He dug the pen into Inspector Jervis's latest bit of dialogue once more and resumed.

'I thought I saw a way of straightening things out. It meant taking a chance, but it was no moment for prudence and caution. Did you read that last book of mine, *Inspector Jervis at Bay*?'

'Well, what with one thing and another, trying to catch up with my Proust and Kafka and all that—'

'Don't apologize. The British Isles are stiff with people who didn't read it. You see them on every side. But there were enough who did to enable me to make a hundred and eleven pounds six and threepence out of it.'

'Nice going.'

'So I took the hundred and put it on an outsider in the Derby. Ballymore.'

'My unhappy lad! Beaten by Moke the Second after a photo finish.'

'Yes, if it had had a longer nose, my troubles would have been at an end.'

'And you have no other means of raising that five hundred?'

'Not that I can see.'

'How about the furniture?'

'I've come to the end of the things I'm allowed to sell. All the rest are heirlooms, except the fake walnut cabinet, of course, Great-Uncle Walter's gift to Hammer Hall.'

'That eyesore!'

'I can sell that without getting slapped into gaol. I'm putting it up for auction soon. It might fetch a fiver.'

'From somebody astigmatic.'

'But, as you are about to point out, that would still leave me short four hundred and ninety-five. Oh, hell! Have you ever robbed a bank, Uncle Fred?'

'Not that I can recall. Why?'

'I was just thinking that that might be the simplest way out. But, with my luck, if I bust the Bank of England, I'd find they hadn't got five hundred quid in the safe. Still, there's always one consolation.'

'What's that?'

'It'll be all the same in a hundred years. And now, if you don't mind buzzing off and leaving me, I'll be getting back to Inspector Jervis.'

'Yes, it's time that I was moving. The Big Chief said I was on no account to fail to go and pay my respects to Beefy Bastable, and I want to have a chat with my old friend Albert Peasemarch. Lots of thread-picking-up to be done. I shall be back in an hour or so and shall then be wholly at your disposal.'

'Not that there's a damn thing you can do.'

'It is always rash to say that about an Ickenham. We are not easily baffled. I agree that your problem undoubtedly presents certain features of interest, but I am confident that after turning it over in my mind I shall be able to find a formula.'

'You and your formulas!'

'All right, me and my formulas. But wait. That is all I say—wait.'

And with a wave of the hand and a kindly warning to his godson not to take any wooden nickels, Lord Ickenham tilted his hat slightly to one side and set off across the park to Hammer Lodge.

# 9

THERE was a thoughtful frown on Lord Ickenham's brow and a pensive look in his eye as he skirted the lake, on the other side of which the grounds of Hammer Lodge lay. A cow was paddling in the shallows, and normally he would have paused to throw a bit of stick at it, but now he hurried on, too preoccupied to do the civil thing.

He was concerned about Johnny. His story would have made it plain to a far less intelligent godfather that the lad was in a spot. He was not on intimate terms with Nannie Bruce, but he was sufficiently acquainted with her personality to recognize the impossibility, once her mind was made up, of persuading her to change it. If Nannie Bruce wanted five hundred pounds cash down, she would get five hundred pounds cash down, or no wedding bells for Officer McMurdo. And as Johnny did not possess five hundred pounds, the situation had all the earmarks of an impasse. It is not too much to say that, though his hat was on the side of his head and his walk as jaunty as ever, Lord Ickenham, as he rang the front door bell of Hammer Lodge and was admitted by his friend Albert Peasemarch, was mourning in spirit.

Butlers come in three sizes—the large, the small, and the medium. Albert Peasemarch was one of the smalls. Short and somewhat overweight for his height, he had a round, moonlike face, in which were set, like currants in a suet dumpling, two brown eyes. A captious critic, seeing, as captious critics do, only the dark side, would have commented on the entire absence from these eyes of anything like a gleam of human intelligence: but to anyone non-captious this would have been amply compensated for by their kindliness and honesty. His circle of friends, while passing him over when they wanted someone to explain the Einstein Theory to them, knew that, if they were in trouble, they could rely on his help. True, this help almost invariably made things worse than they had been, for if there was a way of getting everything muddled up, he got it, but his intentions were excellent and his heart in the right place.

His face, usually disciplined to a professional impassivity, melted into a smile of welcome as he recognized the visitor.

'Oh, good evening, m'lord.'

'Hullo, Bert. You're looking very roguish. Is the old folk at home?'

'Sir Raymond is in his study, m'lord, but a gentleman is with him at the moment—a Mr Carlisle.'

'I know the chap you mean. He's probably trying to sell him a ruby ring. Well, then, if the big shot is tied up in conference, we've nice time for a spot of port in your pantry, and very agreeable it will be after a hot and dirty journey. You haven't run short of port?'

'Oh, no, m'lord. If you will step this way, m'lord.'

'California, as you might say, here I come. This,' said Lord Ickenham some moments later, 'is the real stuff. The poet probably had it in mind when he spoke of the port of heaven. "If the Dons sight Devon, I'll quit the port of heaven an' drum them up the Channel as we drummed them long ago." Sir Henry Newbolt. Drake's Drum. Are you familiar with Drake's Drum? But of course you are. What am I thinking of? I've heard you sing it a dozen times round the old camp fire in our Home Guard days.'

'I was always rather partial to Drake's Drum, m'lord.'

'And how you belted the stuffing out of it! It was like hearing a Siberian wolf-hound in full cry after a Siberian wolf. I remember thinking at the time how odd it is that small men nearly always have loud, deep voices. I believe midgets invariably sing bass. Very strange. Nature's law of compensation, no doubt.'

'Very possibly, m'lord.'

Lord Ickenham, who had been about to sip, lowered his glass with a reproachful shake of the head.

'Now listen, Bert. This "M'lord" stuff. I've been meaning to speak to you about it. I'm a Lord, yes, no argument about that, but you don't have to keep rubbing it in all the time. It's no good kidding ourselves. We know what lords are. Anachronistic parasites on the body of the state, is the kindest thing you can say of them. Well, a sensitive man doesn't like to be reminded every half second that he is one of the untouchables, liable at any moment to be strung up on a lamp post or to have his blood flowing in streams down Park Lane. Couldn't you substitute something matier and less wounding to my feelings?'

'I could hardly call your lordship "Ickenham".'

'I was thinking of "Freddie".'

'Oh, no, m'lord.'

'Then how about "old man" or "cully"?'

'Certainly not, m'lord. If your lordship would not object to "Mr I"?'

'The ideal solution. Well, Bert, how are things in the home now? Not much improvement, I gather from your letters. Our mutual friend still a little terse with the flesh and blood, eh?'

'It is not for me to criticize Sir Raymond.'

'Don't come the heavy butler over me, Bert. This meeting is tiled. You may speak freely.'

'Then I must say that I consider that he treats Madam very badly, indeed.'

'Bellows at her?'

'Almost daily, Mr I.'

'They will bring their court manner into private life, these barristers. I was in court once and heard Beefy cross-examining a meek little man who looked like Bill the Lizard in *Alice in Wonderland*. I forget what the actual words were, but the fellow piped up with some perfectly harmless remark, and Beefy fixed him with a glittering eye and thundered "Come, come, sir, don't attempt to browbeat *me*!" And he's still like that in the home, is he?'

'More so now than ever before. Madam is distressed because Mr

Cosmo has written this book there is so much talk about. She disapproves of its moral tone. This makes her cry a good deal.'

'And he ticks her off?'

'Most violently. Her tears appear to exasperate him. I sometimes feel I can't bear it any longer.'

'Why don't you hand in your portfolio?'

'And leave her? I couldn't.'

Lord Ickenham looked at him keenly. His host's face, usually, like Oily Carlisle's, an expressionless mask, was working with an odd violence that made him seem much more the Home Guardsman of years ago than the butler of today.

'Hullo!' he said. 'What's this?'

Albert Peasemarch remained for a moment in the process of what is commonly known as struggling for utterance. Finding speech at length, he said in a low, hoarse voice very different from the one he employed when rendering Drake's Drum:

'I love her, Mr I.'

It always took a great deal to surprise Lord Ickenham. Where another man, hearing this cry from the heart, might have leaped in his chair and upset his glass of port, he merely directed at the speaker a look full of sympathy and understanding. His personal feeling that loving Phoebe Wisdom was a thing beyond the scope of the most determined Romeo he concealed. It could, apparently, be done.

'My poor old Bert,' he said. 'Tell me all. When did you feel this coming on?'

A dreamy look came into Albert Peasemarch's eye, the look of one who tenderly relives the past.

'It was our rheumatism that first brought us together,' he said, his voice trembling a little.

Lord Ickenham cocked an enquiring eyebrow.

'I'm not sure I quite got that. Rheumatism, did you say?'

'Madam suffers from it in the left shoulder, and I have it in the right leg, and we fell into the habit of discussing it. Every morning Madam would say "And how is your rheumatism, Peasemarch?" and I would tell her, and I would say "How is *your* rheumatism, madam?" and she would tell *me*. And so it went on.'

'I see. Swapping gossip from the lazar house. Yes, I understand. Naturally, if you tell a woman day after day about the funny burning feeling in your right leg, and she tells you about the curious shooting sensation in her left shoulder, it forms a bond.'

'And then last winter . . .'

'Yes—?'

A reverent note crept into Albert Peasemarch's voice. 'Last winter I had influenza. Madam nursed me throughout my illness.'

'Smoothed your pillow? Brought you cooling drinks?'

'And read Agatha Christie to me. And something came right over me, Mr I, and I knew that it was love.'

Lord Ickenham was silent for some moments, sipping his port and turning this revelation over in his mind. It still puzzled him that anyone could have had the divine spark touched off in him by Phoebe Wisdom. In a vague way, though he knew her to be more than a decade younger than himself, he had always regarded her as many years his senior. She looked, he considered, about eighty. But presumably she did not look eighty to Albert Peasemarch, and, even if she did, a woman who for years had kept house for Beefy Bastable was surely entitled to look a hundred.

His heart went out to Albert Peasemarch. Dashed unpleasant it must be, he was feeling, for a butler to fall in love with the chatelaine of the establishment. Having to say 'Yes, madam,' 'Very good, madam,' 'The carriage waits, madam' and all that sort of thing, when every fibre of his being was urging him to tell her that she was the tree on which the fruit of his life hung and that for her sake he would pluck the stars from the sky, or whatever it is that butlers say when moved by the fire within. A state of affairs, Lord Ickenham thought, which would give him personally the pip. He resolved to do all that in him lay—and on these occasions there was always quite a lot that in him lay—to push the thing along and bring sweetness and light into these two at present sundered lives.

'Taken any steps about it?' he asked.

'Oh, no, m'lord, I mean Mr I. It wouldn't be proper.'

'This is no time to mess about, being proper,' said Lord Ickenham bluffly. 'Can't get anywhere if you don't take steps.'

'What do you advise, Mr I?'

'That's more the tone. I don't suppose there's a man alive better equipped to advise you than I am. I'm a specialist at this sort of thing. The couples I've brought together in my time, if placed end to end, not that I suppose one could do it, of course, would reach from Piccadilly Circus to well beyond Hyde Park Corner. You don't know Bill Oakshott, do you? He was one of my clients, my nephew Pongo another. And there was the pink chap down at Mitching Hill, I've forgotten his name, and Polly Pott and Horace Davenport and Elsie Bean the housemaid, oh, and dozens more. With me behind him, the most diffident wooer can get the proudest beauty to sign on the dotted line. In your case, the relationship between you and the adored object being somewhat unusual, one will have to go rather carefully. The Ickenham system, for instance, might seem a little abrupt.'

'The Ickenham system, Mr I?'

'I call it that. Just giving you the bare outlines, you stride up to the subject, grab her by the wrist, clasp her to your bosom and shower burning kisses on her upturned face. You don't have to say much—just "My mate!" or something of that sort, and, of course, in grabbing by the wrist, don't behave as if you were handling a delicate piece of china. Grip firmly and waggle her about a bit. It seldom fails, and I usually recommend it, but in your case, as I say, it might be better to edge into the thing more gradually. I think that as a starter you should bring her flowers every day, wet with the morning dew. And when I say "bring", I don't mean hand them over as if you were delivering a parcel from the stores. Put them secretly in her room. No message. An anonymous gift from a mystery worshipper. That will pique her curiosity. "Hullo!" she will say to herself. "What's all this in aid of?" and at a suitable moment you reveal that they came from you, and it knocks her base over apex. Wait!' said Lord Ickenham. A thought had come like a full-blown rose, flushing his brow. 'I'm seeing deeper into this thing. Isn't there a language of flowers? I'm sure I've read about it somewhere. I mean, you send a girl nasturtiums or lobelias or whatever it may be, and it signifies "There is one who adores you respectfully from afar" or "Watch out, here comes Albert!" or something. You've heard of that?'

'Oh, yes, indeed. There are books on the subject.'

'Get one, and make of it a constant companion.' Lord Ickenham mused for a moment. 'Is there anything else? Ah, yes. The dog. Has she a dog?'

'A cocker spaniel, Mr I, called Benjy.'

'Conciliate that dog, Bert. Omit no word or act that will lead to a *rapprochement* between yourself and it. The kindly chirrup. The friendly bone. The constant pat on the head or ribs, according to the direction in which your tastes lie. There is no surer way to a woman's heart than to get in solid with her dog.'

He broke off. Through the window of the pantry he had seen a gentlemanly figure pass by.

'The boss's conference has concluded,' he said, rising. 'I'd better go and pass the time of day. You won't forget, Bert? An atmosphere of the utmost cordiality where the dog Benjy is concerned, and the daily gift of flowers.'

'Yes, Mr I.'

'Every morning without fail. It's bound to work. Inevitably the little daily dose will have its effect,' said Lord Ickenham, and went along the passage to the study where, he presumed, Sir Raymond Bastable would still be—gloating, possibly, over the ruby ring he had purchased.

His manner was even more preoccupied than it had been when he ignored the paddling cow. So many problems had presented themselves, coming up one after the other. It was never his habit to grumble and make a fuss when this happened, but he did sometimes, as now, feel that the life work he had set himself of spreading sweetness and light—or, as some preferred to put it, meddling in other people's business—was almost more than any man could be expected to undertake singlehanded. In addition to that of his godson Johnny, he now had Albert Peasemarch's tangled love life to worry about, and to promote a union between a butler and the sister of his employer is in itself a whole-time task, calling for all that one has of resolution and ingenuity. And there was, furthermore, the matter of the reformation of Beefy Bastable, whose attitude toward his sister Phoebe, so like that of a snapping turtle suffering from ulcers, he was determined to correct.

A full programme.

Still, 'Tails up, Ickenham. Remember your triumphs in the past,' he was saying to himself. This was not the first time in his career that the going had been sticky.

He was right about Sir Raymond being in the study, but wrong about the ruby ring. His half-brother-in-law was sitting huddled in a chair with his head between his hands, his air that of a man who, strolling along a country lane thinking of this and that, has caught an unexpected automobile in the small of the back, and his outward appearance mirrored perfectly the emotions within. At about three-fifteen on a November afternoon at Oxford, when the University rugby football team were playing Cardiff, a Welshman with a head constructed apparently of ivory or one of the harder metals had once butted Sir Raymond Bastable in the solar plexus, giving him the illusion that the world had suddenly come to an end and judgment day set in with unusual severity. It had happened a matter of thirty years ago, but the episode had never faded from his memory, and until this evening he had always looked on it as the high spot of his life.

Some five minutes previously, when Oily Carlisle, producing Cosmo Wisdom's letter, had revealed its contents and gone off to give him, as he explained, time to think it over, it had been eclipsed.

# 10

Lord Ickenham came into the room, concern in every hair of his raised eyebrows. Many men in his place, beholding this poor bit of human wreckage, would have said to themselves 'Oh, my gosh, another toad beneath the harrow' and ducked out quickly to avoid having to listen to the hard luck story which such toads are always so ready to tell, but to the altruistic peer it never occurred to adopt such a course. His was a big heart, and when he saw a toad not only beneath the harrow but apparently suffering from the effects of one of those gas explosions in London street which slay six, he did not remember an appointment for which he was already late but stuck around and prepared to do whatever lay in his power to alleviate the sufferer's distress.

'Beefy!' he cried. 'My dear old bird, what on earth's the matter? You look like a devastated area.'

It took Sir Raymond some little time to tell him what the matter was, for he had much to say on the subject of the black-hearted villainy of his nephew Cosmo and also a number of pungent remarks to make about Oily Carlisle. As he concluded the recital of their skulduggery, his audience, which he had held spellbound, clicked its tongue. It shocked Lord Ickenham to think that humanity could sink to such depths, and he blamed himself for having allowed this new development to catch him unprepared.

'We should have foreseen this,' he said. 'We should have told ourselves that it was madness to place our confidence in anyone like young Cosmo, a twister compared with whom corkscrews are straight and spiral staircases the shortest line between two points. Seeing that little black moustache of his, we should have refused him the nomination and sought elsewhere for a co-worker. "Never put anything on paper, my boy," my old father used to say to me, "and never trust a man with a small black moustache." And you, my poor Beefy, have done both.'

Sir Raymond's reply was somewhat muffled, for he was having trouble with his vocal cords, but Lord Ickenham understood him to say that it was all his, Lord Ickenham's, fault.

'You suggested him.'

'Surely not? Yes, by Jove, you're right. I was sitting here, you were sitting there, lapping up martinis like a vacuum cleaner, and I said . . . Yes, it all comes back to me. I'm sorry.'

'What's the use of that?'

'Remorse is always useful, Beefy. It stimulates the brain. It has set mine working like a buzz-saw, and already a plan of action is beginning to present itself. You say this fellow went off? Where did he go?'

'How the devil do I know where he went?'

'I ask because I happen to be aware that he has a sensitive skin and is undergoing considerable discomfort because his wife made him put on his winter woollies this morning. I thought he might be in the garden somewhere, stripped to the buff in order to scratch with more authority, in which case his coat would be on the ground or hung from some handy bough, and I could have stolen up, not letting a twig snap beneath my feet, and gone through his pockets. But I doubt if he is the sort of man to be careless with a coat containing important documents. I shall have to try the other plan I spoke of, the one I said was beginning to present itself. Since you last heard from me, I have shaped it out, complete to the last button, and it will, I am convinced, bring home the bacon. You're sure he's coming back?'

'Of course he's coming back, curse him!'

'Through those French windows, no doubt. He would hardly ring the front door bell and have himself announced again. It would confuse Albert Peasemarch and make him fret. All right, Beefy, receive him courteously, ask after his sensitive skin and keep him engaged in conversation till I am with you again.'

'Where are you going?'

'Never mind. When the fields are white with daisies, I'll return,' said Lord Ickenham, and withdrew through the door a minute or so before Oily Carlisle came in through the French windows.

It could scarcely be said that Sir Raymond received Mr Carlisle courteously, unless it is courteous to glare at someone like a basilisk and call him a slimy blackmailer, nor did he enquire after his skin or engage him in conversation. What talk ensued was done by Oily, who was in excellent spirits and plainly feeling that all was for the best in this best of all possible worlds. Cosmo's letter, nestling in his inside coat pocket, made a little crackling sound as he patted it, and it was music to his ears. There was a brisk cheerfulness in his manner as he started talking prices that gashed his companion like a knife.

He had just outlined the tariff and was suggesting that if Sir Raymond would bring out his cheque book and take pen in hand, the whole thing could be cleaned up promptly, neatly and to everybody's satisfaction, when there came to him a sudden doubt as to the world being, as he had supposed, the best of all possible. The door opened, and Albert Peasemarch appeared.

'Inspector Jervis,' he announced, and with an uneasy feeling in his interior, as if he had recently swallowed a heaping tablespoonful of butterflies, Oily recognized, in the tall, slim figure that entered, his fellow-traveller from the station. And noting that his eyes, so genial in the cab, were now hard and his lips, once smiling, tight and set, he quailed visibly. He remembered a palmist at Coney Island once telling him, in return for fifty cents, that a strange man would cross his path and that of this strange man he would do well to beware, but not even the thought that it looked as if he were going to get value for his half dollar was enough to cheer him.

If Lord Ickenham's eyes were hard and his lips set, it was because that was how he saw the role he had undertaken. There were gaps in his knowledge of his godson's literary work, but he had read enough of it to know that when Inspector Jervis found himself in the presence of the criminal classes, he did not beam at them. The eyes hard, the lips set, the voice crisp and official—that was how he envisaged Inspector Jervis.

'Sir Raymond Bastable?' he said. 'Good evening, Sir Raymond, I am from the Yard.'

And looked every inch of it, he was feeling complacently. He was a man who in his time had played many parts, and he took a pride in playing them right. It was his modest boast that there was nothing in existence, except possibly a circus dwarf, owing to his height, or Gina Lollobrigida, owing to her individual shape, which he could not at any moment and without rehearsal depict with complete success. In a single afternoon at The Cedars, Mafeking Road, in the suburb of Mitching Hill, on the occasion when he had befriended the pink chap to whom he had alluded in his talk with Albert Peasemarch, he had portrayed not only an official from the bird shop, come to clip the claws of the resident parrot, but Mr Roddis, owner of The Cedars, and a Mr J. G. Bulstrode, one of the neighbours, and had been disappointed that he was given no opportunity of impersonating the parrot, which he was convinced he would have done on broad, artistic lines.

Oily continued to quail. Not so good, he was saying to himself, not so good. He had never been fond of inspectors, and the time when their society made the smallest appeal to him was when they popped up just as he was concluding an important deal. He did not like the way this one was looking at him and, when he spoke, he liked what he said even less.

'Turn out your pockets,' said Lord Ickenham curtly.

'Eh?'

'And don't say "Eh?" I have been watching this man closely,' said Lord Ickenham, turning to Sir Raymond, whose eyes were bulging like a snail's, 'since I saw him on the station platform in London. His furtive behaviour excited my suspicions. "Picking pockets right and left, that chap," I said to myself. "Helping himself to wallets and what not from all and sundry."'

Oily started, and a hot flush suffused his forehead. His professional pride was piqued. In no section of the community are class distinctions more rigid than among those who make a dishonest living by crime. The burglar looks down on the stick-up man, the stick-up man on the humbler practitioner who steals milk cans. Accuse a high-up confidence artist of petty larceny, and you bring out all the snob in him.

'And when I shared a cab with him to Hammer Hall and discovered on alighting that I was short a cigarette case, a tie pin, a packet of throat pastilles and a fountain pen, I knew that my suspicions had been well founded. Come on, my man, what are we waiting for?'

Oily was still gasping.

'Are you saying I picked pockets? You're crazy. I wouldn't know how.'

'Nonsense. It's perfectly simple. You just dip. It's no use pleading inability. If Peter Piper,' said Lord Ickenham, who on these occasions was always a little inclined to let his tongue run away with him, 'could pick a peck of pickled peppers, I see no reason why you should not be capable of picking a peck of pickled pockets. Has the fellow been left alone in here?' he asked Sir Raymond, who blinked and said he had not.

'Ah? Then he will have had no opportunity of trousering any of your little knick-knacks, even if he still had room for them. But let us see what he has got. It should be worth more than a casual glance.'

'Yes,' said Sir Raymond, at last abreast. He was always rather a slow thinker when not engaged in his profession. 'Turn out your pockets, my man.'

Oily wavered, uncertain what to do for the best. If he had been calmer, it might have struck him that this was a most peculiar inspector, in speech and manner quite unlike the inspectors with whom his professional activities had brought him into contact in his native country, and his suspicions, too, might have been excited. But he was greatly agitated and feeling far from his usual calm self. And perhaps, he was thinking, all English inspectors were like this. He had never met one socially. His acquaintance with Scotland Yard was a purely literary one, the fruit of his reading of the whodunits to which he was greatly addicted.

It was possibly the fact that Sir Raymond was between him and the window that decided him. The Beefy Bastable who had recently celebrated his fifty-second birthday was no longer the lissom athlete of thirty years ago, but he was still an exceedingly tough-looking customer, not lightly to be engaged in physical combat by one who specialized in the persuasive word rather than violence. Drinking in his impressive bulk, Oily reached a decision. Slowly, with a sad sigh as he thought how different it all would have been if his Gertie had been there with her vase of gladioli, he emptied his pockets.

Lord Ickenham appeared surprised at the meagreness of their contents.

'He seems to have cached the swag somewhere, no doubt in a secret spot marked with a cross,' he said. 'But, hullo! What's this? A letter addressed to you, Sir Raymond.'

'You don't say?'

'Written, I should deduce from a superficial glance, by a man with a small black moustache.'

'Well, well.'

'Just what I was going to say myself.'

'Most extraordinary!'

'Very. Will you press a charge against this man for swiping it?'

'I think not.'

'You don't want to see him in a dungeon with dripping walls, getting gnawed to the bone by rats? You string along with the Bard of Avon about the quality of mercy not being strained? Very well. It's up to you, of course. All right, Mr Carlisle, you may go.'

It was at this moment, when everything appeared, as Oily would have put it, to have been cleaned up neatly and to everybody's satisfaction, that the door opened again and Mrs Phoebe Wisdom pottered in, looking so like a white rabbit that the first impulse of any lover of animals would have been to offer her a lettuce.

'Raymond, dear,' she said, 'have you seen my pig?'

For the past half-hour Sir Raymond Bastable had been under a considerable strain, and though relief at the success of his half-brother-in-law's intervention had lessened this, he was still feeling its effects. This sudden introduction of the pig motif seemed to take him into a nightmare world where nothing made sense, and for a moment everything went blank. Swaying a little on his base, he said in a low whisper:

'Your pig?'

'The little gold pig from my charm bracelet. It has dropped off, and I can't find it anywhere. Well, Frederick, how nice to see you after all this time. Peasemarch told me you were here. When did you arrive?'

'I came on the 3.26 train. I'm staying with my godson, Johnny Pearce, at the Hall. You don't look too well, Phoebe. What's the trouble? Not enough yeast?'

'It's this book of Cossie's, Frederick. I can't imagine how he came to write such a book. A bishop denouncing it!'

'Bishops will be bishops.'

'I went up to London yesterday to see him and tell him how upset I was, but he wasn't there.'

'Somewhere else, perhaps?' Lord Ickenham suggested.

Oily had been listening to these exchanges with growing bewilderment. From the first he had thought this Inspector an odd Inspector, but only now was it borne in on him how very odd he was.

'Say, who *is* this guy?' he demanded.

'Hasn't my brother introduced you?' said Phoebe. 'He is my half-sister's husband, Lord Ickenham. *You* haven't seen my pig, have you, Frederick?'

'Phoebe,' said Sir Raymond, 'get out!'

'What, dear?'

'Get out!'

'But I was going to look for my pig.'

'Never mind your pig. Get OUT!' bellowed Sir Raymond in the voice that had so often brought plaster down from the ceiling of the Old Bailey and caused nervous court officials to swallow their chewing gum.

Phoebe withdrew, sobbing softly and looking like a white rabbit that has had bad news from home, and Oily confronted Lord Ickenham. His face was stern, but there was a song in his heart, as there always is in the hearts of men who see defeat turn into victory.

'So!' he said.

'So what?' said Lord Ickenham.

'I'm afraid you're in a lot of trouble.'

'I am? Why is that?'

'For impersonating an officer. Impersonating an officer is a very serious offence.'

'But, my dear fellow, when did I ever impersonate an officer? Wouldn't dream of doing such a thing.'

'The butler announced you as Inspector Jervis.'

'What the butler said is not evidence. Am I to be blamed because a butler tries to be funny? That was just a little private joke we have together.'

'You said you were from the Yard.'

'I referred to the yard outside the kitchen door. I was smoking a cigarette there.'

'You made me turn out my pockets.'

'*Made* you? I *asked* you to, and you very civilly did.'

'Give me that letter.'

'But it is addressed to Sir Raymond Bastable. It belongs to him.'

'Yes,' boomed Sir Raymond, intervening in the debate, 'it belongs to me, and when you talk of serious offences, you foul excrescence, let me remind you that interfering with the mails is one of them. Give me that letter, Frederick.'

Lord Ickenham, who had been edging to the door, paused with his fingers on the handle.

'No, Beefy,' he said. 'Not yet. You must earn this letter.'

'What!'

'I can speak freely before Mr Carlisle, for I could see from the way he winced that your manner toward your sister Phoebe just now distressed him deeply. I, too, have long been wounded by your manner toward your sister Phoebe, Beefy, considering it to resemble far too closely that of one of the less attractive fauna in the Book of Revelations. Correct this attitude. Turn on that brotherly charm. Coo to her like a cushat dove. Take her up to London for dinner and a theatre from time to time, and when addressing her bear in mind that the voice with the smile wins and that you are not an Oriental potentate dissatisfied with the efficiency of an Ethiopian slave. If I learn from Albert Peasemarch, who will be watching you closely, that there has been a marked and substantial improvement, you shall have this letter. Meanwhile, I am going to keep it and hold it over you like the sword of . . . who was the chap? . . . no, it's gone. Forget my own name next,' said Lord Ickenham, annoyed, and went out, shutting the door behind him.

A moment later, it opened again, and his head appeared.

'Damocles,' he said. 'Sword of Damocles.'

The door closed.

# 11

On a sunny morning precisely two weeks after Lord Ickenham had adjusted the sword of Damocles over the head of Sir Raymond Bastable, completely spoiling the latter's day and causing him to entertain toward the sweetness-and-light specialist thoughts of a kind that no one ought to have entertained toward a brother-in-law, even a half one, the door of Brixton prison in the suburbs of London was opened by a uniformed gentleman with a large key, and a young man in a form-fitting navy blue suit emerged. Cosmo Wisdom, his debt to Society paid, was in circulation once more. He was thinner and paler than when last seen, and the first act of the beauty-loving authorities had been to remove his moustache. This, however, was not so great a boon to pedestrians and traffic as it might seem, for he was resolved, now that he was in a position to do so, to grow it again.

The Law of Great Britain is a smoothly functioning automatic machine, providing prison sentences to suit all tastes. You put your crime in the slot, and out comes the appropriate penalty—seven years, as it might be, for embezzling trust funds, six months for carving up a business competitor with a razor, and for being drunk and disorderly and while in that condition assaulting the police fourteen days without the option of a fine. Cosmo had drawn the last of these.

When Oily Carlisle in a moment of unwonted generosity had lent Cosmo twenty pounds, the latter, it may be remembered, receiving these pennies from heaven, had expressed his intention of celebrating. He had done so only too heartily. The thought of the good red gold which would soon be gushing like a geyser from the coffers of his Uncle Raymond had given wings to his feet as he started on his way along the primrose path. There was a sound of revelry by night and, one thing leading to another, in what seemed almost no time at all he was kicking Police Constable Styles of the C division, whose manner when he was trying to steal his helmet had offended him, rather severely in the stomach. Whistles blew, colleagues of the injured officer rallied to the spot, and presently stern-faced men were leading Cosmo off to the local hoosegow with gyves upon his wrists.

It was not a case, in the opinion of the magistrate at Bosher Street police court next morning, which could be met by the mere imposition of a fine. Only the jug, the whole jug and nothing but the jug would show the piefaced young son of a what-not where he got off, he said, though he phrased it a little differently, and he seemed chagrined at not being able to dish out more than those fourteen days. The impression he gave was that if he had been a free agent with no book of the rules to hamper him, Cosmo would have been lucky to escape what is known to the Chinese as the Death Of A Thousand Cuts. You could see that he was thinking that they manage these things better in China, and P.C. Styles, whose stomach was still paining him, thought the same.

The first act of your ex-convict on coming out into the great world after graduating from the Alma Mater is to buy a packet of cigarettes, his second to purchase a morning paper, his third to go and get the substantial lunch of which he has been dreaming ever since he clocked in. During the past two weeks Cosmo, rubbing along on the wholesome but rather meagre prison fare, had given a good deal of thought to the square meal he would have on getting out, and after considering the claims of Barribault's, Mario's, Claridge's, and the Savoy, had decided to give his custom to Simpson's in the Strand, being well aware that at no establishment in London are the meals squarer. As he hastened thither, with the picture rising before him of those white-coated carvers wheeling around their massive joints, his mouth watered and a fanatic gleam came into his eyes, as if he had been a python which has just heard the dinner bell. It was one of those warm summer days when most people find their thoughts turning to cold salmon and cucumber salad, but what he wanted was roast beef, smoking hot, with Yorkshire pudding and floury potatoes on the side, followed by something along the lines of roly-poly pudding and Stilton cheese.

The paper he had bought was the *Daily Gazette*, and he glanced at it in the intervals of shovelling nourishing food into himself like a stevedore loading a grain ship. *Cocktail Time*, he noted with a touch of disapproval, had been dislodged from the front page by a big feature story about a twelve-year-old school-boy who had shaved all his hair off in order to look like Yul Brynner, but it came into its own on page four with a large black headline which read:

FRANK, FORTHRIGHT, FEARLESS
BEGINNING FRIDAY

and beneath this the announcement that *Cocktail Time* was about to appear in the *Daily Gazette* as a serial. 'The sensational novel by Richard Blunt,' said the announcement, adding that this was the pseudonym of Cosmo Wisdom, a prominent young man about town who is, of course, the nephew of the well-known Queen's Counsel, Sir Raymond Bastable.

The roast beef, roly-poly pudding and Stilton cheese had done much to bring Cosmo into a cheerful frame of mind, and the manner in which this manifesto was worded completed the good work. For obviously, if in the eyes of the *Daily Gazette* he was still the author of *Cocktail Time*, it could only mean that his Uncle Raymond, reading that letter, had prudently decided to play for safety and pay the price of secrecy and silence. No doubt, Cosmo felt, there was a communication to that effect waiting at his rooms in Budge Street, Chelsea, and his only regret was that the pangs of hunger had made it impossible for him to go there and read it before making up leeway at Simpson's.

So far, so good. But after he had been gloating happily for some little time over the picture of Uncle Raymond at his desk, pen in hand and writing golden figures in his cheque book, the sunshine was suddenly blotted from his life. It had just occurred to him to speculate on the possible activities of his friend Gordon Carlisle during his enforced absence, and this train of thought was a chilling one. Suppose his friend Gordon Carlisle—shown by his every action to be a man who thought on his feet and did it now—had taken that letter in person to Uncle Raymond, disclosed its contents, got cash down for it and was already on his way back to America, his pockets full of Uncle Raymond's gold. It was fortunate for Cosmo that he had already consumed his roly-poly pudding, for, had he not, it would have turned to ashes in his mouth.

But in envisaging Gordon Carlisle leaning on the rail of an ocean liner, watching porpoises and totting up his ill-gotten gains, he had allowed imagination to mislead him. Oily was not on his way to America. He was at this moment in the process of rising from a table on the opposite side of Chez Simpson, where he had been lunching with his wife Gertie. And though, like Cosmo, he had lunched well, his heart was heavy. There, said those who saw him to each other, went a luncher who had failed to find the blue bird.

Cosmo's inexplicable disappearance had tried Gordon Carlisle sorely. It was holding up everything. Scarcely five minutes after leaving Hammer Lodge his astute brain had grasped what must be done to stabilize the situation, but the scheme he had in mind could not be put into operation without the assistance of Cosmo, and Cosmo had vanished. Every day for the past two weeks Oily had called at Budge Street, hoping for news, and every day he had been sent empty away by a landlady who made no secret of the fact that she was sick of the sight of him. He was in much the same position as a General who, with his strategic plans all polished and ready to be carried out, finds that his army has gone off somewhere, leaving no address.

It is not to be wondered at, therefore, that when, as he made for the door, he heard a voice utter his name and, turning, found himself gazing into the face of the man he had sought so long, his heart leaped up as if he had beheld a rainbow in the sky. Rather more so, in fact, for, unlike the poet Wordsworth, he had never cared much for rainbows.

'Carlisle!' cried Cosmo exuberantly. He was blaming himself for having wronged this man in thought, and remorse lent to his voice something of the warmth which a shepherd exhibits when he sees a lost sheep reporting for duty. 'Sit down, my dear old chap, sit down!'

His dear old chap sat down, but he did so in a reserved and distant manner that showed how deeply he was stirred. Wrath had taken the place of joy in Oily's bosom. Thinking of the strain to which he had been subjected in the last fourteen days, he could not readily forgive. The eye which he fixed on Cosmo was the eye of a man who intends to demand an explanation.

'Mrs Carlisle,' he said curtly, indicating his companion. 'This is the Wisdom guy, sweetie.'

'It is, is it?' said Gertie. Her teeth made a little clicking sound, and as she looked at Cosmo, she, too, seemed to bring a chill into the summer day.

The austerity of their demeanour passed unnoticed by Cosmo. His cordiality and effervescence continued undiminished.

'So here you are!' he said. 'Well?'

Oily had to remember that he was a gentleman before he could trust himself to speak. Words which he had learned in early boyhood were jostling each other in his mind. He turned to his wife.

'He says "Well?"'

'I heard him,' said Gertie grimly.

'"Well?" He sits there and says "Well?" Can you beat it?'

'He's got his nerve,' Gertie agreed. 'He's certainly there with the crust, all right. Listen, you. Where the heck have you been all this time?'

It was an embarrassing question. One likes to have one's little secrets.

'Oh—er—away,' said Cosmo evasively.

The words had the worst effect on his companions. Already cold and austere, they became colder and austerer, and so marked was their displeasure that he was at last forced to realize that he was not among friends.

There was a bottle on the table, and a quick shiver ran down his spine as he observed Mrs Carlisle's hand stray absently in its direction. Knowing what a magnetic attraction bottles had for this woman, when cross, he decided that the moment had come to be frank, forthright and fearless.

'As a matter of fact, I've been in prison.'

'What!'

'Yes. I went on a toot and kicked a policeman, and they gave me fourteen days without the option. I got out this morning.'

A magical change came over the Carlisles, Mr and Mrs. An instant before stern and hostile, they looked at him now with the sympathetic eyes of a Mr and Mrs who understood all. The claims of prison are paramount.

'Oh, so that was it!' said Oily. 'I see. I couldn't think what had become of you, but if you were in the cooler . . .'

'How are they over here?' asked Gertie.

'Eh?'

'The coolers.'

'Oh, the coolers. Not too good.'

'Much the same as back home, I guess. Prison's all right for a visit, I always say, but I wouldn't live there if you gave me the place. Well, too bad they pulled you in, but you're here now, so let's not waste any more time. Give him the over-all picture, Oily.'

'Right away, sweetie. Things have gone and got a mite gummed up, Wisdom. You know a guy called Ickenham?'

'Lord Ickenham? Yes. He married my uncle's half-sister. What about him?'

Oily did not believe in breaking things gently.

'He's got that letter.'

Cosmo, as Police Constable Styles had done two weeks previously, made an odd, gurgling sound like water going down a waste pipe.

'My letter?'

'Yay.'

'Old Ickenham has?'

'Yup.'

'But I don't understand.'

'You will.'

Gordon Carlisle's narrative of the happenings at Hammer Lodge was a lengthy one, and long before it had finished Cosmo's jaw had dropped to its fullest extent. He had got the over-all picture, and his spirits were as low as his jaw.

'But what do we do?' he said hoarsely, seeing no ray of light among the clouds.

'Oh, now that I've contacted you, everything's nice and smooth.'

'Nice?'

'Yay.'

'Smooth?'

'Yup.'

'I don't see it,' said Cosmo.

Oily gave a gentlemanly little chuckle.

'Pretty clear, I'd have said. Fairly simple, seems to me. You just write your uncle another letter, saying you've been thinking it over some more and still feel the same way about letting everybody know that it was him and not you that wrote the book, and you're going to spill the beans in the next couple of days or so. Won't that make him play ball? Of course it will.'

The hearty lunch with which his rather bewildered gastric juices were doing their best to cope had dulled Cosmo's wits a good deal, but they remained bright enough to enable him to grasp the beauty of the scheme.

'Why, of course! It doesn't matter that Ickenham has got the letter, does it?'

'Not a bit.'

'This second one of mine will do the trick.'

'Sure.'

'I'll go home and write it now.'

'No hurry. I see you've got the *Gazette* there. You've read about the serial?'

'Yes. I suppose Saxby sold it to them. I had a letter from a literary agent called Saxby, asking if he could handle the book, and I thought it was a good idea. I told him he could.'

'Well, the first thing you do is go see him and get the money.'

'And the second,' said Gertie, 'is slip Oily his cut. Seventy smackers, if you remember. You owed him fifty, and he loaned you another twenty. Making seventy in all.'

'That's right. It all comes back to me.'

'And now,' said Gertie, speaking with a certain metallic note in her voice, 'it's coming back to Oily. He'll call around at your place in an hour or so and collect it.'

# 12

OLD Mr Howard Saxby was seated at his desk in his room at the Edgar Saxby literary agency when Cosmo arrived there. He was knitting a sock. He knitted a good deal, he would tell you if you asked him, to keep himself from smoking, adding that he also smoked a good deal to keep himself from knitting. He was a long, thin old gentleman in his middle seventies with a faraway unseeing look in his eye, not unlike that which a dead halibut on a fishmonger's slab gives the pedestrian as he passes. It was a look which caused many of those who met him to feel like disembodied spirits, so manifest was it that they were making absolutely no impression on his retina. Cosmo, full though he was of roast beef, roly-poly pudding and Stilton cheese, had the momentary illusion as he encountered that blank, vague gaze that he was something diaphanous that had been hurriedly put together with ectoplasm.

'Mr Wisdom,' said the girl who had led him into the presence.

'Ah,' said Howard Saxby, and there was a pause of perhaps three minutes, during which his needles clicked busily. 'Wisdom, did she say?'

'Yes. I wrote *Cocktail Time*.'

'You couldn't have done better,' said Mr Saxby cordially. 'How's your wife, Mr Wisdom?'

Cosmo said he had no wife.

'Surely?'

'I'm a bachelor.'

'Then Wordsworth was wrong. He said you were married to immortal verse. Excuse me a moment,' murmured Mr Saxby, applying himself to the sock again. 'I'm just turning the heel. Do you knit?'

'No.'

'Sleep does. It knits up the ravelled sleave of care.'

In the Demosthenes Club, where he lunched every day, there was considerable speculation as to whether old Saxby was as pronounced an old lunatic as he appeared to be or merely for some whimsical purpose of his own playing a part. The truth probably came midway between these two contending views. As a boy he had always been inclined to let his mind wander—'needs to concentrate', his school reports had said—and on entering the family business he had cultivated this tendency because he found it brought results. It disconcerts a publisher, talking terms with an agent, when the agent stares fixedly at him for some moments and then asks him if he plays the harp. He becomes nervous, says fifteen per cent when he meant to say ten, and forgets to mention subsidiary rights altogether.

On Cosmo the Saxby manner acted as an irritant. Though meek in the presence of his Uncle Raymond, he had his pride, and resented being treated as if he were some negligible form of insect life that had strayed out from the woodwork. He coughed sharply, and Mr Saxby's head came up with a startled jerk. It was evident that he had supposed himself alone.

'Goodness, you made me jump!' he said. 'Who are you?'

'My name, as I have already told you, is Wisdom.'

'How did you get in?' asked Mr Saxby with a show of interest.

'I was shown in.'

'And stayed in. I see, Tennyson was right. Knowledge comes, but Wisdom lingers. Take a chair.'

'I have.'

'Take another,' said Mr Saxby hospitably. 'Is there,' he asked, struck by a sudden thought, 'something I can do for you?'

'I came about that serial.'

Mr Saxby frowned. A subject had been brought up on which he held strong views.

'When I was a young man,' he said severely, 'there were no cereals. We ate good wholesome porridge for breakfast and throve on it. Then along came these Americans with their Cute Crispies and Crunchy Whoopsies and so forth, and what's the result? Dyspepsia is rife. England riddled with it.'

'The serial in the paper.'

'Putting the beastly stuff in paper makes no difference,' said Mr Saxby, and returned to his sock.

Cosmo swallowed once or twice. The intellectual pressure of the conversation was making him feel a little light-headed.

'I came,' he said, speaking slowly and carefully, 'about that serial story of mine in the *Daily Gazette*.'

Mr Saxby gave a little cry of triumph.

'I've turned the heel! I beg your pardon? What did you say?'

'I came . . . about that serial story of mine . . . in the *Daily Gazette*.'

'You want my opinion of it? I would give it gladly, were it not for the fact that I never read serial stories in newspapers. Years ago I promised my mother I wouldn't, and to that promise I have faithfully adhered. Foolishly sentimental, you will say, pointing out that my mother, who has long been in heaven, would never know, but there it is. One has these rules to live by. And now,' said Mr Saxby, putting his sock away in a drawer and rising, 'I fear I must leave you. I have found your conversation very interesting, most interesting, but at this hour I always take a brisk constitutional. It settles my lunch and allows the digestive processes to work smoothly. If more people took brisk constitutionals after meals, there wouldn't be half the deaths there are, if any.'

He left the room, to return a moment later and regard Cosmo with a vague, benevolent eye.

'Do you play leap-frog?' he asked.

Cosmo, speaking rather shortly, said that he did not.

'You should. Neglect no opportunity to play leap-frog. It is the best of all games and will never become professionalized. Well, goodbye, my dear fellow, so glad to have met you. Look in again, and next time bring your wife.'

For some moments after the old gentleman had shuffled out, the dizzy feeling, as of being in some strange nightmare world, which came upon so many people after a *tête-à-tête* with Howard Saxby, had Cosmo strongly in its grip, and he sat motionless, breathing jerkily from between parted lips. Then torpor gave place to indignation. As Roget would have put it in his excellent Thesaurus, he was angry, wroth, irate, ireful, up in arms, flushed with passion and in high dudgeon, and he intended to make his presence felt. He rose, and pressed the bell on Mr Saxby's desk, keeping his thumb on it so forcefully that the girl who answered the summons did so in something of the manner of an athlete completing a four-minute mile, thinking that at last old Mr Saxby must have had the seizure the office force had been anticipating for years.

'I want to see somebody,' said Cosmo.

Wilting beneath his eye, which was blazing like a searchlight, the underling panted a little, and said:

'Yes, sir.' Then, for one likes to know these things, 'Who?'

'Anyone, anyone, anyone, anyone!'

'Yes, sir,' said the underling, and withdrew. She went to the second door down the passage, and knocked. Roget would have described her as upset, disconcerted, thrown off her centre and rattled (*colloq*), and employees of the Edgar Saxby literary agency when thus afflicted always sought out Barbara Crowe, knowing that they could rely on her for sympathy and constructive counsel.

'Come in,' called a musical voice, a voice like a good brand of Burgundy made audible. 'Why, hullo, Marlene, you look agitated. What's the matter?'

'There's a gentleman in old Mr Saxby's room who says he wants to see someone.'

'Can't he see old Mr Saxby?'

'He isn't there, Mrs Crowe.'

'Hell's bells!' said Barbara. She knew old Mr Saxby's habits. 'Left the poor gentleman flat, has he? All right, I'll go and soothe him.'

She spoke confidently, and her confidence was justified, for at the very first sight of her Cosmo's righteous indignation sensibly diminished. A moment before, he would gladly have put the entire personnel of the Edgar Saxby literary agency to the sword, but now he was inclined to make an exception in favour of this member of it. Here, he could see at a glance, was a nice change from the sock-knitting old museum piece whose peculiar methods of conducting a business talk had turned his thoughts in the direction of mayhem.

It is probable that almost anyone, even one of the Jukes family with two heads, would have looked good to Cosmo after old Mr Saxby, but in sealing Barbara Crowe with the stamp of his approval he was perfectly justified. Lord Ickenham, speaking of this woman to Pongo, had used the adjective 'lovely'. While not quite that, she was undeniably attractive. Brown eyes, brown hair, just the right sort of nose and a wide, humorous mouth that smiled readily and was smiling now. Her personality, too, had a distinct appeal of its own. There was about her a kindly briskness which seemed to say 'Yes, yes, you have your troubles, I can see you have, but leave everything to me.' Fierce authors who came into the Saxby offices like lions always went out like lambs after talking with Barbara Crowe.

'Good afternoon,' she said. 'Is there something I can do for you? They tell me you have been in conference with old Mr Saxby. Very rash of you. What made you ask for him?'

'He wrote to me. He said he wanted to handle my novel *Cocktail Time*.'

'*Cocktail Time*? Good heavens! Are you Cosmo Wisdom?'

'Yes.'

'I know your uncle. My name is Mrs Crowe.'

Not moving much in his Uncle Raymond's circle, Cosmo had never seen Barbara Crowe, but he knew all about her from his mother, and looking at her now he was amazed that anyone, having succeeded in becoming engaged to her, could have let her get away. It confirmed the opinion he had always held that his Uncle Raymond, though possibly possessed of a certain rude skill in legal matters, was in every other respect the world's champion fathead.

'How is he?' asked Barbara.

'Uncle Raymond? Well, I don't see very much of him, but somebody who met him two weeks ago said he seemed worried.'

'Worried?'

'A bit on the jumpy side.'

A cloud passed over Barbara's cheerful face. As Lord Ickenham had indicated, she had by no means thrust Sir Raymond Bastable from her thoughts.

'He *will* overwork. He isn't ill?'

'Oh, no. Just . . . nervous,' said Cosmo, finding the *mot juste*.

There was a momentary silence. Then Barbara reminded herself that she was a conscientious literary agent and this young man not merely the nephew of the man whom for all his fatheadedness she still loved but an author, and an author plainly in need of having his hand held.

'But you didn't come here to talk about your uncle, did you? You came to discuss business of some sort. I don't suppose you got far with old Mr Saxby? No, I thought not. Was he knitting?'

Cosmo winced. Her question had touched an exposed nerve.

'Yes,' he said coldly. 'A sock.'

'How was it coming along?'

'I understood him to say that he had turned the heel.'

'Good. Always the testing part. Once past the heel, you're home. But except for learning that the sock was going well, you did not get much satisfaction out of him, I imagine. Not many of our clients do. Old Mr Saxby likes to come here still and potter about, though supposed to have retired at about the time when Gutenberg invented the printing press, but he is not what you would call an active cog in the machine. Our only authors who ever see him now are those who mistakenly ask for Howard Saxby. I suppose you did?'

'Yes. That was the name on the letter I got.'

'It should have been signed H.S., junior. Young Mr Howard Saxby is old Mr Howard Saxby's son. He runs things here, with as much assistance as I am able to give him. He's away today, so I am your only resource. What did you come about?'

'That serial in the *Daily Gazette*.'

'Oh, yes. A cheque for that was sent to you more than a week ago. Didn't you get it?'

'I've—er—been away.'

'Oh, I see. Well, it's waiting for you at your rooms. And we're hoping to have more good news for you at any moment. The movie end.'

It had never occurred to Cosmo that there was a movie end.

'You think the book might sell to the pictures?'

'Our man in Hollywood seems sure it will. He's been sending significant cables almost daily. The last one, which arrived yesterday, said . . . Yes?'

The girl Marlene had entered, bearing a russet envelope. She looked nervously at Cosmo, and sidled out. Barbara Crowe opened the envelope, and uttered an exclamation.

'Well, of all the coincidences!'

'Eh?'

'That you should have been here when this came and just when I was starting to tell you about the movie prospects. It's from our man in Hollywood, and . . . better sit down. Oh, you are sitting down. Well, hold on to your chair. He says he has now had a firm offer for the picture rights of *Cocktail Time* from the Superba-Llewellyn studio. Would it interest you to hear what it is?'

It would, Cosmo intimated, interest him exceedingly.

'A hundred and five thousand dollars,' said Barbara.

# 13

IT was a stunned and dizzy Cosmo Wisdom who some quarter of an hour later tottered from the premises of the Saxby literary agency, hailed a cab and tottered into it. He was feeling very much as his Uncle Raymond had felt on that faraway afternoon at Oxford when he had taken the Welsh forward to his bosom. But whereas Sir Raymond's emotions on that occasion had been of a sombre nature, those of Cosmo, as he drove to Budge Street, Chelsea, can best be described by the adjective ecstatic. It is not easy to drive in a taxi-cab of the 1947 vintage and feel that you are floating on a pink cloud high up in the empyrean, but he did it. And this in spite of the fact that his head was still hurting him quite a good deal.

At the moment when Barbara opened the cable from the man in Hollywood, he had been tilting his chair back, and the convulsive spasm which had resulted when she talked figures had caused him to take a nasty toss, bumping his occipital bone with considerable force on the side of old Mr Saxby's desk. But, placed right end up again with a civil 'Upsy-daisy', he had speedily forgotten physical discomfort in the rapture and what Roget would have called oblectation (*rare*) of listening to her subsequent remarks.

For this offer from the Superba-Llewellyn studio was, it appeared, not an end but a beginning. The man in Hollywood, she assured him, would not rest on his laurels with a complacent 'That's that.' He was, like so many men-in-Hollywood, a live wire who, once started, went from strength to strength. There would now, she said, come the bumping-up process—the mentioning to a rival studio that S-L were offering a hundred and five thousand dollars, the extracting from the rival studio of a bid of a hundred and fifty thousand, the trotting back to the Superba-Llewellyn with this information and . . .

'Well, you get the idea,' said Barbara.

Cosmo did indeed get the idea, and nearly injured his occipital bone again when this woman, a ministering angel if ever he saw one, went on to speak of one of the agency's clients whose latest work the man in Hollywood had just bumped up to three hundred and fifty thousand. True, he was feeling as he drove to Budge Street, he could not count on *Cocktail Time* bringing in quite as much as that, but even two hundred thousand would be well worth having. It is evidence of the heady effect which these chats about Hollywood have on authors that he had now begun to look on Superba-Llewellyn's original offer with a sort of amused contempt. Why this parsimony, he was wondering. Money was made to spend. Had no one ever told the Superba-Llewellyn studio that you can't take it with you?

But in every ointment there is a fly, in every good thing a catch of some sort. Elated though he was, Cosmo could not but remember that he had written a letter—in his own personal handwriting and signed with his own name—specifically disclaiming the authorship of *Cocktail Time*, and that this letter was in the possession of Lord Ickenham. For the moment, that blot on the peerage was withholding its contents from the public, but who could say how long he would continue to do so? Somehow, by some means, he must get the fatal paper into his hands and burn it, thus destroying the only evidence that existed that the book was the work of another.

It was not too difficult to sketch out a tentative plan to this end. From Oily, in the course of his narrative at Simpson's, he had learned that Lord Ickenham was staying at Hammer Hall, where paying guests were taken in. His first move must obviously be to become one of these paying guests. A vital document like that letter would presumably be hidden somewhere in the old buster's room, for where else in a country house could anyone hide anything? Once on the spot, he would sooner or later find an opportunity of searching that room. In the stories which were his favourite reading people were always searching rooms, generally with excellent results.

It was with his spirits high again that he entered No. II Budge Street. In the hall he encountered his landlady, a Mrs Keating, a gloomy woman whom two weeks of daily visits from Oily had rendered gloomier. Oily often had that effect on people.

'Why, hullo!' she said, plainly surprised at this return to the fold. 'Where you been all this time?'

'Away,' said Cosmo, wondering how often he was going to have to answer this question. 'Staying with friends.'

'You didn't take any luggage.'

'They lent me everything.'

'You're looking thinner.'

Cosmo admitted that he had lost a little weight.

'Tuberculosis, I should say,' said Mrs Keating, brightening a little. 'That's what Keating died of. There's a lot of letters in there for you, and there's been a fellow calling asking for you every day these last two weeks. Carmichael or some such name.'

'Carlisle. I've seen him.'

'Seemed to think I've nothing to do but answer the bell. You be wanting dinner tonight?'

'No, I'm going away again. I just looked in to pack.'

'Odd some folks don't seem able to stay put for two minutes on end. It's this modern restless spirit. Gadding about. I've lived here twenty years and never been further than the King's Road, except to Kensal Green, when Keating was laid to his rest. Wasted away to a shadow, he did, and it wasn't two months before we were wearing our blacks. Tuberculosis it was, same as you've got. Where you going this time?'

'Dovetail Hammer in Berkshire. Forward my letters to Hammer Hall.'

'More work,' said Mrs Keating, and went off to the kitchen to attend to whatever it was on the stove that was making the house smell as if a meal were being prepared for a pack of hounds.

Quite a considerable mail awaited Cosmo in his sitting-room. The table was piled with letters. Most of them had been forwarded from Alfred Tomkins, Ltd, and he read them with enjoyment—an author is always glad to hear from the fans—but the one that pleased him most was the one from the Edgar Saxby literary agency containing that cheque. It was one of those fat, substantial cheques, and he enclosed it in an envelope addressed to his bank. After which, feeling that things were making a good start, he went to his bedroom and began packing. He had filled a large suitcase and was standing on the front steps with it, waiting for a taxi, when Oily arrived—without, he was relieved to see, Sweetie, the bottle addict.

The indications of impending departure which met his eye surprised Oily.

'Where are you going?' he asked.

It was a change from being asked where he had been, but Cosmo made his customary answer.

'Away. Thought I'd have a couple of days at Bournemouth.'

'Why Bournemouth?'

'Why not Bournemouth?' said Cosmo rather cleverly, and Oily appeared to see the justice of this.

'Well, I'm glad I caught you,' he said, having expressed the opinion that his young friend might just as well bury himself alive. Oily was the metropolitan type, never at his ease outside big cities. 'What have you done with the letter?'

Cosmo, rehearsing this scene in the privacy of his bedroom, had decided to be nonchalant. It was nonchalantly that he now replied:

'Oh, the letter? I was going to tell you about that. I've changed my mind. I'm not going to write it.'

'What!'

'No. I think I'll let things stay the way they are. Oh, by the way, I owe you some money, don't I? I wrote a cheque. I've got it somewhere. Yes, here you are. Taxi!' cried Cosmo, waving.

Oily was still standing stunned among the ruins of his hopes and dreams.

'But—'

'It's no good saying "But,"' said Cosmo briskly, 'if you really want to know, I like being the author of *Cocktail Time*. I enjoy getting all these letters from admirers of my work—'

'What do you mean, your work?'

'Well, Uncle Raymond's work. It's the same thing. And being the author of *Cocktail Time* improves my social standing. To give you an instance, I found a note in there from Georgina, Lady Witherspoon, inviting me to one of her Sunday afternoon teas. It isn't everybody by any means whom Georgina, Lady Witherspoon, invites to her Sunday afternoon teas. She runs a sort of salon, and you have to be somebody of importance to get in. I don't feel like throwing away all that just to collect a few hundred pounds or whatever it may be from Uncle Raymond.' Less, probably, he almost said, than the absurd chicken-feed the Superba-Llewellyn people were offering. 'So there you are. Well, goodbye, Carlisle, it's been nice knowing you. I must be off,' said Cosmo, and was, leaving Oily staring blankly after him and asking himself if these things could really be. Even a high-up confidence artist has to expect disappointments and setbacks, of course, from time to time, but he never learns to enjoy them. In the manner of Gordon Carlisle as half an hour later he entered the presence of his wife Gertie there still lingered a suggestion of Napoleon returning from Moscow.

Gertie, having listened frowningly to the tale he had to tell, expressed the opinion that Cosmo was a low-down double-crossing little rat, which was of course quite true.

'There's oompus-boompus going on,' she said.

'Oompus-boompus, sweetie?'

'Yay. Social standing, did he say?'

'That's what he said.'

Gertie emitted what in a less attractive woman would have been a snort.

'Social standing, my left eyeball! When he left us, he was going to see his agent, wasn't he? Well, it's as clear what's happened as if he'd drawn a diagram. The agent told him there's been a movie offer.'

'Gosh!'

'Sure. And a big one, must have been.'

'I never thought of that. You're dead right. It would explain everything.'

'And he isn't going to any Bournemouth—who the hell goes to Bournemouth?—he's going to this Dovetail-what-is-it place to try to snitch that letter off the Ickenham character, because if he can get it and destroy it, there's nothing in the world to prove he didn't write the book. So what we do is go to Dovetail-and-what-have-you and snitch it before he does.'

'I get you. If we swing it, we'll be sitting pretty.'

'In the catbird seat. There we'll be, in the middle, with the Wisdom character bidding for it and the Bastable character bidding for it, and the sky the limit. And it oughtn't to be so hard to find out where the Ickenham character is keeping the thing. We'll go through his room with a fine-tooth comb, and if it isn't there, we'll know he's got it on him. Then all there is to it is beaning him with a blackjack and hunting around in his pockets, see what I mean?'

Oily saw what she meant. She could hardly have been more lucid. He drew an emotional breath, and even the most short-sighted could have seen the lovelight in his eyes.

'What a comfort you are to me, sweetie!' he said.

'I try to be,' said Gertie virtuously. 'I think a wife oughter.'

# 14

IT was two days after the vultures had decided to muster at Hammer Hall that a little procession emerged from the front door of Hammer Lodge, the country seat of Sir Raymond Bastable, Q.C. It was headed by Mrs Phoebe Wisdom, who was followed by the local veterinary surgeon, who was followed by Albert Peasemarch. The veterinary surgeon got into his car, spoke a few parting words of encouragement and good cheer, and drove off. He had been in attendance on Mrs Wisdom's cocker spaniel Benjy, who, as cocker spaniels will, had 'picked up something'. Both Phoebe and Albert, having passed the night at the sick bed, were looking in need of rest and repose, but their morale was high, and they gazed at each other tenderly, like two boys of the old brigade who have been standing shoulder to shoulder.

'I don't know how to thank you, Peasemarch,' said Phoebe.

'It was nothing, madam.'

'Mr Spurrell said that if it had not been for you making the poor angel swallow that mustard and water, the worst would have happened.'

It occurred to Albert Peasemarch as a passing thought that the worst could not have been much worse than what had happened when the invalid reacted to the healing draught. It would, he was convinced, remain for ever photographically lined on the tablets of his memory when a yesterday had faded from its page, just as the eruption of the Old Faithful geyser in Yellowstone Park lingers always in the memory of the tourist who sees it.

'I am glad to have given satisfaction, madam,' he said, remembering a good line taught him by Lord Ickenham's Coggs at the time when he was being coached for the high office he held. And, thinking of Lord Ickenham, he felt how right the clear-seeing peer had been in urging him to spare no effort that would lead to a *rapprochement* between this cocker spaniel and himself. Unless he was greatly mistaken there was a new light in Phoebe's eyes as she gazed at him, the sort of light a knight of King Arthur's Round Table might have observed in the eyes of a damsel in distress, as he dusted his hands after dispatching the dragon which had been causing her annoyance. The vigil of the night had brought them very close together. He found his thoughts turning in the direction of what his mentor had called the Ickenham System. Had the moment come for putting this into operation?

He had the drill, he fancied, pretty clear in his mind. How did it go? Ah, yes. Stride up, grab by wrist, waggle about a bit, say 'My mate!' clasp to bosom and shower burning kisses on upturned face. All quite simple, and yet he hesitated. And, as always happens when a man hesitates, the moment passed. Before he could nerve himself to do something constructive, she had begun to speak of warm milk with a little drop of brandy in it. Mr Spurrell, the veterinary surgeon, had recommended this.

'Will you heat some up in a saucepan, Peasemarch?'

Albert Peasemarch sighed. To put the Ickenham System into operation with any hope of success, a man needs something in the nature of a cue, and cannot hope to give of his best if the saucepan motif is introduced into the conversation. Romeo himself would have been discouraged, if early in the balcony scene Juliet had started talking about saucepans.

'Very good, madam,' he said dully.

'And then you ought to lie down and have a good rest.'

'I was about to suggest the same thing to you, madam.'

'Yes, I am feeling tired. But I want to speak to Lord Ickenham first.'

'I see his lordship is fishing on the lake, madam. Could I take a message?'

'No, thank you very much, Peasemarch. It's something I must say to him personally.'

'Very good, madam,' said Albert Peasemarch, and went off to heat saucepans with the heavy heart of a man conscious of having missed the bus. Possibly there were ringing in his ears the words of James Graham, first Marquis of Montrose:

*He either fears his fate too much*
*Or his deserts are small,*
*That dares not put it to the touch,*
*To win or lose at all.*

Or, of course, possibly not.

What knitting was to old Mr Saxby, fishing was to Lord Ickenham. He had not yet caught anything, nor was he expecting to, but sitting in a punt, watching a bobbing float, with the white clouds drifting across the blue sky above him and a gentle breeze from the west playing about his temples, helped him to think, and happenings at Hammer Hall of late had given him much to think about. The recent muster of the vultures had not escaped his notice, and, even had it done so, the fact that his room had been twice ransacked in the past two days would have drawn it to his attention. Rooms do not ransack themselves. There has to be a motivating force behind the process, and if there are vultures on the premises, one knows where to look for suspects.

Except for the nuisance of having to tidy up after these vultures, their arrival had pleased rather than perturbed Lord Ickenham. He was a man who always liked to have plenty happening around him, and he found the incursion of Cosmo Wisdom, closely followed by that of Gordon Carlisle and wife, a pleasant break in what was at the moment a dull visit. Enjoying the company of his fellows, he was finding himself distinctly short of it at Hammer Hall. He could scarcely, after what had occurred, hobnob with Beefy Bastable; Albert Peasemarch was hard to get hold of; and Johnny Pearce, racked with anxiety about his Belinda, had been for the last week a total loss as a companion.

So on the whole, he reflected, it was probably no bad thing to have a vulture or two about the home. They livened things up. What puzzled him about this current consignment was the problem of what had brought them to Hammer Hall and why, being there, they had ransacked his room. They were apparently searching eagerly for that letter of young Cosmo's, but he could imagine no reason for them to consider it of any value. Like Oily, he had seen immediately that Cosmo could quite easily write another, which would have precisely the same effect as the first. Eccentric blighters, these vultures, he told himself.

Another thing that perplexed him was that they seemed to be on such distant terms with one another. There was no mistaking the coolness that existed between Mr and Mrs Carlisle on the one side and Cosmo Wisdom on the other. One expects vultures, when they muster, to be a chummy bunch, always exchanging notes and ideas and working together for the good of the show. But every time Gordon Carlisle's eye rested on Cosmo, it rested with distaste, and if Cosmo passed Gordon Carlisle in the hall, he did so without appearing to see him. Very curious.

He was roused from these meditations by hearing his name called, and perceived Phoebe standing on the shore. Reluctantly, for he would have preferred to be alone, he drew in his line and rowed to land. Disembarking and seeing her at close quarters, he was a good deal shocked by her appearance. It reminded him of that of women he had seen at Le Touquet groping their way out into the morning air after an all-night session at the Casino.

'My dear Phoebe,' he exclaimed, 'you appear to be coming apart at the seams somewhat, if you don't mind me being personal. Not your bonny self at all. What's happened?'

'I was up all night with Benjy, Frederick. The poor darling was terribly ill. He picked up something.'

'Good Lord, I'm sorry to hear that. Is he all right now?'

'Yes, thanks to Peasemarch. He was wonderful. But I came to talk about something else, Frederick.'

'Anything you wish, my dear. Had you any particular topic in mind?' said Lord Ickenham, hoping that she had not come to resume yesterday's conversation about her son Cosmo and how thin he looked and how odd it was that, visiting Dovetail Hammer, he should be staying at the Hall and not with his mother at the Lodge. He could hardly explain that Cosmo was at the Hall because he wanted to be on the spot, to ransack people's rooms.

'It's about Raymond, Frederick.'

'Oh, Beefy?' said Lord Ickenham, relieved.

'I'm dreadfully worried about him.'

'Don't tell me he has picked up something?'

'I think he is going off his head.'

'Oh, come!'

'Well, there is insanity in the family, you know. George Winstanley ended his days in an asylum.'

'I'm not so well up on George as I ought to be. Who was he?'

'He was in the Foreign Office. He married my mother's second cousin Alice.'

'And went off his onion?'

'He had to be certified. He thought he was Stalin's nephew.'

'He wasn't, of course?'

'No, but it made it very awkward for everybody. He was always sending secret official papers over to Russia.'

'I see. Well, I doubt if the pottiness of a second cousin by marriage is hereditary,' said Lord Ickenham consolingly. 'I don't think you need have any anxiety about Beefy. What gives you the idea that he has not got all his marbles?'

'His what?'

'Why do you think he is *non compos*?'

'It's the way he's behaving.'

'Tell me all.'

Phoebe brushed away the tears that came so readily to her eyes.

'Well, you know how . . . what shall I say . . . how *impatient* dear Raymond has always been with me. It was the same when we were children. He has always had such a keen brain, and I don't think very quickly, and this seemed to exasperate him. He would say something, and I would say "What?" and he would start shouting. Morning after morning he used to make me cry at breakfast, and that seemed to exasperate him more. Well, quite suddenly one day about two weeks ago he changed completely. He became so sweet and kind and gentle that it took my breath away. I'm sure Peasemarch noticed it, for he was so often in the room when it happened. I mean, things like asking after my rheumatism and would I like a footstool and how nice I looked in that green dress of mine. He was a different man.'

'All to the good, I should have thought.'

'I thought so, too, at first. But as the days went by I began to get uneasy. I knew how overworked he always is, and I thought he must be going to have a nervous breakdown, if not something worse. Frederick,' her voice sank to a whisper, 'he sends me flowers! Every morning. I find them in my room.'

'Very civil. I see no objection to flowers in moderation.'

'But it's so *unnatural*. It alarmed me. I wrote to Sir Roderick Glossop about him. You know him?'

'The loony doctor? I should say so. What I could tell you about old Roddy Glossop!'

'He is a friend of the family, and I thought he would be able to advise me. But I didn't send the letter.'

'I'm glad you didn't,' said Lord Ickenham. His handsome face was grave. 'It would have been a floater of the worst description. There is nothing odd about this change in Beefy's attitude, my dear girl. I can give you the explanation in a word. Peasemarch.'

'Peasemarch?'

'He is behaving like this to conciliate Albert Peasemarch. An observant man, he noticed Albert Peasemarch's silent disapproval of the way he used to carry on, and realized that unless he speedily mended his ways, he would be a butler short, and nobody wants to lose a butler in these hard post-war days. As the fellow said—Ecclesiastes, was it?—I should have to check with Nannie Bruce—whoso findeth a butler findeth a good thing. I know that I would go to even greater lengths to retain the services of my Coggs.'

Phoebe's eyes were round. She looked like a white rabbit that is not abreast of things.

'You mean Peasemarch would have given notice?'

'Exactly. You wouldn't have seen him for dust.'

'But why?'

'Unable to stand the strain of watching you being put through the wringer each morning. No man likes to see a fourteen-stone Q.C. hammering the stuffing out of the woman he loves.'

'*Loves?*'

'Surely you must be aware by now that Albert Peasemarch worships the very ground you tread on?'

'But . . . but this is extraordinary!'

'I see nothing remarkable in it. When you don't sit up all night with sick cocker spaniels, you're a very attractive woman, my dear Phoebe.'

'But Peasemarch is a *butler*.'

'Ah, I see what you mean. You are thinking that you have never had a butler in love with you before. One gets new experiences. But Albert Peasemarch is only a synthetic butler. He is a man of property who took to buttling simply in order to be near you, to be able to exchange notes on your mutual rheumatism, to have you rub his chest with embrocation when he had influenza. Do you remember,' said Lord Ickenham, giving rein to his always rather vivid imagination, 'a day about two years ago when Beefy was standing you and me lunch at the Savoy Grill, and I nodded to a man at the next table?'

'No.'

Lord Ickenham was not surprised.

'That man,' he said, 'was Albert Peasemarch. He came to me later—he is an old friend of mine—and asked who you were. His manner was feverish, and it wasn't long before he was pouring out his soul to me. It was love, my dear Phoebe, love at first sight. How, he asked, could he get to know you? I offered to introduce him to Beefy, but he seemed to think that that wouldn't work. He said what he had seen of Beefy had not given him the impression of a man who would invite him to the home for long week-ends and generally give him the run of the place. I agreed with him. Beefy, when you introduce someone to him, is far too prone to say "Haryer, haryer," and then drop the party of the second part like a hot coal. We needed some mechanism whereby Albert Peasemarch could be constantly in your society, giving you the tender look and occasionally heaving the soft sigh, and to a man of my intelligence the solution was obvious. Who, I asked myself, is the Johnny who is always on the spot, the man who sticketh closer than a brother? The butler, I answered myself. Albert Peasemarch, I said, still addressing myself, must become Beefy's butler. No sooner—or not much sooner—said than done. A few simple lessons from Coggs and there he was, all ready to move in.'

Phoebe was still fluttering. The way the tip of her nose wiggled showed how greatly the story had affected her. She said she had never heard of such a thing, and Lord Ickenham agreed that the set-up was unusual.

'But romantic, don't you think?' he added. 'The sort of policy great lovers through the ages would have pursued, if they had happened to think of it. Hullo,' he said, breaking off. 'I'm afraid I must be leaving you, Phoebe.'

He had seen the station cab drive up to the front door and discharge Johnny Pearce from its interior.

'My godson has returned,' he explained. 'He went up to London to give his fiancée lunch, and I am anxious to learn how everything came out. The course of true love has not been running very smooth of late, I understand. Something of a rift within the lute, I gather, and you know what happens when rifts get into lutes. By and by they make the music mute and ever widening slowly silence all. I shall be glad to receive a reassuring bulletin.'

# 15

BESIDE Johnny Pearce, as he stood on the gravel drive, there was lying a battered suitcase. It signified, Lord Ickenham presumed, the advent of another paying guest, and he was delighted that business was booming so briskly. What with himself, this new arrival and the three vultures already in residence, Johnny in his capacity of jovial innkeeper was doing well. Though, now that he was in a position to study him closely, he had doubts as to whether 'jovial' was the right adjective. The young man's face, while not actually haggard, was definitely careworn. He looked like an innkeeper with a good deal on his mind, and when he spoke, his voice was toneless.

'Oh, hullo, Uncle Fred. I've just got back.'

'So I see. And you appear on your travels to have picked up some luggage. Whose suitcase is that?'

'It belongs to a bloke I shared the cab with. I dropped him at the Lodge. He wanted to see Bastable. Saxby he said his name was.'

'Saxby? Was he a fellow in the early forties with a jutting chin and a head like the dome of St Paul's, or a flattened-out septuagenarian who looked as if he had at one time been run over by a steam-roller? The latter? Then it must be Saxby senior, the father of the jutting chinner, I've met him at the Demosthenes Club. How did you get on with him?'

'Oh, all right. Odd sort of chap. Why did he ask me if I played the trombone?'

'One has to say something to keep the conversation going. Do you?'

'No.'

'Well, don't let yourself get an inferiority complex about it. Many of our most eminent public men don't play the trombone. Lord Beaverbrook, for one. Yes, that was old Saxby all right. I recognize his peculiar conversational methods. Every time I meet him, he asks me if I have seen Flannery lately. Who on earth Flannery is I have never been able to ascertain. When I reply that I have not, he says "Ah? And how *was* he?" The day old Saxby makes anything remotely resembling sense, they will set the church bells ringing and proclaim a national holiday. I wonder why he was going to see Beefy. Just a social call, I suppose. The question that intrigues one is why is he here at all. Is he staying with you?'

'Yes.'

'Good. Every little bit added to what you've got makes just a little bit more.'

'He may be staying some time. He's a bird-watcher, he tells me.'

'Indeed? I never saw that side of him. Our encounters have always taken place at the Demosthenes, where the birds are few and far between. I believe the committee is very strict about admitting them. Do you watch birds, Johnny?'

'No.'

'Nor I. If I meet one whose looks I like, I give it a nod and a wave of the hand, but I would never dream of prowling about and goggling at our feathered friends in the privacy of their homes. What a curse he must be to them. I can imagine nothing more unpleasant for a chaffinch or a reed-warbler than to get settled down for the evening with a good book and a pipe and then, just as it is saying to itself "This is the life," to look up and see old Saxby peering at it. When you reflect that strong men wilt when they meet that vague, fishy eye of his, you can imagine what its effect must be on a sensitive bird. But pigeon-holing old Saxby for the moment, what happened when you met Bunny? How was she? Gay? Sparkling?'

'Oh, yes.'

'Splendid. I was afraid that, with your relations a bit strained, she might have given you the Farthest North treatment or, as it is sometimes called, the ice-box formula. Cold. Aloof. The long silence and the face turned away to show only the profile. You relieve my mind considerably.'

'I wish someone would relieve mine.'

'Why, what's wrong? You say she was gay and sparkling.'

'Yes, but it wasn't me she was gay and sparkling with.'

Lord Ickenham frowned. His godson seemed to have dropped again into that habit of his of speaking in riddles, and it annoyed him.

'Don't be cryptic, my boy. Start at the beginning, and let your yea be yea and your nay be nay. You gave her lunch?'

'Yes, and she brought along a blighter called Norbury-Smith.'

Lord Ickenham was shocked and astounded.

'To a lovers' tryst? To what should have been a sacred reunion of two fond hearts after long parting? You amaze me. Did she offer any explanation of what she must have known was a social gaffe?'

'She said he had told her he was at school with me, and she was sure I would like to meet him again.'

'Good God! Smiling brightly as she spoke?'

'Yes, she was smiling quite a lot. Norbury-Smith!' said Johnny bitterly. 'A fellow I thought I'd seen the last of ten years ago. He's a stockbroker now, richer than blazes, and looks like a movie star.'

'Good heavens! Did their relations seem to you cordial?'

'She was all over him. They were prattling away like a couple of honeymooners.'

'Leaving you out of it?'

'I might as well have been painted on the back drop.'

Lord Ickenham drew a sharp breath. His face was grave.

'I don't like this, Johnny.'

'I didn't like it myself.'

'It's the Oh-well-if-you-don't-want-me-there-are-plenty-who-do formula, which too often means that the female of the species, having given the matter considered thought, has decided that she is about ready to call it a day. Do you know what I think, Johnny?'

'What?'

'You'd better marry that girl quick.'

'And bring her here with Nannie Bruce floating about the place like poison gas? We don't have to go into all that again, do we? I wouldn't play such a low trick on her.' Johnny paused, and eyed his companion sourly. 'What', he asked, 'are you grinning about?'

Lord Ickenham patted his arm in a godfatherly manner.

'If,' he said, 'you allude to the gentle smile which you see on my face—I doubt if somebody like Flaubert, with his passion for the right word, would call it a grin—I will tell you why I smile gently. I have high hopes that the dark menace of Nannie Bruce will shortly be removed.'

Johnny found himself unable to share this optimistic outlook.

'How can it be removed? I can't raise five hundred pounds.'

'You may not have to. You see that bicycle propped up near the back door,' said Lord Ickenham, pointing. 'Police Constable McMurdo's Arab steed. He's in the kitchen now, getting down to brass tacks with her.'

'It won't do any good.'

'I disagree with you. I anticipate solid results. I must mention that since I got here I have been seeing quite a bit of Officer McMurdo, and he has confided in me as in a sympathetic elder brother. He unloaded a police constable's unspotted heart on me, and I was shocked to learn on what mistaken lines he had been trying to overcome Nannie Bruce's sales-resistance. He had been arguing with her, Johnny, pleading with her, putting his trust in the honeyed word and the voice of reason. As if words, however honeyed, could melt the obstinacy of a woman whose mother, I am convinced, must have been frightened by a deaf adder. Action, Cyril, I told him—his name is Cyril—is what you need, and I urged him with all the vehemence at my disposal to cut the cackle and try the Ickenham System.'

'What's that?'

'It's a little thing I knocked together in my bachelor days. I won't go into the details now, but it has a good many points in common with all-in wrestling and osteopathy. I generally recommend it to diffident wooers, and it always works like magic. Up against it, the proudest beauty—not that that's a very good description of Nannie Bruce—collapses like a dying duck and recognizes the mastery of the dominant male.'

Johnny stared.

'You mean you told McMurdo to . . . *scrag* her?'

'You put it crudely, but yes, something on those lines. And, as I say, I anticipate the best results. At this very moment Nannie Bruce is probably looking up into Officer McMurdo's eyes and meekly murmuring "Yes, Cyril, dear," "Just as you say, Cyril, dear," "How right you are, Cyril, darling," as he imperiously sketches out his plans for hastening on the wedding ceremony. You might go and listen at the kitchen door and see how things are coming along.'

'I might, yes, but what I'm going to do is have a swim in the lake. I'm sweating at every pore.'

'Keep it clean, my boy. No need to stress the purely physical. Well, if you run into McMurdo, tell him I am anxious to receive his report and can be found in the hammock on the back lawn. Is that the evening paper you have there? I might just glance through it.'

'Before going to sleep?'

'The Ickenhams do not sleep. Anything of interest in it?'

'Only that movie thing.'

'To what movie thing do you allude?'

'About this chap Wisdom's book.'

'*Cocktail Time*?'

'Yes. Have you read it?'

'Every word. I thought it was extremely good.'

'It is. It's the sort of thing I should like to write, and I could do it on my head, only the trouble is that, once you start turning out thrillers, they won't take anything else from you. Odd, a fellow like Wisdom being able to do anything as good as that. He doesn't give one the impression of being very bright, do you think?'

'I agree with you. The book seemed to me the product of a much maturer mind. But you were saying something about a movie thing, whatever that is.'

'Oh, yes. Apparently all the studios in Hollywood are bidding frantically for the picture rights. According to the chap who does the movie stuff in that paper, the least Wisdom will get is a hundred and fifty thousand dollars. Oh, well, some people have all the luck,' said Johnny, and went off to take his swim.

The hammock to which Lord Ickenham had alluded was suspended between two trees in a shady nook some distance from the house, and it was in pensive mood that a few minutes later he lowered himself into it. His godson's words had opened up a new line of thought and, as so often happened to Johnny's Inspector Jervis, he saw all. The mystery of why there was this sudden muster of vultures at Hammer Hall had been solved. The motives of these vultures in seeking to secure the letter which was sewn into the lining of the coat he was wearing were crystal clear.

Obviously, with a hundred and fifty thousand dollars coming to the author of *Cocktail Time*, Cosmo Wisdom was not going to look favourably on the idea of writing a second letter to his Uncle Raymond, disclaiming the authorship of the book, and equally obviously he would strain every nerve to secure and destroy the letter he had already written. And the Carlisle duo would naturally strain every nerve to secure it first and start Sir Raymond and nephew bidding against each other for it. No wonder there was that coolness he had noticed between the vulture of the first part and the vultures of the second. With a hundred and fifty thousand dollars at stake, a coolness would have arisen between Damon and Pythias.

It was a mistake on Lord Ickenham's part at this point to close his eyes in order to brood more tensely on the problems this new development had raised, for if you close your eyes in a hammock on a warm summer evening, you are apt to doze off. He had told Johnny that the Ickenhams did not sleep, but there were occasions when they did, and this was one of them. A pleasant drowsiness stole over him. His eyes closed and his breathing took on a gentle whistling note.

It was the abrupt intrusion of a finger between his third and fourth ribs and the sound of a voice that said 'Hey!' that some little while later awakened him. Opening his eyes, he found that Gordon Carlisle was standing on one side of the hammock, his wife Gertie on the other, and he could not fail to notice that in the latter's shapely hand was one of those small but serviceable rubber instruments known as coshes.

She was swinging it negligently, as some dandy of the Regency period might have swung his clouded cane.

# 16

ALTHOUGH there was nothing in the unruffled calm of his manner to show it, Lord Ickenham, as he sat up and prepared to make the party go, was not at his brightest and happiest. He had that self-reproachful feeling of having been remiss which comes to Generals who wake up one morning to discover that they have carelessly allowed themselves to be outflanked. With conditions as they were at Hammer Hall, he should, he told himself, have known better than to loll in hammocks out of sight and earshot of friends and allies. The prudent man, aware that there are vultures in every nook and cranny of the country house he is visiting, watches his step. Failing to watch his, he had placed himself in the sort of position his godson Johnny's Inspector Jervis was always getting into. It was rarely in a Jonathan Pearce novel of suspense that Inspector Jervis did not sooner or later find himself seated on a keg of gunpowder with a lighted fuse attached to it or grappling in a cellar with one of those disagreeable individuals who are generally referred to as Things.

However, though recognizing that this was one of the times that try men's souls, he did his best to ease the strain.

'Well, well, well,' he said heartily, 'so there you are! I must have dropped off for a moment, I think. One is reminded of the experience of the late Abou ben Adhem, who, as you may recall, awoke one night from a deep dream of peace to find an angel at his bedside, writing in a book of gold. Must have given him a nasty start, I have always thought.'

The interest of Oily and his bride in Abou ben Adhem appeared to be slight. Neither showed any disposition to discuss this unusual episode in his life. Mrs Carlisle, in particular, indicated unmistakably that her thoughts were strictly on business.

'Shall I bust him one?' she said.

'Not yet,' said Oily.

'Quite right,' said Lord Ickenham cordially. 'There is, in my opinion, far too much violence in the world today. I deprecate it. Do you read Mickey Spillane?'

This attempt, too, to give the conversation a literary turn proved abortive.

'Gimme,' said Oily. His manner was curt.

'I beg your pardon?'

'You heard. Remember making me turn out my pockets?'

'I don't like the word "making". There was no compulsion.'

'Oh, no? Well, there is now. Let's inspect what you've got in your pockets, Inspector Jervis.'

'Why, of course, my dear fellow, of course,' said Lord Ickenham with a cheerful willingness to oblige which should have lessened the prevailing tension, if not removed it altogether, and in quick succession produced a handkerchief, a cigarette case, a lighter, the notebook in which he jotted down great thoughts when they occurred to him, and a small button which had come off his shirt. Oily regarded the collection with a jaundiced eye, and looked at his wife reproachfully.

'He hasn't got it on him.'

Gertie, with her woman's intuition, was not so easily baffled.

'You poor simp, do you think he'd carry it around in his pocket? It's sewn into his coat or sum'pn.'

This being actually the case, Lord Ickenham was conscious of a passing regret that Gordon Carlisle had not selected a less intelligent mate. Had he led to the altar something more in the nature of a dumb blonde, the situation would have been greatly eased. But he continued to do his best.

'What is it you are looking for?' he asked genially. 'Perhaps I can help you.'

'You know what I'm looking for,' said Oily. 'That letter.'

'Letter? Letter?' Lord Ickenham's face cleared. 'Oh, the *letter*? My dear fellow, why didn't you say so before? You don't suppose I would keep an important document like that on me? It is, of course, lodged at my banker's.'

'Oh, yeah?' said Oily.

'Oh, yeah?' said his wife, and it was abundantly evident that neither had that simple faith which we are assured is so much better than Norman blood. 'Oily!'

'Yes, sweetie?'

'Why *not* let me bust him one?'

It had become borne in on Lord Ickenham more and more that the situation in which his negligence had placed him was one of considerable embarrassment, and he was not finding it easy to think what to do next. Had he been able to rise to his feet, a knowledge of ju-jitsu, acquired in his younger days and, though a little rusty, still efficient, might have served him in good stead, but his chances of being allowed to exhibit this skill were, he realized, slight. Even under the most favourable conditions, a hammock is a difficult thing to get out of with any rapidity, and the conditions here were definitely unfavourable. It was impossible to ignore that cosh. So far, Gordon Carlisle had discouraged his one-tracked-minded wife's wistful yearning to bust him one with it, but were he to give the slightest indication of wishing to leave his little nest, he was convinced that the embargo would be lifted.

Like the youth who slew the Jabberwock, he paused awhile in thought. His problem, he could see, resembled that of his godson Johnny Pearce, in being undoubtedly one that presented certain features of interest, and he was conscious of feeling a little depressed. But it was not long before he was his old debonair self again, his apprehensions removed and the sun smiling through once more. Looking past his two companions, he had seen something that brought the roses back to his cheek and made him feel that, even though he be in a hammock, you cannot keep a good man down.

'I'll tell you—' he began.

Oily, his manner even curter than before, expressed a wish to be handed Lord Ickenham's coat.

'I'll tell you where you of the criminal classes, if you do not mind me so describing you, make your mistake, and a very serious mistake it is, too. You weave your plots and schemes, you spend good money on coshes, you tip-toe with them to people's bedsides, but there is something you omit. You don't allow for the United States Marines.'

'Gimme that coat.'

'Never mind my coat for the moment,' said Lord Ickenham. 'I want to tell you about the United States Marines. I don't know if you are familiar with the procedure where these fine fellows are concerned. To put it in a word, they arrive. The thing generally works out somewhat after this fashion. A bunch of bad men are beleaguering a bunch of good men in a stockade or an embassy or wherever it may be and seem to be getting along splendidly, and then suddenly the bottom drops out of everything and all is darkness, disillusionment and despair. Looking over their shoulders, they see the United States Marines arriving, and I don't suppose there is anything that makes bad men, when beleaguering someone, sicker. The joy goes out of their lives, the sun disappears behind the clouds, and with a muffled "Oh dear, oh dear, oh dear!" they slink away to their underground dens, feeling like thirty cents. The reason I bring this up,' said Lord Ickenham, hurrying his remarks to a conclusion, for he could see that his audience was becoming restive, 'is that, if you glance behind you, you will notice that the United States Marines are arriving now.'

And with a friendly finger he drew their attention to Police Constable McMurdo, who, dressed in the authority of helmet and blue uniform, was plodding across the lawn toward them, the evening sun gleaming on his substantial official boots.

'I speak as a layman,' he said, 'but I believe the correct thing to do at a moment like this is to say "Cheese it, the cops!" and withdraw with all speed. What a fine, big fellow he is, is he not? Ah, Cyril, were you looking for me?'

'Yes, m'lord. Mr Pearce said I should find you here. But if your lordship is occupied—'

'No, it's quite all right,' said Lord Ickenham, sliding from the hammock. 'We had finished our little talk. I am sure Mr and Mrs Carlisle will excuse me. *Au revoir*, Mr Carlisle. Mrs Carlisle, I kiss your hand. At least, I don't, but you know what I mean. I am wholly at your disposal, Cyril.'

Police Constable McMurdo was a large man with an agreeable, if somewhat stolid and unintellectual face, heavily moustached toward the centre. He had a depressed and dejected look, and the cause of his mental distress was not far to seek, for while one of his cheeks was the normal pink of the rural constable, the other had taken on a bright scarlet hue, seeming to suggest that a woman's hand had recently landed on it like a ton of bricks. In his hot youth, Lord Ickenham, peering into the mirror, had sometimes seen his own cheek looking like that, and he needed no verbal report to tell him what must have happened at the late get-together in the kitchen.

'You bring bad news, I fear,' he said sympathetically, as they made their way to the house. 'The Ickenham System didn't work?'

'No, it didn't.'

Lord Ickenham nodded understandingly.

'It doesn't sometimes. One has to budget for the occasional failure. From the evidence submitted to my notice, I take it that she busted you one.'

'Rrrr!' said Officer McMurdo, with feeling. 'I thought my head had come off!'

'I am not surprised. These nannies pack a wicked punch. How did you leave things?'

'She said if I ever acted that way again, she'd never speak to me as long as she lived.'

'I wouldn't worry too much about that. She didn't break off relations?'

'She nearly broke me.'

'But not her troth. Excellent. I thought she wouldn't. Women try to kid us that they don't like ardour, but they do. I'll bet at this very moment she is pacing the kitchen floor, whispering "What a man!" and wishing you would play a return engagement. You wouldn't consider having another pop? Striking while the iron is hot, as it were?'

'I wouldn't, no.'

'Then we must think of some other way of achieving the happy ending. I will devote my best thought to your problem.'

And also, added Lord Ickenham to himself, to the problem of how to find a safe place to put that letter. The recent conference had left him convinced that the sooner such a place was found, the better. A far duller man than he would have been able to divine from the attitude of the Carlisle family that things were hotting up.

Not that he objected. He liked things to hot up.

# 17

OLD Mr Saxby, looking like something stationed in a corn field to discourage crows, stood on the lawn of Hammer Lodge, raking the countryside with his binoculars. At the moment when he re-enters this chronicle they were focused on the island in the middle of the lake.

The explanation of his presence in Dovetail Hammer, which Lord Ickenham had found mystifying, is a simple one. He was there at a woman's behest. Returning to the office after that brisk constitutional of his, he had been properly ticked off by Barbara Crowe for his uncouth behaviour to Cosmo Wisdom and sternly ordered by her to proceed without delay to Hammer Hall and apologize to him.

'No, a letter will *not* do,' said Barbara severely. 'Especially as you would be sure to forget to post it. You must go to him in person and grovel. Lick his shoes. Kiss the hem of his garment. Cosmo Wisdom has to be conciliated and sucked up to. He's a very important person.'

'He's a squirt.'

'A squirt maybe, but he wrote *Cocktail Time*, on its ten per cent of the proceeds of which the dear old agency expects to be able to afford an extra week at the seaside this year. So none of your larks, young Saxby. I shall want to hear on your return that he has taken you to his bosom.'

There was nothing Mr Saxby, whose view of Cosmo's bosom was a dim one, wanted less than to be taken to it, but he always did what Barbara Crowe told him to, even when it involved getting his hair cut, and he had set out obediently for Dovetail Hammer, consoling himself with the thought that a few days in the country, with plenty of birds to watch, would not be unpleasant. Nice, too, being next door to Bastable. He always enjoyed hobnobbing with Bastable.

Sir Raymond, who did not derive the same uplift from their hobnobbings, received him, when he was ushered into his presence by Albert Peasemarch, with a marked sinking sensation. Learning that his old clubmate was not proposing to make Hammer Lodge his headquarters but would be staying at the Hall, he brightened considerably, took him out on to the lawn to see the view and, finding that he had left his pipe behind, went back to fetch it. He now returned, and found the old gentleman, as has been stated, scrutinizing the island on the lake through his binoculars.

'Watching birds?' he asked, with the heartiness of a man assured that he is not going to have to put Howard Saxby senior up for an indefinite stay.

'Not so much birds,' said Mr Saxby, 'as that chap Scriventhorpe.'

'Chap who?'

'Scriventhorpe. Flannery's friend. I've met him with you at the club. I think you told me he was your son or your brother or something.'

Sir Raymond collected his wits, which, as so often happened when he was conversing with Howard Saxby senior, had been momentarily scattered.

'Do you by any chance mean Ickenham?'

'Didn't I say Ickenham?'

'You said Scriventhorpe.'

'Well, I meant Ickenham. Nice fellow. I don't wonder Flannery's fond of him. He's on that island over there.'

'Oh?' said Sir Raymond without enthusiasm. The only news about his half-brother-in-law that would have brought a sparkle to his eyes would have been that he had fallen out of a boat and was going down for the third time.

'He's tacking to and fro,' proceeded Mr Saxby. 'Now he's crouching down. Seems to be looking for something. No, I see what he's doing. He's not looking for something, he's hiding something. He's got a paper of some kind in his hand, and he seems to be burying it.'

'What!'

'Odd,' said Mr Saxby. 'He jumped up just then and hurried off. Must have gone back to his boat. Yes, here he comes. You can see him rowing away.'

Sir Raymond had never expected that any observation of this club-mate of his would thrill him to the core, but that was what this one had done. He felt as if he had been reclining in an electric chair and some practical joker had turned on the juice.

The problem of what his relative by marriage had done with the fatal letter was one which for two weeks and more had never been out of Sir Raymond Bastable's thoughts. He had mused on it while shaving, while bathing, while breakfasting, while lunching, while taking his afternoon's exercise, while dining, while putting on his pyjamas of a night and while dropping off to sleep. The obvious solution, that Lord Ickenham had hidden it in his bedroom, he rejected. With determined bedroom searchers like Cosmo Wisdom and Mr and Mrs Gordon Carlisle on the premises, such a policy would be madness. He would have thought of some really ingenious place of concealment—a hollow tree, perhaps, or a crevice in some wall. That he would bury the document on an island, like a pirate of the Spanish Main disposing of his treasure, had never occurred to Sir Raymond. Yet to anyone familiar with Frederick Ickenham's boyish outlook on life, how perfectly in character it seemed.

Quivering, he grabbed at his companion's arm, and Mr Saxby quivered, too, for the grip of those fevered fingers had affected him like the bite of a horse. He also said 'Ouch!'

Sir Raymond had no time to waste listening to people saying 'Ouch!' He had seen Lord Ickenham bring his boat to shore, step out of it and disappear in the direction of the house, and he was feeling, as did Brutus, that there is a tide in the affairs of men, which, taken at the flood, leads on to fortune.

'Quick!' he cried.

'When you say "Quick!"' began Mr Saxby, but got no further, for he was being hurried to where the boat lay at a pace that made speech difficult for a man who was getting on in years. He could not remember having whizzed along like this, touching the ground only here and there, since the afternoon sixty-three years ago when, a boy of twelve, he had competed at a village sports meeting in the choirboys' hundred-yard race, open to all those whose voices had not broken by the second Sunday in Epiphany.

It was only natural, therefore, that as Sir Raymond bent to the oars, putting his back into it like a galley slave of the old school, silence should have prevailed in the boat. Mr Saxby was trying to recover his breath, and Sir Raymond was thinking.

The problem that confronted him, the one that so often bothers murderers, was what to do with the body—viz: Mr Saxby's. He had brought the old gentleman along because, having witnessed Lord Ickenham's activities, he would be able to indicate the spot where the treasure lay, but now he was asking himself if this had not been a mistake. There are men—the salt of the earth—who, if they see you searching islands on lakes, preserve a tactful silence and do not ask for explanations, but Mr Saxby, he was convinced, was not one of these. He belonged rather to the more numerous class who want to know what it is all about, and Sir Raymond had no desire for a co-worker of this description. Explanations would be foreign to his policy. By the time they reached their destination he had arrived at the conclusion that the less Mr Saxby saw of what was going on, the better.

'You stay in the boat,' he said, and Mr Saxby thought it a good idea. He was still in the process of trying to recover his breath, and was well content to be spared further exercise for the moment. His stamina was not what it had been in his choirboy days.

'Woof!' he said, meaning that he fully concurred, and Sir Raymond set out into the interior alone.

Alone, that is to say, except for the swan which was at the moment taking it easy in the undergrowth beside the bijou residence where its mate was nesting. It was unexpectedly meeting this swan that had caused Lord Ickenham to revise his intention of burying the letter on the island and take to his boat with all possible speed. The Ickenhams were brave, but they knew when and when not to be among those present.

For some minutes after his companion's departure Mr Saxby, whose breathing apparatus had now returned to normal, gave himself up to thought. But though nothing could be fraught with greater interest than a detailed list of the things he thought about, it is better perhaps to omit such a list and pass on to the moment when he felt restored enough to take up his binoculars again. It was as he scanned the mainland through these that he observed Cosmo Wisdom smoking a cigarette on the gravel outside the front door of the Hall, and the sight reminded him that he was a man with a mission. Long ere this, he felt guiltily, he should have been seeking the young squirt out and kissing the hem of his garment, in accordance with Barbara Crowe's directions.

Though what there was to kiss hems of garments about, he was thinking, as, having completely forgotten Sir Raymond Bastable's existence, he started to row ashore, was more than he could tell you. Young squirt barges in on a fellow while he is knitting his sock and needs every ounce of concentration for the successful turning of the heel. Fellow receives him with the utmost cordiality and civility, though most men, interrupted at such a moment, would have bitten his head off, and they chat pleasantly for a while of this and that. Finally, having threshed out all the matters under discussion, fellow bids squirt a courteous farewell, and goes for his brisk constitutional. Nothing wrong with that, surely? But Barbara Crowe seemed to think there was, and women had to be humoured. As he rowed, he was throwing together in his mind a few graceful expressions of apology which he thought would meet the case.

These, a few minutes later, he delivered with an old-world charm. Their reception was what a dramatic critic would have called adequate. Cosmo did not take him to his bosom, but, the wound to his dignity apparently more or less healed, he offered him a cigarette, and they smoked in reasonable amity for a time, while Mr Saxby, always informative on his favourite subject, spoke at considerable length of birds he had watched. It was mid-way through a description of the peculiar behaviour of a sand martin he had once known in Norfolk—impossible to insert here owing to considerations of space—that he broke off suddenly and said:

'Bless my soul!'

'Now what?' said Cosmo rather sharply. He was finding Mr Saxby on sand martins a little trying.

'Exactly,' said Mr Saxby. 'What? You may well ask. There was something Barbara Crowe told me to tell you, and I've forgotten what it was. Now what could it have been? You don't happen to know, do you?'

At the name Barbara Crowe Cosmo had given a start. For the first time since their conversation had begun he was feeling that this Edwardian relic might be on the verge of saying something worth listening to.

'Was it about the movie end?' he said eagerly.

'The what?'

'Has there been another offer for the film rights of my book?'

Mr Saxby shook his head.

'No, it was nothing like that. Have you written a book?'

'I wrote *Cocktail Time*.'

'Never heard of it,' said Mr Saxby cordially. 'I'll tell you what I'll do. I'll go in and telephone her. She is sure to remember what it was. She has a memory like a steel trap.'

When he returned, he had a slip of paper in his hand, and was beaming.

'You were perfectly right,' he said. 'It *was* connected with what you call the movie end. I wrote it down, so that I should not forget it again. She said . . . Do you know Mrs Crowe?'

'I've met her.'

'Charming woman, though she bullies me unmercifully. Makes me get my hair cut. You don't know what the trouble was between her and your uncle, do you?'

'No.'

'They were engaged.'

'Yes.'

'She broke it off.'

'Yes.'

'Well, who can blame her? I wouldn't want to marry young Bastable myself.'

Cosmo spurned the gravel with an impatient foot.

'What did she *say*?'

'Ah, that we shall never know. What *do* women say on these occasions? Take back your ring and letters, do you think, or something of that sort?'

'About the movie end.'

'Oh, the movie end? Yes, as I told you, I have her very words here.' He peered at the paper. 'She said "Have you apologized?" and I said "Yes, I had apologized," and she said "Did he take you to his bosom?" and I said, "No, the young squirt did not take me to his bosom, but he gave me a cigarette," and she said "Well, tell him that Medulla-Oblongata-Glutz have offered a hundred and fifty thousand, and our man in Hollywood has gone back to Superba-Llewellyn to bump them up." Does that convey anything to you?'

Cosmo inhaled deeply.

'Yes,' he said. 'It does.'

And suddenly Mr Saxby, for all his fishy eye and flattened-out-by-a-steam-roller appearance, looked almost beautiful to him.

Sir Raymond Bastable, meanwhile, questing hither and thither like a Thurber bloodhound, had begun to regret that he had not availed himself of his shipmate's co-operation. Having no means of knowing whereabouts on this infernal island Mr Saxby had seen Lord Ickenham tacking to and fro and crouching down, he was in the position of one who hunts for pirate gold without the assistance of the yellowing map which says 'E. by N.20,' '16 paces S.' and all that sort of thing, and anyone who has ever hunted for pirate gold will tell you what a handicap this is. The yellowing map is of the essence.

The island was rather densely wooded—or perhaps under-growthed would be a better term—and was rich in spiky shrubs which caught at his ankles and insects which appeared to look on the back of his neck as the ideal rallying ground. 'Let's all go round to the back of Bastable's neck' seemed to be the cry in the insect world. He had become very hot and thirsty, and there was a hissing sound in his ears which he did not like. It suggested to him that his blood pressure was getting out of control. He was always a little nervous about his blood pressure.

It was as he straightened himself after his thirty-second attempt to find one of those spots, so common in fiction, where you can see, if you look closely, that the earth here has been recently disturbed, that he found he had wronged his blood pressure. This hissing sound had proceeded not from it but from the lips of a fine swan which had emerged from a bush behind him and was regarding him with unmistakable menace. There are moments when, meeting a swan, we say to ourselves that we have found a friend. This was not one of them. The chances of any fusion of soul between the bird and himself were, he could see at a glance, of the slightest.

It is always important at times like this to understand the other fellow's point of view, and the swan could certainly have made out a case for itself. With the little woman nesting in the vicinity and wanting to be alone with her eggs, it is not to be wondered at that it found intruders unwelcome. Already it had had to take a strong line with Lord Ickenham, and now, just as it was thinking that the evil had been stamped out, along came another human pest. It was enough to try the patience of any swan, and one feels that the verdict of history will be that in making hissing noises, staring bleakly, spreading its wings to their fullest extent and scrabbling the feet to indicate the impending frontal attack this one was perfectly justified. Swans, as every ornithologist knows, can be pushed only so far.

Sir Raymond, like Lord Ickenham, was not a pusillanimous man. If burglars had broken into Hammer Lodge, he would have sprung to the task of hitting them over the head with his niblick, and he had frequently looked traffic policemen in the eye and made them wilt. But the stoutest-hearted may well quail before an angry swan. It is possible that Sir Raymond, as he now started to withdraw, thought that he was doing so at a dignified walk, but actually he was running like a choirboy intent on winning the hundred yards dash. His one idea was to return as speedily as possible to the boat in which Mr Saxby was awaiting him.

Reaching the waterfront with something of the emotions of Xenophon's Ten Thousand when they won through to the sea, he was disconcerted to find that Mr Saxby was not awaiting him. Nor was there any boat. He saw what the poet Tennyson has described as the shining levels of the lake, but could detect nothing that would enable him to navigate them. And the hissing sound which he had wrongly attributed to his blood pressure was coming nearer all the time. The swan was not one of those swans that abandon a battle half fought. When it set its hand to the plough, it did not readily sheathe the sword. Casting a hasty glance behind him, Sir Raymond could see it arriving like a United States Marine.

It was a time for quick thinking, and he thought quickly. A split second later he was in the water, swimming strongly for the shore.

At the moment when he was making this dash for life, his sister Phoebe was up in her bedroom, trying her hair a new way.

It has so often been the chronicler's melancholy task to introduce this woman into his narrative in a state of agitation and tears that he finds it pleasant now to be able to show her gay and happy. Not even Sherlock Holmes, seeing her as she stood at her mirror, would have been able to deduce that she had been up all night with a sick cocker spaniel. Her eye was bright, her manner bumps-a-daisy. She was humming a light air.

Nor is this to be wondered at. Lord Ickenham's sensational revelation of the fire that burned in the bosom of Albert Peasemarch would alone have been enough to lift her to the heights, and on top of that had come his comforting assurance that her brother Raymond was not, as she had supposed, a candidate for the ministrations of Sir Roderick Glossop. Nothing, except possibly the discovery that the ground on which she treads is worshipped by a butler for whom she has long entertained feelings deeper and warmer than those of ordinary friendship, can raise a woman's spirits more than the knowledge that the brother who is the apple of her eye is, in spite of appearances, in full possession of his marbles. One can understand Phoebe Wisdom humming light airs. A weaker woman would have sung.

The mirror was in the window that looked over the lake and, glancing past it as she turned to examine the new hair-do in profile, she found her eye attracted to something singular that was going on in the water. A seal was there, swimming strongly for the shore, and this surprised her, for she had not supposed that there would be seals in an inland lake.

Nor were there. As she watched the creature emerge at journey's end, she saw that she had formed a wrong impression of its species. It was, as Mr Saxby would have said, not so much a seal as her brother Raymond. He was dressed, as always in the country, in a sports coat, grey flannel trousers and a coloured shirt.

She stared, aghast. Her old fears had swept back over her. Do men who have got all their marbles go swimming in lakes with their clothes on? Very seldom, Phoebe felt, and feared the worst.

# 18

At the hour of eight forty-five that night Lord Ickenham might have been observed—and was observed by Rupert Morrison, the landlord, licensed to sell ales, wines and spirits, who was polishing glasses behind the counter—sitting in the saloon bar of the village inn, the Beetle and Wedge, with a tankard of home-brew, watching television. Except for an occasional lecture by the vicar on his holiday in the Holy Land, illustrated with lantern slides, there was not a great deal of night life in Dovetail Hammer. The Beetle and Wedge's television set afforded the local pleasure-seekers about their only means of hitting the high spots after sundown.

The statement that Lord Ickenham was watching television is perhaps one calculated to mislead. His eyes, it is true, were directed at the screen, but what was going on there, apparently in a heavy snowstorm, made no impression on his mind. His thoughts were elsewhere. He was reviewing the current crisis in his affairs and turning stones and exploring avenues with a view to deciding how to act for the best.

Although it was his boast that the Ickenhams were not easily baffled, he could not conceal it from himself that the dislocation of his plans by the recent swan had left him in no slight quandary. With a bird as quick on the draw as that doing sentry-go there, burying the letter on the island in the lake was obviously not within the sphere of practical politics, and with two Carlisles and a Cosmo Wisdom prowling and prowling around in the manner popularized by the troops of Midian, any alternative place for its bestowal would have to be a very safe one. It is proof of the knottiness of the problem with which he was wrestling that in a moment of weakness he actually considered doing what he had tried to persuade the sceptical Carlisles that he had done and depositing the document with his bank.

A good deal shocked that he should even for an instant have contemplated a policy so tame and unworthy of an Ickenham, he turned his attention to the television screen. It might, he felt, enable him to come back to the thing with a fresh mind if he gave that mind a temporary rest.

They were doing one of those spy pictures tonight, a repeat performance, and he was interested to observe that by an odd coincidence the hero of it was in precisely the same dilemma as himself. Circumstances had placed this hero—D'Arcy Standish of the Foreign Office—in possession of papers which, if they fell into the hands of an unfriendly power, would make a third world war inevitable, and he was at the moment absolutely dashed if he could think how to hide them from the international spies who were surging around him, all right on their toes and up-and-coming. It was with a sympathetic eye that Lord Ickenham watched D'Arcy running about in circles and behaving generally like a cat on hot bricks. He knew just how the poor chap felt.

And then suddenly he started, violently, as if he had seen a swan entering the saloon bar, and sat up with a jerk, the home-brew trembling in his grasp.

'Egad!' he said.

'M'lord?' said Rupert Morrison.

'Nothing, my dear fellow,' said Lord Ickenham. 'Just Egad.'

As the saloon bar was open for saying Egad in at that hour, Mr Morrison made no further comment. He jerked a thumb at the screen.

'See what he's done?' he said, alluding to D'Arcy Standish. 'He wants to keep those papers safe from all those spies, so he's given 'em to his butler to take care of.'

Lord Ickenham said Yes, he had noticed.

'I call that clever.'

'Very clever.'

'Never occurs to 'em that the butler could have 'em,' proceeded Mr Morrison, who had seen the drama the previous week, 'so they keep after the fellow same as before. Thinking *he's* got 'em. See? But he hasn't. See?'

Lord Ickenham said he saw.

'They burgle his house and trap him in a ruined mill and chase him through the sewers,' Mr Morrison continued, giving the whole plot away, 'and all the time he hasn't got the papers, the butler's got 'em. Made me laugh, that did.'

'I'm not surprised. Have you a telephone here? I wonder if I might use it for a moment,' said Lord Ickenham.

Some minutes later, a fruity voice caressed his ear. Albert Peasemarch's mentor, Coggs, had advised making the telephone-answering voice as fruity as possible in the tradition of the great butlers of the past.

'Sir Raymond Bastable's residence. Sir Raymond's butler speaking.'

'*Not* the Albert Peasemarch there has been so much talk about?'

'Oh, good evening, Mr I. Do you wish to speak to Sir Raymond?'

'No, Bert, I wish to speak to you. I'm at the pub. Can you come here without delay?'

'Certainly, Mr I.'

'Fly like a youthful hart or roe over the hills where spices grow,' said Lord Ickenham, and presently the Beetle and Wedge's picturesque saloon bar was made additionally glamorous by the presence of Albert Peasemarch and his bowler hat. ('Always wear a bowler, chum. It's expected of you'—Coggs.)

'Bert,' said Lord Ickenham, when Rupert Morrison had supplied the ales he was licensed to sell and had withdrawn once more into the background, 'I hated to have to disturb your after-dinner sleep, but I need you in my business. You are probably familiar with the expression "Now is the time for all good men to come to the aid of the party." Well, this is where you do it. Let me start the conversational ball rolling by asking you a question. Do you take an active interest in world politics?'

Albert Peasemarch considered this.

'Not very active, Mr I. What with cleaning the silver and brushing the dog—'

'I know, I know. Your time is so full. Let me put it another way. You realize that there are such things as world politics and that a certain section of the community has the job of looking after them?'

'Oh, yes, Mr I. Diplomats they call them.'

'Diplomats is right. Well—can we be overheard?'

'Not unless someone's listening.'

'I'll whisper.'

'I'm a little deaf in the right ear.'

'Then I'll whisper into your left ear. Well, as I was about to say, the thing to bear in mind is that these diplomats can't get anywhere without papers. No, no,' said Lord Ickenham, as his old friend mentioned that he always read the *Daily Mirror* at breakfast, 'I don't mean that sort of paper, I mean documents. A diplomat without documents is licked from the start. He might just as well turn it up and go back to his crossword puzzle. And you know what I mean when I say documents.'

'Secret documents?'

'Exactly. You follow me like a bloodhound. A diplomat must have secret documents, and he gives these secret documents to trusted underlings to take care of, warning them on no account to let any international spies get their hooks on them. "Watch out for those international spies!" is the cry in what are called the chancelleries.'

This seemed reasonable to Albert Peasemarch.

'You mean if these spies got them, they would start creating?'

'Precisely. Throwing their weight about like nobody's business and making a third world war inevitable.'

'Coo! That would never do, would it?'

'I can imagine nothing more disagreeable. Remember those chilly nights in the Home Guard? I haven't been really warm since. You wouldn't want to go through all that again, would you?'

'I certainly wouldn't.'

'Nor I. Not even for the sake of hearing you sing Drake's Drum round the camp fire. Another beer, Bert?'

'Thank you, Mr I. Though I really shouldn't. I have to watch my figure.'

'If the document now in my possession falls into the hands of the gang that are after it, you won't have any figure to watch. It'll be distributed in little pieces over the countryside.'

To this Albert Peasemarch was prevented from replying immediately by the arrival of Mr Morrison, bringing up supplies. When the cupbearer had retired and he was able to speak, he did so in the awed voice of a man who is wondering if he can believe his ears.

'What was that, Mr I? Did you say *you* had a document in your possession?'

'You bet I have, Bert. And it's a pippin.'

'But how—?'

'—did it come into my possession? Very simply. I'm not sure if I ever mentioned to you, when we were comrades of the Home Guard, that I was in the Secret Service. Did I?'

'Not that I can recall, Mr I.'

'Probably slipped my mind. Well, I am, and not long ago the head man sent for me. "Number X 3476," he said—the boys call me Number X 3476—"you see this document. Top secret, if ever there was one. Guard it day and night," he said, "and don't let those bounders get a smell of it." He was referring, of course, to the international spies.'

Albert Peasemarch drank beer like a man in a trance, if men in trances do drink beer.

'Cor lumme, stone the crows!' he said.

'You may well say "Cor lumme, stone the crows!" In fact, if anything, "Cor lumme, stone the crows" rather understates it.'

Albert Peasemarch drank some more beer, like another man in another trance. His voice, when he spoke, showed how deeply he was intrigued. Like so many of those with whom Lord Ickenham conversed, he was finding new horizons opening before him.

'These spies, Mr I. Are there many of them?'

'More than you could shake a stick at. Professor Moriarty, Doctor Fu Manchu and The Ace of Spades, to name but three. And every one of them the sort of chap who would drop cobras down your chimney or lace your beer with little-known Asiatic poisons as soon as look at you. And the worst of it is that they have got on to it that this document is in my possession, and it is only a question of time before they start chivvying me through the sewers.'

'You won't like that.'

'Exactly the feeling I had. And so, Bert,' said Lord Ickenham, getting down to the *res*, 'I have decided that the only thing to do is to pass the document on to you and let you take care of it.'

Albert Peasemarch was aware of a curious gulping sound. It reminded him of something. Then he knew what it reminded him of, the preliminary gurglings of the dog Benjy before reacting to that dose of mustard and water. It was only after listening to this odd sound for a moment or two that he realized that it was he who was making it.

'You see the devilish cleverness of the idea, Bert. The blighters will be non-plussed. When they chivvy me through the sewers, they'll just be chasing rainbows.'

'But, Mr I!'

A look compounded of astonishment and incredulity came into Lord Ickenham's face. It was as though he had been a father disappointed in a loved son or an uncle in a loved nephew.

'Bert! Your manner is strange. Don't tell me you are faltering? Don't tell me you are jibbing at taking on this simple assignment? No, no,' said Lord Ickenham, his face clearing. 'I know you better than that. We old Home Guarders don't draw back when we are asked to serve the country we love, do we? This is for England's sake, Bert, and I need scarcely tell you that England expects that every man will do his duty.'

Albert Peasemarch, having gulped again, more like the dog Benjy than ever, raised a point of order.

'But I don't want to be chased through sewers, Mr I.'

'You won't be. I'll attend to the sewer sequence. How on earth are they to know that you have got the thing?'

'You don't think they'll find out?'

'Not a chance. They aren't clairvoyant.'

That a struggle was going on in Albert Peasemarch's soul was plainly to be seen by anyone watching his moonlike face. Lord Ickenham could detect it with the naked eye, and he waited anxiously for the referee's decision. It came after a long pause in four words, spoken in a low, husky voice, similar in its intonation to a voice from the tomb.

'Very well, Mr I.'

'You'll do it? Splendid. Capital. Excellent. I knew you wouldn't fail me. Well, it's no good me giving you the thing now, for the very walls have eyes, so I'll tell you how we'll work it. Where's your bedroom?'

'It's off my pantry.'

'On the ground floor. Couldn't be better. I'll be outside your window at midnight on the dot. I will imitate the cry of the white owl—the white owl, remember, not the brown—and the moment you hear me hooting, you slip out and the document changes hands. It will be in a plain manilla envelope, carefully sealed. Guard it with your life, Bert.'

Albert Peasemarch's manner betrayed a momentary uneasiness.

'How do you mean, my life?'

'Just an expression. Well, that cleans it up, I think, does it not? All you have to do is sit tight and say nothing. And now I ought to be leaving you. We must not be seen together. Hark!' said Lord Ickenham. 'Did you hear a low whistle? No? Then all is well. I thought for a moment those fellows might be lurking outside.'

Albert Peasemarch's uneasiness increased.

'You mean they're *here*, Mr I? Around these parts?'

'In dozens, my dear fellow, in positive droves. Dovetail Hammer has international spies the way other beauty spots have green fly and wasps. Still, it all adds to the spice of the thing, does it not?' said Lord Ickenham, and went out, leaving Albert Peasemarch staring with haggard eyes at the bottom of his empty tankard, a prey to the liveliest emotion.

Pongo Twistleton, had he been present, would have understood this emotion. He, too, had often experienced that stunned feeling, as if the solid earth beneath his feet had disintegrated, which was so apt to come to those who associated with the fifth Earl of Ickenham, when that fine old man was going good. And Pongo, in Albert Peasemarch's place, would have pursued precisely the same policy which now suggested itself to the latter.

'Another of the same, please, Mr M,' he said, and Rupert Morrison once more became the human St Bernard dog.

The results were instantaneous—indeed, magical would scarcely be too strong a word. Until now, the chronicler has merely hinted at the dynamic properties of the Beetle and Wedge home-brew. The time has come to pay it the marked tribute it deserves. It touched the spot. It had everything. It ran like fire through Albert Peasemarch's veins and made a new man of him. The careworn, timorous Albert Peasemarch ceased to be, and in his place there sat an Albert Peasemarch filled to the brim with the spirit of adventure. A man of regular habits, he would normally have shrunk from playing a stellar role in an E. Phillips Oppenheim story, as he appeared to be doing now, but with the home-brew lapping up against his back teeth he liked it. 'Bring on your ruddy spies!' about summed up his attitude.

He had had his tankard refilled for the fourth time and was telling himself militantly that any spies who attempted to get fresh with him would do so at their own risk, when the door of the saloon bar opened and Johnny Pearce and Cosmo Wisdom came in.

It was obvious at a glance that neither was in festive mood. Johnny was thinking hard thoughts about his old school-fellow, Norbury-Smith, whose attitude toward Belinda Farringdon at lunch had seemed to him far too closely modelled on that of a licentious clubman of the old silent films, and Cosmo was brooding on the letter, asking himself how it could be detached from Lord Ickenham's keeping and unable at the moment to see any means of achieving the happy ending. It was with a distrait listlessness that they put in their order for home-brew.

Rupert Morrison delivered the elixir, and looked regretfully at the television set, which was now deep in one of those parlour games designed for the feeble-minded trade. D'Arcy Standish had gone off the air ten minutes ago.

'You've missed the picture, Mr Pearce,' he said.

'Picture? What picture?'

'The spy picture that was on the TV just now. It's where this Foreign Office gentleman has these important papers,' began Mr Morrison, falling easily into his stride, 'and these spies are after them, so he gives them to his butler . . .'

'I saw it last week,' said Johnny. 'It was lousy. Absolute drivel,' he said, leaving no doubt as to how he felt about it. So much of his work had been turned down for television that he had become a stern critic of that medium.

'I do so agree with you, sir,' said Mr Morrison. Actually he had thoroughly enjoyed the picture and would gladly have sat through it a third time, but an innkeeper has to suppress his private feelings and remember that the customer is always right. 'Silly, I thought it. As if any gentleman would give an important paper to a butler to take care of. It just couldn't happen.'

'Oh, couldn't it?' said Albert Peasemarch, rising—a little unsteadily—and regarding the speaker with a glazed but compelling eye.

It is only a man of exceptional self-restraint who is able to keep himself from putting people right when they begin talking ignorantly on subjects on which he happens to be well-informed, especially if he has just had four goes of the Beetle and Wedge home-brew. Knowing that these three were not international spies—in whose presence he would naturally have been more reticent—Albert Peasemarch had no compunction in intervening in the debate and speaking freely.

'Oh, couldn't it?' he said. 'Shows what a fat lot you know about it, Mr M. It may interest you to learn that a most important paper or document has been entrusted to me this very night by a gentleman who shall be nameless, with instructions to guard it with my life. And I'm a butler, aren't I? You should think before you speak, Mr M. I will now,' said Albert Peasemarch, with the air of a kindly uncle unbending at a children's party, 'sing Drake's Drum.'

And having done so, he slapped his bowler hat on his head and took his departure, walking with care, as if along a chalk line.

# 19

THE sun was high in the sky next day when Cosmo, approaching it by a circuitous route, for he had no desire to run into his Uncle Raymond, arrived at the back door of Hammer Lodge and walked in without going through the formality of ringing the bell. He was all eagerness for a word with Albert Peasemarch on a subject very near his heart.

It was the opinion of his late employer, J. P. Boots of Boots and Brewer, export and import merchants, an opinion he had often voiced fearlessly, that Cosmo Wisdom was about as much use to a business organization as a cold in the head, and in holding this view he was substantially correct. But a man may be a total loss at exporting and importing, and still have considerable native shrewdness. Though a broken reed in the eyes of J. P. Boots, Cosmo was quite capable of drawing conclusions and putting two and two together, and on the previous night he had done so. Where Johnny Pearce and Rupert Morrison, listening to Albert Peasemarch, had classified his observations as those of a butler who has had one over the eight, Cosmo had read between the lines of that powerful speech of his. He had divined its inner significance. The nameless gentleman was Lord Ickenham and the paper or document the fatal letter. It stuck out, he considered, a mile. As he hurried to Hammer Lodge, he did not actually say 'Yoicks!' and 'Tally ho!' but that was what he was thinking.

He found Albert Peasemarch in his pantry having his elevenses, two hard-boiled eggs and a bottle of beer. Butlers always like to keep their strength up with a little something in the middle of the morning, and at the moment of Cosmo's entry Albert Peasemarch was finding his in need of all the keeping up it could get. The one defect of the Beetle and Wedge's home-brew is that its stimulus, so powerful over a given period, does not last. Time marches on, and the swashbuckling feeling it induces wears off. Albert Peasemarch, who on the previous night had gone out of the saloon bar like a lion, had come into his pantry this morning like a lamb, and a none too courageous lamb, at that. It is putting it crudely to say that he had cold feet, but the expression unquestionably covers the facts. He was all of a twitter and inclined to start at sudden noises. His reaction to the sudden noise of Cosmo's 'Good morning', spoken in his immediate rear, was to choke on a hard-boiled egg with a wordless cry and soar from his seat in the direction of the ceiling.

His relief on finding that it was not Professor Moriarty or The Ace of Spades who had spoken was extreme.

'Oh, it's you, Mr C,' he gasped, as his heart, which had crashed against his front teeth, returned slowly to its base.

'Just thought I'd look in for a chat,' said Cosmo. 'Do go on with your egg. Don't mind me.'

It was the beer rather than the egg that appealed to Albert Peasemarch at the moment. He quaffed deeply, and Cosmo proceeded.

'You certainly pulled old Morrison's leg last night with that yarn of yours about the secret document,' he said, chuckling amusedly. 'He believed every word of it. Can you beat it? Never suspected for a moment that you were just kidding him,' said Cosmo, and broke into a jolly laugh. Very droll, he seemed to suggest, it had been, the whole thing.

There was a pause, and during that pause, though it lasted but an instant, Albert Peasemarch decided to tell all. He was in the overwrought state of mind that makes a man yearn for a confidant with whom he can share the burden that has been placed upon him, and surely Mr I would agree that it was perfectly all right letting Cosmo Wisdom, the child of his half-sister by marriage, in on the ground floor. If Cosmo had still had his little black moustache, he might have hesitated, but, as we have seen, the aesthetic authorities of Brixton prison had lost no time in shaving it off. Gazing into his now unblemished face, Albert Peasemarch could see no possible objection to cleansing his bosom of the perilous stuff which was weighing on his heart. If you cannot confide in the son of the woman you love, in whom can you confide?

'But I wasn't, Mr C.'

'Eh?'

'I wasn't kidding him.'

Cosmo's hand flew to the barren spot where his moustache had been. At times when he was dumbfounded he always twirled it. That he was dumbfounded now was plainly to be seen. He stared incredulously at Albert Peasemarch.

'Now you're pulling *my* leg.'

'No, really, Mr C.'

'You don't mean it's true?'

'Every word of it.'

'Well, I'm blowed!'

'It was like this, Mr C. His lordship sent for me—'

'His lordship?'

'Lord Ickenham, sir.'

'You don't mean he's mixed up in this?'

'It's his document I'm taking care of, the one that was entrusted to him by the head of the Secret Service, of which he is a member.'

'Old Ickenham's in the Secret Service?'

'He is, indeed.'

Cosmo nodded.

'By Jove, yes, so he is. I remember him telling me. One forgets these things. Let's have the whole story from start to finish.'

When Albert Peasemarch had concluded his narrative, Cosmo went through the motion of twirling his lost moustache again.

'I see,' he said slowly. 'So that's how it is. He's left you holding the baby.'

'Yes, sir.'

'It looks to me as if you were in a bit of a spot.'

Albert Peasemarch assented. That, he said, was how it looked to him, too.

'I don't suppose these international spies stick at much.'

'No, sir.'

'If they get on to it that you've got that document, the mildest thing they'll do is shove lighted matches between your toes.' Cosmo mused for a space. 'Look here,' he said, struck with a happy thought. 'Why don't you give it to *me*?'

Albert Peasemarch stared.

'You, sir?'

'It's the only way,' said Cosmo, becoming more and more enthusiastic about the idea. 'Put yourself in the place of these spies. They'll soon find out old Ickenham hasn't got this document, and then they'll start asking themselves what he's done with it, and it won't take them long to realize that he must have handed it on to someone. Then what'll they say? They'll say "To who?"'

'Whom,' murmured Albert Peasemarch mechanically. He was rather a purist. He shuddered a little, for those last words had reminded him of Lord Ickenham imitating the cry of the white owl.

'And they'll pretty soon answer that. They know you and he are friends.'

'Old comrades. Home Guard.'

'Exactly. It'll be obvious to them that he must have given the thing to you.'

Again Albert Peasemarch was reluctantly reminded of his old comrade giving his owl impersonation. He spoke with an increase of animation, for the scheme was beginning to appeal to him.

'I see what you mean, Mr C. They'd never suspect that you had it.'

'Of course they wouldn't. I hardly know old Ickenham. Is it likely he'd give important documents to a fellow who's practically a stranger? Whatever this paper is, it will be as safe with me as if it were in the Bank of England.'

'It's certainly an idea, Mr C.'

'Where is the thing?'

'In my bedroom, sir.'

'The first place spies would look. Go and get it.'

Albert Peasemarch went and got it. But though Cosmo extended a hand invitingly, he did not immediately place the envelope in it. His air was that of a man who lets 'I dare not' wait upon 'I would', as so often happens with cats in adages.

'There's just one thing, Mr C. I must have his lordship's permission.'

'What!'

'Can't make a move like this without consulting his lordship. But it won't take a jiffy to step over to the Hall and get his okay. Five minutes at the outside,' said Albert Peasemarch, reaching for his bowler hat.

It sometimes happens at the Beetle and Wedge that a customer, demanding home-brew and licking his lips at the prospect of getting it, is informed by the voice of doom, speaking in the person of Rupert Morrison, that he has already had enough and cannot be served. On such occasions the customer has the feeling that the great globe itself has faded, leaving not a wrack behind, and that, as in the case of bad men interrupted in their activities by the United States Marines, all is darkness, disillusionment and despair. Such a feeling came to Cosmo Wisdom now. This unforeseen check, just as he had been congratulating himself on having fought the good fight and won it, induced a sudden giddiness and swimming of the head, so that his very vision was affected and he seemed to see two Albert Peasemarches with two round faces reaching for a brace of bowler hats.

Was there, he asked himself desperately, no way out, no means of persuading this man to skip the red tape?

There was. Beside the remains of the two hard-boiled eggs, which in that sudden spasm of spiritual anguish had seemed to him for an instant four hard-boiled eggs, there stood a pepper pot. To snatch this up and project its contents into Albert Peasemarch's face was with Cosmo the work of a moment. Then, leaving the suffering man to his sneezing, he shot out into the great open spaces, where he could be alone, in his pocket the only proof that existed that he was not the author of *Cocktail Time*, for the motion picture rights of which the Superba-Llewellyn studio would, he hoped, shortly be bumped up to an offer of two hundred thousand dollars.

But in assuming that in the great open spaces he would be alone, he was mistaken. Scarcely had he reached them, when a voice that might have been that of an ancient sheep spoke at his elbow.

'Well met by moonlight, proud Wisdom,' it bleated, and spinning on his axis he perceived old Mr Saxby.

'Oh, hullo,' he said, when able to articulate. 'Nice morning, isn't it? The sun and all that. Well, goodbye.'

'Let us not utter that sad word,' said Mr Saxby. 'Are you on your way to the Hall? I will walk with you.'

It was a pity that Cosmo had never taken any great interest in birds, for he was afforded now an admirable opportunity of adding to his information concerning their manners and habits. In considerable detail Mr Saxby spoke of hedge sparrows he had goggled at in their homes and meadow pipits he had surprised while bathing, and, had Cosmo been an ornithologist, he would have found the old gentleman's conversation absorbing. But, like so many of us, he could take meadow pipits or leave them alone, and it was with something of the feeling he had had when released from Brixton prison that at long last he saw the human porous plaster potter off on some business of his own.

It was in the hall of Johnny Pearce's ancestral home that this happened, and at the moment of Mr Saxby's departure he was standing beside one of the comfortable, if shabby, armchairs which were dotted about in it. Into this he now sank. The nervous strain to which he had been subjected, intensified by the society of the late bird *aficionado*, had left him dazed. So much so that it was several minutes before he realized that he ought not to be just sitting here like this, he should be acting. The letter was still in his pocket, undestroyed. He took it out, and removed its manilla wrapping. First and foremost on the agenda paper was the putting of it to the flames—not the tearing of it up and depositing it in the wastepaper basket, for a torn-up letter can be pieced together.

There was a table beside the chair, on it an ashtray and matches. He reached for these, and was in the very act of striking one, when he became aware of a wave of some exotic scent that seemed to proceed from behind him, the sort of scent affected by those mysterious veiled women who are always stealing Naval Treaties from Government officials in Whitehall. Turning sharply, he perceived Mrs Gordon Carlisle, and with considerable emotion noted that she was holding, and in the act of raising, one of those small but serviceable rubber instruments known as coshes. At her side, on his face the contented look of one who feels that his affairs are in excellent hands, stood her husband.

It was almost immediately after this that the roof fell in, and Cosmo knew no more. J. P. Boots, in his sardonic way, would have said that he had not known much even before that.

# 20

'NICE work, sweetie,' said Mr Carlisle, viewing the remains with satisfaction. 'Just behind the ear, that's the spot.'

'Never known it to fail,' said Gertie.

'He isn't dead, is he?'

'Oh, I shouldn't think so.'

'Just as well, maybe. Gimme the letter. And,' added Oily urgently, 'gimme that blackjack.'

'Eh?'

'Someone's coming. We've got to ditch them quick.'

'Slip 'em in your pocket.'

'And have them frisk me and find them there? Talk sense.'

'Yay, I see what you mean.' Gertie's eyes flickered about the hall. 'Look. Dump 'em in that thing over there.'

She alluded to the imitation walnut cabinet, the legacy of Johnny Pearce's Great-Uncle Walter, which had always so jarred on Lord Ickenham, and Oily approved of the suggestion. He darted across the hall, opened and slammed one of the drawers, dusted his hands and returned, just as Johnny appeared.

Johnny was on his way to get a breath of fresh air after a chat with

Nannie Bruce about the new cook, concerning whose short-comings, more marked in her opinion even than those of the one who had held office two weeks previously, she had unburdened her mind in a speech containing at least three extracts from Ecclesiastes. He was in a sombre mood, having had his fill of Nannie Bruce, Ecclesiastes and paying guests, and the sight of one of these last apparently asleep in a chair would have left him uninterested, had not Cosmo at this moment slumped to the floor. A man who takes in paying guests can ignore them when they are vertical. When they become horizontal, he has to ask questions.

'What's all this?' he said, an observation which should more properly have been left to Police Constable McMurdo, who was down the passage, talking to Nannie. He had been hanging about outside the door of Johnny's study for some twenty minutes in the hope of finding an opportunity of pleading with her.

Gertie was swift to supply the desired information.

'Seems to me the guy's had some kind of a fit.'

Oily said that that was the way it looked to him, too.

'My husband and I was passing through on our way to our room, when he suddenly keeled over. With a groan.'

'More a gurgle, sweetie.'

'Well, with whatever it was. Could have been a death rattle, of course.'

Johnny frowned darkly. Life these days, he was thinking, was just one damn thing after another. First Nannie with her cooks and Ecclesiastes, then Norbury-Smith, from whom no good woman was safe, and now this groaning, gurgling or possibly death-rattling paying guest. Had even Job, whose troubles have received such wide publicity, ever had anything on this scale to cope with?

He raised his voice in a passionate bellow.

'Nannie!'

Nannie Bruce appeared, followed by Officer McMurdo, whose air was that of a police constable who has not been making much headway.

'Nannie, phone for Doctor Welsh. Tell him to come over right away. Mr Wisdom's had a fit or something. And for heaven's sake don't start yammering about what your biblical friend would have thought of the situation. Get a move on!'

Officer McMurdo looked at him with a wistful admiration. That was telling her, he felt. That was the way to talk to the other sex. Nannie Bruce, who did not hold this view, bridled.

'There is no necessity to shout at me, Master Jonathan, *nor* to make a mock of the holy scriptures. And I disagree with you when you say that Mr Wisdom has had a fit. Look at the way he's lying, with his legs straight out. My Uncle Charlie suffered from fits, and he used to curl up in a ball.' She went to where Cosmo lay, scrutinized him closely and ran an expert finger over his head. 'This man,' she said, 'has been struck with a blunt instrument!'

'What!'

'There's a lump behind his ear as big as a walnut. It's a matter for the police, such,' said Nannie Bruce, eyeing Officer McMurdo coldly, 'as they are. Still, when you say telephone for Doctor Welsh, that's sense. I'll go and do it at once.'

She departed on her errand with the dignity of a woman who does not intend to be ordered about but is willing to oblige, and long before she had disappeared Police Constable McMurdo's notebook was out and his pencil licked and poised.

'Ho!' he said. 'This throws a different light on the matter. I will now proceed to look into it. The great thing here is to ascertain who's responsible for this.'

'Ecclesiastes,' said Johnny bitterly, and Constable McMurdo's pencil leaped like a live thing. As far as was within the power of a man with a face like his, he was looking keen and alert. He eyed Johnny sharply.

'Have you evidence to support that charge, Mr Pearce?'

'No. It was just a suggestion.'

'I should like the address of the suspect Ecclesiastes.'

'I'm afraid I can't help you there.'

'Is he a juvenile delinquent?'

'More elderly than that, I should say.'

The constable pondered.

'I'm beginning to think you're right, sir. As I piece together the jig-saw puzzle, what happened was this. The gentleman was sitting here, dozing as the expression is, and the front door opens and in walks Ecclesiastes.

To hit him on the napper with a blunt instrument, him being asleep, would be an easy task.'

Oily intervened in his suavest manner.

'I scarcely see how your theory can be correct, officer. My wife has told you that as we were passing through the hall, we saw Mr Wisdom—'

'Keel over,' said Gertie.

'Exactly. With a gurgle.'

'Or groan.'

'With a groan or gurgle.'

'Like as if somep'n had gone wrong with the works.'

'Precisely. You remember her mentioning it to you.'

'Not to me she didn't mention it.'

'Ah, no, it was to Mr Pearce before you came in. We both received the impression that he had had a fit.'

'Then why isn't he curled up in a ball?'

'There you take me into deep waters, constable.'

'And how do you account for the lump behind his ear, as big as a walnut?'

'That surely is very simply explained. He struck his head against the side of the chair as he was—'

'Keeling over,' said Gertie.

'As he was keeling over. It is far more probable—'

What was far more probable he did not get around to mentioning, for at this moment Cosmo Wisdom stirred, groaned (or gurgled), and sat up. He looked about him with what the poet has called a wild surmise, and said:

'Where am I?'

'Hammer Hall, Dovetail Hammer, Berks, sir,' Officer McMurdo informed him, and would have added the telephone number, if he had remembered it. 'If you'll just lie nice and quiet and relax, the doctor will be here in a moment. You've had some kind of fit or seizure, sir. This gentleman, Mr—'

'Carlisle.'

'This gentleman, Mr Carlisle, was passing through the hall, accompanied by Mrs Carlisle—'

The mention of that name brought memory flooding back to Cosmo. The past ceased to be wrapped in mist. He rose, clutched the chair with one hand, and with the forefinger of the other pointed accusingly.

'She hit me!'

'Sir?'

'That Carlisle woman. She hit me with a cosh. And,' said Cosmo, feeling feverishly through his pockets, 'she and that blasted husband of hers have stolen a very valuable paper from me. Grab them! Don't let them get away.'

Oily's eyebrows rose. He did not smile, of course, for the occasion was a serious one where levity would have been out of place, but his mouth twitched a little.

'Well, really, officer! One makes allowances for a sick man, but . . . well, really!'

Johnny Pearce's attention had been wandering. His thoughts had drifted back to that luncheon. Had he or had he not seen Norbury-Smith squeeze Belinda Farringdon's hand? At a certain point in the meal when Norbury-Smith's foot had collided with his under the table, had that foot's objective been Belinda Farringdon's shoe?

Aware now of raised voices, he came out of his reverie.

'What's the argument?' he enquired.

Constable McMurdo brought him abreast. This gentleman here, he said, had made a statement charging that lady there with having biffed him on the napper with a cosh. It did not, he added, seem plausible to *him*.

'Delicately nurtured female,' he explained.

Johnny could not quite see eye to eye with him in this view. In the stories he wrote you could never rule out females as suspects because they were delicately nurtured. Not once but on several occasions Inspector Jervis had been laid out cold by blondes of just that description. They waited till his back was turned and then let him have it with the butt end of a pistol or a paperweight. He looked at Gertie dubiously.

It was Oily who saw the way of proving his loved one's innocence.

'This is all very absurd,' he said in his gentlemanly way, 'but the thing can be settled, it seems to me, quite simply. If my wife struck Mr Wisdom with a . . . what was the word you used, officer?'

'Cosh, sir.'

'Thank you. I think you must mean what in my native country we call a blackjack. You know what a blackjack is, sweetie?'

'I've heard of 'em.'

'They are used a good deal by the criminal classes. Well, as I was saying, if my wife struck Mr Wisdom with an implement of this description, it is presumably either in her possession or mine. You will probably agree with me that Mrs Carlisle, wearing, as you see, Bermuda shorts and a shirt, would scarcely be able to conceal a weapon of any size on her person, so all that remains is for you to search me, officer. Frisk, is, I believe, the technical expression, is it not, ha, ha. Frisk me, constable, to the bone. You see,' he said, when the arm of the law had apologetically done so, 'not a thing! So we return to our original conclusion that Mr Wisdom had a fit.'

Police Constable McMurdo scratched his head.

'Why wasn't he curled up in a ball?'

'Ah, there, as I said before, you take me into deep waters. No doubt this gentleman will be able to tell you,' said Oily, as Nannie Bruce returned, ushering in Doctor Welsh with his black bag.

# 21

THE hall emptied soon after Doctor Welsh's arrival, like a theatre when the show is over. The doctor supported Oily's theory that Cosmo must have struck his head on the side of the chair, exercised his healing arts and, assisted by Johnny, helped the injured man to his room. Mr and Mrs Carlisle, confident that the walnut cabinet held their secret well, went up to theirs. When Lord Ickenham came in from the stroll he had been taking in the park, only Officer McMurdo was present. He was standing by the chair, eyeing it with professional intentness. Lord Ickenham greeted him with his customary geniality.

'Ah, Cyril, old friend. A very hearty good morning to you, my merry constable. Or,' he went on, peering more closely, 'are you so dashed merry? I don't believe you are. You seem to me to have a stern, official air, as if you had seen somebody moving pigs without a permit or failing to abate a smoky chimney. Has a crime wave broken out in these parts?'

Officer McMurdo was only too glad to confide in one for whose IQ he had a solid respect. What he was registering in his mind as the Wisdom case had left him puzzled.

'That's just what I'd like to ascertain, m'lord. Strange things have been happening at Hammer Hall. I still can't see why he wasn't curled up in a ball.'

'I beg your pardon? That one rather got past me.'

'Mr Wisdom, m'lord. When you have a fit, you curl up in a ball.'

'Oh, do you? Nice to know the etiquette. But what makes you think he had had a fit?'

'That's what the doctor said. He was lying on the floor with his legs straight out.'

'Was he, indeed? Quaint fellows, these doctors. Never know what they'll be up to next.'

'You misunderstand me, m'lord. It wasn't Doctor Welsh that was lying on the floor, it was Mr Wisdom. And Mr Carlisle made a statement that . . . I've got it all in my notebook . . . half a jiffy, yes, here we are . . . made a statement that he and Mrs Carlisle was passing through the hall and observed Mr Wisdom fall out of his chair and knock his head on the side of it, causing a lump behind the ear as big as a walnut. Some sort of a fit, they thought. But mark this, m'lord. On regaining consciousness, Mr Wisdom in his turn issued a statement, accusing Mrs Carlisle of striking him on the napper with a cosh.'

'What!'

'Yes, m'lord. Makes it sort of hard to sift the evidence and arrive at conclusions, don't it? If he'd been curled up in a ball, I'd say there was little credence to be attached to his words, but seeing that his legs was straight out, well, one sort of wonders if there might not be something in it. On the other hand, is it likely that a delicately nurtured female would go biffing—'

He broke off, and his face, which had been like that of a bloodhound on the trail, assumed the expression of a lovelorn sheep. Another delicately nurtured female, in the person of Nannie Bruce, had entered. She gave him a haughty look, and addressed Lord Ickenham.

'Your lordship is wanted on the telephone, m'lord. Sir Raymond Bastable from the Lodge. It's the third time this morning he's rung up, asking for your lordship.'

As Lord Ickenham went down the passage to Johnny's study, where the telephone was, he was conscious of a throbbing about the temples and a dazed feeling usually induced only by the conversation of old Mr Saxby. Officer McMurdo's story had left him bewildered. It was obvious to him, sifting, as the constable would have said, the evidence, that for some reason Mrs Gordon Carlisle had applied that cosh of hers to the skull of Cosmo Wisdom—busted him one, as she would have put it—but why had she done so? Because she disliked the young man? In a spirit of girlish exuberance? Or just because one had to do something to fill in the time before lunch? Better, he felt, to dismiss the problem from his thoughts and not try to fathom her mental processes. These vultures acted according to no known laws.

Arrived in Johnny's sanctum, he took up the receiver, and jumped several inches when a voice suggestive of a lion at feeding time roared in his ear drum.

'Frederick! Where the devil have you been all this while?'

'Just out, Beefy,' said Lord Ickenham mildly. 'Roaming hither and thither and enjoying the lovely sunshine. I hear you've been trying to get me. What's your trouble?'

As far as could be gathered from aural evidence, Sir Raymond appeared to be choking.

'I'll tell you what my trouble is! Do you know what I saw in the paper this morning?'

'I think I can guess. It was in yesterday's evening paper.'

'About *Cocktail Time*? About these people offering a hundred and fifty thousand for the picture rights?'

'Yes. It's a lot of money.'

'A lot of money! I should say it was a lot of money. And all going into that blasted Cosmo's pocket unless you do the decent thing, Frederick.'

'Spread sweetness and light, you mean? It is always my aim, Beefy.'

'Then for God's sake give me that letter of his. It's the only proof there is that I wrote the book. Frederick,' said Sir Raymond, and his voice had taken on a pleading note, 'you can't hold out on me. You must have heard from Phoebe by this time that my behaviour toward her these last two weeks has been . . . what's the word?'

'Angelic?'

'Yes, angelic. Ask Peasemarch if I've once so much as raised my voice to her. Ask anybody.'

'No need to institute enquiries, Beefy. It is all over Dovetail Hammer that your attitude where Phoebe is concerned has been that of one brushing flies off a sleeping Venus. Several people have told me that they mistook you in a dim light for the Chevalier Bayard.'

'Well, then?'

'But will this happy state of things last?'

'Of course it will.'

'I have your word for that as a man of honour and an old Oxford rugger blue?'

'Certainly. Wait a minute. Do you see what I've got here?'

'Sorry, Beefy, my vision's limited.'

'A bible, and I'm prepared to swear on it—'

'My dear old man, your word is enough. But aren't you forgetting something? How about your political career?'

'Damn my political career! I don't want a political career, I want a hundred and fifty thousand dollars.'

'All right, Beefy. You can relax. The money's yours. Go and fetch Albert Peasemarch and put him on the phone.'

'Do *what*?'

'So that I can tell him to hand that letter over to you. I had to put it in his charge, for bad men are after it and one never knows if the United States Marines won't sooner or later be caught asleep at the switch. Ring up again when you've got him. I don't want to sit here holding the instrument.'

Lord Ickenham hung up, and went back to the hall, hoping for further conversation with Officer McMurdo. But the constable had vanished, possibly to go about his professional duties but more probably to resume his wooing. The only occupant of the hall was old Mr Saxby, who was sitting in the chair recently vacated by Cosmo. He regarded Lord Ickenham with the eye of a benevolent codfish.

'Ah, Scriventhorpe,' he said. 'Nice to run into you. Have you seen Flannery lately?'

'I'm afraid I haven't.'

'Indeed? And how was he looking? Well, I hope? He suffers a little from sciatica. Is this your first visit to Hammer Hall?'

'No, I often come here. Johnny Pearce is my godson.'

'I used to be somebody's godson once, but many years ago. He has a nice place.'

'Very.'

'And some nice things. But I don't like that imitation walnut cabinet.'

'It's an eyesore, of course. Johnny's getting rid of it.'

'Very sensible of him. You remember what Flannery always says about fake antiques.'

Before Lord Ickenham was able to learn what that mystic man's views were on the subject indicated, Nannie Bruce appeared.

'Sir Raymond Bastable on the telephone, m'lord.'

'Oh, yes. Excuse me.'

'Certainly, certainly. Have you,' Mr Saxby asked Nannie Bruce, as Lord Ickenham left them, 'ever been to Jerusalem?'

'No, sir.'

'Ah. You must tell me all about it some time,' said Mr Saxby.

It is doubtful if even Miss Bruce's Uncle Charlie, at the peak of one of his celebrated fits, could have exhibited a greater agitation than did Sir Raymond Bastable when embarking on this second instalment of his telephone conversation with his half-brother-in-law. His visit to Albert Peasemarch's pantry, where that unfortunate stretcher-case was still sneezing, had left him—we must once more turn to Roget and his Thesaurus for assistance—unhappy, infelicitous, woebegone, dejected, heavy-laden, stricken and crushed. It is not easy for a man who is sneezing all the time to tell a story well, but Albert Peasemarch had told his well enough to enable Sir Raymond to grasp its import, and it had affected him like a bomb explosion. This, he said to Lord Ickenham, after he had informed him in a flood of molten words what he thought of his nephew Cosmo, was the end.

'The end,' he repeated, choking on the words. 'The young reptile must have burned the thing by now. Oh, hell and damnation!'

It was probably injudicious of Lord Ickenham to tell him at this moment not to worry, for the kindly advice, judging from the sounds proceeding from the Bastable end of the wire, seemed to have had the worst effects. But there were solid reasons for his doing so. In a flash he had divined the thought behind Mrs Gordon Carlisle's apparently inexplicable behaviour in busting Cosmo Wisdom one with her cosh. In supposing that she had merely been indulging some idle whim, busting just because it seemed a good idea to her at the time, he saw that he had done the woman an injustice. It was from the soundest business motives that she had raised that lump as big as a walnut behind Cosmo's ear.

'Listen,' he said, and started to place the facts before his relative by marriage, hampered a good deal at the outset by the latter's refusal to stop talking.

When he had finished, there was a pause of some moments, occupied by Sir Raymond in making a sort of gargling noise.

'You mean,' he said, becoming articulate, 'that that bounder Carlisle has got the letter?'

'Exactly. So now everything's fine.'

There was another pause. Sir Raymond appeared to be praying for strength.

'Fine?' he said, in a strange, low, husky voice. 'Did you say fine?'

'I did. He will be coming to see you about it shortly, I imagine, so what I want you to do, Beefy, is to step out into the garden and gather some frogs. About half a dozen. To put down the back of his neck,' explained Lord Ickenham. 'You remember what a sensitive skin he has. We grab him and decant the frogs. I shall be vastly surprised if after the third, or possibly fourth, frog has started to do the rock 'n roll on his epidermis, he is not all eagerness to transfer the letter to you. Years ago, when I was a child, a boy named Percy Wilberforce threatened that unless I gave him my all-day sucker, he would put frogs down my back. He got it F.O.B. in three seconds. Even then I was about as intrepid as they come, but I could not face the ordeal. And if an Ickenham weakened like that, is it likely that a Gordon Carlisle will prove more resolute? Off you go, Beefy, and start gathering. Put them in a paper bag,' said Lord Ickenham, and returned to the hall.

He found Mr Saxby pottering about in the vicinity of the walnut cabinet.

'Ah, Scriventhorpe. Back again? I've been having a look at this thing, and it's worse than I thought it was. It's a horrible bit of work. Flannery would hate it. I found something odd in one of the drawers,' said Mr Saxby. 'You don't happen to know what this is?'

Lord Ickenham looked at the object he was holding up, and started.

'It's a cosh.'

'Cosh, did you say?'

'That's right.'

'The word is new to me. What are its uses?'

'Delicately nurtured females bust people one with it.'

'Indeed? Most interesting. I must tell Flannery that when I see him. By the way,' Mr Saxby proceeded, 'I also found this letter addressed to Bastable.'

Lord Ickenham drew a deep breath, the sort of breath a gambler draws who has placed the last of his money on a number at the roulette table and sees it come up.

'May I look at it?' he said, his voice shaking a little. 'Thank you. Yes, you're quite right. It is addressed to Bastable. Perhaps I had better take charge of it. I shall be seeing him soon, and can give it to him. Curious it turning up in that cabinet.'

'A letter of Flannery's once turned up inside the Christmas turkey.'

'Indeed? Strange things happen in this disturbed post-war era, do they not? Rather a lesson to the dear old chap not to eat turkey. Excuse me,' said Lord Ickenham. 'I have to telephone.'

It was Phoebe who answered his ring.

'Oh, hullo, Phoebe,' he said. 'Is Raymond there?'

'He went out into the garden, Frederick. Shall I fetch him?'

'No, don't bother. Just give him a message. Tell him to stop gathering frogs.'

'Stop *what*?'

'Gathering frogs.'

'There must be something wrong with this wire. You sound as if you were telling me to tell Raymond to stop gathering frogs.'

'I am.'

'*Is* he gathering frogs?'

'He told me he was going to.'

'But *why* is he gathering frogs?'

'Ah, who can say? These eccentric barristers, you know. Probably just felt a sudden urge. Goodbye, Phoebe. Where are you at the moment?'

'I'm in Raymond's study.'

'Well, don't forget that Albert Peasemarch worships the very carpet you are standing on,' said Lord Ickenham.

He was humming a gay snatch of melody as he replaced the receiver, for there was no room for doubt in his mind that all things were working together for good. With the letter which had been leaping from vulture to vulture like the chamois of the Alps from crag to crag safely in his coat pocket, he was feeling at the top of his form. Something attempted, something done, had earned a mild cigar, and he was smoking it on the drive and thinking how pleasant it was to be away from Mr Saxby, when he found that he was not. The old gentleman came pottering along, having apparently popped up through a trap.

'Oh, Scriventhorpe.'

'Hullo, Saxby. I was just saying to myself how nice it would be if you were with me.'

'I have been looking for you, Scriventhorpe. I thought it would interest you to hear . . . A water ousel!'

'Worth hearing, are they, these water ousels?'

'There is a water ousel over there. I must go and look at it in a moment. What I started to say was that I thought it would interest you to hear that that beastly walnut cabinet has gone.'

'Has done what?'

'A couple of men came and took it away after you left. I understand it is to be put up for auction.'

Lord Ickenham started. One of those sudden inspirations of his had come to him.

'Put up for auction, eh?'

'So they told me. But I doubt if anyone in his senses would give more than a pound or two for it,' said Mr Saxby, and toddled away, binoculars in hand, to look at his water ousel.

As a rule, men whom old Mr Saxby relieved of his company were conscious of a wave of relief, coupled with a determination not to let him corner them again in a hurry, but Lord Ickenham hardly noticed that he had gone. His whole attention was riveted on a picture which had risen before his mind's eye, the picture of Beefy and Gordon Carlisle bidding furiously against each other for the imitation walnut cabinet, the proceeds of the winning bid to go to Jonathan Twistleton Pearce, that impoverished young man who had to have five hundred pounds in order to marry his Belinda. Knowing Beefy and knowing Gordon Carlisle—their deep purses and their iron resolve to get hold of the fateful letter—he was confident that considerably more than five hundred of the best and brightest would accrue to Jonathan Twistleton Pearce's bank account.

Though there are, of course, drawbacks to everything. In order to achieve this desirable end it would be necessary for him to depart a little from the truth and inform Beefy that the letter was in the cabinet, but he was a man who rather blithely departed from the truth when the occasion called. An altruist whose mission it is to spread sweetness and light is entitled to allow himself a certain licence.

# 22

THE auction sale was to be held in the village hall, a red-brick monstrosity erected in the eighties by the Victorian Pearce who had bought that walnut cabinet, and after lunch on the big day Lord Ickenham, in order to avoid old Mr Saxby, who was showing an increasing disposition to buttonhole him and talk about Flannery, had taken his cigar to his godson's study, feeling that there, if anywhere, a man might be safe. Johnny, his objective a heart-to-heart talk with Belinda Farringdon, had gone up to London in a car borrowed from Mr Morrison of the Beetle and Wedge, looking grim and resolute. It was his intention to take a firm line about this Norbury-Smith nonsense.

It was cool and peaceful in the study, with its french windows opening on the terrace, but on the fifth Earl's face, as he sat there, a frown might have been observed, as though sombre thoughts were troubling him. Nor would anyone who formed this impression have been in error. He was thinking of Beefy Bastable, that luckless toy of Fate who—for one of his wealth and determination could not fail to outbid Oily Carlisle at their coming contest—would shortly be parting with several hundred pounds for an imitation walnut cabinet worth perhaps fifty shillings.

Chatting with Oily while reclining in the hammock, Lord Ickenham, it will be recalled, had laid considerable stress on the spiritual agonies suffered by the dregs of society when they see the United States Marines arriving. Those of Sir Raymond on opening that cabinet and finding no letter in it would, he could not but feel, be even keener. There is a type of man who, however rich he be, has a sturdy distaste for paying out large sums of money for nothing, and it was to this section of humanity that the eminent barrister belonged. Lord Ickenham mourned in spirit for his old friend's distress. Too bad, he felt, that when you started spreading sweetness and light, you so often found that there was not enough to go round and that somebody had to be left out of the distribution.

On the other hand, if nobody was there to bid against Oily, carrying out the manoeuvre known to Barbara Crowe's man-in-Hollywood as bumping him up, the cabinet would be knocked down to that gentlemanly highbinder for about ten shillings, which would not greatly further the interests of a Jonathan Pearce who needed five hundred pounds. The occasion, in a word, was one of those, so common in this imperfect world, where someone has to get the short end of the stick, and only Beefy was available for the role. Lord Ickenham could see clearly enough that it was necessary to sacrifice Beefy for the good of the cause but that did not mean that he had to be happy about it.

To distract himself for a moment from his sad thoughts, he picked up the copy of that morning's *Daily Gazette* which Johnny had left lying on the floor beside his desk, and began to glance through it. It was a paper he had never much admired, and he was not surprised that he found little to intrigue him on pages one, two and three. But on page four the interest quickened. His attention was arrested by one of those large headlines in which this periodical specialized.

FRANK, FORTHRIGHT, FEARLESS

it said, and beneath this:

COCKTAIL TIME
Our Powerful New Serial

by
COSMO WISDOM
Begin It Today

There was also, inset, a photograph of Phoebe's ewe lamb, all shifty eyes and small black moustache, which might have been that of some prominent spiv who had been detained by the police for questioning in connection with the recent drug-ring raids.

'Cor lumme, stone the crows!' whispered Lord Ickenham, borrowing from Albert Peasemarch's non-copyright material. The scales had fallen from his eyes.

Until this moment it had never occurred to him to regard Cosmo Wisdom in the light of a potential bidder for the cabinet. He had supposed him to be, if not penniless, certainly several hundred poundsless. It was obvious that he must now revise this view. He knew little of the prices prevailing in the marts of literature, but it was to be presumed that for a serial as frank, forthright and fearless as *Cocktail Time* a paper like the *Gazette*, making more money than it knew what to do with and always on the look-out for a chance of giving it away to someone, would have loosened up on a pretty impressive scale. Cosmo, in other words, so recently a biter of ears for ten bobs to see him through till next Saturday, was plainly in the chips. If on this sunny summer afternoon his hip pocket was not filled to bursting with the right stuff, he, Lord Ickenham, would be dashed.

What, then, could be a happier thought than to substitute the opulent young man for Beefy?

And scarcely had he reached this most satisfactory solution of his problem when, glancing out of the french window, he saw the opulent young man in person. He was pacing the terrace with bent head and leaden feet, like a Volga boatman.

And if anyone might excusably have impersonated a Volga boatman, it was Cosmo Wisdom at this juncture. Behind the left ear of the head he was bending there was a large lump, extremely painful if he made any sudden movement, and this alone would have been enough to lower the *joie de vivre*. But far worse than physical distress was the mental anguish caused by the thought that the letter which meant everything to him was now in the custody of Oily Carlisle. It is scarcely to be wondered at that when he heard a voice call his name and, raising his bent head, saw Lord Ickenham beaming at him from the study window, his manner was not cordial. It was, indeed, rather like that of a timber wolf with its foot in a trap.

'Just come in here for a moment, will you, Cosmo? I want to speak to you.'

'What about?'

'Nothing that can be shouted from the house tops or yelled on terraces. I won't keep you long,' said Lord Ickenham as his young friend stepped through the french windows. 'It's about that letter.'

Cosmo's scowl darkened. He had no wish to talk about that letter.

'It is, is it?' he said unpleasantly. 'Well, you're wasting your time. I haven't got it.'

'I am aware of that. Mr Carlisle has it.'

'Curse him!'

'Certainly, if you wish. I don't like the fellow myself. We must baffle that man, Cosmo, before he can start throwing his weight about. You don't need to peer into any crystal ball to inform yourself of what the future holds in store, if this letter remains in his possession. Not much of that Hollywood largess of yours will be left after he has staked out his claim, for if ever a man believed in sharing the wealth, it is this same Carlisle. He must be foiled and frustrated.'

'A fat lot of good saying that,' said Cosmo, speaking even more unpleasantly than before. 'How the devil can I foil and frustrate him?'

'Listen attentively and I will tell you.'

The effect of Lord Ickenham's brief résumé of the position of affairs on Cosmo was to cause him to start convulsively. And as anything in the nature of a convulsive start makes a man who has recently been struck on the head by a woman's gentle cosh feel as if that head had a red-hot skewer thrust through it, he uttered a yelp of agony, like a Volga boatman stung by a wasp.

'I know, I know,' said Lord Ickenham, nodding sympathetically. 'The after effects of being bust one do linger, don't they? As a young man, in the course of a political argument in a Third Avenue saloon in New York,

I was once struck squarely on the topknot by a pewter tankard in the capable hands of a gentleman of the name of Moriarty—no relation of the Professor, I believe—and it was days before I was my old bright self again.'

Cosmo was staring, open-mouthed.

'You mean the letter's in that cabinet?'

'Carlisle certainly put it there.'

'How do you know?'

'I have my ways of getting to know things.'

'And it's up for auction?'

'Precisely.'

'I'll go and bid for it!'

'Exactly what I was about to suggest. You will, of course, have to be prepared to bid high. Carlisle is not going to let the thing go without a struggle. But, what with this serial and everything, I imagine that you are rolling in money these days, and a few hundred pounds here and there mean nothing to you. How is your voice?'

'Eh?'

'Say "Mi-mi". Excellent,' said Lord Ickenham. 'Like a silver bell. The auctioneer will hear your every word. So off you go. Bid till your eyes bubble, my boy, and may heaven speed your efforts.'

And now, he was saying to himself, as Cosmo hurried away and a distant howl told that he had incautiously jerked his head again, to find some simple ruse which would remove Beefy from the centre of things. The village hall must not see Beefy this summer afternoon.

It was seldom that Lord Ickenham sought for inspiration in vain. Why, of course, he was thinking a few moments later. Yes, that would do it. How simple these things always were, if you just sat back and closed your eyes and let the little grey cells take over. It needed but a quick telephone call to Albert Peasemarch, instructing him to lock Beefy up in the wine cellar, and the situation would be stabilized.

He was about to reach for the instrument, glowing as men do when their brains are working well, when it rang its bell at him in the abrupt way telephones have. He took up the receiver.

'Hullo?' he said.

It was Phoebe who replied. As nearly always, she appeared agitated.

# 23

'OH, Frederick!' she said, panting like a white rabbit heated in the chase.

'Hullo, Phoebe, my dear,' said Lord Ickenham. 'What's the matter? You seem upset.'

There was a brief pause while she seemed to contemplate the adjective, weighing it as Roget might have done if someone had suggested admitting it into his Thesaurus.

'Well, not upset exactly. But I don't know if I am standing on my head or my heels.'

'Sift the evidence. At which end of you is the ceiling?'

'Oh, don't be silly, Frederick. You know what I mean. Oh dear, I do hope Cossie will approve of this step I'm taking. I mean, it isn't as if I were a young girl. I'm nearly fifty, Frederick. He may think it odd.'

'That you are joining the chorus at the Hippodrome?'

'Whatever are you talking about?'

'Isn't that what you are trying to tell me?'

'Of course it isn't. I'm going to marry again.'

The receiver jumped in Lord Ickenham's right hand, the cigar in his left. This was big stuff. Any popular daily paper would have used it without hesitation as its front page feature story.

'Bert?' he exclaimed. 'Has Bert at last cast off his iron restraint and spoken? Are you going to be Lady Peasemarch?'

'Mrs Peasemarch.'

'For a while, no doubt, yes. But a man of Bert's abilities is bound to get knighted sooner or later. My dear Phoebe, this is news to warm the cockles of the heart. They don't come any truer and stauncher than Bert. You know what Ecclesiastes said about him? He said . . . No, sorry, it's gone for the moment, but it was something very flattering. There's only one thing you have to watch out for with Albert Peasemarch, the Drake's Drum side of him. Be careful that he doesn't sing it during the wedding ceremony.'

'What, dear?'

'I was saying that if, as you stand at the altar, Bert starts singing Drake's Drum, give him a nudge.'

'We are going to be married at a registrar's.'

'Oh, then that's all right. These registrars are good sports. Yours will probably join in the chorus. What does Raymond think of the proposed union?'

'We haven't told him yet. Albert thought it would be better if he finished his month first.'

'Very sensible. It will save Beefy a lot of embarrassment. It's always difficult for a man to be really at his ease with his butler, if he knows the latter is engaged to be married to his sister. A certain constraint when Bert was handing the potatoes would be inevitable. But aren't we skipping some of the early chapters? Tell me how it all happened. Be frank, forthright and fearless.'

'Well—'

'Yes?'

'I was trying to think where to begin. Well, I had gone to Albert's pantry to talk to him about poor little Benjy, who is ever so much better, you will be glad to hear. Albert says his nose is quite cold.'

'I remember it used to get very cold in our Home Guard days.'

'What, dear?'

'You were saying that Albert Peasemarch's nose was cold.'

'No, no, Benjy's.'

'Oh, Benjy's? Well, that's fine, isn't it?'

'And then we got talking, and something Albert said made me think of Raymond. I don't mean I've ever *not* thought of Raymond, but this something Albert said reminded me of what you had said the other day, about him not having got all his marbles.'

'I said he *had* got all his marbles.'

'Oh, did you? I thought you said he hadn't, and it worried me terribly. Thinking of George Winstanley, you know. Because Raymond has been behaving so very oddly this last week or two. I don't mean so much giving me flowers and asking after my rheumatism, but I do think it was strange of him to go swimming in the lake with all his clothes on.'

'Did he do that?'

'I saw him from my window.'

'According to Shakespeare, Julius Caesar used to swim with all his clothes on.'

'But he didn't gather frogs.'

'No, you have a point there. One finds it very difficult to see why Beefy should have wanted to gather frogs. Puzzled me a good deal, that.'

'You must admit that I had enough to worry me.'

'Oh, quite.'

'It seemed to me so dreadfully sad.'

'I don't wonder.'

'And I couldn't help it. I broke down and sobbed. And the next thing I knew, Albert was striding up to me and seizing me by the wrist and pulling me about till I felt quite giddy. And then he said "My mate!" and clasped me to him and—'

'Showered burning kisses on your upturned face?'

'Yes. He told me later that something seemed to snap in him.'

'I believe that often happens. Well, I couldn't be more pleased about this, Phoebe. You have done wisely in linking your lot with Bert's. Instinct told you you were on a good thing, and you very sensibly pushed it along. The ideal husband. Where is Bert, by the way? In his pantry?'

'I think so. He was giving Benjy beef extract.'

'Will you bring him to the phone. I would have speech with him.'

'You want to congratulate him?'

'That, of course. But there is also a little business matter I would like to discuss with him. Just one of those things that crop up from time to time. Oh, Bert,' said Lord Ickenham some moments later, 'I've been hearing the great news. Felicitations by the jugful, my old comrade, and a million wishes for your future happiness. Very interesting to learn that yet another success has to be chalked up to the Ickenham System. It seldom fails, if you remember to waggle with sufficient vigour, as I understand you did. The preliminary waggle is everything. That was probably where Cyril McMurdo went wrong. Well, I suppose you're walking on air and strewing roses from your bowler hat?'

'I do feel extremely grateful for my good fortune, Mr I.'

'I bet you do. There's nothing like getting married. It's the only life, as Brigham Young and King Solomon would tell you, if they were still with us. And now here's something I was wanting to ask you. I wonder if plighting your troth has affected you as plighting mine many years ago affected me. I remember that I was filled with a sort of yeasty benevolence that embraced the whole human race. I wanted to go about doing acts of kindness to everybody I met. Do you feel the same?'

'Oh yes, Mr I. I feel just like that.'

'Splendid! Because there's a little routine job I would like you to do for me. Will your future wife be on the premises during the next hour or so?'

'I shouldn't think so, Mr I. She went off to this sale in the village hall, and wasn't expecting to get back too soon.'

'Excellent. Then there will be no one to hear his cries.'

'Cries, Mr I?'

'The big chief's. I want you to lock him up in the wine cellar, Bert, and I imagine he'll shout a good deal. You know how people do, when you lock them in wine cellars.'

It seemed to be Lord Ickenham's fate these days to extract from those with whom he conversed on the telephone what Mr and Mrs Carlisle called groans or gurgles, though for the sound that now came over the wire a precisian might have preferred the term 'gulp'. Whatever its correct classification, it indicated plainly that his words had made a deep impression on Albert Peasemarch. In the manner in which he spoke there was more than a suggestion of Phoebe Wisdom at her most emotional.

'Do *what* to Sir Raymond, did you say, Mr I?'

'Lock him in the wine cellar. I wouldn't call him Sir Raymond, though, now that you are linked to him in such sentimental bonds. It's time you were thinking of him as Ray or Beefy. Well, that's all, Bert. Carry on.'

'But, Mr I!'

Lord Ickenham frowned. Wasted, of course, on a Peasemarch who could not see him.

'You have a rather annoying habit, Bert, when I ask you to do some perfectly simple thing for me, of saying "But, Mr I",' he said, a little stiffly. 'It's just a mannerism, I know, but I wish you wouldn't. What's on your mind?'

'Well, the question it occurred to me to ask was—'

'Yes?'

'*Why* do you want me to lock Sir Raymond in the wine cellar?'

Lord Ickenham clicked his tongue.

'Never mind why. You know as well as I do that the Secret Service can't give reasons for every move it makes. If I were to tell you why, and it got about through some incautious word of yours, a third world war would be inevitable. And I seem to remember you saying that you were opposed to the idea of a third world war.'

'Oh, I am, Mr I. I wouldn't like it at all. But—'

'That word again!'

'But what I was going to say was How do I go about it?'

'My dear fellow, there are a hundred ways of luring a man into a wine cellar. Tell him you would like his opinion on the last lot of claret. Ask him to come and inspect the ginger ale, because you're afraid the moths have been at it. That part of the thing presents no difficulty. And the locking-in will be equally simple. You just shimmer off while his back is turned and twiddle the key. A child of four could do it. A child of three,' said Lord Ickenham, correcting himself. 'Drake would have done it without missing a drum beat. Snap into it, Bert, and give me a ring when you're through.'

It was some ten minutes later that the telephone bell rang. When Albert Peasemarch spoke, it was in the subdued voice of a nervous novice who had just done his first murder.

'Everything has been attended to, Mr I.'

'He's in storage?'

'Yes, Mr I.'

'Capital! I knew I could rely on you not to bungle it. We of the Home Guard don't bungle. It wasn't so hard, was it?'

'Not hard, no—'

'But it has taken it out of you a little, no doubt,' said Lord Ickenham sympathetically. 'Your pulse is high, your breathing is stertorous and there are floating spots before your eyes. Well, go and lie down and have a nice nap.'

Albert Peasemarch coughed.

'What I was thinking I'd do, Mr I, was take the bus to Reading and catch the train to London, and spend the next week or two there. I would prefer not to encounter Sir Raymond until some little time has elapsed.'

'From what you were able to gather through the closed door, he seemed annoyed, did he?'

'Yes, Mr I.'

'I can't imagine why. I know dozens of men who would think it heaven to be locked in a wine cellar. Still, no doubt you're right. Time, the great healer, and all that sort of thing. Then this is goodbye for the moment, Bert. A thousand thanks. I will see that word of what you have done reaches the proper quarter. And if you're in London long enough, I'll look you up and we'll have a night out together.'

Well pleased, Lord Ickenham replaced the receiver and went on to the terrace. He had been there a few minutes, finishing his cigar and enjoying the peace of the summer afternoon, when a car came by and drew up at the front door. Fearing that this might be the County paying a formal call, he had recoiled a step and was preparing to make a dive for safety, when the occupant of the car alighted, and he saw that it was Barbara Crowe.

# 24

Lord Ickenham would probably have been deeply offended if he had been told that in any circumstances his mind could run on parallel lines with that of Cosmo Wisdom, a young man whose intelligence he heartily despised, but it is undoubtedly the fact that the sight of Barbara Crowe set him thinking, as Cosmo had done, what a consummate ass Raymond Bastable had been to let this woman go. In her sports dress, with the little green hat that went with it, she was looking more attractive than ever, and nothing could have been more warming to the heart than the smile she gave him as he hailed her.

'Why, Freddie,' she said, 'what on earth are you doing here?'

'I am staying with Johnny Pearce, my godson, while my wife is in Scotland. She wanted me to go with her, but I would have none of it. So, having some foolish prejudice against letting me run loose, as she calls it, in London, she dumped me on Johnny. But what brings you to these parts?'

'I've come to see Cosmo Wisdom about making some appearances on television. And Howard Saxby junior wants me to bring Howard Saxby senior back. He's afraid he'll fall into the lake or something. This place of your godson's is a kind of pub, isn't it?'

'Johnny takes in paying guests, yes.'

'I'd better book a room.'

'Plenty of time. I want to talk to you, Barbara. Let us go and seat ourselves under yonder tree. What I was hoping when I saw you get out of that car,' said Lord Ickenham, having settled her in a deck chair and dropping into one himself, 'was that you had come to see Beefy Bastable.'

Barbara Crowe started.

'Raymond? What do you mean? Is he here?'

'Not actually in Johnny's dosshouse. He lives at the Lodge across the park. We might look in on him later. Not just now, for I know he will be occupied for the next hour or so, but after you have had a wash and brush-up.'

Barbara's cheerful face lost some of its cheerfulness.

'This is a bit awkward.'

'Why?'

'He'll think I'm pursuing him.'

'Of course he will, and a very good thing, too. It will give him the encouragement he sorely needs. He'll say to himself, "Well, dash my buttons, I thought I'd lost her, but if she comes legging it after me like this, things don't look so sticky after all." It will make his day. And from that to restoring relations to their old footing will be but a step. Why,' asked Lord Ickenham, 'do you laugh in that hollow, hacking way?'

'Well, don't you think it's funny?'

'Not in the least. What's funny?'

'The idea you seem to have that Raymond still cares for me.'

'My dear girl, he's potty about you.'

'What nonsense! He's never been near me or phoned me or written to me since . . . it happened.'

'Of course he hasn't. You don't realize what a sensitive plant Beefy is. You see him in court ripping the stuffing out of witnesses, and you say to yourself, "H'm! A tough guy!" little knowing that at heart he is . . . what are those things that shrink? . . . violets, that's the word I was after . . . little knowing that at heart he is a shrinking violet. He's not a coarse-fibred chap like me. Every time my Jane broke our engagement, I hounded her with brutal threats till she mended it again, but Beefy would never do that. Delicacy is his dish. He would assume that when you gave him the old heave-ho, it meant that you didn't want to have any more to do with him, and, though it was agony, he kept away. He should have known that little or no importance is to be attached to these lovers' tiffs. That hacking laugh again! What amuses you?'

'Your calling it a tiff.'

'I believe that is the expression commonly used. If it wasn't a tiff, what was it?'

'A terrific row. A pitched battle, which culminated in my calling him a pompous old stuffed shirt.'

'I wouldn't have thought Beefy would have objected to that. He must know that he is a pompous old stuffed shirt.'

Barbara Crowe blazed into sudden fury.

'He isn't anything of the sort! He's a lamb.'

'A *what?*'

'He's the most wonderful man there ever was.'

'That is your considered opinion?'

'Yes, Frederick Altamont Cornwallis Twistleton, that is my considered opinion.'

Lord Ickenham gave a satisfied nod.

'So, as I suspected, the flame of love still burns! It does, does it not?'

'Yes, it does.'

'One word from him, and you would follow him to the ends of the earth?'

'Yes, I would.'

'Well, he won't be going there, not at the moment, anyway. My dear Barbara, this is extremely gratifying. If that's how things are at your end, we ought to be able to fix this up in no time in a manner agreeable to all parties. I wasn't sure how you felt. I knew, of course, that Beefy loved you. That habit of his, when he thinks he is alone, of burying his face in his hands and muttering "Barbara! Barbara."'

'He always called me "Baby".'

Lord Ickenham started.

'*Beefy* did?'

'Yes.'

'You're sure?'

'Quite sure.'

'Well, you know best. I wouldn't have thought . . . but that is neither here nor there. Then no doubt it was "Baby! Baby!" that he was muttering. It doesn't really matter. The salient point is that he muttered. Well, I must say everything looks pretty smooth now.'

'Does it?'

'Surely? Here, as I see it, are two sundered hearts it will be very simple to bring together.'

'Not so simple as you think.'

'What seems to be the difficulty?'

'The difficulty, my dear Freddie, is that he is determined that Phoebe shall share our little nest, and I'm equally determined that she shan't. That's the real rock we split on.'

'He wanted Phoebe to live with you?'

'Yes. There's a parsimonious streak in Raymond. I suppose it comes from having been so hard up when he was starting at the Bar. He was desperately hard up, you know, before he got going. When I suggested that our married life would run much more smoothly if he gave Phoebe a couple of thousand a year and told her to go off and take a flat in Kensington, or a villa in Bournemouth or whatever she fancied, he said he couldn't possibly afford it. And, as they say, one word led to another. Do you ever lose your temper, Freddie?'

'Very seldom. I'm the equable type.'

'I wish I were. When moved, I spit and scratch. He kept saying things like "We must be practical" and "Women never realize that men are not made of money", and I couldn't take it. That was when I called him a pompous old stuffed shirt. Yes?' said Barbara coldly. 'Why are *you* laughing in that hollow, hacking way?'

'I doubt if those are the right adjectives to describe my little ripple of mirth. They suggest gloom and bitterness, and I am anything but gloomy and bitter. I laughed—musically and with an infectious lilt—because it always entertains me to see people creating, as Albert Peasemarch would say, when there is no necessity.'

'No necessity?'

'None whatever.'

'God bless you, Frederick Ickenham. And who is Albert Peasemarch?'

'An intimate friend of mine. To tell you all about him—his career, his adventures by flood and field, his favourite breakfast food and so on—would take too long. What will probably interest you most is the fact that he will very shortly be marrying Phoebe.'

'What!'

'Yes. They fixed it up this afternoon. The expression you are probably groping for,' suggested Lord Ickenham, seeing that his companion was struggling to find speech, 'is "Cor lumme, stone the crows!"—It is the one Bert Peasemarch uses when in the grip of some powerful emotion.'

Barbara found speech.

'He's marrying *Phoebe?*'

'This surprises you?'

'Well, it isn't everybody who would want to marry Phoebe, is it? Who is this humble hero?'

'Beefy's butler. Or perhaps, after what he was saying to me on the telephone just now, I should put an "ex" before the word.'

'Phoebe's marrying a *butler?*'

'Somebody's got to, or the race of butlers would die out. And Bert will be a notable improvement on the late Algernon Wisdom. You spoke?'

'I said, "Quick, Freddie—your handkerchief!"'

'Cold in the head?'

'Crying. Tears of joy. Oh, Freddie!'

'I thought you might possibly be pleased about it.'

'Pleased! Why, this solves everything.'

'Things have a way of getting solved when an Ickenham takes a hand in them.'

'You mean, you worked it?'

'I think something I said to Phoebe, some casual remark about Albert Peasemarch worshipping the ground she trod on, may have been not without its influence.'

'Freddie, I'm going to kiss you.'

'There is nothing I would enjoy more, but if you will glance over your shoulder, you will see that we are about to have Howard Saxby senior with us. This frequently happens here. Whatever Hammer Hall's short-comings, there is never any stint of Howard Saxby senior. I have been wondering what has been keeping him away. It is not often that he denies one his society for such a lengthy period. Hullo, Saxby.'

'Ah, Scriventhorpe.'

'Cigarette?'

'No, thank you,' said Mr Saxby, taking needles and a ball of wool from his pocket. 'I would prefer to knit. I'm roughing out a sweater for my little grandson. An ambitious project, but I think something ought to come of it!'

'That's the spirit. Here's Barbara Crowe.'

'So I see. It's an extraordinary thing. I was saying to myself, as I came up, "That woman has quite a look of Barbara Crowe." I understand now why there was such a resemblance. What are you doing here, Barbara?'

'I've come to take you home, young Saxby.'

'I don't want to go home.'

'Howard junior says you must.'

'Then I suppose I'll have to. When did you arrive?'

'About ten minutes ago.'

'I am sorry I was not here to greet you. I have been down at the village hall, watching that sale. You should have been there, Scriventhorpe. That cabinet . . .'

Lord Ickenham sat up alertly.

'How much did it fetch?'

'I wish you would not bark at me like that,' said Mr Saxby a little peevishly. 'You've made me drop a stitch. I was telling you about the sale, was I not? It was replete with interest. You have often accused me, Barbara,' Mr Saxby proceeded, 'of being eccentric, and there may be something in the charge, for others have told me the same. But real eccentricity, eccentricity in the fullest sense of the term, flourishes only in Dovetail Hammer. I must begin by saying—you will forgive me, Scriventhorpe, for going over ground which is already familiar to you—that there was recently on these premises an imitation walnut cabinet which was an offence to the eye and worth at the most a few pounds. It was included in this sale of which I speak, and judge of my astonishment—'

'How much did it fetch?' said Lord Ickenham.

Mr Saxby gave him a cold look.

'And judge of my astonishment when, after several other objects of equal horror had been put up and knocked down for a few shillings, this cabinet was displayed, and I heard a voice say "Fifty pounds".'

'Ha!'

'I wish you wouldn't say "Ha!" in that abrupt way. I've dropped another stitch. It was the voice of that American fellow who is staying at the Hall. Carstairs is, I think, the name.'

'Carlisle.'

'Indeed? Flannery knows a man named Carlisle. You've probably heard him speak of him. A most interesting life he has had, Flannery says, with curious things constantly happening to him. He was once bitten by a rabbit.'

'You don't say?'

'So Flannery assures me. An angora. It turned on him and sank its teeth in his wrist while he was offering it a carrot.'

'Probably on a diet,' said Lord Ickenham, and Mr Saxby agreed that this might have been so.

'But we must not allow ourselves to get mixed up,' he proceeded. 'It was not that Carlisle, the one who was bitten by a rabbit, who said "Fifty pounds", but this other Carlisle, who is staying at the Hall and has never, to the best of my knowledge, been bitten by a rabbit. He said "Fifty pounds", and I was still gasping with astonishment, when another voice said "A hundred". It was that young fellow who was in my office the other day, Barbara, the squirt, the one you sent me here to apologize to. Though what there was to apologize about . . . However, what is his name? I've forgotten.'

'Cosmo Wisdom.'

'Ah, yes. Connected somehow with the motion picture industry. Well, he said "A hundred pounds"!'

'And to cut a long story short,' said Lord Ickenham.

Mr Saxby never cut long stories short.

'I could scarcely credit my senses. I must emphasize once again that this beastly cabinet would have been dear at five pounds. Sometimes you will see an imitation walnut cabinet that looks reasonably attractive. Some quite good work done in that line, if you know where to find it.

But this one had no redeeming features. And yet these two eccentrics persisted in bidding against each other for it, and might have gone on for ever, had not a peculiar interruption occurred. I don't know if either of you are acquainted with Bastable's sister?'

'We know her well,' said Barbara. 'Do get on, young Saxby. Phoebe Wisdom is Freddie's wife's half-sister.'

'Is that so? Who is Freddie?'

'This is Freddie.'

'Oh, really? Did you say Wisdom?'

'Yes.'

'Related in any way to the squirt?'

'His mother.'

'Then I understand everything. She was saving him from himself.'

'Doing what?'

'Preventing him throwing away his money on a cabinet no man of discernment would willingly have been found dead in a ditch with. For as the bidding reached a certain point—'

'What point?' asked Lord Ickenham.

'—this woman, bathed in tears, approached the squirt, accompanied by the village policeman, and after, so I gathered from her manner, pleading with him and trying in vain to use a mother's influence to stop him making a fool of himself signalled to the policeman to lead him away, which he did. So Carstairs got the cabinet.'

'How much for?' said Lord Ickenham.

'Well,' said Mr Saxby, rising, 'I think I will go and take a bath. I got very warm and sticky in that village hall. There was practically no ventilation.'

'Hi!' cried Lord Ickenham.

'You were calling me?' said Mr Saxby, turning.

'How much did Carlisle pay for the cabinet?'

'Oh, didn't I tell you that?' said Mr Saxby. 'I fully intended to. Five hundred pounds.'

He pottered away, and Lord Ickenham expended his breath in a deep sigh of satisfaction. Barbara Crowe shot an enquiring look at him.

'Why are you so interested in this cabinet, Freddie?'

'It belonged to my godson, who was in urgent need of five hundred pounds. Now he's got it.'

'Was it really worth nothing?'

'Practically nothing.'

'Then why did Cosmo Wisdom and that other man bid like that for it?'

'It's a long story.'

'Your stories are never too long.'

'Bless my soul, I remember my niece Valerie saying that to me once. But she spoke with a nasty tinkle in her voice. It was on the occasion when she found me at Blandings castle, posing—from the best motives—as Sir Roderick Glossop. Did I ever tell you about that?'

'No. And you can save up these reminiscences of your disreputable past for another time. What I want to hear now is about this cabinet. Don't ramble off on to other subjects like old Mr Saxby.'

'I see. You would like it short and crisp. You would wish me, as I was saying to Johnny the other day, to let my Yea be Yea and my Nay be Nay?'

'I would.'

'Then here it comes,' said Lord Ickenham.

It was, as he had predicted, a long story, but it gripped his audience throughout. There was no wandering of attention on Barbara Crowe's part to damp a raconteur's spirits. At each successive twist and turn of the plot her eyes seemed to grow wider. It was some moments after he had finished before she spoke. When she did, it was with a wealth of feeling.

'Cor lumme, stone the crows!' she said.

'I was expecting you to say that,' said Lord Ickenham. 'I must remember, by the way, to ask Albert Peasemarch what the meaning of the expression is. What crows? And why stone them? I have met men who, when moved, have said "Cor chase my Aunt Fanny up a gum tree!", which seems to me equally cryptic. However, this is not the time to go into all that. I anticipated that you would react impressively to my revelation, for it is of course a sensational tale. Are you feeling faint?'

'Not faint, no, but I think I'm entitled to gasp a bit.'

'Or gurgle. Quite.'

'Fancy Toots writing that book! I wouldn't have thought he had it in him.'

Lord Ickenham clicked his tongue.

'Haven't you been listening? I said the author of *Cocktail Time* was Raymond Bastable.'

'I used to call him Toots.'

'You did?'

'I did.'

'How perfectly foul! And he used to call you Baby?'

'He did.'

'How utterly loathsome! It makes one realize that half the world never knows how the other half lives. Well, you'll soon be calling him that revolting name again. If, that is to say, what I have told you has not killed your love.'

'What do you mean?'

'Lots of people recoil in horror from *Cocktail Time*. The bishop did. So did Phoebe. So, according to Beefy, did about fifty-seven publishers before he finally landed it with the Tomkins people. It doesn't diminish your love for him to know that he is capable of writing a book like that?'

'It does not. If anything was needed to deepen my love for Beefy, as you call him—'

'Better than calling him Toots.'

'—it is the discovery that he has a hundred and fifty thousand dollars coming to him from the movie sale of the first thing he ever wrote. Golly! Think what we'll get for the next one!'

'You feel there will be a next one?'

'Of course there will. I'll see to that. I'm going to make him give up the Bar—I've always hated him being a barrister—and concentrate on his writing. We'll live in the country, where he can breathe decent air and not ruin his lungs by sitting all day in stuffy courts. Have you ever been in the Old Bailey?'

'Once or twice.'

'I believe you can cut the atmosphere there with a spoon. They carve it up in slices and sell it as rat poison. And living in the country, he'll get his golf every day and bring his weight down. He had put on weight terribly the last time I saw him. I suppose he's worse than ever now.'

'He is far from streamlined.'

'I'll adjust that,' said Barbara grimly. 'Do you know when I first saw Raymond? When I was ten. One of my uncles took me to see the Oxford and Cambridge match, and there he was, looking like a Greek god. My uncle introduced me to him after the game, and I got his autograph and fell in love with him there and then. Gosh, he was terrific!'

'You plan to pare him down to the Beefy of thirty years ago?'

'Well, not quite that, perhaps, but some of that too, too solid flesh is certainly going to melt. And now,' said Barbara, rising from her deck chair, 'I think I'll follow our Mr Saxby's excellent example and have a bath. What's the procedure about clocking in here? Do I see your godson and haggle about terms?'

'He's gone to London. You conduct the negotiations with his old nurse. And I'd better come and help you through the ordeal. She's rather formidable.'

If there was a touch of smugness in Lord Ickenham's demeanour as he returned to his deck chair after piloting Barbara Crowe through her interview with Nannie Bruce, it would have been a stern judge who would not have agreed that that smugness was excusable. He had set out for Dovetail Hammer with the intention of spreading sweetness and light among the residents of that inland Garden of Eden, and in not one but several quarters he had spread it like a sower going forth sowing. Thanks to his efforts, Barbara would get her Toots, and Beefy would get his Baby, plus all that lovely cash from the cornucopias of Hollywood. Johnny had got his five hundred pounds, Albert Peasemarch his Phoebe, and it would not be long presumably before Cyril McMurdo got his Nannie Bruce. It was true that both Mr and Mrs Carlisle were at the moment probably feeling a little short of sweetness and light, but, as has already been pointed out, there is seldom enough of that commodity to go round. No doubt in due season they would be able to console themselves with the thought that money is not everything and that disappointments such as they had suffered are sent to us to make us more spiritual.

After perhaps half an hour had elapsed, his meditations were interrupted by the arrival of Johnny Pearce, who approached him on foot, having returned his borrowed car to the Beetle and Wedge. His manner,

Lord Ickenham was amused to see, was gloomy. He would soon, as Barbara had put it, adjust that.

'Hullo, Johnny.'

'Hullo, Uncle Fred.'

'Back again?'

'Yes, I'm back.'

'Everything all right?'

'Well, yes and no.'

Lord Ickenham frowned. His objection to his godson's habit of talking in riddles has already been touched on.

'What do you mean, Yes and No? Did you square things with Bunny?'

'Oh, yes. We're getting married next week. At the registrar's.'

'Business is certainly brisk in the registraring industry these days. And I suppose you're asking yourself what the harvest will be when she settles down here with Nannie?'

'Yes, that's what's worrying me.'

'It need worry you no longer, my dear boy. Do you know what happened at that sale this afternoon? You will scarcely credit it, but that cabinet of yours fetched five hundred pounds.'

Johnny collapsed into the deck chair in which Barbara Crowe had sat.

'What!' he gasped. 'You're kidding!'

'Not at all. That was the final bid, five hundred pounds. Going, going, gone, and knocked down to Mr Gordon Carlisle. So all you have to do now is go to Nannie . . . Why', asked Lord Ickenham, breaking off and regarding his godson with amazement, 'aren't you skipping like the high hills? Well, I suppose you could hardly do that, sitting in a deck chair, but why aren't you raising your eyes thankfully to heaven and giving three rousing cheers?'

It was some moments before Johnny was able to speak.

'I'll tell you why I'm not giving three rousing cheers,' he said, and laughed in a way which Lord Ickenham recognized as hollow and hacking. 'That sale was the vicar's jumble sale. I contributed the cabinet to it, glad to get rid of the beastly thing. So not a penny of the five hundred quid comes to me. It will be applied to the renovation and repair of the church heating system, which, I understand,' said Johnny, with another hollow, hacking laugh, 'needs a new boiler.'

# 25

Mr Saxby, feeling greatly refreshed after his bath, came out into the cool evening air and started to toddle across the park. He had decided not to resume the knitting of his grandson's sweater, which could very well wait till the quiet period after dinner, but to stroll over to Hammer Lodge and tell his friend Bastable about the auction sale. It would, he thought, interest him. For though Bastable had probably never seen that cabinet, whose peculiar foulness was the point of his story, he was convinced that he could describe it sufficiently vividly to make him appreciate the drama of what had occurred.

Nothing happened when he reached the Lodge and rang the front door bell. The butler appeared to be away from his post, down at the Beetle and Wedge perhaps or possibly out having a round of golf. But things like that never deterred Mr Saxby. The door being open, he walked in, and having done so, raised his voice and bleated:

'Bastable! BASTable!'

And from somewhere in the distance there came an answering shout. It seemed to proceed from the depths of the house, as though the shouter were in the cellar. Very strange, Mr Saxby felt. What would Bastable be doing in a cellar? And then the obvious solution presented itself. He was having a look at his wine. The good man loves his wine, and it is only natural that he should go down from time to time to see that all is well with it.

'Bastable,' he said, arriving at the cellar door.

'Who's that?' a muffled voice replied.

'Saxby.'

'Thank God! Let me out!'

'Do what?'

'Let me *out*.'

'But why don't you *come* out?'

'The door's locked.'

'Unlock it.'

'The key's on your side.'

'You're perfectly correct. So it is.'

'Well, turn it, man, turn it.'

Mr Saxby turned it, and there emerged an incandescent figure at the sight of which Albert Peasemarch, had he been present, would have trembled like one stricken with an ague. Lord Ickenham had spoken of men of his acquaintance who would thoroughly have enjoyed being locked up in a wine cellar. Sir Raymond Bastable did not belong to this convivial class. He was, as Gordon Carlisle had put it, when speaking of his wife Gertie, vexed.

'Where's Peasemarch?' he said, glaring about him with reddened eyes.

'Who?'

'Peasemarch.'

'I don't think I know him. Nice fellow?'

Sir Raymond continued to glare to left and right, as if expecting something to materialize out of thin air. As the missing member of his staff did not so materialize, he glared at Mr Saxby.

'How did you get in?'

'I walked in.'

'He didn't let you in?'

'Who didn't?'

Sir Raymond tried another approach.

'Did you see a round little bounder with a face like a suet pudding?'

'Not to my recollection. Who is this round bounder?'

'My butler. Peasemarch. I want to murder him.'

'Oh, really? Why is that?'

'He locked me in that damned cellar.'

'Locked you in the cellar?' bleated Mr Saxby, toiling in the rear as his companion, snorting with visible emotion, led the way to his study. 'Are you sure?'

'Of course I'm sure,' said Sir Raymond, sinking into an armchair and reaching for his pipe. 'I've been there for hours, with nothing to smoke. A-a-a-ah!' he said, puffing out a great cloud.

Tobacco rarely fails to soothe, but you have to give it time. The mixture of Sir Raymond's choice was slow in producing any beneficent effects. As he finished his first pipeful and prepared to light a second, his eyes were still aflame and those emotional snorts continued to proceed from him like minute guns. In a voice which would have been more musical if he had not been shouting all the afternoon, he sketched out the plans he had formed for dealing with Albert Peasemarch, should fate eventually throw them together again.

'I shall strangle him very slowly with my bare hands,' he said, rolling the words round his tongue as if they were vintage port. 'I shall kick his spine up through that beastly bowler hat he wears. I shall twist his head off at the roots. He got me to that cellar saying he wanted me to look at the last lot of claret, and when I went over to look at it, he nipped out, locking the door behind him.'

It was a simple tale, simply told, but it gripped Mr Saxby from the start. He uttered a curious high cry which he had probably picked up from some wild duck of his acquaintance.

'How extremely odd. I have never heard of a butler locking anyone in a wine cellar. I knew one once, many years ago, who kept tropical fish, but that', said Mr Saxby, who could reason clearly when he gave his mind to it, 'is not, of course, quite the same thing. Do you know what I think, Bastable? Do you know the conviction that recent happenings in Dovetail Hammer have forced on me? It is that there is something in the air here that breeds eccentricity. You see it on all sides. Take the auction sale this afternoon.'

It was agony to Sir Raymond to be reminded of the auction sale, and once again there surged up in him a passionate desire to twist Albert Peasemarch's head off at the roots. But curiosity overcame his reluctance to speak of it.

'What happened?' he asked huskily.

Mr Saxby slid into his narrative with the polished ease of one who even at the Demosthenes, where the species abounds, was regarded as something unusual in the way of club bores. Members who could sit without flinching through Sir Roderick Glossop's stories about his patients or old Mr Lucas-Gore's anecdotes of Henry James, paled beneath their tan when Howard Saxby senior started to tell the tale.

'I must begin by saying,' he began by saying, 'that at Hammer Hall, where, as you know, I am now residing, though my son tells me I must return home, so I shall shortly be leaving, and sorry to go, I assure you, for apart from your delightful society, Bastable, there is a wealth of bird life in these parts which an ornithologist like myself finds richly rewarding—'

'Get on,' said Sir Raymond.

Mr Saxby looked surprised. He had supposed that he was getting on.

'At Hammer Hall, as I was about to say,' he resumed, 'there is—or was—an imitation walnut cabinet, the property of my host Mr Pearce . . . Do you know Mr Pearce?'

'Slightly.'

'Well, this imitation walnut cabinet belonged to him, and it stood in the hall, facing you as you entered through the front door. I stress this, because it was impossible, as you went in and out, not to see the beastly thing, and it had given me some bad moments. I want to impress upon you, Bastable, that this loathsome cabinet was entirely worthless, for that is the core and centre of my story. This afternoon I was relieved to hear that it was being included in the auction sale which was held at the village hall, for words cannot tell you the effect which the sight of that revolting object had on a sensitive eye. It was—'

'I know all about the cabinet,' said Sir Raymond. 'Get on.'

'You do bustle me so, my dear fellow. Men at the club do the same thing, I never know why. Well, this cabinet came up for auction, and judge of my amazement when I heard Carlisle—not the Carlisle who was bitten by an angora rabbit but the one who is staying at the Hall—bid fifty pounds. But more was to come. The next moment, a squirt of the name of Cosmo Wisdom, whom you have probably not met, had bid a hundred. And so it went on. A cabinet, I must again emphasize, of no value whatsoever. Can you wonder that I say that the air of Dovetail Hammer breeds eccentricity? Are you in pain, Bastable?'

Sir Raymond was, and he had been unable to check a groan. The way the story appeared to be heading, it looked to him as though the blow-out or punch of it was going to be that his frightful nephew had won the cabinet, which would be the end of all things.

'Get on,' he said dully.

'How you do keep saying "Get on"! But I think I see what is in your mind. You want to know how it all ended. Well, I always think it spoils a good story to hurry it, but if you must have it in a nutshell, what happened was that just as Carlisle bid five hundred pounds, the squirt's mother with the assistance of the village policeman removed him from the scene, so the distressing cabinet was knocked down to Carlisle at that figure.'

Sir Raymond puffed out a relieved cloud of smoke. Everything was . . . well, not perhaps all right, but much more nearly all right than it might have been. He knew Gordon Carlisle to be a man who had his price. That price would undoubtedly be stiff, but to secure Cosmo's letter he was prepared to pay stiffly. Yes, things, he felt, looked reasonably bright.

'So Carlisle got the cabinet?'

'I told you he did,' said Mr Saxby. 'But when you say "So Carlisle got the cabinet?" as if that were the important thing, it seems to me that you are missing the whole point of my story. It is immaterial which of the two eccentrics made the higher bid, what is so extraordinary is that they were bidding at all in fifties and hundreds for this entirely worthless object. It bears out what I was saying to Barbara Crowe just now—'

Sir Raymond sat up with a jerk. His pipe fell from his mouth in a shower of sparks. Mr Saxby regarded it with a shake of the head.

'That's how fires get started,' he said reprovingly.

'Barbara Crowe?'

'Though Boy Scouts start them, I believe, by rubbing two sticks together. How, I have never been able to understand. Why two sticks, rubbed together, should—'

'Is Barbara Crowe *here?*'

'She was when I went to take my bath. Looking very well, I thought.'

As Sir Raymond picked up his pipe, strange emotions were stirring within him—exultation one of them, tenderness another. There could be only one reason for Barbara's arrival in Dovetail Hammer. She had come to see him, to try to effect a reconciliation. She was, in short, making what is known as the first move, and it touched him deeply that anyone as proud as she could have brought herself to do it. All the old love, so long kept in storage, as if it had been something Albert Peasemarch had locked up in a wine cellar, came popping out as good as new, and in spite of the presence in it of men like Gordon Carlisle and his nephew Cosmo the world seemed to him a very pleasant world indeed.

That strange tenderness grew. He could see now how wrong had been the stand he had taken about Phoebe sharing their home. Of course a bride would not want her home shared by anyone, let alone a woman like his sister Phoebe. Wincing a little, he resolved that, even if it meant paying out the two thousand pounds a year she had mentioned, Barbara must be alone with him in their little nest.

He had just reached this admirable decision, when Lord Ickenham came in through the french windows, and paused, momentarily disconcerted, at the sight of Mr Saxby. He had come to talk to Sir Raymond privately, and there was nothing in Howard Saxby senior's manner to suggest that he did not intend to remain rooted to the spot for hours.

But he had always been a quick thinker. There were ways of removing this adhesive old gentleman, and it took him but an instant to select the one he knew could not fail.

'Oh, there you are, Saxby,' he said. 'I was looking for you. Flannery wants to see you.'

Mr Saxby gave an interested bleat.

'Flannery? Is he here?'

'Just arrived.'

'Why didn't you bring him along?'

'He said he wanted to see you on some private matter.'

'It must be something to do with those Amalgamated Rubber shares.'

Sir Raymond, who had been daydreaming about little nests, came out of his reverie.

'Who's Flannery?'

'He's on the stock exchange. He looks after my investments.'

'They could be in no safer hands,' said Lord Ickenham, with a curious little thrill of satisfaction as he realized that the mists had at last cleared away and he now knew who Flannery was. 'I wouldn't keep him waiting. Beefy,' he went on, as Mr Saxby ambled off, making remarkably good time for a man of his years, 'I come bearing news which will, unless I am greatly mistaken, send you gambolling about the house and grounds like a lamb in springtime. But before going into that,' he said, cocking an interested eyebrow, 'I would like, if I may do so without giving offence, to comment on your personal appearance. Possibly it is my imagination, but you give me the idea of being a bit more dusty than usual. Have you been rolling in something, or do you always have cobwebs in your hair?'

A cloud marred the sunniness of Sir Raymond's mood. This reminder that he was sharing the same planet with Albert Peasemarch caused a purple flush to spread over his face.

'You'd have cobwebs in your hair, if you'd been in a cellar all the afternoon,' he said warmly. 'Do you know where Peasemarch is?'

'I was chatting with him on the phone not long ago, and he told me he was going to London for a week or two, presumably to stay with his sister, who has a house at East Dulwich. I was surprised at his leaving you so suddenly. No unpleasantness, I trust?'

Sir Raymond breathed heavily.

'He locked me in the cellar, if you call that unpleasantness.'

Lord Ickenham seemed staggered, as a man might well be at hearing such sensational words.

'Locked you in the cellar?'

'The wine cellar. If Saxby hadn't come along, I'd be there still. The man's insane.'

'One of the mad Peasemarches, you think? I'm not so sure. I admit that his behaviour was peculiar, but I believe I can understand it. Owing to a singular piece of good fortune which has just befallen him, Albert

Peasemarch is a bit above himself this afternoon. Needing an outlet for his high spirits and feeling that he had to do something by way of expressing himself, he chose this unusual course. Where you or I in similar circumstances would have opened a bottle of champagne or gone about giving small boys sixpences, Peasemarch locked you in the cellar. It's just a matter of how these things happen to take you. I suppose he thought you would laugh as heartily as he at the amusing little affair.'

'Well, he was wrong,' said Sir Raymond, still breathing heavily. 'If Peasemarch were here and I could get my hands on him, I would take him apart, limb by limb, and dance on his fragments.'

Lord Ickenham nodded.

'Yes, I can see your side of the thing. Well, when I meet him, I will let him know that you are displeased, and you will certainly get a letter of apology from him, for there is good stuff in Albert Peasemarch and no one is quicker than he to admit it when he knows he has acted mistakenly. But we must not waste precious moments talking of Albert Peasemarch, for there are other and far more important matters that call for our attention. Prepare yourself for a surprise, Beefy. Barbara Crowe is here.'

'It isn't a surprise.'

'You knew?'

'Saxby told me.'

'And what steps do you propose to take?'

'I'm going to tell her I've been a fool.'

'Doesn't she know?'

'And I'm going to marry her, if she'll still have me.'

'Oh, she'll have you, all right. I could tell that by the way, every time I mentioned your name, she buried her face in her hands and murmured "Toots! Toots!"'

'She did?' said Sir Raymond, much moved.

'Brokenly,' Lord Ickenham assured him.

'You know what the trouble was,' said Sir Raymond, removing a cobweb from his left eyebrow. 'She didn't want Phoebe living with us.'

'Very naturally.'

'Yes, I see that now. I'm going to give her two thousand pounds a year and tell her to go off and take a flat somewhere.'

'A sound and generous decision.'

'Or do you think she might settle for fifteen hundred?' said Sir Raymond wistfully.

Lord Ickenham considered the question.

'If I were you, Beefy, I would cross that bridge when you come to it. For all you know, Phoebe may be getting married herself.'

Sir Raymond stared.

'Phoebe?'

'Yes.'

'My sister Phoebe?'

'Stranger things have happened.'

For an instant it seemed that Sir Raymond was about to say 'Name three', but he merely gave a grunt and brushed away another cobweb. Lord Ickenham studied him with a thoughtful eye. He was debating within himself whether or not this was a suitable moment to reveal to the barrister-novelist that he was about to become allied by marriage to the East Dulwich Peasemarches. He decided that it was not. It is only an exceptionally mild and easy-tempered man who can receive with equanimity the news that his sister will shortly be taking for better or for worse a butler who has recently locked him in the wine cellar. Apprised of the impending union, it seemed highly probable to Lord Ickenham that Sir Raymond Bastable would follow in the footsteps of Nannie Bruce's Uncle Charlie and curl up in a ball. He turned to another matter, one to which ever since his momentous talk with Johnny Pearce he had been devoting his powerful mind.

'Well, I'm delighted, my dear fellow, that all is well again between you and Barbara,' he said. 'If there is one thing that braces me up, it is to see two sundered hearts come together, whether it be in springtime or somewhat later in the year. Oh, blessings on the falling out that all the more endears, as the fellow said. But there's one thing you must budget for, Beefy, when you marry Barbara, and this may come as something of a shock to you. You will have to be prepared to start work on another book.'

'What!'

'Well, of course.'

'But I can't.'

'You'll have to. If you think you can write a novel and sell it for a hundred and fifty thousand dollars and marry a literary agent and not have her make you sit down on your trouser seat and write another, you sadly underestimate the determination and will to win of literary agents. You won't have a moment's peace till you take pen in hand.'

Sir Raymond's lower jaw had fallen to its fullest extent. He stared into the future and was appalled by what he saw.

'But I can't, I tell you! It nearly killed me, writing *Cocktail Time*. You haven't any conception what it means to sweat your way through one of these damned books. I daresay it's all right for fellows who are used to it, but for somebody like myself . . . I'd much rather be torn to pieces with red-hot pincers.'

Lord Ickenham nodded.

'I thought that might possibly be your attitude. But I see a way out of the difficulty. Ever hear of Dumas?'

'Who?'

'Alexandre Dumas. *The Three Musketeers. Count of Monte Cristo.*'

'Oh, Dumas? Yes, of course. Everybody's read Dumas.'

'You're wrong. They just think they have. What they were really getting was the output of his corps of industrious assistants. He was in rather the same position as you. He wanted the money, as much of it as he could gouge out of the reading public, but he strongly objected to having to turn out the stuff. So he assigned the rough spadework—the writing of his books—to others.'

Hope leaped into Sir Raymond's haggard eyes. There flooded over him a relief similar to that which he had experienced when hearing Mr Saxby's voice outside the cellar door. It was as though spiritual United States Marines had arrived.

'You mean I could get someone else to write the infernal thing?'

'Exactly. And who more suitable than my godson, Johnny Pearce?'

'Why, of course! He's an author, isn't he?'

'Been one for years.'

'Would he do it?'

'Nothing would please him more. Like Dumas, he needs the money. Fifty-fifty would be a fair arrangement, I think?'

'Yes, that seems reasonable.'

'And of course he would have to have something down in advance. A refresher you call it at the Bar, don't you? Five hundred pounds suggests itself as a suitable figure. Just step to your desk, Beefy, and write him a cheque for that amount.'

Sir Raymond stared.

'You want me to give him five hundred pounds?'

'In advance of royalties.'

'I'm not going to give him any five hundred pounds.'

'Then I, on my side, am not going to give you that letter of young Cosmo's. I quite forgot to mention, Beefy, that shortly after our Mr Carlisle placed it in the cabinet, I found and removed it. I have it in my pocket now,' said Lord Ickenham, producing it. 'And if', he added, noting that his companion had begun to stir in his chair and seemed to be gathering himself for a spring, 'you are thinking of rising and busting me one and choking it out of me, let me mention that I have a rudimentary knowledge of ju-jitsu, amply sufficient to enable me to tie you into a lover's knot which it would take you hours and hours to get out of. Five hundred pounds, Beefy, payable to Jonathan Twistleton Pearce.'

There was a silence, during which a man might have uttered the words 'Jonathan Twistleton Pearce' ten or perhaps twelve times, speaking slowly. Then Sir Raymond heaved himself up. His manner was not blithe. Roget, asked to describe it, would have selected some term such as 'resigned' or 'nonresisting' or possibly 'down on his marrowbones (*slang*)', but it was plain, when he spoke, that he had made his decision.

'How do you spell Pearce?' he said. 'P-e-a-r-c-e or P-i-e-r-c-e?'

The shadows were lengthening across the grass as Ickenham started to saunter back through the park to Hammer Hall, the cheque in his pocket which would bring wedding bells to Belinda Farringdon, his godson Johnny, Nannie Bruce and Officer Cyril McMurdo—unless, of course, they were all going to be married at the registrar's, in which event there would be no bells. It was one of those perfect days which come from three to five times in an English summer. The setting sun reddened the waters of the lake, westward the sky was ablaze with green and gold and amethyst and purple, and somewhere a bird, probably an intimate friend of Mr Saxby's, was singing its evensong before knocking off for the night.

Everywhere was peace and gentle stillness, and it made Lord Ickenham think how jolly it would be to be in London.

He had become a little tired of country life. Well enough in its way, of course, but dull . . . humdrum . . . nothing ever happening. What he needed to tone up his system was a night out in the pleasure-seeking section of the metropolis in the society of some congenial companion.

Not his nephew Pongo. You couldn't dig Pongo out nowadays. Marriage had turned him into a sober citizen out of tune with the hopes and dreams of a man who liked his evenings lively. Ichabod was the word that sprang to the lips when the mind dwelt on Pongo Twistleton, and for a moment, looking back on the days when a telephone call had always been enough to bring his nephew out with, as the expression is, a whoop and a holler, Lord Ickenham was conscious of a slight depression.

Then he was his bright self again. He had remembered that in his little red book in his bedroom at the Hall he had the address of Albert Peasemarch.

What pleasanter than to go to Chatsworth, Mafeking Road, East Dulwich, imitate the cry of the white owl, tell Albert Peasemarch to put on his bowler hat, and, having checked that bowler hat in the cloakroom of some gay restaurant, to plunge with him into London's glittering night life?

Which, he was convinced, would have much to offer to two young fellows up from the country.

# SERVICE WITH A SMILE

# 1

## · I ·

The morning sun shone down on Blandings Castle, and the various inmates of the ancestral home of Clarence, ninth Earl of Emsworth, their breakfasts digested, were occupying themselves in their various ways. One may as well run through the roster just to keep the record straight.

Beach, the butler, was in his pantry reading an Agatha Christie; Voules, the chauffeur, chewing gum in the car outside the front door. The Duke of Dunstable, who had come uninvited for a long visit and showed no signs of ever leaving, sat spelling through *The Times* on the terrace outside the amber drawing-room, while George, Lord Emsworth's grandson, roamed the grounds with the camera which he had been given on his twelfth birthday. He was photographing—not that the fact is of more than mild general interest—a family of rabbits down by the west wood.

Lord Emsworth's sister, Lady Constance, was in her boudoir writing a letter to her American friend James Schoonmaker. Lord Emsworth's secretary, Lavender Briggs, was out looking for Lord Emsworth. And Lord Emsworth himself, accompanied by Mr Schoonmaker's daughter Myra, was on his way to the headquarters of Empress of Blandings, his pre-eminent sow, three times silver medallist in the Fat Pigs class at the Shropshire Agricultural Show. He had taken the girl with him because it seemed to him that she was a trifle on the low-spirited side these days, and he knew from his own experience that there was nothing like an after-breakfast look at the Empress for bracing one up and bringing the roses back to the cheeks.

'There is her sty,' he said, pointing a reverent finger as they crossed the little meadow dappled with buttercups and daisies. 'And that is my pigman Wellbeloved standing by it.'

Myra Schoonmaker, who had been walking with bowed head, as if pacing behind the coffin of a dear and valued friend, glanced listlessly in the direction indicated. She was a pretty girl of the small, slim, slender type, who would have been prettier if she had been more cheerful. Her brow was furrowed, her lips drawn, and the large brown eyes which rested on George Cyril Wellbeloved had in them something of the sadness one sees in those of a dachshund which, coming to the dinner table to get its ten per cent, is refused a cut off the joint.

'Looks kind of a plugugly,' she said, having weighed George Cyril in the balance.

'Eh? What? What?' said Lord Emsworth, for the word was new to him.

'I wouldn't trust a guy like that an inch.'

Enlightenment came to Lord Emsworth.

'Ah, you have heard, then, how he left me some time ago and went to my neighbour, Sir Gregory Parsloe. Outrageous and disloyal, of course, but these fellows will do these things. You don't find the old feudal spirit nowadays. But all that is in the past, and I consider myself very fortunate to have got him back. A most capable man.'

'Well, I still say I wouldn't trust him as far as I can throw an elephant.'

At any other moment it would have interested Lord Emsworth to ascertain how far she could throw an elephant, and he would have been all eager questioning. But with the Empress awaiting him at journey's end he was too preoccupied to go into the matter. As far as he was capable of hastening, he hastened on, his mild eyes gleaming in anticipation of the treat in store.

Propping his back against the rail of the sty, George Cyril Wellbeloved watched him approach, a silent whistle of surprise on his lips.

'Well, strike me pink!' he said to his immortal soul. 'Cor chase my aunt Fanny up a gum tree!'

What had occasioned this astonishment was the fact that his social superior, usually the sloppiest of dressers and generally regarded as one of Shropshire's more prominent eyesores, was now pure Savile Row from head to foot. Not even the *Tailor and Cutter*'s most acid critic could have found a thing to cavil at in the quiet splendour of his appearance. Enough to startle any beholder accustomed to seeing him in baggy flannel trousers, an old shooting coat with holes in the elbows, and a hat which would have been rejected disdainfully by the least fastidious of tramps.

It was no sudden outbreak of foppishness that had wrought this change in the ninth earl's outer crust, turning him into a prismatic sight at which pigmen blinked amazed. As he had explained to Myra Schoonmaker on encountering her mooning about in the hall, he was wearing the beastly things because he was going to London on the 10.35 train, because his sister Connie had ordered him to attend the opening of Parliament. Though why Parliament could not get itself opened without his assistance he was at a loss to understand.

A backwoods peer to end all backwoods peers, Lord Emsworth had a strong dislike for London. He could never see what pleasure his friend Ickenham found in visiting that frightful city. The latter's statement that London brought out all the best in him and was the only place where his soul could expand like a blossoming flower and his generous nature find full expression bewildered him. Himself he wanted nothing but Blandings Castle, even though his sister Constance, his secretary Lavender Briggs and the Duke of Dunstable were there and Connie, over-riding his veto, had allowed the Church Lads' Brigade to camp out by the lake. Many people are fond of church lads, but he was not of their number, and he chafed at Connie's highhandedness in letting loose on his grounds and messuages what sometimes seemed to him about five hundred of them, all squealing simultaneously.

But this morning there was no room in his mind for morbid thoughts about these juvenile pluguglies. He strongly suspected that it was one of them who had knocked his top hat off with a crusty roll at the recent school treat, but with a visit to the Empress in view he had no leisure to brood on past wrongs. One did not think of mundane things when about to fraternize with that wonder-pig.

Arriving at her G.H.Q., he beamed on George Cyril Wellbeloved as if on some spectacle in glorious technicolor. And this was odd, for the O.C. Pigs, as Myra Schoonmaker had hinted, was no feast for the eye, having a sinister squint, a broken nose acquired during a political discussion at the Goose and Gander in Market Blandings, and a good deal of mud all over him. He also smelt rather strongly. But what enchanted Lord Emsworth, gazing on this son of the soil, was not his looks or the bouquet he diffused but his mere presence. It thrilled him to feel that this prince of pigmen was back again, tending the Empress once more. George Cyril might rather closely resemble someone for whom the police were spreading a drag-net in the expectation of making an arrest shortly, but nobody could deny his great gifts. He knew his pigs.

So Lord Emsworth beamed, and when he spoke did so with what, when statesmen meet for conferences, is known as the utmost cordiality.

'Morning, Wellbeloved.'

'Morning, m'lord.'

'Empress all right?'

'In the pink, m'lord.'

'Eating well?'

'Like a streak, m'lord.'

'Splendid. It is so important,' Lord Emsworth explained to Myra Schoonmaker, who was regarding the noble animal with a dull eye, 'that her appetite should remain good. You have of course read your Wolff-Lehmann and will remember that, according to the Wolff-Lehmann feeding standards, a pig, to enjoy health, must consume daily nourishment amounting to fifty-seven thousand eight hundred calories, these to consist of proteids four pounds five ounces, carbohydrates twenty-five pounds.'

'Oh?' said Myra.

'Linseed meal is the secret. That and potato peelings.'

'Oh?' said Myra.

'I knew you would be interested,' said Lord Emsworth. 'And of course skimmed milk. I've got to go to London for a couple of nights, Wellbeloved. I leave the Empress in your charge.'

'Her welfare shall be my constant concern, m'lord.'

'Capital, capital, capital,' said Lord Emsworth, and would probably have gone on doing so for some little time, for he was a man who, when he started saying 'Capital', found it hard to stop, but at this moment a new arrival joined their little group, a tall, haughty young woman who gazed on the world through harlequin glasses of a peculiarly intimidating kind. She regarded the ninth earl with the cold eye of a governess of strict views who has found her young charge playing hooky.

'Pahdon me,' she said.

Her voice was as cold as her eye. Lavender Briggs disapproved of Lord Emsworth, as she did of all those who employed her, particularly Lord Tilbury of the Mammoth Publishing Company, who had been Lord Emsworth's predecessor. When holding a secretarial post, she performed her duties faithfully, but it irked her to be a wage slave. What she wanted was to go into business for herself as the proprietress of a typewriting bureau. It was the seeming impossibility of ever obtaining the capital for this venture that interfered with her sleep at night and in the daytime made her manner more than a little forbidding. Like George Cyril Wellbeloved, whose views were strongly communistic, which was how he got that broken nose, she eyed the more wealthy of her circle askance. Idle rich, she sometimes called them.

Lord Emsworth, who had been scratching the Empress's back with the ferrule of his stick, an attention greatly appreciated by the silver medallist, turned with a start, much as the Lady of Shalott must have turned when the curse came upon her. There was always something about his secretary's voice, when it addressed him unexpectedly, that gave him the feeling that he was a small boy again and had been caught by the authorities stealing jam.

'Eh, what? Oh, hullo, Miss Briggs. Lovely morning.'

'Quate. Lady Constance desiah-ed me to tell you that you should be getting ready to start, Lord Emsworth.'

'What? What? I've plenty of time.'

'Lady Constance thinks othahwise.'

'I'm all packed, aren't I?'

'Quate.'

'Well, then.'

'The car is at the door, and Lady Constance desiah-ed me to tell you—'

'Oh, all right, all right,' said Lord Emsworth peevishly, adding a third 'All right' for good measure. 'Always something, always something,' he muttered, and told himself once again that, of all the secretarial assistants he had had, none, not even the Efficient Baxter of evil memory, could compare in the art of taking the joy out of life with this repellent female whom Connie in her arbitrary way had insisted on engaging against his strongly expressed wishes. Always after him, always harrying him, always popping up out of a trap and wanting him to *do* things. What with Lavender Briggs, Connie, the Duke and those beastly boys screaming and yelling beside the lake, life at Blandings Castle was becoming insupportable.

Gloomily he took one last, lingering look at the Empress and pottered off, thinking, as so many others had thought before him, that the ideal way of opening Parliament would be to put a bomb under it and press the button.

## · II ·

The Duke of Dunstable, having read all he wanted to read in *The Times* and given up a half-hearted attempt to solve the crossword puzzle, had left the terrace and was making his way to Lady Constance's sitting-room. He was looking for someone to talk to, and Connie, though in his opinion potty, like all women, would be better than nothing.

He was a large, stout, bald-headed man with a jutting nose, prominent eyes and a bushy white moustache of the type favoured by regimental sergeant majors and walruses. In Wiltshire, where he resided when not inviting himself for long visits to the homes of others, he was far from popular, his standing among his neighbours being roughly that of a shark at a bathing resort—something, that is to say, to be avoided on all occasions as nimbly as possible. A peremptory manner and an autocratic disposition combined to prevent him winning friends and influencing people.

He reached his destination, went in without knocking, found Lady Constance busy at her desk, and shouted 'Hoy!'

The monosyllable, uttered in her immediate rear in a tone of voice usually confined to the hog-calling industry of western America, made Lady Constance leap like a rising trout. But she was a hostess. Concealing her annoyance, not that that was necessary, for her visitor since early boyhood had never noticed when he was annoying anyone, she laid down her pen and achieved a reasonably bright smile.

'Good morning, Alaric.'

'What do you mean, good morning, as if you hadn't seen me before today?' said the Duke, his low opinion of the woman's intelligence confirmed. 'We met at breakfast, didn't we? Potty thing to say. No sense to it. What you doing?'

'Writing a letter.'

'Who to?' said the Duke, never one to allow the conventions to interfere with his thirst for knowledge.

'James Schoonmaker.'

'Who?'

'Myra's father.'

'Oh, yes, the Yank I met with you in London one day,' said the Duke, remembering a tête-à-tête luncheon at the Ritz which he had joined uninvited. 'Fellow with a head like a pumpkin.'

Lady Constance flushed warmly. She was a strikingly handsome woman, and the flush became her. Anybody but the Duke would have seen that she resented this loose talk of pumpkins. James Schoonmaker was a very dear friend of hers, and she had sometimes allowed herself to think that, had they not been sundered by the seas, he might one day have become something more. She spoke sharply.

'He has not got a head like a pumpkin!'

'More like a Spanish onion, you think?' said the Duke, having weighed this. 'Perhaps you're right. Silly ass, anyway.'

Lady Constance's flush deepened. Not for the first time in an association which had lasted some forty years, starting in the days when she had worn pigtails and he had risked mob violence by going about in a Little Lord Fauntleroy suit, she was wishing that her breeding did not prohibit her from bouncing something solid on this man's bald head. There was a paper-weight at her elbow which would have fitted her needs to a nicety. Debarred from physical self-expression by a careful upbringing at the hands of a series of ladylike governesses, she fell back on hauteur.

'Was there something you wanted, Alaric?' she asked in the cold voice which had so often intimidated her brother Clarence.

The Duke was less susceptible to chill than Lord Emsworth. Coldness in other people's voices never bothered him. Whatever else he had been called in the course of his long life, no one had ever described him as a sensitive plant.

'Wanted someone to talk to. Seems impossible to find anyone to talk to in this blasted place. Not at all sure I shall come here again. I tried Emsworth just now, and he just yawped at me like a half-wit.'

'He probably didn't hear you. You know how dreamy and absent-minded Clarence is.'

'Dreamy and absent-minded be blowed! He's potty!'

'He is not!'

'Of course he is. Do you think I don't know pottiness when I see it? My old father was potty. So was my brother Rupert. So are both my nephews. Look at Ricky. Writes poetry and sells onion soup. Look at Archie. An artist. And Emsworth's worse than any of them. I tell you he just yawped at me without uttering, and then he went off with that girl Clarissa Stick-in-the-mud.'

'Myra Schoonmaker.'

'Same thing. She's potty, too.'

'You seem to think everybody potty.'

'So they are. Very rare to meet anyone these days with the intelligence of a cockroach.'

Lady Constance sighed wearily.

'You may be right. I know so few cockroaches. What makes you think that Myra is mentally deficient?'

'Can't get a word out of her. Just yawps.'

Lady Constance frowned. She had not intended to confide her young guest's private affairs to a man who would probably spread them far and near, but she felt that the girl's reputation for sanity should be protected.

'Myra is rather depressed just now. She has had an unfortunate love affair.'

This interested the Duke. He had always been as inquisitive as a cat. He blew his moustache up against his nose and allowed his eyes to protrude.

'What happened? Feller walk out on her?'

'No.'

'She walk out on him?'

'No.'

'Well, somebody must have walked out on someone.'

Lady Constance felt that having said so much she might as well tell all. The alternative was to have the man stand there asking questions for the rest of the morning, and she wanted to finish her letter.

'I put a stop to the thing,' she said curtly.

The Duke gave his moustache a puff.

'You did? Why? None of your ruddy business, was it?'

'Of course it was. When James Schoonmaker went back to America, he left her in my charge. I was responsible for her. So when I found that she had become involved with this man, there was only one thing to do, take her away to Blandings, out of his reach. He has no money, no prospects, nothing. James would never forgive me if she married him.'

'Ever seen the chap?'

'No. And I don't want to.'

'Probably a frightful bounder who drops his aitches and has cocoa and bloaters for supper.'

'No, according to Myra, he was at Harrow and Oxford.'

'That damns him,' said the Duke, who had been at Eton and Cambridge. 'All Harrovians are the scum of the earth, and Oxonians are even worse. Very wise of you to remove her from his clutches.'

'So I thought.'

'That's why she slinks about the place like a funeral mute, is it? You ought to divert her mind from the fellow, get her interested in somebody else.'

'The same idea occurred to me. I've invited Archie to the castle.'

'Archie who?'

'Your nephew Archie.'

'Oh, my God! That poop?'

'He is not a poop at all. He's very good-looking and very charming.'

'Who did he ever charm? Not me.'

'Well, I am hoping he will charm her. I'm a great believer in propinquity.'

The Duke was not at his best with long words, but he thought he saw what she was driving at.

'You mean if he digs in here, he may cut this bloater-eating blighter out? Girl's father's a millionaire, isn't he?'

'Several times over, I believe.'

'Then tell young Archie to get after the wench with all speed,' said the Duke enthusiastically. His nephew was employed by the Mammoth Publishing Company, that vast concern which supplies the more fat-headed of England's millions with their daily, weekly and monthly reading matter, but in so minor a capacity that he, the Duke, was still obliged to supplement his salary with an allowance. And if there was one thing that parsimonious man disliked, it was supplementing people's salaries with allowances. The prospect of getting the boy off his payroll was a glittering one, and his eyes bulged brightly as he envisaged it. 'Tell him to spare no effort,' he urged. 'Tell him to pull up his socks and leave no stone unturned. Tell him . . . Oh, hell! Come in, curse you.'

There had been a knock at the door. Lavender Briggs entered, all spectacles and efficiency.

'I found Lord Emsworth, Lady Constance, and told him the car was in readiness.'

'Oh, thank you, Miss Briggs. Where was he?'

'Down at the sty. Would there be anything furthah?'

'No thank you, Miss Briggs.'

As the door closed, the Duke exploded with a loud report.

'Down at the sty!' he cried. 'Wouldn't you have known it! Whenever you want him, he's down at the sty, gazing at that pig of his, absorbed, like somebody watching a strip-tease act. It's not wholesome for a man to worship a pig the way he does. Isn't there something in the Bible about the Israelites worshipping a pig? No, it was a golden calf, but the principle's the same. I tell you . . .'

He broke off. The door had opened again. Lord Emsworth stood on the threshold, his mild face agitated.

'Connie, I can't find my umbrella.'

'Oh, Clarence!' said Lady Constance with the exasperation the head of the family so often aroused in her, and hustled him out towards the cupboard in the hall where, as he should have known perfectly well, his umbrella had its home.

Left alone, the Duke prowled about the room for some moments, chewing his moustache and examining his surroundings with popping eyes. He opened drawers, looked at books, stared at pictures, fiddled with pens and paper-knives. He picked up a photograph of Mr Schoonmaker and thought how right he had been in comparing his head to a pumpkin. He read the letter Lady Constance had been writing. Then, having exhausted all the entertainment the room had to offer, he sat down at the desk and gave himself up to thoughts of Lord Emsworth and the Empress.

Every day in every way, he was convinced, association with that ghastly porker made the feller pottier and pottier. And, in the Duke's opinion, he had been quite potty enough to start with.

## • III •

As the car rolled away from the front door, Lord Emsworth inside it clutching his umbrella, Lady Constance stood drooping wearily with the air of one who has just launched a battleship. Beach, the butler, who had been assisting at his employer's departure, eyed her with respectful sympathy. He, too, was feeling the strain that always resulted from getting Lord Emsworth off on a journey.

Myra Schoonmaker appeared, looking, except that she was not larded with sweet flowers, like Ophelia in Act Four, Scene Five, of Shakespeare's well-known play *Hamlet*.

'Oh, hello,' she said in a hollow voice.

'Oh, there you are, my dear,' said Lady Constance, ceasing to be the battered wreck and becoming the hostess. 'What are you planning to do this morning?'

'I don't know. I might write a letter or two.'

'I have a letter I must finish. To your father. But wouldn't it be nicer to be out in the open on such a lovely day?'

'Oh, I don't know.'

'Why not?'

'Oh, I don't know.'

Lady Constance sighed. But a hostess has to be bright, so she proceeded brightly.

'I have been seeing Lord Emsworth off. He's going to London.'

'Yes, he told me. He didn't seem very happy about it.'

'He wasn't,' said Lady Constance, a grim look coming into her face. 'But he must do his duty occasionally as a member of the House of Lords.'

'He'll miss his pig.'

'He can do without her society for a couple of days.'

'And he'll miss his flowers.'

'There are plenty of flowers in London. All he has to do . . . Oh, Heavens!'

'What's the matter?'

'I forgot to tell Clarence to be sure not to pick the flowers in Hyde Park. He will wander off there, and he will pick the flowers. He nearly got arrested once for doing it. Beach!'

'M'lady—?'

'If Lord Emsworth rings up tomorrow and says he is in prison and wants bail, tell him to get in touch immediately with his solicitors. Shoesmith, Shoesmith, Shoesmith and Shoesmith of Lincoln's Inn Fields.'

'Very good, m'lady.'

'I shan't be here.'

'No, m'lady. I quite understand.'

'He's sure to have forgotten their name.'

'I will refresh his lordship's memory.'

'Thank you, Beach.'

'Not at all, m'lady!'

Myra Schoonmaker was staring at her hostess. Her voice trembled a little as she said:

'You won't be here, Lady Constance?'

'I have to go to my hairdresser's in Shrewsbury, and I am lunching with some friends there. I shall be back for dinner, of course. And now I really must be going and finishing that letter to your father. I'll give him your love.'

'Yes, do,' said Myra, and sped off to Lord Emsworth's study, where there was a telephone. The number of the man she loved was graven on her heart. He was staying temporarily with his old Oxford friend, Lord Ickenham's nephew, Pongo Twistleton. But until now there had been no opportunity to call it.

Seated at the instrument with a wary eye on the door, for though Lord Emsworth had left, who knew that Lavender Briggs might not pop in at any moment, she heard the bell ringing in distant London, and presently a voice spoke.

'Darling!' said Myra. 'Is that you, darling? This is me, darling.'

'Darling!' said the voice devoutly.

'Darling,' said Myra, 'the most wonderful thing has happened, darling. Lady Constance is having her hair done tomorrow.'

'Oh, yes?' said the voice, seeming a little puzzled, as if wondering whether it would be in order to express a hope that she would have a fine day for it.

'Don't you get it, dumb-bell? She has to go to Shrewsbury, and she'll be away all day, so I can dash up to London and we can get married.'

There was a momentary silence at the other end of the wire. One would have gathered that the owner of the voice had had his breath taken away. Recovering it, he said:

'I see.'

'Aren't you pleased?'

'Oh, rather!'

'Well, you don't sound as if you were. Listen, darling. When I was in

London, I did a good deal of looking around for registry offices, just in case. I found one in Milton Street. Meet me there tomorrow at two sharp. I must hang up now, darling. Somebody may come in. Goodbye, darling.'

'Goodbye, darling.'

'Till tomorrow, darling.'

'Right ho, darling.'

'Goodbye, darling.'

And if they're listening in at the Market Blandings exchange, thought Myra, as she replaced the receiver, that'll give them something to chat about over their tea and crumpets.

# 2

## • 1 •

'And now,' said Pongo Twistleton, crushing out his cigarette in the ash tray and speaking with a note of quiet satisfaction in his voice, 'I shall have to be buzzing along. Got a date.'

He had been giving his uncle, Lord Ickenham, lunch at the Drones Club, and a very agreeable function he had found it, for the other, who like Lord Emsworth had graced the opening of Parliament with his presence, had been very entertaining on the subject of his experiences. But what had given him even more pleasure than his relative's mordant critique of the appearance of the four pursuivants, Rouge Croix, Bluemantle, Rouge Dragon and Portcullis, as they headed the procession, had been the stimulating thought that, having this engagement, he ran no risk at the conclusion of the meal of being enticed by his guest into what the latter called one of their pleasant and instructive afternoons. The ordeal of sharing these in the past had never failed to freeze his blood. The occasion when they had gone to the dog races together some years previously remained particularly green in his memory.

Of Frederick Altamont Cornwallis Twistleton, fifth Earl of Ickenham, a thoughtful critic had once said that in the late afternoon of his life he retained, together with a juvenile waistline, the bright enthusiasms and fresh, unspoiled outlook of a slightly inebriated undergraduate, and no one who knew him would have disputed the accuracy of the statement. As a young man in America, before a number of deaths in the family had led to his succession to the title, he had been at various times a cowboy, a soda jerker, a newspaper reporter and a prospector in the Mojave Desert, and there was not a ranch, a drug-store, a newspaper office or a sandy waste with which he had been connected that he had not done his best to enliven. His hair today was grey, but it was still his aim to enliven, as far as lay within his power, any environment in which he found himself. He liked, as he often said, to spread sweetness and light or, as he sometimes put it, give service with a smile. He was a tall distinguished-looking man with a jaunty moustache and an alert and enterprising eye. In this eye, as he turned it on his nephew, there was a look of disappointment and reproach, as if he had expected better things from one of his flesh and blood.

'You are leaving me? Why is that? I had been hoping for—'

'I know,' said Pongo austerely. 'One of our pleasant and instructive afternoons. Well, pleasant and instructive afternoons are off. I've got to see a man.'

'About a dog?'

'Not so much about a dog as—'

'Phone him and put him off.'

'I can't.'

'Who is this fellow?'

'Bill Bailey.'

Lord Ickenham seemed surprised.

'He's back, is he?'

'Eh?'

'I was given to understand that he had left home. I seem to remember his wife being rather concerned about it.'

Pongo saw that his uncle had got everything mixed up, as elderly gentlemen will.

'Oh, this chap isn't really Bill. I believe he was christened Cuthbert. But if a fellow's name is Bailey, you've more or less got to call him Bill.'

'Of course, noblesse oblige. Friend of yours?'

'Bosom. Up at Oxford with him.'

'Tell him to join us here.'

'Can't be done. I've arranged to meet him in Milton Street.'

'Where's that?'

'In South Kensington.'

Lord Ickenham pursed his lips.

'South Kensington? Where sin stalks naked through the dark alleys and only might is right. Give this man a miss. He'll lead you astray.'

'He won't jolly well lead me astray. And why? Because for one thing he's a curate and for another he's getting married. The rendezvous is at the Milton Street registry office.'

'You are his witness?'

'That's right.'

'And who is the bride?'

'American girl.'

'Nice?'

'Bill speaks well of her.'

'What's her name?'

'Schoonmaker.'

Lord Ickenham leaped in his seat.

'Good heavens! Not little Myra Schoonmaker?'

'I don't know if she's little or not. I've never seen her. But her name's Myra all right. Why—do you know her?'

A tender look had come into Lord Ickenham's handsome face. He twirled his moustache sentimentally.

'Do I know her! Many's the time I've given her her bath. Not recently, of course, but years ago when I was earning my living in New York. Jimmy Schoonmaker was my great buddy in those days. I don't get over to God's country much now, your aunt thinks it better otherwise, and I've often wondered how he was making out. He promised, when I knew him, to become a big shot in the financial world. Even then, though comparatively young, he was able to shoot a cigar across his face without touching it with his fingers, which we all know is the first step to establishing oneself as a tycoon. I expect by this time he's the Wolf of Wall Street, and is probably offended if he isn't investigated every other week by a Senate commission. Well, it all seems very odd to me.'

'What's odd?'

'His daughter getting married at a registry office. I should have thought she would have had a big choral wedding with bridesmaids and bishops and all the fixings.'

'Ah, I see what you mean.' Pongo looked cautiously over his shoulder. No one appeared to be within earshot. 'Yes, you would think so, wouldn't you? But Bill's nuptials have got to be solemnized with more than a spot of secrecy and silence. The course of true love hasn't been running too smooth. Hell-hounds have been bunging spanners into it.'

'What hell-hounds would those be?'

'I should have said one hell-hound. You know her. Lady Constance Keeble.'

'What, dear old Connie? How that name brings back fragrant memories. I wonder if you recall the time when you and I went to Blandings Castle, I posing as Sir Roderick Glossop, the loony doctor, you as his nephew Basil?'

'I recall it,' said Pongo with a strong shudder. The visit alluded to had given him nightmares for months.

'Happy days, happy days! I enjoyed my stay enormously, and wish I could repeat it. The bracing air, the pleasant society, the occasional refreshing look at Emsworth's pig, it all combined to pep me up and brush away the cobwebs. But how does Connie come into it?'

'She forbade the banns.'

'I still don't follow the scenario. Why was she in a position to do so?'

'What happened was this. She and Schoonmaker are old pals—I got all this from Bill, so I assume we can take it as accurate—and he wanted his daughter to have a London season, so he brought her over here and left her in Lady C.'s charge.'

'All clear so far.'

'And plumb spang in the middle of their London season Lady C. discovered that the beazel was walking out with Bill. Ascertaining that he was a curate, she became as sore as a gumboil.'

'She does not like curates?'

'That's the idea one gets.'

'Odd. She doesn't like me, either. Very hard to please, that woman. What's wrong with curates?'

'Well, they're all pretty hard up. Bill hasn't a bean.'

'I begin to see. Humble suitor. Curious how prejudiced so many people are against humble suitors. My own case is one in point. When I was courting your Aunt Jane, her parents took the bleakest view of the situation, and weren't their faces red when one day I suddenly became that noblest of created beings, an Earl, a hell of a fellow with four christian names and a coronet hanging on a peg in the downstairs cupboard. Her father, scorning me because I was a soda-jerker at the time, frequently, I believe, alluded to me as "that bum", but it was very different when I presented myself at his Park Avenue residence with a coronet on the back of my head and a volume of Debrett under my arm. He gave me his blessing and a cigar. No chance of Bill Bailey becoming an earl, I suppose?'

'Not unless he murders about fifty-seven uncles and cousins.'

'Which a curate, of course, would hesitate to do. So what was Connie's procedure?'

'She lugged the poor wench off to Blandings, and she's been there ever since, practically in durance vile, her every movement watched. But this Myra seems to be a sensible, level-headed girl, because, learning from her spies that Lady C. was to go to Shrewsbury for a hair-do and wouldn't be around till dinner time, she phoned Bill that she would be free that day and would nip up to London and marry him. She told him to meet her at the Milton Street registry office, where the project could be put through speedily and at small expense.'

'I see. Very shrewd. I often think these runaway marriages are best. No fuss and feathers. After all, who wants a lot of bishops cluttering up the place? I often say, when you've seen one bishop, you've seen them all.' Lord Ickenham paused. 'Well,' he said, looking at his watch. 'I suppose it's about time we were getting along. Don't want to be late.'

Pongo started. To his sensitive ears this sounded extremely like the beginning of one of their pleasant and instructive afternoons. In just such a tone of voice had his relative a few years earlier suggested that they might look in at the dog races, for there was, he said, no better way of studying the soul of the people than to mingle with them in their simple pastimes.

'We? You aren't coming?'

'Of course I'm coming. Two witnesses are always better than one, and little Myra—'

'I can't guarantee that she's little.'

'And Myra, whatever her size, would never forgive me if I were not there to hold her hand when the firing squad assembles.'

Pongo chewed his lower lip, this way and that dividing the swift mind.

'Well, all right. But no larks.'

'My dear boy! As if I should dream of being frivolous on such a sacred occasion. Of course, if I find this Bill Bailey of yours unworthy of her, I shall put a stopper on the proceedings, as any man of sensibility would. What sort of a chap is he? Pale and fragile, I suppose, with a touch of consumption and a tendency to recite the collect for the day in a high tenor voice?'

'Pale and fragile, my foot. He boxed three years for Oxford.'

'He did?'

'And went through the opposition like a dose of salts.'

'Then all should be well. I expect I shall take the fellow to my bosom.'

His expectation was fulfilled. The Rev. Cuthbert Bailey met with his instant approval. He liked his curates substantial, and Bill proved to be definitely the large economy size, the sort of curate whom one could picture giving the local backslider the choice between seeing the light or getting plugged in the eye. Amplifying his earlier remarks, Pongo on the journey to Milton Street had told his uncle that in the parish of Bottleton East, where he had recently held a cure of souls, Bill Bailey had been universally respected, and Lord Ickenham could readily appreciate why. He himself would have treated with the utmost respect any young man so obviously capable of a sweet left hook followed by a snappy right to the button. A captious critic might have felt on seeing the Rev. Cuthbert that it would have been more suitable for one in holy orders to have looked a little less like the logical contender for the world's heavyweight championship, but it was impossible to regard his rugged features and bulging shoulders without an immediate feeling of awe. Impossible, too, not to like his manifest honesty and simplicity. It seemed to Lord Ickenham that in probing beneath the forbidding exterior to the gentle soul it hid his little Myra had done the smart thing.

They fell into pleasant conversation, but after the first few exchanges it was plain to Lord Ickenham that the young man of God was becoming extremely nervous. Nor was the reason for this difficult to divine. Some twenty minutes had elapsed, and there were still no signs of the bride-to-be, and nothing so surely saps the morale of a bridegroom on his wedding day as the failure of the party of the second part to put in an appearance at the tryst.

Ten minutes later, Bill Bailey rose, his homely features registering anguish.

'She isn't coming?'

Lord Ickenham tried to comfort him with the quite erroneous statement that it was early yet. Pongo, also anxious to be helpful, said he would go out and cock an eye up and down the street to see if there were any signs of her. His departure from the room synchronized with a hollow groan from the suffering young man.

'I must have put her off!'

Lord Ickenham raised a sympathetic but puzzled eyebrow.

'I don't think I understand you. Put her off? How?'

'By the way I spoke on the phone. You see, I was a bit doubtful of this idea of hers. It didn't seem right somehow that she should be taking this terrifically important step without thinking it over. I mean, I've so little to offer her. I thought we ought to wait till I got a vicarage.'

'I follow you now. You had scruples?'

'Yes.'

'Did you tell her so?'

'No, but she must have noticed something odd in my voice, because she asked me if I wasn't pleased.'

'To which you replied—?'

'"Oh, rather!"'

Lord Ickenham shook his head.

'You should have done better than that. Or did you say "Oh, ra-a-a-ther!" emphasizing it and dragging it out, as it were? Joyously, if you know what I mean, with a sort of lilt in the voice?'

'I'm afraid I didn't. You see—'

'I know. You had scruples. That's the curate in you coming out. You must fight against this tendency. You don't suppose Young Lochinvar had scruples, do you? You know the poem about Young Lochinvar?'

'Oh, yes. I used to recite it as a kid.'

'I, too, and to solid applause, though there were critics who considered that I was better at "It wath the schcooner Hesperuth that thailed the thtormy thea". I was rather short on front teeth in those days. But despite these scruples you came to this marriage depot.'

'Yes.'

'And the impression you have given me is that your one desire is to have the registrar start doing his stuff.'

'Yes.'

'You overcame your scruples?'

'Yes.'

'I quite understand. I've done the same thing myself. I suppose if the scruples I've overcome in my time were laid end to end, they would reach from London to Glasgow. Ah, Pongo,' said Lord Ickenham, as his nephew appeared in the doorway. 'Anything to report?'

'Not a thing. Not a single female as far as the eye could reach. I'll tell you what occurred to me, Bill, as I was scanning the horizon.'

'Probably the very thing that has just occurred to me,' said Lord Ickenham. 'You were thinking that Lady Constance must have changed her mind about going to Shrewsbury for that hair-do.'

'That's right. And with her on the premises, the popsy—'

Bill's rugged features registered displeasure.

'I wish you wouldn't call her a popsy.'

'With her on the premises, your ball of worsted would naturally be unable to make her getaway. You'll probably receive a letter tomorrow explaining the situation and making arrangements for the next fixture.'

'Yes, that must be it,' said Bill, brightening a little. 'Though you'd have thought she would have wired,' he added, sinking into the depths again.

Lord Ickenham patted his burly shoulder paternally.

'My dear chap! How could she? The Market Blandings post office is two miles from the castle and, as Pongo says, her every movement is watched. She'll be lucky if she gets so much as a letter through the lines without having it steamed open and intercepted. If I were you, I wouldn't worry for a moment.'

'I'll try not to,' said Bill, heaving a sigh that shook the room. 'Well, anyway, there's no sense in hanging around here. This place gives me the creeps. Thanks for coming along, Pongo. Thanks for coming along, Lord Ickenham. Sorry your time was wasted.'

'My dear fellow, time is never wasted when it is passed in pleasant company.'

'No. No. There's that, of course. Well, I'll be off.'

As the door closed behind him, Lord Ickenham sighed, not so vigorously as Bill had done but with a wealth of compassion. He mourned in spirit for the young cleric.

'Too bad,' he said. 'It is always difficult for a bridegroom to key himself up to going through the wedding ceremony, an ordeal that taxes the stoutest, and when he's done it and the bride doesn't meet him half way, the iron enters into the soul pretty deeply. And no knowing when the vigilance of the authorities will be relaxed again, I suppose, if ever. You don't make prison breaks easily when Connie is holding the jailer's keys.'

Pongo nodded. He, too, mourned in spirit for his stricken friend.

'No,' he said. 'I'm afraid Bill's in a spot. And what makes the situation stickier is that Archie Gilpin's at Blandings.'

'Who?'

'The Duke of Dunstable's nephew.'

'Ricky Gilpin's brother?'

'That's right. You ever met him?'

'Never. I know Dunstable, of course, and I know Ricky, but this Archibald is a sealed book to me. Who told you he was at Blandings?'

'He did. In person. I ran into him yesterday and he said he was off there on the afternoon train. Pretty sinister, it seemed to me.'

'Why is that?'

'Well, dash it, there he'll be closeted with the girl, and who knows she won't decide to switch from Bill to him? He's a very good-looking bloke. Which you can't say Bill is.'

'No, I would call Bill's an interesting rather than a beautiful face. He reminds me a little of one of my colleagues on the Wyoming ranch where I held a salaried position in my younger days as a cow-puncher, of whom another of my colleagues, a gifted phrasemaker, said that he had a face that would stop a clock. No doubt Bill has stopped dozens. But surely the little Myra I used to wrap in a bath towel and dandle on my knee can't have grown up into the sort of girl who attaches all that importance to looks.'

'You never know. Girls do go for the finely-chiselled. And apart from his looks, he's an artist, and there's something about artists that seems to act on the other sex like catnip on cats. What's more, I happen to know, because I met a fellow who knows a chap who knows her, that Archie's girl has just broken their engagement.'

'Indeed?'

'A girl called Millicent Rigby. Archie works on one of those papers Lord Tilbury runs at the Mammoth Publishing Company, and she's Tilbury's secretary. This fellow told me that the chap had told him that he had had it direct from the Rigby wench that she had handed Archie the black spot. You see what that means?'

'Not altogether.'

'Use your bean, Uncle Fred. You know what you do when your girl gives you the push. You dash off and propose to another girl, just to show her she isn't the only onion in the stew.'

Lord Ickenham nodded. It was many years since he had acted in the manner described, but he, too, had lived in Arcady. 'Ah, youth, youth!' he was saying to himself, and he shuddered a little as he recalled the fearful female down Greenwich Village way, all beads and bangles and matted hair, at whose sandalled feet he had laid his heart the second time Pongo's Aunt Jane had severed relations with him.

'Yes, I follow you now. This does make Archibald a menace, and one cannot but feel a certain anxiety for Bill. Where can I find him, by the way?'

'He's staying with me at my flat. Why?'

'I was thinking I might look in on him from time to time and try to cheer him up. Take him to the dog races, perhaps.'

Pongo quivered like an aspen. He always quivered like an aspen when reminded of the afternoon when he had attended the dog races in Lord Ickenham's company. Though on that occasion, as his uncle had often pointed out, a wiser policeman would have been content with a mere reprimand.

## • II •

The canny peer of the realm, when duty calls him to lend his presence to the ceremony of the opening of Parliament, hires his robes and coronet from that indispensable clothing firm, the Brothers Moss of Covent Garden, whose boast is that they can at any time fit anyone out as anything and have him ready to go anywhere. Only they can prevent him being caught short. It was to their emporium that, after leaving his nephew, Lord Ickenham repaired, carrying a suitcase. And he had returned the suitcase's contents and paid his modest bill, when there entered, also carrying a suitcase, a tall, limp, drooping figure, at the sight of which he uttered a glad cry.

'Emsworth! My dear fellow, how nice to run into you again. So you too are bringing back your sheaves?'

'Eh?' said Lord Emsworth, who always said 'Eh?' when anyone addressed him suddenly. 'Oh, hullo, Ickenham. Are you in London?'

Lord Ickenham assured him that he was, and Lord Emsworth said so was he. This having been straightened out,

'Were you at that thing this morning?' he said.

'I was indeed,' said Lord Ickenham, 'and looking magnificent. I don't suppose there is a peer in England who presents a posher appearance when wearing the reach-me-downs and comic hat than I do. Just before the procession got under way, I heard Rouge Croix whisper to Bluemantle, "Don't look now, but who's that chap over there?", and Bluemantle whispered back, "I haven't the foggiest, but evidently some terrific swell." But it's nice to get out of the fancy dress, isn't it, and it's wonderful seeing you, Emsworth. How's the Empress?'

'Eh? Oh, capital, capital, capital. I left her in the care of my pigman Wellbeloved, in whom I have every confidence.'

'Splendid. Well, let's go and have a couple for the tonsils and a pleasant chat. I know a little bar round the corner,' said Lord Ickenham, who, wherever he was, always knew a little bar round the corner. 'You have rather a fatigued air, as if putting on all that dog this morning had exhausted you. A whisky with a splash of soda will soon bring back the sparkle to your eyes.'

Seated in the little bar round the corner, Lord Ickenham regarded his companion with some concern.

'Yes,' he said. 'I was right. You don't look your usual bonny self. Very testing, these Openings of Parliament. Usually I give them a miss, as no doubt you do. What brought you up today?'

'Connie insisted.'

'I understand. There are, I should imagine, few finer right-and-left-hand insisters than Lady Constance. Charming woman, of course.'

'Connie?' said Lord Emsworth, surprised.

'Though perhaps not everybody's cup of tea,' said Lord Ickenham, sensing the incredulity in his companion's voice. 'But tell me, how is everything at Blandings Castle? Jogging along nicely, I hope. I always look on that little shack of yours as an earthly Paradise.'

It was not within Lord Emsworth's power to laugh bitterly, but he uttered a bleating sound which was as near as he could get to a bitter laugh. The description of Blandings Castle as an earthly Paradise, with his sister Constance, the Duke, Lavender Briggs, and the Church Lads' Brigade running around loose there, struck him as ironical. He mused for a space in silence.

'I don't know what to do, Ickenham,' he said, his sombre train of thought coming to its terminus.

'You mean now? Have another.'

'No, no, thank you, really. It is very unusual for me to indulge in alcoholic stimulant so early in the day. I was referring to conditions at Blandings Castle.'

'Not so good?'

'They are appalling. I have a new secretary, the worst I have ever had. Worse than Baxter.'

'That seems scarcely credible.'

'I assure you. A girl of the name of Briggs. She persecutes me.'

'Get rid of her.'

'How can I? Connie engaged her. And the Duke of Dunstable is staying at the castle.'

'What, again?'

'And the Church Lads' Brigade are camping in the park, yelling and squealing all the time, and I am convinced that it was one of them who threw a roll at my top hat.'

'Your top hat? When did you ever wear a top hat?'

'It was at the school treat. Connie always makes me wear a top hat at the school treat. I went into the tent at teatime to see that everything was going along all right, and as I was passing down the aisle between the tables, a boy threw a crusty roll at my hat and knocked it off. Nothing will persuade me, Ickenham, that the culprit was not one of the Church Lads.'

'But you have no evidence that would stand up in a court of law?'

'Eh? No, none.'

'Too bad. Well, the whole set-up sounds extraordinarily like Devil's Island, and I am not surprised that you find it difficult to keep the upper lip as stiff as one likes to see upper lips.' A strange light had come into Lord Ickenham's eyes. His nephew Pongo would have recognized it. It was the light which had so often come into them when the other was suggesting that they embark on one of their pleasant and instructive afternoons. 'What you need, it seems to me,' he said, 'is some rugged ally at your side, someone who will quell the secretary, look Connie in the eye and make her wilt, take the Duke off your hands and generally spread sweetness and light.'

'Ah!' said Lord Emsworth with a sigh, as he allowed his mind to dwell on this utopian picture.

'Would you like me to come to Blandings?'

Lord Emsworth started. His pince-nez, which always dropped off his nose when he was deeply stirred, did an adagio dance at the end of their string.

'Would you?'

'Nothing would please me more. When do you return there?'

'Tomorrow. This is very good of you, Ickenham.'

'Not at all. We earls must stick together. There is just one thing. You won't mind if I bring a friend with me? I would not ask you, but he's just back from Brazil and would be rather lost in London without me.'

'Brazil? Do people live in Brazil!'

'Frequently, I believe. This chap has been there some years. He is connected with the Brazil nut industry. I am a little sketchy as to what his actual job is, but I think he's the fellow who squeezes the nuts in the squeezer, to give them that peculiar shape. I may be wrong, of course. Then I bring him with me?'

'Certainly, certainly, certainly. Delighted, delighted.'

'A wise decision on your part. Who knows that he may not help the general composition? He might fall in love with the secretary and marry her and take her to Brazil.'

'True.'

'Or murder the Duke with some little-known Asiatic poison. Or be of assistance in a number of other ways. I'm sure you'll be glad to have him about the place. He is house-broken and eats whatever you're having yourself. What train are you taking tomorrow?'

'The 11.45 from Paddington.'

'Expect us there, my dear Emsworth,' said Lord Ickenham. 'And not only there, but with our hair in a braid and, speaking for myself, prepared to be up and doing with a heart for any fate. I'll go and ring my friend up now and tell him to start packing.'

## · III ·

It was some hours later that Pongo Twistleton, having a tissue-restorer before dinner in the Drones Club smoking-room, was informed by the smoking-room waiter that a gentleman was in the hall, asking to see him, and a shadow fell on his tranquil mood. Too often when gentlemen called asking to see members of the Drones Club, their visits had to do with accounts rendered for goods supplied, with the subject of remittances which would oblige cropping up, and he knew that his own affairs were in a state of some disorder.

'Is he short and stout?' he asked nervously, remembering that the representative of the Messrs Hicks and Adrian, to whom he owed a princely sum for shirtings, socks and underlinen, could be so described.

'Far from it. Tall and beautifully slender,' said a hearty voice behind him. 'Svelte may be the word I am groping for.'

'Oh, hullo, Uncle Fred,' said Pongo, relieved. 'I thought you were someone else.'

'Rest assured that I am not. First, last and all the time yours to command Ickenham! I took the liberty of walking in, my dear Pongo, confident that I would receive a nephew's welcome. We Ickenhams dislike to wait in halls. It offends our pride. What's that you're having? Order me one of the same. I suppose it will harden my arteries but I like them hard. Bill not with you tonight?'

'No. He had to go to Bottleton East to pick up some things.'

'You have not seen him recently?'

'No, I haven't been back to the flat. Do you want me to give you dinner?'

'Just what I was about to suggest. It will be your last opportunity for some little time. I'm off to Blandings Castle tomorrow.'

'You're . . . *what*?'

'Yes, after I left you I ran into Emsworth and he asked me to drop down there for a few days or possibly longer. He's having trouble, poor chap.'

'What's wrong with him?'

'Practically everything. He has a new secretary who harries him. The Duke of Dunstable seems to be a fixture on the premises. Lady Constance has pinched his favourite hat and given it to the deserving poor, and he lives in constant fear of her getting away with his shooting jacket with the holes in the elbows. In addition to which, he is much beset by Church Lads.'

'Eh?'

'You see how full my hands will be, if I am to help him. I shall have to devise some means of ridding him of this turbulent secretary—'

'Church Lads?'

'—shipping the Duke back to Wiltshire, where he belongs, curbing Connie and putting the fear of God into these Church Lads. An impressive programme, and one that would be beyond the scope of a lesser man. Most fortunately I am not a lesser man.'

'How do you mean, Church Lads?'

'Weren't you ever a Church Lad?'

'No.'

'Well, many of the younger generation are. They assemble in gangs in most rural parishes. The Church Lads' Brigade they call themselves. Connie has allowed them to camp out by the lake.'

'And Emsworth doesn't like them?'

'Nobody could, except their mothers. No, he eyes them askance. They ruin the scenery, poison the air with their uncouth cries, and at the recent school treat, so he tells me, knocked off his top hat with a crusty roll.'

Pongo shook his head censoriously.

'He shouldn't have worn a topper at a school treat,' he said. He was remembering functions of this kind into which he had been lured at one time and another by clergymen's daughters for whose charms he had fallen. The one at Maiden Eggesford in Somerset, when his great love for Angelica Briscoe, daughter of the Rev. P. P. Briscoe, who vetted the souls of the peasantry in that hamlet, had led him to put his head in a sack and allow himself to be prodded with sticks by the younger set, had never been erased from his memory. 'A topper! Good Lord! Just asking for it!'

'He acted under duress. He would have preferred to wear a cloth cap, but Connie insisted. You know how persuasive she can be.'

'She's a tough baby.'

'Very tough. Let us hope she takes to Bill Bailey.'

'Does what?'

'Oh, I didn't tell you, did I? Bill is accompanying me to Blandings.'

'What!'

'Yes, Emsworth very kindly included him in his invitation. We're off tomorrow on the 11.45, singing a gypsy song.'

Horror leaped into Pongo's eyes. He started violently, and came within an ace of spilling his martini with a spot of lemon peel in it. Fond though he was of his Uncle Fred, he had never wavered in his view that in the interests of young English manhood he ought to be kept on a chain and seldom allowed at large.

'But my gosh!'

'Something troubling you?'

'You can't . . . what's the word . . . you can't subject poor old Bill to this frightful ordeal.'

Lord Ickenham's eyebrows rose.

'Well, really, Pongo, if you consider it an ordeal for a young man to be in the same house with the girl he loves, you must have less sentiment in you than I had supposed.'

'Yes, that's all very well. His ball of fluff will be there, I agree. But what good's that going to do him when two minutes after his arrival Lady Constance grabs him by the seat of the trousers and heaves him out?'

'I anticipate no such contingency. You seem to have a very odd idea of the sort of thing that goes on at Blandings Castle, my boy. You appear to look on that refined home as a kind of Bowery saloon with bodies being hurled through the swing doors all the time, and bounced along the sidewalk. Nothing of that nature will occur. We shall be like a great big family. Peace and good will everywhere. Too bad you won't be with us.'

'I'm all right here, thanks,' said Pongo with a slight shudder as he recalled some of the high spots of his previous visit to the castle. 'But I still maintain that when Lady Constance hears the name Bailey—'

'But she won't. You don't suppose a shrewd man like myself would have overlooked a point like that. He's calling himself Cuthbert Meriwether. I told him to write it down and memorize it.'

'She'll find out.'

'Not a chance. Who's going to tell her?'

Pongo gave up the struggle. He knew the futility of arguing, and he had just perceived the bright side to the situation—to wit, that after tomorrow more than a hundred miles would separate him from his amiable but hair-bleaching relative. The thought was a very heartening one. Going by the form book, he took it for granted that ere many suns had set the old buster would be up to some kind of hell which would ultimately stagger civilization and turn the moon to blood, but what mattered was that he would be up to it at Lord Emsworth's rural seat and not in London. How right, he felt, the author of the well-known hymn had been in saying that peace, perfect peace is to be attained only when loved ones are far away.

'Let's go in and have some dinner,' he said.

# 3

## · I ·

One of the things that made Lord Emsworth such a fascinating travelling companion was the fact that shortly after the start of any journey he always fell into a restful sleep. The train bearing him and guests to Market Blandings had glided from the platform of Paddington station, as promised by the railway authorities, whose word is their bond, at 11.45, and at 12.10 he was lying back in his seat with his eyes closed, making little whistling noises punctuated at intervals by an occasional snort. Lord Ickenham, accordingly, was able to talk to the junior member of the party without the risk, always to be avoided when there is plotting afoot, of being overheard.

'Nervous, Bill?' he said, regarding the Rev. Cuthbert sympathetically. He had seemed to notice during the early stages of the journey a tendency on the other's part to twitch like a galvanized frog and allow a sort of glaze to creep over his eyes.

Bill Bailey breathed deeply.

'I'm feeling as I did when I tottered up the pulpit steps to deliver my first sermon.'

'I quite understand. While there is no more admirably educational experience for a young fellow starting out in life than going to stay at a country house under a false name, it does tend to chill the feet to no little extent. Pongo, though he comes from a stout-hearted family, felt just as you do when I took him to Blandings Castle as Sir Roderick Glossop's nephew Basil. I remember telling him at the time that he reminded me of Hamlet. The same moodiness and irresolution, coupled with a strongly marked disposition to get out of the train and walk back to London. Having become accustomed to this kind of thing myself, so much so that now I don't think it quite sporting to go to stay with people under my own name, I have lost that cat-on-hot-bricks feeling which I must have had at one time, but I can readily imagine that for a novice an experience of this sort cannot fail to be quite testing. Your sermon was a success, I trust?'

'Well, they didn't rush the pulpit.'

'You are too modest, Bill Bailey. I'll bet you had them rolling in the aisles and carried out on stretchers. And this visit to Blandings Castle will, I know, prove equally triumphant. You are probably asking yourself what I am hoping to accomplish by it. Nothing actually constructive, but I think it essential for you to keep an eye on this Archibald Gilpin of whom I have heard so much. Pongo tells me he is an artist, and you know how dangerous they are. Watch him closely. Every time he suggests to Myra an after-dinner stroll to the lake to look at the moonlight glimmering on the water—and on the Church Lads' Brigade too, of course, for I understand that they are camping out down there—you must join the hikers.'

'Yes.'

'That's the spirit. And the same thing applies to any attempt on his part to get the . . . popsy is the term you use, is it not?'

'It is not the term I use. It's the term Pongo uses, and I've had to speak to him about it.'

'I'm sorry. Any attempt on his part, I should have said, to get the girl you love into the rose garden must be countered with the same firmness and resolution. But I can leave that to you. Tell me, how did you two happen to meet?'

A rugged face like Bill Bailey's could never really be a mirror of the softer emotions, but something resembling a tender look did come into it. If their host had not at this moment uttered a sudden snort rather like that of Empress of Blandings on beholding linseed meal, Lord Ickenham would have heard him sigh sentimentally.

'You remember that song, the Limehouse Blues?'

'It is one I frequently sing in my bath. But aren't we changing the subject?'

'No, what I was going to say was that she had heard the song over in America, and she'd read that book *Limehouse Nights*, and she was curious to see the place. So she sneaked off one afternoon and went there. Well, Limehouse is next door to Bottleton East, where my job was, and I happened to be doing some visiting there for a pal of mine who had sprained an ankle while trying to teach the choir boys to dance the carioca, and I came along just as someone was snatching her bag. So, of course, I biffed the blighter.'

'Where did they bury the unfortunate man?'

'Oh, I didn't biff him much, just enough to make him see how wrong it is to snatch bags.'

'And then?'

'Well, one thing led to another, sort of.'

'I see. And what is she like these days?'

'You know her?'

'In her childhood we were quite intimate. She used to call me Uncle Fred. Extraordinarily pretty she was then. Still is, I hope?'

'Yes.'

'That's good. So many attractive children lose their grip and go all to pieces in later life.'

'Yes.'

'But she didn't?'

'No.'

'Still comely, is she?'

'Yes.'

'And you would die for one little rose from her hair?'

'Yes.'

'There is no peril, such for instance as having Lady Constance Keeble look squiggle-eyed at you, that you would not face for her sake?'

'No.'

'Your conversational method, my dear Bill,' said Lord Ickenham, regarding him approvingly, 'impresses me a good deal and has shown me that I must change the set-up as I had envisaged it. I had planned on arrival at the castle to draw you out on the subject of Brazil, so that you could hold everybody spellbound with your fund of good stories about your adventures there and make yourself the life of the party, but I feel now that that is not the right approach.'

'Brazil?'

'Ah, yes, I didn't mention that to you, did I? I told Emsworth that there was where you came from.'

'Why Brazil?'

'Oh, one gets these ideas. But I was saying that I had changed my mind about featuring you as a sparkling raconteur. Having had the pleasure of conversing with you, I see you now as the strong, silent man, the fellow with the far-away look in his eyes who rarely speaks except in monosyllables. So if anybody tries to pump you about Brazil, just grunt. Like our host,' said Lord Ickenham, indicating Lord Emsworth, who was doing so. 'A pity in a way, of course, for I had a couple of good stories about the Brazilian ants which would have gone down well. As I dare say you know, they go about eating everything in sight, like Empress of Blandings.'

The sound of that honoured name must have penetrated Lord Emsworth's slumbers, for his eyes opened and he sat up, blinking.

'Did I hear you say something about the Empress?'

'I was telling Meriwether here what a superb animal she was, the only pig that has ever won the silver medal in the Fat Pigs class three years in succession at the Shropshire Agricultural Show. Wasn't I, Meriwether?'

'Yes.'

'He says Yes. You must show her to him first thing.'

'Eh? Oh, of course. Yes, certainly, certainly, certainly,' said Lord Emsworth, well pleased. 'You'll join us, Ickenham?'

'Not immediately, if you don't mind. I yield to no one in my appreciation of the Empress, but I feel that on arrival at the old shanty what I shall need first is a refreshing cup of tea.'

'Tea?' said Lord Emsworth, as if puzzled by the word. 'Tea? Oh, tea? Yes, of course, tea. Don't take it myself, but Connie has it on the terrace every afternoon. She'll look after you.'

## · II ·

Lady Constance was alone at the tea-table when Lord Ickenham reached it. As he approached, she lowered the cucumber sandwich with which she had been about to refresh herself and contrived what might have passed for a welcoming smile. To say that she was glad to see Lord Ickenham would be overstating the case, and she had already spoken her mind to her brother Clarence with reference to his imbecility in inviting him—with a friend—to Blandings Castle. But, as she had so often had to remind herself when coping with the Duke of Dunstable, she was a hostess, and a hostess must conceal her emotions.

'So nice to see you again, Lord Ickenham. So glad you were able to come,' she said, not actually speaking from between clenched teeth, but far from warmly. 'Will you have some tea, or would you rather . . . Are you looking for something?'

'Nothing important,' said Lord Ickenham, whose eyes had been flitting to and fro as if he felt something to be missing. 'I had been expecting to see my little friend, Myra Schoonmaker. Doesn't she take her dish of tea of an afternoon?'

'Myra went for a walk. You know her?'

'In her childhood we were quite intimate. Her father was a great friend of mine.'

The rather marked frostiness of Lady Constance's manner melted somewhat. Nothing would ever make her forget what this man in a single brief visit had done to the cloistral peace of Blandings Castle while spreading sweetness and light there, but to a friend of James Schoonmaker much had to be forgiven. In a voice that was almost cordial she said:

'Have you seen him lately?'

'Alas, not for many years. He has this unfortunate habit so many Americans have of living in America.'

Lady Constance sighed. She, too, had deplored this whim of James Schoonmaker's.

'And as my dear wife feels rightly or wrongly that it is safer for me not to be exposed to the temptations of New York but to live a quiet rural life at Ickenham Hall, Hants, our paths have parted, much to my regret. I knew him when he was a junior member of one of those Wall Street firms. I suppose he's a monarch of finance now, rolling in the stuff?'

'He has been very successful, yes.'

'I always predicted that he would be. I never actually saw him talking into three telephones at the same time, for he had not yet reached those heights, but it was obvious that the day would come when he would be able to do it without difficulty.'

'He was over here not long ago. He left Myra with me. He wanted her to have a London season.'

'Just the kindly sort of thing he would do. Did she enjoy it?'

Lady Constance frowned.

'I was unfortunately obliged to take her away from London after we had been there a few weeks. I found that she had become involved with a quite impossible young man.'

There was shocked horror in Lord Ickenham's 'Tut-tut!'

'She insisted that they were engaged. Absurd, of course.'

'Why absurd?'

'He is a curate.'

'I have known some quite respectable curates.'

'Have you ever known one who had any money?'

'Well, no. They don't often have much, do they? I suppose a curate who was quick with his fingers would make a certain amount out of the Sunday offertory bag, but nothing more than a small, steady income. Did Myra blow her top?'

'I beg your pardon?'

'Is she emotionally disturbed at being parted from the man of her choice?'

'She seems depressed.'

'What she needs is young society. How extremely fortunate that I was able to bring my friend Meriwether with me.'

Lady Constance started. She had momentarily forgotten his friend Meriwether.

'Emsworth took him off to look at the Empress, feeling that it would have a tonic effect after the long railway journey. You'll like Meriwether.'

'Indeed?' said Lady Constance, who considered this point a very moot one. She was strongly of the opinion that any associate of Frederick, fifth Earl of Ickenham, would be as unfit for human consumption as that blot on the peerage himself. The slight flicker of friendliness resulting from the discovery that he had at one time been on cordial terms with the man who meant so much to her had died away, and only the memory of his last visit to the castle remained. She wished she did not remember that visit so clearly. Like quite a number of those whose paths Lord Ickenham had crossed, she wanted to forget the past. Pongo Twistleton would have understood how she felt.

'You have known Mr Meriwether a long time?' she said.

'From boyhood. His boyhood, of course, not mine.'

'He comes from Brazil, I hear.'

'Yes, like Charley's Aunt. But—' Here Lord Ickenham's voice took on a grave note, '—on no account mention Brazil to him, if you don't mind. It was the scene of the great tragedy of his life. His young wife fell into the Amazon and was eaten by an alligator.'

'How dreadful!'

'For her, yes, though not of course for the alligator. I thought I had better give you this word of warning. Pass it along, will you? Oh, hullo, Dunstable.'

The Duke had lumbered on to the terrace and was peering at him in his popeyed way.

'Hullo, Ickenham. You here again?'

'That's right.'

'You've aged.'

'Not spiritually. My heart is still the heart of a little child.'

'Pass what along?'

'Ah, you overhead what I was saying? I was speaking of my friend Meriwether, whom Lady Constance very kindly invited here with me.'

It would be too much, perhaps, to say that Lady Constance snorted at this explanation of Bill's presence in the home, but she unquestionably sniffed. She said nothing, and ate a cucumber sandwich in rather a marked manner. She was thinking that she would have more to say to her brother Clarence on this subject when she got him alone.

'What about him?'

'I was urging Lady Constance not to speak to him of Brazil. Will you remember this?'

'What would I want to speak to him of Brazil for?'

'You might on learning that that was where he had spent much of his life. And if you did, a faraway look would come into his eyes and he would grunt with pain. His young wife fell into the Amazon.'

'Potty thing to do.'

'And was eaten by an alligator.'

'Well, what else did the silly ass expect would happen? Connie,' said the Duke, dismissing a topic that had failed from the start to grip him. 'Stop stuffing yourself with food and come along. Young George wants to take some pictures of us with his camera. He's out on the lawn with Archibald. You met my nephew, Archibald?'

'Not yet,' said Lord Ickenham. 'I am looking forward eagerly to making his acquaintance.'

'You're *what*?' said the Duke incredulously.

'Any nephew of yours.'

'Oh, I see what you mean. But you can't go by that. He's not like me. He's potty.'

'Indeed?'

'Got less brain than Connie here, and hasn't the excuse for pottiness that she has, because he's not a woman. Connie's hoping he'll marry the Stick-in-the-Mud girl, though why any girl would want to tie herself up with a poop like that, is more than I can imagine. He's an artist. Draws pictures. And you know what artists are. Where is the Tiddlypush girl, Connie? George wants her in the picture.'

'She went down to the lake.'

'Well, if she thinks I'm going there to fetch her, she's mistaken,' said the Duke gallantly. 'George'll have to do without her.'

## · III ·

On a knoll overlooking the lake there stood a little sort of imitation Greek temple, erected by Lord Emsworth's grandfather in the days when landowners went in for little sort of imitation Greek temples in their grounds. In front of it there was a marble bench, and on this bench Myra Schoonmaker was sitting, gazing with what are called unseeing eyes at the Church Lads bobbing about in the water below. She was not in the gayest of spirits. Her brow, indeed, was as furrowed and her lips as drawn as they had been three days earlier when she had accompanied Lord Emsworth to the Empress's sty.

A footstep on the marble floor brought her out of her reverie with a jerk. She turned and saw a tall, distinguished-looking man with grey hair and a jaunty moustache, who smiled at her affectionately.

'Hullo there, young Myra,' he said.

He spoke as if they were old friends, but she had no recollection of ever having seen him before.

'Who are you?' she said. The question seemed abrupt, and she wished she had thought of something more polished.

A reproachful look came into his eyes.

'You usedn't to say that when I soaped your back. "Nobody soaps like you, Uncle Fred," you used to say, and you were right. I had the knack.'

The years fell away from Myra, and she was a child in her bath again.

'Well!' she said, squeaking in her emotion.

'I see you remember.'

'Uncle Fred! Fancy meeting you again like this after all these years. Though I suppose I ought to call you Mr Twistleton.'

'You would be making a serious social gaffe, if you did. I've come a long way since we last saw each other. By pluck and industry I've worked my way up the ladder, step by step, to dizzy heights. You may have heard that a Lord Ickenham was expected at the castle today. I am the Lord

Ickenham about whom there has been so much talk. And not one of your humble Barons or Viscounts, mind you, but a belted Earl, with papers to prove it.'

'Like Lord Emsworth?'

'Yes, only brighter.'

'I remember now Father saying something about your having become a big wheel.'

'He in no way overstated it. How is he?'

'He's all right.'

'Full of beans?'

'Oh, yes.'

'More than you are, my child. I was watching you sitting there, and you reminded me of Rodin's Penseur. Were you thinking of Bill Bailey?'

Myra started.

'You don't—?'

'Know Bill Bailey? Certainly I do. He's a friend of my nephew Pongo's and to my mind as fine a curate as ever preached a sermon.'

The animation which had come into the girl's face at this reunion with one of whom she had such pleasant memories died away, to be replaced by a cold haughtiness like that of a princess reluctantly compelled to give her attention to the dregs of the underworld.

'You're entitled to your opinion, I suppose,' she said stiffly. 'I think he's a rat.'

It seemed to Lord Ickenham that he could not have heard correctly. Young lovers, he knew, were accustomed to bestow on each other a variety of pet names, but he had never understood 'rat' to be one of them.

'A *rat*?'

'Yes.'

'Why do you call him that?'

'Because of what he did.'

'What was that?'

'Or didn't do, rather.'

'You speak in riddles. Couldn't you make it clearer?'

'I'll make it clearer, all right. He stood me up.'

'I still don't get the gist.'

'Very well, then, if you want the whole story. I phoned him that I was coming to London to marry him, and he didn't show up at the registry office.'

'What!'

'Had cold feet, I suppose. I ought to have guessed from the way he said "Oh, rather", when I asked him if he wasn't pleased. I waited at the place for hours, but he never appeared. And he told me he loved me!'

It was not often that Lord Ickenham was bewildered, but he found himself now unequal to the intellectual pressure of the conversation.

'He never appeared? Are we talking of the same man? The one I mean is an up-and-coming young cleric named Bill Bailey, in whose company I passed fully three-quarters of an hour yesterday at the registry office. I was to have been one of his witnesses, lending a tone to the thing.'

Myra stared.

'Are you crazy?'

'The charge has sometimes been brought against me, but there's nothing in it. Just exuberant. Why do you ask?'

'He can't have been at the registry office. I'd have seen him.'

'He's hard to miss, I agree. Catches the eye, as you might say. But I assure you—'

'At the registry office in Wilton Street?'

'Say that again.'

'Say what again?'

'Wilton Street.'

'Why?'

'I wanted to test a theory that has just occurred to me. I think I have the solution of this mystery that has been perplexing us. Someone, especially if a good deal agitated, hearing somebody say "Wilton" over the telephone, could easily mistake it for "Milton". Some trick of the acoustics. It was at the Milton Street registry office that Bill, my nephew Pongo and I kept our vigil. We all missed you.'

The colour drained from Myra Schoonmaker's face. Her eyes, as they stared into Lord Ickenham's, had become almost as prominent as the Duke's.

'You don't mean that?'

'I do, indeed. There were we, waiting at the church—'

'Oh, golly, what an escape I've had!'

Lord Ickenham could not subscribe to this view.

'Now there I disagree with you. My acquaintance with Bill Bailey has been brief, but as I told you, it has left me with a distinctly favourable impression of him. A sterling soul he seemed to me. I feel the spiritual needs of Bottleton East are safe in the hands of a curate like that. Don't tell me you've weakened on him?'

'Of course I've not weakened on him.'

'Then why do you feel that you have had an escape?'

'Because I came back here so mad with him for standing me up, as I thought, that when Archie Gilpin proposed to me I very nearly accepted him.'

Lord Ickenham looked grave. These artists, he was thinking, work fast.

'But you didn't?'

'No.'

'Well, don't. It would spoil Bill's visit. And I want him to enjoy himself at Blandings Castle. But I didn't tell you about that, did I? It must have slipped my mind. I've brought Bill here with me. Incognito, of course. I thought you might like to see him. I always strive, when I can, to spread sweetness and light. There have been several complaints about it.'

# 4

## · I ·

It was the practice of Lord Ickenham, when visiting a country house to look about him, before doing anything else, for a hammock to which he could withdraw after breakfast and lie thinking deep thoughts. Though, like Abou ben Adhem a man who loved his fellow men, he made it an invariable rule to avoid them after the morning meal with an iron firmness, for at that delectable hour he wished to be alone to meditate. Whoever wanted to enjoy the sparkle of his conversation had to wait till lunch, when it would be available to all.

Such a hammock he had found on the lawn of Blandings Castle, and on the morning after his arrival he was reclining in it at peace with all the world. The day was warm and sunny. A breeze blew gently from the west. Birds chirped, bees buzzed, insects droned as they went about the various businesses that engage the attention of insects in the rural districts. In the stable yard, out of view behind a shrubbery, somebody—possibly Voules the chauffeur—was playing the harmonica. And from a window in the house, softened by distance, there sounded faintly the tap-tap-tap of a typewriter, showing that Lavender Briggs, that slave of duty, was at work on some secretarial task and earning the weekly envelope. Soothed and relaxed, Lord Ickenham fell into a reverie.

He had plenty to occupy his mind. As a man who specialized in spreading sweetness and light, he was often confronted with problems difficult of solution, but he had seldom found them so numerous. As he mused on Lady Constance, on Lavender Briggs, on the Duke of Dunstable and on the Church Lads, he could see, as he had told Pongo, that his hands would be full and his ingenuity strained to the uttermost.

He was glad, this being so, that he had not got to worry about Bill Bailey, who had relieved whatever apprehensions he may have had by fitting well into the little Blandings circle. True, Lady Constance had greeted him with a touch of frost in her manner, but that was to be expected. The others, he had been happy to see, had made him welcome, particularly Lord Emsworth, to whom he appeared to have said just the right things about the Empress during yesterday evening's visit to her residence. Lord Emsworth's approval did not, of course, carry much weight at Blandings Castle, but it was something.

It was as he lay meditating on Lord Emsworth that he observed him crossing the lawn and sat up with a start of surprise. What had astonished him was not the other's presence there, for the proprietor of a country house has of course a perfect right to cross lawns on his own premises, but the fact that he was wet. Indeed, the word 'wet' was barely adequate. He was soaked from head to foot and playing like a Versailles fountain.

This puzzled Lord Ickenham. He was aware that his host sometimes took a dip in the lake, but he had not known that he did it immediately after breakfast with all his clothes on, and abandoning his usual policy of allowing nothing to get him out of his hammock till the hour of the midday cocktail, he started in pursuit.

Lord Emsworth was cutting out a good pace, so good that he remained out of earshot, and he had disappeared into the house before Lord Ickenham reached it. The latter, shrewdly reasoning that a wet man would make for his bedroom, followed him there. He found him in the nude, drying himself with a bath towel, and immediately put the question which would have occurred to anyone in his place.

'My dear fellow, what happened? Did you fall into the lake?'

Lord Emsworth lowered the towel and reached for a patched shirt.

'Eh? Oh, hullo, Ickenham. Did you say you had fallen into the lake?'

'I asked if you had.'

'I? Oh, no.'

'Don't tell me that was merely perspiration you were bathed in when I saw you on the lawn?'

'Eh? No, I perspire very little. But I did not fall into the lake. I dived in.'

'With your clothes on?'

'Yes, I had my clothes on.'

'Any particular reason for diving? Or did it just seem a good idea at the time?'

'I had lost my glasses.'

'And you thought they might be in the lake?'

Lord Emsworth appeared to realize that he had not made himself altogether clear. For some moments he busied himself with a pair of trousers. Having succeeded in draping his long legs in these, he explained.

'No, it was not that. But when I am without my glasses, I find a difficulty in seeing properly. And I had no reason to suppose that the boy was not accurate in his statement.'

'What boy was that?'

'One of the Church Lads. I spoke to you about them, if you remember.'

'I remember.'

'I wish somebody would mend my socks,' said Lord Emsworth, deviating for a moment from the main theme. 'Look at those holes. What were we talking about?'

'This statement-making Church Lad.'

'Oh yes. Yes, quite. Well, the whole thing was very peculiar. I had gone down to the lake with the idea of asking the boys if they could possibly make a little less noise, and suddenly one of them came running up to me with the most extraordinary remark. He said, "Oh, sir, please save Willie!"'

'Odd way of starting a conversation, certainly.'

'He was pointing at an object in the water, and putting two and two together I came to the conclusion that one of his comrades must have fallen into the lake and was drowning. So I dived in.'

Lord Ickenham was impressed.

'Very decent of you. Many men who had suffered so much at the hands of the little blisters would just have stood on the bank and sneered. Was the boy grateful?'

'I can't find my shoes. Oh yes, here they are. What did you say?'

'Did the boy thank you brokenly?'

'What boy?'

'The one whose life you saved.'

'Oh, I was going to explain that. It wasn't a boy. It turned out to be a floating log. I swam to it, shouting to it to keep cool, and was very much annoyed to find that my efforts had been for nothing. And do you know what I think, Ickenham? I strongly suspect that it was not a genuine mistake on the boy's part. I am convinced that he was perfectly well aware that the object in the water was not one of his playmates and that he had deliberately deceived me. Oh yes, I feel sure of it, and I'll tell you why. When I came out, he had been joined by several other boys, and they were laughing.'

Lord Ickenham could readily imagine it. They would, he supposed, be laughing when they told the story to their grandchildren.

'I asked them what they were laughing at, and they said it was at something funny which had happened on the previous afternoon. I found it hard to credit their story.'

'I don't wonder.'

'I feel very indignant about the whole affair.'

'I'm not surprised.'

'Should I complain to Constance?'

'I think I would do something more spirited than that.'

'But what?'

'Ah, that wants thinking over, doesn't it? I'll devote earnest thought to the matter, and if anything occurs to me, I'll let you know. You wouldn't consider mowing them down with a shotgun?'

'Eh? No, I doubt if that would be advisable.'

'Might cause remark, you feel?' said Lord Ickenham. 'Perhaps you're right. Never mind. I'll think of something else.'

## · II ·

When a visitor to a country house learns that his host, as to the stability of whose mental balance he has long entertained the gravest doubts, has suddenly jumped into a lake with all his clothes on, he cannot but feel concern. He shakes his head. He purses his lips and raises his eyebrows. Something has given, he says to himself, and strains have been cracked under. It was thus that the Duke of Dunstable reacted to the news of Lord Emsworth's exploit.

It was from the latter's grandson George that he got the story. George was a small boy with ginger hair and freckles, and between him and the Duke there had sprung up one of those odd friendships which do sometimes spring up between the most unlikely persons. George was probably the only individual in three counties who actually enjoyed conversing with the Duke of Dunstable. If he had been asked wherein lay the other's fascination, he would have replied that he liked watching the way he blew his moustache about when he talked. It was a spectacle that never wearied him.

'I say,' he said, coming on to the terrace where the Duke was sitting, 'have you heard the latest?'

The Duke, who had been brooding on the seeming impossibility of getting an egg boiled the way he liked it in this blasted house, came out of his thoughts. He spoke irritably. Owing to his tender years George had rather a high voice, and the sudden sound of it had made him bite his tongue.

'Don't come squeaking in my ear like that, boy. Blow your horn or something. What did you say?'

'I asked if you'd heard the latest?'

'Latest what?'

'Front page news. Big scoop. Grandpapa jumped into the lake.'

'What are you talking about?'

'It's true. The country's ringing with it. I had it from one of the gardeners who saw him. Grandpapa was walking along by the lake, and suddenly he stopped and paused for a moment in thought. Then he did a swan dive,' said George, and eyed the moustache expectantly.

He was not disappointed. It danced like an autumn leaf before a gale.

'He jumped into the lake?'

'That's what he did, big boy.'

'Don't call me big boy.'

'Okay, chief.'

The Duke puffed awhile.

'You say this gardener saw him jump into the water?'

'Yes, *sir.*'

'With his clothes on?'

'That's right. Accoutred as he was, he plungéd in,' said George, who in the preceding term at his school had had to write out a familiar passage from Shakespeare's *Julius Caesar* fifty times for bringing a white mouse into the classroom. 'Pretty sporting, don't you think, an old egg like Grandpapa?'

'What do you mean—old egg?'

'Well, he must be getting on for a hundred.'

'He is the same age as myself.'

'Oh?' said George, who supposed the Duke had long since passed the hundred mark.

'But what the deuce made him do a thing like that?'

'Oh, just thought he would, I suppose. Coo—I wish I'd been there with my camera,' said George, and went on his way. And a few moments later, having pondered deeply on this sensational development, the Duke rose and stumped off in search of Lady Constance. What he had heard had convinced him of the need for a summit meeting.

He found her in her sitting-room. Lavender Briggs was with her, all spectacles and notebook. It was part of her secretarial duties to look in at this hour for general instructions.

'Hoy!' he boomed, like something breaking the sound barrier.

'Oh, Alaric!' said Lady Constance, startled and annoyed. 'I do wish you would knock.'

'Less of the "Oh, Alaric!"' said the Duke, who was always firm with this sort of thing, 'and where's the sense in knocking? I want to talk to you on a matter of the utmost importance, and it's private. Pop off, you,' he said to Lavender Briggs. He was a man who had a short way with underlings. 'It's about Emsworth.'

'What about him?'

'I'll tell you what about him, just as soon as this pie-faced female has removed herself. Don't want her muscling in with her ears sticking up, hearing every word I say.'

'You had better leave us, Miss Briggs.'

'Quate,' said Lavender Briggs, withdrawing haughtily.

'Really, Alaric,' said Lady Constance as the door closed, speaking with the frankness of one who had known him for a lifetime, 'you have the manners of a pig.'

The Duke reacted powerfully to the criticism. He banged the desk with a hamlike hand, upsetting, in the order named, an inkpot, two framed photographs and a vase of roses.

'Pig! That's the operative word. It's the pig I came to talk about.'

Lady Constance would have preferred to talk about the inkpot, the two photographs and the vase of roses, but he gave her no opportunity. He had always been a difficult man to stop.

'It's at the bottom of the whole thing. It's a thoroughly bad influence on him. Stop messing about with that ink and listen to me. I say it's the pig that has made him what he is today.'

'Oh, dear! Made whom what he is today?'

'Emsworth, of course, ass. Who do you think I meant? Constance,' said the Duke in that loud, carrying voice of his, 'I've told you this before, and I tell it to you again. If Emsworth is to be saved from the loony bin, that pig must be removed from his life.'

'Don't shout so, Alaric.'

'I will shout. I feel very strongly on the matter. The pig is affecting his brain, not that he ever had much. Remember the time when he told me he wanted to enter it for the Derby?'

'I spoke to him about that. He said he didn't.'

'Well, I say he did! Heard him distinctly. Anyway, be that as it may, you can't deny that he's half way round the bend, and I maintain that the pig is responsible. It's at the root of his mental unbalance.'

'Clarence is not mentally unbalanced!'

'He isn't, isn't he? That's what you think. How about what happened this morning? You know the lake?'

'Of course I know the lake.'

'He was walking beside it.'

'Why shouldn't he walk beside the lake?'

'I'm not saying he shouldn't walk beside the lake. He can walk beside the lake till his eyes bubble, as far as I'm concerned. But when it comes to jumping in with all his clothes on, it makes one think a bit.'

'What!'

'That's what he did, so young George informs me.'

'With his *clothes* on?'

'Accoutred as he was.'

'Well, really!'

'Don't know why you seem so surprised. It didn't surprise me. I was saddened, yes, but not surprised. Been expecting something like this for a long time. It's just the sort of thing a man would do whose intellect had been sapped by constant association with a pig. And that's why I tell you that the pig must go. Eliminate it, and all may still be well. I'm not saying that anything could make Emsworth actually sane, one mustn't expect miracles, but I'm convinced that if he hadn't this pig to unsettle him all the time, you would see a marked improvement. He'd be an altogether brighter, less potty man. Well, say something, woman. Don't just sit there. Take steps, take steps.'

'What steps?'

'Slip somebody a couple of quid to smuggle the ghastly animal away somewhere, thus removing Emsworth from its sphere of influence.'

'My dear Alaric!'

'It's the only course to pursue. He won't sell the creature, though if I've asked him once, I've asked him a dozen times. "I'll give you five hundred pounds cash down for that bulbous mass of lard and snuffle," I said to him. "Say the word," I said, "and I'll have the revolting object shipped off right away to my place in Wiltshire, paying all the expenses of removal." He refused, and was very offensive about it, too. The man's besotted.'

'But you don't keep pigs.'

'I know I don't, not such a silly ass, but I'm prepared to pay five hundred pounds for this one.'

Lady Constance's eyes widened.

'Just to do Clarence good?' she said, amazed. She had not credited her guest with this altruism.

'Certainly not,' said the Duke, offended that he should be supposed capable of any such motive. 'I can make a bit of money out of it. I know someone who'll give me two thousand for the animal.'

'Good gracious! Who . . . Oh, Clarence!'

Lord Emsworth had burst into the room, plainly in the grip of some strong emotion. His mild eyes were gleaming through their pince-nez, and he quivered like a tuning-fork.

'Connie,' he cried, and you could see that he had been pushed just so far. 'You've got to do something about these infernal boys!'

Lady Constance sighed wearily. This was one of those trying mornings.

'What boys? Do you mean the Church Lads?'

'Eh? Yes, precisely. They should never have been let into the place. What do you think I just found one of them doing? He was leaning over the rail of the Empress's sty, where he had no business to be, and he was dangling a potato on a string in front of her nose and jerking it away when she snapped at it. Might have ruined her digestion for days. You've got to do something about it, Constance. The boy must be apprehended and severely punished.'

'Oh, Clarence!'

'I insist. He must be given a sharp lesson.'

'Changing the subject,' said the Duke, 'will you sell me that foul pig of yours? I'll give you six hundred pounds.'

Lord Emsworth stared at him, revolted. His eyes glowed hotly behind their pince-nez. Not even George Cyril Wellbeloved could have disliked dukes more.

'Of course I won't. I've told you a dozen times. Nothing would induce me to sell the Empress.'

'Six hundred pounds. That's a firm offer!'

'I don't want six hundred pounds. I've got plenty of money, plenty.'

'Clarence,' said Lady Constance, also changing the subject, 'is it true that you jumped into the lake this morning with all your clothes on?'

'Eh? What? Yes, certainly. I couldn't wait to take them off. Only it was a log.'

'What was a log?'

'The boy.'

'What boy?'

'The log. But I can't stand here talking,' said Lord Emsworth impatiently, and hurried out, turning at the door to repeat to Lady Constance that she must do something about it.

The Duke blew his moustache up a few inches.

'You see? What did I tell you? Definitely barmy. Reached the gibbering stage, and may get dangerous at any moment. But I was speaking about this fellow who'll give two thousand for the porker. I used to know him years ago when I was a young man in London. Pyke was his name then. Stinker Pyke we used to call him. Then he made a packet by running all those papers and magazines and things and got a peerage. Calls himself Lord Tilbury now. You've met him. He says he's stayed here.'

'Yes, he was here for a short time. My brother Galahad used to know him. Miss Briggs was his secretary before she came to us.'

'I'm not interested in Miss Briggs, blast her spectacles.'

'I merely mentioned it.'

'Well, don't mention it again. Now you've made me forget what I was going to tell you. Oh, yes. I ran into Stinker at the club the other day, and we got talking and I said I was coming to Blandings, and the subject of the pig came up. It appears that he keeps pigs at his place in Buckinghamshire, just the sort of potty thing he would do, and he has coveted this ghastly animal of Emsworth's ever since he saw it. He specifically told me that he would give me two thousand pounds to add it to his piggery.'

'How extraordinary!'

'Opportunity of a lifetime.'

'Clarence must be made to see reason.'

'Who's going to make him? I can't. You heard him just now. And you won't pinch the creature. The thing's an impasse. No co-operation, that's what's wrong with this damned place. Very doubtful if I'll ever come here again. You'll miss me, but that can't be helped. Only yourself to blame. I'm going for a walk,' said the Duke, and proceeded to do so.

## • III •

Lord Emsworth was a man with little of the aggressor in his spiritual make-up. He believed in living and letting live. Except for his sister Constance, his secretary Lavender Briggs, the Duke of Dunstable and his younger son Frederick, now fortunately residing in America, few things were able to ruffle him. Placid is the word that springs to the lips.

But the Church Lads had pierced his armour, and he found resentment growing within him like some shrub that has been treated with a patent fertilizer. He brooded bleakly on the injuries he had suffered at the hands of these juvenile delinquents.

The top-hat incident he could have overlooked, for he knew that when small boys are confronted with a man wearing that type of headgear and there is a crusty roll within reach, they are almost bound to lose their calm judgement. The happy laughter which had greeted him as he emerged from the lake had gashed him like a knife, but with a powerful effort he might have excused it. But in upsetting Empress of Blandings' delicately attuned digestive system by dangling potatoes before her eyes and jerking them away as she snapped at them they had gone too far. As Hamlet would have put it, their offence was rank and smelled to heaven. And if heaven would not mete out retribution to them—and there was not a sign so far of any activity in the front office—somebody else would have to attend to it. And that somebody, he was convinced, was Ickenham. He had left Ickenham pondering on the situation, and who knew that by this time his fertile mind might not have hit on a suitable method of vengeance.

On leaving Lady Constance's boudoir, accordingly, he made his way to the hammock and bleated his story into the other's ear. Nor was he disappointed in its reception. Where a man of coarser fibre might have laughed, Lord Ickenham was gravity itself. By not so much as a twitch of the lip did he suggest that he found anything amusing in his host's narrative.

'A potato?' he said, knitting his brow.

'A large potato.'

'On a string?'

'Yes, on a string.'

'And the boy jerked it away?'

'Repeatedly. It must have distressed the Empress greatly. She is passionately fond of potatoes.'

'And you wish to retaliate? You think that something in the nature of a counter move is required?'

'Eh? Yes, certainly.'

'Then how very fortunate,' said Lord Ickenham heartily, 'that I can put you in the way of making it. I throw it out merely as a suggestion, you understand, but I know what I would do in your place?'

'What is that?'

'I'd bide my time and sneak down to the lake in the small hours of the morning and cut the ropes of their tent, as one used to do at the Public Schools Camp at Aldershot in the brave days when I was somewhat younger. That, to my mind, would be the retort courteous.'

'God bless my soul!' said Lord Emsworth.

He spoke with sudden animation. Forty-six years had rolled away from him, the forty-six years which had passed since, a junior member of the Eton contingent at the Aldershot camp, he had been mixed up in that sort of thing. Then he had been on the receiving, not the giving, end. Some young desperadoes from a school allergic to Eton had cut the ropes of the guard tent in which he was reposing, and he could recall vividly his emotions on suddenly finding himself entangled in a cocoon of canvas. His whole life—some fifteen years at that time—had passed before him, and in suggesting a similar experience for these Church Lads Ickenham, he realized, had shown his usual practical good sense.

For a moment his mild face glowed. Then the light died out of it. Would it, he was asking himself, be altogether prudent to embark on an enterprise of which Connie must inevitably disapprove? Connie had an uncanny knack of finding out things, and if she were to trace this righteous act of vengeance to him . . .

'I'll turn it over in my mind,' he said. 'Thank you very much for the suggestion.'

'Not at all,' said Lord Ickenham. 'Ponder on it at your leisure.'

# 5

## · 1 ·

The Duke's walk took him to the Empress's sty, and he lit a cigar and stood leaning on the rail, gazing at her as she made a late breakfast.

Except for a certain fullness of figure, the Duke of Dunstable and Empress of Blandings had little in common. There was no fusion between their souls. The next ten minutes accordingly saw nothing in the nature of an exchange of ideas. The Duke smoked his cigar in silence, the Empress in her single-minded way devoted herself to the consumption of her daily nourishment amounting to fifty-seven thousand five hundred calories.

Lord Emsworth would not have believed such a thing possible, but the spectacle of this supreme pig was plunging the Duke in gloom. It was not with admiration that he gazed upon her, but with a growing fury. There, he was saying to himself, golloped a Berkshire sow which, if conveyed to his Wiltshire home, would mean a cool two thousand pounds added to his bank balance, and no hope of conveying her. The thought was like a dagger in his heart.

His cigar having reached the point where, if persevered with, it would burn his moustache, he threw it away, straightened himself with a peevish grunt and was about to leave the noble animal to her proteids and carbohydrates, when a voice said 'Pahdon me', and turning he perceived the pie-faced female whom he had so recently put in her place.

'Get out of here!' he said in his polished way, 'I'm busy.'

Where a lesser woman would have quailed and beaten an apologetic retreat, Lavender Briggs stood firm, her dignified calm unruffled. No man, however bald his head or white his moustache, could intimidate a girl who had served under the banner of Lord Tilbury of the Mammoth Publishing Company.

'I would like a word with Your Grace,' she said in the quiet, level voice which only an upbringing in Kensington followed by years of secretarial college can produce. 'It is with refahrence,' she went on, ignoring the purple flush which had crept over her companion's face, 'to this pig of Lord Emsworth's. I chanced to overhear what you were saying to Lady Constance just now.'

A cascade of hair dashed itself against the Duke's Wellingtonian nose.

'Eavesdropping, eh? Listening at keyholes, what?'

'Quate,' said Lavender Briggs, unmoved by the acidity of his tone. In her time she had been spoken acidly to by experts. 'You were urging Lady Constance to pay somebody to purloin the animal. To which her reply'—she consulted a shorthand note in her notebook—'was "My dear Alaric!", indicating that she was not prepare-ahed to consid-ah the idea-h. Had you made the suggestion to me, you would not have received such a dusty answer.

'Such a what?'

A contemptuous light flickered for an instant behind the harlequin glasses. Lavender Briggs moved in circles where literary allusions were grabbed off the bat, and the other's failure to get his hands to this one aroused her scorn. She did not actually call the Duke an ill-read old bohunkus, but this criticism was implicit in the way she looked at him.

'A quotation. "Ah, what a dusty answer gets the soul when hot for certainties in this our life." George Meredith, "Modern Love", stanza forty-eight.'

The Duke's head had begun to swim a little, but with the sensation of slight giddiness had come an unwilling respect for this goggled girl. Superficially all that stanza forty-eight stuff might seem merely another indication of the pottiness which was so marked a feature of the other sex, but there was something in her manner that suggested that she had more to say and that eventually something would emerge that made sense. This feeling solidified as she proceeded.

'If we can come to some satisfactory business arrangement, I will abstract the pig and see that it is delivered at your address.'

The Duke blinked. Whatever he had been expecting, it was not this. He looked at the Empress, estimating her tonnage, then at Lavender Briggs, in comparison so fragile.

'You? Don't be an ass. You couldn't steal a pig.'

'I should, of course, engage the service of an assistant to do the rough work.'

'Who? Not me.'

'I was not thinking of Your Grace.'

'Then who?'

'I would prefer not to specify with any greatah exactitude.'

'See what you mean. No names, no pack-drill?'

'Quate.'

A thoughtful silence fell. Lavender Briggs stood looking like a spectacled statue, while the Duke, who had lighted another cigar, puffed at it. And at this moment Lord Emsworth appeared, walking across the meadow in that jerky way of his which always reminded his friends and admirers of a mechanical toy which had been insufficiently wound up.

'Hell!' said the Duke. 'Here comes Emsworth.'

'Quate,' said Lavender Briggs. It was obvious to her that the conference must be postponed to some more suitable time and place. Above all else, plotters require privacy. 'I suggest that Your Grace meet me later in my office.'

'Where's that?'

'Beach will direct you.'

The secretary's office, to which the butler some quarter of an hour later escorted the Duke, was at the far end of a corridor, a small room looking out on the Dutch garden. Like herself, it was tidy and austere, with no fripperies. There was a desk with a typewriter on it, a table with a tape-recording machine on it, filing cabinets against the walls, a chair behind the desk, another chair in front of it, both hard and business-like, and—the sole concession to the beautiful—a bowl of flowers by the window. As the Duke entered, she was sitting in the chair behind the desk, and he, after eyeing it suspiciously as if doubtful of its ability to support the largest trouser-seat in the peerage, took the other chair.

'Been thinking over what you were saying just now,' he said. 'About stealing that pig for me. This assistant you were speaking of. Sure you can get him?'

'I am. Actually, I shall requiah two assistants.'

'Eh?'

'One to push and one to pull. It is a very large pig.'

'Oh, yes, see what you mean. Yes, undoubtedly. As you say, very large pig. And you can get this second chap?'

'I can.'

'Good. Then that seems to be about it, what? Everything settled, I mean to say.'

'Except terms.'

'Eh?'

'If you will recall, I spoke of a satisfactory business arrangement? I naturally expect to be compensated for my services. I am anxious to obtain capital with which to start a typewriting bureau.'

The Duke, a prudent man who believed in watching the pennies, said, 'A typewriting bureau, eh? I know the sort of thing you mean. One of those places full of machines and girls hammering away at them like a lot of dashed riveters. Well, you don't want much money for that,' he said, and Lavender Briggs, correcting this view, said she wanted as much as she could get.

'I would suggest five hundred pounds.'

The Duke's moustache leaped into life. His eyes bulged. He had the air of one who is running the gamut of the emotions.

'Five . . . *what*?'

'You were thinking of some lesser fig-ah?'

'I was thinking of a tenner.'

'Ten pounds?' Lavender Briggs smiled pityingly, as if some acquaintance of hers, quoting Horace, had made a false quantity. 'That would leave you with a nice profit, would it not?'

'Eh?'

'You told Lady Constance that you had a friend who was prepared to pay you two thousand pounds for the animal.'

The Duke chewed his moustache in silence for a moment, regretting that he had been so explicit.

'I was pulling her leg,' he said, doing his best.

'Oh?'

'Harmless little joke.'

'Indeed? I took it au pied de la lettre.'

'Au what de what?' said the Duke, who was as shaky on French as he was on English literature.

'I accepted the statement at its face value.'

'Silly of you. Thought you would have seen that I was just kidding her along and making a good story out of it.'

'That was not the impression your words made on me. When'—she consulted her notebook—'when I heard you say "I know someone who'll give me two thousand for the animal", I was quate convinced that you meant precisely what you said. Unfortunately at that moment Lord Emsworth appeared and I was obliged to move from the door, so did not ascertain the name of the friend to whom you referred. Otherwise, I would be dealing with him directly and you would not appear in the transaction at all. As matters stand, you will be receiving fifteen hundred pounds for doing nothing—from your point of view, I should have supposed, a very satisfactory state of aff-ay-ars.'

She became silent. She was thinking hard thoughts of Lord Emsworth and feeling how like him it was to have intruded at such a vital moment. Had he postponed his arrival for as little as half a minute, she would have learned the identity of this lavish pig-lover and would have been able to dispense with the middle man. A momentary picture rose before her eyes of herself, armed with a stout umbrella, taking a full back swing and breaking it over her employer's head. Even though she recognized this as but an idle dream, it comforted her a little.

The Duke sat chewing his cigar. There was, he had to admit, much in what she said. The thought of parting with five hundred pounds chilled him to his parsimonious marrow, but after all, as she had indicated, the remaining fifteen hundred was nice money and would come under the general heading of velvet.

'All right,' he said, though it hurt him to utter the words, and Lavender Briggs' mouth twitched slightly on the left side, which was her way of smiling.

'I was sure you would be reasonable. Shall we have a written agreement?'

'No,' said the Duke, remembering that one of the few sensible remarks his late father had ever made was 'Alaric, my boy, never put anything in writing'. 'No, certainly not. Written agreement, indeed! Never heard a pottier suggestion in my life.'

'Then I must ask you for a cheque.'

As far as it is possible for a seated man to do so, the Duke reeled.

'What, in advance?'

'Quate. Have you your cheque-book with you?'

'No,' said the Duke, brightening momentarily. For an instant it seemed to him that this solved everything.

'Then you can give it me tonight,' said Lavender Briggs. 'And meanwhile repeat this after me. I, Alaric, Duke of Dunstable, hereby make a solemn promise to you, Lavender Briggs, that if you steal Lord Emsworth's pig, Empress of Blandings, and deliver it to my home in Wiltshire, I will pay you the sum of five hundred pounds.'

'Sounds silly.'

'Nevertheless, I must insist on a formal agreement, even if only a verbal one.'

'Oh, all right.'

The Duke repeated the words, though still considering them silly. The woman had to be humoured.

'Thank you,' said Lavender Briggs, and went off to scour the countryside for George Cyril Wellbeloved.

## · II ·

George Cyril was having his elevenses in the tool-shed by the kitchen garden when the rich smell of pig which he always diffused enabled her eventually to locate him. As she entered, closing the door behind her, he lowered the beer bottle from his lips in some surprise. He had seen her around from time to time and knew who she was, but he had not the pleasure of her acquaintance, and he was wondering to what he owed the honour of this visit.

She informed him, but not immediately, for there were what are called pourparlers to be gone through first.

'Wellbeloved,' she said, starting to attend to these, 'I have been making inquiries about you in Market Blandings, and everyone to whom I have mentioned your name tells me that you are thoroughly untrustworthy, a man without scruples of any sort, who sticks at nothing and will do anything for money.'

'Who—me?' said George Cyril, blinking. He had frequently had much the same sort of thing said to him before, for he moved in outspoken circles, but somehow it seemed worse and more wounding coming from those Kensingtonian lips. For a moment he debated within himself the advisability of dotting the speaker one on the boko, but decided against this. You never know what influential friends these women had. He contented himself with waving his arms in a passionate gesture which caused the aroma of pig to spread itself even more thickly about the interior of the shed. 'Who—me?' he said again.

Lavender Briggs had produced a scented handkerchief and was pressing it to her face.

'Toothache?' asked George Cyril, interested.

'It is a little close in here,' said Lavender Briggs primly, and returned to the pourparlers. 'At the Emsworth Arms, for instance, I was informed that you would sell your grandmother for twopence.'

George Cyril said he did not have a grandmother, and seemed a good deal outraged by the suggestion that, if that relative had not long since gone to reside with the morning stars, he would have parted with her at such bargain-basement rates. A good grandmother should fetch at least a couple of bob.

'At the Cow and Grasshopper they told me you were a—petty thief of the lowest description.'

'Who—me?' said George Cyril uneasily. That, he told himself, must be those cigars. He had not supposed that suspicion had fallen on himself regarding their disappearance. Evidently the hand had not moved sufficiently quickly to deceive the eye.

'And the butler at Sir Gregory Parsloe's, where I understand you were employed before you returned to Lord Emsworth, said you were always pilfering his cigarettes and whisky.'

'Who—me?' said George Cyril for the fourth time, speaking now with an outraged note in his voice. He had always thought of Binstead, Sir Gregory's butler, as a pal and, what is more, a staunch pal. And now this. Like the prophet Zachariah, he was saying to himself, 'I have been wounded in the house of my friends.'

'Your moral standards have thus been established as negligible. So I want you,' said Lavender Briggs, 'to steal Lord Emsworth's pig.'

Another man, hearing these words, might have been stunned, and certainly a fifth 'Who—me?' could have been expected, but in making this request of George Cyril Wellbeloved the secretary was addressing one who in the not distant past actually had stolen Lord Emsworth's pig. It was a long and intricate story, reflecting great discredit on all concerned, and there is no need to go into it now. One mentions it merely to explain why George Cyril Wellbeloved did not draw himself to his full height and thunder that nothing could make him betray his position of trust, but merely scratched his chin with the beer bottle and looked interested.

'Pinch the pig?'

'Precisely.'

'Why?'

'Never mind why.'

George Cyril did mind why.

'Now use your intelligence, miss,' he pleaded. 'You can't come telling a man to go pinching pigs without giving him the gruff about why he's doing it and who for and what not. Who's after that pig this time?'

Lavender Briggs decided to be frank. She was a fair-minded girl and saw that he had reason on his side. Even the humblest hired assassin in the Middle Ages probably wanted to know, before setting out to stick a poignard into someone, whom he was acting for.

'The Duke of Dunstable,' she said. 'You would be requiahed to take the animal to his house in Wiltshire.'

'Wiltshire?' George Cyril seemed incredulous. 'Did you say Wiltshire?'

'That is where the Duke lives.'

'And how do we get to Wiltshire, me and the pig? Walk?'

Lavender Briggs clicked her tongue impatiently.

'I assume that you have some disreputable friend who has a motor vehicle of some kind and is as free from scruples as yourself. And if you are thinking that you may be suspected, you need have no uneasiness. The operation will be carried through early in the morning and nobody will suppose that you were not asleep in bed at the time.'

George Cyril nodded. This was talking sense.

'Yes, so far so good. But aren't you overlooking what I might call a technical point? I can't pinch a pig that size all by myself.'

'You will have a colleague, working with you.'

'I will?'

'Quate.'

'Who pays him?'

'He will not requiah payment.'

'Must be barmy. All right, then, we've got that straight. We now come to the financial aspect of the thing. To speak expleasantly, what is there in it for me?'

'Five pounds.'

'*Five?*'

'Let us say ten.'

'Let us ruddy well say fifty.'

'That is a lot of money.'

'I like a lot of money.'

It was a moment for swift decisions. Lavender Briggs shared the Duke's views on watching the pennies, but she was a realist and knew that if you do not speculate, you cannot accumulate.

'Very well. No doubt I can persuade the Duke to meet you on the point. He is a rich man.'

'R!' said George Cyril Wellbeloved, so far forgetting himself as to spit out of the side of his mouth. 'And how did he get his riches? By grinding the face of the poor and taking the bread out of the mouths of the widow and the orphan. But the red dawn will come,' he said, warming up to his subject. 'One of these days you'll see blood flowing in streams down Park Lane and the corpses of the oppressors hanging from lamp-posts. And His Nibs of Dunstable'll be one of them. And who'll be there, pulling on the rope? Me, and happy to do it.'

Lavender Briggs made no comment on this. She was not interested in her companion's plans for the future, though in principle she approved of suspending Dukes from lamp-posts. All she was thinking at the moment was that she had concluded a most satisfactory business deal, and like a good business girl she was feeling quietly elated. She stood to make four hundred and fifty pounds instead of five hundred, but then she had always foreseen that there would be overheads.

The conference having been concluded and terms arranged, George Cyril Wellbeloved felt justified in raising the beer bottle to his lips, and the spectacle reminded her that there was something else that must be added.

'There is just one thing,' she said. 'No more fuddling yourself with alcoholic liquor. This is a very delicate operation which you will be undertaking, and we cannot risk failure. I want you bright and alert. So no more drinking.'

'Except beer, of course.'

'No beer.'

If George Cyril had not been sitting on an upturned wheelbarrow, he would have reeled.

'No beer?'

'No beer.'

'When you say no beer, do you mean no *beer*?'

'Quate. I shall be keeping an eye on you, and I have my way of finding out things. If I discover that you have been drinking, you will lose your fifty pounds. Do I make myself clear?'

'Quate,' said George Cyril Wellbeloved gloomily.

'Then that is understood,' said Lavender Briggs. 'Keep it well in mind.'

She left the shed, glad to escape from its somewhat cloying atmosphere, and started to return to the house. She was anxious now to have a word with Lord Ickenham's friend Cuthbert Meriwether.

## · III ·

Lying in his hammock, a soothing cigarette between his lips and his mind busy with great thoughts, Lord Ickenham became aware of emotional breathing in his rear and realized with annoyance that his privacy had been invaded. Then the breather came within the orbit of his vision and he saw that it was not, as for an instant he had feared, the Duke of Dunstable, but only his young friend, Myra Schoonmaker. He had no objection to suspending his thinking in order to converse with Myra.

It seemed to him, as he rose courteously, that the child was steamed up about something. Her eyes were wild, and there was in her manner a suggestion of the hart panting for cooling streams when heated in the chase. And her first words told him that his diagnosis had been correct.

'Oh, Uncle Fred! The most awful thing has happened!'

He patted her shoulder soothingly. Those who brought their troubles to him always caught him at his best. Such was his magic that there had been times—though not on the occasion of their visit to the dog races—when he had even been able to still the fluttering nervous system of his nephew Pongo.

'Take a hammock, my dear, and tell me all about it,' he said. 'You mustn't let yourself get so agitated. I have no doubt that when we go into it we shall find that whatever is disturbing you is simply the ordinary sort of thing you have to expect when you come to Blandings Castle. As you have probably discovered for yourself by now, Blandings Castle is no place for weaklings. What's on your mind?'

'It's Bill.'

'What has Bill been doing?'

'It's not what he's been doing, poor lamb, it's what's being done to him. You know that secretary woman?'

'Lavender Briggs? We're quite buddies. Emsworth doesn't like her, but for me she has a rather gruesome charm. She reminds me of the dancing mistress at my first kindergarten, on whom I had a crush in my formative years. Though when I say crush, it wasn't love exactly, more a sort of awed respect. I feel the same about Lavender Briggs. I had a long chat with her the other day. She was telling me she wanted to start a typewriting bureau, but hadn't enough capital. Why she should have confided in me, I don't know. I suppose I have one of those rare sympathetic natures you hear about. A cynic would probably say that she was leading up to trying to make a touch, but I don't think so. I think it was simply . . . Swedish exercises?' he asked, breaking off, for his companion had flung her arms out in a passionate gesture.

'Don't *talk* so much, Uncle Fred!'

Lord Ickenham felt the justice of the rebuke. He apologized.

'I'm sorry. A bad habit of mine, which I will endeavour to correct. What were you going to say about La Briggs?'

'She's a loathsome blackmailer!'

'She's *what?* You astound me. Who—or, rather, whom—is she blackmailing?'

'Bill, the poor angel. She's told him he's got to steal Lord Emsworth's pig.'

It took a great deal to make Lord Ickenham start. These words, however, did so. The rule by which he lived his life was that the prudent man, especially when at Blandings Castle, should be ready at all times for anything, but he had certainly not been prepared for this. His was a small moustache, not bushy and billowy like the Duke's, and it did not leap as the Duke's would have done, but it quivered perceptibly. He stared at his young friend as at a young friend who has had a couple.

'What on earth do you mean?'

'I'm telling you. She says Bill has got to steal Lord Emsworth's pig. I don't know who's behind her, but somebody wants it and she's working for him, and she's drafted my poor darling Bill as her assistant.'

Lord Ickenham whistled softly. Never a dull moment at Blandings Castle, he was thinking. At first incredulous, he now saw how plausible the girl's story was. People who employ people to steal pigs know that the labourer is worthy of his hire, and the principal in this venture, whoever he was, would undoubtedly reward Lavender Briggs with a purse of gold, thus enabling her to start her typewriting bureau. All that was plain enough, and one could understand the Briggs enthusiasm for the project, but there remained the perplexing problem of why she had selected the Rev. Cuthbert Bailey as her collaborator. Why, dash it, thought Lord Ickenham, they hardly knew one another.

'But why Bill?'

'You mean why *Bill*?'

'Exactly. Why is he the people's choice?'

'Because she's got the goods on him. Shall I tell you the whole thing?'

'It would be a great help.'

Prefacing her remarks with the statement that if girls like Lavender Briggs were skinned alive and dipped in boiling oil, this would be a better and sweeter world, Myra embarked on her narrative.

'Bill was out taking a stroll just now, and she came along. He said, "Oh, hello. Nice morning."'

'And she said "Quate"?'

'No, she said, "I should like a word with you, Mr Bailey."'

'Mr *Bailey*? She knew who he was?'

'She's known from the moment he got here. Apparently when she lived in London, she used to mess about in Bottleton East, doing good works among the poor and all that, so of course she saw him there and recognized him when he showed up at the castle. Bill's is the sort of face one remembers.'

Lord Ickenham agreed that it did indeed stamp itself on the mental retina. He was looking grave. Expecting at the outset to be called on to deal with some trifling girlish malaise, probably imaginary, he saw that here was a major crisis. If defied, he realized, Lavender Briggs would at once take Lady Constance into her confidence, with the worst results. Hell has no fury like a woman scorned, and very few like a woman who finds that she has been tricked into entertaining at her home a curate at the thought of whom she has been shuddering for weeks. Unquestionably Lady Constance would take umbrage. There would be pique on her part, and even dudgeon, and Bill's visit to Blandings Castle would be abruptly curtailed. In a matter of minutes the unfortunate young pastor of souls would be slung out of this Paradise on his ear like Lucifer, son of the morning.

'And then?'

'She said he had got to steal the pig.'

'And what did he say?'

'He told her to go to hell.'

'Strange advice from a curate.'

'I'm just giving you the rough idea.'

'Quate.'

'Actually, he said Lord Emsworth was his host and had been very kind to him, and he was very fond of him and he'd be darned if he'd bring his grey hairs in sorrow to the grave by pinching his pig, and apart from that what would his bishop have to say, if the matter was drawn to his attention?'

Lord Ickenham nodded.

'One sees what he meant. Curates must watch their step. One false move, like being caught stealing pigs, and bang goes any chance they may have had of rising to become Princes of the Church. And she—?'

'Told him to think it over, the—'

Lord Ickenham raised a hand.

'I know the word that is trembling on your lips, child, but don't utter it. Let us keep the conversation at as high a level as possible. Well, I agree with you that the crisis is one that calls for thought. I wonder if the simplest thing might not be for Bill just to fold his tent like the Arabs and silently steal away.'

'You mean leave the castle? Leave me?'

'It seems the wise move.'

'I won't have him steal away!'

'Surely it is better to steal away than a pig?'

'I'd die here without him. Can't you think of something better than that?'

'What we want is to gain time.'

'How can we? The—'

'Please!'

'The woman said she had to have his answer tomorrow.'

'As soon as that? Well, Bill will have to consent and tell her that she must give him a couple of days to nerve himself to the task.'

'What's the good of that?'

'We gain time.'

'Only two days.'

'But two days during which I shall be giving the full force of the Ickenham brain to the problem, and there are few problems capable of standing up to that treatment for long. They can't take it.'

'And when the two days are up and you haven't thought of anything?'

'Why, then,' admitted Lord Ickenham, 'the situation becomes a little sticky.'

# 6

## · 1 ·

Among other notable observations, too numerous to mention here, the poet Dryden (1631–1700) once said that mighty things from small beginnings grow, and all thinking men are agreed that in making this statement he called his shots correctly.

If a fly had not got into his bedroom and started buzzing about his nose in the hearty way flies have, it is improbable that Lord Emsworth would have awoken on the following morning at twenty minutes to five, for he was as a rule a sound sleeper who seldom failed to enjoy his eight hours. And if he had not woken and been unable to doze off again, he would not have lain in bed musing on the Church Lads. And if he had not mused on the Church Lads, he would not have recalled Lord Ickenham's advice of the previous day. Treacherous though his memory habitually was, it all came back to him.

Sneak down to the lake in the small hours of the morning and cut the ropes of the boys' tent, Ickenham had said, and the more he examined the suggestion, the more convinced he became that this was the manly thing to do. These fellows like Ickenham, he told himself, cautious conservative men of the world, do not make snap decisions; they think things over before coming to a conclusion, and when they tell you how to act, you know that by following their instructions you will be acting for the best.

No morning hour could be smaller than the present one, and in his library, he knew, there was a paper-knife of the type with which baronets get stabbed in the back in novels of suspense, and having cut his finger on it only two days ago he had no doubts of its fitness for the purpose he had in mind. Conditions, in short, could scarcely have been more favourable.

The only thing that held him back was the thought of his sister Constance. No one knew better than he how high was her standard of behaviour for brothers, and if the pitiless light of day were to be thrown on the crime he was contemplating, she would undoubtedly extend herself. She could, he estimated, be counted on for at least ten thousand words of rebuke and recrimination, administered in daily instalments over the years. In fact, as he put it to himself, for he was given to homely phrases, he would never hear the end of it.

If Connie finds out . . . he thought, and a shudder ran through him.

Then a voice seemed to whisper in his ear.

'She won't find out,' said the voice, and he was strong again. Filled with the crusading spirit which had animated ancestors of his who had done well at the battles of Acre and Joppa, he rose from his bed and dressed, if putting on an old sweater and a pair of flannel trousers with holes in the knees could be called dressing. When he reached the library his mood was definitely that of those distant forebears who had stropped their battle-axes and sallied out to fight the Paynim.

As he left the library, brandishing the paper-knife as King Arthur had once brandished the sword Excalibur, a sudden hollowness in his interior reminded him that he had not had his morning cup of tea. Absent-minded though he was, he realized that this could be remedied by going to the kitchen. It was not a part of the castle which he ever visited these days, but as a boy he had always been in and out—in when he wanted cake and out when the cook caught him getting it, and he had no difficulty in finding his way there. Full of anticipation of the happy ending, for though he knew he had his limitations he was pretty sure that he could boil a kettle, he pushed open the familiar door and went in, and was unpleasantly surprised to see his grandson George there, eating eggs and bacon.

'Oh, hullo, Grandpa,' said George, speaking thickly, for his mouth was full.

'George!' said Lord Emsworth, also speaking thickly, but for a different reason. 'You are up very early.'

George said he liked rising betimes. You got two breakfasts that way. He was at the age when the young stomach wants all that is coming to it.

'Why are you up so early, Grandpapa?'

'I . . . er . . . I was unable to sleep.'

'Shall I fry you an egg?'

'Thank you, no. I thought of taking a little stroll. The air is so nice and fresh. Er—goodbye, George.'

'Goodbye, Grandpapa.'

'Little stroll,' said Lord Emsworth again, driving home his point, and withdrew, feeling rather shaken.

## • II •

The big story of the cut tent ropes broke shortly before breakfast, when a Church Lad who looked as if he had had a disturbed night called at the back premises of the castle asking to see Beach. To him he revealed the position of affairs, and Beach dispatched an underling to find fresh rope to take the place of the severed strands. He then reported to Lady Constance, who told the Duke, who told his nephew Archie Gilpin, who told Lord Ickenham, who said, 'Well, well, well! Just fancy!'

'The work of an international gang, do you think?' he said, and Archie said Well, anyway, the work of somebody who wasn't fond of Church Lads, and Lord Ickenham agreed that this might well be so.

Normally at this hour he would have been on his way to his hammock, but obviously the hammock must be postponed till later. His first task was to seek Lord Emsworth out and offer his congratulations. He was feeling quite a glow as he proceeded to the library, where he knew that the other would have retired to read *Whiffle On The Care Of The Pig* or some other volume of porcine interest, his invariable procedure after he had had breakfast. It gratified the kindly man to know that his advice had been taken with such excellent results.

Lord Emsworth was not actually reading when he entered. He was sitting staring before him, the book on his lap. There are moments when even Whiffle cannot hold the attention, and this was one of them. It would be too much, perhaps, to say that remorse gripped Lord Emsworth, but he was undoubtedly in something of a twitter and wondering if that great gesture of his had been altogether well-advised. His emotions were rather similar to those of a Chicago business man of the old school who has rubbed out a competitor with a pine-apple bomb and, while feeling that that part of it is all right, cannot help speculating on what the F.B.I. are going to do when they hear about it.

'Oh—er—hullo, Ickenham,' he said. 'Nice morning.'

'For you, my dear Emsworth, a red-letter morning. I've just heard the news.'

'Eh?'

'The place is ringing with the story of your exploit.'

'Eh?'

'Now come,' said Lord Ickenham reproachfully. 'No need to dissemble with me. You took my advice, didn't you, and pulled a sword of Gideon on those tented boys? And I imagine that you are feeling a better, cleaner man.'

Lord Emsworth was looking somewhat more guilty and apprehensive than good, clean men usually do. He peered through his pince-nez at the wall, as if suspecting it of having ears.

'I wish you wouldn't talk so loudly, Ickenham.'

'I'll whisper.'

'Yes, do,' said Lord Emsworth, relieved.

Lord Ickenham took a seat and sank his voice.

'Tell me all about it.'

'Well—'

'I understand. You are a man of action, and words don't come to you easily. Like Bill Bailey.'

'Bill Bailey?'

'Fellow I know.'

'There was a song called "Won't You Come Home, Bill Bailey?" I used to sing it as a boy.'

'It must have sounded wonderful. But don't sing it now. I want to hear all about your last night's activities.'

'It was this morning.'

'Ah, yes, that was the time I recommended, wasn't it? With dawn pinking the eastern sky and the early bird chirping over its early worm. I had a feeling that you would be in better shape under those romantic conditions. You thoroughly enjoyed it, no doubt?'

'I was terrified, Ickenham.'

'Nonsense. I know you better than that.'

'I was. I kept thinking what my sister Constance would say, if she found out.'

'She won't find out.'

'You really think so?'

'How can she?'

'She does find out things.'

'But not this one. It will remain one of those great historic mysteries like the Man in the Iron Mask and the *Mary Celeste*.'

'Have you seen Constance?'

'For a moment.'

'Was she—er—upset?'

'One might almost say she split a gusset.'

'I feared as much.'

'But that's nothing for you to worry about. Your name never came up. Suspicion fell immediately on the boy who cleans the knives and boots. Do you know him?'

'No, we have never met.'

'Nice chap, I believe. Percy is his name, and apparently his relations with the Church Lads have been far from cordial. They tell me he is rather acutely alive to class distinctions and being on the castle payroll has always looked down on the Church Lads as social inferiors. This has led to resentment, thrown stones, the calling of opprobrious names and so forth, so that when the authorities were apprised of what had happened, he automatically became the logical suspect. Taken into the squad room and grilled under the lights, however, he persisted in stout denial and ultimately had to be released for lack of evidence. That is the thing that is baffling the prosecution, the total lack of evidence.'

'I'm glad of that.'

'You ought to be.'

'But I keep thinking of Constance.'

'You're not afraid of her?'

'Yes, I am. You have no notion how she goes on about a thing. On and on and on. I remember coming down to dinner one night when we had a big dinner party with a brass paper-fastener in my shirt front, because I had unfortunately swallowed my stud, and she kept harping on it for months.'

'I see. Well, I'm sure you need have no uneasiness. Why should she suspect you?'

'She knows I have a grievance against these boys. They knocked off my top hat at the school treat and teased the Empress with a potato on a string. She may put two and two together.'

'Not a chance,' said Lord Ickenham heartily. 'I'm sure you're in the clear. But if she does start anything, imitate the intrepid Percy and stick to stout denial. You can't beat it as a general policy. Keep telling yourself that suspicion won't get her anywhere, she must have proof, and she knows perfectly well that there is none that would have a hope of getting past the Director of Public Prosecutions. If she pulls you in and wants you to make a statement, just look her in the eye and keep saying "Is zat so?" and "Sez you", confident that she can never pin the rap on you. And if she tries any funny business with a rubber hose, see your lawyer. And now I must be leaving you. I am long overdue at my hammock.'

Left alone, Lord Emsworth, though considerably cheered by these heartening words, still did not feel equal to resuming his perusal of *Whiffle On The Care Of The Pig*. He sat staring before him, and so absorbed was he in his meditations that the knock on the door brought him out of his chair, quivering in every limb.

'Come in,' he quavered, though reason told him that this could not be his sister Constance, come to ask him to make a statement, for Connie would not have knocked.

It was Lavender Briggs who entered. In her bearing, though he was too agitated to observe it, there was an unaccustomed jauntiness, a jauntiness occasioned by the fact that after dinner on the previous night the Duke had handed her a cheque for five hundred pounds and she was going to London for the night to celebrate. There are few things that so lend elasticity to a girl's step as the knowledge that in the bag swinging from her right hand there is a cheque for this sum payable to herself. Lavender Briggs was not actually skipping like the high hills, but she came within measurable distance of doing so. On her way to the library she had been humming a morceau from one of the avant-garde composers and sketching out preliminary plans for that typewriting bureau for which she now had the requisite capital.

Her prospects, she felt, were of the brightest. She could think offhand of at least a dozen poets and as many whimsical essayists in her own circle of friends who were always writing something and having to have it typed. Shade her prices a little in the first month or so, and all these Aubreys and Lionels and Lucians and Eustaces would come running, and after them—for the news of good work soon gets around—the general public. Every red-blooded man in England, she knew, not to mention the red-blooded women, was writing a novel and would have to have top copy and two carbons.

It was consequently with something approaching cheeriness that she addressed Lord Emsworth.

'Oh, Lord Emsworth, I am sorry to disturb you, but Lady Constance has given me leave to go to London for the night. I was wondering if there was anything I could do for you while I am there?'

Lord Emsworth thanked her and said No, he could not think of anything, and she went her way, leaving him to his thoughts. He was still feeling boneless and had asked himself for the hundredth time if his friend Ickenham's advice about stout denial could be relied on to produce the happy ending, when a second knock on the door brought him out of his chair again.

This time it was Bill Bailey.

'Could I see you for a moment, Lord Emsworth?' said Bill.

## · III ·

Having interviewed Lavender Briggs and given her permission to go to London for the night, Lady Constance had retired to her boudoir to look through the letters which had arrived for her by the morning post. One of them was from her friend James Schoonmaker in New York, and she was reading it with the pleasure which his letters always gave her, when from the other side of the door there came a sound like a mighty rushing wind, and Lord Emsworth burst over the threshold. And she was about to utter a rebuking 'Oh, Clarence!', the customary formula for putting him in his place, when she caught sight of his face and the words froze on her lips.

He was a light mauve in colour, and his eyes, generally so mild, glittered behind their pince-nez with a strange light. It needed but a glance to tell her that he was in one of his rare berserk moods. These occurred perhaps twice in each calendar year, and even she, strong woman though she was, always came near to quailing before them, for on these occasions he ceased to be a human doormat whom an 'Oh, Clarence!' could quell and became something more on the order of one of those high winds which from time to time blow through the state of Kansas and send its inhabitants scurrying nimbly to their cyclone cellars. When the oppressed rise and start setting about the oppressor, their fury is always formidable. One noticed this in the French Revolution.

'Where's that damned Briggs woman?' he demanded, snapping out the words as if he had been a master of men and not a craven accustomed to curl up in a ball at the secretary's lightest glance. 'Have you seen that blasted female anywhere, Constance? I've been looking for her all over the place.'

Normally, Lady Constance would have been swift to criticize such laxity of speech, but until his belligerent mood had blown over she knew that the voice of authority must be silent.

'I let her go to London for the night,' she replied almost meekly.

'So you did,' said Lord Emsworth. He had forgotten this, as he forgot most things. 'Yes, that's right, she told me. I'm going to London, she said, yes, I remember now.'

'Why do you want Miss Briggs?'

Lord Emsworth, who had shown signs of calming down a little, returned to boiling point. His pince-nez flew off his nose and danced at the end of their string, their practice whenever he was deeply stirred.

'I'm going to sack her!'

'What!'

'She doesn't stay another day in the place. I've just been sacking Wellbeloved.'

It would be putting it too crudely to say that Lady Constance bleated, but the sound that proceeded from her did have a certain resemblance to the utterance of a high-strung sheep startled while lunching in a meadow. She was not one of George Cyril Wellbeloved's warmest admirers, but she knew how greatly her brother valued his services and she found it incredible that he should voluntarily have dispensed with them. She could as readily imagine herself dismissing Beach, that peerless butler. She shrank a little in her chair. The impression she received was that this wild-eyed man was running amok, and there shot into her mind those ominous words the Duke had spoken on the previous afternoon. 'Definitely barmy,' he had said. 'Reached the gibbering stage and may become dangerous at any moment.' It was not too fanciful to suppose that that moment had arrived.

'But, Clarence!' she cried, and Lord Emsworth, who had recovered his pince-nez, waved them at her in a menacing manner, like a retarius in the Roman arena about to throw his net.

'It's no good sitting there saying "But, Clarence!"' he said, replacing the pince-nez on his nose and glaring through them. 'I told him he'd got to be out of the place in ten minutes or I'd be after him with a shot-gun.'

'But, Clarence!'

'Don't keep saying that!'

'No, no, I'm sorry. I was only wondering why.'

Lord Emsworth considered the question. It seemed to him a fair one.

'You mean why did I sack him? I'll tell you why I sacked him. He's a snake in the grass. He and the Briggs woman were plotting to steal my pig.'

'What!'

'Are you deaf? I said they were plotting to steal the Empress.'

'But, Clarence!'

'And if you say "But, Clarence!" once more, just once more,' said Lord Emsworth sternly, 'I'll know what to do about it. I suppose what you're trying to tell me is that you don't believe me.'

'How can I believe you? Miss Briggs came with the highest testimonials. She is a graduate of the London School of Economics.'

'Well, apparently the course she took there was the one on how to steal pigs.'

'But, Clarence!'

'I have warned you, Constance!'

'I'm sorry. I meant you must be mistaken.'

'Mistaken be blowed! I had the whole sordid story from the lips of Ickenham's friend Meriwether. He told it me in pitiless detail. According to him, some hidden hand wants the Empress and has bribed the Briggs woman to steal her for him. I would have suspected Sir Gregory Parsloe as the master-mind behind the plot, only he's in the South of France. Though he could have made the preliminary arrangements by letter, I suppose.'

Lady Constance clutched her temples.

'Mr Meriwether?'

'You know Meriwether. Large chap with a face like a gorilla.'

'But how could Mr Meriwether possibly have known?'

'She told him.'

'*Told* him?'

'That's right. She wanted him to be one of her corps of assistants, working with Wellbeloved. She approached him yesterday and said that if he didn't agree to help steal the Empress, she would expose him. Must have been a nasty shock to the poor fellow. Not at all the sort of thing you want to have women coming and saying to you.'

Lady Constance, who had momentarily relaxed her grip on her temples, tightened it again. She had an uneasy feeling that, unless she did so, her head would split.

'Expose him?' she whispered hoarsely. 'What do you mean?'

'What do I mean? Oh, I see. What do I mean? Yes, quite. I ought to have explained that, oughtn't I? It seems that his name isn't Meriwether. It's something else which I've forgotten. Not that it matters. The point is that the Briggs woman found out somehow that he was here under an alias, as I believe the expression is, and held it over him.'

'You mean he's an impostor?'

Lady Constance spoke with a wealth of emotion. In the past few years Blandings Castle had been peculiarly rich in impostors, notable among them Lord Ickenham and his nephew Pongo, and she had reached saturation point as regarded them, never wanting to see another of them as long as she lived. A hostess gets annoyed and frets when she finds that every second guest whom she entertains is enjoying her hospitality under a false name, and it sometimes seemed to her that Blandings Castle had impostors the way other houses had mice, a circumstance at which her proud spirit rebelled.

'Who is this man?' she demanded. 'Who is he?'

'Ah, there I'm afraid you rather have me,' said Lord Emsworth. 'He told me, but you know what my memory's like. I do remember he said he was a curate.'

Lady Constance had risen from her chair and was staring at him as if instead of her elder brother he had been the Blandings Castle spectre, a knight in armour carrying his head in his hand, who was generally supposed to be around and about whenever there was going to be a death in the family. Ever since she had discovered that Myra Schoonmaker had formed an attachment to the Reverend Cuthbert Bailey, any mention of curates had affected her profoundly.

'What! What did you say?'

'When?'

'Did you say he was a curate?'

'Who?'

'Lord Ickenham's friend, Mr Meriwether.'

'Oh, ah, yes, quite, Mr Meriwether, to be sure.' Lord Emsworth's fury had expended itself, and he was now his amiable, chatty—or, as some preferred to call it, gibbering—self once more. 'Yes, he's a curate, he tells me. He doesn't look like one, but he is. That was why he refused to be a party to the purloining of my pig. Being in holy orders, his conscience wouldn't let him. I must say I thought it very civil of him to come and warn me of the Briggs woman's foul plot, knowing that it would mean her exposing him to you and you cutting up rough. But he said he had these scruples, and they wouldn't allow him to remain silent. A splendid young man, I thought, and very sound on pigs. Odd, because I didn't know they had pigs in Brazil, or curates either, for that matter. By the way, I've just remembered his name. It's Bailey. You want to keep this very clear, or you'll get muddled. He's got two names, one wrong, the other right. His wrong name's Meriwether, and his right name's Bailey.'

Lady Constance had uttered a wordless cry. She might have known, she was feeling bitterly, that Lord Ickenham would never have brought a friend to Blandings Castle unless with some sinister purpose. That much could be taken as read. But she had never suspected that even he would go to such lengths of depravity as to introduce the infamous Bailey into her home. So that, she told herself, was why Myra Schoonmaker had suddenly become so cheerful recently. Her lips tightened. Well, she was reflecting grimly, it would not be long before Blandings Castle saw the last of Lord Ickenham and his clerical friend.

'Yes, Bailey,' said Lord Emsworth. 'The Reverend Cuthbert Bailey. I was telling Ickenham just now that there was a song years ago called "Won't You Come Home, Bill Bailey?" I used to sing it as a boy. But why he should have brought the chap here under the name of Meriwether and told me he was in the Brazil-nut industry, I can't imagine. Silly kind of thing to do, wouldn't you say? I mean, if a fellow's name's Bailey, why call him Meriwether? And why say he's come from Brazil when he's come from Bottleton East? Doesn't make sense.'

'Clarence!'

'About that song,' said Lord Emsworth. 'Very catchy tune it had. The verse escapes me—in fact, I don't believe I ever sang it—but the chorus began "Won't you come home, Bill Bailey, won't you come home?" Now, how did the next line go? Something about "the whole day long", and you had to make the "long" two syllables. "Lo-ong", if you follow me.'

'Clarence!'

'Eh?'

'Go and find Lord Ickenham.'

'Lord who?'

'Ickenham.'

'Oh, you mean Ickenham. Yes, certainly, of course, delighted. I think he usually goes and lies in that hammock on the lawn after breakfast.'

'Well, ask him if he will be good enough to leave his hammock, if it is not inconveniencing him, and come and see me immediately,' said Lady Constance.

She sank into her chair, and sat there breathing softly through the nostrils. A frozen calm had fallen on her. Her lips had tightened, her eyes were hard, and even Lord Ickenham, intrepid though he was, might have felt, had he entered at this moment, a pang of apprehension at the sight of her, so clearly was her manner that of a woman about to say to her domestic staff, 'Throw these men out, and see to it that they land on something sharp.'

# 7

## · I ·

Breakfast concluded, the Duke of Dunstable had gone to the terrace, where there was a comfortable deck-chair in the shade of a spreading tree, to smoke the first cigar of the day and read his *Times*. But scarcely had he blown the opening puff of smoke and set eye to print when his peace was destroyed by the same treble voice which had disturbed him on the previous day. Once more it squeaked in his ear, and he saw that he had been joined by Lord Emsworth's grandson George, who, as on the former occasion, had omitted to announce his presence by blowing his horn.

He did not strike the lad, for that would have involved rising from his seat, but he gave him an unpleasant look. Intrusion on his sacred after-breakfast hour always awoke the fiend that slept in him.

'Go away, boy!' he boomed.

'You mean "Scram!", don't you, chum?' said George, who liked to get these things right. 'But I want to confer with you about this tent business.'

'What tent business?'

'That thing that happened last night.'

'Oh, that?'

'Only it wasn't last night, it was this morning. A mysterious affair. Have you formed any conclusions?'

The Duke stirred irritably. He was regretting the mistaken kindness that had led him to brighten Blandings Castle with his presence. It was the old story. You said to yourself in a weak and sentimental moment that Emsworth and Connie and the rest of them led dull lives and needed cheering up by association with a polished man of the world, so you sacrificed yourself and came here, and the next thing you knew everyone was jumping into lakes and charging you five hundred pounds for stealing pigs and coming squeaking in your ear and so on and so forth—in short, making the place a ruddy inferno. He gave an animal snarl, and even when filtered through his moustache the sound was impressive, though it left George unmoved. To George it merely seemed that his old friend had got an insect of some kind in his thoracic cavity.

'What do you mean, have I formed any conclusions? Do you think a busy man like myself has time to bother himself with these trifles? Scram, boy, and let me read my paper.'

Like most small boys, George had the quiet persistence of a gadfly. It was never easy to convince him that his society was not desired by one and all. He settled himself on the stone flooring beside the Duke's chair in the manner of one who has come to stay. Limpets on rocks could have picked up useful hints from him in the way of technique.

'This is a lot hotter news than anything you'll read in the paper,' he squeaked. 'I have a strange story to relate.'

In spite of himself, the Duke found that he was becoming mildly interested.

'I suppose you know who did it, hey?' he said satirically.

George shrugged a shoulder.

'Beyond the obvious facts that the miscreant was a Freemason, left-handed, chewed tobacco and had travelled in the east,' he said, 'I have so far formed no conclusion.'

'What on earth are you talking about?'

'I only put that in to make it sound better. As a matter of fact, it was Grandpapa.'

'What do you mean, it was Grandpapa? Who was Grandpapa?'

'The miscreant.'

'Are you telling me that your grandfather—'

Words failed the Duke. His opinion of Lord Emsworth's I.Q. was, as we know, low, but he was unable to credit him with the supreme pottiness necessary for the perpetration of an act like the one they were discussing. Then, thinking again, he felt that there might be something in what the boy said. After all, from making an exhibition of oneself by maundering over a pig to sneaking out at daybreak and cutting tent ropes is but a step.

'What makes you think that?' he said, now definitely agog.

George would have liked to say, 'You know my methods. Apply them,' but it would have wasted time, and he was anxious to get on with his story.

'Shall I tell it you from the beginning, omitting no detail, however slight?'

'Certainly, certainly,' said the Duke, and would have added, 'I am all ears,' if the expression had been familiar to him. He wished the boy had a voice in a rather lower register, but in consideration of the importance of what he had to communicate he was willing to be squeaked at.

George marshalled his thoughts.

'I was in the kitchen at five o'clock this morning—'

'What were you doing there at such an hour?'

'Oh, just looking around,' said George guardedly. He knew that there was a school of thought that disapproved of these double breakfasts of his, and nothing to be gained by imparting information which might be relayed to Lady Constance, the head of that school. 'I sort of happened to go in.'

'Well?'

'And I hadn't been there more than about a couple of ticks when Grandpapa entered. He had a knife on his person.'

'A knife?'

'A whacking great scimitar.'

'How do you mean, on his person?'

'Well, actually he was brandishing it. His manner was strange, and there was a wild glitter in his eyes. So I said to myself, "Ho!"'

'You said what?'

'Ho!'

'Why "Ho!"?'

'Well, wouldn't you have said "Ho!"?'

The Duke considered the question, and saw that the lad had a point there.

'No doubt I should have been surprised,' he admitted.

'So was I. That's why I said "Ho!"'

'To yourself?'

'Of course. You can't go about saying "Ho!" to people out loud. So when he went out, I followed him.'

'Why?'

'Use your loaf, big boy,' pleaded George. 'You know my methods. Apply them,' he said, happy to get it in at last. 'I wanted to see what he was up to.'

'Of course. Yes, quite understandable. And—?'

'He headed for the lake. I trickled after him, taking advantage of every inch of cover, and he made a beeline for that tent and started sawing away at the ropes.'

A sudden suspicion darted into the Duke's mind. He puffed a menacing moustache.

'If this is some silly joke of yours, young man—'

'I swear it isn't. I tell you I was watching him the whole time. He didn't see me because I was well concealed behind a neighbouring bush, but I was an eye-witness throughout. Did you ever read *The Hound Of The Baskervilles*?'

For an instant the Duke received the impression that the pottiness of Lord Emsworth had been inherited by his grandson, with an assist from the latter's father, the ninth Earl's elder son, Lord Bosham, whom he knew to be one of England's less bright minds. You don't, he reasoned, read hounds, you gallop after them on horses, shouting 'Yoicks!' or possibly 'Tally-ho!' Then it occurred to him that the lad might be referring to some book or other. He inquired whether this was so, and received an answer in the affirmative.

'I was thinking of the bit where Holmes and Watson are lurking in the mist, waiting for the bad guy to start things moving. It was rather like that, only there wasn't any mist.'

'So you saw him clearly?'

'With the naked eye.'

'And he was cutting the ropes?'

'With the naked knife.'

The Duke relapsed into a gloomy silence. Like many another thinker before him, he was depressed by the reflection that nothing ever goes just right in this fat-headed world. Always there is the fatal snag in the path that pulls you up sharp when the happy ending seems in sight.

A man of liberal views, he had no objection whatsoever to a little gentlemanly blackmail, and here, you would have said, the luck of the Dunstables had handed him the most admirable opportunity for such blackmail. All he had to do was to go to Lord Emsworth, tell him that his sins had found him out, demand the Empress as the price of his silence, and the wretched man would have no option but to meet his terms. The thing was a walkover. In the bag, as he believed the expression was nowadays.

Such had been his thoughts as he listened to the boy's story, but now despondency had set in. The whole project, he saw, became null and void because of one small snag—that proof of the crime depended solely on the unsupported word of the witness George. If Emsworth, as he was bound to do, pleaded not guilty to the charge, who was going to believe the testimony of a child with ginger hair and freckles, whose reputation as a teller of the truth had never been one to invite scrutiny? His evidence would be laughed out of court, and he would be dashed lucky if he were not sent to bed without his supper and deprived of his pocket money for months and months.

Engrossed in these sombre thoughts, he was only dimly aware that the squeaky voice was continuing to squeak. It seemed to be saying something about motion pictures, a subject in which he had never taken even a tepid interest.

'Shut up, boy, and pop off,' he grunted.

'But I thought you'd like to know,' said George, pained.

'If you think I want to hear about a lot of greasy actors grinning on a screen, you are very much mistaken.'

'But this wasn't a greasy, grinning actor, it was Grandpapa.'

'What's that?'

'I was telling you I took pictures of Grandpapa with my camera.'

The Duke quivered as if he had been the sea monster he rather closely resembled and a harpoon had penetrated his skin.

'In the act of cutting those ropes?' he gasped.

'That's right. I've got the film upstairs in my room. I was going to take it into Market Blandings this afternoon to have it developed.'

The Duke quivered again, his emotion such that he could scarcely speak.

'You must do nothing of the sort. And you must not say a word of this to anyone.'

'Well, of course I won't. I only told you because I thought you'd think it was funny.'

'It is very far from funny. It is extremely serious. Do you realize what would happen when the man developed that film, as you call it, and recognized your grandfather?'

'Coo! I never thought of that. You mean he'd blow the gaff? Spread the story hither and thither? Squeal on him?'

'Exactly. And your grandfather's name in the county would be—'

'Mud?'

'Precisely. Everyone would think he was potty.'

'He *is* rather potty.'

'Not so potty as he would seem if that film were made public. Dash it, they'd certify him without blinking an eye.'

'Who would?'

'The doctors, of course.'

'You mean he'd be put in a loony bin?'

'Exactly.'

'Coo!'

George could see now why his companion had said it was serious. He was very fond of Lord Emsworth, and would have hated to find him winding up in a padded cell. He felt in his pocket and produced a bag of acid drops, always a great help to thought. Chewing one of these, he sat pondering in silence. The Duke resumed his remarks.

'Do you understand what I am saying?'

George nodded.

'I dig you, Chief.'

'Don't say "I dig you" and don't call me "chief". Bring the thing to me, and I'll take care of it. It's not safe in the hands of a mere child like you.'

'Okay, big boy.'

'And don't call me big boy,' said the Duke.

## • II •

There was a contented smile on Lord Ickenham's face as he settled himself in his hammock after leaving Lord Emsworth. It gratified him to feel that he had allayed the latter's fears and eased his mind. Nothing like a pep talk, he was thinking, and he was deep in a pleasant reverie when a voice spoke his name and he perceived Lord Emsworth at his side, drooping like a tired lily. Except when he had something to prop himself against, there was always a suggestion of the drooping floweret about the master of Blandings Castle. He seemed to work on a hinge somewhere in the small of his back, and people searching for something nice to say of him sometimes described him as having a scholarly stoop. Lord Ickenham had become accustomed to this bonelessness and no longer expected his friend to give any evidence of possessing vertebrae, but the look of anguish on his face was new, and it shocked him. He rose from the hammock with a lissom leap, full of sympathy and concern.

'Good heavens, Emsworth! What's the matter? Is something wrong?'

For some moments it seemed as though speech would prove beyond the ninth earl's powers and that he would continue indefinitely to give his rather vivid impersonation of a paralysed deaf mute. But eventually he spoke.

'I've just seen Dunstable,' he said.

Lord Ickenham remained perplexed. The situation did not appear to him to have been clarified. He, personally, would always prefer not to see the Duke, a preference shared by the latter's many acquaintances in Wiltshire and elsewhere, but it did not disturb him unduly when he had to, and he found it strange that his companion should be of less stern stuff.

'Unavoidable, don't you think, when he's staying in the house?' he said. 'There he is, I mean to say, and you can't very well help running into him from time to time. But perhaps he said something to upset you?'

The anguished look in Lord Emsworth's eyes became more anguished. It was as if the question had touched an exposed nerve. He gulped for a moment, reminding Lord Ickenham of a dog to which he was greatly attached, which made a similar sound when about to give up its all after a too busy day among the fleshpots.

'He said he wanted the Empress.'

'Who wouldn't?'

'And I've got to give her to him.'

'You've *what*?'

'The alternative was too terrible to contemplate. He threatened, if I refused, to tell Constance that it was I who cut those tent ropes.'

Lord Ickenham began to feel a little impatient. He had already told his man, in words adapted to the meanest intelligence, what course to pursue, should suspicion fall upon him.

'My dear fellow, don't you remember what I said to you in the library? Stick to stout denial.'

'But he has proof.'

'Proof?'

'Eh? Yes, proof. It seems that my grandson George took photographs of me with his camera, and Dunstable now has the film in his possession. And I gave George that camera for his birthday! "This will keep you out of mischief, George, my boy," I remember saying. Out of mischief!' said Lord Emsworth bitterly, his air that of a grandfather regretting that he had ever been so foolish as to beget a son who in his turn would beget a son of his own capable of using a camera. There were, he was feeling, far too many grandsons in the world and far too many cameras for them to take pictures of grandfathers with. His view of grandsons was, in short, at the moment jaundiced, and as, having told his tale, he moved limply away, he was thinking almost as harshly of George as of the Duke of Dunstable.

Lord Ickenham returned to his hammock. He always thought more nimbly when in a recumbent position, and it was plain to him that a considerable amount of nimble thinking was now called for. Hitherto, his endeavours to spread sweetness and light and give service with a smile had been uniformly successful, but a man whose aim in life it is to do the square thing by his fellows is never content to think with modest pride of past triumphs; it is the present on which he feels the mind must be fixed, and it was to Lord Emsworth's problem that he gave the full force of his powerful intellect.

It was a problem which undoubtedly presented certain points of interest, and at the moment he confessed himself unable to see how it was to be solved. Given the unhappy man's panic fear of having Lady Constance's attention drawn to his recent activities, there seemed no course for Lord Emsworth to pursue but to meet the Duke's terms. It was one of those occasions, more frequent in real life than on the television and motion picture screens, when the bad guy comes out on top and the good guy gets the loser's end. The Duke of Dunstable might not look like a green bay tree, but everything pointed to the probability of him flourishing like one.

He was musing thus, and had closed his eyes in order to muse the better, when a stately figure approached the hammock and stood beside it. Shrewdly realizing that there was but the slimmest chance of her brother Clarence remembering to tell Lord Ickenham that his presence was desired in her boudoir, Lady Constance had rung for Beach and sent him off to act as a substitute messenger. The butler coughed respectfully, and Lord Ickenham opened his eyes.

'Pardon me for disturbing you, m'lord—'

'Not at all, Beach, not at all,' said Lord Ickenham heartily. He was always glad to chat with this pillar of Blandings, for a firm friendship had sprung up between them during his previous sojourn at the castle, and this second visit had cemented it. 'Something on your mind?'

'Her ladyship, m'lord.'

'What about her?'

'If it is convenient to you, m'lord, she would be glad to see you for a moment in her boudoir.'

This struck Lord Ickenham as unusual. It was the first time his hostess had gone out of her way to seek his company, and he was not sure that he liked the look of things. He had never considered himself psychic, but he was conscious of a strong premonition that trouble was about to raise its ugly head.

'Any idea what she wants?'

Butlers rarely display emotion, and there was nothing in Beach's manner to reveal the sympathy he was feeling for one who, in his opinion, was about to face an ordeal somewhat comparable to that of the prophet Daniel when he entered the lions' den.

'I rather fancy, m'lord, her ladyship wishes to confer with you on the subject of Mr Meriwether. With reference to the gentleman's name being in reality the Reverend Cuthbert Bailey.'

Once in his cowboy days Lord Ickenham, injudiciously standing behind a temperamental mule, had been kicked by the animal in the stomach. He felt now rather as he had felt then, though only an involuntary start showed that he was not his usual debonair self.

'Oh,' he said thoughtfully. 'Oh. So she knows about that?'

'Yes, m'lord.'

'How did you come to get abreast?'

'I was inadvertently an auditor of his lordship's conversation with her ladyship. I chanced to be passing the door, and his lordship had omitted to close it.'

'And you stopped, looked and listened?'

'I had paused to tie my shoelace,' said Beach with dignity. 'I found it impossible not to overhear what his lordship was saying.'

'And what was he saying?'

'He was informing her ladyship that Miss Briggs, having discovered Mr Meriwether's identity, was seeking to compel the gentleman to assist her in her project of stealing his lordship's pig, but that Mr Meriwether refused to be a party to the undertaking, having scruples. It was in the course of his remarks on this subject that his lordship revealed that Mr Meriwether was not Mr Meriwether, but Mr Bailey.'

Lord Ickenham sighed. In principle he approved of his young friend's rigid code of ethics, but there was no denying that that high-mindedness of his could be inconvenient, lowering as it did his efficiency as a plotter. The ideal person with whom to plot is the furtive, shifty-eyed man who stifled his conscience at the age of six and would not recognize a scruple if you served it up to him on an individual blue plate with béarnaise sauce.

'I see,' he said. 'How did Lady Constance take this piece of hot news?'

'She appeared somewhat stirred, m'lord.'

'One sees how she might well be. And now she wants to have a word with me?'

'Yes, m'lord.'

'To thresh the thing out, no doubt, and consider it from every angle. Oh, what a tangled web we weave, Beach, when first we practise to deceive.'

'We do, indeed, m'lord.'

'Well, all right,' said Lord Ickenham, rising. 'I can give her five minutes.'

## • III •

The time it had taken Beach to deliver his message and Lord Ickenham to make the journey between lawn and boudoir was perhaps ten minutes, and with each of those minutes Lady Constance's wrath had touched a new high. At the moment when her guest entered the room she had just been thinking how agreeable it would be to skin him with a blunt knife, and the genial smile he gave her as he came in seemed to go through her nervous system like a red-hot bullet through butter. 'My tablets—Meet it is I set it down that one may smile and smile and be a villain. At least, I'm sure it may be so in Blandings Castle,' she was saying to herself.

'Beach says you want to see me, Lady Constance,' said Lord Ickenham, smiling another affectionate smile. His manner was that of a man looking forward to a delightful chat on this and that with an attractive woman, and Lady Constance, meeting the smile head on, realized that in entertaining the idea of skinning him with a blunt knife she had been too lenient. Not a blunt knife, she was thinking, but some such instrument as the one described by the poet Gilbert as looking far less like a hatchet than a dissipated saw.

'Please sit down,' she said coldly.

'Oh, thanks,' said Lord Ickenham, doing so. His eye fell on a photograph on the desk. 'Hullo, this face seems familiar. Jimmy Schoonmaker?'

'Yes.'

'Taken recently?'

'Yes.'

'He looks older than he used to. One does, of course, as the years go on. I suppose I do, too, though I've never noticed it. Great chap, Jimmy. Did you know that he brought young Myra up all by himself after his wife died? With a certain amount of assistance from me. The one thing he jibbed at was giving her her bath, so he used to call me in of an evening, and I would soap her back, keeping what the advertisements call a safe suds level. It was a little like massaging an eel. Bless my soul, how long ago it seems. I remember once—'

'Lord Ickenham!' Lady Constance's voice, several degrees below zero at the outset, had become even more like that of a snow queen. The hatchet that looked like a dissipated saw would not have seemed to her barely adequate. 'I did not ask you to come here because I wished to hear your reminiscences. It was to tell you that you will leave the castle immediately. *With*,' added Lady Constance, speaking from between clenched teeth, 'your friend Mr Bailey.'

She paused, and was conscious of a feeling of flatness and disappointment. She had expected her words to bathe this man in confusion and shatter his composure to fragments, but he had not turned a hair of his neatly brushed head. He was looking at another photograph. It was that of Lady Constance's late husband, Joseph Keeble, but she gave him no time to ask questions about it.

'Lord Ickenham!'

He turned, full of apology.

'I'm sorry. I'm afraid I let my attention wander. I was thinking of the dear old days. You were saying that you were about to leave the castle, were you not?'

'I was saying that *you* were about to leave the castle.'

Lord Ickenham seemed surprised.

'I had made no plans. You're sure you mean me?'

'And you will take Mr Bailey with you. How dare you bring that impossible young man here?'

Lord Ickenham fingered his moustache thoughtfully.

'Oh, Bill Bailey. I see what you mean. Yes, I suppose it was a social solecism. But reflect. I meant well. Two young hearts had been sundered in springtime . . . well, not in springtime, perhaps, but as near to it as makes no matter, and I wanted to adjust things. I'm sure Jimmy would have approved of the kindly act.'

'I disagree with you.'

'He wants his ewe lamb to be happy.'

'So do I. That is why I do not intend to allow her to marry a penniless curate. But there is no need to discuss it. There are—'

'You'll be sorry when Bill suddenly becomes a bishop.'

'—good trains—'

'Why did I not push this good thing along, you'll say to yourself.'

'—throughout the day. I recommend the 2.15,' said Lady Constance. 'Good morning, Lord Ickenham. I will not keep you any longer.'

A nicer-minded man would have detected in these words a hint—guarded, perhaps, but nevertheless a hint—that his presence was no longer desired, but Lord Ickenham remained glued to his chair. He was looking troubled.

'I agree that you are probably right in giving this plug to the 2.15 train,' he said. 'No doubt it is an excellent one. But there are difficulties in the way of Bill and me catching it.'

'I see none.'

'I will try to make myself clearer. Have you studied Bill Bailey at all closely during his visit here? He's an odd chap. Wouldn't hurt a fly in the ordinary way, in fact I've known him not to do so—'

'I am not interested in Mr—'

'But, when driven to it, ruthless and sticking at nothing. You might think that, being a curate, he would suppress those photographs, and of course I feel that that is what he ought to do. But even curates can be pushed too far, and I'm afraid if you insist on him leaving the castle, however luxurious the 2.15 train, that that is how he will feel he is being pushed.'

'Lord Ickenham!'

'You spoke?'

'*What* are you talking about?'

'Didn't I explain that? I'm sorry. I have an annoying habit of getting ahead of my story. I was alluding to the photographs he took of Beach and saying that, if driven out into the snow, he will feel so bitter that he will give them wide publicity. Vindictive, yes, and not at all the sort of thing one approves of in a clerk in holy orders, but that is what will happen, I assure you.'

Lady Constance placed a hand on a forehead which had become fevered. Not even when conversing with her brother Clarence had she ever felt so marked a swimming sensation.

'Photographs? Of Beach?'

'Cutting those tent ropes and causing alarm and despondency to more Church Lads than one likes to contemplate. But how foolish of me. I didn't tell you, did I? Here is the thing in a nutshell. Bill Bailey, unable to sleep this morning possibly because love affects him that way, started to go for a stroll, saw young George's camera lying in the hall, picked it up with a vague idea of photographing some of the local fauna and was surprised to see Beach down by the lake, cutting those ropes. He took a whole reel of him and I understand they have come out splendidly. May I smoke?' said Lord Ickenham, taking out his case.

Lady Constance did not reply. She seemed to have been turned into a pillar of salt, like Lot's wife. It might have been supposed that, having passed her whole life at Blandings Castle, with the sort of things happening that happened daily in that stately but always somewhat hectic home of England, she would have been impervious to shocks. Nothing, one would have said, would have been able to surprise her. This was not so. She was stunned.

Beach! Eighteen years of spotless buttling, and now this! If she had not been seated, she would have reeled. Everything seemed to her to go black, including Lord Ickenham. He might have been an actor, made up to play Othello, lighting an inky cigarette with a sepia lighter.

'Of course,' this negroid man went on, 'one gets the thought behind Beach's rash act. For days Emsworth has been preaching a holy war against these Church Lads, filling the listening air with the tale of what he has suffered at their hands, and it is easy to understand how Beach, feudally devoted to him, felt that he could hold himself back no longer. Out with the knife and go to it, he said to himself. It will probably have occurred to you how closely in its essentials the whole set-up resembles the murder of the late St Thomas à Becket. King Henry, you will remember, kept saying, "Will no one rid me of this turbulent priest?" till those knights of his decided that something had to be done about it. Emsworth, perhaps in other words, expressed the same view about the Church Lads, and Beach, taking his duties as a butler very seriously, thought that it was part of them to show the young thugs that crime does not pay and that retribution must sooner or later overtake those who knock top hats off with crusty rolls at school treats.'

Lord Ickenham paused to cough, for he had swallowed a mouthful of smoke the wrong way. Lady Constance remained congealed. She might have been a statue of herself commissioned by a group of friends and admirers.

'You see how extremely awkward the situation is? Whether or not Emsworth formally instructed Beach to take the law into his hands, we shall probably never know, but it makes very little difference. If those photographs are given to the world, it is inevitable that Beach, unable to bear the shame of exposure, will hand in his portfolio and resign office, and you will lose the finest butler in Shropshire. And there is another thing. Emsworth will unquestionably confess that he inflamed the man and so was directly responsible for what happened, and one can see the County looking very askance at him, pursing their lips, raising their eyebrows, possibly even cutting him at the next Agricultural Show. Really, Lady Constance, if I were you, I think I would reconsider this idea of yours of giving Bill Bailey the old heave-ho. I will leave the castle on the 2.15, if you wish, though sorry to go, for I like the society here, but Bailey, I'm afraid, must stay. Possibly in the course of time his winning personality will overcome your present prejudice against him. I'll leave you to think it over,' said Lord Ickenham, and with another of his kindly smiles left the room.

For an appreciable time after he had gone Lady Constance sat motionless. Then, as if a sudden light had shone on her darkness, she gave a start. She stretched out a hand towards the pigeonholes on the desk, in which reposed notepaper, envelopes, postcards, telegraph forms and cable forms. Selecting one of the last named, she took pen in hand, and began to write.

James Schoonmaker
1000 Park Avenue
New York

She paused a moment in thought. Then she began to write again: 'Come immediately. Most urgent. Must see you . . .'

## · IV ·

It is always unpleasant for a man of good will to be compelled, even from the best motives, to blacken the name of an innocent butler, and his first thought after he has done so is to make amends. Immediately after leaving Lady Constance, therefore, Lord Ickenham proceeded to Beach's pantry, where with a few well-chosen words he slipped a remorseful five-pound note into the other's hand. Beach trousered the money with a stately bow of thanks, and in answer to a query as to whether he had any knowledge of the Reverend Cuthbert Bailey's whereabouts said that he had seen him some little time ago entering the rose garden in company with Miss Schoonmaker.

Thither Lord Ickenham decided to make his way. He was sufficiently a student of human nature to be aware that, when two lovers get together in a rose garden, they do not watch the clock, and he presumed that, if Bill and Myra had been there some little time ago, they would be there now. They would, he supposed, be discussing in gloomy mood the former's imminent departure from Blandings Castle, and he was anxious to relieve their minds. For there was no doubt in his own that Lady Constance, having thought things over, would continue to extend her hospitality to the young cleric. Her whole air, as he left her, had been that of a woman unable to see any alternative to the hoisting of the white flag.

He had scarcely left the house when he saw that he had been mistaken. So far from being in the rose garden, Myra Schoonmaker was on the gravel strip outside the front door, and so far from being in conference with Bill, she was closeted, as far as one can be closeted in the open air, with the Duke of Dunstable's nephew, Archie Gilpin. As he appeared, Archie Gilpin moved away, and as Myra came towards him, he saw that her face was sombre and her walk the walk of a girl who can detect no silver lining in the clouds. This did not cause him concern. He had that to tell which would be a verbal shot in the arm and set her dancing all over the place and strewing roses from her hat.

'Hullo there,' he said.

'Oh, hullo, Uncle Fred.'

'You look pretty much down among the wines and spirits, young Myra.'

'That's the way I feel.'

'You won't much longer. Where's Bill?'

The girl shrugged her shoulders.

'Oh, somewhere around, I suppose. I left him in the rose garden.'

Lord Ickenham's eyebrows shot up.

'You *left* him in the rose garden? Not a lovers' tiff, I hope?'

'If you like to call it that,' said Myra. She kicked moodily at a passing beetle, which gave her a cold look and went on its way. 'I've broken our engagement.'

It was never easy to disconcert Lord Ickenham, as his nephew Pongo would have testified. Even on that day at the dog races his demeanour, even after the hand of the Law had fallen on his shoulder, had remained unruffled. But now he could not hide his dismay. He looked at the girl incredulously.

'You've broken the engagement?'

'Yes.'

'But why?'

'Because he doesn't love me.'

'What makes you think that?'

'I'll tell you what makes me think that,' said Myra passionately. 'He went and told Lord Emsworth who he was, knowing that Lord Emsworth was bound to spill the beans to Lady Constance, and that Lady Constance would instantly bounce him. And why did he do it, you ask? Because it gave him the excuse to get away from me. I suppose he's got another girl in Bottleton East.'

Lord Ickenham twirled his moustache sternly. He had often in the course of his life listened patiently to people talking through their hats, but he was in no mood to be patient now.

'Myra,' he said. 'You ought to have your head examined.'

'Oh, yes?'

'It would be money well spent. I assure you that if all the girls in Bottleton East came and did the dance of the seven veils before him, Bill Bailey wouldn't give them a glance. He told Emsworth who he was because his conscience wouldn't let him do otherwise. The revelation was unavoidable if he was to make his story of the Briggs' foul plot convincing, and he did not count the cost. He knew that it meant ruin and disaster, but he refused to stand silently by and allow that good man to be deprived of his pig. You ought to be fawning on him for his iron integrity, instead of going about the place breaking engagements. I have always held that the man of sensibility should be careful what he says to the other sex, if he wishes to be numbered among the preux chevaliers, but I cannot restrain myself from telling you, young M. Schoonmaker, that you have behaved like a little half-wit.'

Myra, who had been staring at the beetle as if contemplating having another go at it, raised a startled head.

'Do you think that was really it?'

'Of course it was.'

'And he wasn't just jumping at the chance of getting away from me?'

'Of course he wasn't. I tell you, Bill Bailey is about as near being a stainless knight as you could find in a month of Sundays. He's as spotless as they come.'

A deep sigh escaped Myra Schoonmaker. His eloquence had convinced her.

'Half-wit,' she said, 'is right. Uncle Fred, I've made a ghastly fool of myself.'

'Just what I've been telling you.'

'I don't mean about Bill. I could have put that right in a minute. But I've just told Archie Gilpin I'll marry him.'

'No harm that I can see in confiding your matrimonial plans to Archie Gilpin. He'll probably send you a wedding present.'

'Oh, don't be so dumb, Uncle Fred! I mean I've just told Archie I'll marry *him*!'

'What, *him*?'

'Yes, *him*.'

'Well, fry me for an oyster! Why on earth did you do that?'

'Oh, just a sort of gesture, I suppose. It's what they used to write in my reports at Miss Spence's school. "She is often too impulsive", they used to say.'

She spoke despondently. Ever since that brief but fateful conversation with Archie, an uneasy conviction had been stealing over her that in a rash moment she had started something which she would have given much to stop. Her emotions were somewhat similar to those of a nervous passenger on a roller coaster at an amusement park who when it is too late to get off feels the contraption gathering speed beneath him.

It was not as if she even liked Archie Gilpin very much. He was all right in his way, a pleasant enough companion for a stroll or a game of tennis, but until this awful thing had happened he had been something completely negligible, just some sort of foreign substance that happened to be around. And now she was engaged to him, and the announcement would be in *The Times*, and Lady Constance would be telling her how pleased her father would be and how sensible it was of her to have realized that that other thing had been nothing but a ridiculous infatuation, and she could see no point in going on living. She was very much inclined to go down to the lake and ask one of the Church Lads if he would care to earn a shilling by holding her head under water till the vital spark expired.

'Oh, Uncle Fred!' she said.

'There, there!' said Lord Ickenham.

'Oh, Uncle Fred!'

'Don't talk, just cry. There is nothing more therapeutic.'

'What shall I do?'

'Break it off, of course. What else? Tell him it's been nice knowing him, and hand him his hat.'

'But I can't.'

'Nonsense. Perfectly easy thing to bring into the conversation. You're strolling with him in the moonlight. He says something about how jolly it's going to be when you and he are settled down in your little nest, and you say, "Oh, I forgot to tell you about that. It's off." He says, "What!" You say, "You heard," and he reddens and goes to Africa.'

'And I go to New York.'

'Why New York?'

'Because that's where I'll be shipped back to in disgrace when they hear I've broken my engagement to a Duke's nephew.'

'Don't tell me Jimmy's a stern father?'

'That would make him stern enough. He's got a thing about the British aristocracy. He admires them terrifically.'

'I don't blame him. We're the salt of the earth.'

'He would insist on taking me home, and I'd never see my angel Bill again, because he couldn't possibly afford the fare to New York.'

Lord Ickenham mused. This was a complication he had not taken into his calculations.

'I see. Yes, I appreciate the difficulty.'

'Me, too.'

'This opens up a new line of thought. You'd better leave everything to me.'

'I don't see that you can do anything.'

'That is always a rash observation to make to an Ickenham. As I once remarked to another young friend of mine, this sort of situation brings out the best in me. And when you get the best in Frederick Altamont Cornwallis Twistleton, fifth Earl of good old Ickenham, you've got something.'

# 8

## • 1 •

If you go down Fleet Street and turn into one of the side streets leading to the river, you will find yourself confronted by a vast building that looks something like a county jail and something like a biscuit factory. This is Tilbury House, the home of the Mammoth Publishing Company, that busy hive where hordes of workers toil day and night, churning out reading matter for the masses. For Lord Tilbury's numerous daily and weekly papers are not, as is sometimes supposed, just Acts of God; they are produced deliberately.

The building has its scores of windows, but pay no attention to those on the first two floors, for there are only editors and things behind them. Concentrate the eye on the three in the middle of the third floor. These belong to Lord Tilbury's private office, and there is just a chance, if you wait, that you may catch a glimpse of him leaning out to get a breath of air, than which nothing could be more calculated to make a sightseer's day.

This morning, however, you would have been out of luck, for Lord Tilbury was sitting motionless at his desk. He had been sitting there for some little time. There were a hundred letters he should have been dictating to Millicent Rigby, his secretary, but Millicent remained in the outer office, undictated to. There were a dozen editors with whom he should have been conferring, but they stayed where they were, unconferred with.

He was deep in thought, and anyone seeing him would have asked himself with awe what it was that was occupying that giant mind. He might have been planning out some pronouncement which would shake the chancelleries, or pondering on the most suitable line to take in connection with the latest rift in the Cabinet, or even, for he took a personal interest in all his publications, considering changes in the policy of *Wee Tots*, the journal which has done so much to mould thought in the British nursery. In actual fact, he was musing on Empress of Blandings.

In the life of every successful man there is always some little something missing. Lord Tilbury had wealth and power and the comforting knowledge that, catering as he did for readers who had all been mentally arrested at the age of twelve, he would continue to enjoy these indefinitely, but he had not got Empress of Blandings: and ever since the day when he and that ornament of her sex had met he had yearned to add her to his Buckinghamshire piggery. That was how the pig-minded always reacted to even the briefest glance at the Empress. They came, saw, gasped and went away unhappy and discontented, ever after, to move through life bemused, like men kissed by goddesses in dreams.

His sombre thoughts were broken in upon by the ringing of the telephone. Moodily he took up the receiver.

'Hoy!' shouted a voice in his ear, and he had no difficulty in identifying the speaker. He had a wide circle of acquaintances, but the Duke of Dunstable was the only member of it who opened conversations with this monosyllable in a booming tone reminiscent of a costermonger calling attention to his blood oranges. 'Is that you, Stinker?'

Lord Tilbury frowned. There were only a few survivors of the old days who addressed him thus. Even in the distant past he had found the name distasteful, and now that he had become a man of distinction, it jarred upon him even more gratingly. In addition to frowning, he also swelled a good deal. He was a short, stout man who swelled readily when annoyed.

'Lord Tilbury speaking,' he said curtly, emphasizing the first two words. 'Well?'

'What?' roared the Duke. He was a little deaf in the right ear.

'Well?'

'Speak up, Stinker. Don't mumble.'

Lord Tilbury raised his voice to an almost Duke-like pitch.

'I said "Well?".'

'Well?'

'Yes.'

'Damn silly thing to say,' said the Duke, and Lord Tilbury's frown deepened.

'What is it, Dunstable?'

'Eh?'

'What *is* it?'

'What is what?'

'What do you want?' Lord Tilbury rasped, the hand gripping the receiver about to crash it back on to its cradle.

'It's not what I want,' bellowed the Duke. 'It's what you want. I've got that pig.'

'What!'

'What?'

Lord Tilbury did not reply. He had stiffened in his chair and presented the appearance of somebody in a fairy story who had had a spell cast upon him by the local wizard. His silence offended the Duke, never a patient man.

'Are you there, Stinker?' he roared, and Lord Tilbury thought for a moment that his ear drum had gone.

'Yes, yes, yes,' he said, removing the receiver for a moment in order to massage his ear.

'Then why the devil don't you utter?'

'I was overcome.'

'What?'

'I could hardly believe it. You have really persuaded Emsworth to sell you Empress of Blandings?'

'We came to an arrangement. Is that offer of yours still open?'

'Of course, of course.'

'Two thousand, cash down?'

'Certainly.'

'What?'

'I said Certainly.'

'Then you'd better come here and collect the animal.'

'I will. I'll—'

Lord Tilbury paused. He was thinking of all the correspondence he should have been dictating to Millicent Rigby. Could he neglect this? Then he saw the solution. He could take Millicent Rigby with him. He pressed a bell. His secretary entered.

'Where do you live, Miss Rigby?'

'Shepherd Market, Lord Tilbury.'

'Take a taxi, go and pack some things for the night, and come back here. We're driving down to Shropshire.' He spoke into the telephone. 'Are you there, Dunstable?'

Something not unlike an explosion in an ammunition dump made itself heard at the other end of the line.

'Are *you* there, blast your gizzard? What's the matter? Can't get a word out of you.'

'I was speaking to my secretary.'

'Well, don't. Do you realize what these trunk calls cost?'

'I'm sorry. I am motoring down immediately. Where can I see you? I don't want to come to the castle.'

'Put up at the Emsworth Arms in Market Blandings. I'll meet you there.'

'I'll be waiting for you.'

'What?'

'I said I'll be waiting for you.'

'What?'

Lord Tilbury gritted his teeth. He was feeling hot and exhausted. That was the effect the other's telephone technique often had on people.

## · II ·

Lavender Briggs had caught the 12.30 train at Paddington. It set her down on the platform of Market Blandings station shortly after four.

The day was warm and the journey had been stuffy and somewhat exhausting, but her mood was one of quiet contentment. She had enjoyed every minute of her visit to the metropolis. She had deposited the Duke's cheque. She had dined with a group of earnest friends at the Crushed Pansy, the restaurant with a soul, and at the conclusion of the meal they had all gone on to the opening performance at the Flaming Youth Group Centre of one of those avant-garde plays which bring the scent of boiling cabbage across the footlights and in which the little man in the bowler hat turns out to be God. And she was confident that when she saw him the Reverend Cuthbert Bailey would have made up his mind, rather than be unmasked, to lend his services to the purloining of Lord Emsworth's pig. It seemed to her that a cup of tea was indicated by way of celebration, and she made her way to the Emsworth Arms. There were other hostelries in Market Blandings—one does not forget the Goose and Gander, the Jolly Cricketers, the Wheatsheaf, the Waggoner's Rest, the Beetle and Wedge and the Stitch in Time—but the Emsworth Arms was the only one where a lady could get a refined cup of tea with buttered toast and fancy cakes. Those other establishments catered more to the George Cyril Wellbeloved type of client and were content to say it with beer.

At the Emsworth Arms, moreover, you could have your refreshment served to you in the large garden which was one of the features of Market Blandings. Dotted about with rustic tables, it ran all the way down to the river, and there were few of the rustic tables that did not enjoy the shade of a spreading tree or a clump of bushes. The one Lavender Briggs selected was screened from view by a green mass of foliage, and she had chosen it because she wanted complete privacy in which to meditate on the very satisfactory state of her affairs. Elsewhere in the garden one's thoughts were apt to be interrupted by family groups presided over by flushed mothers telling Wilfred to stop teasing Katie or Percival to leave off making faces at Jane.

She had finished the cakes and the buttered toast and was sipping her third cup of tea, when from the other side of the bushes, where she had noticed a rustic table similar to her own, a voice spoke. All it said was 'Two beers', but at the sound of it she stiffened in her chair, some sixth sense telling her that if she listened, she might hear something of interest. For it was the Duke's voice that had shattered the afternoon stillness, and there was only one thing that could have brought the Duke to Market Blandings, the desire for a conference with the mystery man who was prepared to go as high as two thousand pounds to acquire Lord Emsworth's peerless pig.

A moment later a second voice spoke, and if Lavender Briggs had stiffened before, she stiffened doubly now. The words it had said were negligible, something about the warmth of the day, but they were enough to enable her to recognize the speaker as her former employer, Lord Tilbury of the Mammoth Publishing Company. She had taken too much dictation from those august lips in the past to allow of any misconception.

Rigid in her chair, she set herself to listen with, in the Duke's powerful phrase, her ears sticking up.

## · III ·

Conversation on the other side of the bushes was for awhile desultory. With a waiter expected back at any moment with beer, two men who have serious matters to discuss do not immediately plumb the deeps, but confine themselves to small talk. Lord Tilbury said once more that the day was warm, and the Duke agreed. The Duke said he supposed it had been even warmer in London, and Lord Tilbury said Yes, much warmer. The Duke said it wasn't the heat he minded so much as the humidity, and Lord Tilbury confessed that it was the humidity that troubled him also. Then the beer arrived, and the Duke flung himself on it with a grunt. He must have abandoned rather noticeably the gentlemanly restraint which one likes to see in Dukes when drinking beer, for Lord Tilbury said:

'You seem thirsty. Did you walk from the castle?'

'No, got a lift. Bit of luck. It's a warm day.'

'Yes, very warm.'

'Humid, too.'

'Very humid.'

'It's the humidity I don't like.'

'I don't like the humidity, either.'

Silence followed these intellectual exchanges. It was broken by a loud chuckle from the Duke.

'Eh?' said Lord Tilbury.

'What?' said the Duke. 'Speak up, Stinker.'

'I was merely wondering what it was that was amusing you,' said Lord Tilbury frostily. 'And I wish you wouldn't call me Stinker. Somebody might hear.'

'Let them.'

'What the devil are you giggling about?' demanded Lord Tilbury, as a second chuckle followed the first. He had never been fond of the Duke of Dunstable, and he felt that having to put up with his society, after a fatiguing journey from London, was a heavy price to pay even for Empress of Blandings.

The Duke was not a man who made a practice of disclosing his private affairs to every dashed Tom, Dick and Harry, and at another time and under different conditions would have been blowed if he was going to let himself be pumped by Stinker Pyke, or Lord Tilbury, as he now called himself. He mistrusted these newspaper fellers. You told them something in the strictest confidence, and the next thing you knew it was spread all over the gossip page with a six-inch headline at the top and probably a photograph of you, looking like someone the police were anxious to question in connection with the Dover Street smash-and-grab raid.

But he was now fairly full of the Emsworth Arms beer, and, as everybody who has tried it knows, there is something about the home-brewed beer purveyed by G. Ovens, landlord of the Emsworth Arms, that has a mellowing effect. What G. Ovens put into it is a secret between him and his Maker, but it acts like magic on the most reticent. With a pint of this elixir sloshing about inside him, it seemed to the Duke that it would be churlish not to share his happiness with a sympathetic crony.

'Just put one over on a blasted female,' he said.

'Lady Constance?' said Lord Tilbury, jumping to what suggested itself to him as the obvious conclusion. His visit to Blandings Castle had been a brief one, but it had enabled him to become well acquainted with his hostess.

'No, not Connie. Connie's all right. Potty, but a good enough soul. This was Emsworth's secretary, a frightful woman of the ghastly name of Briggs. Lavender Briggs,' said the Duke, as if that made it worse.

Something stirred at the back of Lord Tilbury's mind.

'Lavender Briggs? I had a secretary named Briggs, and I seem to have a recollection of hearing someone address her as Lavender.'

'Beastly name.'

'And quite unsuited to a woman of her appearance, if it's the same woman. Is she tall and ungainly?'

'Very.'

'With harlequin glasses?'

'If that's what you call them.'

'Large feet?'

'Enormous.'

'Hair like seaweed?'

'Just like seaweed. And talks rot all the time about dusty answers.'

'I never heard her do that, but from your description it must be the same woman. I sacked her.'

'You couldn't have done better.'

'She had a way of looking at me as if I were some kind of worm, and I frequently caught her sniffing. Well, I wasn't going to put up with that sort of thing. She was an excellent secretary as far as her work was concerned, but I told her she had to go. So she is with Emsworth now? He has my sympathy. But you were saying that you had—ah—put one over on her. How was that?'

'It's a long story. She tried to get five hundred pounds out of me.'

Lord Tilbury seemed for a moment bewildered. Then he understood. He was a quick-witted man.

'Breach of promise, eh? Odd that you should have been attracted by a hideous woman like Lavender Briggs. Her glasses alone, one would have thought . . . However, there is no accounting for these sudden infatuations, though one would have expected a man of your age to have had more sense. No fool like an old fool, as they say. Well, if she could prove this breach of promise—had letters and so forth—I think you got off cheap, and it should be a valuable lesson to you.'

There is just this one thing more to be said about G. Ovens' home-brewed beer. If you want to preserve that mellow fondness for all mankind which it imparts, you have to go on drinking it. The Duke, having had only a single pint, was unable to retain the feeling that Lord Tilbury was a staunch friend from whom he could have no secrets. He was conscious of a vivid dislike for him, and couldn't imagine why a gracious sovereign had bestowed a barony on a man like that. Lavender Briggs, leaning forward, alert not to miss a word, nearly fell out of her chair, so loud was the snort that rang through the garden. When the Duke of Dunstable snorted, he held back nothing but gave it all he had.

'It wasn't breach of promise!'

'What was it, then?'

'If you want to know, she said she knew where she could lay her hands on a couple of willing helpers who would pinch Emsworth's pig for me, so I engaged her services, and she demanded five hundred pounds for the job, cash down in advance, and I gave her a cheque for that sum.'

'Well, really!'

'What do you mean, Well, really? She wouldn't settle for less.'

'Then so far it would seem that she is the one who has put something over, as you express it.'

'That's what she thought, but she was mistaken. Immediately after coming to that arrangement I spoke of with Emsworth I got in touch with my bank and stopped the cheque. I telephoned the blighters and told them I'd scoop out their insides with my bare hands if they coughed up so much as a penny of it. I'd like to see her face when it comes back marked "Refer to drawer".'

It seemed to Lord Tilbury that from somewhere near at hand, as it might have been from behind those bushes near which he was sitting, there had come a sudden gasping sound as if uttered by some soul in agony, but he paid little attention to it. He was following a train of thought.

'So you have not had to pay anything for the pig?'

'Not a bean.'

'Then you ought to let me have it cheaper.'

'You think so, do you? Well, let me tell you, Stinker,' said the Duke, who had been deeply offended by his companion's remark about old fools, 'that my price for that pig has gone up. It's three thousand now.'

'What!'

'That's what it is. Three thousand pounds.'

A sudden hush seemed to have fallen on the garden of the Emsworth Arms. It was as though it and everything in it had been stunned into silence. Birds stopped chirping. Butterflies froze in mid-flutter. Wasps wading in strawberry jam paused motionless, as if they were having their photographs taken. And the general paralysis extended to Lord Tilbury. It was an appreciable time before he spoke. When he did, it was in the hoarse voice of a man unable to believe that he has heard correctly.

'You're joking!'

'Like blazes I'm joking.'

'You expect me to pay three thousand pounds for a pig?'

'If you want the ruddy pig.'

'What about our gentlemen's agreement?'

'Gentlemen's agreements be blowed. If you care to meet my terms, the porker's yours. If you don't, I'll sell it back to Emsworth. No doubt he'll be glad to have it, even if the price is stiff. I'll leave you to think it over, Stinker. No skin off my nose,' said the Duke, 'whichever way you decide.'

# 9

## • 1 •

A man who has built up a vast business, starting from nothing, must of necessity be a man capable of making swift decisions, and until this moment Lord Tilbury had never had any difficulty in doing so. His masterful handling of the hundred and one problems that arise daily in a concern like the Mammoth Publishing Company was a byword in Fleet Street.

But as he sat contemplating the dilemma on the horns of which the Duke's parting words had impaled him, he was finding it impossible to determine what course to pursue. The yearning to enrol the Empress under his banner was very powerful, but so also was his ingrained dislike for parting with large sums of money. There was, and always had been, something about signing his name to substantial cheques that gave him a sort of faint feeling.

He was still weighing this against that and balancing the pros and cons, when a shadow fell on the sunlit turf before him and he became aware that his reverie had been intruded on. Something female was standing beside the rustic table, and after blinking once or twice he recognized his former secretary, Lavender Briggs. She was regarding him austerely through her harlequin glasses.

If Lavender Briggs' gaze was austere, it had every reason for being so. No girl enjoys hearing herself described as tall and ungainly with large feet and hair like seaweed, especially if the description is followed up by the revelation that the five hundred golden pounds on which she had been counting to start her off as a proprietress of a typewriting bureau have gone with the wind, never to return. If she had not had a business proposition to place before him, she would not have lowered herself by exchanging words with this man. She would much have preferred to hit him on the head with the tankard from which the Duke had been refreshing himself. But a business girl cannot choose her associates. She has to take them as they come.

'Good afternoon, Lord Tilbury,' she said coldly. 'If you could spay-ah me a moment of your time.'

To any other caller without an appointment the owner of the Mammoth Publishing Company would have been brusque, but Lord Tilbury could not forget that this was the girl who had come within an ace of taking five hundred pounds off the Duke of Dunstable, and feeling as he did about the Duke he found his surprise at seeing her mingled with an unwilling respect. It would be too much to say that he was glad to see her, for he had hoped to continue wrestling undisturbed with the problem which was exercising his mind, but if she wanted a moment of his time, she could certainly have it. He even went so far as to ask her to take a seat, which she did. And having done so she came, like a good business woman, straight to the point.

'I heard what the Duke of Dunstable was saying to you,' she said. 'This mattah of Lord Emsworth's pig. His demand for three thousand pounds was preposterous. Quate absurd. Do not dream of yielding to his terms.'

Lord Tilbury found himself warming to this girl. He still felt that the words in which he had described her hair, feet and general appearance had been well chosen, but we cannot all be Miss Americas and he was prepared to condone her physical defects in consideration of this womanly sympathy. Beauty, after all, is but skin deep. The main thing a man should ask of the other sex is that their hearts be in the right place, as hers was. 'Preposterous' . . . 'Quate absurd' . . . The very expressions he would have chosen himself.

On the other hand, it seemed to him that she was overlooking something.

'But I want that pig.'

'You shall have it.'

Enlightenment dawned on Lord Tilbury.

'Why, of course! You mean you'll—er—'

'Purloin it for you? Quate. My arrangements are all made and can be put into effect immediately.'

Lord Tilbury could recognize efficiency when he saw it. Here, he perceived, was a girl who thought on her feet and did it now. A genial glow suffused him. Almost as sweet as the thought of obtaining possession of the Empress was the knowledge that, to employ the latter's phrase, he would be putting one over on the Duke.

'Provided,' Lavender Briggs went on, 'that we agree on terms. I should requiah five hundred pounds.'

'Later, you mean?'

'Now, I mean. I know you always carry your cheque-book with you.'

Lord Tilbury gulped. Then the momentary sensation of nausea passed. Nothing could make him enjoy writing a cheque for five hundred pounds, but there are times when a man has to set his teeth and face the facts of life.

'Very well,' he said, a little huskily.

'Thank you,' said Lavender Briggs a few moments later, placing the slip of paper in her bag. 'And now I ought to be getting back to the castle. Lady Constance may be wanting me for something. I will go and telephone for the station cab.'

The telephone by means of which residents of the Emsworth Arms put themselves in touch with the station cab (Jno Robinson, propr.) was in the bar. Proceeding thither, Lavender Briggs was about to go in, when she nearly collided with Lord Ickenham, coming out.

## · II ·

Lord Ickenham had come to the bar of the Emsworth Arms because the warmth of the day had made him want to renew his acquaintance with G. Ovens' home-brew, of which he had many pleasant memories. It would have been possible—indeed, it would have been more seemly—for him to have taken tea on the terrace with Lady Constance, but he was a kindly man and something told him that after their recent get-together his hostess would prefer to be spared anything in the nature of peaceful co-existence with him. Moments come in a woman's life, he knew, when her prime need is a complete absence of Ickenhams.

He was glad to see Lavender Briggs. He was a man who made friends easily, and in the course of this visit to the castle, something approaching a friendship had sprung up between himself and her. And though he disapproved of her recent activities, he could understand and sympathize with the motives which had actuated them. He was a broad-minded man, and it was his opinion that a girl who needs five hundred pounds to set herself up in business for herself is entitled to stretch a point or two and to forget, if only temporarily, the lessons which she learned at her mother's knee. Thinking these charitable thoughts and knowing the reception that awaited her at Blandings Castle, he was happy to have this opportunity of warning her against completing her journey there.

'Well, well,' he said. 'So you're back?'

'Yayess. I caught the twelve-thirty train.'

'I wonder how it compares with the two-fifteen.'

'I beg your pardon?'

'Just a random thought. It was simply that I have heard the two-fifteen rather highly spoken of lately. Did you have a nice time in London?'

'Quate enjoyable, thank you.'

'I hope I didn't stop you going into that bar for a quick one?'

'I was merely intending to telephone for the station cab to take me to the castle.'

'I see. Well, I wouldn't. Are you familiar with the poem "Excelsior"?'

'I read it as a child,' said Lavender Briggs with a little shiver of distaste. She did not admire Longfellow.

'Then you will recall what the old man said to the fellow with the banner with the strange device. "Try not the pass," he said. "Dark lowers the tempest overhead." That is what an old—or, rather, elderly but wonderfully well-preserved—man is saying to you now. Avoid station cabs. Lay off them. Leave them alone. You are better without them.'

'I don't know what you mean!'

'There are many things you do not know, Miss Briggs,' said Lord Ickenham gravely, 'including the fact that you have got a large smut on your nose.'

'Oh, have I?' said Lavender Briggs, opening her bag in a flutter and reaching hurriedly for her mirror. She plied the cleansing tissue. 'Is that better?'

'Practically perfect. I wish I could say as much for your general position.'

'I don't understand.'

'You will. You're in the soup, Miss Briggs. The gaff has been blown, and the jig is up. The pitiless light of day has been thrown on your pig-purloining plans. Bill Bailey has told all.'

'What!'

'Yes, he has squealed to the F.B.I. Where you made your mistake was in underestimating his integrity. These curates have scruples. The Reverend Cuthbert Bailey's are the talk of Bottleton East. Your proposition revolted him, and only the fact that you didn't offer him any kept him from spurning your gold. He went straight to Lord Emsworth and came clean. That is why I suggest that you do not telephone for station cabs in that lighthearted way. Jno Robinson would take you to your destination for a reasonably modest sum, no doubt, but what would you find there on arrival? A Lord Emsworth with all his passions roused and flame coming out of both nostrils. For don't deceive yourself into thinking that he will be waiting on the front doorstep with a "Welcome to Blandings Castle" on his lips. In his current role of sabre-toothed tiger he would probably bite several pieces out of your leg. I have seldom seen a man who had got it so thoroughly up his nose.'

Lavender Briggs' jaw had fallen. So, slipping from between her nerveless fingers, had her bag. It fell to earth, and from it there spilled a powder compact, a handkerchief, a comb, a lipstick, a match box, an eyebrow pencil, a wallet with a few pound notes in it, a small purse containing some shillings, a bottle of digestive pills, a paperback copy of a book by Albert Camus and the Tilbury cheque. A little breeze which had sprung up sent the last-named fluttering across the road with Lord Ickenham in agile pursuit. He recovered it, glanced at it, and brought it back to her, his eyebrows raised.

'Your tariff for stealing pigs comes high,' he said. 'Who's Tilbury? Anything to do with Tilbury House?'

There was good stuff in Lavender Briggs. Where a lesser woman would have broken down and wept, she merely hitched up her fallen jaw and tightened her lips.

'He owns it,' she said, taking the cheque. 'I used to be his secretary. Lord Tilbury.'

'Oh, that chap? Good heavens, what are you doing?'

'I'm tearing up his cheque.'

Lord Ickenham stopped her with a horrified gesture.

'My dear child, you mustn't dream of doing such a thing. You need it in your business.'

'But I can't take his money now.'

'Of course you can. Stick to it like glue. He has far too much money, anyway, and it's very bad for him. Look on adhering to this five hundred as a kindly act in his best interests, designed to make him a better, deeper man. It may prove a turning point in his life. I would take five hundred pounds off Tilbury myself, if only I could think of a way of doing it. I should feel it was my duty. But if you have scruples, though you haven't any business having any, not being a curate, look on it as a loan. You could even pay him interest. Not too much, of course. You don't want to spoil him. I would suggest a yearly fiver, accompanied, as a pretty gesture, by a bunch of white violets. But you can think that over at your leisure. The problem that presents itself now, it seems to me, is Where do you go from here? I take it that you will wish to return to London, but you don't want another stuffy journey in the train. I'll tell you what,' said Lord Ickenham, inspired. 'We'll hire a car. I'll pay for it, and you can reimburse me when that typewriting bureau of yours gets going. Don't forget the bunch of white violets.'

'Oh, Lord Ickenham!' said Lavender Briggs devoutly. 'What a help you are!'

'Help is a thing I am always glad to be of,' said Lord Ickenham in his courteous way.

## · III ·

As he turned from waving a genial hand at the departing car and set out on the two-mile walk back to the castle, Lord Ickenham was feeling the gentle glow of satisfaction which comes to a man of goodwill conscious of having acted for the best. There had been a moment when his guardian angel, who liked him to draw the line somewhere, had shown a disposition to become critical of his recent activities, whispering in his ear that he ought not to have abetted Lavender Briggs in what, in the guardian angel's opinion, was pretty raw work and virtually tantamount to robbery from the person, but he had his answer ready. Lavender Briggs, he replied in rebuttal, needed the stuff, and when you find a hard-up girl who needs the stuff, the essential thing is to see that she gets it and not to be fussy about the methods employed to that end.

This, moreover, he pointed out, was a special case. As he had reminded La Briggs, it was imperative for the good of his soul that Lord Tilbury should receive an occasional punch in the bank balance, and to have neglected this opportunity of encouraging his spiritual growth would have been mistaken kindness. His guardian angel, who could follow a piece of reasoning all right if you explained it carefully to him, apologized and said he hadn't thought of that. Forget the whole thing, the guardian angel said.

With the approach of evening the day had lost much of its oppressive warmth, but Lord Ickenham kept his walking pace down to a quiet amble, strolling in leisurely fashion and pausing from time to time to inspect the local flora and fauna: and he had stopped to exchange a friendly glance with a rabbit whose looks he liked, when he became aware that there were others more in tune than himself with the modern spirit of rush and bustle. Running footsteps sounded from behind him, and a voice was calling his name. Turning, he saw that the Duke of Dunstable's nephew, Archie Gilpin, was approaching him at a high rate of m.p.h.

With Archie's brother Ricky, the poet, who supplemented the meagre earnings of a minor bard by selling onion soup in a bar off Leicester Square, Lord Ickenham had long been acquainted, but Archie, except for seeing him at meals, he scarcely knew. Nevertheless, he greeted him with a cordial smile. The urgency of his manner suggested that here was another fellow human being in need of his advice and counsel, and, as always, he was delighted to give it. His services were never confined to close personal friends.

'Hullo there,' he said. 'Getting into training for the village sports?'

Archie came to a halt, panting. He was a singularly handsome young man. Pongo at the Milton Street registry office had described him as good-looking, but Lord Ickenham, now that he had met him, considered this an understatement. Tall and slim and elegant, he looked like a film star of the better type. He also, Lord Ickenham was sorry to see, looked worried, and he prepared to do all that was in his power to brighten life for him.

Archie seemed embarrassed. He ran a hand through his hair, which was longer than Lord Ickenham liked hair to be. A visit to a hairdresser would in his opinion have done this Gilpin a world of good. But artists, he reminded himself, are traditionally shy of the scissors, and to do the lad justice he did not wear sideburns.

'I say,' said Archie, when he had finished panting. 'Could you spare me a moment?'

'Dozens, my dear fellow. Help yourself.'

'I don't want to interrupt you, if you're thinking about something.'

'I am always thinking about something, but I can switch it off in a second, just like that. What seems to be the trouble?'

'Well, I'm in a bit of a jam, and my brother Ricky once told me that if ever I got into a jam of any kind, you were the man to get me out of it. When it comes to fixing things, he said, you have to be seen to be believed.'

Lord Ickenham was gratified as any man would have been. One always likes a word of praise from the fans.

'He probably had in mind the time when I was instrumental in getting him the money that enabled him to buy that onion soup bar of his. Oddly enough, it was not till I had it explained to me by my nephew Pongo that I knew what an onion soup bar was. My life is lived in the country, and we rustics so soon get out of touch. Pongo tells me these bars abound in the Piccadilly Circus and Leicester Square neighbourhoods of London, staying open all night and selling onion soup to the survivors of bottle parties. It sounds the ideal life. Is Ricky still gainfully employed in that line?'

'Oh, rather. But may I tell you about my jam?'

Lord Ickenham clicked an apologetic tongue.

'Of course, yes. I'm sorry. I'm afraid we old gaffers from the country have a tendency to ramble on. When I start talking you must stop me, even if you haven't heard it before. This jam of yours, you were saying. Not a bad jam, I trust?'

Once more, Archie Gilpin ran a hand through his hair. The impression he conveyed was that if the vultures gnawing at his bosom did not shortly change their act, he would begin pulling it out in handfuls.

'It's the dickens of a jam. I don't know what to do about it. Have you ever been engaged to two girls at the same time?'

'Not to my recollection. Nor, now I come to think of it, do I know of anyone who has, except of course King Solomon and the late Brigham Young.'

'Well, that's what I am.'

'You? Engaged to two girls? Half a second, let me work this out.'

There was a pause, during which Lord Ickenham seemed to be doing sums in his head.

'No,' he said at length. 'I don't get it. I am aware that you are betrothed to my little friend Myra Schoonmaker, but however often I tot up the score, that only makes one. You're sure you haven't slipped up somewhere in your figures?'

Archie Gilpin's eye rolled in a fine frenzy, glancing from heaven to earth, from earth to heaven, though one would more readily have expected that sort of thing from his poetic brother.

'Look here,' he said. 'Could we sit down somewhere? This is going to take some time.'

'Why, certainly. There should be good sitting on that stile over there. And take all the time you want.'

Seated on the stile, his deportment rather like that of a young Hindu fakir lying for the first time on the traditional bed of spikes, Archie Gilpin seemed still to find a difficulty in clothing his thoughts in words. He cleared his throat a good deal and once more disturbed his hair with a fevered hand. He reminded Lord Ickenham of a nervous after-dinner speaker suddenly aware, after rising to his feet, that he has completely forgotten the story of the two Irishmen, Pat and Mike, on which he had been relying to convulse his audience.

'I don't know where to begin.'

'At the beginning, don't you think? I often feel that that is best. Then work through the middle and from there, taking your time, carry on to the end.'

This appeared to strike Archie Gilpin as reasonable. He became a little calmer.

'Well, it started with old Tilbury. You know I had a job on one of old Tilbury's papers?'

'Had?'

'He fired me last week.'

'Too bad. Why was that?'

'He didn't like a caricature I'd drawn of him.'

'You shouldn't have shown it to him.'

'I didn't, not exactly. I showed it to Millicent. I thought she would get a laugh out of it.'

'Millicent?'

'His secretary. Millicent Rigby. Girl I was engaged to.'

'That you *were* engaged to?'

'Yes. She broke it off.'

'Of course, yes,' said Lord Ickenham. 'I remember now that Pongo told me he had met a fellow who knew a chap who was acquainted with Miss Rigby, and she had told him—the chap, not the fellow—that she had handed you the pink slip. What had you done to incur her displeasure? You showed her this caricature, you say, but why should that have offended her? Tilbury, if I followed you correctly, was its subject, not she.'

A curious rumbling sound told Lord Ickenham that his companion had uttered a hollow groan. It occurred to him, as the other's hand once more shot to his head, that if this gesture was to be repeated much oftener, Archie, like Lady Constance, would have to go to Shrewsbury for a hair-do.

'Yes, I know. Yes, that's right. But I ought to have mentioned that, thinking Tilbury was out at lunch, I went and showed it to her in his office. I put it on his desk, and we were looking at it with our heads together.'

'Ah,' said Lord Ickenham, beginning to understand. 'And he wasn't out at lunch? He came back?'

'Yes.'

'Saw your handiwork?'

'Yes.'

'Took umbrage?'

'Yes.'

'And erased your name from the list of his skilled assistants?'

'Yes. It was his first move. And later on Millicent ticked me off in no uncertain manner for being such a fool as to bring the thing into the old blighter's office, because anyone but a perfect idiot would have known that he was bound to come in, and hadn't I any sense at all, and . . . Oh, well, you know what happens when a girl starts letting a fellow have it. One word led to another, if you know what I mean, and it wasn't long before she was breaking the engagement and telling me she didn't want to see or speak to me again in this world or the next. She didn't actually return the ring, because I hadn't given her one, but apart from that she made the thing seem pretty final.'

Lord Ickenham was silent for a moment. He was thinking of the six times his Jane had done the same thing by him years ago, and he knew how the other must be feeling.

'I see,' he said. 'Well, my heart bleeds for you, my poor young piece of human wreckage, but this bears out what I was saying, that the sum total of your fiancées is not two, but one. It's nice to have got that straight.'

Another hollow groan escaped Archie Gilpin. His hand rose, but Lord Ickenham caught it in time.

'I wouldn't,' he said. 'Don't touch it. It looks lovely.'

'But you don't know what happened just now. You could have knocked me down with a toothpick. I was coming along by the Emsworth Arms, and I saw her.'

'Miss Rigby?'

'Yes.'

'Probably a mirage.'

'No, she was there in the flesh.'

'What in the world was she doing in Market Blandings?'

'Apparently old Tilbury came here for some reason . . .'

Lord Ickenham nodded. He knew that reason.

' . . . and he brought her with him, to do his letters. She had popped out for a breath of air, and I came along, and we met, face to face, just about opposite the jubilee Memorial watering-trough in the High Street.'

'Dramatic.'

'I was never so surprised in my life.'

'I can readily imagine it. Was she cold and proud and aloof?'

'Not by a jugful. She was all over me. Remorse had set in. She said she was sorry she had blown a fuse, and wept a good deal and . . . well, there we were, so to speak.'

'You folded her in your embrace, no doubt?'

'Yes, quite a good deal, actually, and the upshot of the whole thing was that we got engaged again.'

'You didn't mention that you were engaged to Myra?'

'No, I didn't get around to that. The subject didn't seem to come up, somehow.'

'I quite understand. So the total is two, after all. You were perfectly right, and I apologize. Well, well!'

'I don't see what you're grinning about.'

'Smiling gently would be a more exact description. I was thinking how absurdly simple these problems are, when you give your mind to them. The solution here is obvious. You must at once tell Myra to make no move in the way of buying the trousseau and pricing wedding cakes, because they won't be needed.'

Only a sudden clutch at the rail on which he was seated prevented Archie Gilpin from falling off the stile. It seemed for a moment that he was about to reach for his hair again, but he merely gaped like a good-looking codfish.

'Tell her it's all off, you mean?'

'Precisely. Save the girl a lot of unnecessary expense.'

'But I can't. I admit that I asked her to marry me because I was feeling pretty bitter about Millicent and had some sort of rough idea of showing her—'

'That she was not the only onion in the stew?'

'Something on those lines. And I was considerably relieved when she turned me down. A narrow escape, I felt I'd had. But now that on second thoughts she's decided that she's in favour of the scheme, I don't see how I can possibly just stroll in and tell her I've changed my mind. Well, dash it, is a shot like that on the board? I ask you!'

'You mean that once a Gilpin plights his troth, it stays plighted? A very creditable attitude to take, though it's a pity you plight it so often. But if you are thinking you may break that gentle heart, have no uneasiness. I can state authoritatively that, left to herself, she wouldn't marry you with a ten-foot pole.'

'Then why did she tell me she would?'

'For precisely the reason that made you propose to her. Relations were strained between her and her betrothed, just as they were between you and Miss Rigby, and she did it as what is known as a gesture. She thought, in a word, that that would teach him.'

'She's got a betrothed?'

'And how! You know him. My friend Meriwether.'

'Good Lord!' Archie Gilpin seemed to blossom like a rose in June. 'Well, this is fine. You've eased my mind.'

'A pleasure.'

'Now one begins to see daylight. Now one knows where one is. But, look here, we don't want to do anything . . . what's the word?'

'Precipitate?'

'Yes, we want to move cautiously. You see, on the strength of getting engaged to the daughter of a millionaire I'm hoping to extract a thousand quid from Uncle Alaric.'

Lord Ickenham pursed his lips.

'From His Grace the pop-eyed Duke of Dunstable? No easy task. His one-way pockets are a byword all over England.'

Archie nodded. He had never blinded himself to the fact that anyone trying to separate cash from the Duke of Dunstable was in much the same position as a man endeavouring to take a bone from a short-tempered wolf-hound.

'I know. But I have a feeling it will come off. When I told him I was engaged to Myra, he was practically civil. I think he's ripe for the touch, and I've simply got to get a thousand pounds.'

'Why that particular sum?'

'Because that's what Ricky wants, to let me into his onion soup business. He's planning to expand, and has to have more capital. He said that if I put in a thousand quid, I could have a third share of the profits, which are enormous.'

'Yes, so Pongo told me. I got the impression of dense crowds of bottle-party addicts charging into Ricky's bar night after night like bisons making for a water-hole.'

'That's right, they do. There's something about onion soup that seems to draw them like a magnet. Can't stand the muck myself but there's no accounting for tastes. Here's the set-up, as I see it,' said Archie, with mounting enthusiasm. 'We coast along as we are at present, Myra engaged to me, me engaged to Myra, and Uncle Alaric fawning on me and telling me I can have anything I want, even unto half his kingdom. I get the thousand quid. Myra gives me the push. I slide off and marry Millicent. Myra marries this Meriwether chap, and everybody's happy. Any questions?'

A look of regret and pity had come into Lord Ickenham's face. It pained him to be compelled to act as a black frost in this young man's garden of dreams, but he had no alternative.

'Myra can't give you the push.'

Archie stared. It seemed to him that this kindly old buster, until now so intelligent, had suddenly lost his grip.

'Why not?'

'Because the moment she did, she would be shipped back to America in disgrace and would never see Bill Bailey again.'

'Who on earth's Bill Bailey?'

'Oh, I forgot to tell you, didn't I? That—or, rather, the Reverend Cuthbert Bailey—is Meriwether's real name. He is here incognito because Lady Constance has a deep-seated prejudice against him. He is a penniless curate, and she doesn't like penniless curates. It was to remove Myra from his orbit that she took her away from London and imprisoned her at Blandings Castle. Let her break the engagement, and she'll be back in New York before you can say What ho.'

Silence fell. The light had faded from the evening sky, and simultaneously from Archie Gilpin's face. He sat staring bleakly into the middle distance as if the scenery hurt him in some tender spot.

'It's a mix-up,' he said.

'It wants thinking about,' Lord Ickenham agreed. 'Yes, it certainly wants thinking about. We must turn it over in our minds from time to time.'

# 10

## · I ·

The Duke of Dunstable was not a patient man. When he had business dealings with his fellows, he liked those fellows to jump to it and do it now, and as a general rule took pains to ensure that they did so. But in the matter of Lord Tilbury and the Empress he was inclined to be lenient. He quite understood that a man in the position of having to make up his mind whether or not to pay three thousand pounds for a pig, however obese, needs a little time to think it over. It was only on the third day after the other's return to London that he went to the telephone and having been placed in communication with him opened the conversation with his customary 'Hoy!'

'Are you there, Stinker?'

If the Duke had not been a little deaf in the right ear, he might have heard a sound like an inexperienced motorist changing gears in an old-fashioned car. It was the proprietor of the Mammoth Publishing Company grinding his teeth. Sometimes, when we hear a familiar voice, the heart leaps up like that of the poet Wordsworth when he beheld a rainbow in the sky. Lord Tilbury's was far from doing this. He resented having his morning's work interrupted by a man capable of ignoring gentlemen's agreements and slapping an extra thousand pounds on the price of pigs. When he spoke, his tone was icy.

'Is that you, Dunstable?'

'What?'

'I said, Is that you?'

'Of course it's me. Who do you think it was?'

'What do you want?'

'What?'

'I said What do you want? I'm very busy.'

'What?'

'I said I am very busy.'

'So am I. Got a hundred things to do. Can't stand talking to you all day. About that pig.'

'What about it?'

'Are you prepared to meet my terms? If so, say so. Think on your feet, Stinker.'

Lord Tilbury drew a deep breath. How fortunate, he was feeling, that Fate should have brought him and Lavender Briggs together and so enabled him to defy this man as he ought to be defied. He had heard nothing from Lavender Briggs, but he presumed that she was at Blandings Castle, working in his interests, framing her subtle schemes, and strong in this knowledge he proceeded to answer in the negative. This took some time for in addition to saying 'No' he had to tell the Duke what he thought of him, indicating one by one the various points on which his character diverged from that of the ideal man. Whether it was right of him to call the Duke a fat old sharper whose word he would never again believe, even if given on a stack of Bibles, is open to debate, but he felt considerably better when he had done so, and it was with the feeling of having fought the good fight that several minutes later he slammed down the receiver and rang for Millicent Rigby to come and take dictation.

Nothing that anyone could say to him, no matter how derogatory, ever had the power to wound the Duke. After that initial 'No', indeed, he had scarcely bothered to listen. He could see that it was just routine stuff. All he was thinking, as he came away from the telephone, was that he would now sell the Empress back to Lord Emsworth, who he knew would prove co-operative, and he was proceeding in search of him when a loud squeak in his rear told him that little George was with him again.

'Hullo, big boy,' said George.

'How often have I told you not to call me big boy?'

'Sorry, chum, I keep forgetting. I say, frightfully exciting about Myra, isn't it?'

'Eh?'

'Getting engaged to Archie Gilpin.'

In the interest of his conversation with Lord Tilbury, the Duke had momentarily forgotten that his nephew had become betrothed to the only daughter of a millionaire. Reminded of this, he beamed, as far as it was within his ability to beam, and replied that it was most satisfactory and that he was very pleased about it.

'Her father arrives tomorrow.'

'Indeed?'

'Gets to Market Blandings station, wind and weather permitting, at four-ten. Grandpapa's gone to London to meet him, all dressed up. He looked like a city slicker.'

'You must not call your grandfather a city slicker,' said the Duke, too happy at the way his affairs were working out for a sterner rebuke. He paused, for a sudden thought had struck him, and George, about to inquire whose grandfather he *could* call a city slicker, found himself interrupted. 'What made him get all dressed up and go to London to meet this feller?' he asked, for he knew how much his host disliked the metropolis and how great was his distaste for putting on a decent suit of clothes and trying to look like a respectable human being.

'Aunt Connie told him he jolly well had to or else. He was as sick as mud.'

The Duke puffed at his moustache. His nosiness where other people's affairs were concerned was intense, and Connie's giving this Yank what amounted to a civic welcome intrigued him. It meant something, he told himself. It couldn't be that she was trying to sweeten the feller in the hope of floating a loan, for she had ample private means, bequeathed to her by her late husband, Joseph Keeble, who had made a packet out East, so it must be that she entertained towards him feelings that were deeper and warmer than those of ordinary friendship, as the expression was. He had never suspected this, but it occurred to him now that when a woman keeps a photograph of a man with a head like a Spanish onion on her writing table, it means that her emotions are involved, in all probability deeply. There was that occasion, too, when he had joined them at luncheon at the Ritz. Their heads, he remembered, had been very close together. By the time he had succeeded in shaking off George, declining his invitation to come down to the lake and chat with the Church Lads, he was convinced that he had hit on the right solution, and he waddled off to find Lord Ickenham and canvass his views on the subject. He was not fond of Lord Ickenham, but there was nobody else available as a confidant.

He found him in his hammock, pondering over the various problems which had presented themselves of late, and lost no time in placing the item on the agenda paper.

'I say, Ickenham, this fellow who's coming here tomorrow. This chap Stick-in-the-mud.'

'Schoonmaker. Jimmy Schoonmaker.'

'You know him?'

'One of my oldest friends. I shall like seeing him again.'

'So will somebody else.'

'Who would that be?'

'Connie, that's who. Let me tell you something, Ickenham. I was in Connie's room yesterday, having a look round, and there was a cable on the writing table. "Coming immediately", it said, and a lot more I've forgotten. It was signed Schoonmaker, and was obviously a reply to a cable from her, urging him to come here. Now why was she in such a sweat to get the feller to Blandings Castle, you ask.'

'So I do. Glad you reminded me.'

'I'll tell you why. It sticks out a mile. She's potty about the chap. Sift the evidence. In spite of his having a head like a Spanish onion, she keeps his photograph on her writing table. She sends him urgent cables telling him to come immediately. And what is even more significant, she makes Emsworth put on a clean collar and go all the way to London to meet him. Why, dash it, she didn't do that for *me*! Would she go to such lengths if she wasn't potty about the . . . Get out, you!'

He was addressing Beach, who had approached the hammock and uttered a discreet cough.

'What you want?'

'I was instructed by her ladyship to inquire of his lordship if he would be good enough to speak to her ladyship in her ladyship's boudoir, your Grace,' said Beach with dignity. He was not a man to be put upon by Dukes, no matter how white-moustached.

'Wants to see him, does she?'

'Precisely, your Grace.'

'Better go and find out what it's all about, Ickenham. Remember what I was saying. Watch her closely!' said the Duke in a hissing whisper. 'Watch her like a hawk.'

There was a thoughtful look in Lord Ickenham's eye as he crossed the lawn. This new development interested him. He was aware how sorely persecuted Lord Emsworth was by his sister Constance—the other's story of the brass paper-fastener had impressed him greatly—and he had hoped by his presence at the castle to ease the strain for him a little, but he had never envisaged the possibility of actually removing her from the premises. If Lady Constance were to marry James Schoonmaker and go to live with him in America, it would be the biggest thing that had happened to Lord Emsworth since his younger son Frederick had transferred himself to Long Island City, N.Y., as a unit of the firm of Donaldson's Dog Biscuits, Inc. There is no surer way of promoting human happiness than to relieve a mild man of the society of a sister who says, 'Oh, Clarence!' to him and sees life in the home generally as a sort of Uncle Tom's Cabin production, with herself playing Simon Legree and her brother in the supporting role of Uncle Tom.

Of course, it takes two to make a romance, and James Schoonmaker had yet to be heard from, but Lord Ickenham regarded his old friend's instant response to Lady Constance's cable as distinctly promising. A man in Jimmy's position, a monarch of finance up to his eyes all the time in big deals, with barely a moment to spare from cornering peanuts or whatever it might be, does not drop everything and come bounding across the

Atlantic with a whoop and a holler unless there is some great attraction awaiting him at the other end. It would be a good move, he decided, when Jimmy arrived, to meet him at Market Blandings station, hurry him off to the Emsworth Arms and fill him to the brim with G. Ovens' home-brewed beer. Mellowed by that wonder fluid, he felt, it was more than likely that he would cast off reserve, become expansive and give a sympathetic buddy what George Cyril Wellbeloved would have called the griff.

Lady Constance was seated at her writing table, tapping the woodwork with her fingers, and Lord Ickenham had the momentary illusion, as always when summoned to her presence, that time had rolled back in its flight and that he was once more vis-à-vis with his old kindergarten mistress. The great question in those days had always been whether or not she would rap him on the knuckles with a ruler, and it was with some relief that he noted that the only weapon within his hostess's reach was a small ivory paper-knife.

She was not looking cordial. Her air was that of somebody who, where Ickenhams were concerned, could take them or leave them alone. A handsome woman, though, and one well calculated to touch off the spark in the Schoonmaker bosom.

'Please sit down, Lord Ickenham.'

He took a chair, and Lady Constance remained silent for a moment. She seemed to be searching for words. Then, for she was never a woman who hesitated long when she had something to say, even when that something verged on the embarrassing, she began.

'Myra's father is arriving tomorrow, Lord Ickenham.'

'So I had heard. I was saying to Dunstable just now how much I shall enjoy seeing him again after all these years.'

A slight frown on Lady Constance's forehead seemed to suggest that his emotions did not interest her.

'I wonder if Jimmy's put on weight. He was inclined to bulge when I last saw him. Wouldn't watch his calories.'

Nor, said the frown, was she in a mood to discuss Mr Schoonmaker's poundage.

'He has come because I asked him to. I sent him an urgent cable.'

'After we had had our little talk?'

'Yes,' said Lady Constance, shuddering as she recalled that little talk. 'I intended to put the whole matter in his hands and advise him to take Myra back to America immediately.'

'I see. Did you say so?'

'No, I did not, and I am particularly anxious that he shall know nothing of her infatuation. It would be difficult to explain why I had allowed Mr Bailey to stay on at the castle.'

'Very difficult. One can see him raising his eyebrows.'

'On the other hand, I must give him some reason why I sent that cable, and I wanted to see you, Lord Ickenham, to ask if you had anything to suggest.'

She sank back in her chair, stiffened in every limb. Her companion was beaming at her, and his kindly smile affected her like a blow in the midriff. She was in a highly nervous condition, and the last thing she desired was to be beamed at by a man whose very presence revolted her finer feelings.

'My dear Lady Constance,' said Lord Ickenham buoyantly, 'the matter is simple. I have the solution hot off the griddle. You tell him that his daughter has become engaged to Archie Gilpin and you wanted him to look in and give the boy the once-over. Perfectly natural thing to suggest to an affectionate father. He would probably have been very hurt, if you hadn't cabled him. That solves your little difficulty, I think?'

Lady Constance relaxed. Her opinion of this man had in no way altered, she still considered him a menace to one and all and his presence an offence to the pure air of Blandings Castle, but she was fair enough to admit that, however black his character might be, and however much she disliked having him beam at her, he knew all the answers.

• II •

The 11.45 train from Paddington, first stop Swindon, rolled into Market Blandings station, and Lord Emsworth stepped out, followed by James R. Schoonmaker of Park Avenue, New York, and The Dunes, Westhampton, Long Island.

American financiers come in all sizes, ranging from the small and shrimp-like to the large and impressive. Mr Schoonmaker belonged to the latter class. He was a man in the late fifties with a massive head and a handsome face interrupted about half way up by tortoiseshell-rimmed spectacles. He had been an All-American footballer in his youth, and he still looked capable of bucking a line, though today he would have done it not with a bull-like rush but with an authoritative glance which would have taken all the heart out of the opposition.

His face, as he emerged, was wearing the unmistakable look of a man who has had a long railway journey in Lord Emsworth's company, but it brightened suddenly when he saw the slender figure standing on the platform. He stared incredulously.

'Freddie! Well, I'll be darned!'

'Hullo there, Jimmy.'

'You here?'

'That's right.'

'Well, well!' said Mr Schoonmaker.

'Well, well, well!' said Lord Ickenham.

'Well, well, well, *well*!' said Mr Schoonmaker.

Lord Emsworth interrupted the reunion before it could reach the height of its fever. He was anxious to lose no time in getting to the haven of his bedroom and shedding the raiment which had been irking him all day. His shoes, in particular, were troubling him.

'Oh, hullo, Ickenham. Is the car outside?'

'Straining at the leash.'

'Then let us be off, shall we?'

'Well, I'll tell you,' said Lord Ickenham. 'I can readily understand your desire to hasten homeward and get into something loose—'

'It's my shoes, principally.'

'They look beautiful.'

'They're pinching me.'

'The very words my nephew Pongo said that day at the dog races, and his statement was tested and proved correct. Courage, Emsworth! Think of the women in China. You don't find them beefing because their shoes are tight. But what I was about to say was that Jimmy and I haven't seen each other for upwards of fifteen years, and we've a lot of heavy thread-picking-up to do. I thought I'd take him to the Emsworth Arms for a quick one. You'd enjoy a mouthful of beer, Jimmy?'

'Ah!' said Mr Schoonmaker, his tongue flickering over his lips.

'So we'll just bung you into the car and walk over later.'

The process of bunging Lord Emsworth into a car was never a simple one, for on these occasions his long legs always took on something of the fluid quality of an octopus's tentacles, but the task was accomplished at last, and Lord Ickenham led his old friend to a table in the shady garden where all those business conferences between Lord Tilbury, the Duke of Dunstable and Lavender Briggs had taken place.

'Ah!' said Mr Schoonmaker again some little time later, laying down his empty tankard.

'Have another?'

'I think I will,' said Mr Schoonmaker, speaking in the rather awed voice customary with those tasting G. Ovens' homebrewed for the first time. He added that the beverage had a kick, and Lord Ickenham agreed that its kick was considerable. He said he thought G. Ovens put some form of high explosive in it, and Mr Schoonmaker agreed that this might well be so.

A considerable number of threads had been picked up by this time, and it seemed to Lord Ickenham that it would not be long now before he would be able to divert the conversation from the past to the present. From certain signs he saw that the homebrewed was beginning to have its beneficent effect. Another pint, he felt, should be sufficient to bring his companion to the confidential stage. In one of the cosy talks he had had with George Cyril Wellbeloved before Lord Emsworth had driven him with a flaming sword from his garden of Eden, the pigman had commented on the mysterious properties of a quart of the Ovens output, speaking with a good deal of bitterness of the time when that amount of it had caused him to reveal to Claude Murphy, the local constable, certain top secrets which later he would have given much to have kept to himself.

The second pint arrived, and Mr Schoonmaker quaffed deeply. His journey had been a stuffy one, parching to the throat. He looked about him approvingly, taking in the smooth turf, the shady trees and the silver river that gleamed through them.

'Nice place, this,' he said.

'Rendered all the nicer by your presence, Jimmy,' replied Lord Ickenham courteously. 'What brought you over here, by the way?'

'I had an urgent cable from Lady Constance.' A thought struck Mr Schoonmaker. 'Nothing wrong with Mike, is there?'

'Not to my knowledge. Nor with Pat. Mike who?'

'Myra.'

'I didn't know she was known to the police as Mike. You must have started calling her that after my time. No, Myra's all right. She's just got engaged.'

Mr Schoonmaker started violently, always a dangerous thing to do when drinking beer. Having stopped coughing and dried himself off, he said:

'She has? What made her do that?'

'Love, Jimmy,' said Lord Ickenham with a touch of reproach. 'You can't expect a girl not to fall in love in these romantic surroundings. There's something in the air of Blandings Castle that brings out all the sentiment in people. Strong men have come here without a thought of matrimony in their minds and within a week have started writing poetry and carving hearts on trees. Probably the ozone.'

Mr Schoonmaker was frowning. He was not at all sure he liked the look of this. His daughter's impulsiveness was no secret from him.

'Who is the fellow?' he demanded, not exactly expecting to hear that it was the boy who cleaned the knives and boots, but prepared for the worst. 'Who is this guy she's got engaged to?'

'Gilpin is the name, first name Archibald. He's the nephew of the Duke of Dunstable,' said Lord Ickenham, and Mr Schoonmaker's brow cleared magically. He would have preferred not to have a son-in-law called Archibald, but he knew that in these matters one has to take the rough with the smooth, and he had a great respect for Dukes.

'Is he, by golly! Well, that's fine.'

'I thought you'd be pleased.'

'When did this happen?'

'Oh, recently.'

'Odd that Lady Constance didn't mention it in her cable.'

'Probably wanted to keep the expense down. You know what they charge you per word for cables, and a penny saved is a penny earned. Do you call her Lady Constance?'

'Of course. Why not?'

'Rather formal. You've known her a long time.'

'Yes, we've been friends for quite a while, very close friends as a matter of fact. She's a wonderful woman. But there's a sort of cool aristocratic dignity about her . . . a kind of aloofness . . . I don't know how to put it, but she gives you the feeling that you'll never get to first base with her.'

'And you want to get to first base with her?' said Lord Ickenham, eyeing him narrowly. Mr Schoonmaker had just finished his second pint, and something told him that this was the moment for which he had been waiting. It was after his second pint that George Cyril Wellbeloved had poured out his confidences to Constable Claude Murphy, among them his personal technique for poaching pheasants.

For an instant it seemed that Mr Schoonmaker would be reticent, but the Ovens home-brewed was too strong for him. A pinkness spread itself over his face. The ears, in particular, were glowing brightly.

'Yes, I do,' he said, glaring a little as if about to ask Lord Ickenham if he wanted to make something of it. 'Why shouldn't I?'

'My dear fellow, I'm not criticizing. I'm all sympathy and understanding. Any red-blooded man would be glad to get to first base with Connie.'

Mr Schoonmaker started.

'Do you call her Connie?'

'Of course.'

'How do you manage it?'

'Just comes naturally.'

'I wish it did to me.' Mr Schoonmaker looked into his tankard, saw that it was empty and heaved a long sigh. 'Yes, sir, I wish I had your nerve. Freddie, if I could get that woman to marry me, I'd be the happiest man on earth.'

With the exception, Lord Ickenham thought, as he laid a gentle hand on his friend's arm, of her brother Clarence.

'Now you're talking, Jimmy. Relay that information to her. Women like to hear these things.'

'But I told you. I haven't the nerve.'

'Nonsense. A child of six could do it, provided he hadn't got the dumb staggers.'

Mr Schoonmaker sighed again. G. Ovens' home-brewed tends as a rule to induce joviality—sometimes, as in the case of George Cyril Wellbeloved, injudicious joviality—but it was plain that today it had failed of its mission.

'That's just what I have got. When I try to propose to her, the words won't come. It's happened a dozen times. The sight of that calm aristocratic profile wipes them from my lips.'

'Try not looking at her sideways.'

'I'm not in her class. That's the trouble. I'm aiming too high.'

'A Schoonmaker is a fitting mate for the highest in the land.'

'Who says so?'

'I say so.'

'Well, I don't. I know what would happen. She'd be very nice about it, but she would freeze me.'

Lord Ickenham, who had removed his hand from the arm, replaced it.

'Now there I'm sure you're wrong, Jimmy. I happen to be certain that she loves you. Connie has few secrets from me.'

Mr Schoonmaker stared.

'You aren't telling me she told you she did?'

'Not in so many words, of course. You could hardly expect that, even to an old friend like myself. But that way she has of drawing her breath in sharply and looking starry-eyed whenever your name is mentioned is enough to show me how things stand. The impression I received was of a woman wailing for her demon lover. Well, perhaps not actually wailing, but making quite a production number of it. I tell you I've seen her clench her hands till the knuckles stood out white under the strain, just because your name happened to come up in the course of conversation. I'm convinced that if you were to try the Ickenham system, you couldn't fail.'

'The Ickenham system?'

'I call it that. It's a little thing I knocked together in my bachelor days. It consists of grabbing the girl, waggling her about a bit, showering kisses on her upturned face and making some such remark as "My mate!". Clench the teeth of course, while saying that. It adds conviction.'

Mr Schoonmaker's stare widened.

'You expect me to do that to *Lady Constance*?'

'I see no objection.'

'I do.'

'Such as—?'

'I couldn't even get started.'

'Where's your manly courage?'

'I don't have any, not where she's concerned.'

'Come, come. She's only a woman.'

'No, she isn't. She's Lady Constance Keeble, sister of the Earl of Emsworth, with a pedigree stretching back to the Flood, and I can't forget it.'

Lord Ickenham mused. He recognized the fact that an obstacle had arisen, but a few moments' thought told him that it was not an impasse.

'What you need, Jimmy, is a pint or two of May Queen.'

'Eh?'

'It is a beverage which I always recommend to timorous wooers when they find a difficulty in bringing themselves to try the Ickenham system. Its full name is "Tomorrow'll be of all the year the maddest, merriest day, for I'm to be Queen of the May, mother, I'm to be Queen of the May", but the title is generally shortened for purposes of convenience in ordinary conversation. Its foundation is any good dry champagne, to which is added liqueur brandy, kummel and green chartreuse, and I can assure you it acts like magic. Under its influence little men with receding chins and pince-nez have dominated the proudest beauties and compelled them to sign on the dotted line. I'll tell Beach to see that you get plenty of it before and during dinner tonight. Then you take Connie out on the terrace under the moon and go into the Ickenham routine, and I shall be vastly surprised if we don't shortly see an interesting announcement in *The Times*.'

'H'm.' Mr Schoonmaker weighed the suggestion, but it was plain that he was none too enthusiastic about it. 'Grab her?'

'That's it.'

'Waggle her about?'

'That's the idea.'

'And say "My mate!"?'

'Unless there is some other turn of phrase which you prefer,' said Lord Ickenham, always ready to stretch a point. 'You needn't stick too closely to the script if you feel like gagging, but on no account tamper with the business. That is of the essence.'

## · III ·

On the morning following his old friend's arrival, Lord Ickenham had settled himself in his hammock when a husky voice spoke his name and he found Mr Schoonmaker at his side. Sitting up and directing a keen glance at him, he did not like what he saw. James Schoonmaker was looking pale and careworn, and there was in his bearing no suggestion whatsoever that he was the happiest man on earth. He looked, indeed, far more like that schooner Hesperus of which Lord Ickenham in his boyhood had recited so successfully, on the occasion when it swept like a sheeted ghost to the reef of Norman's Woe. Give him a skipper and a little daughter whom he had taken to bear him company, thought Lord Ickenham, and he could have made straight for the reef of Norman's Woe, and no questions asked.

But he was too well-bred to put this sentiment into words. Instead, he affected an eager animation which he was far from feeling.

'Jimmy! I was hoping you would come along. Have you good news to report? Everything pretty smooth? I start saving up for the wedding present?'

Mr Schoonmaker shook his head and simultaneously uttered a sharp cry of anguish. As Lord Ickenham had suspected, he was in no shape to shake heads. To the dullest eye it would have been plain that this hand across the sea was in the grip of a hangover of majestic proportions.

'That May Queen is kind of powerful stuff,' said Mr Schoonmaker, endorsing this view.

'It sometimes brings regrets with the dawning of a new day,' Lord Ickenham agreed. 'It's the chartreuse mostly, I think. Still, if it has produced results . . .'

'But it hasn't.'

'Come, come, Jimmy. With my own eyes I saw you lead Connie out on to the terrace, and the moon was shining like billy-o.'

'Yes, and what happened? What always happens, and what's always going to happen. I lost my nerve.'

Lord Ickenham sighed. This was a set-back, and though he knew that these disappointments are sent to us to make us more spiritual, he could never bring himself to like them.

'You didn't ask her to marry you?'

'I didn't come within a mile of it.'

'What *did* you talk about? The weather?'

'We talked about Mike and this boy she's engaged to. I asked her why she hadn't mentioned him in her cable.'

'What did she say to that?'

'She said she wanted to wait till I could see him for myself. Seems strange.'

'Nothing strange about it. She could hardly tell you that she sent the cable because she couldn't endure being away from you for another minute. Modesty forbade.'

For a moment Mr Schoonmaker brightened.

'You really think that was it?'

'Of course it was. She loves you with every fibre of her being. She's crazy about you. So cheer up, Jimmy, and have another pop when you're feeling better. My experience is that a May Queen hangover soon wears off after one has had a little sleep. Try this hammock.'

'Don't you want it?'

'Your need is greater than mine.'

'Well, thanks,' said Mr Schoonmaker. The momentary brightness seemed to ooze out of him as he climbed into the hammock, leaving him the pessimist he had been. He heaved a sigh. 'Of course, you're all wrong, Freddie. There's no hope for me. I know when I'm licked.'

'Scarcely the spirit of '76.'

'She would never consider me for a moment. We don't play in the same league. Oh well,' said Mr Schoonmaker, heaving another sigh, 'there's always one's work.'

A sudden gleam came into Lord Ickenham's eye. It was as if a thought had occurred to him.

'What are you working on now, Jimmy? Something big, of course?'

'Fairly big. Do you know Florida?'

'Not very well. My time in America was spent out west and in New York.'

'Then you probably don't know Jupiter Island.'

'I've heard of it. Sort of a winter home from home for millionaires, isn't it?'

'That kind of idea. Club, golf links, tennis, bathing. You rent a cottage for the season.'

'And pay pretty high for it, no doubt?'

'Yes, it comes high. This thing I'm promoting is the same sort of set-up farther down the coast. The Venus Island Development Corporation, it's called. There'll be a fortune in it.'

'You aren't looking for capital, I suppose?'

'No difficulty there. Why?'

'I was only thinking, Jimmy, that as your daughter is marrying his nephew, it would be a graceful act to let the Duke in on the ground floor. He's rolling in money, but he can always do with a bit more. There's something about the stuff that fascinates him.'

Mr Schoonmaker was on the verge of sleep, but he was sufficiently awake to reply that he would be glad to do the Duke this good turn. He thanked Lord Ickenham for the suggestion and Lord Ickenham said he always made a point of doing his day's kind deed. His mother, he said, had been frightened by a Boy Scout.

'I expect to pass through this world but once, Jimmy. Any good thing, therefore, that I can do, let me do it now, as the fellow said. How's the hammock?'

Mr Schoonmaker snored gently, and Lord Ickenham went off to have a word with the Duke.

# 11

## · I ·

The Duke of Dunstable was sitting on the terrace, and not only on the terrace but on top of the world with a rainbow round his shoulder. Counting his blessings one by one, he was of the opinion that he had never had it so good. He had not yet approached Lord Emsworth in the matter of the Empress, but he knew that when he did he would be in the pleasant position of dealing in a seller's market. And he had the comforting thought that, whatever the figure arrived at, it would be all clear profit, with none of the distasteful necessity of paying agent's commission. The recollection of how nearly he had come to parting with that five hundred pounds to Lavender Briggs still made him shudder.

And in addition to this, showing that when Providence starts showering its boons on a good man, the sky is the limit, his nephew Archibald, until now a sad burden on his purse, was engaged to be married to the only daughter of a millionaire. How the young poop had done it, he was at a loss to understand, but there it was, and so deep was his contentment that when Lord Ickenham dropped into a chair beside him, he did not even puff at his moustache. He disliked Lord Ickenham, considering him a potty sort of feller whose spiritual home was a padded cell in some not too choosy lunatic asylum, but this morning he was the friend of all the world.

Lord Ickenham was looking grave.

'Hope I'm not interrupting you, Dunstable, if you were doing the crossword puzzle.'

'Not at all,' said the Duke amiably. 'I was only thinkin' a bit.'

'I'm afraid I've come to give you more food for thought,' said Lord Ickenham, 'and not very agreeable thought, either. It's very saddening, don't you feel, how people change for the worse as the years go on?'

'Who does? I don't.'

'No, not you. You always maintain a safe suds level. I was thinking of poor Schoonmaker.'

'What's poor about him?'

There was a look of pain on Lord Ickenham's face. He was silent for a moment, musing, or so it seemed, on life's tragedies.

'Everything,' he said. 'When I knew James Schoonmaker fifteen years ago in New York, he was a man with a glittering future, and for a time, I understand, he did do extremely well. But that's all in the past. He's gone right under.'

'Under what?' said the Duke, who was never very quick at the uptake.

'He's a pauper. Down to his last thirty cents. Please don't mention this to anyone, but he's just been borrowing money from me. It was a great shock.'

The Duke sat up. This time he did not neglect to puff at his moustache. It floated up like a waterfall going the wrong way.

'But he's a millionaire!'

Lord Ickenham smiled sadly.

'That's what he'd like you to believe. But I have friends in New York who keep me posted from time to time about the fellows I used to know there, and they have told me his whole story. He's down to his last dollar, and his bankruptcy may be expected at any moment. You know how it is with these American financiers. They over-extend themselves. They bite off more than they can chew, and then comes the inevitable smash. A fiver means a lot to Schoonmaker at this moment. A tenner was what he wanted just now, and I gave it to him, poor devil. I hadn't the heart to refuse. This is strictly between you and me, of course, and I wouldn't like it to be spread about, but I thought I ought to warn you about him.'

The Duke's eyes were protruding like a snail's. His moustache was in a constant state of activity. Not even little George had ever seen it giving so sedulously of its best.

'Warn me? If the feller thinks he's going to get tuppence out of *me*, he'll be disappointed.'

'He's hoping for more than tuppence. I'm afraid he's planning to try to talk you into putting up money for some wildcat scheme he's got. As far as I could make out, it's some sort of land and building operation down in Florida. The Venus Island Development Corporation he calls it. The very name sounds fishy, don't you think? Venus Island, I mean to say! There probably isn't such a place. What's worrying me is that you may feel tempted to invest, because he'll make the thing sound so good. He's very plausible. But don't dream of doing it. Be on your guard.'

'I'll be on my guard,' said the Duke, breathing heavily.

Lord Ickenham waited a moment in case the other might wish to thank his benefactor, but as he merely continued to breathe heavily, he made his way back to the hammock. He found Mr Schoonmaker sitting up and looking brighter. He was glad to hear that his nap had done him good.

'Headache gone?'

Mr Schoonmaker considered this.

'Well, not *gone*,' he said. He was a man who liked exactness of speech. 'But it's a lot better.'

'Then what I wish you would do, Jimmy, is go and see the Duke and tell him all about that Venus Island thing of yours. I've just been talking to him, and oddly enough, he was saying he wished he could find some business opportunity which would give him the chance of having a little flutter. He's a great gambler at heart.'

Mr Schoonmaker disapproved of his choice of words. A man with a hangover of the dimensions of the one from which he was suffering finds it difficult to bridle, but he did his best.

'Gambler? What do you mean, gambler? The Venus Island Development Corporation's as sound as Fort Knox.'

'I'm sure it is,' said Lord Ickenham soothingly. 'Impress that on him. Give him a big sales talk.'

'Why?' said Mr Schoonmaker, still ruffled. 'I don't want his money.'

'Of course you don't. You'll be doing him a great favour by allowing him to buy in. But for goodness' sake don't let him see that. You know how proud these dukes are. They hate to feel under an obligation to anyone. Seem eager, Jimmy.'

'Oh, all right,' said Mr Schoonmaker grudgingly. 'Though it's funny, having to wheedle someone into accepting shares in something that'll quadruple his money in under a year.'

'We'll have a good laugh about it later,' Lord Ickenham assured him. 'You'll find him on the terrace,' he said. 'I told him you might be looking in.'

He nestled into the vacated hammock, and was in the process of explaining to his guardian angel, who had once more become critical, that there is no harm in deviating from the truth a little, if it is done in a good cause, and that the interview which Mr Schoonmaker was about to have with the Duke of Dunstable, though possibly wounding to his feelings, would make him forget his headache, when he became aware of Archie Gilpin at his side.

Archie was looking as beautiful as ever, but anxious.

'I say,' he said. 'I saw you talking to Uncle Alaric.'

'Yes, we had a chat.'

'What sort of mood is he in?'

'He seemed to me a little agitated. He was annoyed because an attempt was being made to get money out of him.'

'Oh, my God!'

'Or, rather, he was expecting such an attempt to be made. That always does something to the fine old man. Did you ever read a book called *The Confessions Of Alphonse*, the reminiscences of a French waiter? No, I suppose not, for it was published a number of years ago, long before you were born. At one point in it Alphonse says "Instantly as a man wishes to borrow money of me, I dislike him. It is in the blood. It is more strong than me." The Duke's like that.'

Archie Gilpin reached for his hair and was busy for awhile with the customary scalp massage. There was a bleakness in his voice when at length he spoke.

'Then you wouldn't recommend an immediate try for that thousand?'

'Not whole-heartedly. But what's your hurry?'

'I'll tell you what's my hurry. I had a letter from Ricky this morning. He says he can only give me another week to raise the money. If I don't give it him by then, he'll have to get somebody else, he says.'

'A nuisance, I agree. That kind of ultimatum is always unpleasant. But much may happen in a week. Much, for that matter, may happen in a day. My advice to you—'

But Archie was not destined to receive that advice, which would probably have been very valuable, for at this moment Mr Schoonmaker appeared, and he sidled off. The father of his betrothed, now that he had made his acquaintance, always gave him a sort of nervous feeling akin to what are sometimes called the heeby-jeebies and he was never completely at his ease in his presence. It was the tortoiseshell-rimmed spectacles principally that did it, he thought, though possibly the square jaw contributed its mite.

Mr Schoonmaker stood looming over the hammock like a thunder-cloud.

'You and your damned Dukes!' he said and Lord Ickenham raised his eyebrows.

'My dear Jimmy! It may be my imagination, but a certain half-veiled something in your manner seems to suggest that your conference with Dunstable was not an agreeable one. What happened? Did you broach the subject of the Venus Island Development Corporation?'

'Yes, I did,' said Mr Schoonmaker, taking time out for a snort similar in its resonance to the shot heard round the world. 'And he acted as if he thought I was some sort of con. man. Did you tell him I'd borrowed money from you?'

Lord Ickenham's eyes widened. He was plainly at a loss.

'Borrowed money from me? Of course not.'

'He said you did.'

'How very extraordinary. How much am I supposed to have lent you?'

'Ten pounds.'

'What a laughable idea! The sort of sum a man like you leaves on the plate for the waiter when he's had lunch. What on earth can have put that into his head?' Lord Ickenham's face cleared. 'I'll tell you what I think must have misled him, Jimmy. I remember now that I was talking to him about the old days in New York, when we were both young and hard up and I would sometimes sting you for a trifle and you would sometimes sting me for a trifle, according to which of us happened to have anything in his wallet at the moment, and he got it all mixed up. Very muddle-headed man, the Duke. His father, I believe, was the same. So were his sisters and his cousins and his aunts. Well, I must say the thought of someone of your eminence panhandling me for a tenner is a very stimulating one. It isn't everyone who gets his ear bitten by a millionaire. How did you leave things with Dunstable?'

'I told him he was crazy and came away.'

'Very proper. And what are you planning to do now?'

A faint blush spread itself over Mr Schoonmaker's face.

'I thought I might go and see if Lady Constance would like a stroll in the park or something.'

'Connie,' Lord Ickenham corrected. 'You won't get anywhere if you don't think of her as Connie.'

'I won't get anywhere if I do,' said Mr Schoonmaker morosely.

The morning was now pleasantly warm and full of little soothing noises, some contributed by the local insects, others by a gardener who was mowing a distant lawn, and it was not long after Mr Schoonmaker's departure before Lord Ickenham's eyes closed and his breathing became soft and regular. He was within two breaths of sleep, when a voice spoke.

'Hoy!' it said, and he sat up.

'Hullo, Dunstable. You seem upset.'

The Duke's eyes were popping, and his moustache danced in the breeze.

'Ickenham, you were right!'

'About what?'

'About that Yank, that feller Stick-in-the-mud. Not ten minutes after you'd warned me he was going to do it, he came to me and started trying to get me to put up money for that Tiddlypush Island scheme of his.'

Lord Ickenham gave a low whistle.

'You don't say!'

'That's what he did.'

'So soon! One would have expected him to wait at least till he had got to know you a little better. He was very plausible, of course?'

'Yes, very.'

'He would be. These fellows always specialize in the slick sales talk. You weren't taken in, I hope?'

'*Me*?'

'No, of course not. You're much too level-headed.'

'I sent him off with a flea in his ear, by Jove!'

'I see. I don't blame you. Still, it's very embarrassing.'

'Who's embarrassed? I'm not.'

'I was only thinking that as your nephew is going to marry his daughter . . .'

The Duke's jaw fell.

'Good God! I'd forgotten that.'

'I should try to bear it in mind from now on, if I were you, for it is a matter that affects you rather deeply. It's lucky you're a rich man.'

'Eh?'

'Well, you're going to have to support Archie and the girl, and not only them but Schoonmaker and his sisters. I believe he has three of them.'

'I won't do it!'

'Can't let them starve.'

'Why not?'

'You mean you think we all eat too much nowadays? Quite true, but it won't do you any good if they go about begging crusts of bread and telling people why. Can't you see the gossip columns in Tilbury's papers? They'd really spread themselves.'

The Duke clutched at the hammock, causing Lord Ickenham to oscillate and feel a little seasick. He had overlooked this angle, and none knew better than he how blithely, after what had occurred between them, the proprietor of the Mammoth Publishing Company would spring to the task of getting a certain something of his own back.

A thought struck him.

'Why should Archibald beg crusts of bread?'

'Wouldn't you, if suffering from the pangs of hunger?'

'He has a salaried position.'

'No longer.'

'Eh?'

'They handed him his hat.'

'His hat? How do you mean, his hat?'

'Putting it another way, his services were dispensed with last week.'

'What!'

'So he told me.'

'He never said anything about it to me.'

'Probably didn't want to cause you anxiety. He's a very considerate young man.'

'He's a poop and a waster!'

'I like his hair, though, don't you? Well, that's how matters stand, and I'm afraid it's going to cost you a lot of money. I don't see how you're going to do it under two or three thousand a year. For years and years and years. Great drain on your resources. What a pity it isn't possible for you just to tell Archie to break the engagement. That would solve everything. But of course you can't do it.'

'Why can't I? It's an excellent idea. I'll go and find him now, and if he raises the slightest objection, I'll kick his spine up through his hat.'

'No, wait. You still haven't got that toehold on the situation which I should like to see. You're forgetting the breach of promise case.'

'What breach of promise case?'

Lord Ickenham's manner was that of a patient governess explaining a problem in elementary arithmetic to a child who through no fault of its own had been dropped on the head when a baby.

'Isn't it obvious? If Archie were to break the engagement, the girl's first move would be to start an action for breach of promise. Even if the idea didn't occur to her independently, a man like Schoonmaker would see that she did it, and the jury would give her heavy damages without leaving the box. Archie tells me he has written her any number of letters.'

'How can he have written her letters when they're staying in the same dashed house?'

'Notes would perhaps be a better term. Fervid notes slipped into her hand by daylight or pushed under her door at night. You know what lovers are.'

'Sounds potty.'

'But is frequently done, I believe, when the heart is young.'

'He may not have mentioned marriage.'

'I wouldn't build too much on that. I know he asked me once how to spell "honeymoon", which shows the trend his thoughts were taking. You can't speak of honeymoons in a letter to a girl without laying up trouble for yourself. When you consider what a mere reference to chops and tomato sauce did to Mr Pickwick—'

'Who's Mr Pickwick?'

'Let it pass. I'm only saying that when those notes are read out in court, you'll be for it.'

'Why, me? If Archibald is fool enough to get involved in a breach of promise case, blast his idiotic eyes. I don't have to pay his damages.'

'It won't look well in the gossip columns, if you don't. He's your nephew.'

The Duke uttered a bitter curse on all nephews, and Lord Ickenham agreed that they could be trying, though his own nephew Pongo, he said, held the view that all the trouble in the world was caused by uncles.

'I can see only one ray of hope.'

'What's that?' asked the Duke, who was unable to detect even one. His prominent eyes gleamed a little. He was saying to himself that this feller Ickenham might be potty, but apparently he had lucid intervals.

'It may be possible to buy the girl off. We have this in our favour, that she isn't in love with Archie.'

'Who could be in love with a poop like that?'

'Hers is rather a sad case. You know Meriwether?'

'The feller with the face?'

'A very accurate description. He has a heart of gold, too, but you don't see that.'

'What about him?'

'He is the man she wants to marry.'

'Meriwether is?'

'Yes.'

'Then why did she get engaged to Archibald?'

'My dear Dunstable! A girl whose father is on the verge of bankruptcy has to look out for herself. She isn't in a position to let her heart rule her head. When she has the opportunity of becoming linked by marriage to a man like you, you can't expect her not to grab it.'

'That's true.'

'She would much prefer not to make a marriage of convenience, but she sees no hope of happiness with the man she loves. What stands in the way of her union to Meriwether is money.'

'Hasn't he got any? You told me he came from Brazil. Fellers make money in Brazil.'

'He didn't. A wasting sickness struck the Brazil nuts, and he lost all his capital.'

'Silly ass.'

'Your sympathy does you credit. Yes, his lack of money is the trouble. And the reason I think Myra Schoonmaker would jump at any adequate offer is that he has just got the chance of buying into a lucrative onion soup business.'

The Duke started as if stung. The last three words always stirred him to his depths.

'My nephew Alaric runs an onion soup business.'

'No, really?'

'That's what he does. Writes poetry and sells onion soup. It embarrasses me at the club. Fellers come up to me and ask, "What's that nephew of yours doing now?", thinking I'm going to say he's in the diplomatic service or something, and I have to tell them he's selling onion soup. Don't know which way to look.'

'I can understand your emotion. The stuff is very nourishing, I believe, but, as far as I know, no statue has ever been erected to a man who sold onion soup. Still, there's lots of money in it, and this chap I'm speaking of is doing so well that he wants to expand. He has offered Meriwether a third share in his business for a thousand pounds. So if you were to offer the girl that . . .'

'A thousand pounds?'

'That's what Meriwether told me.'

'It's a great deal of money.'

'That's why the chap wants it.'

The Duke pondered. His was a slow mind, and it was only gradually that he ever grasped a thing. But he had begun to see what this Ickenham feller was driving at.

'You think that if I give the girl a thousand pounds, she'll pass it on to this gargoyle chap, and then she'll hand Archibald his hat and marry the gargoyle?'

'Exactly. You put it in a nutshell.'

A sudden healing thought came to the Duke. It was that if he bought the dashed girl off for a thousand and got three thousand from Emsworth for that appalling pig, he would still be comfortably ahead of the game. If it had been within his power to give people grateful looks, he would have given Lord Ickenham one, for it appeared to him that he had found the way.

'I'll go and write the cheque now,' he said.

• II •

It seemed to Lord Ickenham, drowsing in his hammock after the Duke's departure, that an angel voice was speaking his name, and he speculated for a moment on the possibility of his having been snatched up to heaven in a fiery chariot without noticing it. Then reason told him that an angel, punctilious as all angels are, would scarcely on so brief an acquaintance be addressing him as Uncle Fred, and he sat up, brushing the mists of sleep from his eyes, to see Myra Schoonmaker standing beside him. She was looking as attractive as always, but her clothes struck him as unsuitable for a morning in the country.

'Hullo, young Myra,' he said. 'Why all dressed up?'

'I'm going to London. I came to ask if there was any little present I could bring you back.'

'Nothing that I can think of except tobacco. What's taking you to London?'

'Father has given me a big cheque and wants me to go and buy things.'

'A kindly thought. You don't seem very elated.'

'Not much to be elated about these days. Everything's such a mess.'

'Things will clear up.'

'Says you!'

'I would call the outlook rather promising.'

'Well, I don't know where you get that idea, but I wish you would sell it to Bill. He needs a bracer.'

'Morale low?'

'Very low. He's all jumpy. You know how you feel when you're waiting for something to explode.'

'Apprehensive?'

'That's the word. He can't understand why Lady Constance has said nothing to him.'

'Was he expecting a chat with her?'

'Well, wouldn't you in his place? He told Lord Emsworth who he was, and Lord Emsworth must have told her.'

'Not necessarily. Perhaps he forgot.'

'Could he forget a thing like that?'

'There is no limit to what Emsworth can forget, especially when he's distracted about his pig.'

'What's wrong with the pig? She looked all right to me when I saw her last.'

'What's wrong is that the Duke has taken her from him.'

'How?'

'It's a long story. I'll tell you about it some other time. What train are you catching?'

'The ten-thirty-five. I wanted Bill to sneak down to the station and come with me. I thought we might get married.'

'Very sensible. Wouldn't he?'

'No. He had scruples. He said it would be a low trick to play on Archie.'

Lord Ickenham sighed.

'Those scruples! They do keep popping up, don't they? Tell him to relax. Archie's dearest wish is to marry a girl named Millicent Rigby. He's engaged to her.'

'But he's engaged to me.'

'He's engaged to both of you. Very awkward situation for the poor boy.'

'Then why doesn't he just break it off?'

'He wants to get a thousand pounds out of the Duke to buy into an onion soupery, and he felt that if he jilted the daughter of a millionaire, his chances would be slim. His only course seemed to him to be to sit tight and hope for the best. And you can't break the engagement because Jimmy would take you back to America. Until this morning the situation was an extraordinarily delicate one.'

'What happened this morning?'

'The Duke somehow or other got the curious idea that your father was on the verge of bankruptcy, and he saw himself faced with the prospect of having to support not only you and Archie but the whole Schoonmaker family. His distaste for this was so great that he left me just now to go and write a cheque for a thousand pounds, payable to you. He hopes to buy you off.'

'Buy me *off*?'

'So that you won't sue Archie for breach of promise. When you see him, accept the cheque in full settlement, endorse it to Archie, and pay it into his bank. You'll just have time, if the train isn't late. Be sure to do it today. The Duke has a nasty habit of stopping cheques. Then, if you explain the situation to him, it is possible that Bill might see his way to joining you on that 10.35 train, and you and he could look in at the registry office tomorrow, being very careful this time to choose the same one. It would wind everything up very neatly.'

There was a silence. Myra drew a deep breath.

'Uncle Fred, did you work this?'

Lord Ickenham seemed surprised.

'Work it?'

'Did you tell the Duke Father was broke?'

Lord Ickenham considered.

'Well, now you mention it,' he said, 'it is just possible that some careless word of mine may have given him that impression. Yes, now that I think back, I believe I did say something along those lines. It seemed to me to come under the head of spreading sweetness and light. I thought I would be making everybody happy, except perhaps the Duke.'

'Oh, Uncle Fred!'

'Quite all right, my dear.'

'I'm going to kiss you.'

'Nothing to stop you, as far as I can see. Tell me,' said Lord Ickenham, when this had been done, 'do you think you can now overcome those scruples of Bill's?'

'I'll overcome them.'

'Just as well, perhaps, that he'll be leaving Blandings Castle. Never outstay your welcome, I always say. Then all that remains is to write a civil note to Lady Constance, thanking her for her hospitality, placing the facts before her and hoping that this finds her in the pink, as it leaves you at present. Give it to Beach. He'll see that she gets it. Why the light laugh?'

'It was more a giggle. I was thinking I'd like to see her face, when she reads it.'

'Morbid, but understandable. I'm afraid she may not be too pleased. There is always apt to be that trouble when you start spreading sweetness and light. You find there isn't enough to go around and someone has to be left out of the distribution. Very difficult to get a full hand.'

## · III ·

In supposing that, having given audience to the Duke, Mr Schoonmaker, Archie Gilpin and Myra, he would now be allowed that restful solitude which was so necessary to him when digesting the morning eggs and bacon, Lord Ickenham was in error. This time it was not an angel voice that interrupted his slumber, but more of a bleat, as if an elderly sheep in the vicinity had been endowed with speech. Only one man of his acquaintance bleated in just that manner, and he was not surprised, on assuming an upright pose, to find that it was Lord Emsworth who had been called to his attention. The ninth earl was drooping limply at his side, as if some unfriendly hand had removed his spinal column.

Having become reconciled by now to being in the position of a French monarch of the old régime holding a levee, Lord Ickenham showed no annoyance, but greeted him with a welcoming smile and said that it was a nice day.

'The sun,' he said, indicating it.

Lord Emsworth looked at the sun, and gave it a nod of approval.

'I came to give you something.'

'The right spirit. It's not my birthday, but I am always open to receive presents. What sort of something?'

'I'm sorry to say I've forgotten.'

'Too bad.'

'I shall remember it in time, I expect.'

'I'll count the minutes.'

'And there's something I wanted to tell you.'

'But you've forgotten it?'

'No, I remember that. It is about the Empress. I have been thinking it over, Ickenham, and I have decided to buy the Empress from Dunstable. I admit I hesitated for awhile, because his price was so stiff. He is asking three thousand pounds.'

It took a great deal to disturb Lord Ickenham's normal calm, but at these words he could not repress a gasp.

'Three thousand *pounds*! For a pig?'

'For the Empress,' Lord Emsworth corrected in a reverent voice.

'Kick him in the stomach!'

'No, I must have the Empress, no matter what the cost. I am lost without her. I'm on my way to see her now.'

'Who's attending to her wants now that Wellbeloved's gone?'

'Oh, I've taken Wellbeloved back,' said Lord Emsworth, looking a little sheepish, as a man will who has done the weak thing. 'I had no alternative. The Empress needs constant care and attention, and no pigman I have ever had has understood her as Wellbeloved does. But I gave him a good talking to. And do you know what he said to me? He said something that shocked me profoundly.'

Lord Ickenham nodded.

'These rugged sons of the soil don't always watch their language. They tend at times to get a bit Shakespearian. What did he call you?'

'He didn't call me anything.'

'Then what shocked you?'

'What he said. He said that Briggs woman who bribed him to steal the Empress was in the pay of Dunstable. It was Dunstable she was working for. I was never so astounded in my life. Should I tax him about it, do you think?'

'In the hope of making him shave his price a bit?' Lord Ickenham shook his head. 'I doubt if that would get you anywhere. He would do what I always advise everyone to do, stick to stout denial. All you have to go on is Wellbeloved's word, and that would not carry much conviction. I like George Cyril Wellbeloved and always enjoy exchanging ideas with him, but I wouldn't believe his word if he brought it to me on a plate with watercress round it. On this occasion he probably deviated from the policy of a lifetime and told the truth, but what of that? You know and I know that Dunstable is a man who sticks at nothing and would walk ten miles in the snow to chisel a starving orphan out of tuppence, but we are helpless without proof. If only he had written some sort of divisional orders, embodying his low schemes in a letter, it would be—'

'Oh!' said Lord Emsworth.

'Eh?' said Lord Ickenham.

'I've just remembered what it was I came to give you,' said Lord Emsworth, feeling in his pocket. 'This letter. It got mixed up with mine. Well, I'll be getting along and seeing the Empress. Would you care to come?'

'Come? Oh, I see what you mean. I think not, thanks. Later on, perhaps.'

Lord Ickenham spoke absently. He had opened the letter, and a glance at the signature had told him that its contents might well be fraught with interest.

His correspondent was Lavender Briggs.

# 12

The door of Lady Constance's boudoir flew open and something large and spectacled shot out, so rapidly that it was only by an adroit *pas seul* that Beach, who happened to be passing at the moment, avoided a damaging collision.

'Oops!' said Mr Schoonmaker, for the large spectacled object was he. 'Pardon me.'

'Pardon me, sir,' said Beach.

'No, no, pardon me,' said Mr Schoonmaker.

'Very good, sir,' said Beach.

He was regarding this man who had so nearly become his dancing partner with a surprise which he did not allow to appear on his moonlike features, for butlers are not permitted by the rules of their guild to look surprised. Earlier in the day he had viewed Mr Schoonmaker with some concern, thinking that his face seemed pale and drawn, as if he were suffering from a headache, but now there had been a magical change and it was plain that he had made a quick recovery. The cheeks glowed, and the eyes, formerly like oysters in the last stages of dissolution, were bright and sparkling. Exuberant was the word Beach would have applied to the financier, if he had happened to know it. He had once heard Lord

Ickenham use the expression 'All spooked up with zip and vinegar', and it was thus that he was mentally labelling Mr Schoonmaker now. Unquestionably spooked up, was his verdict.

'Oh, Beach,' said Mr Schoonmaker.

'Sir?' said Beach.

'Lovely day.'

'Extremely clement, sir.'

'I'm looking for Lord Ickenham. You seen him anywhere?'

'It was only a few moments ago that I observed his lordship entering the office of Lord Emsworth's late secretary, sir.'

'Late?'

'Not defunct, sir. Miss Briggs was dismissed from her post.'

'Oh, I see. Got the push, did she? Where is this office?'

'At the far end of the corridor on the floor above this one. Should I escort you there, sir?'

'No, don't bother. I'll find it. Oh, Beach.'

'Sir?'

'Here,' said Mr Schoonmaker, and thrusting a piece of paper into the butler's hand he curvetted off like, thought Beach, an unusually extrovert lamb in springtime.

Beach looked at the paper, and being alone, with nobody to report him to his guild, permitted himself a sharp gasp. It was a ten-pound note, and it was the third piece of largesse that had been bestowed on him in the last half hour. First, that charming young lady, Miss Schoonmaker, giving him a missive to take to her ladyship, had accompanied it with a fiver, and shortly after that Mr Meriwether had pressed money into his hand with what looked to him like a farewell gesture, though he had not been notified that the gentleman was leaving. It all seemed very mysterious to Beach, though far from displeasing.

Mr Schoonmaker, meanwhile, touching the ground only at odd spots, had arrived at Lavender Briggs' office. He found Lord Ickenham seated at the desk, and burst immediately into speech.

'Oh, Freddie. The butler told me you were here.'

'And he was quite right. Here I am, precisely as predicted. Take a chair.'

'I can't take a chair, I'm much too excited. You don't mind me walking about the room like this? I wanted to see you, Freddie. I wanted you to be the first to hear the news. Do you remember me telling you that if I could get Lady Constance to be my wife, I'd be the happiest man on earth?'

'I remember. Those were your very words.'

'Well, I am.'

Something of the bewilderment recently exhibited by Beach showed itself on Lord Ickenham's face. This was a totally unexpected development. A shrewd judge of form, he had supposed that only infinite patience and a compelling series of pep talks would have been able to screw this man's courage to the sticking point and turn him, as he appeared to have been turned, into a whirlwind wooer. Very unpromising wedding bells material his old friend had seemed to him in the previous talks they had had together, and he had almost despaired of bringing about the happy ending. For if a suitor's nerve fails him every time he sees the adored object sideways, it is seldom that he can accomplish anything constructive. Yet now it was plain that something had occurred to change James Schoonmaker from the timorous rabbit he had been to a dasher with whom Don Juan would not have been ashamed to shake hands. It struck him instantly that there could be but one solution of the mystery.

'Jimmy, you've been at the May Queen again.'

'I have not!'

'You're sure?'

'Of course I'm sure.'

'Well, I'm glad to hear that, for it is not a practice I would recommend so early in the day. And yet you tell me that you have been proposing marriage with, I am glad to hear, great success. How did you overcome that diffidence of yours?'

'I didn't have to overcome it. When I saw her sitting there in floods of tears, all my diffidence vanished. I felt strong and protective. I hurried to where she sat.'

'And grabbed her?'

'Certainly not.'

'Waggled her about?'

'Nothing of the kind. I bent over her and took her hand gently in mine. "Connie," I said.'

'Connie?'

'Certainly.'

'At last! I knew you would get around to it sooner or later. And then?'

'She said, "Oh, James!"'

'Well, I don't think much of the dialogue so far, but perhaps it got brighter later on. What did you say after that?'

'I said, "Connie, darling. What's the matter?"'

'One can understand how you must have been curious to know. And what was the matter?'

Mr Schoonmaker, who had been pacing the floor in the manner popularized by tigers at a zoo, suddenly halted in midstride, and the animation died out of his face as though turned off with a switch. He looked like a man suddenly reminded of something unpleasant, as indeed he had been.

'Who's this guy Meriwether?' he demanded.

'Meriwether?' said Lord Ickenham, who had had an idea that the name would be coming up shortly. 'Didn't Connie tell you about him?'

'Only that you brought him here.'

Lord Ickenham could understand this reticence. He recalled that his hostess, going into the matter at their recent conference, had decided that silence was best. It would have been difficult, as she had said, were she to place the facts before her betrothed, to explain why she had allowed Bill to continue enjoying her hospitality.

'Yes, I brought him here. He's a young friend of mine. His name actually is Bailey, but he generally travels incognito. He's a curate. He brushes and polishes the souls of the parishioners of Bottleton East, a district of London, where he is greatly respected. I'll tell you something about Bill Bailey, Jimmy. I have an idea he's a good deal attracted by your daughter Myra. Not easy to tell for certain because he wears the mask, but I wouldn't be at all surprised if he wasn't in love with her. One or two little signs I've noticed. Poor lad, it must have been a sad shock for him when he learned that she's going to marry Archie Gilpin.'

Mr Schoonmaker snorted. This habit of his of behaving like a bursting paper bag was new to Lord Ickenham. Probably, he thought, a mannerism acquired since his rise to riches. No doubt there was some form of unwritten law that compelled millionaires to act that way.

'She isn't,' said Mr Schoonmaker.

'Isn't what?'

'Going to marry Archie Gilpin. She eloped with Meriwether this morning.'

'You astound me. Are you sure? Where did you hear that?'

'She left a note for Connie.'

'Well, this is wonderful news,' said Lord Ickenham, his face lighting up. 'I'm not surprised you're dancing about all over the place on the tips of your toes. He's a splendid young fellow. Boxed three years for Oxford and, so I learn from a usually reliable source, went through the opposition like a dose of salts. I congratulate you, Jimmy.'

Mr Schoonmaker seemed to be experiencing some difficulty in sharing his joyous enthusiasm.

'I call it a disaster. Connie thinks so, too—that's why she was in floods of tears. And she says you're responsible.'

'Who, me?' said Lord Ickenham, amazed, not knowing that the copyright in those words was held by George Cyril Wellbeloved. 'What had I got to do with it?'

'You brought him here.'

'Merely because I thought he looked a little peaked and needed a breath of country air. Honestly, Jimmy,' said Lord Ickenham, speaking rather severely, 'I don't see what you're beefing about. If I hadn't brought him here, he wouldn't have eloped with Myra, thus causing Connie to burst into floods of tears, thus causing you to lose your diffidence and take her hand gently in yours and say "Connie, darling." If it hadn't been for these outside stimuli, you would still be calling her Lady Constance and wincing like a salted snail every time you saw her profile. You ought to be thanking me on bended knee, unless the passage of time has made you stiff in the joints. What's your objection to Bill Bailey?'

'Connie says he hasn't a cent to his name.'

'Well, you've enough for all. Haven't you ever heard of sharing the wealth?'

'I don't like Myra marrying a curate.'

'The very husband you should have wished her. The one thing a financier wants is a clergyman in the family. What happens next time the Senate Commission has you on the carpet and starts a probe? You say "As proof of my respectability, gentlemen, I may mention that my daughter is married to a curate. You don't find curates marrying into a man's family if there's anything fishy about him," and they look silly and apologize. And there's another thing.'

'Eh?' said Mr Schoonmaker, who had been musing.

'I said there was another thing you ought to bear in mind. Have you considered what would have happened if Myra had married the Duke of Dunstable's nephew? You would never have got Dunstable out of your hair. A Christmas present would have been expected yearly. You would have had to lunch with him, dine with him, be constantly in his society. He would have come over to New York to spend long visits with you. The children, if any, would have had to learn to call him "Uncle Alaric". I think you've been extraordinarily lucky, Jimmy. Imagine a life with Dunstable like a sort of Siamese twin.'

It is possible that Mr Schoonmaker would have had much to say in reply to this, for Lord Ickenham's reasoning, though shrewd, had not wholly convinced him that everything was for the best in the best of all possible worlds, but at this moment the air was rent by a stentorian 'Hoy!' and they perceived that the Duke of Dunstable was in their midst.

'Oh, *you're* here?' said the Duke, pausing in the doorway and giving Mr Schoonmaker a nasty look.

Mr Schoonmaker, returning the nasty look with accrued interest, said he was.

'I hoped you'd be alone, Ickenham.'

'Jimmy was just going, weren't you, Jimmy? This is your busy day, isn't it? A thousand things to attend to. So what,' said Lord Ickenham, as the door closed, 'can I do for you, Dunstable?'

The Duke jerked a thumb at the door.

'Has he been trying to touch you?'

'Oh, no. We were just talking.'

'Oh?'

The Duke transferred his gaze to the room, regarding it with dislike and disapproval. It had unpleasant memories for him. He took in the desk, the typewriter, the recording machine and the chairs with a smouldering eye. It was in this interior set, he could not but remember, that that woman with the spectacles had so nearly deprived him of five hundred pounds.

'What you doing here?' he asked, as if revolted to find Lord Ickenham in such surroundings.

'In Miss Briggs' office? I had a letter from her this morning asking me to look in and attend to a number of things on her behalf. She left, if you recall, in rather a hurry.'

'Why did she write to you?'

'I think she felt that I was her only friend at Blandings Castle.'

'You a friend of hers?'

'We became reasonably matey.'

'Then I'd advise you to choose your friends more carefully, that's what I'd advise you. Matey, indeed!'

'You don't like the divine Briggs?'

'Blasted female.'

'Ah, well,' said Lord Ickenham tolerantly, 'we all have our faults. Even I have been criticized at times. But you were going to tell me what you wanted to see me about.'

The Duke, who had been scowling at the typewriter, as if daring it to start something, became more composed. A curious gurgling noise suggested that he had chuckled.

'Oh, that? I just came to say that everything's all right.'

'Splendid. What's all right?'

'About the pipsqueak.'

'What pipsqueak would that be?'

'The Tiddlypush girl. She took the cheque.'

'She did?'

'In full settlement.'

'Well, that's wonderful news.'

'So there won't be any breach of promise case. She's gone to London.'

'Yes, I saw her for a moment before she left. You bought her off, did you?'

'That's what I did. "Here you are," I said, and I dangled the cheque in front of her. She didn't hesitate. Grabbed at it like a seal going after a slice of fish. I knew she would. They can't resist the cash. I've just been telling Archibald that she has . . . what's that expression you used when you told me he'd been sacked from that job of his?'

'Handed him his hat?'

'That's right. I told him she's handed him his hat.'

'Was he very distressed?'

'Didn't seem to be.'

'Easy come, easy go, he probably said to himself.'

'I shouldn't wonder. He's gone to London, too.'

'On the same train as Miss Schoonmaker?'

'No, he went in that little car of his. Said he was going to take a friend to dinner. Fellow of the name of Rigby.'

'Ah yes, he has spoken to me of his friend Rigby. I believe they are very fond of each other.'

'Chap must be a silly ass if he's fond of a poop like Archibald.'

'Oh, we all have our likes and dislikes. You'll be leaving soon yourself, I take it?'

'Me? Why?'

'Well, it won't be very comfortable for you here now that Emsworth knows it was you who engaged Miss Briggs to steal his pig. Creates a strain, that sort of thing. Tension. Awkward silences.'

The Duke gaped. The shock had been severe. If a meteorite had entered through the open window and struck him behind one of his rather prominent ears, he might have been more taken aback, but not very much so. When he was able to speak, which was not immediately, he said:

'What . . . what you talking about?'

'Isn't it true?'

'Of course it's not true.'

Lord Ickenham clicked his tongue reprovingly.

'My dear Dunstable, I am always a great advocate of stout denial, but I'm afraid it is useless here. Emsworth has had the whole story from George Cyril Wellbeloved.'

The Duke was still feeling far from at his best, but he rallied sufficiently to say 'Pooh!'

'Who's going to believe him?'

'His testimony is supported by Miss Briggs.'

'Who's going to believe her?'

'Everybody, I should say. Certainly Emsworth, for one, after he hears this record.'

'Eh?'

'I told you I had received a letter from the divine Briggs this morning. In it she asked me to turn on her tape recording machine . . . this is the tape recording machine . . . because, she said, that would give the old bounder . . . I fancy she meant you . . . something to think about. I will now do so,' said Lord Ickenham. He pressed the button, and a voice filled the room.

'I, Alaric, Duke of Dunstable, hereby make a solemn promise to you, Lavender Briggs . . .'

The Duke sat down abruptly. His jaw had fallen, and he seemed suddenly to have become as boneless as Lord Emsworth.

'. . . that if you steal Lord Emsworth's pig, Empress of Blandings, and deliver it to my home in Wiltshire, I will pay you five hundred pounds.'

'That,' said Lord Ickenham, 'is you in conference with La Briggs. She naturally took the precaution of having this instrument working at the time. It's always safer with these verbal agreements. Well, I don't know what view you take of the situation, but it seems to me that you and Emsworth are like two cowboys in the Malemute Saloon who have got the drop on each other simultaneously. You have young George's film, he has this Scotch tape or whatever it's called. I suggest a fair exchange. Or would you rather I brought Emsworth in here and played this recording to him? It's not a thing I would recommend. One feels that the consequences would be extremely unpleasant for you.'

The Duke froze, appalled. The feller was right. Let this get about, and not only would his name be a hissing and a byword, so that when he invited himself to houses in the future, his host and hostess would hasten to put their valuables away in a stout box and sit on the lid, but Emsworth would bring an action against him for conspiracy or malice aforethought or whatever it was and mulct him in substantial damages. With only the minimum of hesitation he thrust a hand in his pocket and produced the spool which had never left his person since little George had given it to him.

'Here you are, blast you!'

'Oh, thanks. Now everybody's happy. Emsworth has his pig, Myra her Bill, Archie his Millicent Rigby.'

The Duke started.

'His *what* Rigby?'

'Oh yes, I should have told you that, shouldn't I? He's gone to London to marry a very nice girl called Millicent Rigby, at least he says she's very nice, and he probably knows. By the way, that reminds me. There's one thing I wish you would clear up for me before you go. Why was it that you were so anxious that Archie shouldn't marry Myra Schoonmaker? It has puzzled me from the first. She's charming, and apart from being charming she's the heiress of one of the richest men in America. Don't you like heiresses?'

The Duke's moustache had become violently agitated. He was not normally quick-witted, but he had begun to suspect that fishy things had been going on. If this Ickenham had not been deliberately misleading him, he was very much mistaken.

'You told me Schoonmaker was broke!'

'Surely not?'

'You said he touched you for a tenner.'

'No, no, I touched *him* for a tenner. That may be where you got confused. What would a man like James Schoonmaker be doing, borrowing money from people? He's a millionaire, so Bradstreet informs us.'

'Who's Bradstreet?'

'The leading authority on millionaires. A sort of American Debrett. Bradstreet is very definite on the subject of James Schoonmaker. Stinking rich is, I believe, the expression it uses of him.'

The Duke continued to bend his brain to the problem. He was more convinced than ever that he had been deceived.

'Then why did she take that cheque?'

'Ah, that we shall never know. Just girlish high spirits, do you think?'

'I'll give her girlish high spirits!'

'I'll tell you a possible solution that has occurred to me. She knew that Archie was planning to get married and needed money, so being a kind-hearted girl she took the cheque and endorsed it over to him. Sort of a wedding present from you. Where are you going?'

The Duke had lumbered to the door. He paused with a hand on the handle, regarded Lord Ickenham balefully.

'I'll tell you where I'm going. I'm going to get to the telephone and stop that cheque.'

Lord Ickenham shook his head.

'I wouldn't. I still have the tape, remember. I was just about to give it to you, but if you are going to stop cheques, I shall have to make an agonizing reappraisal.'

There was a silence, as far as silence was possible in a small room where the Duke was puffing at his moustache.

'You shall have it tomorrow night after the cheque has gone through. It's not that I don't trust you, Dunstable, it's simply that I don't trust you.'

The Duke breathed stertorously. He did not like many people, but he searched his mind in vain for somebody he disliked as much as he was disliking his present companion.

'Ickenham,' he said, 'you are a low cad!'

'Now you're just trying to be nice. I bet you say that to all the boys,' said Lord Ickenham, and rising from his chair he went off to tell Lord Emsworth that though he had lost Lavender Briggs and was losing a sister and the Duke of Dunstable, he would be gaining a pig which for three years in succession had won the silver medal in the Fat Pigs class at the Shropshire Agricultural Show.

There was a smile on his handsome face, the smile it always wore when he had given service.